Let Me Be The One

Tina J

This novel is a work of fiction. Any resemblances to actual events, real people, living or dead, organizations, establishments or locales are products of the author's imagination. Other names, characters, places, and incidents are used fictionally.

Because of the dynamic nature of the Internet, any web address or links contained in this book may have changed since publication, and may no longer be valid.

Warning:

This book is strictly Urban Fiction and the story is **NOT REAL**!

Characters will not behave the way you want them to; nor will they react to situations the way you think they should. Some of them may be drug addicts, kingpins, savages, thugs, rich, poor, ho's, sluts, haters, bitter ex-girlfriends or boyfriends, people from the past and the list can go on and on. That is what Urban Fiction mostly consists of. If this isn't anything you foresee yourself interested in, then do yourself a favor and don't read it because it's only going to piss you off. ☺☺

Also, the book will not end the way you want so please be advised that the outcome will be based solely on my own thoughts and ideas. I hope you enjoy this book that y'all made me write. Thanks so much to my readers, supporters, publisher and fellow authors and authoress for the support. 😮😮

Author Tina J

More books from me:

The Thug I Chose 1, 2 & 3

A Thin Line Between Me and My Thug 1 & 2

I Got Luv For My Shawty 1 & 2

Kharis and Caleb: A Different Kind of Love 1 & 2

Loving You Is A Battle 1 & 2 & 3

Violet and The Connect 1 & 2 & 3

You Complete Me

Love Will Lead You Back

This Thing Called Love

Are We In This Together 1,2 &3

Shawty Down To Ride For a Boss 1, 2 &3

When A Boss Falls in Love 1, 2 & 3

Let Me Be The One 1 & 2

We Got That Forever Love

Aint No Savage Like The One I Got 1&2

A Queen and A Hustla 1, 2 & 3

Thirsty For A Bad Boy 1&2

Hassan and Serena: An Unforgettable Love 1&2

Caught Up Loving A Beast 1, 2 & 3

A Street King And His Shawty 1 & 2

I Fell For The Wrong Bad Boy 1&2

I Wanna Love You 1 & 2

Addicted to Loving a Boss 1, 2, & 3

I Need That Gangsta Love 1&2

Creepin With The Plug 1 & 2

All Eyes On The Crown 1,2&3

When She's Bad, I'm Badder: Jiao and Dreek, A Crazy Love Story 1,2&3

Still Luvin A Beast 1&2

Her Man, His Savage 1 & 2

Marco & Rakia: Not Your Ordinary, Hood Kinda Love 1,2 & 3

Feenin For A Real One 1, 2 & 3

A Kingpin's Dynasty 1, 2 & 3

What Kinda Love Is This: Captivating A Boss 1, 2 & 3

Frankie & Lexi: Luvin A Young Beast 1, 2 & 3

A Dope Boys Seduction 1, 2 & 3

My Brother's Keeper 1. 2 & 3

C'Yani & Meek: A Dangerous Hood Love 1, 2 & 3

When A Savage Falls for A Good Girl 1, 2 & 3

Eva & Deray 1 & 2

Blame It On His Gangsta Luv 1 & 2

Chapter 1

Essence

This nigga had really gotten on my damn nerves inviting another one of his damn family members to crash here. I kept telling him this wasn't no damn hotel.

My man, Stacy, and I had been together for a little over seven years and we had mostly all his relatives stay with us. His two uncles, three aunts, a few cousins, and his ratchet ass trifling sister June, who I had to beat the fuck up.

I had come home from work early and this bitch was fucking some old ass man in my bed. He had to have been in his late forties and her ass was only twenty. I know age ain't nothing but a number but damn.

I whooped her ass so bad my man had to take her to the hospital and then pay her five thousand dollars to say she got jumped. A bitch like me didn't care if I got arrested. That was straight up disrespectful.

Nobody in the family was mad at me because she had done it in their houses, too. June was the ho of all hoes. She didn't care if you had a girl or wife. Bitches like her needed to stay away from married people.

Stacy knew I couldn't stand her ass, so when we had our barbecues, he made sure if she came, she was wherever he was. Anytime I glanced over at her, I had a flashback and wanted to jump on her again.

This weekend Stacy's brother was coming to stay with us for a month until his house was finished. I'd met him a few times when we took trips out to California. He was in jail for the first five years we were together on some bullshit charge, as Stacy put it. He refused to leave California without getting his restitution.

I didn't know all the details of what happened; I just knew the state of California had to pay his ass almost forty million dollars. Shit, I wouldn't have left until I got my money, either. He got his check a few months ago and gave my man ten million of it. He had an account set up for his sister with five in it, but their mom was the account holder so anything she needed, their mom had to get it.

He and Stacy had talked about opening a few clubs and a skating rink. You know, the normal shit to invest so money would always come in. I was cool with that but I told Stacy there wouldn't be any fucking strip clubs, that's for sure. I'd heard too many stories about men investing in them and how the shit broke up their families. Not me, not mine.

Stacy and I had met at the bar one night. My best friend, April, and I were bored as hell and decided to go play pool. There weren't many people inside, which was a good thing. She and I watched the two guys go back and forth on their game while we sat on the stools drinking beer and talking. As we waited our turn, the dude who was playing kept smiling at me and drinking his beer.

"What's up, ma? You see something you like?" he smiled and showed off his gold grill on the bottom row of his teeth. I couldn't lie and say I wasn't staring because he was fine as hell.

He had a low cut Caesar-style haircut, he was brown-skinned, his eyes were brown, and he had a goatee. His muscles were flexing through his t-shirt and dude was rocking some expensive ass clothes, jewelry, and sneakers. Shit, I wasn't a name brand type of chick, but everything about him screamed money.

"Maybe," I smiled and lifted my drink up.

"Ok. What you going to do about it?"

I didn't really know how to respond to his question. I looked at April who was grinning and shaking her head.

"Yeah bitch, what you going to do about it?"

"Bitch, I don't know. I've never been with a man before."

"Girl, you had boyfriends in high school. Cut it out," she whispered over to me.

"Yeah, but they were school boyfriends. It's not like I ever went out on dates or anything. Shit, I don't even know how to kiss."

"He doesn't know that. Get your scary ass up and go over there. That's what your ass gets for staring."

I felt like I was hyperventilating. My palms were sweaty as hell and my feet wouldn't move from the barstool. Here I was, a twenty-two-year-old virgin that had no idea what to do with a man; yet, I was about to go kick it with him.

As I was about to get up, I saw some dude whisper in

his ear. He shook his head, dropped the pool stick, and left.

"Thank goodness, bitch. I had no idea what I was going to say when I got close to him."

"You don't have to say anything right now. Plug your number in my phone and we can figure it out later." He was breathing on the back of my neck and handed me the phone. I put my number in and turned around to hand it back. I hadn't realized he was that close. My lips found his, and before I knew it, he'd put his hands around the back of my neck and pulled me in closer. His tongue parted my lips and danced with mine. I had no idea what I was doing and I think he knew. He stopped and looked me up and down and smirked.

"Yeah, I'm going to have fun with you."

"Huh? What's that supposed to mean?"

"It means I know your secret and you're mine," he pecked my lips and walked away.

"Oh shit bitch, you think he knows I'm a virgin?" I asked April, who was cracking up.

"Yup. Shit, I could tell by the way you kissed him. You looked crazy as hell. You act like you couldn't open your mouth and when you did, your tongue was everywhere." I put my head down in embarrassment.

"Wow. It was that bad, huh?"

"Yup. It's ok. Like he said, he's about to have fun with you."

"Whatever. Let's get this game going."

I picked my pool stick up and tried to focus on my game. The only thing I could focus on was that man. I didn't know his name, where he was from, or if he would even call me. Oh well, if it's meant to be it will be.

Chapter 2

Stacy

"Hey baby," I said to Essence when I answered my phone.

"Do we really have to allow another family member to stay here?"

"Bye Essence."

"Stacy, you better not hang up on me."

"Essence, I'm on my way home. We can talk when I get there."

I put the phone in my pocket and continued watching the woman box up the eight-carat, yellow diamond engagement ring I'd gotten my girl. Yeah, Essence was my heart and there wasn't a woman around that could take it from her. Many had tried, but none succeeded.

I'd met Essence at the bar with her friend and my son's godmother, April. The night we met, and she kissed me, I could tell she had no idea what she was doing. That told me she hadn't been with the right nigga to show her, or she was a virgin. I figured it was the latter because she tensed up when I touched her.

It took me a week before I called her because I was so wrapped up in buying my new house and I'd just cleaned up my last million dollars. Yup, I was a drug dealer-just like most niggas. However, I made a promise to myself that I would be out the game by the time I was twenty-five.

No one knew I sold drugs because I wasn't the corner type of guy, and I didn't sell crack or coke. I sold heroin and prescription drugs. My boy was a doctor and he and I went into business together. At first, we didn't think we would make that much money, but when you're selling to rich folks, you can charge them anything you want. They'll pay thousands of dollars to get that fix.

Anyway, the only person who knew was my brother and even he was pissed. My mom was a teacher and my dad was a bus driver for Academy Buses. They made decent money and gave us whatever we wanted. I appreciated everything they did, but I knew once I had a family and settled down, I didn't want them to need for anything.

The day I ran into Essence at the bar was no

coincidence. I’d known all about her and planned on meeting up with her eventually. I was cool with her brother, and every now and then we would meet up at the bar and shoot some pool. He talked about his sister all the time and how she needed to meet the right guy because all she did was sit in the house. He showed me a photo of her and I knew I had to get her.

Essence was at least five foot three and she had a brown caramel complexion with light brown eyes. Her body was average, but her hips and thighs had a nigga wanting to be buried between them every day.

After we spoke on the phone a few times, she agreed to meet up with me for dinner. This woman was smart, beautiful, a little hood, and had dreams to open up a community center.

I loved everything about her and no one could hold a torch to her in the bedroom. Yes, she was a virgin when I met her, but I showed her how to please me. After a while, she started trying new things she saw online, completely turning me out. My baby was a freak and there was nothing she wouldn't do in the bedroom.

****

I pulled up to my house and saw the lights were out, except in the kitchen. She walked outside in just a short ass robe and some slippers.

"Why are you out here with nothing on?" I turned my body to get out the truck but she stopped me and unbuckled my jeans.

"Because this is our house and the next one is a mile away. Plus, I want to give my man some pleasure."

She stroked my man until she saw he was awake, then kissed the tip.

"Why you playing?"

"This is my dick. I can do what I want," she grinned, put me in her mouth, and started sucking my soul out. Her mouth had my dick so wet I tried not to bust but it was impossible.

"Fuck, baby."

"That's right. Let me taste you. Mmmmm, just how I like it."

That dirty talk did it. I shot so much down her throat I

didn't know when I would stop.

“Damn, I didn't even get to play with my balls or anything,” she said, wiping her mouth with the back of her hand.

“Shit, Essence. It's been a week since we last had sex. What did you expect?”

“I'm sorry. You know when my period comes, I can't do nothing about it.”

“Yeah, ok.” I had already jumped out my truck and was standing behind her. I had her put one leg up on the step of my Ford -F150 while I devoured her pussy. My baby had a taste to her so sweet I could never get enough. I would make her cum over and over just to taste her.

“Stacy, I'm cumming baby. Awwww shit.” Her knees started buckling and she grabbed the seat to catch herself.

“I love you so much, Stacy.” she moaned in my ear as I fucked her standing up. She caught my rhythm and we went at it as if we were in the bedroom.

“I love you too, Essence. Damn, your pussy looks real good creaming all over my dick like that. I was staring at myself go in and out while I hit it from the back. Not too long after, we both climaxed.

"You know I just got you pregnant, right?" I turned her around and tied the robe in front of her.

"It's ok. I want my daughter now." She smiled and strutted her sexy ass in the house. I locked up and followed her to the shower.

"Are you sure you're ready? I mean, the last time I came in you, you had a fit."

"That was because Stacy Jr. was only four weeks old. Luckily, I got on the pill. But I haven't taken the pill in the last month."

"Why didn't you tell me?"

"I shouldn't have to. You don't pull out anyway, so why did it matter?"

I smacked her on the ass and fucked her into a coma. I made sure to let off each time in hopes that she would get pregnant. We were still young and I wanted some more babies running around, and so did my parents.

I was the only one in a steady relationship and they

loved the hell out of Essence. You would think my mom birthed her and not me by the way she took her side. My girl could do no wrong in my mom's eyes and she played on that shit all the time.

****

"Stacy, I want this to be the last relative to live here. I know they're your family, but I feel like they're using you." Essence was getting our son, SJ, ready for school.

"I know but Kane isn't like that. He has his own money and wanted to stay in a hotel."

"I'm fine with him, baby. It's the rest of your family."

I couldn't argue with her because she was right. It was always something with my family. The last straw was her catching my sister fucking some man in our bed. She made me buy an entire new bedroom set after that happened. She put a hurting on my sister and I didn't even care. Of course, my sister stopped speaking to me, but that didn't last long because she needed money, as usual.

My brother gave both of us money, and even though I didn't need it, he wouldn't take no for an answer. I put it in my son's bank account because my wife and I shared one, and we had millions.

"The pool people will be here tomorrow to make sure everything is right for the party. Also, the DJ wants to stop by so he can figure out where he wants to set up his equipment, and the caterers will be here early that morning too."

"Damn baby, you hooking my brother up, huh?"

"No. I'm hooking you up for your brother. If I leave you to do it, he will have hot dogs and hamburgers and no one would be able to use the pool."

"Whatever."

"Yeah, whatever my ass."

"Thank you, baby," I kissed her forehead and took our son to school.

Chapter 3

Kane

I stepped off the plane and was ready to kiss the ground. I was happy as hell to be back in New Jersey. My family wasn't expecting me until Saturday morning, but I refused to stay in Cali any longer. I had my boy Derrick pick me up and take me by my brother's first.

Derrick and I had been boys since we were in middle school. We lived next door to each other and his mom and my mom were friends. We were considered the nerdy thugs. That meant we were smart as hell, but still hood. Our education was always top priority with us, and the streets came second. As my brother said, we didn't need to sell drugs because we had everything we wanted, but you know boys are hardheaded as hell. Derrick was the brains of our little weed operation and I was more of the corner type of guy.

At first, we sold to all our friends, but the more money we made, the more people we sold to. We sold to teachers, lawyers, parents, and a host of others. This went on for years without our parents finding out. Unless they knew but never said anything. The amount of money we made, one would call us kingpins, but that wasn't the case.

The person we worked for was my brother’s best friend, Stan. He took us under his wing, taught us everything he knew, and let us keep eighty percent of our money. He said he had money for three lifetimes and wanted to make sure we could come up like him.

Anyway, I was dealing with this chick named Erica who I took to California with me for a vacation. This woman had my daughter and was going to be my wife. I had the ring and planned on proposing to her the night I got arrested.

We were in a restaurant having dinner when some Feds and California's finest came in and arrested me. They claimed I was some man that had been on the America’s Most Wanted posters. I tried over and over to tell them it wasn't me, but they gave zero fucks. They held me in the interrogation room for hours and even had a picture of the guy. This nigga looked just like me. But I knew I didn't have a twin, so how was it possible?

The person was charged with five murders, two counts

of conspiracy to commit murder, and some other shit. Erica had come to see me a few times when I was locked up, but after a year I didn't see her anymore. She wouldn't take my calls and I had to have my brother get my daughter Lexi and bring her to see me.

It took five years for them to realize I was the wrong person and that's only because they found the person over in Cuba. My lawyer ate their asses up in court. They never fingerprinted me to see if it was a match. They never checked my alibis or the fact that I was on vacation with my girl. When my lawyer filed the suit, they had no choice but to settle.

No one knew I was coming back after I was released because I stayed two years waiting for my suit to go through. Now here I am, standing on my brother's doorstep.

"Oh my God, Kane. Stacy, get down here!" Essence yelled and gave me a hug. I loved her like a sister. My brother would bring her to visit along with my daughter and nephew twice a month. She was a good girl and that's what my brother needed. Shit, that's what every man needed.

"Uncle Kane!" My nephew ran up to me and jumped in

my arms.

"You're getting big. How old are you now?"

"I'm five. How old are you?"

"Younger than your daddy." I put him down and there was my daughter running from the back.

"Daddy!" she screamed with tears coming down her face.

"Hey, baby girl."

"I love you. Can you stay here?" She was holding my neck extra tight.

"Yes. I'm here to stay."

"Come let me show you my room."

"Your room?" Stacy and Essence just looked at me and shook their heads.

"Yes. Mommy didn't want me anymore, so I stay here. Well, I have a room here, at Grandma's and Pop Pop's, and even April has a room for me and SJ at her house."

"Who is April?"

"April is my best friend and also SJ's godmother," Essence told me.

“Ok. Why does she have a room for my daughter?”

“Ugh, you better not let April hear you say that.” Essence walked away talking shit.

“What you mean?”

“Man, when Erica left Lexi with us two years ago, she cried for days. No one could get her to stop. The day April came over to see if she could help, she took Lexi for a ride and brought her back two days later.”

I gave him the side eye because why would they allow someone outside of the family to keep my child.

“Nah, it's not even like that. You know I wouldn't allow anyone to take her I didn't trust,” Stacy said, already knowing what I was about to say.

“Do you know I went over there with SJ and these two were having a girl’s day? I was pissed because I wasn't invited,” Essence came back in rolling her eyes.

“Daddy, she was the only one who wanted me when mommy left.”

“Don't say that.”

“Aunty Essence and Uncle Stacy had SJ, and Grandma

and Pop Pop are too old. She doesn't have any kids, so she told me I was her daughter now. You have to see her, daddy. She's so pretty and she doesn't have a man either."

"Ok, Lexi. That's enough," Essence told her. I smiled when she told me another woman had stepped in to be her mom, even though I didn't know her. That right there had me wanting to meet her and show her my appreciation, and I'm not talking about sex.

"This is my room."

Her room was huge with pink and white everything. She had a Queen-sized bedroom set and a plush rug. Toys were everywhere along with an iPad, Beats headphones and a ton of other stuff. Her closet had more clothes than a six-year-old should have. And the shoes and sneakers were ridiculous.

"Uncle Kane, come see my room."

SJ's room was just as big with black and silver everywhere. He had a Queen-sized bedroom set with an iPad too, a PlayStation 4, and an Xbox One. I wasn't sure he even knew how to play those things yet. His sneaker collection was official with every Jordan out there, along with Timbs and some other shit.

"Damn, these kids got way too much shit."

"I know, right," Stacy said while taking Derrick and me into his man cave to smoke. I stayed down there for an hour or so with them catching me up on everything that had been going on. Most of it I knew, since my brother had told me.

"Why didn't you tell me about this April chick?"

"Lexi asked me not to. She said that since she was her new mom, she wanted to be the first to tell you."

"So who is this chick?"

"Yo', shorty bad as hell," Derrick said as he started describing her.

"She's light-skinned with a few freckles on her face. She has to be at least five foot five with a nice shape. Her hair hangs down to the middle of her back and yes, it's hers and she has all her teeth."

We all started laughing when he said that. Derrick had been known to fuck with chicks that could be walking with one leg and a kickstand. He didn't care as long as he got the pussy.

"Sounds like a winner. Why haven't you tried to hit it?"

"Nah, she's cool people. I look at her like a little sister ever since she started helping with my niece." He considered my daughter his niece since we were so close.

"Well, I guess it's time to meet her."

"A word of advice when you meet her," Stacy said, putting the blunt out.

"What's up?"

"April isn't your average chick. She cool as hell, quiet, and sometimes shy but she doesn't tolerate disrespect and the minute you get on her bad side, you can forget about her ever speaking to you again."

"Damn, it's like that?"

"Yup. That's probably why her ass stay single," Derrick laughed.

"Oh hell no. Don't be down here talking shit about my girl. You know she single because these niggas out here can't handle a real woman who be about her shit."

"That's right baby, tell them."

"Here Stacy go with that punk shit. We can be talking about anything, but the second she comes in here, it's whatever she says." Essence mushed Derrick upside his head.

"That's right, bro. A happy wife makes a happy life," Stacy said, kissing Essence on the cheek. We all went upstairs and that's when I saw my mom and pops coming through the door.

"Awww, my baby is home." My mom had tears in her eyes and so did my dad. I missed the hell out of them. They'd visited me just as much as my brother and Essence.

"I'm home for good." I told them and made sure to spend more time with all of them because I missed a whole lotta time.

****

It was a little after nine by the time everyone left and I was exhausted. I thought about going out, but my daughter and nephew wanted me to stay the night with them in their little clubhouse they made in the living room.

"Goodnight, daddy. I'm glad you're home."

"Me too, uncle Kane."

"Goodnight you two. I love you and I'm happy to be home." I laid on the couch while those two slept in the sleeping bag on the floor.

The next morning, I helped Essence get the kids ready for school and jumped in the shower right after. I was going to see the spot Stacy had for the new club, and then we were going to the store to pick up the stuff for the BBQ.

"Kane, I need you or Stacy to get the kids off the bus this afternoon."

"I'll be here."

"Ok. I'll see you guys later." She gave me a hug, and of course these two freaks had a make out session in front of me.

"Bye Essence. Damn, I'm sure you were getting it in last night."

"Whatever."

"Y'all had the music up loud as hell. What else is there to say?" She stuck her tongue out and went out the door.

"Let's go, man. We got to get your ass some pussy so you can stop hating," Stacy chuckled on the way out the door.

Chapter 4

April

I was on my way to pick up the last of the kids on my bus route. Yes, I drive a school bus and I love it. I'm a certified substitute and I have my Bachelor's in Criminal Justice. I am getting my Master's in Social Work online because I promised my best friend Essence, I would work with her at the community center Stacy had built for her two years ago. He gave her whatever she wanted and the love they had towards one another made me want a man. But I wasn't going to look for one.

"Hey my little babies."

"Mommy April, I'm not a baby," Lexi said, stepping on the bus.

"Me either," SJ said. I always picked them up from their after-school programs after I dropped the last set of kids off. I pulled up to their house and I didn't see any cars in the driveway.

"There's no one here. You guys are going to come with me to the hair salon until Stacy gets off." Both of them put their earphones back on and started playing on their iPads.

I was getting ready to pull off when somebody pulled up in front of the bus in a brand new, white 2016 Jaguar XF. The door opened and out stepped the most handsome man I'd seen in a long time.

He was tall and light-skinned with green eyes. His muscles were popping out of his t-shirt, and his lips were nice and juicy. Whoever he was, you could tell he had money from the jewelry in his ears, on his wrist, and around his neck. I never seen him before, but I could say he had me lusting a little. I rolled my down window to see what he wanted.

"Why would you block me in?" I immediately snapped. I don't even know why, because this man did nothing to me but make me wish I were home so that I could fantasize about him.

"Damn, I didn't even get to say anything and you snapping already."

"What do you want?"

"I'm here to get my daughter and nephew off the bus."

I looked at him like he was crazy. Essence's brother

didn't have any kids and Stacy's brother was in California.

"Ugh, that's my daughter and her father lives in another state. As far as my godson, I know damn well he's not getting off either. You need to move that ugly ass car so I can leave."

He laughed and picked his phone up. He talked to someone then put it on speaker.

"April, that's my brother. You can let the kids off with him. Essence was supposed to call you and tell you he would be there."

"Well, she didn't."

"Now can I have the kids?" he asked and walked over to the door. I opened it and he stepped on.

"Ugh, get your ass off my bus."

"Daddy! I didn't know you were going to be here," Lexi snatched all her stuff up, kissed my cheek, and jumped in his arms. SJ did the same thing and jumped off the last step like he did every day. I went to shut the door when he turned around and flashed a million-dollar smile.

"Thank you for taking care of my daughter. I really appreciate it," he handed me an envelope and took the kids to his car. I couldn't move until he did, so I opened the envelope up and saw a check for two hundred and fifty thousand dollars. Was this nigga crazy? I know Essence said his lawsuit was for a lot of money, but I didn't want anything from him. I took my seat belt off and hopped out the bus.

"Ugh, I think you forgot this." He looked down at it and smiled.

"Is your name April?"

"Yes."

"Then I didn't forget anything. It belongs to you for helping with my daughter."

"It was no bother. But I can't accept this," I handed it back to him and started walking back to the bus.

"You can and you will."

I turned around and stared in his face. I snatched the envelope from him and walked over to his car. Lexi rolled the window down and I handed her the envelope. He sat in the car, looking down at his phone. I guess he didn't realize I gave it to her because he pulled off when I left. I ran to the bus and pulled off. I saw he stopped in the middle of the road and my phone started ringing.

"Girl, why don't you just take the money?"

"I don't want it, Essence." She blew out a breath and told me she would call me back. A minute later, I saw him pull off. I guess she told him what I said.

"You didn't even tell me he was taking the kids off the bus," I yelled in the phone when she called me back.

"I forgot to call you. He came over yesterday and I got sidetracked. But girl, he fine as hell isn't he?"

"Hell yeah. Damn, I didn't know he was that fine up close."

"Yeah, well be prepared to see him all the time."

"Why is that?"

"Because he'll be staying with us for a month until his house is ready."

"That's ok. I can look without touching." She and I stayed on the phone for a while.

I parked the bus in my driveway, jumped in my 2015 Altima, and went to the shop in Neptune to get my hair done. Essence and I were going to some club called Level 10 out in

Orange, NJ.

After the shop, I picked up some Taco Bell on the way home and went to my closet to find something to wear. You were supposed to dress up to go to this club, but the first time we went people were dressed in whatever they wanted. I wasn't about to go all out this time when the people there didn't.

I put on a denim short romper with some black wedges. My hair hung down my back and I wore some lip-gloss and eyeliner.

I drove over to Essence house and blew the horn because I didn't feel like getting out. She stepped out rocking a black dress with silver heels and her makeup and hair were on fleek, too.

"Stacy let you out dressed like that."

"Hell no. Bitch, he downstairs getting high with his brother and Derrick. You know damn well I wouldn't be able to leave the house." We both laughed and headed to our destination.

It took us about forty minutes to get there. Thank

goodness the line wasn't that long yet. We paid for VIP so that we didn't have a bunch of people hovering over us. A few of our other girls came over to our section when they saw us.

The music was playing, the drinks were flowing, and the niggas were everywhere. I started feeling a little tipsy, but I swore I heard the DJ give a shout out to Kane and his brother Stacy. Essence looked at me with this sneaky ass grin on her face.

"Bitch, you knew they were coming here?"

She put her hands up in surrender. I watched the bitches flock to their VIP section. I mean, they were all over Kane like he was a damn celebrity and he loved that shit.

"Damn, that nigga fine as hell," Sherri said. She was one of the other chicks that Essence rolled with.

The DJ started playing *Back to Sleep* by Chris Brown and all of us jumped on the dance floor. We were all screaming, "*Fuck you back to sleep*" with our hands in the air when I felt someone staring at me. I looked around and it was Stacy's brother. He had a drink in his hand and a chick in front of him trying to get his attention.

"I'm about to fuck with your brother-in-law," I yelled in Essence's ear.

"Don't do it to him, girl."

"He wants to stare. I'm going to give him something to stare at."

"Ok, now. Don't hurt him."

I went to the DJ and asked him to play *Slow Dance* by Keri Hilson. When the song came on, I heard the DJ announce that Kane had a treat coming his way. I'd been taking pole and exotic dancing classes but never performed in front of anyone. This will be my first time.

The music started playing and everyone watched me seductively stroll over to him. Our eyes locked and he moved the chick out of the way that was on his lap.

Put your arms around me boy, I got something to show you, tonight,

And you know I need your undivided attention baby, ain't no other girl can rock your world like I, so, rewind, make this moment last forever, feels like your body's calling me, but I don't want to come on too strong, but something happens when we slow dance.

I stood in front of him and my body moved with the beat. I pushed him back on the chair and straddled his lap. I leaned all the way back and allowed my bottom half to grind on his dick. I felt how hard he was getting, lifted myself up, bent down and shook my ass in his face. I had him stand back on his feet, lifted one of my legs and rested it on his shoulder. I did so much freaky shit to him I surprised myself.

"Yo, you better take her ass home tonight," I heard some guy yell out. As the song came to an end, I pulled his face to mine and licked his lips with my tongue. He tried to put his tongue in my mouth. I moved back and shook my finger in his face.

"No thanks. That was a welcome home gift for you," I kissed his cheek and walked out of their VIP section.

"Damn. Now that's the type of welcome home gift I want to come home to," the DJ said on the microphone, making everybody yell out.

"You didn't have to do him like that," Sherri said, sipping her drink.

"You're right. But maybe that will stop him from staring.

"Ugh, no it didn't. Here he comes."

"Let me talk to you for a minute," he took my hand in his and had me walk outside with him. People kept speaking and welcoming him home.

"Why did you do that?"

"Oh. You didn't like it?"

"I didn't say that, but what you do for me should be in private." I threw my head back laughing.

"That's a one-time thing boo. You were staring and it's your welcome home gift."

"I appreciate it, but I don't ever want to see you shaking your ass like that for me in public, or for anyone else."

"You're bugging."

I tried to leave and he grabbed me. I tried to push myself away from him, but his lips found mine. He separated them and made our tongues dance to a beat I'd never heard. I couldn't front, this man's kissing game had my panties wet as hell. I had my arms around his neck and didn't want to let go.

"You're mine from now on." I just shook my head. We both went back inside and went our separate ways.

"What the hell, girl?"

I picked my drink up and listened to Essence and Sherri go back and forth about her trying to get with Kane. I felt him staring most of the night, and even though I knew this wouldn't go anywhere, I fantasized about how it would be to have a man. It'd been so long I forgot what it felt like to even wake up next one.

****

My alarm had gone off around nine because I'd promised Essence I would do some running around with her. I threw on a sundress with sandals and my sunglasses.

I went to her house, knocked on the door, and to my surprise, ran into Kane walking some chick out the house. His eyes grew big when he saw me. I smiled and spoke to him and the chick. He didn't owe me shit, but this right here let me know he wasn't where I needed to be.

"What's up, April?" He came in the kitchen and grabbed some food from the pan I assumed Essence had cooked.

"Nothing much. I see you enjoyed your night?"

"You can say that, but it wasn't with who I wanted it to be with," he smirked and placed eggs and bacon on a piece of bread.

"I'm sure you had a variety of choices last night. Who was the woman you would've chosen?"

"You."

"Boy, you don't even know me."

He put his fork down and walked around the island to where I was sitting. He parted my legs and stood between them.

"I'm far from a boy and I don't have to know you to tell you I like what I see and what I've heard about you."

"You're only saying that because I danced for you."

"That dance definitely had my dick brick hard. But one thing about me that you'll learn soon enough is, I always, and let me emphasize, always. I ALWAYS get what I want."

He lifted my chin and covered my mouth with his. I felt his hands sliding up my dress to touch my center. The panties I had on were being moved to the side by his fingers.

“Mmmmm. Not gonna happen partner,” I pushed him away from me.

“It will happen. Give it time, baby girl.”

He kissed my cheek and went back to finish eating. I know my face was bright red from blushing and I was positive if I hadn’t moved him, he would’ve had me face down, ass up in the room. Essence walked in the kitchen and glanced at both of us.

“It’s about time.” I said rolling my eyes. I needed to get out of there fast.

“Yeah ok. It looks like I should’ve taken a little longer. Your nipples are hard and I can see the lust in your eyes.”

When she said that, my mouth fell open. Kane was smiling hard as hell.

“I can’t stand you. Let’s go,” I snatched her hand and dragged her out to my car.

“What?” she tried to use an innocent voice.

“What my ass. You tried to call me out in front of him. You’re supposed to be my friend. Where the fuck they do that at?” I looked over and the bitch was just about crying from laughing so hard.

"It's about time somebody got your celibate ass hot and bothered. Girl, you know he's been away for a long time. He has nothing but time and energy to give. I'm sure he will *knock the dust off that pussy*," she said, mocking Smokey from *Friday*.

"Fuck you, bitch."

"You better hurry up and lock him down. You know Sherri was stalking the shit out of him last night. Do you know the bitch had the nerve to text me like five times already this morning? Asking me does he have a girl? Is he staying at my house? Can she come over? Would I be mad if she fucked him in my house?"

"No the fuck she didn't ask you that."

"Bitch, yes. I told that bitch do not text my phone with no nonsense like that."

"I've never known Sherri to be that thirsty over a nigga."

"That's because she hasn't been. But she knows that not only does he have money and respect, but he has power and she wants to be the queen of his kingdom. She's right in thinking he's the man to help her get that status, but I'm not sure she's the one for him."

"Is it really that serious?"

"For her it is."

I shook my head and continued driving. I didn't know Sherri like that because she was more of Essence's friend than mine. Essence and I had been best friends for years, but when you work and go to school, you meet different people and that's what happened. She's cool when we go out but I don't trust her, and never have. She fucks with Erica, who is Kane's baby mother on a regular. So, her trying to get at Kane shows me she is definitely a grimy bitch.

Chapter 5

Kane

April can play that hard roll all she wants but I know she wants a nigga, just like that thirsty bitch Sherri does. I peeped home girl last night at the club stalking me. I noticed her watch me get up to use the bathroom after April danced for me and gestured for her to come follow me. There was a bathroom with a few stalls and then there was a private one. I knocked on the door and when no one answered. I guided her inside.

"What's up? Why are you watching me like I'm your man?" I asked, while I was taking a piss. She stood their looking at my dick with lust in her eyes. I finished, zipped my jeans up, and washed my hands. Home girl was still standing there with her mouth hanging open.

"I think you're very sexy and I want to get to know you better."

She pushed me up against the wall and lifted her shirt over her head. My dick instantly bricked up, but I couldn't take it there with her. I didn't have any condoms and I didn't fuck in public bathrooms unless it was with my girl and we were on some freaky shit. That way, it didn't matter if I strapped up because she was my woman.

"Not here. Put your number in my phone and I promise you'll hear from me."

She put her shirt back on and took my phone to store her number. I opened the door and Stacy was standing there waiting to use it. He looked at her, then me, then back at her, and started laughing. I sent Sherri upstairs and waited for my brother to finish.

"She ain't waste no time, did she?" Stacy came out of the bathroom and tossed his paper towel in the trash. He hated touching doorknobs after he washed his hands. He would dry his hands off and open the door with the paper towel. I didn't say anything because I was the same way. If there were no paper towels, we would use our shirt. Call us crazy, but everybody didn't wash their hands. This world was full of nasty motherfuckers.

"Nah, I didn't even let it go down like that."

"I bet she tried it."

"Yeah, she did, but I didn't have a cover and I'm not having kids with no one else that ain't my wife or close to being her."

"I hear you." We went back to our seats and enjoyed the rest of the night.

When I saw April coming in while I was escorting whatever her name was out the door this morning, I was shocked. It's not like I was busted for cheating or anything. It had me feeling some sort of way because I kissed her last night, which surprised me because I never ever put my lips on a woman. I didn't know how many dicks they'd sucked before me, and I didn't want any nasty ass cold sores on my mouth.

For some reason, the way April's lips felt made me want to kiss her forever. I tasted the liquor and lip-gloss she had on. I was adamant about making her mine. I just didn't want to hurt her, so I'd decided to leave her alone until I was ready to commit.

I could tell when I was between her legs in the kitchen, she would be the type of woman that was going to make me work to get the pussy. I needed to get all the fucking out my system, then step to her correctly. Don't get me wrong, though. If she offered, I would definitely take it.

"Where you about to go?" I heard Stacy asking on my way out the door.

"I'm going by Erica's house. She got my number, probably from ma, when she heard I was home. I want to hear what the fuck she has to say."

"Nigga, do you need me to go with you? I'm not about to go bail you out of jail."

"Nah, I'm good. I probably just fuck her one more time for old time's sake anyway." My brother laughed and went in the kitchen.

****

I pulled up to some mini-mansion out in Shrewsbury and parked in the front. The house was something I would live in, but it had too many damn trees in the front. I rang the doorbell and had to catch my balance when Erica jumped in my arms. She hugged me tight then pulled back to kiss me. I turned my head and put her down. These chicks were bugging with trying to play this kissing game.

"Really, Kane?"

She stood there with her hands on her hips looking sexy as hell. Erica was a beautiful Dominican chick with a body these women out here were killing themselves to get. She only stood about five-foot-four and had brown eyes, but for some reason they were blue today. Her chest was always a D size and she had no stomach. Looking at her you would never know she'd had a kid. She was the woman I'd planned on marrying until she bounced a year after I got locked up.

You see, I told Erica when I first got locked up to move on with her life because I didn't know how long I was going to be on lockdown. She told me that's not what she wanted and that she could wait.

After the first year, the visits stopped, no more letters came, and she changed her phone number. I thought that she'd finally taken my advice and moved on. I was ok with that, but what I had a major problem with was the fact she passed my daughter off to my brother and his wife to go shack up with the next nigga. I may not have wanted my daughter around another nigga, but I wouldn't stop her mother from being happy, either.

Last year, my brother came to see me and told me the foul shit she had going on. Erica was an ex-stripper going to school by the time she and I had met. I appreciated her hustle to try and better herself and stay out of strip clubs.

We hit it off and I paid all her school tuition and took care of her. Eventually, she got pregnant and lost the urge to finish school and instead sat back, spending my money. That was never a problem since she was going to be my wife. The day I got arrested in California she told me she was pregnant again. The conversation was never finished because the Feds came in.

"Really."

"Are you going to come in?"

She stepped aside for me. The house was nice on the inside as far as the decorations, but it was dirty as hell. Clothes were everywhere, along with trash in the living room and kitchen. I didn't understand this because she'd never lived like this when I was around. I shook my head as she walked in front of me, switching extra hard.

"Whose house is this?"

"Mine."

"Yours? Where did you get this kind of money from?"

"Does it matter?"

"Not really."

I knew it wasn't my money, because even though she was about to be my wife, the fact remained that she wasn't. I never told her where my stash was and because of it, I still had it, along with my lawsuit money.

She opened up the bedroom door, and believe it or not, this was the only place that was spotless. The king-sized bed was made with some satin sheets and a comforter folded over at the bottom. The floor looked freshly vacuumed and the dressers didn't have anything on them but a few beauty products.

I sat down on the bed, pulled the black and mild from behind my ear, and lit it. She went in the bathroom, and a few minutes later came out dressed in her birthday suit. I couldn't front, her body was still bad as hell. She stepped in front of me and kneeled down. I blew smoke out my mouth as I watched her unbuckle my jeans and pull my man out. She always knew how to give good head, so I was about to enjoy this moment.

"Suck that dick like you missed it." She moved her head down and my entire dick disappeared.

"Yeah, just like that. Make my dick cum." I leaned back and closed my eyes when I felt my nut coming to the top. The chick I'd slept with last night didn't know how to suck my dick so this right here had a nigga gone. I didn't moan out or give her any indication I was about to cum and let it spit down her throat.

"Hold the fuck up," I said when she slid down on my still erect dick.

"Don't you like the way I feel?" she said, grinding in circles on my shit.

"Shit, Erica! I need to put a condom on."

"A condom for what, baby? I'm your daughter's mother," she whispered in my ear and popped harder on me. I had to be strong and stop this before it went any further. Oh, I was going to continue to fuck her, but not without being covered. I had no idea who she'd been sleeping with, or if she had something. I got a clean bill of health before I came from

California, and there was no way I was about to let any woman out here change my status.

I lifted her up, snatched a condom out my pocket, slid it on, and had her screaming to the High and Mighty. I beat that pussy up so bad she got up and fell to the floor.

"Dammit, Kane. You didn't have to be so rough. What happened to making love to me?" I laughed as I tossed the condom in the toilet. I noticed some blood on it and shook my head. She wasn't ready for the beating I just gave her.

"You're not my girl. Why would I make love to you?"

"You don't have to be someone's man to not be rough in bed."

"You're right. If you want to know why I fucked you and didn't take my time, that's different. But you asked me why I didn't make love to you."

"How is it different, Kane?"

"It's different because when I make love to a woman, I put my all in it. I make sure I hit spots she didn't even know existed until she loses her breath. I love staring into her eyes and watching the facial expression she makes when I'm doing it. There's also that intense feeling and connection she and I will have while we're taking each other to another place. I'm letting her know I'm in love with everything about her and pleasing her is my top priority." She sucked her teeth.

"Taking my time is still like fucking just not as fast, and I could care less if I'm hitting every spot. You will get what you get and be happy with it. I'm surprised you're asking me that when you, of all people, know that firsthand." She rolled her eyes.

"You're not in love with me anymore, Kane?"

"I will always have love for you because you had my daughter, but how can a man be in love with a woman who gave her kid away? Now that I think about it, where is the baby you claimed you were pregnant with before I went to jail?"

"Why the fuck do you care?"

"Bitch, because if you had another baby by me, I wanna know why you didn't mention it." I was standing over her in the bed.

"I got rid of it Kane. You know if I had another baby your family would've told you."

"That's some foul shit, Erica." I started walking out the door.

"How is that foul? Huh? You were in jail and I didn't want to raise another baby alone," She was following behind me, screaming.

"You wouldn't have been alone. You know I had money and my family would've helped you, just like they did with Lexi. Don't come to me with that bullshit."

"Your family was not the child's father, you were."

"You know what Erica? You selfish as fuck. I wish I would've known that before I let my seeds off in you."

"I'm coming to get Lexi today."

"I wish the fuck you would. Plus, she has a mother who loves and takes good care of her when you dropped her off." I knew that would hurt her.

"No other bitch is going to have my daughter calling her mommy. Not even Essence stuck up ass."

"I'm gonna act like you didn't say that."

"Why not?"

"If it weren't for Essence and my brother taking her in,

where would she have gone? My parents were done raising their kids. They would've taken her if they had to but you put my family in a position to raise a child that wasn't theirs. Yes, she is mine, but I was out of commission and where were you? Right here being a selfish bitch."

"Whatever. She is still my child and I'm coming for her."

"You know what Erica, I'm going to allow you to spend time with her and get to know her better. If, and only if, she decided she wants to come home to you, then we'll share custody. But I want you to remember two things," I walked up on her so she could feel my breath.

"One, the reason you want her back better be because you really love and miss her and not because you think I'm giving you money. And two, she won't step foot in this house until you clean it up."

"Like I said," she tried to get away and I backed her up against the wall.

"And like I said, until you can abide by what the fuck I just said, you better not step foot in my brother's house."

"You're talking about me having her live with someone else and you are doing the same thing."

"You're a dumb bitch. I stay there too, until I get a new place. Unlike you, my daughter is my top priority."

I slammed the door in her face and continued walking to my car. What was supposed to be me getting a quick nut and enjoying the rest of my day turned into her pissing me off and making me want to kill her. How the fuck did she get rid of my kid and not even tell me? That's some crazy shit.

Chapter 6

Erica

When Kane left, I ran upstairs to jump in the shower and get dressed. I was taking my ass over to Essence's house and see who the hell this woman was so-called raising my daughter. Yeah, I gave her to his brother, but that's because I'd met a dude who didn't want any kids. I knew I wasn't shit, but truth be told, I never wanted kids in the first place. Kane had so much money and power, all I wanted to do was spend it and be treated like royalty. Unfortunately, he got knocked on some bogus charge and I found myself alone, raising a child I didn't want.

That girl was his pride and joy and believe it or not, I was jealous of how much he loved her. I never had to share my man's love and to see it happen with a baby, and not another woman, made me feel like shit. I probably should've spoken to him about it, but I didn't want to sound like a nagging bitch. His mother hated me and his brother's girlfriend always turned her nose up at me. I never did anything to them so I had no idea why they had animosity towards me.

I threw some black jeans on and a red shirt with some black red bottom shoes. My hair was in a ponytail and I put some makeup on.

"Where you going?" I heard his voice coming in the room.

"I'm about to go pick Lexi up. I'll be back in an hour."

He pulled me down on his lap and put his pinky finger to my nose. I loved this man like crazy. I didn't even have to ask for the white girl. He would always know when it was needed.

"You need me to go with you? I know that punk ass nigga Kane home."

"Nah, baby. I'm just picking her up and coming back. Can you call the maid service and have them come straighten up? Your boys left a mess downstairs."

"I got you babe." He lifted me up and smacked me on my ass.

"See you in a few."

I rode over to Stacy's house and saw that Kane wasn't home. I knocked on the door and some high yellow bitch I didn't know opened it. I looked her up and down. I'm no lesbian chick, but the girl was bad as hell.

She had on a sundress that clung to her body, showing off her shape. Her hair was flowing down her back and she didn't have a lot of makeup on; yet, she was still gorgeous. Yeah, I was hating on her already. I knew if Kane saw her, he would try and wife her up because she was definitely his type.

I may have a man, but he didn't hold as much power and respect as Kane. Nor did he have that kind of money. If Kane told me he wanted to be with me tomorrow, I would be out.

"Can I help you?" she said and smiled. *Damn, she even has a nice smile.* I couldn't believe I was standing here staring at this woman and getting mad because she was prettier than me. I instantly caught an attitude and pushed past her.

"Hold the fuck up." She caught me off-guard with that response. I turned around and she was putting her hair up in a ponytail.

"You're going to step your ass back outside and tell me what you're here for, or I'm about to beat that ass." She kicked her wedges off and started towards me.

"Erica." She stopped when Essence called my name.

"You know this bitch?" she said, still staring me down.

"Yeah that's-"

"Mommy," Lexi came running in and jumped in my arms. I saw the look on the face of the girl who'd opened the door. It was like she was hurt and wanted to say something but kept it to herself.

"Does Kane know you're here?" Essence asked me with her arms folded up.

"It's ok, auntie. Daddy doesn't mind if mommy comes to see me."

"Lexi, I came to take you home with me." Her eyes lit up and she took off running and screaming that she'd be back with her stuff.

"Now you wait a fucking minute Erica. I don't know what type of game you're playing, but Kane hasn't said anything to me about you coming to get her."

"Essence I'm her mother. I don't need permission to take her."

"Let me call him then and see what he has to say about it."

"Be my guest. But you see, after I fucked him not too long ago, he left his phone. Be a doll and make sure he gets it." I tossed it on the couch and saw the chick roll her eyes and Essence picked the house phone up.

"Yes, can you send an officer to my house? I have a woman here trying to kidnap my niece without her father's permission." I couldn't believe she called the cops on me.

"Tsk, tsk, tsk. Essence you should know better than that. You know the cops aren't going to be any help." Just as I said that, I saw two officers walking in. Damn they got here fast as hell. But in this white neighborhood they lived in, I see why.

"What's the problem, ma'am?"

I listened to Essence tell the officer she's been taking care of my daughter for the last six years and how I just came by to take her back.

"Do you have any custody or guardianship papers?" the officer asked and Essence shook her head no.

"I understand your concern and frustration right now,

Ms. Miller, but unless you have court documents proving you're her guardian, her mother has every right to take her."

"You're kidding me, right?" the other chick said.

"No, sweetie, he's not. Lexi is my child and if I want her to come home with me, she can. Now if you'll excuse us, we have a date at the park."

"Mommy, we're going to the park? Am I living with you again? Can my daddy come by and visit?" She was dropping question after question, pissing me the fuck off. Granted, I didn't really want her, but if this was the only way to keep Kane around, then it was what it was. I took her to the park, and then we went to the mall to get something to eat like I promised. It was getting late and my high was coming down.

I was pulling into my driveway and noticed Kane was sitting outside his car. I was scared as hell and called 911. I gave them my address and kept them on the phone.

"Hey daddy." She went running to him. He picked her up and put her in his car.

"Kane, that's my daughter and the cops said I can take her."

“Is this some type of fucking joke to you, Erica? You haven’t seen or talked to her in years. Then you go to my brother’s house and think its ok to take her.”

“Kane, I have seen her.” I only saw her if I ran into one of them and they had her. I would play the devoted mother, but I made sure I never brought her home with me. Actually, I was surprised she remembered who I was when I got there. But they say a child always knows their mother.

“Get the fuck out my face Erica. I told you when your house is clean and I check it out along with whatever nigga you fuck with, then she can come over. Until then, my daughter is coming him with me.”

“The house is clean and she’s not going anywhere.” I started smelling myself when I heard the cop sirens getting closer. He looked around me and had a devilish grin on his face.

“Oh, you called the cops on me?”

“Yup. I knew you would try some dumb shit.” The cops got out the car and I watched Kane take Lexi out the car.

“Why are the cops here daddy?”

"Don't worry about it baby. I'm coming to get you in the morning. I don't care who she calls."

He kissed her cheek, got in his car, and sped off. I thought the cops would chase him, but they didn't. I brought her in the house and Glenn was sitting on the couch in just some boxers. I introduced him to my daughter and told her to go find one of the rooms she wanted to stay in. I needed to get high and right now she was in the way.

****

Weeks went by and Kane was persistent in getting Lexi back. The only thing was he had just gotten out of prison and the judge was giving him a hard time. He was allowed to visit her at my house on Saturdays only. I let him take her whenever he felt like it, though. My man acted like he wasn't beat for her to stay with us. I really wasn't either, but a bitch was about to get paid.

"It's time Erica," I heard him say. I had been ignoring his ass for a week. I knew what he wanted, but there was no way.

"No Glenn. I think you should leave and not come

back."

"Oh, you don't want me anymore?"

"I can't be with a man who is making a request like that. You need help."

I felt his fist connect with my jaw and I swear it was broken. He'd smacked me around a few times before, but nothing like this. I felt his feet connecting to my ribs over and over. I must've passed out because I woke up to my daughter crying for her dad.

"Daddy come save me. Where is my daddy?" I tried to get up and go in her room, but my body was refusing me. I was able to move slowly and slide across the ground and to her room, which, thank goodness was next door.

"Shut up little girl, and put it in your mouth," I heard when I pushed the door open.

"No!" I watched him smack her then force it in her mouth. She instantly vomited and so did I. He turned around and came to where I was.

"Get your ass up and clean my dick off since the little bitch threw up on it."

He dragged me back in the room and I heard my daughter scream out for me. I didn't care what he did to me as long as he left my daughter alone.

"Call your father, Lexi," I yelled out and he went running to her room.

"If you even think about mentioning this to your dad, or anyone else, I will kill you, him, and your mother," I heard him yelling while I laid there feeling like I was dying. What the hell did I get my daughter into? Trying to be spiteful, I probably just traumatized her for the rest of her life. Kane was going to kill me if he found out and at this moment, I deserved it.

Chapter 7

April

Ever since the day that stupid bitch of a mother came and took Lexi away, I'd been so depressed. She wasn't my daughter, but I loved that little girl and SJ as if they were my own. I would lay my life on the line for them. Essence had told me Kane was bringing her over a few days out the week. I would stop by and see her, but then the mother would call requesting her to come back home because they had so-called plans.

Kane was distraught over the fact Erica was being this petty because he didn't want her. All he wanted to do was sit back and take care of his daughter and businesses. The shit his baby momma was doing had him going crazy.

Today was the barbeque that was planned for when he first got home. Unfortunately, the day after he came home, the shit happened with Erica. He was a little relieved she was allowing her to come today. He and I had become cool and we would talk on the phone late nights. He would ask me things about Lexi growing up over the last couple years.

The love that man had for his daughter was genuine and every man who had a child could take pointers. Of course, his nasty ass would flirt, but I paid him no mind. Well, I tried not to anyway. I found myself falling for him, but no one knew besides Essence and I wanted to keep it that way

Essence had called and asked me to stop by the store and pick up some liquor and a few other things. I pulled up at her house and stepped out of my car in my white shorts that came to my thighs and a yellow halter-top. I hated those high-waisted jeans and shorts, so I opted out for ones that were different, but just as cute. I had on some yellow knee-high shoes that strapped all the way up. My hair was down and my makeup was non-existent. I didn't like that shit, but occasionally I wore eyeliner.

I walked in the house and there were people everywhere, inside and out. Stacy came in and gave me a hug, and Essence pulled me to the side.

"I know you don't care, but Sherri is here and for some reason Kane is being attentive to her. I'm not sure if they're a couple, because when I asked her, she smiled and walked away."

"It's ok, sis. All he and I did was kiss. No feelings were attached to that kiss, so I'm good."

She gave me the side eye. I loved how my best friend looked out for me. She and I sat up on the phone discussing that kiss just the other day. I told her how much I enjoyed it and was feeling him. If Kane ever tried to kick it to me, I would probably go with it. I could see why she told me before I saw them, and I totally respected it.

"Essence I'm about to go outside. You coming?"

She picked her cup up and followed behind me. There were people swimming, dancing, and laid back on the lawn chairs. I spotted Kane laid back on one of them with Sherri between his legs. A twinge of jealousy shot through me. I damn sure wished it were me, but I wasn't going to hate on Sherri because he chose her. I would never hate on another woman over a man. Well, I can't stand Erica, but that's for a different reason.

"Hey, April," Sherri called out and Kane turned his head. I saw him lick his lips and look me up and down. If I were a grimy bitch, I would wait until she wasn't looking and have him meet me in the house.

"Hey Sherri. Hi Kane. Aren't you two cozy?" Essence and I sat next to them. Kane lifted himself up a little and Sherri looked as if she was bothered by it.

"What's up, April?" I heard someone clear their throat, and of course it was Sherri.

"Since the crew is here, I want to be the first to tell you that Kane and I are a couple now."

I saw his face and I could tell he was mad that she'd announced it. He excused himself and told her to go with him.

"Let's go be nosy," Essence said, hopping up off the chair and grabbing me with her.

"Yo, why the fuck would you tell them we're a couple?" You could hear Kane yelling from the room.

"Why not? We've been sleeping together for the past few weeks and you basically live with me. You told me I couldn't sleep with anyone else, so what's the big deal?"

"The big deal is if I didn't ask you to be my girl, don't go around claiming me. I don't care if you fuck with other niggas. You be making shit up for real. Yeah, I been fucking you, but there's a million bitches out there I can sleep with. Look, it's obvious you're feeling this sleeping together situation more than I am. We need to take a break."

"What?"

"I'm not into you like that and I doubt if I ever will be. You need to find a man that will be with you for the long run."

"Kane, hold up."

"What?" You could still hear them arguing.

"Well, alright then."

I looked at Essence and we both busted out laughing. Everyone was looking around to see where it was coming from. They stopped when they heard it was Kane's voice. No one got involved when it came to him for some reason.

"All the shit she talks and he ain't even claiming her ass."

"You ain't shit, April."

"Hey. I call it how I see it," I put my hands up and headed back in the kitchen to grab something else to drink.

I was sitting down talking to some guy who was fine as

hell. He was brown-skinned with dreads, had a nice smile, and his muscles were busting out his tank top. We were chopping it up when Kane finally came back out. Sherri was still following behind him like a lost puppy. That nigga must have the bomb dick if she's on his ass.

"Let me talk to you right quick April."

I glanced up at him and used my hand to shield the sun from my eyes. Sherri had her arms folded like she had an attitude.

"What's up Kane? Everything ok?" Me not knowing why he asked to speak to me in such a rude manner was bothering me.

"Yeah, I just need to talk to you about Lexi." Once he said that, I jumped up and excused myself from the guy.

"I'll call you later," I told the dude and he nodded. I felt Kane burning a hole in my back as we walked in the house.

"Yo, go the fuck back outside. I don't need you following me around," he barked at Sherri and she did what he said.

He led me in one of the other rooms and stepped out.

He came back a few minutes later with a towel and some clothes. He asked me to stay in the room because he wanted to speak to me about something dealing with his daughter. I was mad as hell I listened to his ass, because when he came out dripping, my pussy was so wet I had to excuse myself to clean up.

"I have that effect on all the women." I stuck my middle finger up and sat next to him on the bed.

"What you want with your ignorant ass?"

"You."

I turned my head to look at him and he moved in closer. He separated my lips once again with his tongue and took over. He sucked on my top lip, then bottom. He sucked on my tongue, and then kissed me hungrily again. I had no business allowing this man to do anything with me, being I'd just heard Sherri say they were together.

He pulled my body on top of his in a straddling position. He kissed and sucked on my neck and removed my halter-top. His hands were caressing my breasts so gently, I didn't want him to stop.

“Let me taste you,” he whispered in my ear. I should’ve said no, but my body was saying something else. He stood up with me on his lap and flipped me over on my back.

“Kane this is not right. You were just with the other chick.”

He ignored me, kissed on my stomach, and slid my shorts and panties down at the same time. His tongue glided up and down my lips and I felt my body about to give him what he wanted. He pushed my legs back and smiled as he stared at it. I was about to say something, but his mouth went back to work and caused me to shut my own.

“Kane. We have to stop,” I said and tried to move back. He had a death grip on my legs as he pulled out my two-year orgasm without my permission. My body was jerking and the second it stopped, he pulled out another one, and another one. I had the pillow over my head to keep from screaming. I wasn’t about to let people hear me like they’d heard him and Sherri arguing.

“I knew your pussy was worth the wait,” he whispered in my ear and before I was able to say something, he had already torn down my wall and welcomed himself into my tunnel. I couldn't lie, he was huge, and the width of it stretched me out. But when I got used to it, he took me to a place I hadn't been in a long time.

"Kane."

"Yeah baby."

"We have to stop," I moaned in his ear as I said it.

"I'm not about to stop fucking my woman."

He lifted my legs back and went deeper. I couldn't hold out any longer. I bit down on his shoulder and released all my juices on him.

"April, you know you're my woman now," he told me as he watched himself go in and out.

"You have someone."

"That bitch is a jump-off. I told you I was coming back for you and I always get what I want. And you're what I want."

"But Kane-"

"Stop fighting it April. No one is going to look at you twice once I make it known." I felt him getting harder which meant he's about to cum.

"I'm cumming again Kane."

"Me too. Cum with me."

He pounded harder and faster. We both came at the same time and laid there, drenched in sweat. We heard a knock at the door. He threw his pants on and went to answer it.

"Put some covers on." I did what he said and just laid there.

"Open the door nigga," I heard Essence say before she made her way in with us. He shut the door back and locked it.

"Did you two just fuck?"

"Yo, beat it Essence," he said, putting his shirt on. I went to get up and he came to where I was.

"Where you going?"

"Damn nigga, can she wash her pussy?"

"Essence, don't make me fuck you up."

"I'm going to wash up."

"I still wanna talk to you, and since Essence is in here with her nosy ass, she may as well listen too."

He was taking the sheets off the bed and Essence was bringing him a new set when I came out the bathroom. I was putting my shoes on when Sherri came busting in the room drunk. Kane was mad as hell.

"What y'all doing in here? And damn April, somebody fucked your neck up with those two hickeys."

I ran back in the bathroom to look. I bet Kane did it on purpose. I came back out and she was sitting on his lap and he didn't move her. See, this was the foolery I didn't want to deal with. How was he going to tell me I'm his girl and have some chick sitting on his lap?

"Sherri, we were in here talking about a private family matter. Can you excuse us for a minute?" Essence said, rolling her eyes at Kane.

"Kane hurry up. I wanna fuck," she tried to kiss him and he turned his head.

"Why don't you ever kiss me?" She was clearly drunk and starting to get in her feelings.

"I don't kiss a chick unless she's my girl. I told you that before. Why are you in here embarrassing yourself? Get the fuck outta here." I didn't understand that because he kissed me the first night we went out and I did that dance for him.

"Kane stop acting like that. You just told me I was your girl when we were arguing in the other room. Why you keep changing up on me?"

"Oh he did, huh? Sherri, I think you and him make a great couple. Hopefully, you two will settle down, have kids, and get married."

"I know right. The good thing is I'm already with him and pregnant. All I have to do now is get him to marry me." The look on Kane's face was priceless and should've been framed.

"Wow, Kane. You wasted no time," Essence said and grabbed me up out the room. I could hear him calling me, but I was in my own feelings. The tears started falling and I couldn't get to my car fast enough. Essence knew how I was and blocked him at the door until I'd had enough time to pull off.

"You ok, sis?" Essence said when I answered the phone.

"Yeah, I'm good. I don't know why I expected him to be different. I deserved what I got because she had him first. I had no business sleeping with that man."

"April right now he is cursing her ass out."

She put the phone to where they were, and I could hear him saying she wasn't his girl and it can't be his baby because he always strapped up. I didn't give a fuck. This entire situation was messy and all I wanted to do was go home, sip on some wine, and go to sleep.

****

I pulled up at the convenience store to grab some lottery tickets. I wasn't rich like my friends. I had a good paying job, but I didn't have any money in my bank account for a rainy day that's for sure. I was hoping to win the mega millions, or even the Powerball, so I could bounce.

I came out the store and heard crying coming from the side of it. I went to see who it was with my pepper spray in my hand and lost it when I noticed the person.

"Lexi?"

She looked up with tears in her eyes and reached for me. I picked her up and she winced out in pain. I put her in the front seat and that's when I saw the blisters on her lip and the bruises on her body. I picked my phone up to call Kane, but she stopped me.

"Please don't call my daddy."

"Lexi, I have to get you to the hospital. What happened to you baby?" I felt myself crying looking at her.

"He's going to kill us if I tell. Please don't call him."

She was crying, I was crying. I didn't know what to do. The only thing that was on my mind was getting her help. I called my mother and asked her to meet me at the hospital around the corner from her house. My mom lived an hour away from me. I knew it was going to take a long time to get to her, but I had to. My mom was the supervisor of nurses at the hospital, and I knew they wouldn't ask questions if she brought her in.

"Oh my God, April! What happened to her?" My mom had two nurses out there when I pulled in the ER.

They rushed Lexi inside and I told my mom all that I knew. We sat at the hospital for over an hour before the doctor came out and asked my mom and I to go into the family room. She told him I was her daughter and Lexi was her granddaughter.

I told him how she was supposed to be staying the night

with a friend and called me to pick her up. My phone started going off back to back from Essence and Kane. I wasn't sure if they knew, so I shut it off.

"Ms. Brown, your granddaughter is a victim of sexual abuse."

I passed out on the floor. I woke up to my mom and the doctor fanning me and offering me water.

"Ms. Brown, whoever did this to her had herpes and that's what the blisters are on her mouth. She also had slight vaginal bleeding, but her hymen wasn't broken. Her ribs are bruised and will take some time healing."

"WHAT?"

"I have to inform you that we did a rape kit on her but because I know your mom, I didn't contact social services."

"Thank you."

"Ms. Brown, whoever did this to her needs to be taken care of right away and put in jail? If you can get Lexi to talk, please let the authorities know before he can do this to another kid."

"How the hell could someone do this to a kid? She's

only six?"

"The person who did this must be a sick individual. I gave her a shot of penicillin and she is on a strong dose of pain medication. I want to keep her overnight, but I'm afraid someone will call Social Services on you. I am going to give your mom strict instructions on taking care of her. I will stop by, if that's ok, at your mom's house in a few days to check on her." My mom nodded her head.

"Can I see her?" I wiped my eyes and stood up.

"Yes. I am going to get the prescription written in your name because we both know you're not her mother." I was surprised when he said it.

"Oh girl relax. This is the man I've been dating, and he knows I don't have grandkids yet." I felt a sense of relief.

"Why didn't you say that in the beginning?"

We all laughed and he led us to Lexi. She was sleeping so peacefully. I wanted to call her father, but I'd promised I wouldn't.

We got the discharge papers and he carried her to the car for me. My mom told me to follow her home because it was too late to drive. Thank goodness I was off work for the summer. Here it was May, and I didn't have to go back until September. I planned on staying here the entire time to get my mind right.

Chapter 8

Kane

That bitch Sherri pissed me all the way off screaming out she was my girl and pregnant by me. I saw the way April looked when she said it and the hurt was all over her face. I had just sexed her down and now some chick claimed I said the same thing to her.

I could see jealousy in Sherri's face as she watched my girl put her shoes on. I also knew her ass wasn't fucking drunk, either. This wasn't the first time she'd pulled that stunt. That's why it was in the best interest for both of us to separate. I'd tried to run after April, but Essence blocked me and I didn't wanna push her. I told Sherri to get her shit and bounce.

"What the fuck you want and why isn't my daughter here yet?" I barked in the phone at Erica's stupid ass.

I had court on Monday and it was guaranteed that the judge was giving me full custody. It was hard at first because I was a convicted felon and my record hadn't been expunged yet. I had to pay q lotta money, but my daughter was worth it.

The reason I wanted to talk to April was because lately

Lexi had been acting very distant and I didn't know why. I knew the type of relationship they had and I wanted her to see if she could get it out of her.

"She's gone, Kane." I removed the phone from my ear.

"Who's gone?" I had a feeling but I needed her to say it in order for me to believe it. The barbeque was over and it was only Essence, Stacy, Derrick, and me in the house straightening up. We were all supposed to hit the strip club.

"Lexi. Kane, she's gone."

"What the fuck you mean she's gone?"

I saw everyone stop moving when I said it. I ran out the house and jumped in my car. I got to her house in less than ten minutes and she lived twenty minutes away. I hopped out and didn't notice that my brother and them were behind me. The cops were listening to Erica tell them how she had been in the shower because they had just come home. Then she'd gone downstairs to cook dinner. She never checked on Lexi because she assumed, she was in her room. When she went to get her for dinner, that's when she'd noticed she was missing. I knew her dumb ass was lying because the bitch didn't cook nor did it smell like any food was cooking. Lexi also knew not to wonder out alone, so who was she fooling?

"What the fuck really happened, Erica?" I yanked her dumb ass up when the cops left.

"I don't know Kane. I was in the shower and-"

"Don't tell me what you told the cops. Tell me the fucking truth."

She told me she was asleep and when she woke up Lexi was gone. I told Essence to call April and ask her to meet at my brother's, but she said there was no answer. I tried calling her until I'd noticed she'd shut the phone off.

All of us took separate cars and searched all over the city for her. I put a flyer with her picture on it, Essence posted it on Facebook and hundreds of people shared it. Not only was my daughter missing, but April had just dropped off the face of the earth too.

*****

It had been two months since my daughter disappeared and we still had no leads. I refused to give up. I still hadn't heard from April and I'm sure it's because she was hurt by what Sherri's stupid ass said. I was so used to speaking to her every night and now it was no communication at all.

My family was stressed out just as much as I was over Lexi being gone. You would think with the Facebook post and flyers out someone would have seen her but no one has. It made me believe whoever had Lexi took her into another state or was hiding her very well.

"You're going to find her," Sherri said. I laid back on the hotel bed because she was not allowed at my house and felt her sit on top of me. I was stressed the fuck out and about to give her the dick when my phone rang. I smiled when I noticed it was April.

"Yo, where are you?"

"Hello to you, too."

Her voice was sexy as hell in the phone. I knew I was feeling her from all the late-night phone calls. She was cool and always listened to me talk without any judgment. I'd had plans on taking her out and making her my woman, but things had changed.

"Stop playing. I got a lot of shit going on and I need

you right now." Sherri scrunched her face up, but I gave zero fucks at this moment.

"Kane, I'm sending you an address and I need you to get here as fast as you can without killing yourself. Bring Stacy, Essence, SJ, and your parents."

"Why do I need to bring all of them?"

"Trust me. You will need all the support you can get for what you find out."

"Alright. Send it to my phone."

"Kane."

"Yeah."

"Be careful."

"I will."

I caught myself smiling when she said that. I hit everybody up and told them we were leaving in twenty minutes. I had to drop Sherri off and pick my parents up. When I got there, my dad said he wanted to drive his car down to the address. If you'd asked me, I'd thought April called and set that up.

We got to the house an hour and a half later. Some

woman opened the door and resembled April like crazy. She called April down and disappeared.

"Hey guys."

"Bitch, you pregnant?" I heard Essence whisper and grinned. If she was, I knew damn sure it was mine.

"Hell no."

She shut the door and we all sat down in the living room. Her mom came back and introduced herself and then some guy came out introducing himself as a doctor. We were all nervous as hell, but my mom was the only one who seemed ok. *Does she know what's going on?* The doctor asked who everyone was and asked if we knew someone named Lexi. My heart immediately dropped when he asked that.

"Kane, you are going to have to be calm or this isn't going to work," April said to me in a low voice.

"What isn't going to work? What the fuck is going on?"

"Daddy."

Everybody turned to Lexi and she was coming in the room crying and reaching for me. I felt my eyes watering and ran to pick her up.

"Daddy missed you so much."

I hugged her so tight she was crying for me to put her down. Everyone did the same thing once I let go.

"April, you had my daughter this entire time and didn't say two fucking words? Do you know how hard we've been looking for her? What type of fuck shit you on?" I pulled my gun out and pointed it at her. My mom snatched Lexi and SJ up and went in the other room.

"Get that gun out my face, *right now*," she stood up and stared me in my eyes.

"Not until you tell me why you kidnapped my daughter."

"If I may, sir. If April didn't take your daughter when she did, I'm afraid she wouldn't be here." I pointed the gun at him.

"What are you talking about?"

"Put the gun down, bro," Stacy said and lowered my arm. April smacked the shit outta me.

"Don't you ever pull a gun out on me! Sit your ass down so I can tell you what the fuck really happened. You over here pulling a gun out on me and I'm the one that saved our daughter. I should smack you again."

She was talking shit but I liked how she said our daughter. She sat there and told me about the day she found her, how she had to take her to the hospital, and then how she promised my daughter she would keep her safe and not tell. I felt the tears rolling down my face as I heard she was sexually assaulted.

"Daddy are you ok now?"

"Yes, baby. Can you tell daddy what happened?"

"He said he would kill us if I told."

That shit hurt me to my soul after she told me what the nigga did to her. He violated her in the worst way and he was about to feel my wrath.

We stayed there a little longer and everyone left, but no one would allow me to go in their car. I didn't mind because I was able to spend time with my daughter.

"Come here, Kane," I heard April call out. She was on the back porch watching SJ and Lexi play.

"She's going to be ok. My mom has a therapist coming

to see her three times a week, and each day she's getting better.

"April, I appreciate everything you did for her. I swear I owe you my life for rescuing our daughter, but you should've called me."

"I wanted to keep her trust. I'm sorry."

"I'm sorry for pulling a gun out on you. I know you're the last person that would fuck me over."

"I'm pregnant Kane." I looked over at her with a grin on my face.

"Why did you tell Essence no?"

"I wanted you to know first. My mom doesn't even know yet."

"Are you keeping it?"

"I don't believe in abortions. Kane, I don't expect you to be with me just because I'm carrying your baby. I don't want you to think I need your money or anything from you. I just want you to be in the baby's life like you are with Lexi.

"I'm going to be in both of your lives so get ready for it."

She laughed and laid her head on my shoulder. We let

the kids stay out there a little longer to tire themselves out. April had both of them take showers and then eat dinner. After they went to bed, April was downstairs cleaning up and I was sitting on the couch, flipping though the television.

"Hi Kane," her mom took a seat next to me.

"Hi, Ms. Brown. I know I said it before, but I appreciate you helping April with Lexi."

"Oh please. You don't have to thank me. I've known Lexi for years and she's like my grandbaby. But that's not what I came in here for."

"Oh no."

"No. I want to know what's going on with you and my daughter. Now that she's pregnant, I'm hoping you stick around."

"No disrespect Ms. Brown, but April will never be alone. That's my girl and our daughter. Yes, I say our daughter because she has taken care of her for years when I couldn't, and her deadbeat mother wouldn't. I know it's early, but my feelings for her are very strong. The entire time those two were missing, they were all I thought about. My mother told me when I found the right one, I would know. I know she's the one and I'm not about to let her go." She nodded her head and smiled.

"How did you know she was pregnant? She said she told me first."

"Boy, please. She may have told you first, but I'm her mother. I heard her throwing up late nights and her ass and hips are spreading." I licked my lips when she said that, hoping she didn't catch me. I was definitely tearing her ass up later.

"She is getting thicker." I felt a mush in my head and it was her. I pulled her down on my lap.

"Alright you two. I'm going to my man's house. Lock up behind me and I will see you two tomorrow."

April kissed her mom and told her to call when she got there. I made sure she locked up and followed her upstairs. She had a huge bed and a bathroom in her room.

"Ma, you're about to be a grandma again," I was on the phone with my mother while April took a shower. I'd gotten in before her and I'm glad I did, because she took forever.

"I knew it. When I saw her, she was glowing. You

know all pregnant people have a glow around them. Are you excited? I am. Wait 'til I tell your father."

"Damn, ma. You would think you were having the baby."

"Shit, I'm waiting on Essence to pop out some more, too."

"So is Stacy," I told her, laughing.

"Kane."

"Yeah, ma?"

"She's a great woman. Be good to her."

"I know and I am. I know we haven't known each other that long, but she makes me wanna do better. After the way she protected Lexi, I know she'll do the same with the new baby."

"Good. How are you doing?"

"Ma, I'm trying to stay calm, but when I come back, I can't control what's going to happen."

"Son listen to me. You just found out you're going to be a father again. I know what happened, but right now the cops still think she's missing. Give yourself some time with Lexi and be there for her. She's still scared something is going to happen to you."

"I'll try."

April came out and dropped her towel to lotion up. She put her leg up on the vanity chair. She rubbed the lotion up and down, not paying me any mind.

"Ok, ma. I'm going to hang up now. April is calling me." Her eyes got big.

"Kane, I'm not a dummy. You're trying to feel inside your woman." I took the phone from my ear to make sure I'd heard her correctly.

"Bye, ma," I hung the phone up laughing.

April pushed me back on the bed and told me to move back. All I had on was a towel wrapped around my waist. She removed it and climbed on top. She stuck her tongue in my mouth and grinded on my dick at the same time. Her kisses were soft and sensual as she placed them on my neck and chest. I tried to pull her up when she got to my man, but she took him in without gagging. I watched her spit on it, use one hand to jerk it and the other to massage my balls. I felt like a bitch the way she had me gripping the sheets and saying her name. I didn't give a fuck. If it felt good, I was saying it.

"Give it to me Kane."

"Shit, April. What the fuck?" I wrapped my hand in her hair and pumped in her mouth until I released two months' worth of cum down her throat. My breathing was erratic and it took me a few minutes to get it back to normal. I was glad I hadn't slept with Sherri because what my girl just did was worth the wait.

"Sit on my face."

She moved up and I had her screaming for me to stop. That river she had in between her legs wouldn't stop overflowing and I caught every drop. I helped her slide off my face and climbed on top of her. I eased in slowly, and within minutes we were making love to each other. I made sure to hit every spot until she lost her breath.

"Kane."

"Yeah, baby?" I was stroking her real slow from the back. She sat up while I was still in her and pulled me in for a kiss. Her hand was massaging her clit and my hands were all over her chest.

"I missed you."

"I missed you, too. April, I've never had any pussy so good that I wanted to live in it." She chuckled and threw her ass back.

"I love you, Kane." I stopped stroking and flipped her back over.

"How much?" I grinned and slammed into her with her legs on my shoulder.

"A… Whole… Lot." I kept hitting that spot, making her voice disappear. I felt my dick twitching and went faster.

"Ahhh fuck, April. This is the best pussy I ever had. Damn, baby." I let my seeds swim inside of her. I moved the hair out of her face and kissed her lips.

"I love you too, baby. I'm sorry for the shit at the barbeque. You are the only woman I want to be with."

"You are the only man I want."

"I better be." She hit me in the arm. I felt my dick stiffening up again inside her.

"Can you handle another round?"

"The question is, can you?"

She and I went at it off and on for a few hours. By the time we went to bed, it was after three in the morning. We both showered and slept naked with just a cover. I looked down at her, and surprisingly she was staring up at me.

"Kane can you stay here another day?"

"Anything for you." I kissed her forehead, and in minutes we were both out like a light.

****

The one-day ended up being two weeks that SJ and I stayed there. I didn't mind because we got to know each other better and spent a lot of time with the kids. We took them to the movies, out to eat, bowling, the beach, and anywhere else they wanted to go. I'd planned on staying there as long as my daughter was there but she said she was ready to go back, but not to her mom.

I didn't have full custody of her yet, but the doctor gave me the papers from the ER and his home visits describing what had happened to her. I also got paperwork from the therapist who'd agreed to travel the hour, twice a week, to see her.

I faxed the papers to my lawyers so when I got home, I

would have custody. He'd also contacted the police department and told them Lexi was safe and they could take her off the missing children's list. Kids disappeared daily. I was just glad my girl was the one who found her and not some sick fuck.

"Daddy, where are we?" Lexi asked when we pulled up to the new house. April and SJ were just as shocked.

"This is your new house."

"Does mommy know where this is, or her boyfriend?" I pulled her close to me.

"Lexi that man will never hurt you again. As far as your mom, I don't think it's a good idea for her to know where you are."

"I don't think so either daddy."

We walked up to the door and I grabbed the key from the mailbox. Stacy had been by to make sure the furniture people could get in. I opened the door and Stacy, Essence, my parents, and Derrick all jumped out and said surprise. There was a *Welcome Home Lexi* banner, cake, and gifts for her. She ran and gave everyone a hug.

"Daddy which room is mine?" I led her upstairs and she

started screaming. She had pink everything, a huge television on the wall, and all new electronics. Her closet was stocked with clothes and shoes.

"That's nice, Lexi," SJ said, sounding a little upset. I picked him up and took him next door and he started yelling. His room was decorated in blue and he had the new game systems and electronics, too. I hadn't bought him as many clothes because Essence said her baby ain't going to be living here.

"Why did you do this?" April asked me sitting on the bed in the master bedroom crying. She had the deed to the house in her hand with both of our names on it and the keys to a brand new, 2017 Acura truck that she'd talked about wanting.

"Why not? You're my woman and this is your house."

"But we haven't known each other long."

"It doesn't matter April. You are my daughter's mother. You're going to be wherever we are. You don't like it?"

"I love it but..."

"Once you said you loved it, there was no need to finish. This baby has you being a crybaby. When I first met you, all you did was talk shit. Now I can't stop the waterworks. Give me a kiss." She stood up and kissed me.

"Bitch, if you don't want this Celine bag or these Prada shoes, I will gladly take them off your hands. Hold up, is that a Birkin bag? Oh, hell no. Stacy where the fuck is my bag like this?" Essence went yelling down the steps.

"Baby, I'm not into materialistic things. This stuff cost a lot of money and…"

"And nothing is too good for you. Stop pricing everything and enjoy it. I love you April. You and my kids can spend all my money and I wouldn't care."

"Well, there is one expensive thing I want."

"What's that?"

"I want a Michael Kors watch. I want it in rose gold."

"Baby, that's not expensive."

"Yeah, it is. It's two hundred and fifty dollars."

"Baby, the Birkin bag probably cost the same amount as ten of those watches."

"Oh. Ok. Well, I still want it."

I laughed and told her I was getting her a rose gold

watch, but it was going to be a more expensive one. She may not wanna spend my money, but I damn sure was going to spend it on her.

****

"What up, Stan?" I spoke in the phone, watching April look at her stomach in the mirror. She was three months and we had a doctor's appointment in a few weeks. I walked behind her and rubbed it.

"I need to see you. I'll be there in a few days."

"Time and place and I'm there." After he told me, I hung up and my phone rang again. I rolled my eyes when I saw the caller.

"Where have you been? I've been looking all over for you."

"Sherri, I told you I didn't want you. Ain't shit change."

"Kane just come see me."

"Not a chance. My girl will fuck me up."

"Your girl? When did you get in a relationship?"

"None of your business," April yelled in the phone and

ended the call.

“Block the bitch.” I hit block on my phone to her number and grabbed April’s hand.

“I know you think I’m going to hurt you April, but I’m not. I’m the type of nigga that if I know you’re down for me; nothing any woman can say or do will get in the middle. I just need for you to trust me.”

“I trust you, baby. It’s the chicks I don’t trust. Now come make love to me so I can go to sleep.”

“You’re so damn bossy.”

“Only over my dick,” she grabbed it and went down to please me.

“It’s your dick, huh?” She didn’t answer because her mouth was full.

“Shittt, baby. Hell yeah, it’s your dick. Damn.”

Chapter 9

Sherri

I couldn't believe Kane went out and made some other woman his chick. All the dick sucking and fucking he and I were doing, I just knew he would pick me. I called his phone back over and over thinking it was something wrong with it, when I realized he'd blocked me.

A few days later, I was horny as hell and had no dick to top my night off. I went down to the club and Stacy and Essence were there all hugged up, and their boy Derrick even had somebody with him. I walked over to where they were and Essence offered me a drink.

"Hey Essence. I haven't seen you two out here in a while." Stacy spoke then got up to go somewhere.

"I know. We've been in the house working on baby number two." I could tell she wasn't really feeling me but I didn't do anything to her.

"Oh shit, bitch. I didn't know you were having another one."

"I said working on it, fool." She laughed and took a sip

of water.

Essence and I had met a few years ago when she first came into the bank inquiring about opening the community center. I was the branch manager at the time and gave her the information she needed. She came in a few more times for a loan and to open an account for it. A week later, she came back and said her man surprised her with a vacant lot and had put all the money up for it. She was super excited and hell, so was I. If her man had that kind of money, it meant his friends did, too.

Come to find out her man was the brother to the guy my friend Erica had a baby by. Yup, Erica was my friend and had a baby with Kane. Essence and I stayed in touch and eventually became close. Not as close as her and her bitch friend, April. I couldn't stand her and the fact that she always thought she was better than me. The bitch drove a school bus for a living for God's sake. What type of man would want her?

Anyway, Essence introduced us and at first she appeared to be friendly, but after a while she wasn't coming out with us as much. Essence said it was because she didn't party a lot, but I knew it was over the fact we didn't see eye to eye.

"There's your friend April," I said sarcastically, and she shot me an evil look.

"What?"

"Don't start any shit tonight."

"You know I love April."

I thought her head was going to snap off when I said that. I watched April give Stacy a hug and then Kane whispered something in her ear. If I didn't know any better, I would think they were a couple. She sashayed her ass over to our section.

She had on an orange halter dress with a big belt draped around the middle. Her shoes looked expensive as fuck. I looked down and she had on some red bottoms. The bitch never wore name brand stuff. She had on a diamond necklace that didn't appear to be costume jewelry, and neither did the earrings or tennis bracelet.

"Who the hell laced you, April?"

"Hello to you too Sherri, and my man draped me. I told him it was too much, but he insisted."

I saw her smirk and sit next to Essence. We sat there talking while Kane and Stacy stepped back into VIP. He spoke then sat next to April. She got up to use the bathroom and this nigga asked if she needed him to go with her. I know damn well she's not screwing him. I tossed my drink back and followed her. I guess no one thought anything of it because they didn't follow me.

"You're fucking my man now?" I asked as she washed her hands in the sink.

"Who's your man Sherri?"

"You know who my man is, don't play with me." She grinned and headed towards the door.

"I'm going to ask you again. Who is your man?"

"Kane, bitch. You know he's my man."

"Oh, I didn't know. Maybe you should speak with Kane about whom he's sleeping with. I don't owe you an explanation on anything." She opened the door and walked out. I let my anger get the best of me. I ran out behind her, grabbed her by the back of her hair, swung her around and landed a punch right in her nose.

“No the fuck you didn’t,” she yelled out when she saw blood dripping down. This bitch kicked her shoes off and came at me full force. I tried to block some of her hits, but she was too fast. I felt my body being lifted and was literally thrown across the club where my head hit the wall.

“If you ever put your hands on my girl again, I will kill you,” Kane barked in my ear. So he *was* fucking her. I looked up and Kane had April bridal style carrying her out the club. People were laughing and snapping pictures of me. Essence was walking towards me at full speed. I saw Stacy trying to catch her, but he didn’t make it time. Essence was laying down a beating just as bad as April. I was no match for the two of them.

“That’s enough Essence,” Stacy picked her up and carried her out on his shoulder. She was shouting obscenities at me about how she was going to beat my ass every time she saw me. I got off the floor the best I could and wobbled my ass to the car. I was going to get those bitches if it was the last thing I did.

Chapter 10

Essence

"I'm beating that bitch ass every time I see her Stacy. She had no business putting her hands on April. I hope she didn't lose the baby."

"Calm down, killer."

"I'm serious."

"I know you are." He pulled up at the emergency room and we were about to get out to go in, but he grabbed my arm.

"Essence, I know you wanna go in and check on April, but I need you to handle something in the car right quick." I looked down and he was hard.

"When the hell did that happen?"

"You know what you do to me when you get like that."

I waited for him to get his pants down then climbed on top. Thank goodness I had a dress on. I glided down and rode my man until we both came. He took some napkins out of his glove compartment and wiped me down. We walked in the emergency room like we hadn't just got a quickie.

The nurse told us what room April was in and I noticed

Stacy's hand stiffen up when we walked past some chick. I looked back and she was staring at him with an evil look on her face. I didn't say anything, but you could bet I was going to address it.

"How are you, sis?"

They had her hooked up to the monitor to make sure the baby was ok, and her nose wasn't broken, but it was swollen. Kane was pissed and I didn't blame him. Pregnant or not, Sherri had no right to question April. They were only cool on the strength of me. Kane was whom she should've spoken to.

"You know I'm whooping her ass again," April said, and Kane shook his head.

"You ain't doing shit with my baby in your stomach. I'm going to handle that."

"Yeah, ok. You ain't handling shit unless I'm with you." He leaned in to kiss her.

I saw the same chick staring at Stacy go past April's room a few times. I told them I would be right back. I handed Stacy my stuff and followed the chick into the bathroom.

"Can I help you?"

"No, you cannot."

"There's no need to get smart. I asked you because I saw the look you gave my man when you came in, and the fact that you're passing my sister's room over and over shows me you want him to notice you. I can help you with that if you fill me in on what's going on."

I listened to her tell me she met Stacy at the bar a couple months ago. They were talking one minute and the next, he had her legs in the air in some hotel room. She went on to say the sex lasted a couple weeks and then he just stopped calling and answering her calls. I was mad, but I wasn't going to allow another woman to see me sweat. I told her to come with me and she could ask him herself why he dissed her.

"Hey, baby."

"What's up?" He turned around and all the color drained from his face.

"What's going on Essence, and who is she?" April asked and I saw her sitting up. Kane looked just as confused as April was. He looked at Stacy with the *what the fuck is she doing here* look.

"You can ask him now."

"Stacy, why did you just fuck me and leave me. You said you were going to leave your girl and be with me. What the hell happened?"

"Bitch are you crazy? I never told you any shit like that. I'm not fucking your crazy ass either."

"You're going to sit here and lie."

"Essence, I swear on our son I have never cheated on you. This bitch is crazy."

"Why would she make it up, Stacy?"

I saw her fold her arms and wait for him to answer. I could see him getting angrier and when he got like that, it was hard to get him to calm down.

"I'm telling you right now bitch, if you don't tell my girl the truth, I will choke the life out of you." The bitch had the nerve to hide behind me.

"Stacy there's no need to hide what we did. You may as well tell her. This bitch lifted her shirt up and had a small pouch.

"Stacy tell me right now you didn't get her pregnant."

At that point I could no longer fight the tears I was holding in. I tried not to let the situation get me to cry but hearing him possibly having a baby on the way had my stomach in knots.

I kissed April on the forehead, grabbed my things, and walked out. I didn't have my car and Stacy had the keys. I heard him yelling my name, so I ducked behind some cars. I was hurt, upset, embarrassed, and humiliated.

I'd always felt bad for women who went through this and swore my man would never stray. I guess I was wrong. I called an Uber and took it to my mom's house. She was always at her boyfriend's so I knew she wouldn't be home. I shut my phone off after I sent a text to April.

I sat in the tub and cried my eyes out. I got in the bed and did the same thing until I'd fallen asleep. Him having a baby by another woman was worse than catching him sleeping with her. I didn't think I could raise an outside child. Shit, I didn't think I could be with a cheater either.

****

“Hey baby, what are you doing here? And why was Stacy calling my phone all night looking for you?” my mom asked, lying on the bed with me. She was like my other best friend. I told her what happened and she told me to think about what I wanted to do. She said people make quick choices when they’re angry and end up regretting them.

“Ma, you didn’t tell him I was here did you?”

“No, but you know that man is crazy over you. It’s just a matter of time before he comes over here and ransacks the house trying to find you.” I rolled my eyes.

“Essence, I know what that woman said to you, but maybe you should hear him out. I’m not saying he’s a saint, but I do know he loves you and his family. If he swore on his own son, he may be telling the truth. Think about that.” She shut the door on her way out. I laid there for a while, then made it downstairs where my mom was cooking breakfast.

“Hey sweetie,” her boyfriend Don said when he saw me. He’d been around me since I was fifteen and was more like my dad than my own.

“Hey,” I put my head on his shoulder and stuck some

bacon in my mouth. He put his arm around me and kissed my forehead.

"You know you're my daughter and your mom and I only want what's best for you." I nodded my head.

"I want you to get yourself together and go home."

"But I-"

"No buts, Essy." That's what he always called me when he was about to be serious.

"You don't allow some woman to come in staking claims on your man, and then you believe her off the bat. Not only did you not give Stacy a chance to explain himself, you gave the woman ammunition to break up your home," he said and went to where my mom was.

"That's the problem with these young couples. A woman will come to the wife on some petty shit, and instead of the wife having her man's back, she turns on him. You know damn well that man worships the ground you walk on and is probably scared to death to cheat on you. I know for a fact that man will do anything for you and I also believe if he did it, he would tell you. Stacy has never lied to you once in your relationship. You've told me some things he admitted to when it came to him being back on the streets. He could've lied then, but he didn't. Go home and see what he has to say. If you still think he's lying, then you have a choice to make. But make the choice on something you know for a fact he did, not because some random woman told you." My mom spoke firmly when she spoke. Don stood behind her, kissing on her neck.

"Fine. But me and SJ moving back here if he's lying."

"That's fine. You'll just hear me busting her ass at night," Don said and my mom started laughing.

"Yuk." I took my plate and went upstairs to eat and get dressed. I turned my phone on and I had tons of messages from Stacy asking me to come home. I hopped in the shower and got dressed.

I got to my house and pressed the code on the gate. As I waited for it to open, I noticed a small red car sitting not too far from my house. I backed my car up and rode by it, and it was the woman from the hospital fixing her hair.

"Excuse me. Why are you sitting outside my house?" I asked when I walked over to her car.

"Oh, you're home. Thanks for staying out last night. Stacy and I enjoyed each other."

"Oh yeah? If that's the case, what color is my bedroom?" I thought I was going to lose my shit when she described what my entire house looked like. She even told me she checked on my son while he took a shower to make sure he was still asleep.

"Don't let me catch your ass back over here again."

"You won't. Stacy and I agreed your house was a one-time thing."

I tried to open that bitch's door but she had pulled off. I jumped back in my car and drove up to my house.

Chapter 11

Stacy

When I saw that crazy bitch Lucy in the hospital, I knew she was going to start some shit. Lucy was Stan's sister. Stan was my best friend who had happened to set Kane up in the dope game when we were younger.

Lucy and I used to date about 13 years ago. We were both fifteen and were in love. Well, I was. Lucy was a bad bitch but the only problem was she knew it and used it to her advantage.

She was Dominican, and tall like a model. She stood at about five-foot-eight but that was nothing to my six-foot-two frame. Her hair was long and down her back. She had an ok body when we'd first started messing around but a year after we started fucking, it was like she woke up with a body like a stripper. I don't know if I just didn't pay attention enough because I was with her all the time, but the niggas noticed.

She and I were together for three years when Lucy started feeling herself too much and allowed niggas in her face constantly. Stan and I weren't too happy with the stories we were hearing, but when we asked her she would deny it.

The stories were about her going out with other dudes and sleeping around. She eventually got busted when Stan and I were out doing business and stopped to get something to eat. She was kissing on some nigga and he was basically fucking her in the restaurant. Needless to say, I broke up with her and started doing me.

The break up wasn't bad because we were still pretty young. I started being a hoe and told myself I would never have another girlfriend. That love shit wasn't for me. A few months later, Lucy came to me saying she was pregnant, but we both knew it was a lie and if she was, I wasn't the father. She and I hadn't had sex for a few months prior to the break up.

A few years went by and Lucy was in a bad car accident where she lost her memory. She remembered certain things, and somehow, I was in those memories.

Over the last year, she'd somehow found me and had been stalking the hell out of me. She was showing up at the club, SJ's school, the mall, and other places I would be. I would see her lurking because it was my responsibility to keep my family safe at all times. She would stare and never say anything, like she did last night. I didn't know where the hell the pouch came from in her stomach, because I hadn't touched her.

My girl had me mad as hell automatically believing that bitch instead of her man. I called her all night and even contacted her mom to make sure she was ok. Once her stepdad called and asked me what had happened, he told me she was there with them and that they had let her have it. Yeah, he was mad cool and they loved me.

I would never cheat on Essence. I'm too afraid she would do it back and then my son would lose his mother, because I would damn sure kill her. The love I had for Essence was ten times stronger than the puppy love Lucy and I had.

"Why the fuck was that bitch in the house last night? You really brought another woman in here while our son slept?"

I was happy Essence was home but I was about to rip into her. She slammed the front door and I yoked her ass up by the shirt. No, I'd never put my hands on her, but I did yoke her up when she pissed me off.

"Calm the fuck down. You know damn well SJ stayed the night at my mother's house, and I'm not a grimy ass nigga to have another bitch in your house. Who the fuck told you some shit like that?" I saw the tears falling down her face.

"I pulled up and the same chick was outside the house talking about she was here last night screwing you and she described everything in the house." I let her go and wiped my hands down my face.

"Stacy, if you want to be with someone else, just tell me." She took her shoes off and went upstairs leaving me in my thoughts. I heard the shower running and took it upon myself to get in with her. She turned around and hugged me.

"Essence, when we get out I will explain everything to you," that was all I said.

I picked the washcloth up, lathered the soap on it and then bathed her. Essence was all that I needed in a woman and I couldn't wait until she was my wife. I still hadn't given her the ring because something always came up. But April's birthday was coming up and Kane wanted to throw her a surprise party. He was more than happy to say I could use the platform to propose.

"I love you Essence," I whispered in her ear as I bent her over in the shower and attacked her clit with my mouth.

"I love you too, baby. Oh God, Stacy! I love you so much! Here I cummmm." She let me suck all her juices up and then returned the favor. I had to do a lot of making up with my girl but I knew this Lucy shit had to be taken care of. I was glad Stan was coming into town. He was the only one she would listen to.

After we got out and were dressed to pick SJ up, I filled her in on everything. Of course she was ready to go out and look for her, but I wasn't having it.

We went out to Olive Garden before we picked SJ up, because she claimed that's what she had a taste for. I thought she was pregnant but I was going to wait for her to confirm it.

"How the fuck your brother not going to tell me he found my daughter?" I turned around and Erica's dumb ass was standing there with her arms folded.

"Go somewhere Erica," Essence said and grabbed my hand.

"No. That's my daughter Stacy. He doesn't get to pay a judge off because I'm sure that's what he did to get her. I'm filing a motion to have the case reviewed. I'm getting Lexi back." She was screaming in the restaurant pissing Essence and me off.

"Bitch, if you think my brother is about to let you near Lexi after you let that motherfucker touch and basically rape her, you must be fucking crazy." Her eyes bucked open. I guess she thought we didn't know.

"Yeah bitch, Lexi told us what he did. You tell that motherfucker we're coming for him." She let some fake tears fall down her face.

"You're living on borrowed time too, bitch," Essence said and spit in her face. Erica tried to hit Essence and I tossed her ass to the ground.

"I'm not with him anymore. I just want my daughter back."

"Mark my words, Lexi already has a mother and I can

tell you she will go to war with you over her. If I were you, I would leave it alone before you find yourself on the wrong side of my gun," I whispered in her ear so everyone couldn't hear. She got up off the floor and ran out of the restaurant.

Essence and I stayed talking about the bullshit that had happened. The waitress handed me the bill when we were finished. I opened the door for Essence and started walking to the car.

Boom! Boom! Boom!

The sound of guns was going off as Essence and I were walking out of Olive Garden. I pushed her to the ground, jumped on top of her, and started shooting back. I must've caught one of them because I heard them say he was hit and let's go.

I looked down and there was blood on the sidewalk and it wasn't coming from me. I turned Essence over and she was coughing up blood. I heard people in the background yelling for someone to call 9-1-1 and asking if there was a doctor around.

"Essence stay with me, baby. The ambulance is on the

way."

"I'm trying, Stacy. It hurts so bad."

"I know. Listen, we have to get SJ so hold on." I had tears running down my face as I watched her struggling to stay awake.

"Excuse me. I'm a doctor, let me through." I saw some man pushing through and it was the same one that took care of April the night she'd fought Sherri. He opened his medical bag and looked for where she was shot. I could hear the sirens getting louder. He lifted her shirt and I almost lost it. She had been shot in the side twice and I saw him lift her dress up and she was hit in the leg. He applied pressure to her and gave her a shot of something for the pain.

Once the EMTs pulled up, they put her on the stretcher, and he rode in the back with us. I heard them radio a female gunshot victim was on the way and to prep for emergency surgery.

"Doc, I know you don't know me, but please don't let her die. We have a son and…" I felt myself breaking down.

"What's your name?" he asked me.

“Stacy. Stacy Anderson.”

“Ok, Mr. Anderson. Right now, she is stable. The pain medicine I gave her stopped her from fighting and that’s a good thing, because the more she fought, the harder it was for her to take slow breaths. I know it’s hard to relax when you’ve been shot, but it’s the best thing to do. Most people don’t know that and I’m going to do everything I can to save her.”

“Wait. Are you a surgeon? I saw you in the ER.”

“Yes, I am a trauma doctor and I perform surgeries once in a while. The day your brother came in with his girlfriend, I was on duty upstairs and came down because my girl is a nurse. She said she knew you guys from school, so I made it my business to take care of her.” He looked at me.

“Mr. Anderson, sometimes it’s all about who you know.”

He gave me a smile and jumped off the back when they opened the door. I hopped off and followed them as far as they let me. He promised to come out and let me know the minute she was out.

Chapter 12

April

Lexi was in the room lying down with me watching some cartoons. Kane ran out to get me some Popeye's because I was fiending for it. I loved the way he catered to me. I really loved the way he made love to my body almost every night, too. His touch was always so gentle and he made sure to hit every spot.

I didn't think I could be around him when we first met, because he had an arrogance I hated. I guess once love gets involved, you really can't help it. I thought it was too soon to fall in love, but my mom told me you can't put a stamp on when it will happen. Some find it when they first meet the person, some don't find it at all. I'm just happy I'm experiencing it with someone that loves me just as much as I love him.

"It's about time, daddy. My brother or sister is hungry."

I laughed when she said that. Lexi was happier than we were she was about to be a big sister. He helped her off the bed and we went downstairs to eat.

"Daddy, can I sit next to mommy?" I didn't mind her calling me that, but every time I tried to explain to her that I wasn't trying to take her mommy's place, she didn't want to hear it.

I told Kane he had to speak with her about it but his ass wasn't beat either. He said as long as she wanted to call me that I should let her. He said she knows who her mother is and if she chose to call me mom, not to sweat it. I guess he was right. Lexi was old enough to understand the difference, so I left it alone.

"Damn Lexi, you don't give me no time with my girl," he said, sucking his teeth.

"Daddy stop it. You sleep in the same bed."

"Lexi what did I tell you about being grown?"

"I'm sorry mommy." We finished eating and she helped me clean up.

"What's wrong?" I asked Kane when he came in the kitchen grabbing my hand and scooping Lexi up. He locked the house up and made us get in the car. He was silent the entire time. When we pulled up to the hospital, I really got nervous.

"April, I need you to try and stay calm when we get inside ok?"

"Kane you're scaring me."

"April, Essence was shot three times and-" All I heard was that my sister was shot and nothing else. I tried to run in there, but Kane snatched me up.

"Lexi go over there with grandma. Ma, can you get Lexi?" He took me back out the hospital and hugged me.

"What happened, Kane?"

"Baby, I don't know yet. My mom called when you were downstairs and told me she was shot and we had to get to the hospital. I know she's your friend but April, I need you to try and stay calm for the baby and for Lexi. Seeing you upset made her upset."

"I'm sorry, Kane."

"Don't be sorry. I know the situation is out of control right now, but you are Lexi's mom and she's going to wanna be up under you." I nodded my head and we walked back in.

"I know it's going to be hard, but I'm here if you need me."

"I love you so much, Kane."

"I love you, too."

We sat in the emergency room for what felt like hours waiting for the doctor to come tell us any news about Essence. I was hungry again and Lexi was asleep on my lap. Kane was trying to get Stacy to calm down. He was pacing back and forth, rambling on about how he was going to murder everyone in this town. His clothes were still full of blood and he'd refused to go home.

"The family of Essence Miller."

"Right here," Stacy spoke up without letting the doctor finish. The doctor stood in front of all of us and told us how she was.

"Ms. Miller suffered three gunshot wounds, as I'm sure you know. We were able to remove all the bullets. Unfortunately, the one on her leg hit a major artery and she bled out." Stacy's body fell back in the chair. Her parents were crying and Kane had to hold me up.

"She's going to be in ICU for a while until she wakes up and can move on her own."

"Wait. I thought you said she bled out. Are you saying she's alive?" her mom asked.

"She's alive. I'm sorry if you guys misunderstood what I was saying. Let me start over. Ms. Miller did bleed out but we were able to stop it and stabilize her. One of the bullets grazed her on the side and the other one punctured her lung, causing it to collapse. Her leg is pretty bad and may cause her to walk with a limp. She will need extensive therapy. Otherwise, she should make a full recovery. She is heavily medicated and when they put her in a room, you can go see her."

Stacy gave the doctor a hug and took him down the hall to speak to him. I'm sure to offer him money. We all left the hospital and left Stacy up there. Kane dropped us off and ran by Stacy's house to get him some clothes. There was a shower on the ICU floor.

I helped Lexi put her pajamas on and went to my room to take a shower. I was lying in bed when I heard her screaming. I tried not to run, but I was scared. I opened the door and she was in the corner of her room, hiding.

“What's wrong?” I sat down on the floor next to her. I heard the alarm to the door indicating Kane was back.

"” had a bad dream. He's coming back to get me.” I pulled her close to me and hugged her tight.

“Lexi, that man will never see you again. Your daddy already told you nothing would ever happen to you. The house has cameras everywhere, alarms, and you know daddy would kill anyone for messing with you. I know you're scared Lexi, but no one is going to hurt you again.” I struggled getting up off the floor. I put my hand out to Lexi and told her she could sleep with us. Kane was coming out of the bathroom naked when I opened the door. I closed it quickly so she wouldn't see.

“Why you shut the door? You've seen all this before.” He was under the covers waiting for me. I opened the door wider so he could see Lexi.

“Lexi, let’s go get something to drink and let daddy meet us.”

“Ok. Hurry up, daddy.” She was excited and ran downstairs.

“Damn, April. I wanted to make love to my girl.” I

walked over to him and kissed his lips.

"She had another nightmare, baby."

"I'm going to torture the fuck out of that nigga when I catch him. How many has it been since the last one?"

"It's only been one in the last two weeks. She's getting better Kane. I know you don't see it, but when it first happened, she was having them every night. I don't doubt you will take care of it. I just want you to do it fast. The minute she knows he's gone, the better it will be for her. Him being alive scares her because she believes he still has the ability to get her."

"You know that motherfucker won't be near her again."

"I know Kane, and she knows you won't allow nothing to happen to her. She's not doubting you. It's just the fact of him being alive."

I walked up to him and wrapped my arms around his waist. He turned me to face him and bent down to kiss my stomach.

"Thank you, April."

"Huh? For what?"

"For being you. For taking care of her when I couldn't.

For claiming her as your own and protecting her. I will always love you for that."

"She is a part of you, therefore a part of me. I'm carrying her sibling, so now I have a part of you, too."

"Mommy and daddy, come on. I'm hungry."

"You better hurry up before she starts whining," I told him and grabbed his hand to go downstairs.

Chapter 13

Erica

I wanted to know who the fuck the bitch was claiming my daughter. It couldn't be the one who was at Essence's house that day, because she would've said something. Every time I asked Lexi about it, she would say I was her mommy. Kane had me fucked up if he thought he was keeping my daughter. I may not have wanted her for the right reasons, but the fact still remained that she was my child.

I told the dude I was sleeping with he had to leave. He was no longer allowed around my child. At first, we argued and he knocked me upside the head a few times but once he came to the house and saw the locks were changed he knew I meant it. I probably should've killed him, but then he would've taken the white girl from me and right now I needed it. No, he wasn't living with me but we were still together; only at his place.

"What's up Erica?" Kane said and bum rushed himself through the door. This was his first time here since the day Lexi went missing. I sat on the couch and waited for him to return from checking all the rooms. I'd heard through the grapevine he'd put a bounty out on the dude Glenn.

"Where the fuck is he bitch?" He had the gun to my temple. I started crying and yes they were real tears. If anyone knew Kane, they knew he never pulled a strap and didn't use it.

"He's gone Kane. I kicked him out after he did that to our daughter." He banged my head against the wall. I was dizzy as hell as he let my body drop.

"Lexi is not your daughter Erica."

"Yes she is. Stop saying that."

"Erica, what kind of mother allows a man to try and rape their daughter?"

"I told you I made him leave."

"You dumb bitch. He didn't do it one time. The shit happened more than a few times and Lexi told me you were in the other room."

How the fuck did she know I was home? I tried to pretend I didn't know what was going on. I thought to myself but didn't dare say it out loud.

"There's no need to wonder how she knew you were here. Just know she's the only reason you're still alive."

"And what's that supposed to mean?"

"It means you would be six feet under if I didn't promise her I wouldn't kill you. Mark my words Erica. You and dude's time is coming. I'm going to kill you and make it look like an accident." He walked towards the door.

"Oh yeah. Tell that nigga he can run, but he can't hide. He fucked with the wrong nigga's daughter."

He slammed the door as he walked out. I was scared as hell now. To know at any time, it could be my last day had me worried. I called Glenn up and told him what Kane said. He laughed and told me he wasn't worried about it, but if I know Kane, he should be.

"Come over here and bring your daughter."

I had to take a look in the phone to make sure I wasn't hearing shit. I know he didn't just ask for my child.

"Yeah right. I'll be over there, but my daughter will never see you again."

I hung the phone up and took a shower before going over there. I got there and some dude was in the bedroom screwing the hell out of some chick. She was screaming her head off. Glenn took me in the room, handed me some coke, and fucked me until we both passed out.

****

The next few days were a blur. All Glenn and I did was fuck and get high. He asked me if I wanted to go to the mall and spend some money. I figured we could because it was early in the morning and no one would catch us.

We were holding hands going from store to store when I noticed him stop and grin. I thought he was smiling at some bitch, but in actuality it was the bitch from Essence's house holding my daughter's hand. They were coming out of Footlocker with some bags. I was a tad bit shocked Kane wasn't lurking around.

"Go say hi to your daughter."

He pushed me that way and made sure to stay right next to me. The chick didn't see me but my daughter did, and instantly started trying to hide under her. She was standing behind and holding onto her. You could see her asking what was wrong.

"Lexi aren't you happy to see me?"

The woman looked up and if looks could kill, I would've been dead on sight. I saw Glenn licking his lips at Lexi. I knew then something was really wrong with him.

"I'm going to say this as nice as possible so I don't cause a scene. Move the fuck on," the chick said and made sure to have Lexi behind her. I saw her stomach poking out a bit. Kane done went and got her ass pregnant.

"Bitch, please. I can say hi to my daughter. Matter of fact let's go Lexi. You're coming with me."

"No, no, no, no. April, don't make me," I heard her crying.

"You're not taking her anywhere. I don't give two shits about you birthing her." *So this is the bitch Essence said was playing her mother and would go to war for Lexi.*

"Don't make me call the cops." I was being real smart now. I had every right to take my child and there was nothing she could do about it. She had her phone out texting. I'm sure it was Kane, which meant I didn't have much time.

I reached around her, grabbed Lexi's arm and the bitch punched me dead in the nose. My shit started bleeding instantly. I went to swing again and this bitch started beating my ass. A couple of guys broke it up and that's when I noticed Glenn and Lexi were gone.

"Oh my God. Where is my daughter?" she had the nerve to scream out.

"What did she have on, ma'am?" one of the guys asked her.

"She had on some blue shorts, with a pink shirt and pink and white Jordan's. Oh my God, you have to help me find her. The man who took her is a pedophile. Please help me."

The two men reacted really quickly when she said that. People hated when you said pedophile. I heard the bitch on the phone yelling about the dude taking her. I could tell it was Kane by the way his voice was booming through the phone.

In less than five minutes, there were cops running in the mall with security and other people trying to help find her.

"OH MY GOD. WHAT ARE YOU DOING TO THAT LITTLE GIRL?" Some woman screamed out. Everybody went running to some small hallway. When we got there, Lexi was naked from the waist down and passed out on the floor. Blood was also coming from her mouth. Kane was going to kill me.

I saw the cops calling for an EMT and the chick I'd fought had her lying in her lap while one of the officers took their shirt off to cover Lexi's body.

"What the fuck did you do?" I asked his dumbass when he'd yanked me away from the crowd. He had me walking fast out the mall.

"Nothing she didn't want me to do. You know Lexi loves me."

I looked at this nigga like he was crazy. What the fuck was I doing with someone like him? Is it really love?

"Here" He passed me a bag of coke in the car.

This is definitely why I was still with him.

He drove me back to the house we had been spending time at. As usual, we got high and passed out. A few days later, I crept back home and snuck in my house. I didn't want anyone to see me and tell Kane. I'd just needed to get some clothes and go back to Glenn.

"You let that man violate my daughter again?" I heard when I shut the door. I tried to run back out but Stacy was standing outside waiting. I turned around to see Kane standing there looking like the devil himself.

"Kane, I-"

"SHUT THE FUCK UP, YOU STUPID BITCH. How could you?"

"Kane the bitch was talking shit and we started fighting. If you want to blame anyone, blame her."

He backhanded the fuck out of me. I was shocked because Kane never hit women, and this was the second time he'd laid hands on me. I could hit him with a bat and he still wouldn't strike me.

"That was her mother and she had every right to protect her when you tried to take her. You know damn well you have no rights to her. What were you going to do? Let him have his way with her again?"

"Kane, she started it."

"I don't want to hear that shit. If she wasn't beating your ass, the nigga would have never tried to violate her again."

"Tried to."

"Yeah. He wasn't successful. Thank goodness to the woman who screamed out. What? Are you mad?"

"But she was passed out."

"Yeah, because she kept screaming and crying for her mother April. He punched her in the face and broke her jaw. HER FUCKING JAW, ERICA. SHE IS SIX FUCKING YEARS OLD AND HAS A BROKEN JAW. WHAT THE FUCK IS WRONG WITH YOU?"

I'd started crying because he was right. I was allowing this man to bring so much harm to my baby, and all I cared about was getting high.

"Do you know how much pain you caused my daughter and my woman?"

"I don't give a fuck about her." I stopped and thought about what he'd said.

"Your woman? Oh, I guess that's your baby, too." He chuckled and moved in closer.

"That's definitely my baby and she's going to be my wife. You know what? It doesn't even matter. Where the fuck is he?" I shook my head no.

"You still trying to protect the nigga? You didn't deserve to carry my child. I wish I'd waited for April. I swear I would've never fucked with you." He shot my ass in the leg.

"What the fuck is his address?" I didn't answer and he shot me again in the other leg.

"Ok. Ok." I gave him an address. I sat there on the floor, bleeding out. I watched him and Stacy pour gasoline through the house. Kane lit a match upstairs first and stood there as it started burning.

"Kane please take me to the hospital."

"Nah, bitch. You're about to get exactly what you deserve for all the pain you inflicted on my daughter."

"But I didn't do it."

He had started pouring gasoline on me. He poured more throughout the downstairs but not close to me. I guess he wanted to watch me die before the entire house burned. Stacy was shaking his head. Kane put a piece of duct tape on my mouth.

"You may as well have."

He dropped the match and I felt the flesh of my skin burning. I tried to roll over to put it out, but my legs wouldn't move and the fire was covering my body. Kane stood there watching me die and had no remorse. I started seeing the rest of the house go up in flames and watched the two of them walk out. There was no way I was surviving this. I stopped screaming, and soon my body succumbed to the flames.

Chapter 14

Kane

I watched that stupid bitch burn right along with her house and had no regrets. It took the fire trucks almost ten minutes to get there. I guess because the house was big it took a while for anyone to notice the flames.

I knew the bitch was dead, but I was making sure she didn't somehow get strength to get up. I dropped Stacy back off at the hospital with Essence and ran home to change my clothes before I went back up there myself to check on my daughter and April. The doctors thought it was best for Lexi to stay a few nights to monitor her jaw and run extra tests.

“What are you doing?” I asked April when I walked in and saw her with a suitcase sitting on the couch.

“I'm leaving, Kane.”

I blew my breath and took a seat next to her. I wasn't in the mood for any bullshit and I needed to get back to the hospital.

“What do you mean you're leaving?”

“I'm saying this is not the place for me and I think it's

best for all of us if I stay away." Now she was really pissing me off.

"Where is all this coming from? We were fine this morning. What happened?"

She wiped her eyes and stood up. She had one suitcase that she dragged behind her to the door. I was shocked because she had tons of clothes.

"She blames me."

"What are you talking about? Who blames you?" She walked down the steps outside with her stuff and I snatched it away.

"Lexi."

"Lexi?" She nodded her head

"How the hell does she blame you and she can't even talk right now?"

"I was at the hospital like I've been for the past two days with her. When you left out earlier, she motioned with her hands to get something to write with and some paper. I didn't know what it was for, so I went out to the nurses' station and asked for a pad and a pen. As I was waiting for the stuff, your mom went in the room. I nodded my head and waited for the nurse to bring me the items I asked for." I didn't see a problem here but I'm sure it's coming.

"Anyway, your mom said it was time for her to get washed up. Me not knowing anything was wrong, I get all the stuff she needs out and go help her get up to get in the shower. Only thing is, she put her hand up and told me no."

"No?" I questioned because she's never had an issue with April.

"At first I understood because I figured your mom was there and she wanted her to help. I waited for them to finish and cleaned her bed off. The minute she came out, she rolled her eyes at me."

"WHAT?" Now I was pissed. My daughter was only six going on seven in a few months. She was smart as hell and knew better than to roll her eyes at an adult.

"That's exactly what I said. Anyway, I said something to her and she did it again. Your mom asked me not to chastise her while she was there." I gave her the side eye.

"Yes, your mom."

"To make a long story short, Lexi got up on the bed and wrote on a piece of paper the best she could that she wanted me to leave and not return. To make matters worse, she told me if I don't leave you alone, she will never come live with you again."

"April, you know she's just hurting."

"Kane, your mother asked me to leave and not to come back too."

"April, I'm gonna get to the bottom of this. I don't know why she feels that way and for my mom to get involved is aggravating me more."

"Kane do you blame me, too? I mean, I would never intentionally allow anyone to hurt her. When Erica went to grab her, my first instinct was to whoop her ass. I never thought he would snatch her up. I'm so sorry Kane. I did everything I could to protect her. I told her that man would never bother her again and he did." She was hysterically crying in my arms.

"Look at me April." The tears were running down her face so quick it was hard to wipe them.

"You know damn well I don't blame you. I also know you did everything you could to protect her. If it weren't for you, she may not even be here." I made her look at me.

"There is nowhere in my mind or heart making me feel like you did this on purpose. Lexi is your daughter and she knows you wouldn't bring harm to her. I don't know if she's saying it because she's hurt, but I will be addressing that with her and my mother."

"No, Kane. I don't want any hostility among you and your family. I'll just leave."

I picked her up and carried her back in the house. I sent my mother a text and told her I would be up at the hospital later. I knew Lexi was fine because she'd sent me a picture of her watching television. Right now, I had to focus on my woman.

I started the shower, stripped both of us down, and stepped in. She continued crying as I washed her up. I bent down to kiss her stomach and couldn't find myself getting back up until I'd tasted her sweetness. Her leg was over my shoulder while she held on to my head and the rail. The way she screamed and moaned had me brick hard. I stood up after giving her a few releases.

I shut the water off and led her in the room and laid her down on the bed. I lifted her legs over my shoulder again and pushed myself in. I almost came on contact from how good she felt. The way her juices made the gushing sound showed me she was receiving as much pleasure as I was.

"Kane."

"Yeah, baby." I put her legs down, pulled her up and laid back so she was on top.

"I love you so much," she moaned out and I felt her juices seeping out on me.

"I love you too." She and I pleased one another for over two hours.

I laid behind her after we got back out of the shower, waiting for her to doze off so I could go back to the hospital. I stared at her taking slow breaths as she began falling asleep. April was beautiful and the way she held it down, not only as Lexi's mom, but in the bedroom, there was no way in hell I was allowing her to leave me.

Once I’d noticed she was asleep, I got up and put some clothes on to deal with the shit Lexi and my mom had said to her. I kept checking my phone waiting for Derrick to call and let me know if the address was correct Erica had given us before she met her fate. I couldn’t wait to get this nigga.

****

I walked in the hospital and went to the floor my daughter was on. Thank goodness I had the hospital bracelet on, otherwise I wouldn't have been allowed up since visiting hours had ended. It was a little after nine, but visiting hours were over at eight.

I heard clapping when I walked into my daughter’s room. That's how she greeted me when I came because she couldn't speak. My mother looked up and came to give me a hug, but I declined it.

“Hmm. I see April spoke to you,” she rolled her eyes. My mom loved April, so I didn't understand this change in either one of them.

“Ma, what were you thinking telling April to leave? And why didn't you address the shit Lexi said, well, wrote to her? You know damn well she would never put her in harm's way intentionally."

She didn't say anything and Lexi folded her arms on her chest. I knew it was killing her not to speak and she should be happy. I would probably pop her ass anyway if she got smart.

"Kane, if she would've just walked away." I put my hand up and cut her off.

"Ma, I'm going to stop you right there. And you, I'm going to deal with after I'm done with nana." She rolled her eyes and I grabbed her arm.

"Let me tell you something, little girl. I am your father and this eye rolling shit you got going on stops now. You are six years old and you need to start acting like that. I don't know how much you got away with before I came home, but don't make me beat your ass. Do I make myself clear?" She had tears running down her face, but she nodded that she understood.

"Kane."

"Ma. No disrespect, but don't ever jump in when I'm disciplining my daughter. If you see me abusing her, that's different. I've been gone a long time and I tried to give her the benefit of the doubt, but her mouth is out of control. I'm putting an end to that shit y'all allowed when I wasn't here."

She picked her purse up and was getting ready to leave. I walked out behind her.

"Kane, I can't believe you right now."

"What can't you believe, Ma? Me being a father, or me confronting you about disrespecting my girl. April is pregnant and you know firsthand how much stress can't affect a baby. Are you trying to make her lose the baby with that bullshit?"

"I'm sorry, Kane. I just think that if she-"I cut her off again.

"You think what? That if she grabbed Lexi and walked away he wouldn't have gotten to her?" She nodded her head yes.

"Ok, say she did what you suggested and they were waiting for April at the car and snatched Lexi up? Then what? Or, what if they followed her around the mall and called the cops and Erica pulled the same crap she did before and they took her from April? Huh? Did you think about that? Erica tried to snatch her and she did what she had to. No one knew that nigga was going to do that."

"I didn't look at it that way."

"No, you didn't. It seems like you already had your mind made up. But check this, you're my mother, and that's my girl. What you said to her was wrong and I expect you to make it right."

"You must really love her if you feel the need to check me over her."

"Yes, I do. She's going to be my wife. I don't expect you to love her if that's not your choice, but you will respect her. The same goes for her. What happened to Lexi has everyone in an uproar, but we can't go blaming the one person who claims her as her own just because she didn't handle it the way you think she should've. For you to even go along and agree with Lexi makes the shit even worse. You know that girl loves April, but you are her nana and she's going to agree with you, right or wrong. Make this right, Ma," I told her and left her standing at the elevator.

I would never disrespect my mom, but at that moment,

it called for me to at least put my foot down and make sure she understood as well that I wasn't playing.

I sent a text to April telling her I was staying the night because my mom had left. She didn't send one back and it's probably because she was still sleeping. I looked over at Lexi and she'd dozed off herself. I was digging in her ass tomorrow, too. I couldn't have the three most important women in my life not liking each other over something that was out of everyone's control. I put my feet up and waited for sleep to find me.

Chapter 15

April

I woke up to use the bathroom and noticed Kane wasn't beside me. I figured he was at the hospital. I looked over at the clock and it was a little after seven, so I got up and handled my hygiene. I went in the closet and laughed when I noticed the suitcase I'd packed. I couldn't believe I was going to leave the best thing that had happened to me.

I can't lie, the way he made love to me and said he didn't blame me had me feeling ten times better. I loved Kane and Lexi with all my heart and it was going to be extremely hard if I had to walk away. Kane said he was going to speak to his mom and I hope it didn't cause any problems between them. That's the last thing I wanted.

I went downstairs to make me something to eat when I realized my phone was still upstairs. I was almost five months and the up and down was starting to kill me. I picked the phone up and there was a text from Kane that came through after he'd left last night. He told me he loved me and that he would speak to me today.

I figured he needed some clothes to change into, so I packed him a bag and drove to the hospital. I didn't plan on staying and was going to call him outside the room once I got there. I refused to face his mom after she'd said that to me and I didn't know what was going on with Lexi, but I didn't want to upset her either.

I went to the front desk and told her what room I was going to. I stopped at the gift shop to pick up some get-well balloons and planned on having Kane give them to her instead. I paid for everything and went to the floor they had her on. The nurses all had a look on their face like something wasn't right. I wanted to ask them but I only knew them from the two days I was there.

I went to walk in and stopped when I saw my so-called man locking lips with some woman. Her back was turned so I couldn't make out who she was. I had tears coming down my face. Kane didn't seem to be too worried about me while the two of them exchanged spit. I was shocked because he'd claimed he didn't kiss women unless they were his girl. But I was really surprised when they stopped and the chick turned around.

"Don't mind me. I was just dropping some things off for you to change into."

The look on Kane's face was of shock and Sherri had a smirk on hers. I didn't expect her to react any differently. I wasn't even mad at her because she didn't owe me anything, but he did. I left everything in the room and walked out.

"April."

"Don't say shit to me," I yelled out as I continued walking and pressed the elevator key. He grabbed my arm and I snatched it back. There was nothing he could say that would justify what I saw.

"April, stop. Let me explain."

"There's no explanation for you kissing her."

"What? You mad? I told you before he was my man and I wasn't playing. Yeah, he was mad, we fought, but guess what? He found his way back to me." I gave him the evilest glare.

"Shut the fuck up, Sherri. I didn't find myself anywhere. Stop making shit up to piss her off." She rolled her eyes and put her arms on her chest.

"Just tell me why Kane? That's all I want to know."

"It's because he blames you for what happened to his daughter. Don't you, Kane? Oh, and the fact that his daughter doesn't want you around isn't helping either. What's crazy is I thought you cared about that girl, but I guess you didn't. There's no way in hell he should've been able to touch her."

"You blame me, Kane? Huh? Is what she saying true?"

"April, she came here and told me Erica spoke to her after everything happened and she said you told him to have his way with her."

My mouth hit the floor. I couldn't pick it up even if I tried.

"I didn't want to believe what she said, but then Sherri showed me these text messages between the two of them. How could you, April? You know my daughter is my life."

I was so mad I smacked him across the face and punched him in the stomach. Of course, neither of them fazed him one bit.

"So you believed her? How did you two end up kissing Kane?"

"She came up to me and caught me off-guard. I should've backed up, but I didn't."

"I wish I wasn't so far along that I couldn't terminate this pregnancy. I swear if I could, I would. I hate you with everything in me Kane." I saw the look on his face go from ok to mad.

"You hate me? I should be hating you for allowing something to happen to my child while she was in your care." I put my hand up before he finished.

"If that's what you truly believe, then I know you never really loved me. If you did, there would be nothing anyone could say or show you that could make you turn on me." He got quiet.

"Who was there taking care of her when her own mother neglected her? Huh? I was! Not that bitch who's supposed to be her friend behind you. I was. Who was there when she had those nightmares? I was. Who did she call her mother? Me. Who would go to the end of the earth for that little girl even before I knew of you? Me, nigga."

I was wiping my tears back and yelling. I felt myself getting dizzy and tried calming myself down, but I couldn't.

"Kane don't you ever in your life say that shit to me again. I know she's mad right now, but I am her mother. I am. Not Erica, and not this bitch who's trying to fuck you and make you her man. I am. I will never turn my back on her, but I will turn it on you. Kane if you don't know by now, it's over. I never want to see you again." He snatched my arm and I grabbed it back.

"Too bad. You're pregnant with my kid."

"That's where you're wrong nigga. I won't ever keep my kid away from its father because I'm not that bitch. But I don't have to see or fuck with the father for that to happen. Arrangements will be made for you to spend time with your child. Until then, stay the fuck out of my life." I thought I'd heard enough, until he said those words, I hated for a man to say to me.

"Fuck you bitch." I snapped my head back. The elevator came and left over and over. We were still in the hallway arguing.

"Bitch? Was I a bitch when your punk ass was moaning out my name last night? Was I a bitch when you brought me a house and truck? Or when you put all that money in my bank account? Huh? You know what? It doesn't even matter anymore. I'm sure I'll be every name in the book."

"Get your stupid ass out of here. You standing here talking like you tough. Bitch, I will fuck you up in this hospital, drag your ass out to my car, and drown you in a river. You think you know me, but you have no idea what the fuck I'm capable of. I suggest you shut the fuck up now and get to stepping." At that moment I heard and saw nothing but hate from him.

"Yo, what the fuck Kane?" I heard Stacy yelling from down the hallway. He was walking up with some security dude. I guess someone told him what was going on.

"This bitch was the one who let the nigga close to Lexi."

"Bitch? Kane, since when did you start disrespecting her?"

"When I found out she was the one who got my daughter hurt." I pressed the elevator button again.

"Who told you that shit?" When Kane explained to him everything that Sherri told him, I thought Stacy was going to kill her.

"Tell me you don't believe what that bitch said."

"It doesn't matter Stacy. Trust me when I say he's said more than enough. Tell Essence I'll call her."

"Nah, don't leave April. This bitch right here needs to go."

He pushed Sherri on the elevator and gave her a look daring her to get off. When the doors closed, I glanced around looking for the stairs. Once I found them, I headed towards them while Stacy and Kane went back and forth. I honestly was over the entire situation.

I drove the truck back to the house and grabbed the suitcase I had from the night before. I didn't take anything except under clothes. I looked down at the suitcase and realized it was something he purchased. I took all my stuff out and put it in a garbage bag. I didn't want to take anything he gave me. I called an Uber and left.

I'd made sure to leave the keys to the truck he bought me, the house keys and I made sure I took the deed out and scribbled my name off of it and left it on the table for him to see. Luckily, the lawyer's name was on a card on the refrigerator. I called him and asked for the address to where he was located. I was happy he wasn't busy and could see me right away. I made a stop at the bank on the way too.

"Are you sure you want to do this? I understand you're angry about something he did but-" I put my hand up.

"I'm positive." He handed me a new deed that only had Kane's name on it with a notarized letter stating I wanted my name removed. I also had him come up with documentation to do the same with the truck. I handed him the cashier's check in the amount of five million dollars that Kane had placed in my bank account. If I'd given him a regular check, he probably wouldn't have cashed it. I also closed the account before I left the bank. I was officially done with Kane.

My mom sent me a text telling me she was downstairs in the car. Yup, I called my mom to pick me up.

"I'm sorry things didn't work out for you two. Good luck with the baby," he said and shook my hand.

I know people may say I'm stupid for leaving all that and giving him his money back, but I wanted to make sure we had no ties to one another besides this child. My mom had money and she was happy for me to move back home. It meant she would be around the baby more. *Fuck Kane and good riddance.*

****

The next day, I ended up having to go in the hospital because I was so stressed out my blood pressure kept going up and my heart was having palpitations. They monitored me for a few hours then sent me home on strict bed rest. I wasn't worried about that because my mom was going to make sure I followed instructions.

My mom was pulling in the driveway and that's when we both noticed a black car we had never seen before. The door opened and my brother stepped out. I hadn't seen him in years, but he still looked the same. He was older than me and had a different mom, too. We used to hang out all the time until he started making money and stopped coming by as much. I'd never met any of his friends because we lived far away. The only reason I knew Essence was because she used to live down here too, but moved up north when Stacy asked her to move in.

"Hey sis." He gave me a hug and my mom smacked him in the back of the head.

"Hey ma." He called her his second ma and never addressed her by her name. He gave her a hug, too. Out stepped some badass chick I assumed was his girlfriend. She came over and he introduced her. Just like I thought, it was his girl and they were engaged to be married.

"I see you're expecting. Who's the father?" he asked with an evil look on his face.

"I don't know who he is," I waved him off to go inside and he pulled me back gently.

"I know you weren't out here doing it like that."

"Boy, please. I know who the baby's father is, but right now he's on some other shit. That's why I said I don't know who he is."

"Do I need to fuck him up?"

"Nah. I think after he realizes he fucked up that's going to be enough payback for me."

"What you mean by that?"

"I mean, some shit happened and he took the word of some ho who wanted him to be her man instead of his own woman's. It's only a matter of time before he realizes she lied and he'll be fucked up over it."

"Damn." He shook his head.

"He had a real woman who accepted him with all his flaws and gave me up for a whore. You know, the shit most men do. The only difference is, I'm going to have a front row seat at watching. His brother's girlfriend is my best friend and she's going to tell me everything."

"You're going to have her spy?"

"Nope. It's not spying if the drama is brought to her house. Him and his brothers are best friends and he's always there. Anyway, enough with my problems. Talk to me about the wedding. Are you excited?" I asked him and the chick and opened the door to go inside. My mom offered them to stay for dinner and wouldn't take no for an answer.

****

We were having a nice dinner when my phone started going off. I expected the call to come sooner but I guess he had to calm down.

Kane: *I see you're on your independent shit. You gave back everything and took your name off the house and car. Don't call me when your dumb ass don't have money for diapers and shit.*

Me: *I won't. Have a good day.*

Kane: *You better contact me when you have the baby.*

Me: *Maybe. Maybe not.*

Kane: *Don't play with me April. You don't wanna see the other side of me.*

Me: *I'm not playing and I already have. I'm glad I saw that side of you sooner than later.*

Kane: *Good. Then you know I'm not playing.*

Me: *What do you really want Kane? It's clearly not me. Why don't you go and fuck Sherri. Matter of fact go get her pregnant so you can stop harassing me.*

Kane: *I did last night. I fucked the shit out of her and came in her each time. I know you're going to be on some petty shit so I made sure I would have another kid.*

I was hurt like crazy when he said that. I didn't respond and shut my phone off. Just thinking about him touching her the way he touched me made me sick. I excused myself from the table.

"You ok, sis?"

"Yeah, I'm good. I'll see you guys tomorrow."

"April," he yelled out to me.

"Yeah."

"I love you, sis."

“I love you too, Stan.”

Chapter 16

Sherri

I was happy as hell about the way Kane treated that bitch. Granted, when I first got to the hospital, he called me all kind of bitches and tried to kick me out. He had me by my hair and was moving me out the room when I told him I had a message from Erica saying the reason his daughter was in the hospital was because of April. He let my hair go and snatched the phone out my hand. He went through the messages and his face turned colors as he read them. I rubbed his back and ran my hand over the top of his head. He pulled me in front of him and hugged me at the waist. I could tell he was upset over what had happened, but he would be more upset if he found out I had someone send me the text. The screen only had Erica's name on it and the phone number wasn't shown.

He stood up to walk out, I assumed since his daughter was out of the room getting some test done. The minute he did, I wrapped my arms around his neck and pulled him close to me. I think he was caught up in the moment because he allowed me to kiss him for maybe ten seconds before he moved me back.

By that time it was too late, because April had caught us. I smirked at her dumb ass. He went running behind her, but I guess once she said she hated him he got in his feelings and treated her like she was a bitch off the street. The disrespect towards her was worse than him tossing me across the club the night she and I fought.

That night he called his mom up to stay with his daughter. She seemed confused when she got there and saw me. He took her outside in the hallway. I stood by the door listening to him tell her the information I had given him. I thought she was going to smack him by how mad she was. Evidently, she felt like the situation with his daughter should have been handled differently but in no way did she agree to what I said.

"What the fuck is wrong with you Kane? You're allowing some woman to come up in here and put thoughts in your head. I may not have agreed with how April handled it, but there's no way she gave Lexi to him. Think about what you're saying. You want to go kill the mother of your unborn child, who raised your other child, over some bullshit this chick brought to you. Take your ass home and calm down."

"I don't care what you or anyone else says. If I find out the shit is true, I'm going to wait for her to have the baby, then I'm ending her life."

His mom shook her head as she stepped back in the room. I was acting as if I'd just come out the bathroom. I think his mom knew because she rolled her eyes. I heard some clapping and it was his daughter coming back in the room. She glanced at me, then at her dad and her grandmother like she too was unsure of what was going on.

"The doctor will be in shortly to tell you how the test went."

Evidently, she had bruised ribs and they gave her a cat scan and MRI to make sure nothing was broken.

"Thank you for checking on my granddaughter, but you can go now," his mom said.

"I'll be back Lexi. Ma, put me on speaker when the doctor comes in."

He walked past me and kept going. I thought he was waiting for me, but he got to his car and pulled off. I didn't get in my car fast enough to follow him home. I'd never been to his house, but I knew he'd had one built from the ground up. I went home that night in hopes he would call me, but he never did. I could tell the shit was bothering him when I said his girl gave his daughter to that man. I was going to be the chick waiting for him to get back to his whorish ways and lock him down this time.

****

"Hey Kane. I haven't seen you in a minute," I said and sat down next to him in the VIP section of the club. It had been two weeks since everything had gone down and I hadn't seen him anywhere.

"What up, Sherri. I'm good." He stood up and I followed his sexy ass straight to the bathroom. I don't think he realized I was in there.

"What are you doing in here?" he zipped his pants up and went to the sink to wash his hands. I noticed he was on his way out and still had a paper towel in his hands. I forgot how germophobic he is. I closed the space between us and stood on my tippy toes to kiss him, but he turned his face.

"What's wrong?" I dropped my clutch on the floor and started trying to unbuckle his jeans. He moved my hands, but I kept putting them back. He grabbed me up and stood me in front of him.

"Sherri, I meant what I said when I told you April was my girl and you and I were over."

"I know, but you're not together anymore."

"It doesn't matter. April is still my girl. We are going through something right now, but I won't cheat on her."

"WHAT? How are you going to be with a woman who brought harm to your child?"

"That's the thing Sherri. I saw the text you showed me and you caught me off-guard with it. When I got home and thought about it, I'm not too sure that's what happened. April loves my daughter probably more than she loves me, and I can't find it in my heart to believe she did that."

"Can I at least taste the dick? It's not like you're sticking your dick in me."

I saw him shaking his head with a smirk. I was getting ready to suck his soul out, or so I thought I was.

"Goodbye, Sherri."

He used the paper towel to open the door and left me standing there with my mouth open. How did I end up finding a man who didn't cheat on a girl he wasn't even with anymore? All men fall victim to a chick giving them head. I was slipping.

I went to the sink and wiped my face off with some water. I reached for a paper towel and felt someone standing behind me. I looked up and had no idea who he was, but he wore the biggest grin on his face.

"Seems like we both have something in common." I dried my face off and turned around.

"Who are you and what do we have in common?" I folded my arms across my chest and looked at this fine specimen in front of me.

He was taller than me, brown-skinned with dreads down to the middle of his back. He had hazel eyes and his build was a little muscular, but not much. He had crowns on the top and bottom of his teeth and his clothes appeared to be expensive, but I couldn't tell.

"You want that nigga Kane, and I want something he has. I think if we work together, we can both get what we want."

"What's your name and what do you want from him?"

"One question at a time. My name is not really a concern and what I want is something he holds dear to him. I almost had it, but it slipped though my fingers from people being too nosy."

"Whatever it is why don't you get it now? He's in the club."

"Yeah, but he doesn't have it on him. In due time baby girl, in due time. What you trying to do tonight?" he asked and licked his lips as he eye fucked me.

"Whatever you want me to do."

"That's what I like to hear. Let's roll."

He took my hand and led me out the bathroom. I glanced up in the VIP section and saw him. He was talking to some dude I had never seen before. He locked eyes with me and tapped the dude on the shoulder who turned around and stared at me. Damn, that nigga was fine as hell and screamed money, too. Why do the best-looking men travel in packs? The dude sipped his drink then winked his eye at me. I saw some chick put her arms around him. I told the dude I was leaving with I would meet him outside because I had left something.

"What's up, shorty?" The dude said when I walked in the section pretending to look for my phone.

"Not much. What's up with you?" I stood in front of him licking my lips.

"I can't talk much right now because I have a situation with me. Put your number in here quick and bounce. I'll hit you later."

His demeanor was the same as Kane's and I loved it. Kane didn't play games with women and told you what it was from the beginning. I already knew if you fucked him over he would end your life. He demanded respect and the power he held over these niggas out here made my panties wet. I could see this man had as much power and respect as Kane. Fuck it, if Kane didn't want me, I would definitely kick it with this dude.

"What's your name?" I asked him before he walked away.

"Stan."

"Stan. Hmm, I can't wait to hear from you," I smiled and strutted my ass outside to the other dude I'd met from the bathroom.

Call me what you want, but I was horny. Kane wouldn't give me any and I'd just met Stan. I was about to get my rocks off somewhere.

I got to the dude's house and it was a small ranch with two bedrooms. It wasn't dirty but it wasn't spotless, either. He locked the door and had me go sit in some room to wait. He came in naked and I must say he was well-endowed. I stripped out my clothes and let this man fuck me over and over.

I was putting my clothes on and he stepped out to use the phone. It was well worth it.

"Erica, I don't know where the fuck you are, but I miss you baby. Call me when you get this. Shit, I know I was fucked up when I hit you. Just come back," I heard him saying in the phone. *Nah, it can't be the same Erica, and this can't be the dude she was with that violated Kane's daughter. Or could it be?*

Chapter 17

Essence

It'd been a month since I got shot and Stacy was mad because he had no idea who did it. They discharged me yesterday and made me walk with a cane until I felt better. My side was hit twice and it still hurt to walk because it was close to my hip. Stacy catered to my every need when he was home and would take off like a thief in the night to find out who did it. He was exhausted, and I could tell it was killing him not knowing who had a hit out on me.

If you ask me, I think it was that chick who was in the hospital. He claimed it was his best friend Stan's sister. I still didn't understand how they were best friends when I hadn't met his ass. All this time we'd been together, and I'd never seen nor spoken to him once. I started thinking he was make believe until Stacy told me he was in town and wanted all of us to have dinner.

"When is this dinner baby?" I asked him when he got out of the shower. SJ was at my mom's, and he'd just come home.

“Who knows? Stan always says shit like that and then we never meet up.”

“Why haven't I ever met him?”

“Stan moved right before I met you. There was a lot of heat on him, and the Feds plus the US Marshalls were trying to take him down. He disappeared for a long time. He wants to retire and to be honest, I think he wants Kane to take his spot.”

“Kane. But I thought Kane was done with- He cut me off.

“Kane doesn't know yet. The dinner he wants to have is to announce it.”

“What do you think Kane is going to say?”

“Honestly, I don't know. With the shit going on between him and April, he may just do it. His plan was to open up legit businesses, but now he’ll probably do it."

“That's what his ass gets for treating her like that.”

“Stay out of it, Essence.”

“I am. As soon as I curse his ass the fuck out.”

“Trust me when I say he's heard it from everyone.”

He dropped his towel and stood in front of me. I may

have still been sore, but my mouth wasn't. I consumed all his cum, wiped my face, and laid back.

"Damn, I missed tasting my pussy."

He spread my legs open and went deep-sea diving, headfirst. After he licked me clean, he entered me, and I almost passed out. Stacy was packing in the dick department, and it'd been over a month since we'd been together intimately, and he was ripping my shit open. I handled it like a champ though. He took his time making love to me.

"You ok babe?" he asked, hitting it from the back.

"Yes. I'm cumming. Don't stop!" I yelled out and grabbed his thigh with one hand and the sheet with the other. I felt him a few seconds later doing the same thing. I couldn't move afterwards. I heard him go in the bathroom and turn the water on. He came back and washed me down there.

"I love you, Essence."

"I love you too, Stacy. Don't leave me."

"Why would I leave you?" He rolled me over so I was facing him.

"Because I'm basically crippled now. I can't move

around like before." He sat up on his elbows and stared at me like I said something wrong.

"Essence, you are not crippled, and I don't care if you were in a fucking wheelchair. You are my woman and always will be. I would never leave you for something like that. What type of nigga do you think I am?"

"I'm sorry Stacy. I don't want you to wake up one day and feel like this isn't what you want." He opened the nightstand on the side of his bed and came over to where I was lying. He made me sit up as he got down on one knee. I covered my mouth when he opened the box with a huge yellow diamond in it. I didn't know how many carats it was, and I didn't care.

"Essence, I planned on proposing to you at April's party, but it looks like that won't happen." I laughed.

"The day I met you, I knew you would be my wife. You held a certain innocence that captivated me, and I couldn't explain how. You gave me a son and I probably just got you pregnant again." I smacked his arm.

"Essence, you held me down all these years, and I

know I should've asked you sooner, but I was scared that this wasn't what you wanted. I want you to know I appreciate you and the way you take care of home, SJ, and me. There's no other woman out there I would rather carry my last name then you. Will you marry me?" I had tears running down my face as I shook my head yes.

He placed the ring on my finger and lifted me up to kiss me. I wrapped my legs around him, and his manhood started growing under me. We made love a few more times before we went to sleep.

****

"I can't believe you asked me to marry you," I said, staring at my finger while we drove to my mom's house to pick SJ up.

"I don't see myself with anyone else." He kissed my hand.

"Oh shit man. You finally did it," my stepdad said when we walked in the house. I gave him the side eye.

"What? You know he came and asked me for your hand in marriage. But that was two years ago." I was smiling hard because he'd been waiting to ask me. My mom was ecstatic and already pulling up wedding sites in her phone. Stacy grabbed me from behind and kissed the back of my neck.

“I can't wait until you're my wife.”

“I can't wait to be your wife.” I kissed him and went back to looking with my mom while he, SJ, and my dad went out to play basketball. I picked my phone up to call my best friend since she was the matron of honor anyway.

I opted out of calling April and decided to take the ride down there to see her. I had spoken to her about two days ago, and she was sick as hell and depressed over the Lexi and Kane situation.

I stopped by Kane’s mom’s house and picked Lexi up and told her we were going for a ride. That’s where she had been staying since April had left and the guys were always on the go. She and SJ sat in the back talking. Well, he did most of the talking because she had just gotten her wires out.

We pulled up at April’s mom’s house, and Lexi jumped out before I had even put the car in park. I blew the horn, and when April opened the door, Lexi jumped in her arms and started crying. I took a picture with my phone and sent it to Stacy with the caption: *she missed her mom.*

April had finally put her down and walked in the house with her hand and hand. SJ and I both gave her a hug and followed them into the kitchen. She poured the kids something to drink then sent them outside. April looked like she was losing weight more than she was gaining and her eyes had bags under them. I could tell the break up was taking a toll on her even though she'd claimed to be fine over the phone.

"Don't look at me like that. I just miss them."

"I'm not saying anything, and just so you know, he misses you too."

"Yeah right. That nigga said more than enough to show me I am not where he wants to be."

"Do you really believe the shit you spitting April? I mean, yes he said some mean things but the man loves you, and you know it. I haven't seen him to curse his ass out yet, but Stacy told me he is coming back for you." I saw her smirk a little.

"No thanks. If he can do that once, he can do it again.

Don't get me wrong, of course, I would love to get back with him, but what if he does it again? I can't take that shit twice. I'm not built like those other women out there who can tolerate the disrespect. I'm not knocking them because to each his own, but it's not me." I nodded and took a sip of my drink.

"Oh shit bitch. You're getting married?" She ran over to me and gave me a hug. I forgot that's what we came for.

"Yes, he proposed last night. I wanted to call you, but I also had to see how you were in person."

"Congratulations heffa. I know I'm in the wedding." She folded her arms.

"Ugh, I don't know."

"Bitch what?"

"You know Kane is the best man."

"So the fuck what? I don't have to walk down the aisle with him."

"Girl bye. You know you're the matron of honor." She gave me a huge hug and called the kids in for a snack. They came in, and Lexi stayed up under April. It was like she knew what she said was wrong and wanted to know she was forgiven.

“Mommy April, can I stay here tonight?”

“If she’s staying, so am I,” SJ said. Those two were thick as thieves, and you couldn’t break them up for shit.

“Ugh, you have to ask your father.”

“He misses you mommy.” I saw April start tearing up.

“What makes you say that?”

“I told him I missed you, and I was sorry for what I said, and he said he missed you too. He also told me you were coming home soon, and I had to be patient.”

“He told you that?” April asked Lexi, and she shook her head yes. I saw her waddle her pregnant ass upstairs. She was carrying small, and it was probably from the stress. I left the kids down in the living room and went to grab my cell phone.

“What’s up Essence?” Kane answered on the third ring.

“First of all, I owe you a tongue lashing, but that’s not what I’m calling for.”

“Whatever. Is everything good with the kids?”

“Yes. I’m calling about April.” The phone got silent.

"I'm on my way. What happened to her?" I could hear the car door open and him starting the car.

"Nothing happened to her, you can relax. I'm just calling to tell you Lexi is staying here with her and that you need to make shit right with her." I heard him blow his breath in the phone.

"I know Essence, and I will. I just can't right now. It's a lot of things going on out in these streets, and the best thing for her right now is to be away from me. Her and Lexi are my main concern, and if anything ever happened to either of them, I would lose my fucking mind. No one knows where she is, and I need to keep it that way. Just do me a favor."

"What?"

"Tell her…you know what, never mind. Tell Lexi to call me before she goes to bed." I told him ok and hung the phone up. Kane was without a doubt still in love with her but whatever he had going on in the streets was holding him back. I laid down on the bed with her, and she was wiping her eyes.

"He still loves you April. I don't know what's going on, but that man is not about to let you leave him."

"He has no choice. Fuck him."

"April, I understand you're mad right now, and I don't blame you. This will all be over soon, and he will explain everything to you." She sucked her teeth.

"Look, I'm going to leave now and get on the road. It's a long drive, and my leg starts to hurt when I'm in the car too long. Plus, it's getting dark. Stacy already sent me two messages telling me to bring my ass home. I love you, and I'll call you when I get home," I kissed her cheek and left her sitting on the bed in deep thought. I hope they work shit out. They both getting on my nerves.

Chapter 18

Kane

I know the way I treated April was dead ass wrong, but I did what I had to do under the circumstances. I knew for a fact Sherri lied, and the text was made up. Derrick hit me up right before she'd walked in and told me some chick he was messing with was drunk and told him what Sherri did.

Evidently, they were friends, and she was in on the shit because the dude Erica messed with was friends with her brother. I'm not sure if they knew he did that shit to my daughter, but I needed to make Sherri think I believed her. April was hurt and as bad as I wanted to explain everything to her, I couldn't right now. Stacy even knew what was going on and came downstairs to make it look real.

I stayed away from Sherri after that because I knew she would try to fuck and I wasn't going there with her. When I saw her at the club, I assumed she would try and be there for me after what happened, but all she wanted to do was fuck. I wasn't gonna do April like that. The second she'd laid eyes on Stan, I knew she was going to make him her prey. What her dumb ass didn't know was she was just a pawn in our game.

“Lexi, I know you don't wanna talk about it, but I need you to tell daddy what the guy looks like who did this to you,” I said to her when I walked in her room. She’d just come back from staying with her mother April after a week.

Yes, that’s what I called her because Erica was dead and it was what it was. I was missing the fuck out of my girl, but I couldn’t take the chance of someone finding her.

The only reason Lexi was around was because she stayed with my parents and their house was like Fort Knox. Stacy’s and mine were too but with me leaving throughout the night and Essence trying to get better, we were leaving the kids at my parents’ house until school started-which was a week away.

The way she described him could be any nigga walking the street. I was going to have to find him on my own. Derrick told me he was over the chick’s house, and she had a friend over. The address Erica gave us was to some old people's house. I couldn't believe she still saved that nigga, even in her death.

I gave Lexi a kiss and went downstairs to tell my mom I would be back later tonight or tomorrow.

"Son, I know you feel like what you're doing is right but the longer you wait to tell her the truth, the harder it's going to be to get her back," my mom said and opened the door for me to leave.

"At this point, I don't even know how to make it right."

"Whatever you were about to do, forget it and go see her." I listened to what she said, and as badly as I wanted to see April, I went to the house where Derrick was.

Some chick opened the door, and she must've been a model somewhere. She was flawless in every way. Her ass looked juicy in those jeans and her cleavage hanging out allowed me to guess her chest was at least in the D section. She was pretty and reminded me of Jennifer Lopez a little. She showed me where my boy was, and this chick was on her knees giving him head.

"Really, nigga?"

"What? Shit, I told her to go in the room, but she insisted." The girl lifted her head and waved. She had no shame in her game.

"Come with me," the other chick said, and we sat down in another room. I took the blunt from the back of my ear and lit it. I offered her some, but she declined.

"Do you want something to drink?" I told her sure, and she went to the kitchen. I was coming out from the bathroom and saw home girl pouring something in my drink.

I didn't say shit, walked back in the room and pretended I didn't see her. She handed me my drink and took a sip of hers. I guess I was taking too long to sip because she asked me why I wasn't drinking yet if I was thirsty.

"I will in a few shorty. Let me finish this blunt."

She stood in front of me and removed her shirt first and then her jeans. My dick was fighting me to come out, but I refused. She took her panties off, exposing her freshly shaven kitty and sat on top of me in a straddling position. The minute she did that I grabbed her by the hair with the blunt in my mouth and put my gun to her temple.

"Who told you to put that shit in my drink?" She started tearing up, but I gave zero fucks.

"Tell me right now or your brains will be all over this room."

"Glenn. Glenn told me to do it."

"Who the fuck is Glenn?"

"That's my brother. He said you two were beefing and you're trying to kill him." Then it dawned on me what my boy said the other day about the person being friends with his sister.

"Hold the fuck up," I yelled out and dropped the blunt on the ground. I still had her by the hair and dragged her stupid ass out to the front.

"Pull your dick out that bitch and let's go."

Derrick looked at me and did what I said. He knew if I said that, something must've happened. The other girl was on the phone texting away while Derrick pulled his jeans up. I let off two shots in her forehead.

"Do you know why I wanna kill your brother?" She shook her head no and was trying to remove my hands from her hair.

"The nigga raped my six-year-old daughter more than once. And before you say anything; yes, it is true." She covered her mouth in shock.

"Now, what you're going to do is give me his real address and phone number."

"Not if you're going to kill him."

"Oh, I see you are your brother's keeper." She nodded her head.

"Too bad. The nigga just got you killed." I let a shot off in between her forehead and grabbed the other chick's phone. Just like I'd thought, she was texting someone and telling them shit went left, and they'd needed to hurry up and get there.

Derrick and I wiped down any and everything we had touched and set the shit on fire. We were in the hood, so it would take the fire trucks a while to get there. They could care less about a house burning down.

By the time they got there, the ceiling had already started caving in. I stood there waiting for some niggas to show up and while a few did, I couldn't pinpoint who was down with this Glenn dude.

"What you wanna do?" Stacy asked, walking up behind me with Stan.

"After he finds out his sister was killed, I'm sure he'll come around." I got in my car and made my way to the next destination.

She came to the door, I swooped her up, kicked the door closed and carried her to the room. I stripped her naked and stared at her body. She was perfect to me, and I wanted her to know it. I kissed and caressed her entire body from head to toe. She tried to push my head away when I found her treasure, but I held her hips tighter and went in for the kill.

"Fuck Kane. I can't cum anymore," she yelled out after reaching her third climax. I allowed her to lie there and catch her breath while I took a quick shower. I was about to give this woman everything I had, and I didn't want the smell of fire or death on me when I did.

"Washing her smell off?" she said, and I smirked. She was jealous, and it showed all over her face.

"Yup. I'm about to make love to you and then fuck the shit out of you. I couldn't have another woman on me." She rolled her eyes.

"Come here and sit on my face."

"No Kane. You're not getting no pussy, and you just came from another woman."

"Fine." I stood up in front of her and dropped my towel. I saw the way she bit down on her lip, and I knew that was all it took. She loved giving me head and anytime I stood like this in front of her she would just take it.

"Shit girl, I'm cumming already." She sucked until all my future kids were tumbling down her throat. She stood up and kissed me. I stroked my man back to life and gently tossed her back.

"Open your fucking legs."

"No." She moved back on the bed. I grabbed her ankles, pulled her to the edge, and entered her roughly with no regrets.

"Fuckkkkk Kane. Oh my Gawd, you feel so good." I felt her release in seconds. I continued making love to her until I saw tears rolling down her face. I stopped and kissed each one away. Her legs wrapped around my back, and I could feel her fucking me from underneath.

"Do you still love me?" She didn't answer. I hit her with a deep death stroke, and her head went back, mouth flew open, and her legs started shaking.

"Do you still love me?" She nodded her head yes.

"I can't hear you nodding your head. I hit her with the same stroke again and this time, she screamed out so loud the neighbors had to have heard her.

"Yes, Kane. Yes, baby, I love you. Fuck. I love you so much." I smiled looking down at her facial expression as I drove her crazy.

"I love you too April, and I swear we're going to be together. I just need more time. Can you wait for me?"

"As long as you don't cheat on me."

"Never baby. I told you you're all I need, and I meant it."

"I am?"

"Without a doubt." I continued making love to her throughout the night. I wanted to fuck the shit out of her too but the moment didn't call for that. I would have if she hadn't told me she loved me.

****

I woke up the next day to breakfast in bed courtesy of

my girl. Yes, I was still calling her that even though it seemed otherwise. She went in the bathroom and started the shower. I was hungry as hell but going all this time without sex had me jump right in the shower with her and give her some more. I guess she was just as horny because she was leaking like a river every time.

"I missed you April."

"I missed you too. I know why you did what you did but Kane, don't ever let you disrespecting me like that be the part of any plan. I was so hurt, and you had me thinking all this time you believed her over me." I had explained everything to her last night before we had fallen asleep.

"When you asked me at the house if I blamed you, what did I say?"

"You told me no."

"Ok. I understand how everything played out, but do you really think I would allow you around my daughter if I thought that?"

"I know Kane, but I've never seen you act like that and shit, you were very convincing," she said and wrapped a towel around her.

“April, there will never come a time where I would disrespect you like that. Like you said you were there for Lexi even when Erica wasn’t. You didn’t know either of us, but you still took care of my daughter and kept her safe. I will always be in debt to you for that. No woman will ever be able to take your spot in my life or my heart. You got the shit on lock.” She started crying as usual.

“It’s ok baby,” she said and sat down on the bed. She pulled me in front of her and did her thing. I tried to stop her but like I said, she loved pleasing me orally, and you can’t deny a pregnant woman.

After we’d finished, I got the clothes outta my car and brought them in the house to get dressed.

“Real funny giving me all my shit back,” I said, pulling my shirt over my head.

“Kane, I don’t want your money. All I ever wanted was you and my daughter.”

“That’s why I love you even more. You didn’t care what I had and left with nothing but the clothes on your back.

April, I know you're not with me for the money, but I also need you to know that whatever I give you, it's yours. I'm not the type of nigga to take shit back because we broke up. That's what fuck niggas do."

"But Kane…"

"But Kane nothing. I've told you that before, but you don't listen. Now here's your new bankcard with all the money on it you gave back plus some. Your truck is in the driveway, and I ordered you a new one, but it's at the house."

"Kane."

"Stop it April. When all this shit blows over, you're coming home. There's no way I should have to visit my girl this far, but right now I have no choice."

"Kane." I stopped at the door and turned around. Stacy was blowing the horn telling me to hurry up. I had him come down here to pick me up so I could leave her truck.

"Make sure you teach our son to treat his woman the same way." I ran over to her like a big ass kid.

"I'm having a son. Oh shit! I squirted a boy in you. Fuck baby. You just made me the happiest man on earth right now." I kissed her with so much passion my dick got hard, and I closed the door. Stacy had to wait. She took me in the downstairs bathroom and let me get a quickie from her.

"I love you April and I can't wait until my son gets here. You know Lexi is going to take over though." I kissed her standing in front of the door.

"I know she is. You just make sure you don't yell at her for it."

"April when all this is over I want you to adopt Lexi. Are you ok with that?" She gasped and covered her mouth.

"Are you serious Kane? Oh my God! Of course I will. I mean, she won't have my last name but hell yea I would. Wait, what about her mother? She's not going to go for that."

"What's understood doesn't need to be explained. She won't be a problem. I love you and take care of my son," I told her and walked out before she could ask me what I meant by it.

"It's about time you made up with her." Stacy passed me the blunt he was smoking.

"Yeah, I know. I just got this bad feeling now."

"About?"

"Now that his sister is dead he's going to come for her. I have to try and stay away until we find his ass."

"I understand. But will she?" I leaned my seat back and shut my eyes in hopes to get a nap before we got back. Stan wanted to have his meeting later today, and I think I knew what he wanted. The question is if that's something I felt like getting back into.

Chapter 19

Stan

I know you guys haven't heard much from me so let me introduce myself. As you already know, my name is Stan. Stacy, and I have been best friends since we were kids. Kane is like my little brother, and he'd been working for me until he got arrested some years back in California on some bogus ass charges. I was happy as hell for him when I heard he sued their asses.

I took Kane under my wing because he proved to me time and time again that hustling was in his bones. He and Derrick made me a lot of money even though I let them keep most of it. To me, I was already rich, and wanted to make sure they were eating too.

Right before Kane was locked up one of the cops on my payroll told me the Feds and the US Marshalls were getting ready to take me down. I couldn't allow that to happen since I was making money nationwide, and so was everyone who worked with me. I made myself disappear and never came back until I heard Kane was in town.

I made plans to retire from this lifestyle, and he was the only one I trusted to keep it up and running the same way. I think he had an idea about why I was there but hadn't said anything. He would be correct if he thought that, but I also came to see my sisters.

Lucy and I had the same parents while April and I shared a father. In my eyes, it didn't matter if you shared both parents or not, if you shared one you were a sibling. Fuck all that half-brother, half-sister shit. We came from the same nutsack.

Now I had to deal with Lucy, who was harassing Stacy because the accident she'd had caused her to lose her memory and the only person she remembered was him.

However, she found him and started causing major problems. April was the hood sister that didn't take shit from anyone and never allowed a man to walk over her. The crazy part is neither of them knew about the other. Don't ask me why our parents never mentioned it, and it wasn't my place to do it.

Today would be my first day seeing Lexi since she was born. I was out of state when she was born and saw her a few times when she was at Stacy's parents' house when I slipped in town. I didn't know why I was nervous going over there when I'd known their parents all my life.

My girl, Sean, was holding my hand as we waited for someone to open the door. Yes, she was a female, but her mom wanted her to be named after her dad since he'd passed away a month before she was born.

"You ok baby?" She pecked me on the lips and wiped her lip gloss off.

Sean was very laid back and didn't say much which is what I loved about her, but don't get on her bad side.

She stood about five foot five with a body most women wanted courtesy of the trainer she saw three to four times a week. She was a health fanatic, but she didn't overdo it. She was a general manager at Bank of America and traveled a lot. I thought it would bother me, but it didn't because we traveled together. Whenever she went, I went, and while she worked, I was out making investments.

"I'm good. It's just been a while." The door opened, and Kane's mom just started crying. I knew I wouldn't be able to handle this shit. She was like my mom, and I knew being away and coming back was going to be emotional for her.

“Oh my God, I can't believe you're here.” She hugged me and wouldn't let go. Sean was standing there grinning.

“Nana who is this and why are you crying?” The little girl said.

“Get off my nana. Why are you making her cry?” Some little boy said and started punching me in the leg. I looked down, and it was SJ. I only knew that from all the photos Stacy would send.

“Stop it, you two. This is your uncle, Stan.”

“I don't have an uncle named Stan.” The little girl had her hands on her hips.

“Who you talking to like that? I know Kane doesn't let you talk like that and take your hands off your hips.”

“Hmmm, maybe you are my uncle. You're mean just like my dad and Uncle Stacy. Don't tell my dad or I'm going to tell him you had my nana crying,” she had the nerve to say and fold her arms.

“Girl, get your grown ass in the house,” I scolded her

like she was my kid through gritted teeth. Sean was cracking up.

“I don't know why you're laughing. If that's my uncle, I know he didn't approve of you coming out half-dressed like that.” Sean's entire demeanor changed as she tried to pull her dress down a little.

“Don't pull it down now. Uncle Stan, you better get your girl before a nigga like me take her upstairs.” Her mouth flew open.

“Yo, where the fuck you learn to talk like that?”

“Uncle Kane. That's how he talks to all his hoes. The only one he doesn't talk to like that is Lexi's mom April.”

“April? I thought her mom was Erica.” We walked in the house, and Kane’s mom was just shaking her head.

“She is the woman who had me in her stomach, but my real mother’s name is April. Please don't make me say it again,” Lexi said.

“Ma, how do you deal with this? They need their ass whooped.”

“They're just kids.”

“Ma, you need to correct that or tell their parents. It's going to get worse.”

“Anyway. Uncle Stan don't come in here trying to get us in trouble. We just met you, and you should be playing nice or at least handing over some money for lost time. You definitely got it by the way you shining over there.”

"Stan, I can't take any more. Please make them stop." Sean was damn near in tears laughing so hard.

“Oh, it's funny huh? See how funny it is when you don't get no dick later, “I whispered in her ear. But those nosy ass kids were on it.

“Don't worry. My dad says that all the time to April and when the door closes, they have adult time anyway.” Sean covered her mouth.

“My mom is the same way. My dad tried to tell her that one-day. My mom dropped me off that afternoon and the next day my dad slept all day. I asked if he went out and he said no, he just kept mommy company all night.”

“Ok, that's it. Take y'all little asses upstairs. What the hell ma?” She was shaking her head, and all I could do was laugh. I sent a text to those fools and told them their kids needed military school as soon as possible.

“Wait. Why is your name Sean if you're a girl? Were you changed or something?”

“Changed?” Sean seemed confused.

“You know, where boys are girls now and…”

“Bye Lexi.” Sean was hysterically laughing.

“What the fuck is they teaching this kids in school?” I yelled out after they went upstairs.

“Baby, don't get mad. It was fun. Pretty soon we'll be going through the same thing” I rubbed her stomach and kissed her lips.

We’d just found out she was three months and couldn't wait to start our family. That was one of the reasons I wanted to get out. I would have legit businesses, but the drug world wasn't cutting it for me anymore.

Stacy came shortly after the fiasco with the kids and I met his new fiancé, Essence, and she was gorgeous. Kane came alone because he said the things he had going on he didn't want his pregnant girl around it. I could understand that.

All through dinner, those little shits were quiet as hell. They spoke amongst themselves but all that tough shit they were talking was nowhere to be found.

"Lexi, I know your ass wasn't being grown," Essence said, and she smirked.

"No auntie. I would never."

"Yeah ok. Don't make me get April on the phone." She hopped up out her seat and went to where Essence was.

"Please don't tell her. I won't do it again."

"Hmmm, seems like April got that ass in check, huh?" The little heffa had the nerve to roll her eyes at me and suck her teeth.

"Stan, that little girl is about to beat your ass. Will you leave her alone?" Sean was getting a kick out of all of it.

I stood up, walked over to where she was and kneeled down in front of her. She flinched, and the entire room got quiet. I saw tears start rolling down her eyes and immediately felt bad.

"Why are you jumping Lexi?"

"You're not going to hit me are you?"

"What? Your ass needs a whooping, but I'm not going to put my hands on you."

"He used to hit me if I got smart or didn't listen to him."

"Who did?" She put her head down. I lifted her chin up for her to face me.

"Lexi, look at me. Who hit you?"

"Glenn. He did it all the time, especially when I didn't touch his thing for him."

I heard a loud noise and when I turned around it was Kane who had punched a hole in the wall. I looked over, and Stacy's girl had her own tears running down her face and Sean had a disgusted look on hers. I hadn't told her what had happened because she herself was a victim of sexual abuse as a kid from her stepfather. I didn't want it to bring up bad memories for her.

"He will never touch you again and know your father and all of us are doing everything we can to find him. Trust me, it's just a matter of time before we find him."

"Can you get him fast? My daddy misses Mommy

April, and she can't come home to us until he gone." She was now wiping her eyes.

"Take them out of here." Essence, Sean, and my mom took them out of the kitchen while I went out to the back where Stacy had just taken Kane. He was pacing back and forth with the gun in his hand. He was ready for war, and I couldn't blame him.

"Yo, I'm going to torture the FUCK out of that nigga when I find him." I saw a tear leave his eye, and I can't say I wasn't shocked.

As a new dad, hearing a man violated your child like that is bound to bring your emotions out. I lit the blunt Stacy passed me and handed it to Kane. He needed to calm down before he went out and did something reckless that would cause him to lose everything; including Lexi. I looked down at my phone, and it was my sister, April, calling.

"What's up sis?" I heard a lot of shuffling in the background.

"Hello." I stood up nervous. Kane and Stacy were staring at me. April never butt dialed me so I knew something was wrong.

"Call your nigga on the phone right now or I swear I will shoot that baby out your stomach." I could hear her telling him no then I heard a gunshot.

"FUCKKKKKKKK!" I yelled out making the both of them look at me.

"What's up?"

"I have to go."

"What's going on?"

"Somebody just shot my sister."

"Your sister Lucy?" Stan asked me.

"Nah, my sister on my dad's side." I ran in the house and yelled to Sean that I would be back. I could hear Kane telling them to lock the doors and not to open them for anyone. The look of concern was all over their faces. It was going to feel like the longest drive ever. I could already feel it.

Chapter 20

April

After Kane left earlier, I got dressed and decided to do a little baby shopping. I had a few things here at my moms' house but the crib, stroller, and other big items I had yet to purchase.

I went into Babies'R'us and used a scanner to put on a registry what I'd wanted. I was going to give it to Kane and let him pay for it. I walked around the store a few minutes longer and went to my car. I picked my phone up to call Kane and what do you know? He was calling me at the same time.

"Hey, I was just about to call you." I told him.

"Oh yeah. What's up?"

"Nothing. I was in the baby store ordering the crib and a few other things. I was going to see if you could put the stuff together."

"April, you and my son are coming home, and he already has everything at the house. I know it feels like forever, but baby I need you to trust me."

“I do trust you, Kane. I’m ready to come home now, but since I can’t and don’t know how long before I will, the baby will need something to sleep in.”

“He can sleep with his mother.”

“I know Kane but-”

“Stop being a brat April.” I found myself pouting as I pulled up in the Cherry Hill Mall parking lot.

“Whatever.”

“Do you plan on breastfeeding?” he asked me out of the blue.

“Probably not. I heard it’s good for the baby, but then I heard it hurts.”

“Good. Those are my titties, and I’m the only one who should be sucking on them.”

“I can’t with you Kane.” I closed the door and headed into the mall.

“Where are you?”

“At the mall. I wanted to get me some stretch pants. I can’t fit anything.”

"Alright. The minute you're done I want you to go straight back to your mom's house. I don't like you being in public alone."

"You said no one knows where I am."

"I know baby, but I just want you to be careful. I'm killing everyone if anything happens to you." I smiled because he was really overprotective of me.

"Ok. I'm just running in Old Navy, and I'm leaving."

"I'm at my mom's house having dinner with everyone. You know Lexi and SJ met my brother from another mother and gave him hell. You know he said we should send your daughter to military school." I busted out laughing because she was a piece of work.

"Kane don't you let anybody send my baby away." I was laughing but dead serious.

"Hmmmm, what do I get if I don't?"

"What do you want?"

"You know what I want. Matter of fact, when you get home FaceTime me. I want to see you play with my pussy. That shit sexy as hell."

"Bye Kane. I love you."

"I love you too baby." We hung up, and I ended up staying in the mall much longer then expected.

By the time I got to my car, my feet were killing me. All I wanted to do was take a shower and lie down. Kane was probably going to come in late, and I would at least be ready for him. I loved everything about that man, and I prayed they caught the motherfucker who violated Lexi.

I brought the bags in and did exactly what I said I would. My mom left and told me she would be gone for the night. I locked up and Face Timed Kane, but he didn't answer. I assumed he was on the road to me and didn't hear the phone. I always told him to turn the music down, but he said it soothed him.

The doorbell rang while I was in the kitchen getting something to drink. I looked at the time, and it was a little after seven.

"Long time no see, baby girl," my ex, Demetrius, said and walked in without my permission. I closed my robe and even though I had on a tank top and pajama pants, I still felt naked in front of him.

“What the fuck are you doing here?” I couldn’t stand my ex, and he knew it.

“Let me find out you didn’t miss me.”

“I didn’t. What the fuck do you want?”

“I see you’re expecting.” I started getting nervous when he said that for some reason.

“If you don’t tell me what you’re here for, I’m going to call the cops.” Just as I said it there was a knock at the door. He had the nerve to open it and when he did it was like the air had left my body. The nigga who violated my daughter on more than one occasion was standing in my doorway. I didn’t know if I should run or call the cops. I was frozen in my spot.

“Don’t be scared, April. I can guarantee he won’t touch you.” The nigga walked in and looked around the house as if he was trying to find something or someone.”

“Demetrius, I know damn well you didn’t bring this pedophile rapist in my house.” I saw the surprised look on his face as if he didn’t know.

"What are you talking about April? He's not a rapist or pedophile. You don't remember Glenn? He used to try and follow us around when we were younger." That's when it hit me.

When I dated Demetrius back then, Glenn was a few years younger and always wanted to hang with us. He was my ex's neighbor. I was standing there looking at him, and he had grown a beard, dreads, and had a mouth full of gold teeth. I would've never imagined that was him.

"Demetrius as long as we've been together when have you ever known me to lie. That nigga raped-" was all I got out when a fist connected with my face. The minute he did, I felt my mouth start bleeding and I spit out two teeth. The impact from his hit caused me to stumble, but Demetrius caught me just in time. He sat me down on the couch.

"What the fuck Glenn? Don't ever put your fucking hands on her."

I didn't know why he said that. The reason we broke up was because he was whooping my ass on a regular. I could come home from the store and run past him to use the bathroom, and that would piss him off, making him hit me a few times.

The abuse went on for the entire four years we were together. The only reason I got away from him was because he had gotten a gun charge and had to serve time. While they were arguing back and forth, I dialed Stan's number and left the phone on in my pocket.

"Call your man on the phone or I'm going to shoot your ass in the stomach. He and I have some unfinished business," Glenn said. I told him no, and he let a shot off in the ceiling.

"Her man. I see she's pregnant and all, but I thought she didn't have one."

"Nah, she goes with that nigga Kane." The look on my ex's face showed me he was about to beat my ass.

"Who the fuck is Kane?" He was in my face and spit was flying out. He yoked me up, and I prayed Stan had answered the phone and heard everything going on. I was hoping the sounds weren't muffled.

"Kane is the nigga who killed my sister?"

"Demetrius, you and I were over, and I found someone else. Please just leave." I felt myself crying. I was trying to stay calm so I wouldn't go into early labor.

He snatched me up and dragged me outside. He had me get in some car and drove off. Twenty minutes later he pulled up to some warehouse and made me go inside. I came face to face with the same bitch that lied and said she was sleeping with Stacy. There were about ten men behind her. What the hell was going on?

"What the fuck are you doing here?" She backhanded the shit out of me, and I punched her right in the nose. Her shit started leaking instantly.

"Bitch!" she yelled out, covering her nose.

"Nah, you're the bitch. Demetrius what the hell is going on and why am I here?" No one said a word as they waited for the chick to come back. She came back to me and hit me on the head with the butt of her gun. I thought Demetrius would say something, but he didn't.

"Next time I'm going to kill you," she said and sat on my ex's lap. This shit couldn't be happening right now. First, the pedophile comes to my house and hits me, then I'm dragged to a warehouse where my ex is with the chick Stacy used to be with. What the fuck else could go wrong?

"Lucy what the fuck is going on?" I turned around, and Stan, Kane, Stacy, Derrick, and a few other dudes were standing there.

"Ahhh, my loving brother and my bitch ass ex," she said sarcastically.

"How's your bitch Stacy? Too bad we didn't kill her." Stacy went to charge for her, but Stan held him back.

"April are you ok?" Kane started walking towards me but stopped when he heard a gun click. I felt it on the back of my head, and when I looked it was Glenn. I knew none of them knew it was him, but you can bet I was telling.

"How do you know my sister?" Stan asked him.

"Your sister?" Stacy and Kane said at the same time.

"Yes, we have the same father." I could see the look of confusion on Kane's face.

"Kane, we lost contact and I hadn't heard from him in years. He came back, and you and I weren't talking at first. Anyway, that's my brother, and I guess she's my sister."

"Ok, fuck this stupid ass family reunion. Stan the reason I have this dumb bitch is because I want everything you planned on passing down to her man." I saw Kane's entire face cringe.

"Are you serious right now?" Stan asked her.

"I know you're retiring, and I want the empire."

"WHAT?" he yelled out walking towards her slowly.

"How am I going to give you an empire and you barely have your memory?"

"Oh yeah, about that? I got my memory back a few years ago. I had to play dumb so I could learn everything from you. You assumed I would forget everything I heard, but I didn't."

"Lucy if you told me your memory was back, I would've groomed you for a takeover. Kane don't want the shit but the way you went about this, I'm going to have to say HELL NO to your unstable ass."

“It doesn’t really matter because I have all your contacts and so forth. I know your bank account information and where you are hiding other money.”

“If you know me like you claim to, then you would know I changed everything up, and my contacts all have new numbers and moved to new locations. My bank accounts are in another name and the ones hidden are as well.” Her mouth dropped.

“You see, when you’re the boss of shit, you need to make changes when no one is paying attention. That way when they think they got you by the balls, BAM! You hit them with some real shit.” The look on her face was priceless.

“What the fuck Stan? I’m your sister.”

“That’s right, and you should’ve known better than to go against the grain.” He shot her in the arm. I had never seen anything like it. Blood was gushing out.

Demetrius came walking towards me and put his mouth on mine. Kane fucking lost it. He was beating the shit out of him. It seemed like everything was under control until I saw

Glenn hold his phone up and there was a familiar face on the screen.

"That's right nigga. I'm the motherfucker who has your daughter."

"What?"

"That's right. She's going to be great in bed when she gets older." Kane tried to rush him, but Stacy stopped him.

"I've had someone watching your mothers' house for a week now. The minute the three of you left, I sent my boy there to get her." He showed us a photo of Lexi, and I broke down crying. I had blood coming from my mouth, and my head but the only thing concerning me was him having Lexi.

"Glenn please just let her go. You can take me," I cried out.

"Hell no April. It's me you want, right? Come on nigga. Kill me and you better hope I die because if I don't, you can bet your life I'm coming for you."

As Kane was talking, I stared a little harder at the phone he held up while his hand held the gun. There was something very familiar about the photo.

BOOM! was all I heard and hit the floor. I felt people stomping on me as they tried to get away.

"April, where are you?" I heard Kane yelling, but his voice was too far.

"I'm here Kane. Help me. I think I'm losing the baby." I no longer heard his voice or any other voices. My body was being lifted off the ground, and I was placed in a car. I was going in and out of consciousness.

"Kane get me to the hospital."

"My name ain't Kane bitch," was the last thing I'd heard before I passed completely out.

TO BE CONTINUED…

CPSIA information can be obtained
at www.ICGtesting.com
Printed in the USA
LVHW031815100419
613666LV00003B/179

Biochemistry of Plant Secondary Metabolism

Annual Plant Reviews

A series for researchers and postgraduates in the plant sciences. Each volume in this annual series will focus on a theme of topical importance and emphasis will be placed on rapid publication.

Editorial Board:

Titles in the Series:

1. Arabidopsis
Edited by M. Anderson and J. Roberts.

2. Biochemistry of Plant Secondary Metabolism
Edited by M. Wink.

3. Functions of Plant Secondary Metabolites and their Exploitation in Biotechnology
Edited by M. Wink.

Biochemistry of Plant Secondary Metabolism

Edited by

MICHAEL WINK
Professor of Pharmaceutical Biology
University of Heidelberg
Germany

CRC Press

First published 1999

Published by
Sheffield Academic Press Ltd
Mansion House, 19 Kingfield Road
Sheffield S11 9AS, England

ISBN 1-84127-007-5
ISSN 1460-1494

Published in the U.S.A. and Canada (only) by
CRC Press LLC
2000 Corporate Blvd., N.W.
Boca Raton, FL 33431, U.S.A.
Orders from the U.S.A. and Canada (only) to CRC Press LLC

U.S.A. and Canada only:
ISBN 0-8493-4085-3
ISSN 1097-7570

Printed on acid-free paper in Great Britain by
Bookcraft Ltd, Midsomer Norton, Bath

British Library Cataloguing-in-Publication Data:
A catalogue record for this book is available from the British Library

Library of Congress Cataloging-in-Publication Data:
Biochemistry of plant secondary metabolism / edited by Michael Wink.
p. cm.
Includes bibliographical references and index.
ISBN 0-8493-4085-3 (alk. paper)
1. Plants--Metabolism. 2. Metabolism, Secondary. 3. Botanical chemistry I. Wink, Michael.
QK881.B54 1999
572'.42--dc21 99-11779
CIP

Preface

A characteristic feature of plants is their capacity to synthesise an enormous variety of low molecular weight compounds, the so-called secondary metabolites. Although only 20–30% of higher plants have been investigated so far, several tens of thousands of secondary metabolites have already been isolated and identified. Over the last decade, it has become evident that secondary metabolites are not just waste products or otherwise functionless molecules. In fact, the opposite is the case: most secondary metabolites have an important role in the plants producing them. They may function as signal molecules within the plant, or between the plant producing them and other plants, microbes, herbivores, pollinating or seed-dispersing animals. More often, they serve as chemical defence compounds against herbivorous animals, microbes, viruses or competing plants. Secondary metabolites are therefore ultimately important for the fitness of the plant producing them.

In order to understand the importance of secondary metabolites for plants, we need detailed information on the biochemistry of secondary metabolism and its integration into the physiology and ecology of plants. Important issues include: characterisation of enzymes and genes of corresponding biosynthetic pathways, and of transport and storage mechanisms, and regulation in space/time and compartmentation of both biosynthesis and storage.

In this volume of *Annual Plant Reviews*, we have tried to provide an up-to-date survey of the biochemistry of plant secondary metabolism. A companion volume—M. Wink (ed.) *Functions of Plant Secondary Metabolites and their Exploitation in Biotechnology*—published simultaneously, provides overviews of the modes of action of secondary metabolites and their utilisation in pharmacology as molecular probes, in medicine as therapeutic agents, and in agriculture as biorational pesticides. To achieve a comprehensive and up-to-date summary, we have invited scientists who are specialists in their particular areas to define current thinking. The present volume draws together results from a broad area of plant biochemistry and it cannot be exhaustive on such a large and diverse group of constituents. Emphasis was therefore placed on new results and concepts which have emerged over the last decade.

The volume starts with an overview of the biochemistry, physiology, function and utilisation of plant secondary metabolites, followed by detailed surveys of alkaloids and betalaines, cyanogenic glycosides, glucosinolates and nonprotein amino acids, phenyl propanoids and related compounds, and terpenoids (monoterpenes, sesquiterpenes, sterols, cardiac glycosides and steroid saponins). A chapter is included on the importance of secondary metabolites in taxonomy, as viewed from the perspective of molecular systematics.

The book is designed for use by advanced students, researchers and professionals in plant biochemistry, physiology, molecular biology, genetics, agriculture and pharmacy working in the academic and industrial sectors, including the pesticide and pharmaceutical industries.

The book brought together contributions from friends and colleagues in many parts of the world. In several instances we had to ask two or more colleagues working in a related field to contribute to a common chapter, instead of writing individual chapters. The Publisher and the Editor are aware that this was not an easy task but, as the reader will be able to judge, our authors were successful in rising to the challenge. As Editor, I would like to thank all those who have taken part in the writing and preparation of this book. Special thanks go to the Publisher, Dr Graeme MacKintosh, and his team for their interest, support and encouragement.

I would like to thank my wife, Dr Coralie Wink, for her help in preparation of the index.

Michael Wink
Heidelberg

Contributors

Professor Dr Jonathan Gershenzon	Max-Planck-Institut für Chemische Ökologie, Tatzendpromenade 1a, D-07745 Jena, Germany
Professor Dr Wolfgang Kreis	Lehrstuhl für Pharmazeutische Biologie, FAU Erlangen-Nürnberg, Staudtstrasse 5, D-91058 Erlangen, Germany
Professor Dr Ulrich Matern	Institut für Pharmazeutische Biologie, Philips-Universität Marburg, Deutschhausstrasse 17 A, D-35037 Marburg, Germany
Professor Dr Maike Petersen	Institut für Pharmazeutische Biologie, Philipps-Universität Marburg, Deutschhausstrasse 17 A, D-35037 Marburg, Germany
Dr Margaret F. Roberts	The School of Pharmacy, University of London, 29/39 Brunswick Square, London WC1N 1AX, UK
Professor Dr Dirk Selmar	Botanisches Institut und Botanischer Garten, Technische Universität Braunschweig, Mendelssohnstrasse 4, Postfach 3329, 38092 Braunschweig, Germany
Professor Dr Dieter Strack	Institut für Pflanzenbiochemie, Abt. Sekundärstoffwechsel, Weinberg 3, D-06120 Halle (Saale), Germany
Professor Dr Peter G. Waterman	Centre for Phytochemistry, Southern Cross University, PO Box 157, Lismore NSW 2480, Australia
Professor Dr Michael Wink	Institut für Pharmazeutische Biologie, Universität Heidelberg, Im Neuenheimer Feld 364, D-69120 Heidelberg, Germany

Contents

1 Introduction: biochemistry, role and biotechnology of secondary metabolites

Michael Wink

1.1 Introduction

A characteristic feature of plants is their capacity to synthesize an enormous variety of low molecular weight compounds, the so-called secondary metabolites (SMs). Although only 20–30% of higher plants have been investigated so far, several tens of thousands of SMs have already been isolated and their structures determined by mass spectrometry (electron impact [EI]-MS, chemical ionisation [CI]-MS, fast atom bombardment [FAB]-MS), nuclear magnetic resonance (^{1}H-NMR, ^{13}C-NMR) or X-ray diffraction (Harborne, 1993; DNP, 1996). In Table 1.1, an estimate of the numbers of known secondary metabolites is given. Representative structures are presented in Figure 1.1.

Table 1.1 Number of known secondary metabolites from higher plants

Type of secondary metabolite	No.*
Nitrogen-containing	
Alkaloids	12000
Nonprotein amino acids (NPAAs)	600
Amines	100
Cyanogenic glycosides	100
Glucosinolates	100
Without nitrogen	
Sesquiterpenes**	3000
Monoterpenes**	1000
Diterpenes**	1000
Triterpenes, steroids, saponins**	4000
Tetraterpenes**	350
Flavonoids	2000
Polyacetylenes	1000
Polyketides	750
Phenylpropanoids	500

*approximate number of known structures.
**total number exceeds 22000 at present.

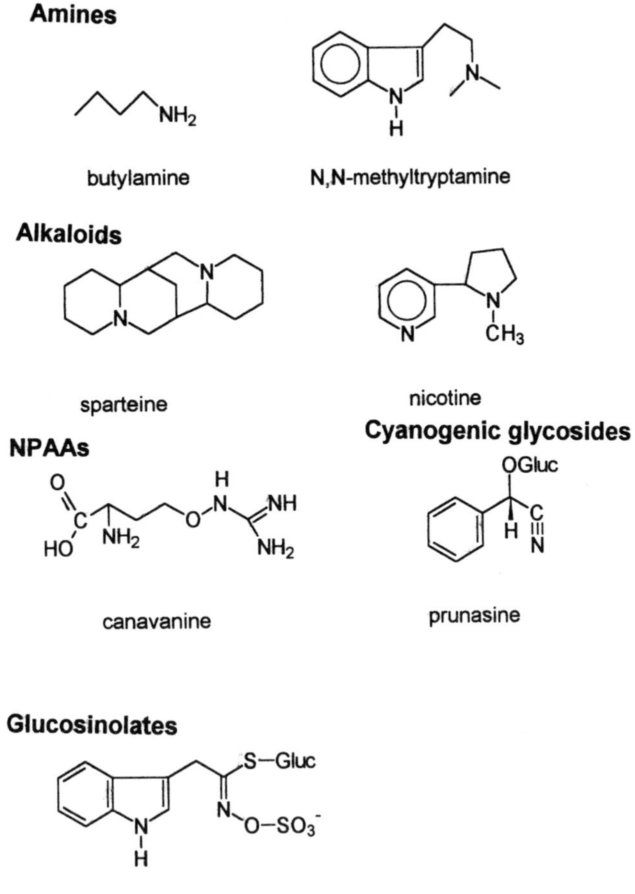

Figure 1.1 Structures of secondary metabolites. Abbreviation: NPAAs, nonprotein amino acids.

1.2 Biosynthesis

Despite the enormous variety of secondary metabolites, the number of corresponding basic biosynthetic pathways is restricted and distinct. Precursors usually derive from basic metabolic pathways, such as glycolysis, Krebs cycle or the shikimate pathway. A schematic overview is presented in Figures 1.2 and 1.3. Plausible hypotheses for the biosynthesis of most SMs have been published (for overviews see Luckner, 1990; Conn, 1981; Bell and Charlwood 1980; Mothes *et al.*, 1985; Dey and Harborne, 1997) that are based, at least, on tracer

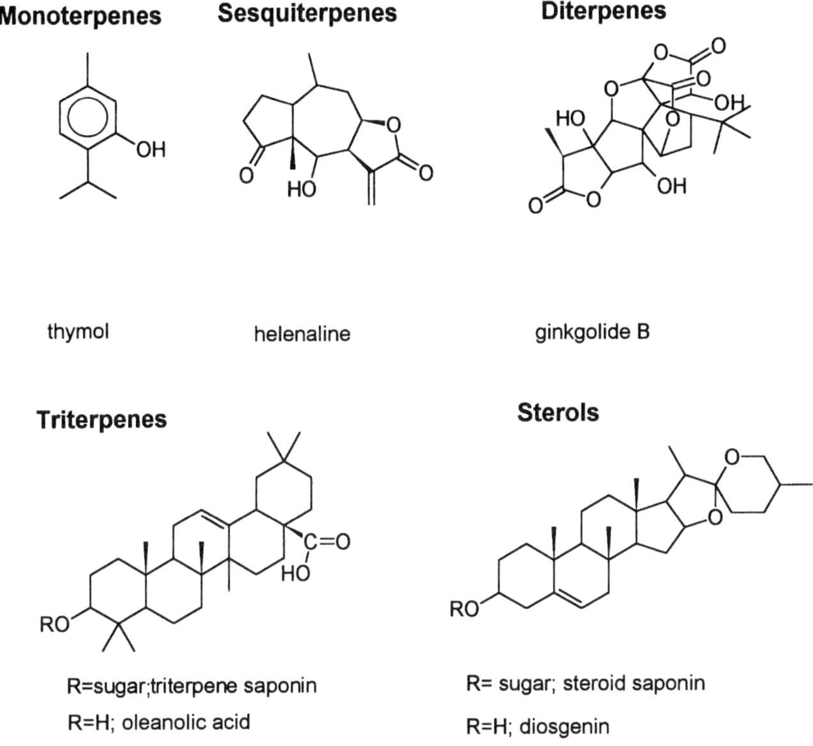

Figure 1.1 (Continued).

experiments. For pathways leading to cyanogenic glycosides, glucosinolates, some alkaloids and nonprotein amino acids (NPAAs), amines, flavonoids and several terpenes, the enzymes which catalyze individual steps have been identified. In pathways leading to isoquinoline, indole, pyrrolidine and tropane alkaloids, flavonoids, coumarins, NPAAs, mono-, sesqui- and triterpenes, some of the genes which encode biosynthetic enzymes have already been isolated and characterized (Kutchan, 1995; Kutchan *et al.*, 1991; Saito and Murakoshi, 1998). Whereas, earlier this century, it was argued that secondary metabolites arise spontaneously or with the aid of nonspecific enzymes, we now have good evidence that biosynthetic enzymes are highly specific in most instances and most have been selected towards this special task (although they often derive from common progenitors with a function in primary metabolism). As a consequence, final products nearly always have a distinct stereochemistry. Only the enzymes that are involved in the degradation of SMs, such as β-glucosidases, esterases and hydrolases, are less substrate-specific.

Tetraterpenes

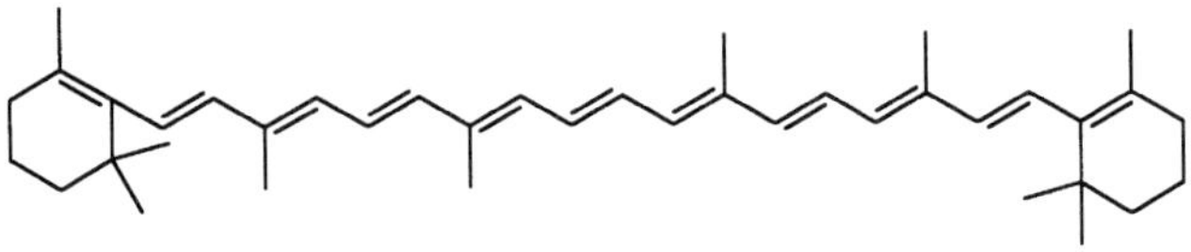

ß-carotene

Anthraquinones

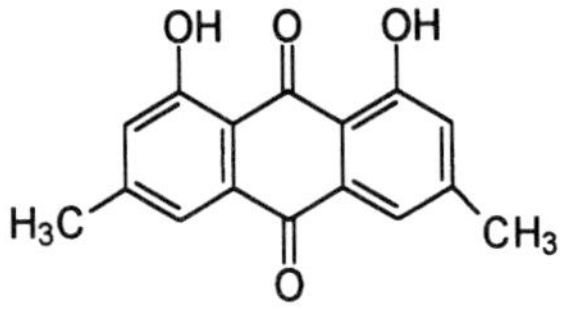

OH O OH

H_3C CH_3

O

emodine

Polyines

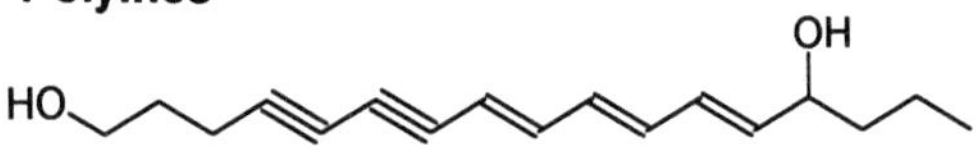

HO OH

cicutoxin

Flavonoids

HO OH OH OH OH O

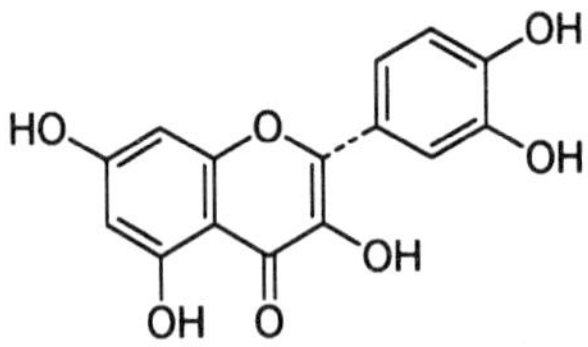

quercetin

Isoflavonoids

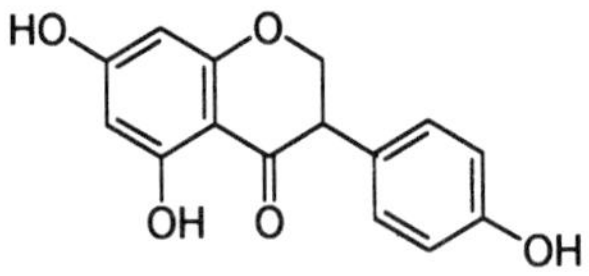

HO O OH O OH

genistein

Anthocyanidins

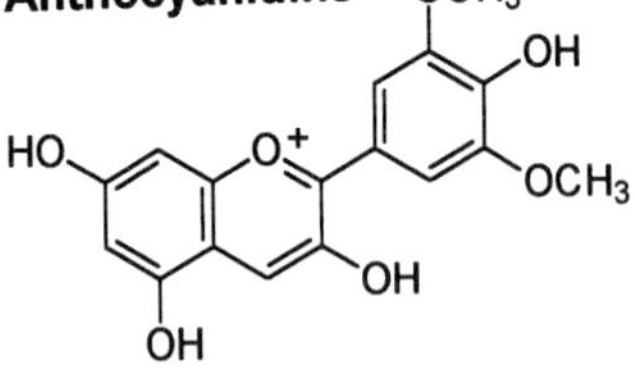

OCH_3 OH HO O^+ OCH_3 OH OH

malvidine

Phenylpropanoids

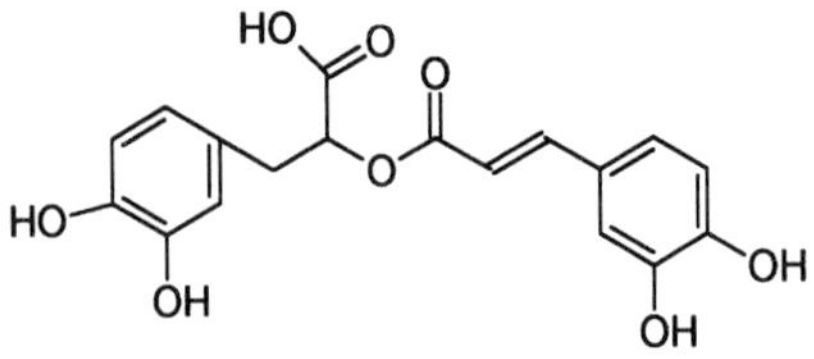

HO O O HO OH OH OH

rosmarinic acid

Figure 1.1 (Continued).

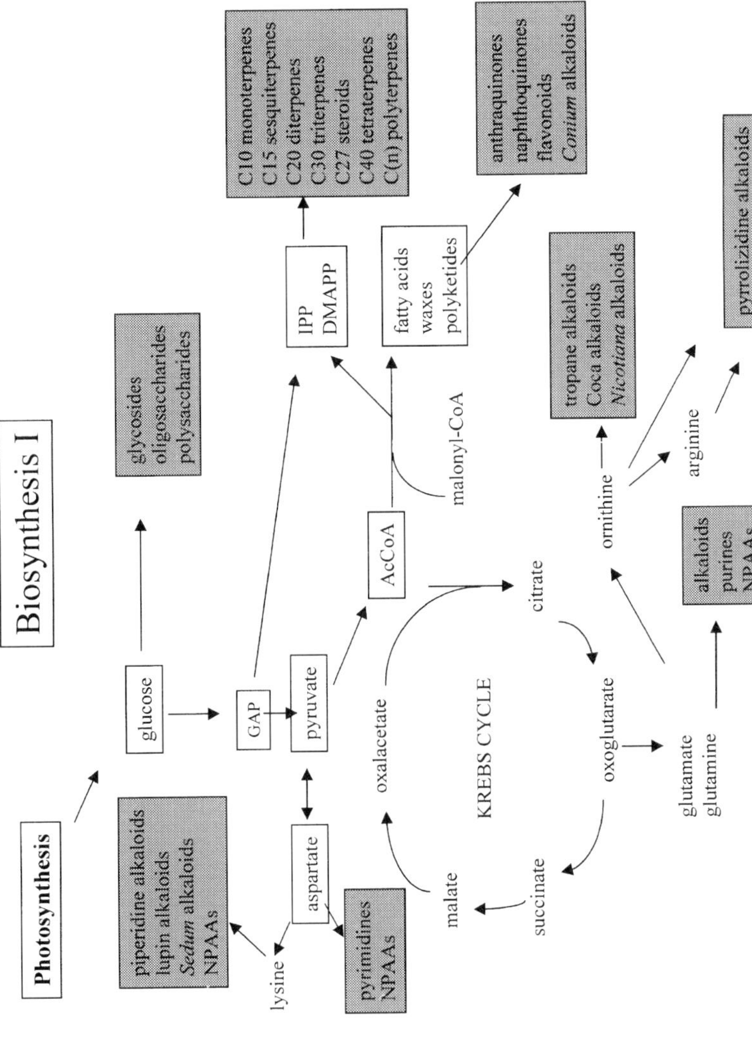

Figure 1.2 Main pathways leading to secondary metabolites. Abbreviations: IPP, isopentenyl diphosphate; DMAPP, dimethyl allyl diphosphate; GAP, glyceraldehyde-3-phosphate; NPAAs, nonprotein amino acids; AcCoA, acetyl coenzyme A.

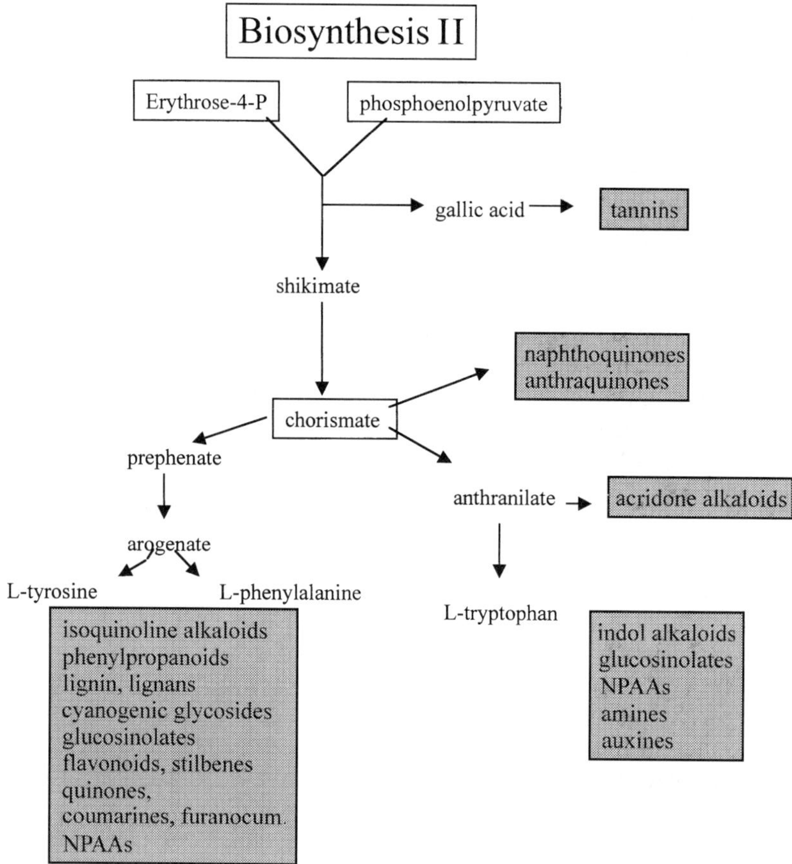

Figure 1.3 Several pathways of secondary metabolites derive from precursors in the shikimate pathway. Abbreviation: NPAAs, nonprotein amino acids.

Some SMs are produced in all tissues but their formation is generally organ-, tissue-, cell- and often development-specific. Although, in most instances, details have not been elucidated, it can be assumed that the genes of secondary metabolism are also regulated in a cell-, tissue- and development-specific fashion (as are most plant genes that have been studied so far).

Sites of biosynthesis are compartmentalized in the plant cell. While most biosynthetic pathways proceed (as least partially) in the cytoplasm, there is evidence that some alkaloids (such as coniine, quinolizidines and caffeine), furano-coumarins and some terpenes (such as monoterpenes, diterpenes, phytol and carotenoids that are formed in the pyruvate/glyceraldehyde phosphate pathway) are synthesized in the chloroplast (Wink and

Hartmann, 1982; Roberts, 1981). Sesquiterpenes, sterols and dolichols are produced in the endoplasmic reticulum or cytosolic compartment. A schematic overview is presented in Figure 1.4. Coniine and amine formation has been localized in mitochondria (Wink and Hartmann, 1981; Roberts, 1981) and steps of protoberberine biosynthesis in vesicles (Amann *et al.*, 1986). Hydroxylation steps are often membrane-bound and the endoplasmic reticulum (ER) is the corresponding compartment, as is also probable for the synthesis of other lipophilic compounds.

The biosyntheses of the major groups of SMs have been reviewed in the present volume: alkaloids (including betalains) by M. Roberts and D. Strack in Chapter 2; cyanogenic glycosides, glucosinolates and NPAAs by D. Selmar in Chapter 3; phenylpropanoids, lignin, lignans, coumarins, furocoumarins, tannins, flavonoids, isoflavonoids and anthocyanins by M. Petersen, D. Strack and U. Matern in Chapter 4; mono-, sesqui- and diterpenes by J. Gershenzon and sterols, cardiac glycosides and steroid saponins by W. Kreis in Chapter 5.

1.3 Transport, storage and turnover

Water soluble compounds are usually stored in the vacuole (Matile, 1978, 1984; Boller and Wiemken, 1986) (Table 1.2) whereas lipophilic substances are sequestered in resin ducts, laticifers, glandular hairs, trichomes, thylakoid membranes or on the cuticle (Wiermann, 1981) (Fig. 1.5).

As mentioned previously, most substances are synthesized in the cytoplasm, the ER or in organelles and, if hydrophilic, they are exported to the vacuole. They have to pass the tonoplast, which is impermeable to many of the polar secondary metabolites. For some alkaloids and flavonoids, a specific transporter has been described, which pumps the compounds into the vacuole (Fig. 1.4). The proton gradient, which is built up by the tonoplast-residing adenosine triphosphatase (ATPase), is used as a driving force (by a so-called proton antiport mechanism) (Deus-Neumann and Zenk, 1984; Mende and Wink, 1987). Alternatively, diverse trapping mechanisms (e.g. isoquinoline alkaloids by chelidonic acid or meconic acid in the latex vesicles of *Chelidonium* or *Papaver,* respectively) can also help to concentrate a particular compound in the vacuole. Moreover, conjugation of secondary metabolites with glutathione in the cytoplasm (Martinoia *et al.*, 1993; Li *et al.*, 1995) and subsequent transportation by an ATP-dependent transporter into the vacuole has been proposed for xenobiotics and some SMs that can be conjugated (for reviews see Wink, 1993, 1997).

Lipophilic compounds will interfere not only with the biomembranes of microbes and herbivores but also with those of the producing plant. In

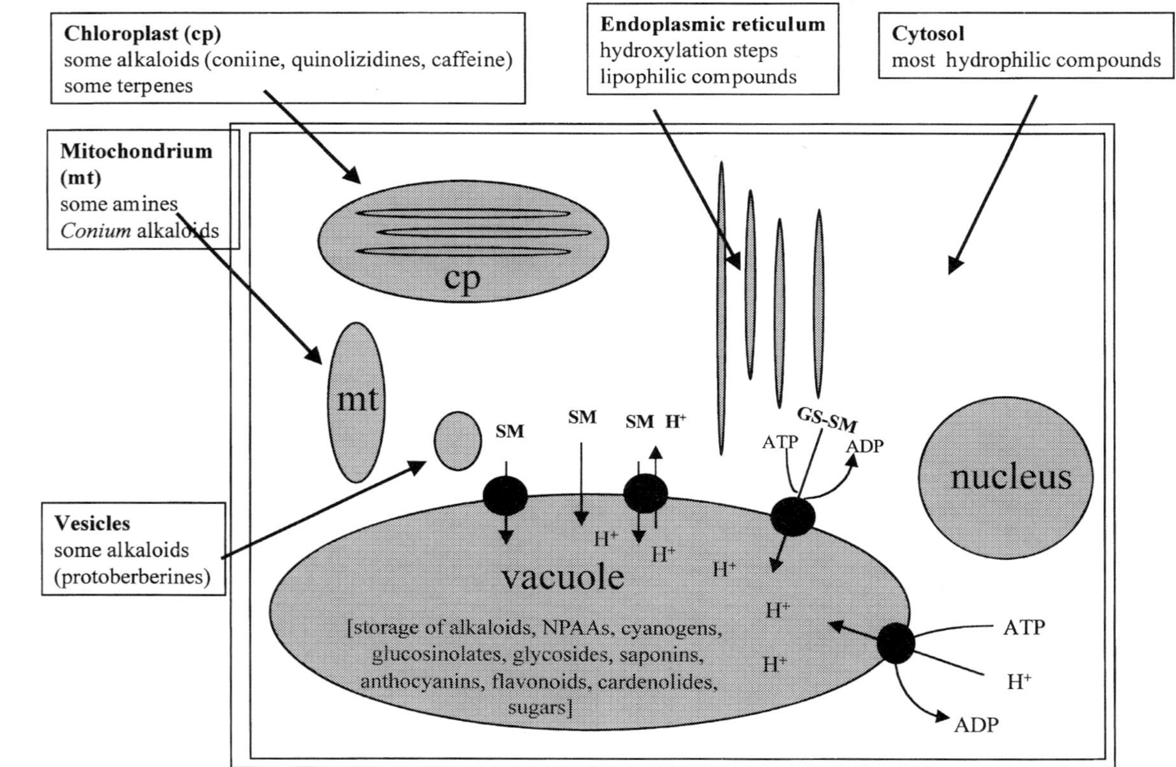

Figure 1.4 Compartmentation of biosynthesis and sequestration. Abbreviations: SM, secondary metabolite; GS-SM, conjugate of SM with glutathione; NPAAs, nonprotein amino acids; ATP, adenosine triphosphate; ADP, adenosine diphosphate.

Table 1.2 Examples for vacuolar sequestration of secondary metabolites (Wink, 1997)

Phenolics	
Anthocyanins	Isoflavone malonyl glycosides
Bergenin	Kaempherol 3,7-*O*-glycoside
Coumaroyl-glycosides (esculin)	Orientin-C-glycosides
Flavonol-glycosides	Pterocarpan malonyl glycosides
Gallic acid	Quercetin-3-triglucoside
7-Glucosyl-pleurostimin	7-Rhamnosyl-6-hydroxyluteolin
Isoflavanone malonyl glycosides	Shikimic acid
Sinapylglycosides	Tricin 5-glucoside
Terpenoids	
Convallatoxin and other cardenolides	Oleanolic acid (3-*O*-glucuronide)
Gentiopicroside	Cardiac glycosides (lanatoside A, C; purpureaglycoside A)
Oleanolic acid (3-*O*-glucoside)	Saponines (avenacosides)
Oligosaccharides	
Gentianose	Gentiobiose
	Stachyose
Nitrogen-containing compounds (excluding alkaloids)	
Cyanogenic glycosides (linamarin)	Glucosinolates
Alkaloids	
Ajmalicine	Noscapine
Atropine	Papaverine
Nicotine	Polyamines
Berberine	(*S*)-Reticuline
Betaine	Sanguinarine
Betalains	Scopolamine
Capsaicin	(*S*)-Scoulerine
Catharanthine	Senecionine-N-oxide
Codeine	Serpentine
Dopamine	Solanidine
Lupanine	Thebaine
Morphine	Vindoline

order to avoid autotoxicity, plants cannot store these compounds in the vacuole but usually sequester them on the cuticle, in dead resin ducts or cells, which are lined not by a biomembrane but by an impermeable solid barrier (Fig. 1.5).

In many instances, the site of biosynthesis is restricted to a single organ, such as roots, leaves or fruits, but an accumulation of the corresponding products can be detected in several other plant tissues. Long distance transport must take place in these instances. The xylem or phloem are likely transport routes but an apoplastic transport can also be involved.

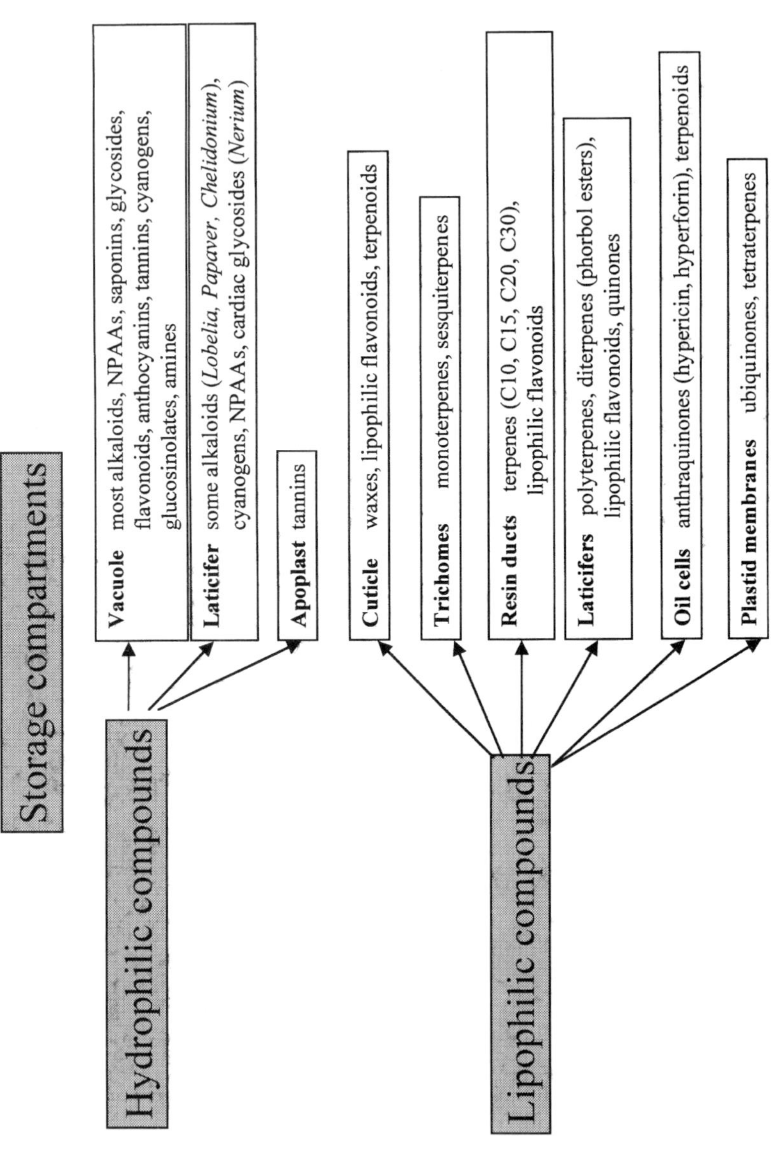

Figure 1.5 Storage compartments for hydrophilic and lipophilic compounds. Abbreviation: NPAAs, nonprotein amino acids.

Table 1.3 summarizes the evidence for xylem and phloem transport of some SMs.

Table 1.3 Examples of xylem and phloem transport of secondary metabolites (SMs)

Compounds	Xylem	Phloem
Quinolizidine alkaloids	–	+
Pyrrolizidine alkaloids	–	+
Aconitine	–	+
Polyhydroxy alkaloids (swainsonine)	–	+
Glucosinolates	–	+
Cardiac glycosides	–	+
Cyanogenic glycosides	–	+
Nicotine	+	–
Tropane alkaloids	+	–

Storage can also be tissue- and cell-specific (Guern *et al.*, 1987). In a number of plants, specific idioblasts have been detected that contain tannins, alkaloids or glucosinolates. More often, SMs are concentrated in trichomes or glandular hairs (many terpenoids in Labiatae, Asteraceae), stinging hairs (many amines in Urticaceae) or the epidermis itself (many alkaloids, flavonoids, anthocyanins, cyanogenic glycosides, coumarins, etc.) (Wiermann, 1981; Wink, 1993, 1997; Wink and Roberts, 1998). Flowers, fruits and seeds are usually rich in SMs, especially in annual plants. In perennial species, high amounts of SMs are found in bulbs, roots, rhizomes and the bark of roots and stems.

Several SMs are not end-products of metabolism but are turned over at a regular rate (Barz and Köster, 1981). During germination, in particular, N-containing SMs, such as alkaloids, NPAAs, cyanogenic glycosides and protease inhibitors, are metabolized and serve as a nitrogen source for the growing seedling (Wink and Witte, 1985). Carbohydrates (e.g. oligosaccharides and lipids) are also turned over during germination. Concentrations of some SMs, such as quinolizidine alkaloids, nicotine, atropine, monoterpenes and phenylpropanoids, vary diurnally; an active interplay between synthesis and turnover is involved in these instances. Turnover of SMs is readily seen in cell suspension cultures (for reviews see Barz and Köster, 1981; Wink, 1997).

It is well-established that profiles of SMs vary with time, space and developmental stage. Since related plant species often show similarities in the profiles of their SMs, they have been used as a taxonomic tool in plant systematics (Harborne and Turner, 1984). However, profiles of closely-related plants quite often differ substantially or those of unrelated plant groups show strong similarities; this clearly shows that SM patterns are not unambiguous systematic markers but that convergent evolution and selective gene expression are common themes. In the present volume, Chapter 6 by M. Wink and P. Waterman summarises the evidence for and against the use of SMs in chemotaxonomy.

1.4 Costs of secondary metabolism

Analogous with other proteins in cells, the enzymes involved in the biosynthesis and transport of SMs show a regular turnover. This means that messenger ribonucleic acid (mRNA) must be regularly transcribed and translated into proteins, even for constitutive compounds. Both transcription and translation require a substantial input of energy in terms of adenosine triphosphate (ATP). Furthermore, the biosynthesis itself is often costly, demanding ATP or reduction equivalents, i.e. nicotinamide adenine dinucleotide phosphate (reduced formed) ($NADPH_2$). In order to exhibit their function as defence or signal compounds, allelochemicals need to be present in relatively high concentrations at the right place and time. Many secondary metabolites are synthesized in the cytoplasm or in cell organelles (Fig. 1.4) but are stored in the vacuole. Energy for the uphill transport across the tonoplast and/or for trapping the metabolite in the vacuole is provided by a H^+-ATPase. If special anatomical differentiations (ducts, gland cells, trichomes) are needed, the formation and maintenance of these structures is also costly. As a consequence, both biosynthesis and sequestration (and the corresponding transcription and translation of related genes and mRNAs) are processes which require substantial amounts of ATP; in other words, it must be costly for plants to produce defence and signal compounds (a schematic overview is presented in Fig. 1.6).

1.5 Role of secondary metabolites and their application in biotechnology

The biosynthesis of secondary metabolites exhibits a remarkable complexity. Enzymes are specific for each pathway and are highly regulated in terms of compartmentation, time and space. The same is true for the mechanisms of accumulation or the site and time of storage. In general, we find that tissues and organs which are important for survival and multiplication, such as epidermal and bark tissues, flowers, fruits and seeds, have distinctive profiles of secondary metabolites, and secondary compounds are abundant in them.

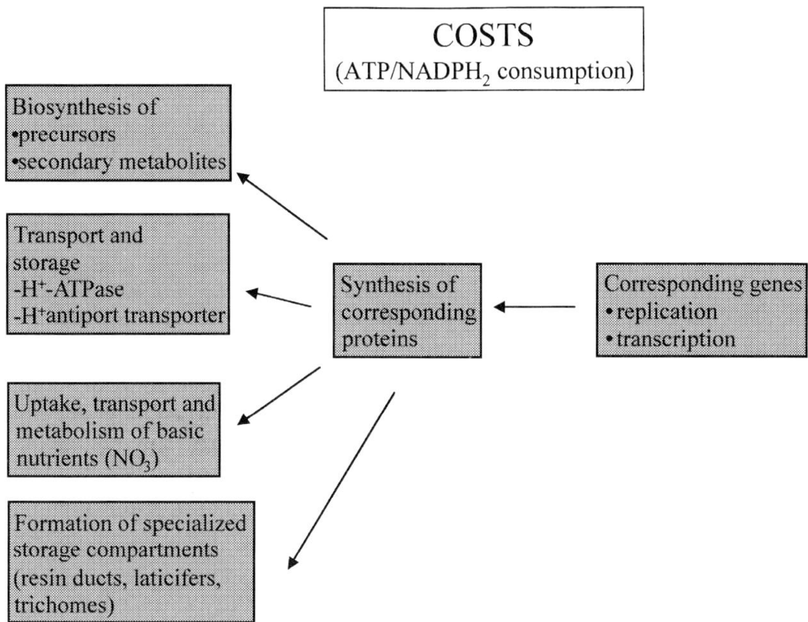

Figure 1.6 Costs of chemical defence and signal compounds. Abbreviations: ATP, adenosine triphosphate; $NADPH_2$, nicotinamide adenine dinucleotide phosphate (reduced form).

All these processes and the corresponding means and structures necessary to express these traits are costly in terms of ATP and NAD(P)H, so it would be highly unlikely that secondary metabolites were waste products or had no function at all, as has been suggested in the older literature. Costly traits without function or advantage usually do not survive in evolution, as plants expressing these traits should perform less well then plants without them. As these metabolites are maintained and diversified in an astounding fashion, it must be assumed that these traits are indeed important, even if their functions are not evident.

During the past few decades, experimental and circumstantial evidence has made it clear that secondary metabolites do indeed have functions that are vital for the fitness of a plant producing them. Main roles are

- Defence against herbivores (insects, vertebrates)
- Defence against fungi and bacteria
- Defence against viruses
- Defence against other plants competing for light, water and nutrients

- Signal compounds to attract pollinating and seed dispersing animals
- Signals for communication between plants and symbiotic micro-organisms (N-fixing Rhizobia or mycorrhizal fungi)
- Protection against UV-light or other physical stress

In order to fulfil these functions, the structures of secondary metabolites have been shaped during evolution so that they can closely interact with molecular targets in cells and tissues or other physiological features in animals or microorganisms. Quite often structures of secondary metabolites resemble endogenous substrates, hormones or neurotransmitters and can thus mimic a response at the corresponding molecular targets. The process leading to these structure similarities could be termed 'evolutionary molecular modelling'.

There is hardly a target in animals or microorganisms for which a natural product does not exist. Thus plants provide a wide array of bioactive substances. This is the reason why so many natural products in biotechnology, pharmacy, medicine and agriculture can be used in so many ways. Using substances that are already known or looking for new ones, hitherto undiscovered compounds or the corresponding genes encoding the genes for their biosynthesis, can be discovered in plants living in deserts or rain forests (bioprospection or gene prospection).

Secondary metabolites often interfere with more than a single molecular target, which is advantageous for the producer, as a toxin might be more efficient if it knocks out two targets instead of one. Furthermore, it will be more difficult for a herbivore or microbe to develop resistance to such a compound, as concomitant resistance at two targets would be required. Plants usually produce a complex mixture of compounds, each of which has its own set of biological activities, which make these mixtures even more powerful as means of defence and protection.

Because of this evolutionary logic, most plants are able to withstand various threats from herbivores, microbes, and the physical environment. Exceptions are many agricultural crops which have been optimised for yield and quite often, their original lines of defence have been selected away, as these metabolites were unpalatable or toxic for humans or its life stock.

The role and function of secondary metabolites as well as their potential biotechnological applications are the topic of volume III of Annual Plant Reviews, '*Functions of Plant Secondary Metabolites and their Exploitation in Biotechnology*'.

References

Amann, M., Wanner, G. and Zenk, M.H. (1986) Purification and characterisation of (*S*)-tetrahydroberberine oxidase from cultured *Coptis japonica* cells. *Phytochemistry*, **37** 979-82.

Barz, W., Köster, J. (1981) Turnover and degradation of secondary products, in *The Biochemistry of Plants*. Vol. 7. Secondary Plant Products (ed. E.E. Conn), Academic Press, Orlando, pp. 35-84.

Bell, E.A. and Charlwood, B.V. (1980) *Secondary Plant Products*. Springer, Heidelberg.

Boller, T. and Wiemken, A. (1986) Dynamics of vacuolar compartmentation. *Annu. Rev. Plant Physiol.*, **37** 137-64.

Conn, E.E. (1981) Secondary Plant Products, in *The Biochemistry of Plants*. Vol. 7, Academic Press, New York.

Deus-Neumann, B. and Zenk, M.H. (1984) A highly selective alkaloid uptake system in vacuoles of higher plants. *Planta*, **162** 250-60.

Dey, P.M. and Harborne, J.B. (1997) *Plant Biochemistry*. Academic Press, San Diego.

DNP (1996) Dictionary of Natural Products. CD-ROM Version 5:1, Chapman and Hall, London, UK.

Guern, J., Renaudin, J.P. and Brown, S.C. (1987) The compartmentation of secondary metabolites in plant cell cultures, in *Cell Culture and Somatic Cell Genetics*. (eds. F. Constabel and I. Vasil), Academic Press, New York, pp. 43-76.

Harborne, J.B. and Turner, B.L. (1984) *Plant Chemosystematics*. Academic Press, London.

Kutchan, T.M. (1995) Alkaloid biosynthesis: the basis for metabolic engineering of medicinal plants. *The Plant Cell*, **7** 1959-70.

Kutchan, T.M., Dittrich, H., Bracher, D. and Zenk, M.H. (1991) Enzymology and molecular biology of alkaloid biosynthesis. *Tetrahedron*, **47** 5945-54.

Li, Z.-S., Zhao, Y. and Rea, P.A. (1995) Magnesium adenosine 5′-triphosphate-energized transport of glutathione-*S*-conjugates by plant vacuolar membrane vesicles. *Plant Physiol.*, **107** 1257-68.

Luckner, M. (1990) *Secondary Metabolism in Microorganisms, Plants and Animals*. Springer, Heidelberg.

Martinoia, E., Grill, E., Tommasini, R., Kreuz, K. and Amrhein, N. (1993) ATP-dependent glutathione-*S*-conjugate export pump in the vacuolar membrane of plants. *Nature*, **364** 247-49.

Matile, P. (1978) Biochemistry and function of vacuoles. *Annu. Rev. Plant Physiol.*, **29** 193-213.

Matile, P. (1980) The 'Mustard oil bomb': compartmentation of myrosinase systems. *Biochem. Physiol. Pflanzen*, **175** 722-31.

Mende, P. and Wink, M. (1987) Uptake of the quinolizidine alkaloid, lupanine, by protoplasts and vacuoles of *Lupinus polyphyllus* cell suspension cultures. *J. Plant Physiol.*, **129** 229-42.

Mothes, K., Schütte, H.R. and Luckner, M. (1985) *Biochemistry of Alkaloids*. Verlag Chemie, Weinheim.

Roberts, M.F. (1981) Enzymic synthesis of coniceine in *Conium maculatum* chloroplasts and mitochondria. *Plant Cell Rep.*, **1** 10-13.

Saito, K. and Murakoshi, I. (1998) Genes in alkaloid metabolism, in *Alkaloids: Biochemistry, Ecological Functions and Medical Applications*. (eds. M.F. Roberts and M. Wink), Plenum, New York, pp. 147-57.

Wiermann, R. (1981) Secondary plant products and cell and tissue differentiation, in *The Biochemistry of Plants*, Vol. 7, 85-116, Academic Press, New York.

Wink, M. (1987) Physiology of the accumulation of secondary metabolites with special reference to alkaloids, in *Cell Culture and Somatic Cell Genetics of Plants*, Vol. 4, Cell Culture in Phytochemistry. (eds. F. Constabel and I. Vasil), Academic Press, San Diego, pp. 17-41.

Wink, M. (1993) The plant vacuole: a multifunctional compartment. *J. Exp. Bot.*, **44** 231-46.

Wink, M. (1997) Compartmentation of secondary metabolites and xenobiotics in plant vacuoles. *Adv. Bot. Res.*, **25** 141-69.

Wink, C. and Hartmann, T. (1981) Properties and subcellular localisation of L-alanine: aldehyde aminotransferase. Concept of an ubiquitous plant enzyme involved in secondary metabolism. *Z. Naturforsch.*, **36c** 625-32.

Wink, M. and Hartmann, T. (1982) Localization of the enzymes of quinolizidine alkaloid biosynthesis in leaf chloroplast of *Lupinus polyphyllus*. *Plant Physiol.*, **70** 74-77.

Wink, M. and Roberts, M.F. (1998) Compartmentation of alkaloid synthesis, transport and storage, in *Alkaloids: Biochemistry, Ecological Functions and Medical Applications* (eds. M.F. Roberts and M. Wink), Plenum, New York, pp. 239-62.

Wink, M. and Witte, L. (1985) Quinolizidine alkaloids as nitrogen source for lupin seedlings and cell suspension cultures. *Z. Naturforsch.*, **40c** 767-75.

Wink, M. and Witte, L. (1991) Storage of quinolizidine alkaloids in *Macrosiphum albifrons* and *Aphis genistae* (Homoptera: Aphididae). *Entomol. Gener.*, **15** 237-54.

2 Biochemistry and physiology of alkaloids and betalains

Margaret F. Roberts and Dieter Strack

2.1 Introduction

The biogenesis of alkaloids has been studied from the beginning of the century, first to determine their structures and subsequently to study their biosynthesis in plants. Detailed hypotheses of alkaloid biosyntheses have been advanced following radio-labelled studies; however, we are still a long way from understanding how most alkaloids are synthesised in plants and how such biosynthesis is regulated. Moreover, there is much to be learned about the chemical ecology of alkaloids, so that we can better understand their roles within the plant.

Alkaloids are an integral part of many medicinal plants and have enjoyed a long and important history in traditional medicine. Our first drugs originated from plant extracts and some important contemporary pharmaceuticals are still either isolated from plants or structurally derived from natural products.

The majority of alkaloids have been found to be derived from amino acids, such as tyrosine, phenylalanine, anthranilic acid, tryptophan/tryptamine, ornithine/arginine, lysine, histidine and nicotinic acid. However, alkaloids may be derived from: purines, i.e. caffeine; 'aminated' terpenoids, i.e. aconite; or the steroidal alkaloids, such as are found in the Solanaceae and Liliaceae. Alkaloids may also be formed from acetate-derived polyketides, where the amino nitrogen is introduced as in the hemlock alkaloid, coniine.

Originally, alkaloids were thought to be essentially plant products; however, these basic compounds also occur in microorganisms and animals. Although, at present, the majority of known alkaloids are amino acid derived, increasing numbers of alkaloids from insects and marine organisms are being discovered that are either terpenoid or polyketide in origin.

Interest in growing and manipulating microorganisms and plants in cell culture for commercial purposes has given impetus to the study of alkaloid biosynthesis and, in particular, to the elucidation of the enzymes involved. It has also brought about renewed interest in the regulation of alkaloid synthesis and in the location and means of sequestration of these substances within the plant.

It was not until the early 1970s that the enzymes associated with alkaloid formation were isolated. Now, however, the enzymes of every step of entire pathways, for instance from tyrosine to berberine and protopine, are known. The relatively few pathways isolated so far clearly indicate that most of the enzymes required are highly specific for a given biosynthetic step. The results of research over the last ten years have helped to revise routes to alkaloid synthesis that were previously hypothesised as a result of feeding radio-labelled precursors to plants. The investigation of enzymes and, more recently, the genes of alkaloid biosynthesis has also helped to answer some of the questions regarding where and at what time during the plant growth cycle the alkaloids are actively made, and has provided an insight into the location of enzymes and alkaloids within the plant and the cell.

The present chapter presents the most recent data in a limited number of areas, where the enzymes of whole pathways and the genes for key enzymes have been isolated. These studies have improved our understanding of the formation, mobilization and sequestration of alkaloids, and their role in plant defence mechanisms (Hashimoto and Yamada, 1994).

For earlier work the reader should consult '*The Alkaloids*' (1950–1997), Academic Press, New York; Pelletier (1983–1996) '*Alkaloids: Chemical and Biological Perspectives*', Volumes 1–8, Pergamon Press, Oxford; and Roberts and Wink (1998) '*Alkaloids: Biochemistry, Ecology and Medical Applications*', Plenum Press, New York.

2.2 Nicotine and tropane alkaloids

In the early 1980s, root cultures of *Nicotiana*, *Hyoscyamus*, *Datura* and *Duboisia* species were found to give high yields of nicotine and tropane alkaloids and have proved useful tools for recent studies of the biosynthetic pathways to these alkaloids. Genetically transformed and untransformed root cultures have been generated and used as models for biosynthetic studies (Rhodes *et al.*, 1990).

2.2.1 Nicotine alkaloids

Nicotiana rustica and *N. tabacum* root cultures principally contain nicotine, which is made from putrescine and nicotinic acid (Fig. 2.1). Putrescine is produced by the decarboxylation of either ornithine or arginine, as a result of the activities of either ornithine (ODC) or arginine decarboxylase (ADC), and is used for the biosynthesis of the polyamines, spermine and spermidine. The conversion of putrescine to *N*-methylputrescine is, therefore, the first committed step of the alkaloidal pathway. *N*-

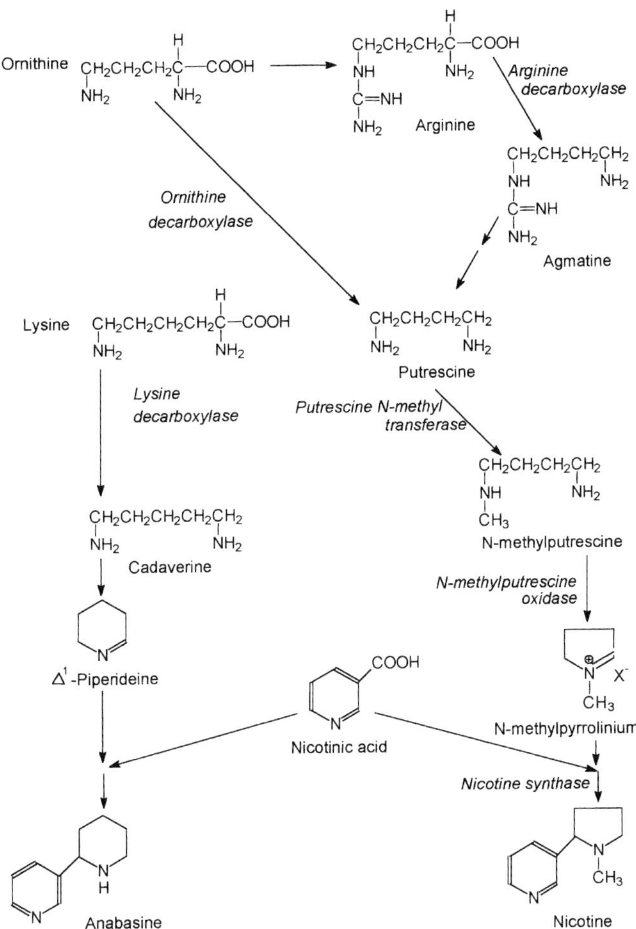

Figure 2.1 Biosynthesis of nicotine and anabasine.

methylpyrrolinium, formed by the oxidative deamination of *N*-methylputrescine, is then condensed with an intermediate derived by the decarboxylation of nicotinic acid. Three specific enzymes, namely, putrescine *N*-methyltransferase (PMT), *N*-methylputrescine oxidase (MPO) and nicotine synthase, are involved. The regulation of these enzymes and the control of flux into the pathway has been the subject of particular study over the last ten years (Friesen and Leete, 1990; Leete, 1990).

2.2.1.1 Regulation of the pyrrolidine alkaloid pathway

Precursor feeding experiments in root cultures of *N. rustica* have indicated that a major limitation in accumulation occurs subsequent to

N-methylpyrrolinium formation. However, small enhancements in alkaloid production are seen with putrescine or agmatine but not with ornithine or arginine, indicating a possible limitation in the supply of putrescine, which may be regulatory (Robins and Walton, 1993; Walton *et al.*,1988). The use of 'suicide' inhibitors of ODC and ADC, namely α-difluoromethylornithine (DFMO) and α-difluoromethylarginine (DFMA) (Robins and Walton, 1993), indicate that arginine is probably the preferred origin of the putrescine incorporated into nicotine. In root cultures, nicotine production and PMT activity are lost if roots are subcultured into media containing phytohormones (Rhodes *et al.*, 1989). This effect is reversible; roots competent in nicotine production being obtained when cells are passaged into phytohormone-free medium. Therefore PMT, rather than ADC or ODC, has been targeted for genetic engineering.

Two enzymes of pyrrolidine alkaloid formation responsible for the conversion of putrescine to the *N*-methylpyrrolinium ion have been investigated in some detail. PMT, partially purified from cultures of *Hyoscyamus niger* and fully characterised from *Datura stramonium*, has been cloned by differential screening of complementary deoxyribonucleic acid (cDNA) libraries from high- and low-nicotine-yielding *Nicotiana tabacum* plants (Hibi *et al.*, 1994). The enzyme shows considerable sequence homology to spermidine synthase but is distinct from this enzyme as it only shows PMT activity when expressed in *Escherichia coli*. *N*-methylputrescine oxidase has been isolated in pure form from *N. tabacum* transformed root cultures (McLauchlan *et al.*, 1993). It is quite widely spread in the Solanaceae, as shown by Western blotting, and is apparently both immunologically (McLauchlan *et al.*, 1993) and kinetically (Hashimoto and Yamada, 1994; Robins and Walton, 1993) related to a wide range of diamine oxidases found in plants. While PMT is important in determining the overall extent to which cultures can make pyrrolidine alkaloids, the level of activity normally found in transformed root cultures of *N. rustica* does not limit the ability of the cultures to accumulate nicotine. Feeding putrescine had some effect on nicotine levels and, therefore, experiments were conducted to try to enhance nicotine formation by engineering the supply of this metabolite (Robins and Walton, 1993).

The *odc* gene obtained from *Saccharomyces cereviseae* was expressed with the enhanced cauliflower mosaic virus 35S protein promoter in transgenic roots of *N. rustica*. The level of ODC was enhanced in several root clones. The level of ODC remained elevated even in the late stationary phase of these cultures, in contrast to control lines. Other enzymes (ADC, PMT and MPO) were not enhanced. The introduced gene appeared to be expressed in a deregulated manner; this was confirmed by showing that

ODC messenger ribonucleic acid (mRNA) was also present at a high level throughout the growth cycle. Some of the *odc*-expressing clones had increased levels of putrescine, in particular *N*-methylputrescine. In addition, the mean nicotine content of the cultures at 14-days-old was increased from 2.28±0.22 to 4.04±0.48 μmol /g fresh mass.

Once the supply of putrescine was enhanced, no larger increases in nicotine were found, presumably because other enzymes contributed, more than previously, to limiting nicotine accumulation. MPO is present at, typically, 2- to 5-fold higher levels than PMT, and therefore PMT may become limiting. Now that the *pmt* gene has been cloned (Hibi *et al.*, 1994), this possibility can be tested directly.

Nicotine biosynthesis also involves the incorporation of nicotinic acid (Fig. 2.1) (Robins *et al.*, 1987) and the availability of this moiety can be as important in nicotine accumulation as that of the putrescine-derived portion. However, the enzyme responsible for the condensation of *N*-methylpyrrolinium with decarboxylated nicotinic acid, nicotine synthase (Friesen and Leete, 1990), was measured at only a very low level of activity, quite inadequate to account for the rates of nicotine accumulation observed in cultures. The molecular analysis of low-nicotine mutants of *Nicotiana tabacum* suggested the presence of regulatory genes (*Nic 1* and *Nic 2*) governing the expression of nicotine biosynthesis (Hibi *et al.*, 1994).

Genetic engineering makes *in vivo* manipulation of the alkaloid mixture possible. Anabasine, a minor alkaloid in some *Nicotiana* species, is derived from lysine via cadaverine, in a pathway parallel to that for the biosynthesis of nicotine (Fig. 2.1). Root cultures of *N. rustica* (Walton *et al.*, 1988) and *N. hesperis* (Walton and Belshaw, 1988) accumulated anabasine when fed cadaverine; the nicotine:anabasine ratio in the former changing from 10:1 to 1:5. Thus, the enhanced anabasine formation was at the expense of nicotine, indicating that the two pathways may be competing for nicotinic acid. However, some steps in each pathway may be catalyzed by the same enzyme. It has been shown that MPO from *N. tabacum* catalyzes the oxidation of both *N*-methylputrescine and cadaverine (Robins and Walton, 1993), with a 34-fold higher affinity for *N*-methylputrescine but a capacity to oxidise cadaverine which is three fold greater. Hence, the occurrence of excess cadaverine might be expected to dominate the reaction, leading to formation of more anabasine and less nicotine.

Walton and co-workers (1988) found that feeding lysine hardly affected the alkaloid ratio, suggesting a deficiency in lysine decarboxylase (LDC). In order to test this, Berlin and co-workers inserted the *ldc* gene from *Hafnia alvei* into transgenic root cultures of *N. glauca* under the control of the cauliflower mosaic virus 35S promoter (Fecker *et al.*, 1992). *N. glauca* root cultures contain only low LDC activity, even though anabasine is accumulated as a major product. Two clones were isolated showing about a six-fold increase of LDC activity. This was accompanied by a ten-fold rise in cadaverine, a two-fold rise in anabasine and a change in the nicotine:anabasine ratio from 75:25 in controls to 60:40 in *ldc* transgenic roots. The experiment clearly demonstrated that anabasine production is limited, in part, by cadaverine supply and provided further evidence for at least one common step in the pathways of nicotine and anabasine production.

2.2.2 The tropane alkaloids

Both untransformed (Hashimoto and Yamada, 1994) and transformed root cultures of *Datura*, *Hyoscyamus*, *Atropa* and *Duboisia* species (Robins and Walton, 1993) accumulate high levels of the tropane alkaloids, hyoscyamine and scopolamine (Fig. 2.2). These medically important tropane alkaloids present not only an interesting biochemical problem but also a realistic target for genetic manipulation. The biosynthetic route to hyoscyamine and scopolamine is now well

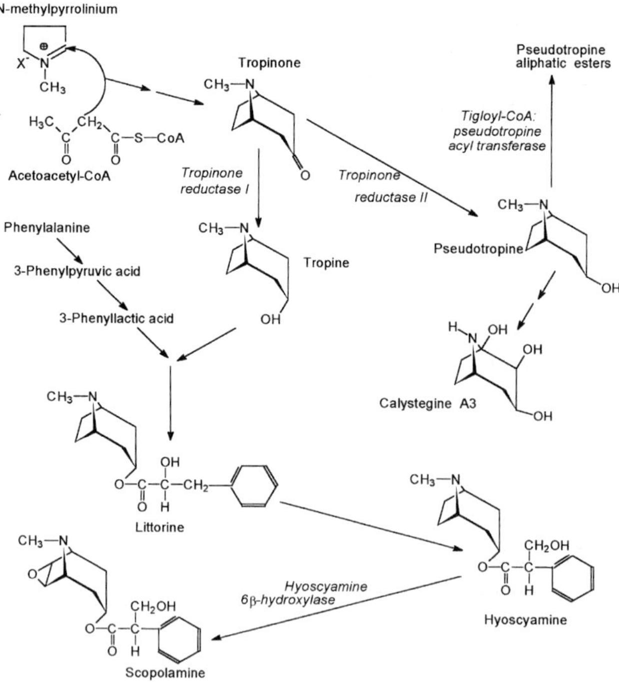

Figure 2.2 Biosynthesis of the tropane alkaloids.

documented. Tropane and pyrrolidine alkaloids have a common biosynthetic pathway to *N*-methylpyrrolinium (Fig. 2.2), the first unique step towards the tropanes being the condensation of *N*-methylpyrrolinium with a C-3 unit to form tropinone (Fig. 2.2). This is stereospecifically reduced to form tropine (tropan-3α-ol), which is esterified with a moiety of phenyllactic acid to form littorine (Robins and Walton, 1993). Recent experiments (Chesters *et al.*, 1996) have shown that D-phenyllactate is converted to tropate by a rearrangement in which, during carboxylate migration, an inversion of configuration occurs at both migration termini to produce hyoscyamine. Further metabolism of hyoscyamine, involving the introduction of a 7β-hydroxyl group followed by oxidation to the 6β,7β-epoxide, results in formation of scopolamine (Robins and Walton, 1993).

2.2.2.1 Regulation of tropane alkaloid production

Recent investigations of the regulation of the tropane alkaloid pathway in *Datura*, *Hyoscyamus* and *Atropa* species have focused on understanding the enzymes involved at the branch-points and in investigating the role these play in regulating the flux into the different groups of products.

The enzymes of hyoscyamine and scopolamine biosynthesis are present throughout much of the growth cycle of both *Datura* (Robins and Walton, 1993) and *Hyoscyamus* (Hashimoto and Yamada, 1994) root cultures. The level of activity present is maximal in rapidly growing tissue but levels of the enzymes ODC, ADC and PMT in *D. stramonium* roots do not greatly exceed the minimum required to synthesise the amounts of alkaloid accumulated *in vivo* (Rhodes *et al.*, 1989). However, levels of the tropinone reductases I and II are much higher than required (Dräger and Schaal, 1994; Portsteffen *et al.*, 1992, 1994). Experiments in feeding various precursors have suggested that, in these root cultures, the esterification of tropine may be crucial in limiting hyoscyamine accumulation (Robins and Walton, 1993).

Tropinone reductases, which catalyse the stereospecific reduction of the keto group of tropinone to 3α- and 3β-hydroxy groups, were analysed in detail by dissection of the peptides and construction of chimeric enzymes. The opposite stereospecificity of the two reductases was ascribed to the carboxy-half of the proteins, to which the substrate tropinone is assumed to bind with reverse orientation in the two enzymes (Hashimoto and Yamada, 1994; Nakajima *et al.*, 1993, 1994). Only tropinone with the 3α-hydroxy group is used to produce hyoscyamine (Leete, 1990). Tropinone with the 3β-hydroxy group forms esters with other acids but these occur only as minor alkaloids.

Some *Hyoscyamus* and *Duboisia* root cultures accumulate scopolamine as a major product (Robins and Walton, 1993). In contrast, only traces of scopolamine were found in *D. stramonium* roots. This implies that the expression of hyoscyamine 6β-hydroxylase (H6H) that forms the 6,7-epoxide is variable and, hence, this enzyme has also been targeted for genetic engineering.

Experiments using radio-labelled precursors have been performed in intact plants, aimed at delineating the tropane pathway (Leete, 1990). Nevertheless, a number of steps remain to be clarified and some inconsistencies in the proposed pathway to the tropanes require resolving.

Robins and Walton (1993), for example, were able to show that 4-*N*-methylornithine was not an intermediate and that the presence of ODC and PMT in excess strongly suggested the route via *N*-methylputrescine, with PMT the first enzyme of the pathway, as in *Nicotiana*.

As in *Nicotiana*, it was debatable whether ADC or ODC might provide the putrescine incorporated. This possibility was tested by growing roots in the presence of DFMO and DFMA (Robins and Walton, 1993) in experiments analogous to those performed in *Nicotiana*. Inhibition of ADC specifically depressed hyoscyamine accumulation and the pools of intermediates, indicating that ADC might be more important for the tropane alkaloid pathway.

Another area of uncertainty concerned the route by which the tropic acid moiety is incorporated. Although early reports claimed to synthesise hyoscyamine from tropine and tropic acid or tropoyl-CoA, these findings were not readily substantiated (Robins and Walton, 1993). A series of experiments in which labelled phenyllactic acids were fed to plants of *D. inoxia* or root cultures of *D. stramonium* confirmed unequivocally that this compound was an intermediate of the pathway (Chesters *et al*., 1994, 1995a,b; Robins *et al*., 1994a; Ansarin and Woolley, 1993, 1994). A recent re-appraisal (Chesters *et al*., 1996) suggested that it is the *S*-isomer that is incorporated.

Other experiments have demonstrated that littorine (the phenyllactoyl ester of tropine) rearranges *in vivo* to hyoscyamine (Robins *et al*., 1994b). Direct rearrangement was demonstrated unequivocally by incorporating three ^{2}H nuclei in the *N*-methyl of the tropinyl portion and two ^{13}C nuclei in the phenyllactoyl moiety.

It was proposed that the rearrangement of littorine to hyoscyamine might occur by a cytochrome P_{450}-catalyzed reaction (Fig. 2.2), and that the minor alkaloids 3α-phenylacetoxytropane and 3α-(2′-hydroxyacetoxy)tropane, which are also formed, are side-products of the mechanism (Robins *et al*., 1995). This particular area of tropane biosynthesis requires further clarification.

The calystegines are also formed from ornithine and, therefore, belong biosynthetically to the tropane alkaloids (Goldmann *et al*., 1992). This has been confirmed by Dräger and co-workers (1994), who fed root cultures of *Atropa belladonna* with ^{15}N-labelled tropinone and obtained good incorporation of isotope. These experiments have cast doubt on the intermediacy of hygrine in the direct pathway to hyoscyamine (Goldman *et al.*, 1992; Dräger *et al.*, 1994; Robins and Walton, 1993). When ^{13}C-labelled hygrine was fed, no incorporation into hyoscyamine or scopolamine could be detected. Feeding other labelled precursors suggested a pathway in which acetoacetate reacts via its C-4 position with *N*-methylpyrrolinium salt to give 4-(1-methyl-2-pyrrolidinyl)-3-oxobutanoate. This intermediate favours cyclization to give 2-carboxy-tropinone, tropinone being formed by decarboxylation (Robins *et al.*, 1997).

As in *Nicotiana*, PMT appears to be regulatory in the pathway. Treating *D. stramonium* root cultures with phytohormones causes dispersion of the cultures, degradative metabolism of tropine and hyoscyamine and a loss of PMT activity. PMT is completely absent in dispersed cultures. Differentiated roots, alkaloid production and PMT activity are fully restored following the removal of phytohormones. Now that a clone for PMT is available, it will be interesting to examine this phenomenon at the molecular level. Robins and Walton (1993) and Hibi and co-workers (1994) have clearly demonstrated that *pmt* expression in *N. tabacum* plants is downregulated by auxin, in agreement with the observed effect of auxins on PMT activity in root cultures (Robins and Walton, 1993; Rhodes *et al.*, 1989). Roots treated with DFMA demonstrated decreased PMT activity (Robins and Walton, 1993) but normal levels were restored by adding agmatine to the cultures. As DFMA treatment results in a loss of agmatine from the system, this effect was interpreted as a possible stimulation of PMT expression by agmatine.

Several enzymes of tropane alkaloid biosynthesis have been purified and characterised from root cultures: namely, putrescine *N*-methyltransferase from *D. stramonium* (Walton *et al.*, 1994) and *H. niger* (Hibi *et al.*, 1992); and tropinone reductases I and II from *Atropa belladonna* (Dräger and Schaal, 1994), *D. stramonium* (Portsteffen *et al.*, 1992, 1994) and *H. niger* (Hashimoto and Yamada, 1994).

Another enzyme involved in the production of minor alkaloids, tigloyl-CoA: pseudotropine acyltransferase, has been purified from roots of *D. stramonium* (Rabot *et al.*, 1995). It catalyzes the transfer to pseudotropine of an acyl group from a range of acyl-CoA thioesters. Esters of pseudotropine do not accumulate significantly in *D. stramonium* roots, although they do appear under abnormal metabolic conditions (Dräger *et al.*, 1992).

Important for the production of scopolamine, hyoscyamine 6β-hydroxylase was the first enzyme of tropane alkaloid metabolism to be purified and remains the most rigorously studied. It was obtained in pure form from *H. niger* root cultures and the preparation showed activity both as the 7β-hydroxylase and as the 6,7β-epoxidase. A clone for H6H was obtained following the purification of enzyme activity. The gene shows some similarity to other hydroxylases, including those involved in oxidative reactions in the formation of ethylene and anthocyanins (Hashimoto and Yamada, 1994).

Detailed study of H6H has allowed the genetic manipulation of scopolamine formation. The alkaloid spectrum of transformed root cultures of *A. belladonna* contains hyoscyamine and scopolamine in a ratio between 10:1 and 5:1 (Robins and Walton, 1993). Following the isolation and introduction of the *h6h* gene into cultures of transformed roots of *A. belladonna*, an engineered root-line was isolated, which showed increased H6H activity and about a two-fold higher accumulation of 7β-hydroxyhyoscyamine and scopolamine. This experiment effectively demonstrated that the ability of these cultures to accumulate hyoscyamine was limited by H6H activity and that, by increasing expression of *h6h*, *A. belladonna* plants almost exclusively contained scopolamine, in contrast to controls (Hashimoto and Yamada,1994).

Since the 6β-hydroxylase is a bifunctional enzyme catalysing two consecutive reactions from hyoscyamine to scopolamine, expression of this single gene could change the alkaloid pattern of the host *A. belladonna* plants and be of commercial benefit. Yun and co-workers (1993) showed that only the single polypeptide is required to carry out both reactions. The *h6h* was inserted into transgenic *N. tabacum* plants. As a result of this single insertion, the plants acquired the ability to biotransform hyoscyamine into scopolamine, showing unequivocally that a single gene product was responsible both for the hydroxylation and epoxidation steps. Species-dependent expression controlled by the promoter of the hyoscyamine 6β-hydroxylase gene was observed in experiments on transgenic plants, using the β-glucuronidase gene as a visible reporter gene (Kanegae *et al.*, 1994). Pericycle-specific accumulation of hyoscyamine 6β-hydroxylase (Hashimoto and Yamada, 1994) was attributed to the 0.8 kb length 5′-flanking region of the gene from *Hyoscyamus niger*. Expression in *E. coli*, in which plant genes were overexpressed, allowed for biotransformation and biosynthesis of alkaloids when feeding appropriate precursors of the tropane alkaloids. Reaction products were accumulated in the medium, suggesting free permeability of the bacterial cell membrane to the products (Hashimoto and Yamada, 1994).

2.2.2.2 Translocation, accumulation and ecology

The correlation between nicotine accumulation and its defensive role in *N. sylvestris* has been convincingly demonstrated. Increased alkaloid production may also be demonstrated by true herbivory. Tobacco plants subjected to leaf damage showed a fourfold increase in the alkaloid content of their undamaged leaves. This resulted from increased alkaloid synthesis and, as a result, a ten fold increase in alkaloids in the xylem. Experimental evidence has indicated that alkaloid induction may be triggered by a phloem translocated signal (Hartmann, 1991 and references therein).

2.3 Pyrrolizidine alkaloids

This group of alkaloids is found in a wide range of families, centred around the Asteraceae and Boraginaceae (Hartmann and Witte, 1995). Their occurrence in many *Senecio* species accounts for the high toxicity of these plants.

The biosynthesis of pyrrolizidine alkaloids has been studied mainly in *Senecio* species (Hartmann,1991). These alkaloids are esters between a necine base, derived from arginine or ornithine via homospermidine (Fig. 2.3) and a necic acid moiety, frequently derived from isoleucine. The

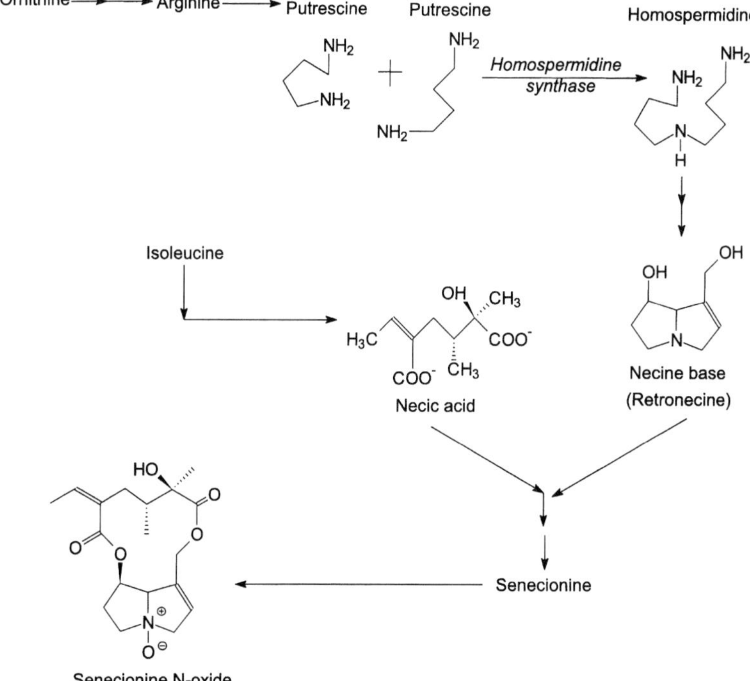

Figure 2.3 Biosynthesis of the pyrrolizidine alkaloid, senecionine-*N*-oxide.

formation of homospermidine from two molecules of putrescine is the first committed step in the pathway, and pyrroline is not an intermediate (Böttcher *et al.*, 1993). Thus, there is a close parallel between this pathway and that described for the tropane alkaloids, with two routes starting from amino acids that provide acidic and alkamine moieties, which are condensed by esterification later in the pathway.

The major product accumulated is senecionine-*N*-oxide (Fig. 2.3), and, since neither suspension cultures nor shoot cultures of *Senecio* form these alkaloids, this suggests that the root is the sole site of biosynthesis (Hartmann, 1994). In root cultures of *Senecio vulgaris*, feeding experiments with a range of ^{14}C-labelled precursors and inhibitors of metabolism showed both ornithine and arginine to be incorporated into senecionine-*N*-oxide (Hartmann, 1991). Experiments with DFMA and DFMO gave results suggesting that, in contrast to *Nicotiana* and *Datura*, label from ornithine is incorporated via arginine. The mechanism for this is not clear. Spermidine and putrescine were found to be rapidly interconverted and both spermine and spermidine reduced the incorporation of label from arginine, suggesting that there is feedback control of agmatine biosynthesis that leads to a depression of alkaloid formation. This interaction between alkaloid and polyamine formation was not apparent in *D. stramonium* roots (Robins and Walton,1993). A higher degree of regulation may be required in this pathway due to the greater demand for putrescine–homospermidine requiring two moles per mole of alkaloid. Senecionine-*N*-oxide is synthesised only in the actively growing parts of root cultures and is not significantly turned over but is slowly transported throughout the root mass. Some limited metabolism occurs during this process, primarily oxidation and acetylation (Hartmann, 1991).

The biosynthesis of the necic acid moiety has, in contrast, received relatively little attention. Label from ^{14}C-isoleucine is effectively incorporated into senecionine-*N*-oxide by root cultures of *S. vulgaris* (Hartmann, 1991).

So far, only one enzyme, homospermidine synthase, has been partially purified and characterised using root cultures of *Eupatorium cannabinum* (Böttcher *et al.*, 1993). Walton and co-workers (1994) found PMT activity in all pyrrolizidine-alkaloid-forming species so far examined; its presence confirms that the biosynthetic route for this group of alkaloids is not via free pyrroline. The enzyme carries out two sequential steps, the first of which is a deaminative oxidation that generates nicotinamide adenine dinucleotide (reduced form) (NADH) and the second of which is a reduction, utilising NADH. This reaction sequence was clearly demonstrated by using chirally-labelled, C1-^{2}H, putrescines (Böttcher *et al.*, 1994). These authors also suggested that spermidine may act, at least in part, as a cosubstrate with putrescine in homospermidine formation.

The apparent rapid interconversion of putrescine and spermidine in these cultures makes this a difficult problem to solve.

However, it has been shown that more than half the aminobutyl moiety of homospermidine comes directly from spermine, and the aminobutyl moiety of spermine is also incorporated directly into the necine base of pyrrolizidine alkaloids (Graser and Hartmann, 1997).

2.3.1 Translocation, accumulation and ecology

The roots have been shown to be the major, if not exclusive, sites of pyrrolizidine alkaloid synthesis, where it occurs preferentially at the root apex, thus coinciding with the sites of active growth. Senecionine-*N*-oxide is produced as a stable product without significant turnover. Pyrrolizidine alkaloids are mobile, being, at least in part, translocated into newly growing aerial tissues, with the highest concentration in the inflorescences, where alkaloid concentrations are 30-fold higher than in the leaves. As soon as root growth stops, synthesis of pyrrolizidine alkaloids ceases. Transport occurs via the phloem and subsequent vacuolisation of the pyrrolizidine alkaloids as salts has been demonstrated. Recent experiments have shown a role for pyrrolizidine alkaloids as part of the plant defence against predation (Hartmann and Witte, 1995 and references therein).

2.4 Benzylisoquinoline alkaloids

Benzylisoquinolines are found within the families of the superorders Magnoliiflorae (i.e. Annonaceae, Eupomatiaceae, Aristolochiaceae, Magnoliaceae, Lauraceae, Monimiaceae and Nelumbonaceae) and Ranunculiflorae (i.e. Berberidaceae, Ranunculaceae, Menispermaceae, Fumariaceae and Papaveraceae). This highly clustered distribution is of interest from a chemotaxonomic point of view, as there are few exceptions, the most notable being the erythrans that occur throughout the genus *Erythrina* (Fabaceae). This group of families contains such alkaloids as: colchicine (a microtubule disrupter and gout suppressant); berberine (an antimicrobial against eye and intestinal infections); morphine (a narcotic analgesic); codeine (a narcotic analgesic and antitussive); and sanguinarine (an antimicrobial used in oral hygiene).

The benzylisoquinolines are formed from two molecules of the aromatic amino acid, tyrosine. In the last ten years, this pathway has been probed at the enzyme and gene level. The recent linking of the phloem-specific expression of tyrosine/Dopa decarboxylase genes with the biosynthesis of the isoquinoline alkaloids in the opium poppy, *Papaver somniferum* (Facchini and De Luca, 1994, 1995), and the association with alkaloid accumulation as part of the plant defence mechanism (Facchini *et al.*, 1996) is of particular interest in furthering our knowledge of the location of alkaloid biosynthesis.

As a result of research over the last ten years, it is now clear that the first committed step in the biosynthesis of isoquinoline is the formation of (*S*)-norcoclaurine. This alkaloid is an important precursor of a variety of pathways that lead to a series of diverse structures within this alkaloid group.

Plant cell cultures established from various isoquinoline-bearing plants have provided useful systems for the study of biosynthetic pathways at the enzyme level. Excellent progress has been made in unravelling the route to (*S*)-norcoclaurine and the sequences leading to some of the more important groups of isoquinolines. Only recently, as a result of investigations into the enzymes of the biosynthetic pathways to morphine, berberine and sanguinarine, have the early steps of the pathway been fully elucidated. These studies have also helped to improve our understanding of the localization at the subcellular level of both enzymes and products (Kutchan, 1995, 1996; Kutchan and Zenk, 1993; Zenk, 1990).

*2.4.1 The formation of (*S*)-norcoclaurine*

Investigations of a number of enzymes involved in tyrosine conversion have suggested that the first committed step in the biosynthesis of benzylisoquinolines involves the condensation of dopamine with 4-hydroxyphenylacetaldehyde to give (*S*)-norcoclaurine, a compound that has proved to be pivotal in the formation of all benzylisoquinoline alkaloids (Fig. 2.4). (*S*)-Reticuline is readily formed from (*S*)-norcoclaurine as a result of a series of hydroxylations and methylations. From intermediates observed *in vivo*, it may be concluded that (*S*)-norcoclaurine is stereospecifically metabolized to (*S*)-reticuline via (*S*)-coclaurine, (*S*)-*N*-methylcoclaurine and (*S*)-3′-hydroxy-*N*-methylcoclaurine. The order in which the various hydroxylations and methylations occur is substantiated by the distribution of radioactivity in the benzylisoquinoline alkaloids of *Berberis stolonifera* cell cultures after feeding [U-^{14}C]-tyrosine (Kutchan and Zenk, 1993; Zenk, 1990).

2.4.2 Biosynthesis of the tetrahydroberberine alkaloids

The enzymatic route to berberine was one of the first to be completely elucidated, with all of the participating enzymes isolated and character-

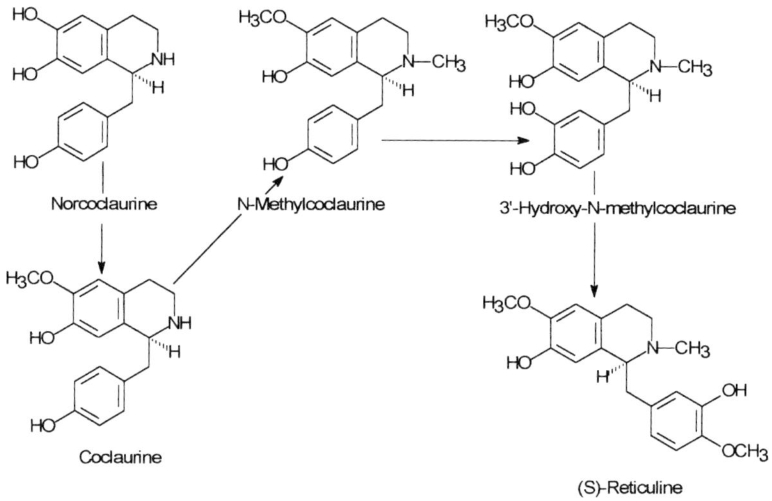

Norcoclaurine

N-Methylcoclaurine

3'-Hydroxy-N-methylcoclaurine

Coclaurine

(S)-Reticuline

Figure 2.4 Formation of (*S*)-reticuline.

ized. The conversion of (*S*)-reticuline to (*S*)-scoulerine by the berberine bridge enzyme may be considered as the first committed step in the production of the tetrahydroprotoberberines and the whole range of alkaloidal types that are derived from this basic skeleton (Fig. 2.5). The

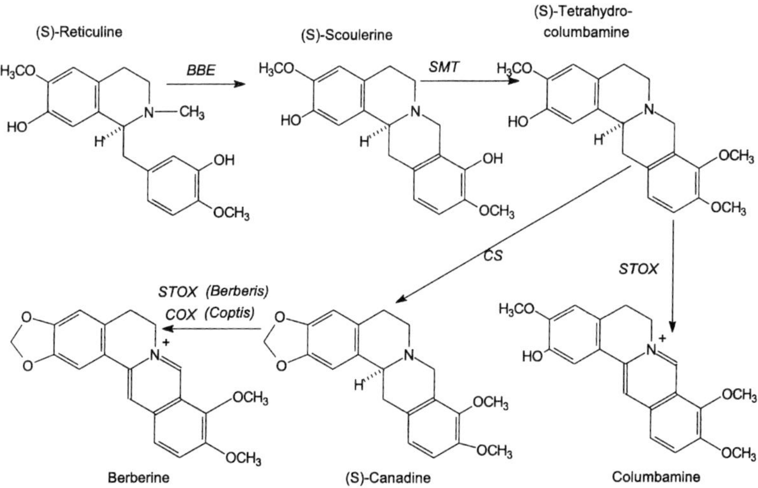

Figure 2.5 Biosynthesis of berberine from (*S*)-reticuline in *Berberis* species and *Coptis japonica*. Abbreviations: *BBE*, berberine bridge enzyme; *SMT*, (*S*)-scoulerine-9-*O*-methyltransferase; *CS*, (*S*)-canadine synthase; *STOX*, tetrahydroberberine oxidase; *COX*, enzyme found in *Coptis japonica*.

berberine bridge enzyme ([*S*]-reticuline:oxygen oxidoreductase [methylene bridge-forming]; E.C. 1.5.3.9.) catalyses the stereospecific conversion of the *N*-methyl group of (*S*)-reticuline into the berberine bridge carbon, C-8 of scoulerine. In *Eschscholzia californica*, this enzyme is found to be elicitor-inducible, which implies that regulation of transcription of this enzyme may regulate benzophenanthridine alkaloid accumulation. Complementary deoxyribonucleic acid encoding the berberine bridge enzyme, overexpressed in insect cell culture, contained covalently attached flavin adenine dinucleotide (FAD) in the molecular cofactor to protein ratio of 1:1.03 (Kutchan and Dittrich, 1995). Translation of the nucleotide sequence of *bbe1* confirmed the presence of a signal peptide that directs the enzyme into the endoplasmic reticulum and then into the smooth vesicles, in which it accumulates. Elicitor-induced transcription of *bbe1* and other inducible genes along the benzophenanthridine alkaloid pathway should help to elucidate the complex defence response signal transduction chain that exists in plants.

The next enzyme in the sequence has been shown to be (*S*)-scoulerine-9-*O*-methyltransferase, which catalyzes the conversion of (*S*)-scoulerine to (*S*)-tetrahydrocolumbamine (Fujiwara *et al.*, 1993). Subsequently, a methylene bridge is formed to yield (*S*)-canadine utilizing the enzyme (*S*)-canadine synthase, a specific methylenedioxy bridge-forming enzyme (Rueffer and Zenk, 1994). (*S*)-canadine can act as a substrate for the tetrahydroberberine oxidase (STOX) enzyme isolated from *Berberis* and may be converted by this enzyme to berberine (Zenk, 1995); however, the oxidase found in *Coptis japonica* (COX) is specific for (*S*)-canadine (Okada *et al.*, 1988; Rueffer and Zenk, 1994). These two oxidases differ, in that STOX contains a flavin and produces 1 mole each of H_2O_2 and water per mole of substrate consumed, whereas COX has a cofactor requirement for iron and produces 2 moles of H_2O_2 per mole of substrate utilised (Okada *et al.*, 1988) (Fig. 2.5). It would appear that either enzyme may be used to oxidise canadine, the type of oxidase being species-dependent. Hence, there is reason not to generalise regarding metabolic pathways, unless enzymatic steps have been elucidated for each species.

The formation of the methylenedioxy bridge in *Berberis* has been found to be caused by the demethylating activity of a peroxidase found within the vesicle. It was also found that the cytochrome P_{450}-requiring enzyme (canadine synthase) from microsomes of *Berberis*, *Thalictrum* and *Coptis* species formed the methylene bridge in (*S*)-tetrahydrocolumbamine but not in the quaternary alkaloid columbamine (Galneder *et al.*, 1988; Zenk, 1995). Because of the substrate-specificity of canadine synthase, the berberine pathway is considered to be that presented in Figure 2.5 (Rueffer and Zenk, 1994). Columbamine, once proposed as an alternative route to berberine, is, however, converted to palmatine by a specific methyltransferase first isolated from *Berberis wilsoniae* cell cultures (Rueffer and Zenk, 1985).

A unique C-O phenolic coupling cytochrome P_{450} enzyme (berbamunine synthase), isolated from *Berberis stolonifera* cell cultures, catalyzes the oxidation of three different chiral benzyltetrahydroisoquinolines, namely, (*S*)-coclaurine, (*R*)-*N*-methylcoclaurine and (*S*)-*N*-methylcoclaurine, leading to the formation of three distinct dimeric products, namely, (*R*,*S*)-berbamunine, (*R*,*S*)-2′-norberbamunine and (*R*,*R*)-guattegaumerine (Stadler and Zenk, 1993). Molecular cloning of the cDNA encoding for berbamunine synthase, utilising cell suspension cultures of *Berberis stolonifera*, has allowed heterologous expression in a functional form in insect cell cultures. This oxidase was accumulated in an active form in insect cell microsomes and accepted electrons from the endogenous NADPH-cytochrome P_{450} reductase (Kraus and Kutchan, 1995).

Important to our understanding of the mechanisms of secondary metabolism was the discovery that all of these enzymes from (*S*)-scoulerine to the production of berberine are firmly associated with vesicles that are thought to be derived from the endoplasmic reticulum. These vesicles appear to be specific sites for the formation of quaternary protoberberine alkaloids. Because of their positive charge, the alkaloids are prevented from leaving the vesicles, and there is some evidence to suggest that they end up in the vacuole when the vesicle membrane fuses with the tonoplast. Tertiary tetrahydrobenzylisoquinolines, such as (*S*)-scoulerine, are able to diffuse freely out of the vesicle to undergo further modifications (Zenk, 1989).

2.4.3 The route to the protopine and benzophenanthridine alkaloids

Another important route stems from the formation of the *N*-methylated moieties of the (*S*)-tetrahydroprotoberberines, which serve as precursors for the protopine, benzophenanthridine, tetrahydrobenzazepines (rhoadines) and spirobenzylisoquinoline alkaloids (Kutchan and Zenk, 1993) (Fig. 2.6). Microsomal, cytochrome P_{450}-dependent enzymes isolated from the cells of *E. californica* convert (*S*)-scoulerine to (*S*)-stylopine by the introduction of methylenedioxy bridges (Bauer and Zenk, 1991). The subsequent *N*-methylation requires *S*-adenosyl-L-methionine:(*S*)-tetrahydro-*cis*-*N*-methyltransferase, and this enzyme has been isolated from the cell cultures of a variety of plants found within the Berberidaceae, Fumariaceae, Menispermaceae, Papaveraceae and Ranunculaceae (Rueffer *et al.*, 1990).

The route to protopine requires oxidation at C-14 of the tetrahydroprotoberberine molecule (Kutchan and Zenk, 1993; Rueffer and

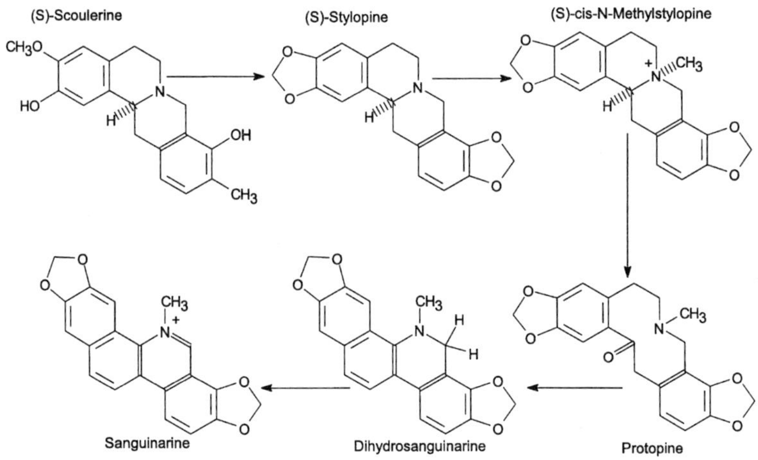

Figure 2.6 Biosynthesis of protopine and the benzophenanthridine alkaloids.

Zenk, 1987b). The enzyme responsible for this oxidation is a microsomal cytochrome P_{450}-NADPH-dependent enzyme that hydroxylates (stereo- and regiospecifically) C-14 of (*S*)-*cis*-*N*-methyltetrahydroprotoberberines, and has been found in a number of cell cultures developed from plants of the Fumariaceae and Papaveraceae. Some of the best activity was observed using cell cultures of *Fumaria officinalis* and *F. cordata*. The protopines may be further metabolised to produce benzazepine and benzophenanthridine alkaloids. Protopine has been found to be a central intermediate in the biosynthesis of the benzophenanthridine, sanguinarine, and also the more highly oxidised alkaloids, such as macarpine (Schumacher and Zenk, 1988). Essential to this conversion is hydroxylation of the tetrahydroprotoberberine skeleton at C-6 and it is this that leads to C-6/N bond fission followed by intramolecular cyclization. Important to these events is the fact that, as acid salts, protopines are not simple *N*-protonated structures. The absence of carbonyl absorption indicates the closure of the ten-membered ring (as shown in Fig. 2.6).

The microsomal enzyme that catalyzes the hydroxylation of protopine has been isolated from *E. californica* and is strictly dependent on NADPH as a reducing factor and on molecular oxygen. Studies with inhibitors have suggested that the enzyme is a cytochrome P_{450}-linked monooxygenase. The enzyme was also found to be specifically present only in plant species that produce benzophenanthridine alkaloids in culture (Kutchan and Zenk, 1993). The dihydro moieties are readily converted to benzophenanthridine alkaloids by an oxidase (Arakawa *et al*., 1992). This latter enzyme, together with a 12-*O*-methyltransferase

(Kammerer *et al.*, 1994), converts dihydrosanguinarine, dihydrochelirubine and dihydromacarpine to sanguinarine, chelirubine and macarpine, respectively.

Dihydrobenzophenanthridine oxidase responds to elicitors implicated in signal transducer mechanisms leading to acquired resistance to pathogens in plants (Ignatov *et al.*, 1996). The route to the benzophenanthridine alkaloids is now clearly defined at the enzyme level. In contrast to the berberine pathway, the enzymes of benzophenanthridine biosynthesis are located in the cytosol.

2.4.4 Biosynthesis of the morphinan alkaloids

The role of reticuline as an intermediate in the biosynthesis of the morphinan alkaloids (Fig. 2.7) was demonstrated by the isolation both of (*S*)- and (*R*)-reticuline from the opium poppy. An excess of the (*S*)-

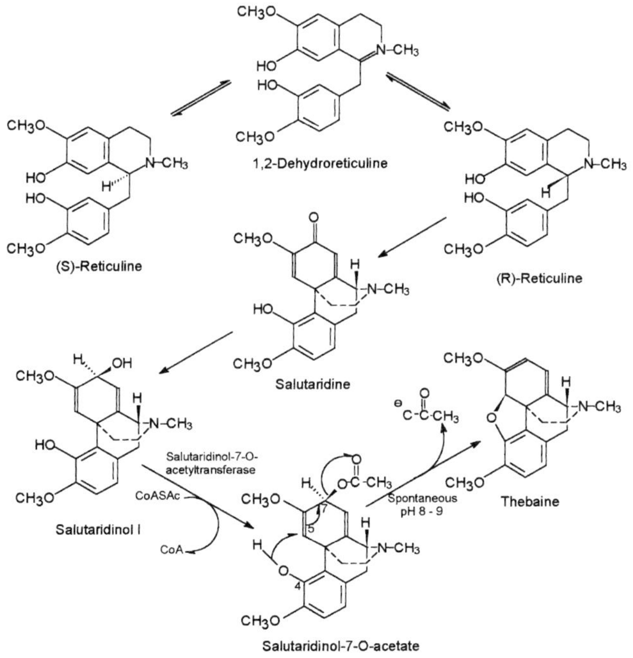

Figure 2.7 Biosynthesis of thebaine via the conversion of (*S*)-reticuline to (*R*)-reticuline.

reticuline over the (*R*)-isomer was found in opium (poppy latex) obtained from the mature plant, in contrast to the roughly equal amounts of these two isomers that occur in poppy seedlings. Both isomers were found to be incorporated into morphine, the major alkaloid isolated from opium, although incorporation of the (*R*)-isomer was slightly more efficient. (*R*)-Reticuline is firmly established in *P. somniferum* as the precursor of the morphinan-type alkaloids (Loeffler and Zenk, 1990). (*S*)-Reticuline, however, is the central intermediate in isoquinoline alkaloid biosynthesis. It has been postulated that (*R*)-reticuline is formed from (*S*)-reticuline by isomerization. This inversion of configuration can be explained by the intermediate formation of the 1,2-dehydroreticulinium ion originating from (*S*)-reticuline, followed by stereospecific reduction to yield the (*R*) counterpart. The 1,2-dehydroreticulinium ion is efficiently incorporated into opium alkaloids and its role as a precursor of the morphinan-type alkaloids has been unequivocally established (De-Eknamkul and Zenk, 1990,1992).

The conversion of (*S*)-reticuline to 1,2-dehydroreticuline has been accomplished using a novel oxidase isolated from cell cultures of plants of the Berberidaceae. This enzyme, (*S*)-tetrahydroprotoberberine oxidase, has previously been shown to catalyze, in the presence of oxygen, the dehydrogenation of (*S*)-tetrahydroprotoberberine (Zenk, 1995). This flavoprotein is compartmentalised in a specific vesicle and can stereospecifically oxidise (*S*)-benzylisoquinolines to their corresponding 1,2-dehydro analogues. Although this enzyme more efficiently oxidises the tetrahydroprotoberberines, it has been shown to occur in *P. somniferum* roots and leaves (Zenk, 1995). The question to be answered is whether, *in vivo*, this is the enzyme primarily responsible for the conversion of (*S*)-reticuline to its iminium ion. The conversion of 1,2-dehydroreticuline to (*R*)-reticuline was brought about by crude cell preparations from young seedlings of *P. somniferum* in the presence of NADPH at pH 8.5. The purified enzyme stereospecifically transfers the pro-*S*-hydride from NADPH to C-1 of the 1,2-dehydroreticuline. The reaction is highly substrate-specific, with no evidence for the reverse reaction. No activity was found either in plants that do not normally synthesise the morphinans or in cell cultures of the genus *Papaver*, i.e. *P. somniferum*, *P. rhoeas*, *P. bracteatum*, *P. feddei* and *P. dubium*, in which the plants do normally synthesise morphinans. The formation of (*R*)-reticuline in this manner enables a narrow range of *Papaver* species to form the morphinandienone alkaloids, morphine, codeine and thebaine, which also possess the (*R*) configuration at the chiral centre.

The next step in the pathway to morphine is the intramolecular condensation of (*R*)-reticuline in a regio- and stereoselective manner to salutaridine, a morphinandienone (De-Eknamkul and Zenk, 1990, 1992). The natural occurrence of salutaridine was confirmed by the isolation of the compound from extracts of opium. The enzyme responsible for this reaction has recently been found to be a highly selective microsomal-bound cytochrome P_{450}-dependent enzyme isolated from young poppy capsules (Zenk *et al.*, 1995; Gerardy and Zenk, 1993). The conversion of salutaridine to salutaridinol with the (7*S*) configuration (Lotter *et al.*, 1992) (Fig. 2.7) by a NADPH-7-oxidoreductase isolated from *P. somniferum* has taken the elucidation of the morphinan pathway a step further (Gerardy and Zenk, 1992, 1993). Salutaridinol possesses the correct configuration for an allylic *syn*-displacement of the activated C-7 hydroxyl by the phenolic C-4 hydroxyl to produce thebaine. A highly substrate-specific enzyme that transfers the acetyl moiety from acetyl coenzyme A (AcCoA) to the 7-OH group of salutaridinol has been discovered and purified to homogeneity. Subsequently, the salutaridine-7-O-acetate that is formed spontaneously closes, at a cellular pH of 8–9, to produce the oxide bridge between C-4 and C-5 and, thus, produce thebaine (Lenz and Zenk, 1994, 1995a).

The sequences from thebaine via various intermediates to morphine, although known from ^{14}C-labelling studies, are as yet poorly understood at the enzyme level (Fig. 2.8). Cell cultures of *P. somniferum* and *Mahonia nervosa* will convert thebaine to codeine, thus proving that these cells have the enzymes necessary for enolether cleavage (Wilhelm and Zenk, 1997). A NADPH-requiring codeinone-reducing enzyme has now been isolated and characterized from cell cultures of *P. somniferum*. Using capsule tissue of differentiated *P. somniferum* plants and applying similar isolation procedures, two isoenzymes were isolated. To determine which isoenzyme is similar to the enzyme isolated from the cell cultures will require the isolation of the appropriate genes. These codeinone reductases (NADPH/NADP$^+$) convert both codeinone to codeine and morphinone to morphine, and are thus of prime importance in the biosynthesis of morphine (Lenz and Zenk, 1995b) (Fig. 2.8). These recent findings mean that most of the enzymes of the metabolic route to morphine have now been isolated.

2.5 Monoterpene indole alkaloids

The monoterpene indole alkaloids have been isolated from three mainly tropical plant families, Loganiaceae, Apocynaceae and Rubiaceae, all of the Gentianales. The indole alkaloids are rich in biologically active constituents, some of which are used as therapeutic agents in medicine, for example, vinblastine and vincristine. These dimeric alkaloids, used in the treatment of leukaemia and Hodgkin's disease and present in small amounts in *Catharanthus roseus* (Apocynaceae), have led to extensive investigation of this plant and cell cultures derived from it. However, neither the formation of vincristine or vinblastine nor vindoline, the major alkaloid of *C. roseus*, was unequivocally found in cell cultures (De

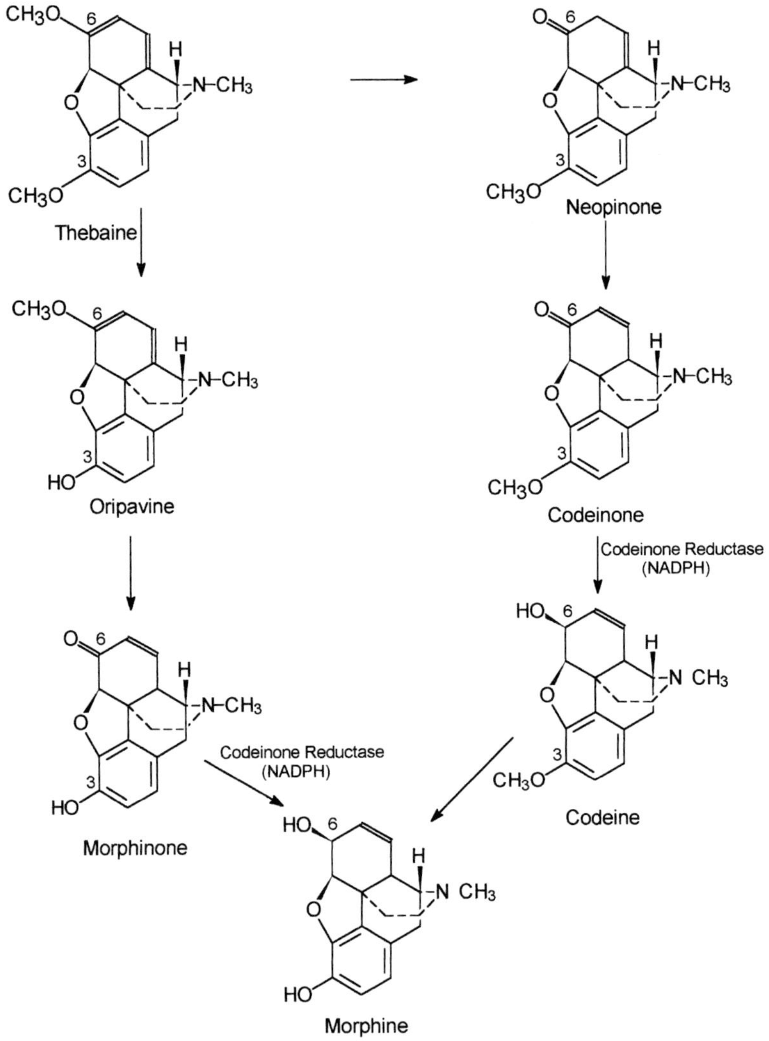

Figure 2.8 Routes of biosynthesis from thebaine to morphine.

Luca, 1993). Cell cultures of *C. roseus*, however, do produce many other indole alkaloids and have proved to be very useful for biochemical studies at the enzyme and gene level (Meijer *et al.*, 1993b).

2.5.1 Biosynthesis of indole alkaloid precursors

Indole alkaloids are derived from tryptophan, which, in the case of the terpenoid indoles, is usually first converted to tryptamine by the enzyme tryptophan decarboxylase (TDC). This enzyme occurs in the cytosol and has been detected in all parts of the developing seedling and in cell cultures of *C. roseus* (De Luca, 1993). It appears to be a pyridoxo-quinoprotein, as two molecules of pyridoxal phosphate and two molecules of covalently bound pyrroloquinoline quinone were found per enzyme molecule (Pennings *et al.*, 1989). A *tdc* cDNA clone has been isolated by immunoscreening of a *C. roseus* cDNA expression library (De Luca, 1993). Its identity was confirmed by expression in *E. coli* and *N. tabacum* (De Luca, 1993; Songstad *et al.*, 1990). TDC is capable of decarboxylating both L-tryptophan and L-tyrosine *in vivo*. The *tdc* occurred as a single copy in *C. roseus* and the protein, when isolated, was found to be similar to that found in parsley and the fruitfly, except that it was found to lack 13 *N*-terminal amino acids compared with TDC from these sources. This suggested a processing of TDC protein in *C. roseus* and *Camptotheca acuminata*, from which it has also been isolated (Goddijn, 1992). However, this cleaved form acts as a functional enzyme and confirms that TDC is a cytosolic enzyme (DeLuca, 1993; Stevens *et al.*, 1993). The 13 *N*-terminal amino acids present in other TDC probably function as a signal peptide for membrane insertion or translocation.

Expression of *tdc* appears to be highly regulated at the transcriptional level. In plants, the highest steady-state *tdc* mRNA levels were observed in roots (Pasquali *et al.*, 1992). In seedlings, the appearance of the *tdc* mRNA was shown to be under developmental control (Roewer *et al.*, 1992), since the gene was UV-inducible, downregulated by auxin and induced by fungal elicitors (Goddijn *et al.*, 1992; Pasquali *et al.*, 1992). The short half-life of *tdc* mRNA (1 h) is another indication that the gene may represent an important regulatory point in alkaloid biosynthesis. TDC protein also has a short half-life (21 h) *in vivo*, and in developing seedlings protein degradation and transcriptional regulation seem to be important controlling factors (Fernandez *et al.*, 1989). Finally, feedback regulation by tyramine could be another mechanism of regulatory control at the level of TDC (Eilert *et al.*, 1987). The *tdc* cDNA driven by the strong cauliflower mosaic virus 35S promoter was introduced into *C. roseus* using *Agrobacterium tumefaciens*. Overexpression did not appear to result in an increase in alkaloid accumulation but enhanced the TDC protein level, TDC activity and tyramine content. Therefore, TDC is not the only rate-limiting step in alkaloid biosynthesis.

Tryptamine condenses with the monoterpene, *seco*-loganin, which is derived from geraniol or nerol by hydroxylation at C-10 with retention of configuration (Fretz and Woggan, 1986; Fretz *et al.*, 1989). The enzyme responsible for this latter reaction is a membrane-bound cytochrome P_{450}-requiring hydroxylase, which was first characterised from *C. roseus* and found with low activity in cell cultures of that plant. Plant cell cultures have been used for further investigation of this enzyme, which appears to have a regulatory effect on alkaloid production; its activity pattern being more closely related to the pattern of indole alkaloid accumulation than that of tryptophan decarboxylase. However, despite the efforts of a number of laboratories, the gene(s) for geraniol-10-hydroxylase (G10H) has yet to be conclusively isolated and characterised (Meijer *et al.*, 1993a). Meijer and co-workers (1993a) found that the NADPH:cytochrome P_{450} reductase is probably encoded by a single copy gene in the *C. roseus* genome, indicating that all cytochrome P_{450} enzyme activity in this plant is dependent on the same reductase enzyme. Steady-state mRNA levels for this reductase observed in *C. roseus* were highest in the flowers, much lower in leaves and stems and intermediate in roots.

In cell cultures, the expression of the reductase mRNA, like the *tdc* and strictosidine synthase (*sss*) genes, was found to be induced by elicitors and downregulated by auxins. G10H was found to be localised in provacuolar membranes and not in the endoplasmic reticulum like many other cytochrome P_{450} enzymes. Interestingly, this enzyme is inhibited by the end-product, alkaloid catharanthine, but not by vindoline and vinblastine. Therefore, feedback regulation may also operate *in vivo*, provided that the catharanthine and G10H are within the same cellular compartment.

A regulatory role for G10H was first proposed by Schiel and co-workers (1987), who observed an increase in the activity of this enzyme when cells were placed in alkaloid-producing medium. The intermediate accumulation of tryptamine and its later incorporation into indole alkaloids, such as ajmalicine, indicated that the coordination of the two precursor pathways for monoterpene indole alkaloid formation are not synchronised (Schiel *et al.*, 1987). The most recent studies have suggested that loganic acid is synthesised from 10-hydroxynerol via 9,10-deoxygeranial by a route involving 10-oxogeranial or 10-oxoneral and iridoidial. In support of this pathway is the isolation of a monoterpene cyclase that converts 10-oxongeranial to iridoidial. The methyltransferase required for the formation of *seco*-loganic acid from loganic acid has been partially purified from young *C. roseus* seedlings (Meijer *et al.*, 1993b and references therein).

2.5.2 *Formation of (*S*)-strictosidine*

Stereospecific condensation between tryptamine and *seco*-loganin is carried out by the enzyme (*S*)-strictosidine synthase and results in the formation of the glucoalkaloid, (*S*)-strictosidine, from which most monoterpene indole alkaloids are derived.

Isolation of the stereospecific strictosidine synthase and formation of strictosidine with the 3α-(*S*) configuration proved conclusively that this was the natural precursor of the terpenoid indole alkaloids. Strictosidine occurs naturally in *Rhazya stricta* and the synthase has been isolated from a number of other species: *Amsonia salicifolia*, *A. tabernaemontana*, *Catharanthus pusillus*, *C. roseus*, *Rauwolfia verticillata*, *R. vomitoria*, *R. serpentina*, *Rhazya orientalis* and *Voacanga africana*. The enzyme has been purified to homogeneity from *R. serpentina* (Hampp and Zenk, 1988). A comparison of the activity of strictosidine synthase from *C. roseus* roots, the only portion of the plant to contain ajmalicine, with that present in plant cell cultures producing the same alkaloid demonstrated that the plant cell cultures are far more metabolically active.

Strictosidine synthase has a number of isoforms but the physiological significance of this is not yet obvious (Pfitzner and Zenk, 1989). However, it has been demonstrated that *sss* occurs as a single copy gene in *C. roseus*, indicating that the reported isoforms of SSS result from post-translational modification of a single precursor (Pasquali *et al.*, 1992).

The cDNA for strictosidine synthase has now been expressed in an enzymatically active form in *E. coli*, *Saccharomyces cereviseae* and cell cultures of the insect *Spodoptera frugiperda* (Kutchan, 1989; Kutchan *et al.*, 1991). Modified cDNA encoded strictosidine synthase from *C. roseus* has been introduced into tobacco plants. Transgenic tobacco plants expressing this construct had 3–22 times greater strictosidine synthase activity than *C. roseus* plants. Ultrastructural immunolocalization demonstrated that strictosidine synthase is a vacuolar protein in *C. roseus* and is correctly targeted to the vacuole in transgenic tobacco (McKnight *et al.*, 1991). Comparison of the terminal amino acid sequence of purified SSS with the protein sequence deduced from *sss* mRNA indicated that the primary translation product contained a signal peptide of 31 amino acids, which appeared to be essential for vacuolar targeting (Pasquali *et al.*, 1992; McKnight *et al.*, 1991)

2.5.3 Deglucosylation of strictosidine

Deglucosylation of strictosidine, a key reaction in the formation of the many types of indole alkaloids, is carried out by two highly specific glucosidases, strictosidine-β-D-glucosidase I and II. They have been isolated from *C. roseus* and a number of other indole alkaloid-containing plants of the Apocynaceae. These specific glucosidases are involved in an essential initial reaction that leads to a complex sequence of events and a series of highly reactive intermediates. Geissoschizine, which is formed from these intermediates (Fig. 2.9), is converted via geissoschizine dehydrogenase to 4,21-dehydrogeissoschizine. The enzyme that removes

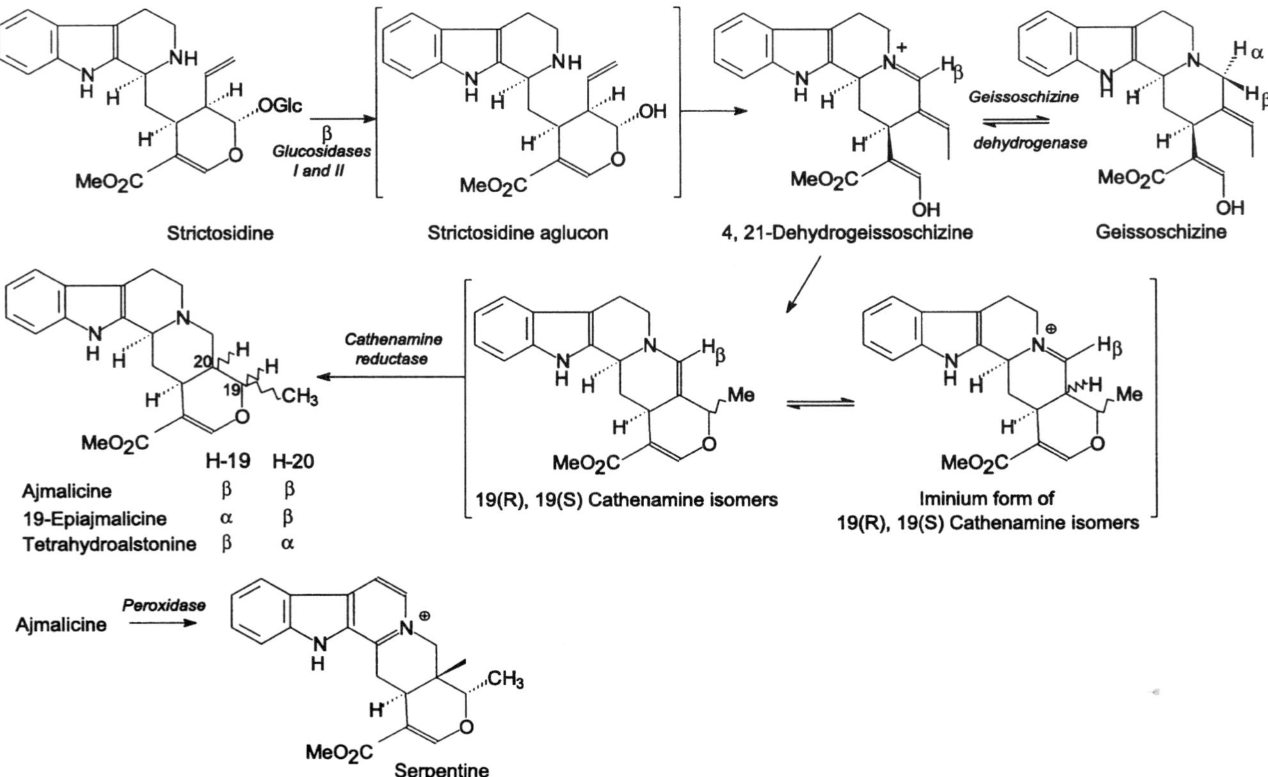

Figure 2.9 Enzymic formation of ajmalicine, 19-epi-ajmalicine and tetrahydroalstonine in *Rauwolfia serpentina.*

the 21α-hydrogen of geissoschizine in an $NADP^+$-dependent reaction has been partially purified from *C. roseus* cell suspension cultures. This enzyme is not thought to be directly involved in ajmalicine production, rather it ensures that geissoschizine is fed back into the pathway. However, geissoschizine and 4,21-dehydrogeissoschizine are key substances in the formation of the Corynanthean (ajmalicine), Sarpagan (ajmaline), Ibogan (catharanthine) and Aspidosperma (vindoline) alkaloids (Stöckigt *et al.*, 1992; Meijer *et al.*, 1993b).

2.5.4 Formation of corynanthe-type alkaloids

Ajmalicine, 19-epi-ajmalicine and tetrahydroalstonine are formed from 4,21-dehydrogeissoschizine via cathenamine (Fig. 2.9). The enzymatic synthesis of these corynanthe-type alkaloids has been investigated using *C. roseus* cell suspension cultures and the enzymes involved have been reviewed by De Luca (1993).

2.5.5 Formation of sarpagan-type alkaloids

Vinorine and ajmaline and the related alkaloid glucoside, raucaffricine, are also formed via a series of enzymatic steps from 4,21-dehydrogeissoschizine (Fig. 2.9). The step from 4,21-dehydrogeissoschizine to the sarpagan structure has not been verified at the enzyme level; however, recent studies have shown that the sarpagine bridge in polyneuridine aldehyde (PNA) (Fig. 2.10) is formed by a microsomal enzyme that requires NADPH and oxygen. Inhibition studies have indicated a cytochrome P_{450}-dependent monooxygenase (Schmidt and Stöckigt, 1995). From structural similarities and the next enzyme in the sequence, it has been proved that PNA is one of the stable intermediates at the beginning of this route. The enzyme that acts on the aldehyde has been well characterized from *R. serpentina* cells and is the specific methylesterase, PNA esterase; the product of the reaction, polyneuridine acid, is highly unstable and decarboxylates to give 16-epi-vellosimine (Stöckigt *et al.*, 1992), which has the correct stereo-requirement for the formation of the ajmaline-type bond (Schmidt and Stöckigt, 1995).

The next step in the sequence to ajmaline is catalyzed by the enzyme, vinorine synthase. Vinorine, a constituent of *Rauwolfia* cell cultures, is an acetylated indolenine alkaloid. Vinorine synthase has a requirement for AcCoA as cosubstrate. The acetyl unit has a stabilizing effect on the indolenine structure. Vinorine is hydroxylated to vomilenine (21-OH-vinorine) by a cytochrome P_{450}-dependent hydroxylase (Falkenhagen and Stöckigt, 1995). This intermediate product is then converted to ajmaline via a series of enzymatic reactions. Firstly, the reduction by an

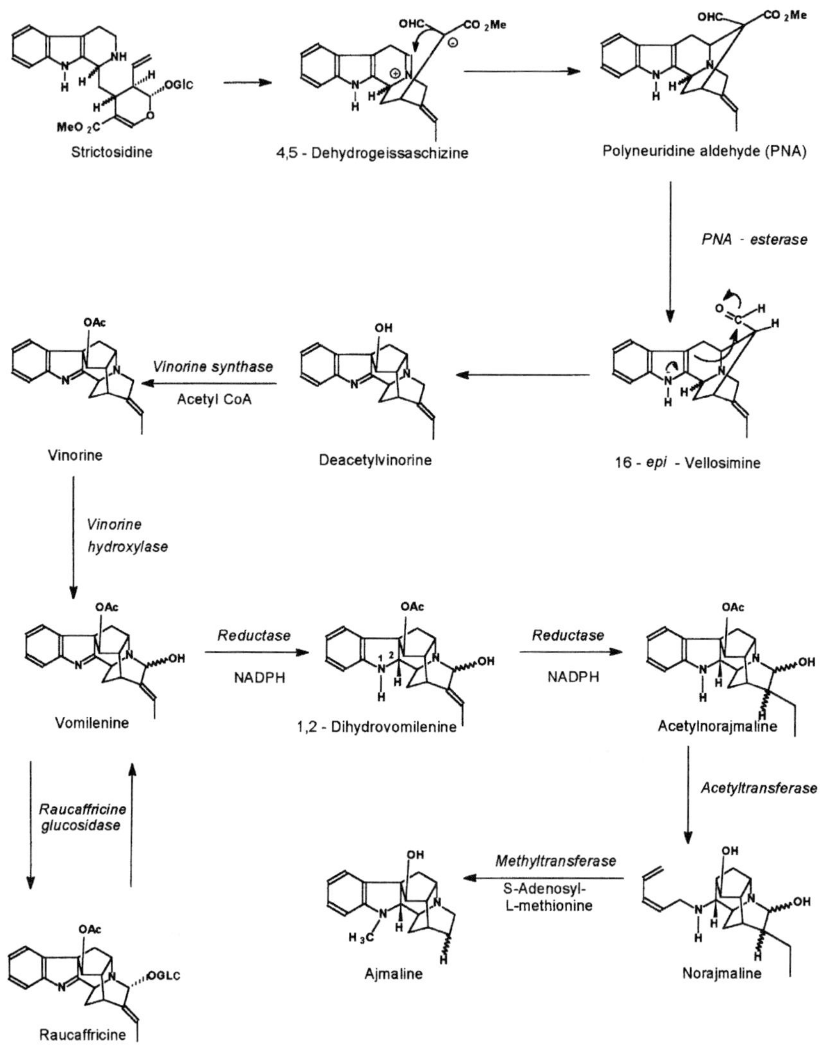

Figure 2.10 Formation of ajmaline and raucaffricine in *Rauwolfia serpentina* cell cultures. Abbreviations: NADPH, nicotinamide adenine dinucleotide phosphate (reduced form); CoA, coenzyme A.

NADPH-requiring reductase to 1,2-dihydrovomilenine, followed by further reduction, also NADPH requiring, to acetylnorajmaline. Deacetylation proceeds with the aid of acetylesterase (specific for the 2β (*R*) configuration) to give norajmaline (Polz *et al.*, 1986). It has high substrate-selectivity and exclusively accepts acetylated ajmaline derivatives with the naturally occurring 2β (*R*)-configuration. The highest enzyme activities were observed in leaves and cell suspension cultures of the tribe Rauwolfieae, which are known to synthesise ajmaline and its congeners. Finally, *N*-methylation occurs to complete the sequence with the production of ajmaline (Fig. 2.10).

In *R. serpentina* cell cultures, vomilenine is converted to its glycoside, raucaffricine (Fig. 2.10), and this has a very significant effect on ajmaline production. In *R. serpentina* cell cultures, raucaffricine levels amounted to 1.2 g/litre medium, whereas ajmaline levels reached only 0.3 g/litre medium (Schübel *et al.*, 1986). It is interesting to note that raucaffricine is a typical constituent of *R. caffra* but has not been isolated from other *Rauwolfia* species. However, in *Rauwolfia* cell cultures the compound is found in all species tested, with a maximum yield in *R. serpentina*. In other words, under these growth conditions the pathway to ajmaline appears to have become deregulated.

2.5.6 Formation of aspidosperma-type alkaloids

Studies performed with *C. roseus* seedlings have suggested that the route from tabersonine to vindoline proceeds by the sequence shown in Figure 2.11. Tabersonine is hydroxlated at C-16, followed by methylation and hydration of the 2,3 double bond, *N*(1)-methylation, hydroxylation at C-4 and 4-O acetylation.

Hydroxlation of tabersonine at C-16 requires a cytochrome P_{450}-mediated monooxygenase. This enzyme was found to be located in the endoplasmic reticulum, was at maximal activity in seedlings at day 9 postimbibition and was induced by light. The leaf-specific distribution of this enzyme in the mature plant is consistent with the localisation of the other enzymes (St-Pierre and De Luca,1995). The methyltransferases required for the formation of 16-methoxytabersonine from tabersonine and desacetoxyvindoline from 16-methoxy-2,3-dihydro-3-hydroxytabersonine have now been isolated and partially purified (Fahn and Stöckigt, 1990; Dethier and De Luca, 1993). These first two steps in vindoline biosynthesis appear to comprise the only enzymes also found in plant cell cultures. Substrate-specificity studies confirm that hydroxylation at C-3 and *N*-methylation are required prior to hydroxylation at position 4 to convert desacetoxyvindoline to deacetylvindoline (De Luca, 1993). The C-4 hydroxylation of 2,3-dihydro-3-hydroxy-*N*(1)-methyltabersonine (desacetoxyvindoline) to the 3,4-dihydroxy derivative, deacetylvindoline, utilises an enzyme that has an absolute requirement for 2-oxyglutarate. Enzymatic activity was enhanced by ascorbate, establishing that the enzyme involved is a 2-oxyglutarate-dependent dioxygenase. This enzyme is specific for position 4 of various alkaloid substrates and has recently been cloned and characterised (Vazquez-Flota *et al.*, 1997). The appearance of 4-hydroxylase activity was shown to be developmentally regulated and is inducible by light treatment of seedlings.

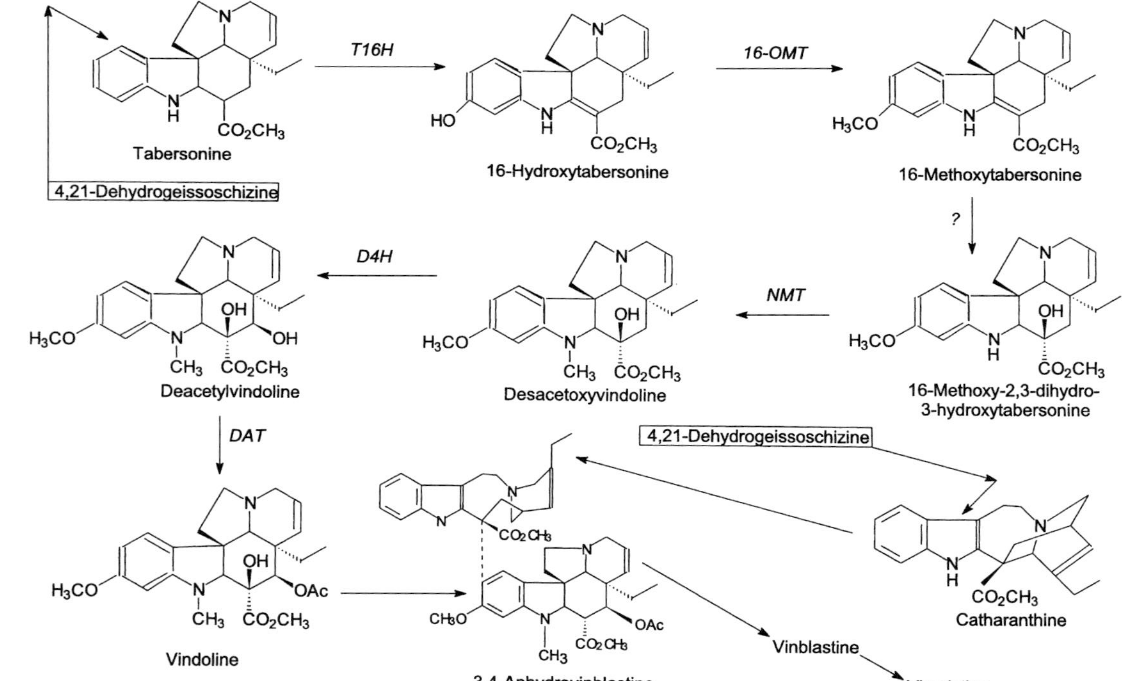

Figure 2.11 Biosynthesis of vindoline, catharanthine and the dimeric alkaloids vinblastine and vincristine. Abbreviations: *T16H*, tabersonine-16-hydroxylase; *16-OMT*, *S*-adenosylmethionine:16-hydroxy-tabersonine-*O*-methyltransferase; *NMT*, *S*-adenosylmethionine:16-methoxy-2,3-dihydro-3-hydroxymethyltabersonine-*N*-methyltransferase; *D4H*, desacetoxy-vindoline-4-dioxygenase; *DAT*, acetylcoenzymeA:4-*O*-deacetylvindoline-4-*O*-acetyl-transferase.

The final step in the formation of vindoline is the acetylation of 4-*O*-deacetylvindoline by a 4-*O*-acetyltransferase. This enzyme has been purified to homogeneity from *C. roseus* leaves (De Luca, 1993).

2.5.6.1 *Developmental control and tissue specificity*

Seedlings grown in the dark produced an early accumulation of tabersonine as a major alkaloid. Transfer of 5-day-old seedlings to the light resulted in the rapid loss of vindoline precursors followed by a more gradual disappearance of tabersonine and the subsequent enhancement of vindoline accumulation. Although light enhanced vindoline biosynthesis, it was not essential (Aerts and De Luca, 1992). The time course of induction indicated that an increase of tryptophan decarboxylase coincided with tabersonine accumulation, whereas increase of AcCoA: deacetylvindoline-*O*-acetyltransferase activity coincided with vindoline accumulation. Results with young seedlings suggested that the enzymes of the tabersonine biosynthetic pathway occur in all plant parts, whereas the last five steps in vindoline biosynthesis are restricted to aerial parts of the plant, and that the whole pathway to vindoline biosynthesis is developmentally regulated (De Luca, 1993).

Further investigations of some of the enzymes involved in vindoline production, using young seedlings of *C. roseus*, showed that while tryptophan decarboxylase (TDC), strictosidine synthase (SS), *N*-methyltransferase (NMT) and *O*-acetyltransferase (OAT) activities appeared early in seedling development, TDC activity was highly regulated and peaked over a 48 h period, achieving a maximum by day 5 postimbibition. Both TDC and SS were present in all tissues of the seedlings. NMT and OAT enzyme activities were induced after TDC and SS had peaked, and these activities could only be found in hypocotyls and cotyledons. TDC, SS and NMT did not require light for induction and OAT enzyme activity increased approximately ten fold after light treatment of dark-grown seedlings (De Luca, 1993). TDC, SS and OAT were found to be cytoplasmic enzymes but NMT was found in the chloroplasts associated with the thylakoid. The participation of the chloroplast in this pathway suggests that the indole alkaloid intermediates enter and exit the compartment during vindoline synthesis (De Luca, 1993). A hypothesis for the compartmentation of terpenoid indole alkaloid biosynthesis in *C. roseus* was given in a paper by Meijer and co-workers (1993b) (Fig. 2.12).

2.5.7 *Dimeric indole alkaloids*

Catharanthine and vindoline condense to form the dimeric alkaloids, vincristine and vinblastine (Fig. 2.11) (for a discussion of this earlier work see Meijer *et al.*, 1993b). Whilst these dimeric alkaloids are not produced

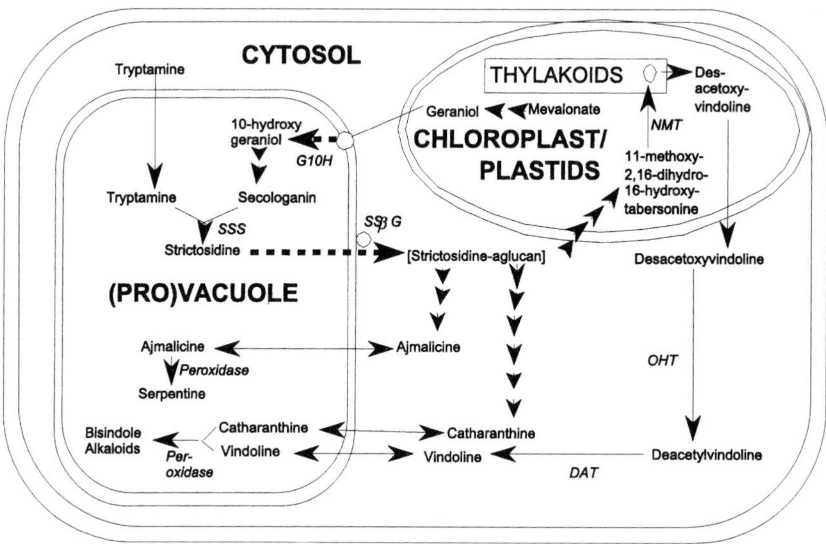

Figure 2.12 A hypothetical view of compartmentation of indole alkaloid biosynthesis in *Catharanthus roseus*. Enzymes located with dashed arrows are hypothetical and circles indicate membrane associated enzymes (after Meijer *et al.*, 1993b). Abbreviations: *GIOH*, geraniol-10-hydroxylase; *NMT*, *S*-adenosyl-L-methionine: 11-methoxy 2, 16-dihydro-16-hydroxytabersonine *N*-methyltransferase; *DAT*, acetylcoenzyme A: deacetylvindoline 17-*O*-acetyltransferase; *OHT*, 2-oxyglutarate-dependent dioxygenase; SSβG: strictosidine-(β)-glucosidase; SSS, strictosidine synthase.

in unorganised cell cultures, they have been found to occur in multiple shoot cultures (Miura *et al.*, 1988). Cell-free extracts from *C. roseus* will convert [2-^{14} C]tryptophan and *seco*-loganin to vindoline (Kutney, 1987). Furthermore, the same cell-free extracts will also couple vindoline and catharanthine to yield the dimeric 3′,4′-anhydrovinblastine, which forms the natural dimeric alkaloids, leurosine, catharine and vinblastine (Fig. 2.11) (Kutney, 1987). The enzyme which brings about the coupling appears to be a peroxidase (Endo *et al.*, 1986; Goodbody *et al.*, 1988). A commercial method for production of vincristine depends on the efficient conversion of 3′,4′-anhydrovinblastine to vinblastine, which has yet to be achieved.

2.6 Ergot alkaloids

The fungus *Claviceps purpurea*, normally parasitic on rye and other cereals, contains alkaloids of a type that is derived, like other indole alkaloids, from tryptophan and, because they are important as medicinal agents, they have been extensively studied.

The naturally occurring ergot alkaloids can be divided into two classes on the basis of their chemical structure: the lysergic acid derivatives and the clavine alkaloids. They all possess the tetracyclic ergoline system. In addition to the sclerotia of *Claviceps*, other fungi and several higher plants can contain ergot alkaloids; some examples of fungi are *Aspergillus fumigatus*, *Rhizopus arrizus*, *Penicillium roqueforti* and *Sclerotium dephinii*, and some examples of higher plants are *Rivea corymbosa* and *Ipomoea tricolor*. The alkaloids from these sources are restricted to low yields and, therefore, for practical purposes *Claviceps* remains the only commercial source. *C. purpurea* in submerged culture is now used to obtain ergotamine and ergocryptine commercially.

The formation of ergot alkaloids from L-tryptophan is well-known (Herbert, 1989). L-Tryptophan condenses with dimethylallylpyrophosphate (DMAPP) to give γ,γ- dimethylallyltryptophan (DMAT), which is modified via chanoclavine-I to give agroclavine and finally elymoclavine (Fig. 2.13). Lysergic acid may be formed from this last alkaloid.

The amide portion of the alkaloid may be a smaller peptide or simple alkylamide, the basic skeleton being called an ergopeptide. Peptidic ergot bases contain lysergic acid and an amide portion reduced to a tricyclic ring system. In the clavine alkaloids, the carboxyl group at C-17 is converted to a group with a lower oxygen state (Fig. 2.13).

The enzyme responsible for the first step in the biosynthesis of these alkaloids is DMAT synthase. This enzyme, which brings about the condensation of L-tryptophan with DMAPP, has been isolated from *C. purpurea* cultures, purified and characterised. The mechanism by which the enzyme works has been probed using a set of analogues of DMAPP and L-tryptophan; it was concluded that the reaction was an electrophilic aromatic substitution similar to that catalyzed by farnesylpyrophosphate synthase. There is a feedback mechanism operative, with inhibition of the enzyme by elymoclavine (Shibuya *et al.*, 1990; Gebler and Poulter, 1992; Gebler *et al.*, 1992). The DMAT formed is methylated using the methyl group of *S*-adenosylmethionine; the activity of the enzyme in cultures roughly parallels that of other ergoline enzymes and has been isolated, purified and characterised. This is, therefore, the second pathway-specific step; however, further reactions are required in the isoprenoid side chain before C-ring formation can take place.

In the conversion of *N*-methyl-DMAT to give chanoclavine-I, there is a potential gap in existing knowledge. The oxygen atoms of both elymoclavine and chanoclavine-I are derived from molecular oxygen (Kobayashi and Floss, 1987). Chanoclavine aldehyde was found as a natural constituent of a blocked mutant strain of *C. purpurea*, which strongly suggested that it was an intermediate on the route to the tetracyclic ergolines. Conformation at the enzyme level is required to validate this hypothesis. Elegant experiments with radio-labelled

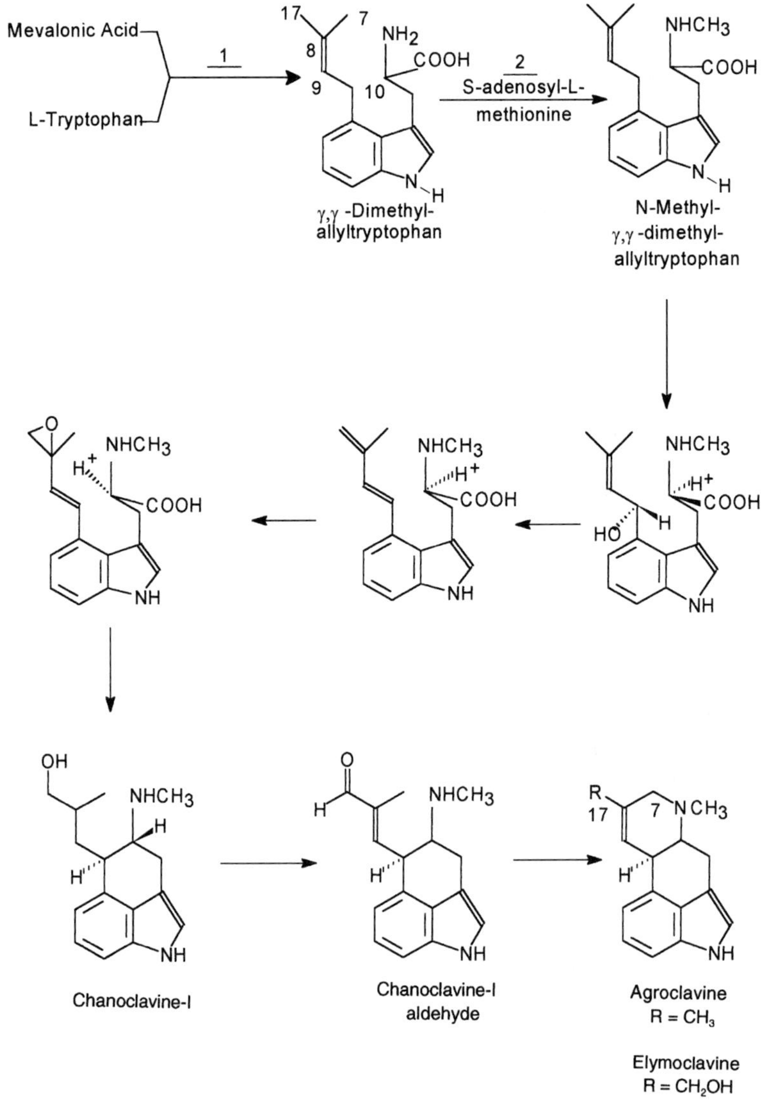

Mevalonic Acid
L-Tryptophan
1
17
7
8
9
10
NH_2
COOH
2
S-adenosyl-L-methionine
$NHCH_3$
COOH
N-H
γ,γ -Dimethyl-allyltryptophan
N-Methyl-γ,γ -dimethyl-allyltryptophan
$NHCH_3$
H^+
COOH
HO
H
NH
OH
Chanoclavine-I
O
H
Chanoclavine-I aldehyde
R
17
7
NCH_3
Agroclavine
R = CH_3
Elymoclavine
R = CH_2OH

Figure 2.13 Biosynthesis of agroclavine and elymoclavine in *Claviceps purpurea* cultures.

precursors suggested that two *cis-trans* isomerizations occur during the conversion of *N*-methyl-DMAT, by ring closure, to agroclavine. The most recent experiments on the formation of the C-ring utilizing deuterated intermediates suggest that the incorporation of *N*-methyl-DMAT into chanoclavine-I is via a mechanism that involves C-10 hydroxylation, followed by 1,4-dehydration and epoxidation at C-7, the terminal double-bond of the resulting diene (Fig. 2.13). The epoxide can then cyclise, with simultaneous decarboxylation and attack of the resulting C-5 anion on C-10 followed by epoxide ring opening to give chanoclavine-I. Whether the decarboxylation occurs in concert with ring closure, as seems most plausible, or as a separate step remains to be determined (Kozikowski *et al.*, 1993).

Chanoclavine-I cyclase catalyzes the conversion of chanoclavine-I and/or chanoclavine-I aldehyde to agroclavine and/or elymoclavine. A requirement for NAD or NADP has been observed. The enzyme's appearance and decline in cultures resembled that of DMAT synthase. The conversion of agroclavine to elymoclavine has been achieved with a cell-free preparation. This enzyme, a microsomal hydroxylase, is NADPH-requiring and the lack of inhibition by ethylenediamine tetra-acetic acid (EDTA) and cyanide suggests a cytochrome P_{450} mono-oxygenase. The enzyme had great activity during maximum alkaloid production (Kim *et al.*, 1981).

Elymoclavine is the precursor of lysergic acid, although the exact mechanism of formation is still unclear. It is assumed that a double-bond shift from $\Delta^{8,9}$ to $\Delta^{9,10}$ occurs at the aldehyde stage and this was confirmed with feeding experiments with the enol acetate of lysergic aldehyde (Fig. 2.13). To form the amide alkaloids, it is suggested that activation of lysergic acid as lysergyl-CoA is required but this remains controversial. A particulate fraction isolated from an ergotamine-producing strain of *C. purpurea* converted elymoclavine to paspalic acid. NADPH was required as was cytochrome P_{450}. A particulate system has also been isolated that converts elymoclavine directly to ergotamine (Maier *et al.*, 1988), suggesting that under normal circumstances paspalic acid is not a free intermediate (Fig. 2.13). This is also borne out by the fact that $^{18}O_2$ is incorporated equally into the carbonyl oxygen of lysergic acid and the oxygen attached to the α-carbon of the alanine of ergotamine. The peptide ergot alkaloids have rather complex structures (Fig. 2.14). The formation of the modified peptide portion of ergotamine involves the conversion of the α-amino acid alanine into the corresponding α-hydroxy-α-amino acid moiety, which then reacts with the carboxyl group of proline to give the unique cyclol structure (Fig. 2.14). This transformation is thought to occur after the formation of the entire lysergyl-tripeptide, i.e. ergotamine (lysergyl-alanyl-phenylalanyl-proline), ergocornine (lysergyl-valyl-valyl-proline) and ergocryptine (lysergyl-alanyl-aminobutyryl-proline).

There are many gaps in our knowledge of the biosynthesis of these alkaloids, despite elegant research using radio-labelled precursors. There is now a real need for more of the enzymes of these sequences to be isolated, so that improvements to commercial production may be effected.

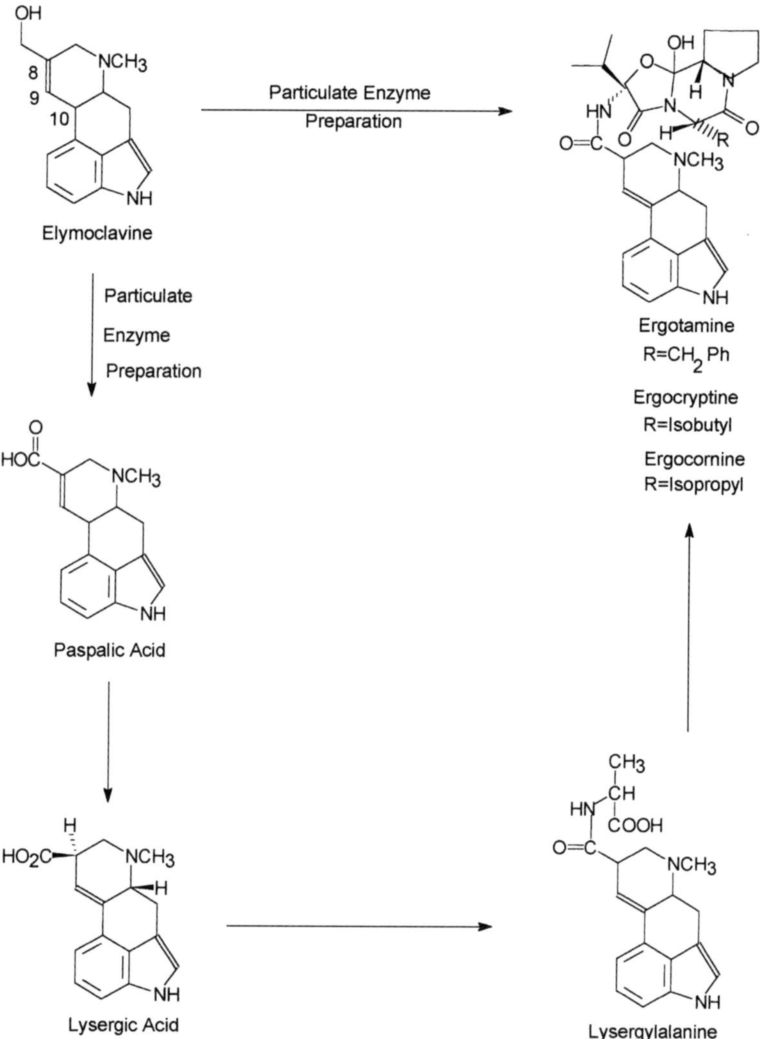

Figure 2.14 Formation of ergotamine alkaloids from elymoclavine.

2.7 Acridone alkaloid biosynthesis

Acridone alkaloids comprise a relatively small group of alkaloids that are found solely in some Rutaceae genera. Some 100 examples of this alkaloid group have been isolated and these include the monomeric acridones and the acridone-coumarin dimers (acrimarines) isolated from

Citrus plants; some binary alkaloids have recently been isolated and described (Takamura *et al.*, 1995).

The monomeric acridone alkaloids are derived from anthranilic acid and acetate via a polyketide. First studies, in which [^{13}C]-acetate was utilised by cell cultures of *Ruta graveolens*, indicated that the C-ring of the acridone nucleus was acetate-derived. Further research revealed that anthranilic acid is specifically incorporated into the A-ring of rutacridone (Baumert *et al.*, 1982).

Cell-free extracts of *R. graveolens* convert anthranilic acid into *N*-methylanthranilate utilizing *S*-adenosyl-L-methionine and a methyltransferase, which has recently been isolated and partially purified from *R. graveolens* cell cultures (Maier *et al.*, 1995). This is the first committed step in the biosynthesis of the rutacridones. The formation of *N*-methylanthraniloyl-CoA from anthranilate utilizing a CoA-ligase (Baumert *et al.*, 1985, 1992) made it possible to study the enzyme that catalyzes the condensation of *N*-methylanthraniloyl-CoA with malonyl-CoA. The product of this reaction, 1,3-dihydroxy-*N*-methylacridone, leads directly to the more complex acridones, such as rutacridone

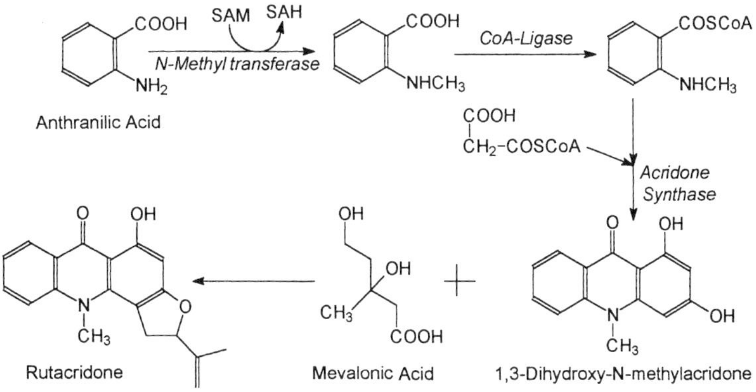

Figure 2.15 Biosynthesis of rutacridone in *Ruta graveolens*. Abbreviations: SAM, *S*-adenosyl-L-methionine; SAH, *S*-adenosyl-L-homocysteine.

(Fig. 2.15) (Baumert *et al.*, 1994). This enzyme has been purified to homogeneity from *R. graveolens*. Complementary deoxyribonucleic acid has been isolated from clones harbouring acridone synthase and introduced into *E. coli*, where high acridone synthase activity was expressed. An insert of roughly 1.4 kb encoded the complete acridone synthase and, although this enzyme expressed no chalcone synthase activity, alignments at both DNA and protein levels corroborated a high degree of homology to chalcone synthase (Junghanns *et al.*, 1995).

Synthesised 1,3-dihydroxy-*N*-methylacridone is readily incorporated into rutacridone by cell-free extracts of *Ruta graveolens* (Maier *et al.*, 1993). It has been hypothesised that the final step in the biosynthesis of these alkaloids requires mevalonic acid (Baumert *et al.*, 1982). The enzyme involved in this step has yet to be elucidated.

The *Ruta* alkaloids are usually found in idioblasts and early experiments using fluorescent microscopy and *Ruta graveolens* showed heavy deposits of acridone alkaloids in the xylem (Wink and Roberts, 1998).

2.8 Purine alkaloids

The biosynthetic pathway from primary metabolism to caffeine is considered to start with the methylation of xanthosine, yielding 7-methylxanthosine. After deribosylation the resulting 7-methylxanthine is further methylated to theobromine and finally to caffeine (Schulthess and Baumann, 1995). The *N*-7-methyltransferase required for the methylation of xanthosine, the key enzyme in caffeine biosynthesis, has recently been isolated (Waldhauser *et al.*, 1997a). The enzymes responsible for the *N*-3 and *N*-1 methylations of 7-methylxanthosine to yield theobromine and caffeine, respectively, have also been isolated. The changes in levels of these enzymes, as well as of theobromine and caffeine, during leaf expansion indicated that each methylation in the sequence required a separate enzyme and these have now been partially separated (Waldhauser *et al.*, 1997b) (Fig. 2.16). The results suggest a role for

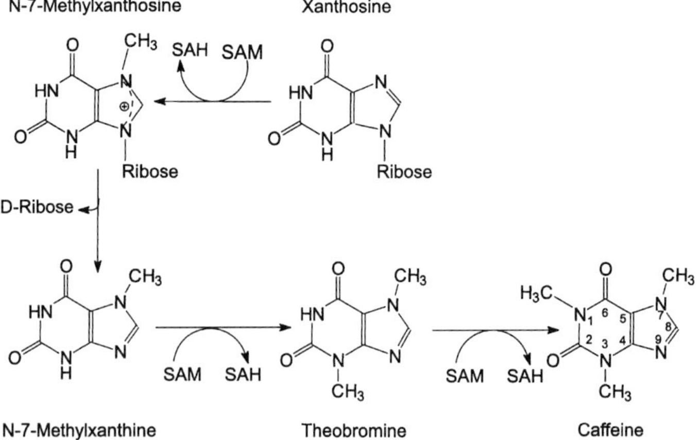

Figure 2.16 Biosynthesis of theobromine and caffeine in *Coffea arabica*. Abbreviations: SAM, *S*-adenosyl-L-methionine; SAH, *S*-adenosyl-L-homocysteine.

these purine alkaloids in defence mechanisms that are strongly correlated with leaf emergence and expansion.

Caffeine and related purines are uncharged under physiological conditions and, due to their dual hydrophilic and lipophilic character, easily penetrate cell-, tissue- and organ-related barriers. In *Coffea arabica*, compartmentation of purine alkaloids, e.g. caffeine, depends exclusively on the physical chemistry of their vacuolar complexation with chlorogenic acid (Waldhauser and Baumann, 1996).

The purine is synthesised and stored in large quantities in the seed. Directly after germination, caffeine remains in the cotyledons surrounding the endosperm and does not migrate to the hypocotyl or root. In older seedlings, caffeine accumulation continues during leaf expansion, and in the mature plant the fruits actively synthesise purine alkaloids as they mature (Aerts and Baumann, 1994).

2.9 Taxol

The novel diterpenoid, taxol (Fig. 2.17), is now well established as a potent chemotherapeutic agent, showing excellent activity against a range of

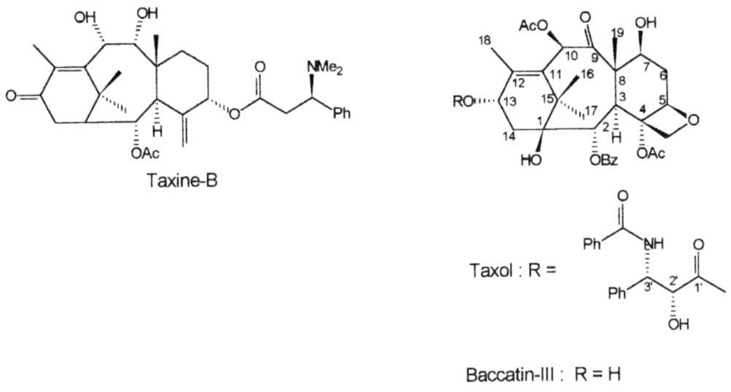

Figure 2.17 Taxine-B, taxol and baccatin III.

cancers, including ovarian and breast cancer. The limited supply of the drug from the original source, the bark of the Pacific yew (*Taxus brevifolia*), prompted intensive efforts to develop alternative means of production from constituents in needles and plant cell culture. Total synthesis is not yet commercially viable and semisynthesis of taxol and its analogue, taxotere, based upon the availability of baccatin III (Fig. 2.17) and other taxane metabolites available from renewable natural sources, has been developed as an interim measure. In considering future routes to these constituents through biotechnology, it is important to understand the pathway for taxol biosynthesis, the enzymes catalyzing the sequence of reactions, especially the slow steps, and the genes encoding the proteins.

2.9.1 Biosynthesis of taxanes

Early work on taxanes (for example, taxane B, Fig. 2.17) has shown that there are several natural taxanes in which the structures analogous to the taxol C-13 side chain are esterified to the 5-hydroxyl group of the diterpene moiety. This, together with the fact that the curvature of the molecule brings the C-13 hydroxyl group into close proximity with the C-5 position, led to the hypothesis that the side chain is first attached to the 5(4) position and then transferred to the C-13 oxygen by intramolecular transesterification (Gueritte-Voegelein *et al.*, 1987). The side chain at C-13 has been found to be derived from phenylalanine by way of β-phenylalanine and phenylisoserine. Recent experiments with tritium and carbon-14-labelled baccatin III and the side chain precursors showed baccatin III to be a precursor of taxol but cast serious doubt on Potier's transesterification theory (Fleming *et al.*, 1994).

The first committed step in the formation of taxol has been shown to involve the cyclisation of geranylgeranyl diphosphate to taxa-4(5),11(12)-diene. The formation of this endocyclic diterpene olefin isomer as a precursor of taxol was unexpected, since the exocyclic isomer, taxa-4(20),11(12)-diene had been predicted as the initial product of the taxol pathway on the basis of metabolite concurrence. The cyclization of geranylgeranyl diphosphate variously labelled with tritium was accomplished using a partially purified taxadiene synthase from *T. brevifolia* stems. From this reaction involving the taxadiene synthase, a stereochemical mechanism has been proposed involving the initial cyclization of geranylgeranyl diphosphate to a transient veticillyl cation intermediate, with the transfer of the C11 α-proton to C7 to initiate transannular B/C-ring closure to the taxenyl cation, followed by deprotonation at C5 to yield the taxa-4(5),11(12)-diene product directly (Fig. 2.18) (Lin *et al.*, 1996).

Concurrently, Eisnreich and co-workers (1996), using cell cultures of *Taxus chinensis* that produce the diterpene, 2α,5α,10β,14β-tetra-acetoxy-4(20),11-taxadiene (taxuyunnanine C) (Fig. 2.18), in 2.6% (dry weight) yield, have suggested that the taxane carbon skeleton is not of mevalonoid origin. Experiments with ^{13}C-labelled glucose and acetate showed the following: 1) the four isopreneoid moieties of taxuyunnanine C have virtually identical labelling patterns; 2) a 2-carbon unit and a 3-carbon unit are diverted to the taxoid intermediate from glucose; 3) the connectivity of the 3-carbon unit is disrupted by a skeletal rearrangement but can still be diagnosed unequivocally by the analysis of long range ^{13}C-^{13}C coupling; and 4) exogenous acetate contributes to the acetyl side

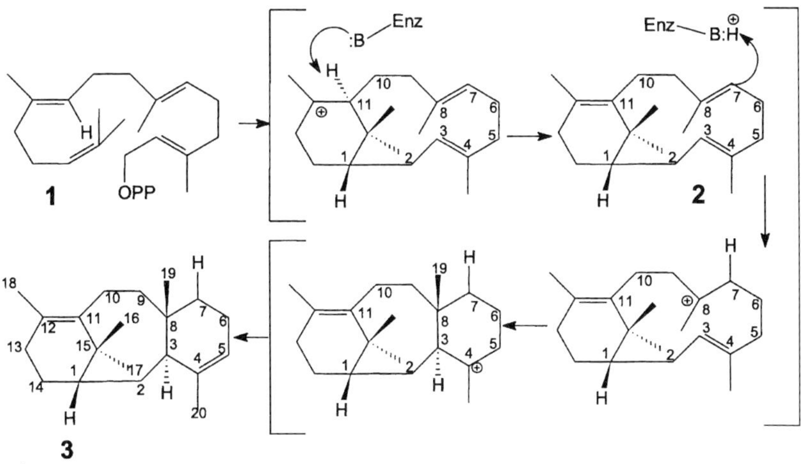

Figure 2.18 Stereochemical mechanism for the cyclisation of geranylgeranyl diphosphate (**1**) via 1*S*-verticilline (**2**), as a transient intermediate, to taxa-4(5), 11(12)-diene (**3**).

chains of taxuyunnanine C but not to the taxane ring system. Biosynthesis via the mevalonate pathway could explain neither the observed contribution of a 3-carbon fragment from glucose to the diterpene nor the label distribution in the isoprenoid moieties.

The assembly of the isoprenoid moiety from a 3-carbon fragment and a 2-carbon fragment from glucose is reminiscent of the alternative isoprenoid pathway reported by Rohmer and co-workers (1993) in the eubacterium, *Zymomonas mobilis*. These authors proposed that the isoprenoid moiety is assembled by condensation of a triose phosphate type compound with activated acetaldehyde derived from the decarboxylation of pyruvate. A subsequent skeletal rearrangement has been proposed to disrupt the connectivity of the 3-carbon unit. However, whilst the data on taxuyunnanine C from [U-$^{13}C_6$]-glucose yielded direct proof of the occurrence of an intramolecular rearrangement in the biosynthesis of isoprenoid precursors, it remains open as to whether the taxoid precursor is assembled from a triose phosphate type compound and activated acetaldehyde. Thus, the ultimate precursor or precursors of the isoprenoid unit in *T. chinensis* is as yet unknown. Hopefully, as the biosynthetic route to taxol is further clarified, this will allow new methods of production to become available.

2.10 Betalains

Betalains constitute a class of taxonomically important water-soluble 'chromoalkaloids', the red-violet betacyanins and the yellow betaxanthins. They are characteristic of all families of the plant order, Caryophyllales, with the exception of the Caryophyllaceae and the Molluginaceae. Members of these two families accumulate anthocyanins, occurring ubiquitously in all other Angiosperms (Steglich and Strack, 1990). Figure 2.19 presents structural schemes of betanidin and a typical anthocyanidin, cyanidin, exhibiting similar light absorption characteristics. Both are the aglycones of various glycosylated structures and their acylated forms.

Cyanidin
λ_{max} 534 nm

Betanidin
λ_{max} 543 nm

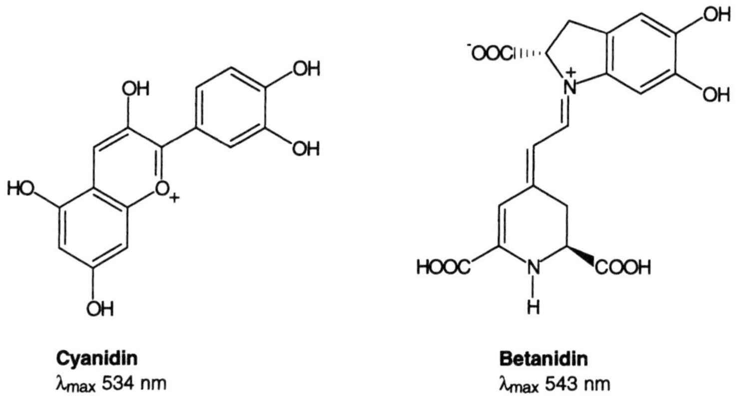

Figure 2.19 Structures of betanidin and a typical anthocyanidin, cyanidin, accumulating as various glycosylated structures and their acylated forms. Both compounds exhibit similar λ_{max} values. Occurrence of these two classes of pigments mutually exclude each other. The betalains are exclusively found in most families of the plant order Caryophyllales, whereas the anthocyanins are ubiquitously distributed in the other families of the Angiosperms.

A well-known example of the occurrence of betalains in higher plants is that of the roots of red beet (*Beta vulgaris* (L.) subsp. *vulgaris*). Unexpectedly, betalains were also detected in some higher fungi (Steglich and Strack, 1990), e.g. the fly agaric (*Amanita muscaria*). Whereas the anthocyanin-analogous functions of these pigments in plant flower and fruit coloration are obvious, their role in pigmentation of vegetative tissues and their occurrence in higher fungi are unknown. In a recent review, Clement and Mabry (1996) indicated the lack of knowledge about the possible importance of anthocyanins and betalains beyond their role in pollination and seed dispersal; but as yet there are no arguments for alternative functions of betalains. Gain and loss of the anthocyanin and betalain pathways remain a mystery (Clement *et al.*, 1994). Both pathways may have diverged prior to the origin of flower pigmentation (Mabry, 1973), or the ability to produce betalains may have evolved subsequent to the loss of anthocyanin formation (Ehrendorfer, 1976). However, the possibility that both classes of pigments may have occurred concurrently in some ancestral plants cannot be excluded (Clement and Mabry, 1996, and references therein).

Betalains have received much attention from the food industry as natural colour additives (Adams *et al.*, 1976; Pourrat *et al.*, 1983). The betacyanins from red beet are used for colouring ice cream, jam and fruit conserves. Earlier interest in betacyanins came from their use in colouring red wine, although this was prohibited by law in 1892 due to the use of the apparently harmful pokeberry, *Phytolacca americana*, extract (Dreiding, 1961).

Research on betalains has received a significant impetus from recent developments in chromatography, spectroscopy, biochemistry and techniques of molecular biology. This has led to a rapid increase in our knowledge about new structures as well as key steps in their biosynthesis. Some new structural features of betalains from plants are reviewed below, resulting primarily from advances in work on their biosynthesis, whilst still being aware of the validity of earlier hypotheses.

2.10.1 Structures

In contrast to the rapid progress in clarifying the structure of anthocyanins early this century, it was only in the 1960s that the nature of betalains was elucidated, mainly by chemical methods. This led to the identification of betanidin by Wyler and co-workers (1963), and of indicaxanthin by Piattelli and co-workers (1964). Both groups of pigments were shown to be immonium derivatives of betalamic acid with *cyclo*-Dopa (betacyanins) and amino acids/amines (betaxanthins). Since then, rapid development of sophisticated techniques in chromatography and spectroscopy has led to the identification of the most complex betanidin conjugates (polyacylated oligoglycosides) known so far from higher plants, such as the betacyanins from *Bougainvillea* bracts (Heuer *et al.*, 1994). Nine betacyanins were identified from red-violet bracts as gomphrenin I (betanidin 6-*O*-glucoside) and derivatives of bougainvillein-v (betanidin 6-*O*-sophoroside), i.e. mono- and diglucosylsophorosides, which are acylated with 4-coumarate and caffeate (mono- and diesters). Figure 2.20 shows the structure of the most complex betanidin conjugate isolated from *Bougainvillea* bracts (for recent reviews concerning betalain structures and methods of structural elucidation, see Steglich and Strack, 1990; Strack *et al.*, 1993; and Strack and Wray, 1994a).

It has only recently been discovered that acylated betacyanins exhibit intramolecular co-pigmentation that may also lead to stabilization of the chromophor, betanidin (Schliemann and Strack, 1998), a phenomenon which is well-known for anthocyanins (Brouillard and Dangles, 1993).

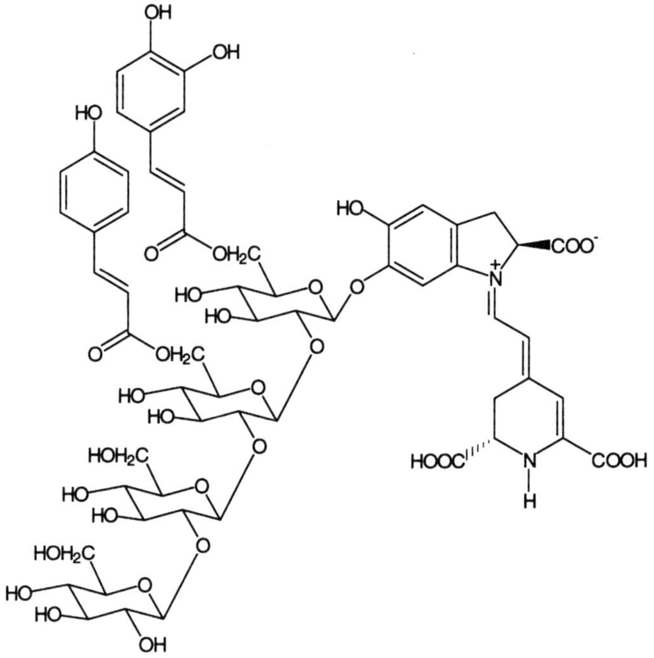

Figure 2.20 Structure of the most complex betanidin conjugate known so far from higher plants, isolated from *Bougainvillea* bracts.

Esterification of the sugar moieties of betanin (betanidin 5-*O*-glucoside), gomphrenin I and bougainvillein-v with hydroxycinnamates leads to bathochromic shifts of light absorption (Heuer *et al.*, 1992, 1994). Nuclear magnetic resonance (NMR) spectroscopic analyses showed ^1H chemical shift differences between gomphrenin I, bougainvillein-v and their respective acylated derivatives (Heuer *et al.*, 1992, 1994), as well as between betanin and lampranthin II (6′-*O*-*E*-feruloylbetanin) (Heuer *et al.*, 1992), indicating molecular association (stacking) of the aromatic acids to betanidin. The attachment of the acylglucosides at C-6 of the *cyclo*-Dopa moiety of betanidin enhances the observed bathochromic shift, which possibly results from a more rigid conformation. This is most interesting when considering the different colours of the red-violet acylated 5-*O*-glucosides of *Bougainvillea* 'Mrs. Butt' (Piattelli and Imperato, 1970a) and the violet-red acylated 6-*O*-glucosides from *B. glabra* (Piattelli and Imperato, 1970b).

An important factor for intramolecular association and, in particular, for structural stabilization is the site of linkage of the hydroxycinnamates to the glycosyl moiety of betacyanins, which has to allow sufficient conformational flexibility on the betanidin skeleton. The binding of the feruloyl residue at the glucuronosyl moiety of a disaccharide in celosianin II apparently leads to a higher flexibility of the acylglycoside moiety, which may effectively protect the aldimine bond against hydrolytic attack (Schliemann and Strack, 1998).

2.10.2 Biosynthesis

Betalain-producing plants are unable to convert dihydroflavonols via flavan-3,4-*cis*-diols to anthocyanidins, whereas the dehydrogenation reactions of dihydroflavonols to flavonols still exist. On the other hand, the formation of flavan-3,4-*cis*-diols (leucoanthocyanidins) seems to be possible, as indicated by the occurrence of leucocyanidin in *Carpobrotus edulis* (Kimler *et al.*, 1970). The lack of the last enzymatic step in the formation of anthocyanidins is, therefore, characteristic of betalain-producing plants, i.e. a dioxygenase-type anthocyanidin synthase with a 2-hydroxylase activity towards leucoanthocyanidins, possibly including two dehydratase reactions. These plants, instead, express a different dioxygenase activity, catalyzing a 4,5-extradiol ring cleavage of Dopa to 4,5-*seco*-Dopa, which subsequently cyclizes to betalamic acid in a spontaneous reaction.

Figure 2.21 presents a scheme of the betalain pathway. The initial key reactions were essentially deduced from feeding experiments with isotopically-labelled tyrosine and Dopa (Hörhammer *et al.*, 1964; Minale *et al.*, 1965; Garay and Towers, 1966), and support the early suggestion of Wyler and co-workers (1963) that both the *cyclo*-Dopa and the betalamic acid moieties of betacyanins are derived from Dopa. By using [^{14}C,^{15}N]-labelled tyrosine, Liebisch and co-workers (1969) unambiguously proved that the entire C_6C_3N-skeleton of this amino acid was incorporated.

Based on genetic studies (cross-breeding) with *Portulaca grandiflora*, Trezzini and Zryd (1990) postulated that only three loci are responsible for betalain biosynthesis. While two loci control the biosynthesis of *cyclo*-Dopa and betalamic acid, the third controls the transport of betalamic acid into the vacuole. They proposed that the formation of betanidin (condensation of *cyclo*-Dopa with betalamic acid) proceeds in the cytoplasm and the formation of betaxanthins (condensation of betalamic acid with an amino acid/amine) takes place spontaneously in the plant vacuole (Trezzini, 1990).

Some of the proposed biosynthetic reactions have only recently been proved by enzymatic studies. It has been suggested that the first enzyme in betalain biosynthesis was a phenol oxidase complex, catalyzing both the conversion of tyrosine to Dopa and the dehydrogenation of the latter to a *o*-quinone (Constabel and Haala, 1968; Stobart and Kinsman, 1977;

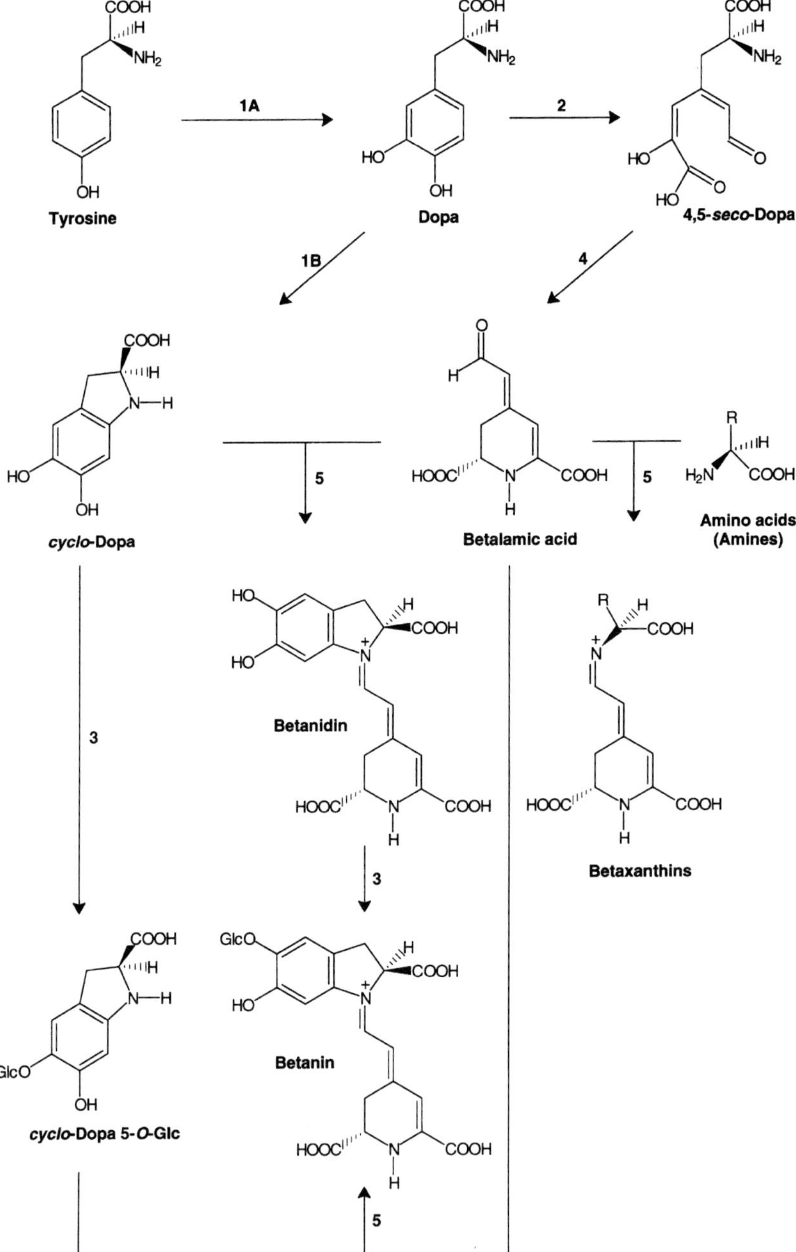

Figure 2.21 Biosynthesis of betalains, involving two 'early' enzymes, the tyrosinase (1A, hydroxylating activity; 1B, oxidising activity) and the Dopa 4,5-dioxygenase (2), and one 'late' enzyme activity, glucosylating *cyclo*-Dopa and/or betanidin (3). Reactions 4 and 5 are considered to proceed spontaneously.

Endress, 1979; Elliott, 1983). This suggestion has been supported by Steiner and co-workers (1996, 1999). They showed that the formation of the *cyclo*-Dopa moiety of betanidin is catalyzed by a tyrosinase in a two-step enzymatic reaction: hydroxylation of tyrosine followed by oxidation of the product, Dopa, yielding Dopaquinone (Steiner *et al.*, 1999). The final formation of *cyclo*-Dopa proceeds via a non-enzymatic ring closure. The enzyme involved in these reactions has been partially purified from betacyanin-producing callus cultures of *Portulaca grandiflora*. It has been characterised as a tyrosinase (EC 1.14.18.1/EC 1.10.3.1) by inhibition experiments with copper-chelating agents (diethyldithiocarbamate and phenylthiocarbamide) and detection of concomitant *o*-diphenol oxidase activity (Steiner *et al.*, 1999). This is in agreement with Joy and co-workers (1995), who isolated two cDNA clones encoding polyphenol oxidases from a suspension culture of *Phytolacca americana* producing betalains. By northern analyses of RNA from various organs of *P. americana* plants, they demonstrated that spatial and temporal expression correlated well with high rates of betalain accumulation in ripening fruits.

The hydroxylating activity of the *P. grandiflora* tyrosinase showed an optimal pH of 5.7 and was specific for L-tyrosine, exhibiting reaction velocities with L-tyrosine and D-tyrosine in a ratio of 1:0.2. Other possible monophenolic substrates were not accepted. The enzyme appeared to be a monomer with a molecular mass of about 53 kDa. Mueller and co-workers (1996) characterised the respective enzyme from the fly agaric. This tyrosinase was apparently not specific for L-tyrosine but also accepted tyramine, 4-hydroxyphenylpropionate and phenol. The enzyme exhibited maximum activity at approximately pH 6.0 and appeared to be a heterodimer of two subunits with molecular masses of 27 and 30 kDa, which is unusual for tyrosinases. These enzyme activities are unique examples of the involvement of a tyrosinase in the biosynthesis of low molecular weight natural products, such as betalains. The role of tyrosinase in the formation of Dopa as an end-product, which accumulates in various plant tissues (Teramoto and Komamine, 1988), or as an intermediate metabolite, for example in the biosynthesis of benzylisoquinoline alkaloids (Rueffer and Zenk, 1987a), has been demonstrated. However, the most obvious function of tyrosinase in plants is to initiate polymerization of the oxidation product of *cyclo*-Dopa, Dopachrome, analogous to the formation of melanin in the skin of animals. A similar function might be ascribed to their involvement in plant defence reactions against insects and microbial pathogens but this has yet to be demonstrated.

The second early enzymatic key reaction in the biosynthesis of betalains is the extradiol ring cleavage of Dopa, leading to betalamic acid. It has been established (Fischer and Dreiding, 1972; Impellizzeri and

Piattelli, 1972) that there is a 4,5-extradiol cleavage of Dopa followed by closure of the dihydropyridine ring by a condensation between the amino and keto groups. An alternative 2,3-cleavage of Dopa could lead, through a dihydroazepine ring closure, to muscaflavin of the fly agaric (Fig. 2.22). Indeed, the postulated Dopa dioxygenase activities have been isolated

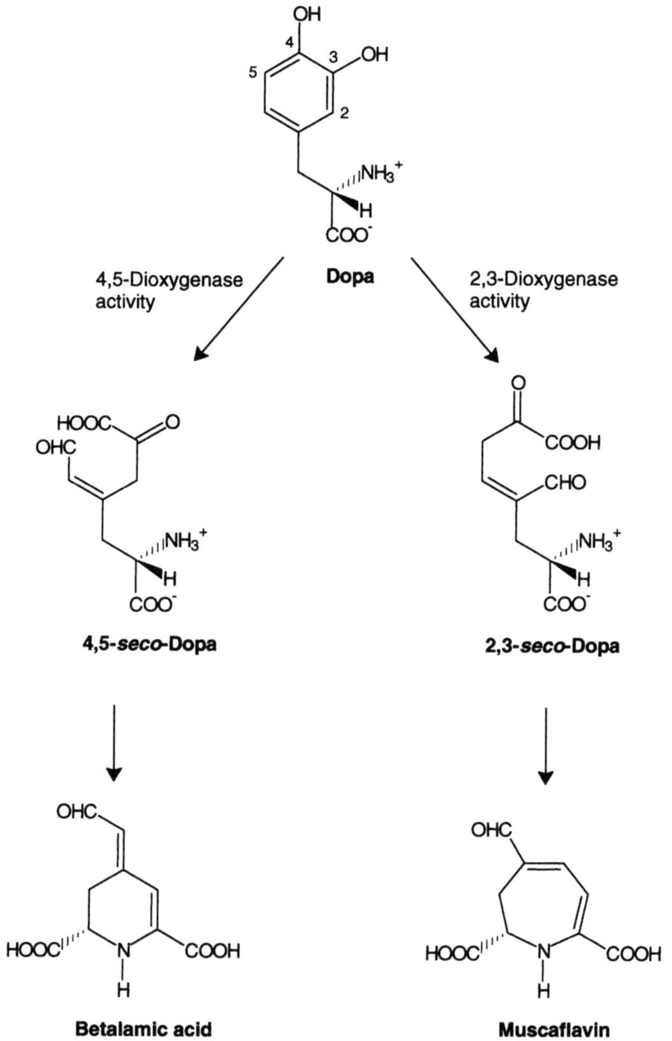

Figure 2.22 Enzymatic Dopa extradiol cleavages leading through spontaneous dihydropyridine ring closure to betalamic acid or dihydroazepine ring closure to muscaflavin. The Dopa dioxygenase from higher fungi catalyzes both ring cleavages, the putative plant enzyme exclusively the 4,5-ring cleavage.

from the fly agaric (Girod and Zryd, 1991; Terradas and Wyler, 1991a) and shown to catalyze the extradiol cleavage leading to betalamic acid and the minor pigment, muscaflavin. In addition, the expected intermediates, 2,3- and 4,5-*seco*-Dopa, were identified in dioxygenase enzyme assays (Terradas and Wyler, 1991a) as well as in *Amanita muscaria* and *Hygrocybe conica* extracts (Terradas and Wyler, 1991b).

The gene encoding the fly agaric Dopa dioxygenase was cloned (Hinz *et al.*, 1997) and expressed in *E. coli* (Mueller *et al.*, 1997a). The recombinant enzyme catalyzed both the 4,5- and the 2,3-extradiol cleavage of Dopa. This was an unexpected result in the light of previous suggestions that the two ring cleavages were catalyzed by two different enzymes (Girod and Zryd, 1991; Terradas and Wyler, 1991a). The cDNA clone encoding the fly agaric Dopa dioxygenase was introduced into white petals of *Portulaca grandiflora*, using particle bombardment (Mueller *et al.*, 1997b). Expression of the clone complemented the betalain pathway in some cells of these petals, indicating that the Dopa extradiol cleavage is the pivotal reaction in betalain biosynthesis. The Dopa dioxygenase activity from betalain-producing higher plants has not yet been demonstrated and attempts to detect the plant enzyme by using antibodies directed against the fly agaric dioxygenase have failed (Mueller *et al.*, 1997a). The authors concluded that the dioxygenases involved in betalain formation in fungi and in plants are different in structure and probably do not share a common evolutionary origin.

Based on the conclusions of Trezzini and Zryd (1990) following their cross-breeding experiments with the model system *Portulaca grandiflora*, only two enzymes are necessary for the biosynthesis of the betacyanin aglycone, betanidin, and the betaxanthins, i.e. tyrosinase and Dopa dioxygenase generating *cyclo*-Dopa and betalamic acid, respectively. According to this model, the subsequent formation of betanidin and betaxanthins (imine formation) should proceed spontaneously, which can easily be demonstrated under *in vitro* conditions (Terradas and Wyler, 1991a). This has been confirmed by recent results from a two-step *in vitro* assay (Schliemann *et al.*, 1998). By combining the Dopa dioxygenase from the fly agaric with the tyrosinase from *Portulaca grandiflora*, the formation of betanidin from Dopa was demonstrated (Schliemann *et al.*, 1998).

Support for the existence of an analogous *in vivo* reaction, at least in the case of betaxanthin formation, came from amino acid feeding experiments with hairy roots and seedlings of *Beta vulgaris* (Hempel and Böhm, 1997). Administration of various amino acids led to the appearance of the corresponding betaxanthins, irrespective of the *S*- or *R*-isomers applied. Following this study, extensive feeding experiments were carried out using *S*- and *R*-isomers of proteinogenic and nonproteinogenic amino acids with hairy roots of *Beta vulgaris* (yellow cultivar) (N. Kobayashi, W. Schliemann, D. Strack, unpublished); these confirmed the lack of amino acid specificity and stereoselectivity in betaxanthin formation. Furthermore, feeding of 2-aminoindan 2-phosphonic acid (AIP), a specific inhibitor of phenylalanine ammonia-lyase (PAL; EC 4.3.1.5) (Zon and Amrhein, 1972), led to an endogenous increase of the phenylalanine level and, thereby, to the formation of the betaxanthin derived from phenylalanine. In addition, by feeding of *cyclo*-Dopa to *Beta vulgaris* seedlings (yellow cultivar), it could be shown that the normally yellow coloured hypocotyls turned red due to the formation of betanidin. The yellow colour of these hypocotyls originates mainly from high concentrations of betalamic acid (N. Kobayashi, W. Schliemann, D. Strack, unpublished), which obviously reacts with *cyclo*-Dopa taken up by the seedlings. In summary, these results indicate that, indeed, the condensation of betalamic acid with amino acids (including *cyclo*-Dopa) or amines in plants is a spontaneous rather than an enzyme-catalyzed reaction. However, this hypothesis still awaits proof. Further studies should prove the spontaneous betaxanthin formation in the plant vacuole, controlled at the site of transport of betalamic acid into the vacuole, as well as the betanidin formation in the plant cytoplasm, as postulated by Trezzini and Zryd (1990).

Considering the complexity of betacyanin structures (Heuer *et al.*, 1994), the 'final enzymes' involved in betacyanin biosynthesis, i.e. glucosyltransferases and acyltransferases, might be as diverse as those in anthocyanin biosynthesis (Strack and Wray, 1994b). Glucosylation of betanidin can proceed at the *cyclo*-Dopa moiety (C-5 and C-6 hydroxyl groups). Feeding experiments using *cyclo*-Dopa and its 5-*O*-glucoside, as well as betanidin, have indicated two possible levels of sugar attachment in the formation of betacyanins, glucosylation of betanidin (Sciuto *et al.*, 1972) or glucosylation of *cyclo*-Dopa prior to condensation with betalamic acid (Sciuto *et al.*, 1974). The latter has been supported by the identification of free *cyclo*-Dopa 5-*O*-glucoside in betacyanin-accumulating red beet roots (Wyler *et al.*, 1984). However, the first description of a glucosyltransferase involved in betalain biosynthesis demonstrated, at least for cell cultures of *Dorotheanthus bellidiformis*, that betanidin is the acceptor for glucose attachment via uridine diphosphate (UDP)-glucose (Heuer and Strack, 1992; Heuer *et al.*, 1996). There are two different regiospecific glucosyltransferases, the UDP-glucose:betanidin 5-*O*- and 6-*O*-glucosyltransferases (5-GT and 6-GT), leading to betanin (betanidin 5-*O*-glucoside) and gomphrenin I (betanidin 6-*O*-glucoside), respectively. Both enzymes have been purified to near homogeneity and characterised (Vogt *et al.*, 1997).

Further glycosylations of betanin and gomphrenin I as well as acylations, mainly with hydroxycinnamates, lead to complex polyacylated oligoglycosides of betanidin. Enzymes responsible for acylation of amaranthin (betanidin 5-*O*-glucuronosylglucoside) to form celosianin I (4-coumaroylamaranthin) and celosianin II (feruloylamaranthin) have been characterised from *Chenopodium rubrum* cell cultures (Bokern *et al.*, 1992). The formation of betacyanins acylated with ferulate has been demonstrated to proceed via 1-*O*-feruloylglucose in eight members from four different families within the Caryophyllales (Bokern *et al.*, 1992). In addition, the respective 1-*O*-acylglucosides regularly co-occur with the acylated betacyanins (Strack *et al.*, 1990). It has not yet been possible to demonstrate the acceptance of the alternative acyldonors, hydroxycinnamoyl-coenzyme A thioesters, in betacyanin acylation. The 1-*O*-hydroxycinnamoylglucose-dependent acylation is presumably the only mechanism of acylation in betacyanin-producing plants. In contrast, most studies on the acyltransferases involved in flavonoid biosynthesis, including anthocyanins, report the acceptance of the coenzyme A ester, for example in the acylation of anthocyanins in *Silene dioica* (Kamsteeg *et al.*, 1980), *Matthiola incana* (Teusch *et al.*, 1987), *Ajuga reptans* (Callebaut *et al.*, 1996) and *Gentiana triflora* (Fujiwara *et al.*, 1997). However, the acceptance of a 1-*O*-acylglucoside has been demonstrated, i.e. the formation of cyanidin hydroxycinnamoyltriglycoside in *Daucus carota* (Gläßgen and Seitz, 1992).

Unexpectedly, purified betanidin glucosyltransferases from *D. bellidiformis*, besides betanidin regioselectively, also accepted highly active flavonoids (Vogt *et al.*, 1997). The 5-GT preferentially catalyzed the transfer of glucose to the C-4′ hydroxyl function of flavonoids (flavonols, flavones, anthocyanidins) with B-ring *ortho*-dihydroxyl groups, with quercetin as the preferred substrate. The 6-GT, instead, catalyzed the glycosylation of the C-3 hydroxyl function of flavonoids (flavonols, anthocyanidins), with cyanidin as the preferred substrate. The speculation of Vogt and co-workers (1997) that these betanidin glucosyltransferases might be phylogenetically-related to flavonoid glucosyltransferases concerns the basic question on the phylogenetic origin of betanidin biosynthesis. The question to be addressed is: are 5-GT and 6-GT phylogenetically-derived from quercetin 4′-*O*- and cyanidin 3-*O*-glucosyltransferases, respectively? The latter implies—in agreement with the hypothesis of Ehrendorfer (1976)—that the biosynthesis of the betacyanins appeared later than the flavonoid pathway in the evolution of higher plants. The discovery of enzymes able to accept substrates of the mutually exclusive anthocyanin and betalain pathways may shed new light on the evolution of both classes of pigments.

Detection of Dopa 4,5-dioxygenase in higher plants and clarification of the level of glucosylation, at betanidin and/or *cyclo*-Dopa, are the last two steps in betalain biosynthesis to be confirmed. Molecular studies are still needed to elucidate the evolutionary mechanisms of the mutual exclusion of the two pathways (Stafford, 1994), one leading to the ubiquitously occurring anthocyanins and the other to the rare betalains.

2.11 Conclusions

These examples of alkaloid biosynthesis serve to indicate how isolation of the enzymes of whole pathways has clarified our understanding of alkaloid biosynthesis and enabled investigations to take place at the molecular level. There is still a need to investigate systems of vesicular transport and alkaloid sequestration. In many instances, little is known about sites of alkaloid synthesis, location of sequestration and means of translocation, although the isolation and heterologous expression of an increasing number of genes is producing new insight into this area. Investigations with plant cell cultures have suggested that, in many plants, alkaloid production is developmentally regulated and this may account for the lack of production of some alkaloids in cell culture. This must be a major area of study in the future if commercial exploitation is to take place.

Acknowledgements

D.S. is grateful to his co-workers, W. Schliemann and T. Vogt, for their contribution to the research reported from Halle and for their critical reading of the manuscript.

General reviews

Brouillard, R. and Dangles, O. (1993) Flavonoids and flower colour, in *The Flavonoids: Advances in Research Since 1986* (ed. J.B. Harborne), Chapman & Hall, London, pp. 565-88.

Clement, J.S., Mabry, T.J., Wyler, H. and Dreiding, A.S. (1994) Chemical review and evolutionary significance of the betalains, in *Caryophyllales, Evolution and Systematics* (eds. H.-D. Behnke and T.J. Mabry), Springer-Verlag, Berlin Heidelberg, pp. 247-61.

De Luca, V. (1993) Enzymology of indole alkaloid biosynthesis, in *Methods in Plant Biochemistry*, Vol. 9 (ed. P.J. Lea), Academic Press, London, pp. 345-67.

Dreiding, A.S. (1961) The betacyanins, a class of red pigments in the Centrospermae, in *Recent Developments in the Chemistry of Natural Phenolic Compounds* (ed. J.B. Harborne), Pergamon Press, Oxford, pp. 194-211.

Hartmann, T. (1991) Alkaloids, in *Herbivores: Their Interactions With Secondary Plant Metabolites*, 2nd Edn. (eds. G.A. Rosenthal and M.R. Berenbaum), Academic Press, San Diego, California.

Hartmann, T. (1994) *Senecio* species: biochemistry of the formation of pyrrolizidine alkaloids in root cultures, in *Biotechnology in Agriculture and Forestry*, Vol. 26 (ed. Y.P.S. Bajaj), Springer-Verlag, Berlin Heidelberg, pp. 339-55.

Hartmann, T. and Witte, L. (1995) Chemistry, biology and chemoecology of the pyrrolizidine alkaloids, in *Alkaloids, Chemical and Biological Perspectives*, Vol. 9 (ed. S.W. Pelletier), Pergamon Press, Oxford, pp. 155-233.

Hashimoto, T. and Yamada, Y. (1994) Alkaloid biogenesis: molecular aspects. *Annu. Rev. Plant Physiol. Plant Mol. Biol.*, **45** 257-85.

Herbert, R.B. (1989) *The Biosynthesis of Secondary Metabolites*, 2nd Edn., Chapman & Hall, London.

Kutchan, T.M. (1995) Alkaloid biosynthesis: the basis for metabolic engineering of medicinal plants. *The Plant Cell*, **7** 1059-70.

Kutchan, T.M. (1996) Heterologous expression of alkaloid biosynthetic genes: a review. *Gene*, **179** 73-81.

Kutchan, T.M. and Zenk, M.H. (1993) Enzymology and molecular biology of benzophenanthridine alkaloid biosynthesis. *J. Plant Res.* (Special Issue), **3** 165-73.

Mabry, T.J. (1973) Is the order Centrospermae monophyletic? in *Chemistry in Botanical Classification* (eds. G. Bends and J. Santesson), Academic Press, London, pp. 275-85.

Pelletier, S.W. (1983-1996) *Alkaloids: Chemical and Biological Perspectives*. Vols. 1-11, Pergamon Press, Oxford.

Rhodes, M.J.C., Robins, R.J., Aird, E.L.H., Payne, J., Parr, A.J. and Walton, N.J. (1989) Regulation of secondary metabolism in transformed root cultures, in *Primary and Secondary Metabolism of Plant Cell Cultures. II.* (ed. W.G.W. Kurz), Springer-Verlag, Berlin Heidelberg, pp. 58-72.

Rhodes, M.J.C., Robins, R.J., Parr, A.J. and Walton, N.J. (1990) Secondary metabolism in transformed root cultures, in *Secondary Products from Plant Tissue Culture* (eds. B.V. Charlwood and M.J.C. Rhodes), Oxford University Press, Oxford, pp. 201-25.

Robins, R.J. and Walton, N.J. (1993) The biosynthesis of tropane alkaloids, in *The Alkaloids*, Vol. 44 (ed. G.A. Cordell), Academic Press, Orlando, pp. 115-87.

Steglich, W. and Strack, D. (1990) Betalains, in *The Alkaloids, Chemistry and Pharmacology* (ed. A. Brossi), Academic Press, London, pp. 1-62.

Stöckigt, J., Lansing, A., Falkenhagen, H., Endreb, S. and Ruyter, C.M. (1992) Plant cell cultures: a source of novel phytochemicals and enzymes, in *Plant Tissue Culture and Gene Manipulation for Breeding and Formation of Phytochemicals* (eds. K. Oono, T. Hirabayashi, S. Kikuchi, H. Handa and K. Kajiwara), Niar, Japan, pp. 277-92.

Strack, D. and Wray, V. (1994a) Recent advances in betalain analysis, in *Caryophyllales, Evolution and Systematics* (eds. H.-D. Behnke and T.J. Mabry), Springer-Verlag, Berlin Heidelberg, pp. 263-77.

Strack, D. and Wray, V. (1994b) The anthocyanins, in *The Flavonoids, Advances in Research Since 1986* (ed. J.B. Harborne), Chapman & Hall, London, pp. 1-22.

Strack, D., Steglich, W. and Wray, V. (1993) Betalains, in *Methods in Plant Biochemistry* (eds. P.M. Dey and J.B. Harborne), Vol. 8, Alkaloids and Sulphur Compounds (ed. P.G. Waterman), Academic Press, London, pp. 421-50.

Teramoto, S. and Komamine, A. (1988) L-Dopa production in plant cell cultures, in *Biotechnology in Agriculture and Forestry* (ed. Y.P.S. Bajaj), Vol. 4, Medicinal and aromatic Plants, Springer-Verlag, Berlin, pp. 209-24.

The Alkaloids (1950–1977) Vols. 1–50, Academic Press, New York.

Wink, M. and Roberts, M.F. (1998) Compartmentation of alkaloid synthesis, transport and storage, in *Alkaloids: Biochemistry, Ecology and Medical Applications* (eds. M.F. Roberts and M. Wink), Plenum Press, New York, pp. 239-62.

Zenk, M.H. (1989) Biosynthesis of alkaloids using plant cell cultures. *Rec. Adv. Phytochem.*, **23** 429-57.

Zenk, M.H. (1990) Plant cell culture: a potential in food biotechnology. *Food Biotechnol.*, **4** 461-70.

Zenk, M.H. (1995) Chasing the enzymes of biosynthesis, in *Organic Reactivity: Physical and Biological Aspects*. The Royal Society of Chemistry, London, UK, pp. 89-109.

References

Adams, J.P., von Elbe, J.H. and Amundson, C.H. (1976) Production of a betacyanine concentrate by fermentation of red beet juice with *Candida utilis*. *J. Food Sci.*, **41** 78-81.

Aerts, R.J. and De Luca, V. (1992) Phytochrome is involved in light-regulation of vindoline biosynthesis in *Catharanthus*. *Plant Physiol.*, **100** 1029-32.

Aerts, R.J. and Baumann, T.W. (1994) Distribution and utilisation of chlorogenic acid in *Coffea* seedlings. *J. Exp. Bot.*, **45** 457-503.

Ansarin, M. and Woolley, J.G. (1993) The obligatory role of phenyllactate in the biosynthesis of tropic acid. *Phytochemistry*, **32** 1183-87.

Ansarin, M. and Woolley, J.G. (1994) The rearrangement of phenyllactic acid in the biosynthesis of tropic acid. *Phytochemistry*, **35** 935-39.

Arakawa, H., Clark, W.G., Psenak, M. and Coscia, C.J. (1992) Purification and characterization of dihydrobenzophenanthridine oxidase from elicited *Sanguinaria canadensis* cell cultures. *Arch. Biochem. Biophys.*, **299** 1-7.

Bauer, W. and Zenk, M.H. (1991) Two methylenedioxy bridge forming cytochrome P_{450}-dependent enzymes are involved in (*S*)-stylopine biosynthesis. *Phytochemistry*, **30** 2953-61.

Baumert, A., Kuzovkina, N.I., Krauss, G., Hieke, M. and Gröger, D. (1982) Biosynthesis of rutacridone in tissue cultures of *Ruta graveolens* (L.). *Plant Cell Rep.*, **1** 168-71.

Baumert, A., Kuzovkina, N. and Gröger, D. (1985) Activation of anthranilic acid and *N*-methylanthranilic acid by cell-free extracts from *Ruta graveolens* tissue cultures. *Planta Med.*, **50** 125-27.

Baumert, A., Porzel, A., Schmidt, J. and Gröger, D. (1992) Formation of 1,3-dihydroxy-*N*-methylacridone from *N*-methylanthranoyl-CoA and malonyl-CoA by cell cultures of *Ruta graveolens*. *Z. Naturforsch.*, **47c** 365-68.

Baumert, A., Maier, W., Gröger, D. and Deutzmann, R. (1994) Purification and properties of acridone synthase from cell suspension cultures of *Ruta graveolens* (L.). *Z. Naturforsch.*, **49c** 26-32.

Bokern, M., Heuer, S. and Strack, D. (1992) Hydroxycinnamic acid transferases in the biosynthesis of acylated betacyanins: purification and characterization from cell cultures of *Chenopodium rubrum* and occurrence in some other members of the Caryophyllales. *Bot. Acta*, **105** 146-51.

Böttcher, F., Adolph, R.-D. and Hartmann, T. (1993) Homospermidine synthase, the first pathway-specific enzyme in pyrrolizidine alkaloid biosynthesis. *Phytochemistry*, **32** 679-89.

Böttcher, F., Ober, D. and Hartmann, T. (1994) Biosynthesis of pyrrolizidine alkaloids: putrescine and spermidine are essential substrates of enzymatic homospermidine formation. *Can. J. Chem.*, **72** 80-85.

Callebaut, A., Terahara, N. and Decleire, M. (1996) Anthocyanin acyltransferases in cell cultures of *Ajuga reptans*. *Plant Sci.*, **118** 109-18.

Chesters, N.C.J.E., O'Hagan, D. and Robins, R.J. (1994) The biosynthesis of tropic acid in plants: evidence for the direct rearrangement of phenyllactate to tropate. *J. Chem. Soc. Perkin Trans.* I, pp. 1159-62.

Chesters, N.C.J.E., O'Hagan, D. and Robins, R.J. (1995a) The biosynthesis of tropic acid: the (*R*)-D-phenyllactyl moiety is processed by the mutase involved in hyoscyamine biosynthesis in *Datura stramonium*. *J. Chem. Soc. Chem. Commun.*, pp. 127-28.

Chesters, N.C.J.E., O'Hagan, D., Robins, R.J., Kastelle, A. and Floss, H.G. (1995b) The biosynthesis of tropic acid: the stereochemical course of the mutase involved in hyoscyamine biosynthesis in *Datura stramonium*. *J. Chem. Soc. Chem. Commun.*, pp. 129-30.

Chesters, N.C.J.E., Walker, K., O'Hagan, D. and Floss, H.G. (1996) The biosynthesis of tropic acid: a re-evaluation of the stereochemical course of the conversion of phenyllactate to tropate in *Datura stramonium*. *J. Am. Chem. Soc.*, **118** 925-26.

Clement, J.S. and Mabry, T.J. (1996) Pigment evolution in the Caryophyllales: a systematic overview. *Bot. Acta*, **109** 360-67.

Constabel, F. and Haala, G. (1968) Recherches sur la formation de pigments dans les tissus de betterave fourragère cultivé *in vitro*. *Colloques Nationaux Centre National de la Recherche Scientifique*, Paris, pp. 223-29.

De-Eknamkul, W. and Zenk, M.H. (1990) Enzymic formation of (*R*)-reticuline from 1,2-dehydroreticuline in the opium poppy plant. *Tetrahedron Lett.*, **34** 4855-58.

De-Eknamkul, W. and Zenk, M.H. (1992) Purification and properties of 1,2-dehydroreticuline reductase from *Papaver somniferum* seedlings. *Phytochemistry*, **31** 813-21.

Dethier, M. and De Luca, V. (1993) Partial purification of a *N*-methyltransferase involved in vindoline biosynthesis in *Catharanthus roseus*. *Phytochemistry*, **31** 663-78.

Dräger, B. and Schaal, A. (1994) Tropinone reduction in *Atropa belladonna* root cultures. *Phytochemistry*, **35** 1441-47.

Dräger, B., Portsteffen, A., Schaal, A., MCCabe, P.H., Peerless, A.C.J. and Robins, R.J. (1992) Levels of tropinone reductase activities influence the spectrum of tropane esters found in transformed root cultures of *Datura stramonium*. *Planta*, **188** 581-86.

Dräger, B., Funck, C., Höhler, A., Mrachatz, G., Portsteffen, A., Schaal, A. and Schmidt, R. (1994) Calystegines as a new group of tropane alkaloids in Solanaceae. *Plant Cell Tiss. Org. Cult.*, **38** 235-40.

Ehrendorfer, F. (1976) Closing remarks: systematics and evolution of centrospermous families. *Plant System. Evol.*, **126** 99-106.

Eilert, U., De Luca, V., Constabel, F. and Kurz, W.G.W. (1987) Elicitor-mediated induction of tryptophan decarboxylase and strictosidine synthase activities in suspension culture of *Catharanthus roseus*. *Arch. Biochem. Biophys.*, **254** 491-97.

Eisnreich, W., Menhard, B., Hylands, P.J. and Zenk, M.H. (1996) Studies on the biosynthesis of taxol: the taxane carbon skeleton is not of mevalonoid origin. *Proc. Natl. Acad. Sci. USA*, **93** 6431-36.

Elliott, D.C. (1983) The pathway of betalain biosynthesis: effect of cytokinin on enzymic oxidation and hydroxylation of tyrosine in *Amaranthus tricolor* seedlings. *Physiol. Plant.*, **59** 428-37.

Endo, T., Goodbody, A., Vukovic, J. and Misawa, M. (1986) Enzymes from *Catharanthus roseus* cell suspension cultures that couple vindoline and catharanthine to form 3′,4′-anhydrovinblastine. *Phytochemistry*, **27** 2147-49.

Endress, R. (1979) Mögliche Beteiligung einer Phenylalaninhydroxylase und einer Tyrosinase bei der Betacyan-Akkumulation in *Portulaca* Kallus. *Biochem. Physiol. Pflanzen*, **174** 17-25.

Facchini, P.J. and De Luca, V. (1994) Differential and tissue specific expression of a gene family for tyrosine/dopa decarboxylase in opium poppy. *J. Biol. Chem.*, **269** 26684-90.

Facchini, P.J. and De Luca, V. (1995) Phloem specific expression of tyrosine/dopa decarboxylase genes and the biosynthesis of isoquinoline alkaloids in opium poppy. *The Plant Cell*, **7** 1811-21.

Facchini, P.J., Johnson, A.G., Poupart, J. and De Luca, V. (1996) Uncoupled defense gene expression and antimicrobial alkaloid accumulation in elicited opium poppy cell cultures. *Plant Physiol.*, **111** 687-97.

Fahn, W. and Stöckigt, J. (1990) Purification of acetyl-CoA: 17-*O*-deacetylvindoline 17-*O*-acetyltransferase from *Catharanthus roseus* leaves. *Plant Cell Rep.*, **8** 613-16.

Falkenhagen, H. and Stöckigt, J. (1995) Enzymic biosynthesis of vomilenine, a key intermediate of the ajmaline pathway, catalysed by a novel cytochrome P_{450}-dependent enzyme from plant cell cultures of *Rauwolfia serpentina*. *Z. Naturforsch.*, **50c** 45-53.

Fecker, L.F., Hillebrandt, S., Rügenhagen, C., Herminghaus, S., Landsmann, J. and Berlin, J. (1992) Metabolic effects of a bacterial lysine decarboxylase gene expressed in hairy root culture of *Nicotiana glauca*. *Biotech. Lett.*, **14** 1035-40.

Fernandez, J.A., Owen, T.G., Kurz, W.G.W. and De Luca, V. (1989) Immunological detection and quantitation of tryptophan decarboxylase in developing *Catharanthus roseus* seedlings. *Plant Physiol.*, **91** 79-84.

Fischer, N. and Dreiding, A.S. (1972) Biosynthesis of betalaines. On the cleavage of the aromatic ring during the enzymatic transformation of dopa into betalamic acid. *Helv. Chim. Acta*, **55** 649-58.

Fleming, P.E., Knaggs, A.R., He, X-G., Mocek, U. and Floss, H.G. (1994) Biosynthesis of taxoids, mode of attachment of the side chain. *J. Am. Chem. Soc.*, **116** 4137-38.

Fretz, H. and Woggon, W.-D. (1986) Regioselectivity and deuterium isotope effects in geraniol hydroxylation by the cytochrome P_{450} monooxygenase from *Catharanthus roseus* (L.). G. Don. *Helv. Chim. Acta*, **69** 1959-70.

Fretz, H., Woggon, W-D. and Voges, R. (1989) The allylic oxidation of geraniol catalysed by cytochrome P_{450} proceeding with retention of configuration. *Helv. Chim. Acta*, **72** 391-400.

Friesen, J.B. and Leete, E. (1990) Nicotine synthase: an enzyme from *Nicotiana* species which catalyses the formation of (*S*)-nicotine from nicotinic acid and 1-methyl-Δ'-pyrrolinium chloride. *Tetrahedron Lett.*, **31** 6295-98.

Fujiwara, H., Takeshita, N., Terano, Y., Fitchen, J.H., Tsujita, T., Katagiri, Y., Sato, F. and Yamada, Y. (1993) Expression of (*S*)-scoulerine 9-*O*-methyltransferase in *Coptis japonica* plants. *Phytochemistry*, **34** 949-54.

Fujiwara, H., Tanakan, Y., Fukui, Y., Nakao, Y., Ashikari, T. and Kusumi, T. (1997) Anthocyanin 5-aromatic acyltransferase from *Gentiana triflora*: purification, characterization and its role in anthocyanin biosynthesis. *Eur. J. Biochem.*, **249** 45-51.

Galneder, E., Rueffer, M., Wanner, G., Tabata, M. and Zenk, M.H. (1988) Alternative final steps in berberine biosynthesis in *Coptis japonica* cell cultures. *Plant Cell Rep.*, **7** 1-4.

Garay, A.S. and Towers, G.H.N. (1966) Studies on the biosynthesis of amaranthin. *Can. J. Bot.*, **44** 231-36.

Gebler, J.C. and Poulter, C.D. (1992) Purification and characterisation of dimethylallyltryptophan synthase from *Claviceps purpurea*. *Arch. Biochem. Biophys.*, **296** 308-13.

Gebler, J.C., Woodside, A.B. and Poulter, C.D. (1992) Dimethylallyltryptophan synthase: an enzyme catalysed electrophilic aromatic substitution. *J. Am. Chem. Soc.*, **114** 7354-60.

Gerardy, R. and Zenk, M.H. (1992) Formation of salutaridine from (*R*)-reticuline by a membrane-bound cytochrome P_{450} enzyme from *Papaver somniferum*. *Phytochemistry*, **32** 79-86.

Gerardy, R. and Zenk, M.H. (1993) Purification and characterization of salutaridine: NADPH-7-oxidoreductase. *Phytochemistry*, **34** 125-32.

Girod, P.-A. and Zryd, J.-P. (1991) Biogenesis of betalains: purification and partial characterization of Dopa 4,5-dioxygenase from *Amanitamuscaria Phytochemistry*, **30** 169-74.

Gläßgen, W.E. and Seitz, H.U. (1992) Acylation of anthocyanins with hydroxycinnamic acids via 1-*O*-acylglucosides by protein preparations from cell cultures of *Daucus carota* (L.). *Planta*, **186** 582-85.

Goddijn, O.J.M. (1992) Regulation of terpenoid indole alkaloid biosynthesis in *Catharanthus roseus*: the tryptophan decarboxylase gene. Ph.D. thesis, Leiden University.

Goddijn, O.J.M., DeKam, R.J., Zanetti, A., Schilperoot, R.A. and Hoge, J.H.C. (1992) Auxin downregulates transcription of the tryptophan decarboxylase gene from *Catharanthus roseus*. *Plant Mol. Biol.*, **18** 1113-20.

Goldmann, A., Milat, A.-L., Ducrot, P.-H., Lallemand, J.-Y., Maille, M., Lepingle, A., Charpin, I. and Tepfer, D. (1992) Tropane derivatives from *Calystegia sepium*. *Phytochemistry*, **29** 2125-27.

Goodbody, A.E., Endo, T., Vukovic, J., Kutney, J.P., Choi, L.S.L. and Misawa, M. (1988) Enzymic coupling of catharanthine and vindoline to form 3′,4′-anhydrovinblastine by horseradish peroxidase. *Planta Med.*, **54** 136-40.

Graser, G. and Hartmann, T. (1997) Biosynthetic incorporation of the aminobutyl group of spermine into pyrrolizidine alkaloids. *Phytochemistry*, **45** 1591-92.

Gueritte-Voegelein, F., Guernard, D. and Potier, P. (1987) Taxol and derivatives: a biogenetic hypothesis. *J. Nat. Prod.*, **50** 9-18.

Hampp, N. and Zenk, M.H. (1988) Homogeneous strictosidine synthase from cell suspension cultures of *Rauvolvia serpentina*. *Phytochemistry*, **27** 3811-15.

Hempel, J. and Böhm, H. (1997) Betaxanthin pattern of hairy roots from *Beta vulgaris* var. *lutea* and its alteration by feeding of amino acids. *Phytochemistry*, **44** 847-52.

Heuer, S. and Strack, D. (1992) Synthesis of betanin from betanidin and UDP-glucose by a protein preparation from cell suspension cultures of *Dorotheanthus bellidiformis* (Burm. f.) N.E.Br. *Planta*, **186** 626-28.

Heuer, S., Wray, V., Metzger, J.W. and Strack, D. (1992) Betacyanins from flowers of *Gomphrena globosa*. *Phytochemistry*, **31** 1801-807.

Heuer, S., Richter, S., Metzger, J.W., Wray, V., Nimtz, M. and Strack, D. (1994) Betacyanins from bracts of *Bougainvillea glabra*. *Phytochemistry*, **37** 761-67.

Heuer, S., Vogt, T., Böhm, H. and Strack, D. (1996) Partial purification and characterization of UDP-glucose:betanidin 5-*O*- and 6-*O*-glucosyltransferases from cell suspension cultures of *Dorotheanthus bellidiformis* (Burm. f.) N.E.Br. *Planta*, **199** 244-50.

Hibi, N., Fujita, T., Hatano, M., Hashimoto, T. and Yamada, Y. (1992) Putrescine *N*-methyltransferase in cultured roots of *Hyoscyamus albus*. *Plant Physiol.*, **100** 826-35.

Hibi, N., Higashiguchi, S., Hashimoto, T. and Yamada, Y. (1994) Gene expression in tobacco low-nicotine mutants. *Plant Cell*, **6** 723-35.

Hinz, U.G., Fivaz, J., Girod, P.-A. and Zryd, J.-P. (1997) The gene coding for the dioxygenase involved in betalain biosynthesis in *Amanita muscaria* and its regulation. *Mol. Gen. Genet.*, **256** 1-6.

Hörhammer, L., Wagner, H. and Fritsche, W. (1964) Zur Biosynthese der Betacyane I. *Biochemische Zeitschrift*, **339** 398-400.

Ignatov, A., Clark, W.G., Cline, S.D., Psenak, M., Krueger, R.J. and Coscia, C.J. (1996) Elicitation of dihydrobenzophenanthridine oxidase in *Sanguinaria canadensis* cell cultures. *Phytochemistry*, **43** 1141-44.

Impellizzeri, G. and Piattelli, M. (1972) Biosynthesis of indicaxanthin in *Opuntia ficus-indica* fruits. *Phytochemistry*, **11** 2499-502.

Joy, R.W., Sugiyama, M., Fukuda, H. and Komamine, A. (1995) Cloning and characterization of polyphenol oxidase cDNAs of *Phytolacca americana*. *Plant Physiol.*, **107** 1083-89.

Junghanns, K.T., Kneusel, R.E., Baumert, A., Maier, W., Gröger, D. and Matern, U. (1995) Molecular cloning and heterologous expression of acridone synthase from elicited *Ruta graveolens* (L.) cell suspension cultures. *Plant Mol. Biol.*, **27** 681-92.

Kammerer, L., De-Eknamkul, W. and Zenk, M.H. (1994) Enzymic 12-hydroxylation and 12-*O*-methylation of dihydrochelirubine in dihydromacarpine formation by *Thalictrum bulgaricum*. *Phytochemistry*, **36** 1409-16.

Kamsteeg, J., Van Brederode, J., Hommels, C.H. and Van Nigtevecht, G. (1980) Identification, properties and genetic control of hydroxycinnamoyl-coenzyme A: anthocyanidin 3-rhamnosyl (1→6) glucoside, 4′-hydroxycinnamoyl transferase isolated from petals of *Silene dioica*. *Biochem. Physiol. Pflanzen*, **175** 403-11.

Kanegae, T., Kajiya, H., Amano, Y., Hashimoto, T. and Yamada, Y. (1994) Species-dependent expression of the hyoscyamine 6β-hydroxylase gene in the pericycle. *Plant Physiol.*, **105** 483-90.

Kim, I.-S., Kim, S.-U. and Anderson, J.A. (1981) Microsomal agroclavine hydroxylase of *Claviceps* species. *Phytochemistry*, **20** 2311-14.

Kimler, L., Mears, J., Mabry, T.J. and Rösler, H. (1970) On the question of the mutual exclusiveness of betalains and anthocyanins. *Taxon.*, **19** 875-78.

Kobayashi, M. and Floss, H.G. (1987) Biosynthesis of ergot alkaloids: origin of the oxygen atoms in chanoclavine I and elymoclavine. *J. Org. Chem.*, **52** 4350-52.

Kozikowski, A.P., Chen, C., Wu, J.-P., Shibuya, M., Kim, C.-G. and Floss, H.G. (1993) Probing alkaloid biosynthesis: intermediates in the formation of ring C. *J. Am. Chem. Soc.*, **115** 2482-88.

Kraus, P.F.X. and Kutchan, T.M. (1995) Molecular cloning and heterologous expression of a cDNA encoding berbamunine synthase, a C-O phenol-coupling cytochrome P_{450} from the higher plant *Berberis stolonifera. Proc. Natl. Acad. Sci. USA*, **92** 2071-75.

Kutchan, T.M. (1989) Expression of enzymatically active cloned strictosidine synthase from the higher plant *Rauvolfia serpentina* in *Escherichia coli. FEBS Lett.*, **257** 127-30.

Kutchan, T.M. and Dittrich, H. (1995) Characterisation and mechanism of berberine bridge enzyme, a covalently flavinylated oxidase of benzophenanthridine alkaloid biosynthesis in plants. *J. Biol. Chem.*, **270** 24475-81.

Kutchan, T.M., Dittrich, H., Bracher, D. and Zenk, M.H. (1991) Enzymology and molecular biology of alkaloid biosynthesis. *Tetrahedron*, **47** 5945-54.

Kutney, J.P. (1987) Studies in plant tissue culture: the synthesis and biosynthesis of indole alkaloids. *Heterocycles*, **25** 617-40.

Leete, E. (1990) Recent developments in the biosynthesis of tropane alkaloids. *Planta Med.*, **56** 339-52.

Lenz, R. and Zenk, M.H. (1994) Closure of the oxide bridge in morphine biosynthesis. *Tetrahedron Lett.*, **35** 3897-900.

Lenz, R. and Zenk, M.H. (1995a) Acetyl coenzyme A: salutaridinol-7-*O*-acetyltransferase from *Papaver somniferum* cell cultures. *J. Biol. Chem.*, **270** 31091-96.

Lenz, R. and Zenk, M.H. (1995b) Purification and properties of codeinone reductase (NADPH) from *Papaver somniferum* plant cell cultures and differentiated plants. *Eur. J. Biochem.*, **233** 132-39.

Liebisch, H.-W., Matschiner, B. and Schütte, H.R. (1969) Beiträge zur Physiologie und Biosynthese des Betanins. *Z. Pflanzenphys.*, **61** 269-78.

Lin, X., Hezari, M., Koepp, A.E., Floss, H.G. and Croteau, R. (1996) Mechanism of taxadiene synthesis, a diterpene cyclase that catalyzes the first step of taxol biosynthesis in Pacific yew. *Biochemistry*, **35** 2968-77.

Loeffler, S. and Zenk, M.H. (1990) The hydroxylation step in the biosynthetic pathway leading from norcoclaurine to reticuline. *Phytochemistry*, **29** 3499-503.

Lotter, H., Gollsitzer, J. and Zenk, M.H. (1992) Revision of the configuration at C-7 of salutaridinol I, the natural intermediate in morphine biosynthesis. *Tetrahedron Lett.*, **33** 2443-46.

McKnight, T.D., Bergey, D.R., Burnett, R.J. and Nessler, C.L. (1991) Expression of enzymatically active and correctly targeted strictosidine synthase in transgenic tobacco plants. *Planta*, **185** 148-52.

McLauchlan, W.R., McKee, R.A. and Evans, D.M. (1993) The purification and immunocharacterisation of *N*-methylputrescine oxidase from transformed root cultures of *Nicotiana tabacum* (L.) cv SC58. *Planta*, **191** 440-45.

Maier, W., Schumann, B. and Gröger, D. (1988) Microsomal oxygenases involved in ergoline alkaloid biosynthesis of various *Claviceps* strains. *J. Basic Microbiol.*, **28** 83-93.

Maier, W., Baumert, A., Schumann, B., Furukawa, H. and Gröger, D. (1993) Synthesis of 1,3-dihydroxy-*N*-methylacridone and its conversion to rutacridone by cell-free extracts of *Ruta graveolens* cell cultures. *Phytochemistry*, **32** 691-98.

Maier, W.D., Baumert, A. and Gröger, D. (1995) Partial purification and characterisation of *S*-adenosyl-L-methinione:anthranilic acid *N*-methyltransferase. *J. Plant Physiol.*, **145** 1-6.

Meijer, A.H., De Wall, A. and Verpoorte, R. (1993a) Purification of the cytochrome P_{450} enzyme, geraniol 10-hydroxylase, from cell cultures of *Catharanthus*. *J. Chromatogr.*, **635** 237-49.

Meijer, A.H., Verpoorte, R. and Hoge, J.H.C. (1993b) Regulation of enzymes and genes involved in terpenoid indole alkaloid biosynthesis in *Catharanthus roseus*. *J. Plant Res.* (Special Issue), **3** 145-64.

Minale, L., Piattelli, M. and Nicolaus, R.A. (1965) Pigments of Centrospermae-IV. On the biogenesis of indicaxanthin and betanin in *Opuntia ficus-indica* Mill. *Phytochemistry*, **4** 593-97.

Miura, Y., Hirata, K., Kurano, N., Miyamoto, K. and Uchida, K. (1988) Formation of vinblastine in shoot cultures of *Catharanthus roseus*. *Planta Med.*, pp. 18-20.

Mueller, L.A., Hinz, U. and Zryd, J.-P. (1996) Characterization of a tyrosinase from *Amanita muscaria* involved in betalain biosynthesis. *Phytochemistry*, **42** 1511-15.

Mueller, L.A., Hinz, U. and Zryd, J.-P. (1997a) The formation of betalamic acid and muscaflavin by recombinant Dopa-dioxygenase from *Amanita*. *Phytochemistry*, **44** 567-69.

Mueller, L.A., Hinz, U., Uzé, M., Sautter, C. and Zryd, J.-P. (1997b) Biochemical complementation of the betalain biosynthetic pathway in *Portulaca grandiflora* by a fungal 3,4-dihydroxyphenylalanine dioxygenase. *Planta*, **203** 260-63.

Nakajima, K., Hashimoto, T. and Yamada, Y. (1993) cDNA encoding tropinone reductase-II from *Hyoscyamus niger*. *Plant Physiol.*, **103** 1465-66.

Nakajima, K., Hashimoto, T. and Yamada, Y. (1994) Opposite stereospecificity of two tropinone reductases is conferred by the substrate-binding sites. *J. Biol. Chem.*, **269** 11695-98.

Okada, N., Shinmyo, A., Okada, H. and Yamada, Y. (1988) Purification and characterisation of (*S*)-tetrahydroberberine oxidase from cultured *Coptis japonica* cells. *Phytochemistry*, **27** 979-82.

Pasquali, G., Goddijn, O.J.M., DeWaal, A., Verpoorte, R., Schilperoot, R.A., Hoge, J.H.C. and Memelink, J. (1992) Coordinated regulation of two indole alkaloid biosynthetic genes from *Catharanthus roseus* by auxin and elicitors. *Plant Mol. Biol.*, **18** 1121-31.

Pennings, E.J.M., Groen, B.W., Duine, J.A. and Verpoorte, R. (1989) Tryptophan decarboxylase from *Catharanthus roseus* is a pyridoxo-quinoprotein. *FEBS Lett.*, **255** 97-100.

Pfitzner, U.M. and Zenk, M.H. (1989) Homogeneous strictosidine synthase isoenzymes from cell suspension cultures of *Catharanthus roseus*. *Planta Med.*, **55** 525-30.

Piattelli, M. and Imperato, F. (1970a) Betacyanins from *Bougainvillea*. *Phytochemistry*, **9** 455-58.

Piattelli, M. and Imperato, F. (1970b) Pigments of *Bougainvillea glabra*. *Phytochemistry*, **9** 2557-60.

Piattelli, M., Minale, L. and Prota, G. (1964) Isolation, structure and absolute configuration of indicaxanthin. *Tetrahedron*, **20** 2325-29.

Polz, L., Schübel, H. and Stöckigt, J. (1986) Characterisation of 2β(*R*)-17-*O*-acetylajmalan: acetylesterase a specific enzyme involved in the biosynthesis of the *Rauwolfia* alkaloid ajmalicine. *Z. Naturforsch.*, **42c** 333-42.

Portsteffen, A., Dräger, B. and Nahrstedt, A. (1992) Two tropinone reducing enzymes from *Datura stramonium* transformed root cultures. *Phytochemistry*, **31** 1135-38.

Portsteffen, A., Dräger, B. and Nahrstedt, A. (1994) The reduction of tropinone in *Datura stramonium* root cultures by two specific reductases. *Phytochemistry*, **37** 391-400.

Pourrat, H., Lejeune, B., Regerat, F. and Pourrat, A. (1983) Purification of red beetroot dye by fermentation. *Biotech. Lett.*, **5** 381-84.

Rabot, S., Peerless, A.C.J. and Robins, R.J. (1995) Tigloyl-CoA:pseudotropine acyl transferase: a novel enzyme of tropane alkaloid biosynthesis. *Phytochemistry*, **39** 315-22.

Robins, R.J., Hamill, J.D., Parr, A.J., Smith, K., Walton, N.J. and Rhodes, M.J.C. (1987) Potential use of nicotinic acid as a selective agent for isolation of high-nicotine-producing lines of *Nicotiana rustica* hairy root cultures. *Plant Cell Rep.*, **6** 122-26.

Robins, R.J., Woolley, J.G., Ansarin, M., Eagles, J. and Goodfellow, B.J. (1994a) Phenyllactic acid but not tropic acid is an intermediate in the biosynthesis of tropane alkaloids in *Datura* and *Brugmansia* transformed root cultures. *Planta*, **194** 86-94.

Robins, R.J., Bachmann, P. and Woolley, J.G. (1994b) Biosynthesis of hyoscyamine involves an intramolecular rearrangement of littorine. *J. Chem. Soc. Perkin Trans. I.*, pp. 615-19.

Robins, R.J., Chesters, N.C.J.E., O'Hagan, D., Parr, A.J., Walton, N.J. and Woolley, J.G. (1995) The biosynthesis of hyoscyamine: the process by which littorine rearranges to hyoscyamine. *J. Chem. Soc. Perkin Trans. I.*, pp. 481-85.

Robins, R.J., Abraham, T., Parr, A.J., Eagles, J. and Walton, N.J. (1997) The biosynthesis of tropane alkaloids *Datura stramonium*: the identity of the intermediate between *N*-methylpyrrolinium salt and tropinone. *J. Am. Chem. Soc.*, **119** 10929-34.

Roewer, I.A., Cloutier, N., Nessler, C.L. and De Luca, V. (1992) Transient induction of tryptophan decarboxylase (TDC) and strictosidine synthase (SS) genes in cell suspension cultures of *Catharanthus roseus. Plant Cell Rep.*, **11** 86-89.

Rohmer, M., Knani, M., Simonin, P., Sutter, B. and Sahmn, H. (1993) Isopreniod biosynthesis in bacteria: a novel pathway for the early steps leading to isopentenyl diphosphate. *Biochem. J.*, **295** 517-24.

Rueffer, M. and Zenk, M.H. (1985) Berberine synthase, the methylenedioxy group-forming enzyme in berberine synthase. *Tetrahedron Lett.*, **26** 201-202.

Rueffer, M. and Zenk, M.H. (1987a) Distant precursors of benzylisoquinoline alkaloids and their enzymatic formation. *Z. Naturforsch.*, **42c** 319-32.

Rueffer, M. and Zenk, M.H. (1987b) Enzymatic formation of protopines by a microsomal cytochrome P_{450} system of *Corydalis vaginans. Tetrahedron Lett.*, **28** 5307-310.

Rueffer, M. and Zenk, M.H. (1994) Canadine synthase from *Thalictrum tuberosum* cell cultures catalyses the formation of the methylenedioxy bridge in berberine synthesis. *Phytochemistry*, **36** 1219-23.

Rueffer, M., Zumstein, G. and Zenk, M.H. (1990) Partial purification and properties of *S*-adenosyl-L-methionine:(*S*)-tetrahydroprotoberberine-*cis*-*N*-methyltransferase from suspension-cultured cells of *Eschscholtzia* and *Corydalis. Phytochemistry*, **29** 3727-33.

St-Pierre, B. and De Luca, V. (1995) A cytochrome, P_{450} monooxygenase, catalyses the first step in the conversion of tabersonine to vindoline in *Catharanthus roseus. Plant Physiol.*, **109** 131-39.

Schiel, O., Witte, L. and Berlin, J. (1987) Geraniol-10-hydroxylase activity and its relation to monoterpene indole alkaloid accumulation in cell suspension cultures of *Catharanthus roseus. Z. Naturforsch.*, **42c** 1075-81.

Schliemann, W. and Strack, D. (1998) Intramolecular stabilization of acylated betacyanins. *Phytochemistry*, **49** 585-88.

Schliemann, W., Steiner, U. and Strack, D. (1998) Betanidin formation from dihydroxyphenylalanine in a model assay system. *Phytochemistry*, **49** 1593-98.

Schmidt, D. and Stöckigt, J. (1995) Enzymic formation of the sarpagan-bridge: a key step in the biosynthesis of sarpagine-ajmalicine-type alkaloids. *Planta Med.*, **61** 254-58.

Schübel, H., Stöckigt, J., Feicht, R. and Simon, H. (1986) Partial purification and characterisation of raucaffricine β-D-glucosidase from plant cell suspension cultures of *Rauwolfia serpentina* Benth. *Helv. Chim. Acta*, **69** 538-47.

Schulthess, B.H. and Baumann, T.W. (1995) Stimulation of caffeine biosynthesis in suspension-cultured coffee cells and the *in situ* existence of 7-methylxanthosine. *Phytochemistry*, **38** 1381-86.

Schumacher, H.-M. and Zenk, M.H. (1988) Partial purification and characterization of dihydrobenzophenanthridine oxidase from *Eschscholtzia californica* cell suspension cultures. *Plant Cell Rep.*, **7** 43-46.

Sciuto, S., Oriente, G. and Piattelli, M. (1972) Betanidin glucosylation in *Opuntia dillenii*. *Phytochemistry*, **11** 2259-62.

Sciuto, S., Oriente, G., Piattelli, M., Impellizzeri, G. and Amico, V. (1974) Biosynthesis of amaranthin in *Celosia plumosa*. *Phytochemistry*, **13** 947-51.

Shibuya, M., Chou, H.-M., Fountoulakis, M., Hassam, S., Kim, S.-U., Kobayashi, K., Otsuka, H., Rogalska, E., Cassady, J.M. and Floss, H.G. (1990) Stereochemistry of the isoprenylation of tryptophan catalysed by 4-(γ,γ-dimethylallyl)tryptophan synthase from *Claviceps*, the first pathway-specific enzyme in ergot alkaloid biosynthesis. *J. Am. Chem. Soc.*, **112** 297-304.

Songstad, D.D., De Luca, V., Brisson, N., Kurz, W.G.W. and Nessler, C.L. (1990) High levels of tryptamine accumulation in transgenic tobacco expressing tryptophan decarboxylase. *Plant Physiol.*, **94** 1410-13.

Stadler, R. and Zenk, M.H. (1993) The purification and characterization of a unique cytochrome P_{450} enzyme from *Berberis stolonifera* plant cell cultures. *J. Biol. Chem.*, **268** 823-31.

Stafford, H.A. (1994) Anthocyanins and betalains: evolution of the mutually exclusive pathways. *Plant Sci.*, **101** 91-98.

Steiner, U., Schliemann, W. and Strack, D. (1996) Assay for tyrosine hydroxylation activity of tyrosinase from betalain-forming plants and cell cultures. *Anal. Biochem.*, **238** 72-75.

Steiner, U., Schliemann, W., Böhm, H. and Strack, D. (1999) Tyrosinase involved in betalain biosynthesis of higher plants. *Planta*, **208** 114-24.

Stevens, L.H., Blom, T.J.M. and Verpoorte, R. (1993) Subcellular localisation of tryptophan decarboxylase, strictosidine synthase and strictosidine glucosidase in cell suspension cultures of *Catharanthus roseus* and *Tabermaemontana divaricata*. *Plant Cell Rep.*, **12** 572-76.

Stobart, A.K. and Kinsman, L.T. (1977) The hormonal control of betacyanin synthesis in *Amaranthus caudatus*. *Phytochemistry*, **16** 1137-42.

Strack, D., Marxen, N., Reznik, H. and Ihlenfeld, H.-D. (1990) Distribution of betacyanins and hydroxycinnamic acid-glucose esters in flowers of the Ruschieae. *Phytochemistry*, **29** 2175-78.

Takamura, Y., Matsushita, Y., Nagareya, N., Abe, M., Takaya, J., Juichi, M., Hashimoto, T., Kan, Y., Takoaka, S., Asakawa, Y., Omura, M., Ito, C. and Furukawa, H. (1995) Citbismine-A, citbismine-B and citbismine-C, new binary acridone alkaloids from Citrus plants. *Chem. Pharm. Bull.*, **43** 1340-45.

Terradas, F. and Wyler, H. (1991a) 2,3- and 4,5-Secodopa, the biosynthetic intermediates generated from L-Dopa by an enzyme system extracted from the fly agaric, *Amanita muscaria* L., and their spontaneous conversion to muscaflavin and betalamic acid, respectively, and betalains. *Helv. Chim. Acta*, **74** 124-40.

Terradas, F. and Wyler, H. (1991b) The *seco*-Dopas, natural pigments in *Hygrocybe conica* and *Amanita muscaria*. *Phytochemistry*, **30** 3251-53.

Teusch, M., Forkmann, G. and Seyffert, W. (1987) Genetic control of hydroxycinnamoyl-coenzyme A: anthocyanidin 3-glycoside-hydroxycinnamoyltransferases from petals of *Matthiola incana*. *Phytochemistry*, **26** 991-94.

Trezzini, G.F. (1990) Génétique des bétalaïnes chez *Portulaca grandiflora* Hook. Thesis, Lausanne.

Trezzini, G.F. and Zryd, J.-P. (1990) *Portulaca grandiflora*: a model system for the study of the biochemistry and genetics of betalain synthesis. *Acta Hortic.*, **280** 581-85.

Vazquez-Flota, F., De Carolis, E., Alarco, A.-M. and De Luca, V. (1997) Molecular cloning and characterization of desacetoxyvindoline-4-hydroxylase, a 2-oxyglutarate-dependent dioxygenase involved in the biosynthesis of vindoline in *Catharanthus roseus* (L.) G. Don. *Plant Mol. Biol.*, **34** 935-48.

Vogt, T., Zimmermann, E., Grimm, R., Meyer, M. and Strack, D. (1997) Are the characteristics of betanidin glucosyltransferases from cell-suspension cultures of *Dorotheanthus bellidiformis* indicative of their phylogenetic relationship with flavonoid glucosyltransferases? *Planta*, **203** 349-61.

Waldhauser, S.S.M. and Baumann, T.W. (1996) Compartmentation of caffeine and related purine alkaloid depends exclusively on the physical chemistry of their vacuolar complex formation with chlorogenic acids. *Phytochemistry*, **42** 985-96.

Waldhauser, S.S.M., Kretschmar, J.A. and Baumann, T.W. (1997a) *N*-methyltransferase activities in caffeine biosynthesis: biochemical characterisation and time course during leaf development of *Coffea arabica. Phytochemistry*, **44** 853-59.

Waldhauser, S.S.M., Gillies, F.M., Crozier, A. and Baumann, T.W. (1997b) Separation of *N*-7-methyltransferase, the key enzyme of caffeine biosynthesis. *Phytochemistry*, **45** 1407-14.

Walton, N.J. and Belshaw, N.J. (1988) The effect of cadaverine on the formation of anabasine from lysine in hairy root cultures of *Nicotiana hesperis. Plant Cell Rep.*, **7** 115-18.

Walton, N.J., Robins, R.J. and Rhodes, M.J.C. (1988) Perturbation of alkaloid production by cadaverine in hairy root cultures of *Nicotiana rustica. Plant Sci.*, **54** 125-31.

Walton, N.J., Peerless, A.C.J., Robins, R.J., Rhodes, M.J.C., Boswell, H.D. and Robins, D.J. (1994) Purification and properties of putrescine *N*-methyltransferase from transformed roots of *Datura stramonium* (L.). *Planta*, **193** 9-15.

Wilhelm, R. and Zenk, M.H. (1997) Biotransformation of thebaine by cell cultures of *Papaver somniferum* and *Mahonia nervosa. Phytochemistry*, **46** 701-708.

Wyler, H., Mabry, T.J. and Dreiding, A.S. (1963) Über die Konstitution des Randenfarbstoffes Betanin: Zur Struktur des Betanidins. *Helv. Chim. Acta*, **46** 1745-48.

Wyler, H., Meuer, U., Bauer, J. and Stravs-Mombelli, L. (1984) Cyclodopa glucoside (=(2*S*)-5-(β-D-glucopyranosyloxy)-6-hydroxyindoline-2-carboxylic acid) and its occurrence in red beet (*Beta vulgaris* var. *rubra* L.). *Helv. Chim. Acta*, **67** 1348-55.

Yun, D.-J., Hashimoto, T. and Yamada, Y. (1993) Expression of hyoscyamine 6β-hydroxylase gene in transgenic tobacco. *Biosci. Biotech. Biochem.*, **57** 502-503.

Zenk, M.H., Gerardy, R. and Stadler, R. (1995) Phenol oxidative coupling of benzylisoquinoline alkaloids is catalyzed by regio- and stereo-selective cytochrome P_{450} linked plant enzymes: salutaridine and berbamunine. *J. Chem. Soc. Chem. Commun.*, pp. 1725-27.

Zont, J. and Amrhein, N. (1992) Inhibitors of phenylalanine ammonia-lyase: 2-aminoindan-2-phosphonic acid and related compounds. *Liebigs Ann. Chem.*, pp. 625-28.

3 Biosynthesis of cyanogenic glycosides, glucosinolates and nonprotein amino acids

Dirk Selmar

3.1 Introduction

The natural products reviewed in this chapter have achieved their popularity largely because their biology and metabolism provide numerous systems to study aspects of biochemistry and the general biology of secondary plant products. The knowledge of liberation of toxic reaction products from nontoxic precursors, known as 'cyanogenesis' and the 'mustard oil bomb', has made a significant contribution to an understanding of major principles in compartmentation as well as to important aspects of ecological biochemistry. In this context, research on nonprotein amino acids, which has contributed decisively to the elucidation of basic principles in the coevolution of plants and herbivores, can also be mentioned (for example, the protection of plants against generalistic herbivores by toxic compounds and the reversal of this protection by specialized herbivores).

The concept of 'channelled biosynthesis' of cyanogenic glucosides, originally developed by Eric Conn's group, is an example of the function of multienzyme complexes, in which the product of one reaction is used directly as the substrate for the subsequent biosynthethic reaction without being liberated from the complex. However, based on the most recent results from Birger Møller's group, showing that this multistep biosynthesis is performed by only two multifunctional cytochrome P_{450} enzymes, the classical term, 'channelled biosynthesis', must obviously be redefined. Research on cyanogenic glucosides has provided new insight into plant biochemisty. Cyanogenic glucosides represent a suitable and effective model system for the investigation of the processes involved in long distance transport of glucosidic natural products. The involvement of diglucosidic cyanogens in translocation processes suggested, for the first time, the necessity for special transport metabolites in the translocation of hydrolysable substances via the apoplasmic space.

Cyanogenic glycosides, glucosinolates and nonprotein amino acids (NPAAs) have attracted only limited attention from pharmacologists and pharmacognosists. For a short time, the cyanogenic glycoside, amygdalin, was examined as a treatment for cancer but this application was abandoned due to the multiple side-effects of cyanide. At the present time, the antitumor activity of glucosinolates and their degradation products are a focus for research on glucosinolates. NPAAs play an increasing role in oligopeptide chemistry with regard to the creation of new pharmacologically active compounds.

Due to their toxic character or the toxicity of their degradation products, cyanogenic glucosides, glucosinolates and NPAAs are considered to be antinutritional. As these natural compounds occur in various concentrations in some food plants, breeding programmes have been designed to create varieties that are either free of these antinutritional factors or contain only low concentrations. At the present time, many researchers are attempting to use biotechnology to achieve this same goal. However, an important requirement for such objectives is a broad and comprehensive understanding of the relevant metabolism, the biochemical reactions involved and the knowledge of their ecological significance. This review will give a brief overview of various aspects of the biology and biochemistry of cyanogenic glucosides, glucosinolates and NPAAs, in order to provide solid information for possible biotechnological approaches.

3.2 Cyanogenic glycosides

3.2.1 General aspects

Cyanogenic plants are characterized by the liberation of hydrogen cyanide (HCN) when plant tissues are damaged and cells have been disrupted. This cyanogenesis is initiated by the loss of cell integrity, leading to contact between cyanogenic glycosides and their hydrolytic enzymes. Cyanogenesis and cyanogenic glycosides are widespread among plants. Nearly 3,000 plant species have been reported to be cyanogenic (Seigler, 1991; Møller and Seigler, 1998). Cyanogenic compounds are also present in a few animals (Nahrstedt, 1996). The HCN liberated from cyanogenic plants is thought to be an important ecological factor, e.g. in plant defence against herbivores, and must be clearly distinguished from low levels of HCN production during ethylene biosynthesis in intact plants (John, 1997). It should be noted that the amounts of HCN produced during ethylene synthesis are several magnitudes lower than those resulting from cyanogenesis following tissue disruption.

In addition to several reviews dealing with general aspects of cyanogenesis and cyanogenic glycosides (Poulton, 1990; Seigler, 1991; Nahrstedt, 1992), other more specialized reviews on cyanogenicity have been published. Among these are reviews on: the occurrence and distribution of cyanogenic glycosides (Nahrstedt, 1987; Hegnauer, 1986); their structures (Nahrstedt, 1987; Møller and Seigler, 1998); their determination (Brinker and Seigler, 1992); their function (Nahrstedt, 1985; Kakes, 1990); their biosynthesis (Møller and Seigler, 1998; Halkier *et al.*, 1988; Conn, 1988); and their occurrence and toxicity in foodstuffs (Nahrstedt, 1993; Poulton, 1989; Jones, 1998). The present chapter summarizes recent progress in research on cyanogenic glucosides, with special emphasis on plant physiological and biochemical aspects.

3.2.2 Structures

Cyanogenic glucosides consist of α-hydroxynitriles, stabilized by glucose. More than 60 different structures are known. The structural differences result from variation in the aglycone and from additional glucosylation of the original glucose moiety. Other cyanogenic glucosides, such as grayanin, xeranthin and prunasin-6′-malonate, are even more complex molecules involving formation of esters with various organic acids. The centre bearing the nitrile group is often chiral. For many structures, both (*R*)- and (*S*)-forms are known. Occasionally, both epimers as well as enantiomers and diastereomers occur in the same plant (Møller and Seigler, 1998). This chapter presents a brief overview of the structural variety of cyanogenic glycosides. For detailed phytochemical information, including the comprehensive presentation of the structural formulae and thorough differentiation between the various optical isomers, the reviews from Møller and Seigler (1998), Seigler (1991) and Nahrstedt (1987, 1992) are recommended.

With the exception of a few special compounds, such as acalyphin and triglochinin (Fig. 3.1), all known cyanogenic glucosides belong to one of the six groups listed in Table 3.1. They are derived from the five protein

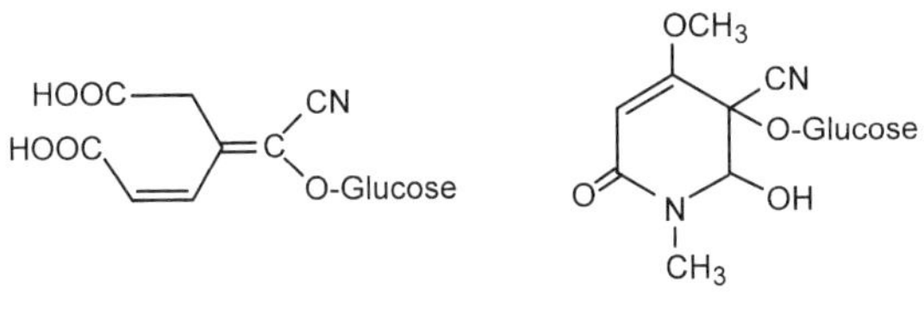

Figure 3.1 Structure of triglochinin and acalyphin.

amino acids, valine, isoleucine, leucine, phenylalanine and tyrosine, and the nonprotein amino acid, cyclopentenylglycine. Whereas hydroxylation of the aglycone is unknown for the linamarin and lotaustralin family, it commonly occurs in the other classes of cyanogenic glycosides. Nevertheless, structural variability results mainly from variations in the

Table 3.1 Cyanogenic glycosides and their precursors

Precursors	Basic structures	Derivatives (examples)
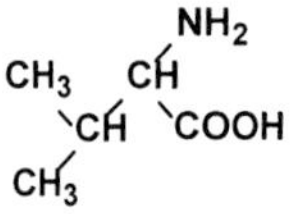 NH_2 CH_3 CH CH COOH CH_3 Valine	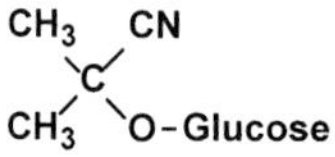 CH_3 CN C CH_3 O-Glucose Linamarin	Linustatin = linamarin-6′glucoside
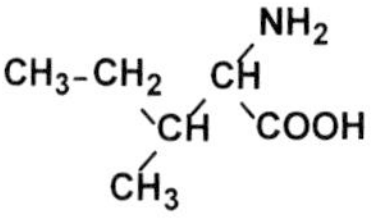 NH_2 CH_3-CH_2 CH CH COOH CH_3 Isoleucine	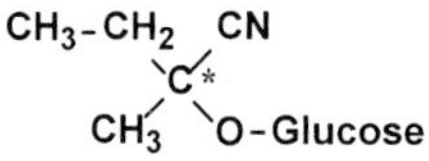 CH_3-CH_2 CN C* CH_3 O-Glucose (*R*)-Lotaustralin (*S*)-Epilotaustralin	Neolinustatin = lotaustralin-6′-glucoside
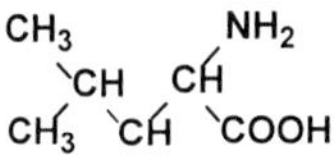 CH_3 NH_2 CH CH CH_3 CH COOH leucine	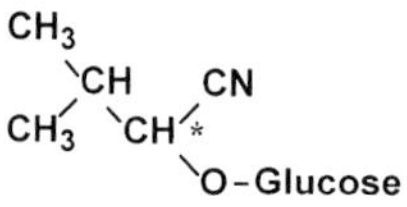 CH_3 CH CN CH_3 CH* O-Glucose (*S*)-Heterodendrin (*R*)-Epiheterodendrin	Proacacipetalin = heterodendrin-2,3-ene Cardiospermin = 4-hydroxy-proacacipetalin Proacaciberin = proacacipetalin-6′-arabinoside
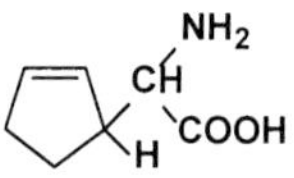 NH_2 CH H COOH Cyclopentenylglycine	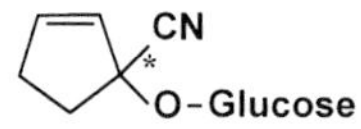 CN * O-Glucose (*R*)-Deidaclin (*S*)-Tetraphyllin A	Taraktophyllin = 4-(*S*)-hydroxydeidaclin Taraktophyllin-6′-rhamnoside Gynocardin = 4-(*S*)-5-(*R*)-tetraphyllin A
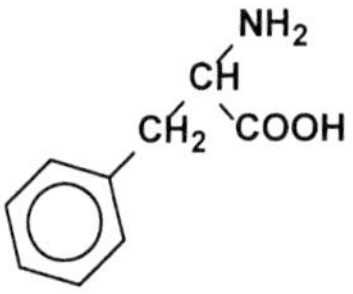 NH_2 CH CH_2 COOH Phenylalanine	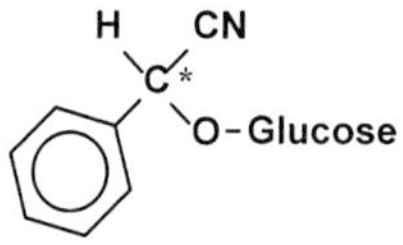 H CN C* O-Glucose (*R*)-Prunasin (*S*)-Sambunigrin	Amygdalin = prunasin-6′glucoside Holocalin = *m*-hydroxyprunasin Prunasin-6′-malonate Vicianin = prunasin- 6′-arabinoside
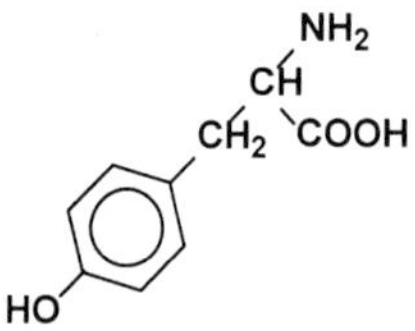 NH_2 CH CH_2 COOH HO Tyrosine	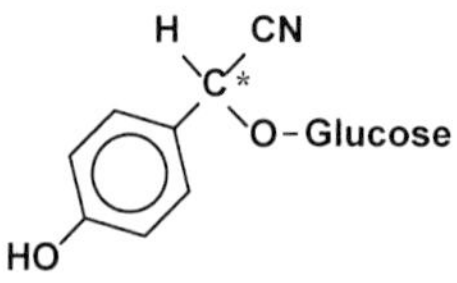 H CN C* O-Glucose HO (*S*)-Dhurrin (*R*)-Taxiphyllin	Proteacin = *p*-glycosyloxy-dhurrin Dhurrin-6′-glucoside Nandinin = 4′-caffeoyl-*p*-glycosyloxy- mandelonitrile

glucosylation and esterification pattern of a small number of basic compounds.

3.2.2.1 Valine- and isoleucine-derived cyanogenic glycosides

In the group of valine- and isoleucine-derived compounds (Table 3.1), apart from the basic glucosides, linamarin and lotaustralin, only the (*S*)-enantiomer of lotaustralin, called epilotaustralin, and the diglucosides, linustatin and neolinustatin, are known. Whereas epilotaustralin has only been detected in *Triticum monococcum* (Pitsch *et al.*, 1984) and in some Passifloraceae species (Olafsdottir *et al.*, 1989), linamarin and lotaustralin are present in a large number of plant families, e.g. Euphorbiaceae, Fabaceae, Linaceae, Mimosaceae and Poaceae. In nearly all of these plants, the concentration of linamarin is far higher (10- to 100-fold) than that of lotaustralin. The latter seems to be—in most plants at least—a byproduct of linamarin biosynthesis. Additionally, the related diglucoside, linustatin, occurs in all linamarin-containing plants so far analyzed (Selmar, 1993a). This compound is thought to be a transport metabolite (see section 3.2.5.2).

3.2.2.2 Leucine-derived cyanogenic glucosides

The cyanogenic glucosides of this group (Table 3.1) are found mainly in the Sapindaceae and Poaceae. Whilst in the Poaceae the (*R*)-enantiomer, epiheterodendrin, is present (Pourmohseni *et al.*, 1993), the various cyanogenic compounds known to occur in the Sapindaceae are derivatives of (*S*)-heterodendrin. Recently, however, Lechtenberg and co-workers (1996) also detected (*R*)-epiheterodendrin in several species of the Rosaceae. In the seeds of some members of the Sapindaceae, cyanogenic lipids are present in addition to cyanogenic glucosides, such as proacacipetalin or cardiospermin, which are desaturated and hydroxylated derivatives of heterodendrin. In cyanogenic lipids (see section 3.2.2.7), the cyanohydrin corresponding to proacacipetalin is stabilized by esterification with a fatty acid (Seigler, 1973).

3.2.2.3 Cyclopentenylglycine-derived cyanogenic glycosides

Various derivatives of deidaclin are found in the Passifloraceae, Flacourtiaceae and Turneraceae. Hydroxylation of the C4-atom of the aglycone creates a second chiral centre, resulting in numerous enantiomers and diastereomers. A comprehensive overview of these compounds and their occurrence is given by Olafsdottir and co-workers (1989) and by Nahrstedt (1992). Apart from a sulfate ester of tetraphyllin B, various further glycosylated derivatives, such as the taraktophyllin-rhamnoside, are known (Jaroszewski and Fog, 1989; Spencer and Seigler, 1985).

3.2.2.4 Phenylalanine-derived cyanogenic glycosides

Amygdalin, first isolated by Liebig and Wöhler from bitter almonds, is the best known cyanogenic glucoside. It represents a glucosyl-derivative of prunasin (Table 3.1). Both compounds are found in the leaves and seeds of many Rosaceae. In addition, prunasin occurs in several other families, e.g. Asteraceae, Convolvulaceae, Lamiaceae and Fabaceae (for review see Nahrstedt, 1987). As mentioned above, the corresponding diglucosides are thought to be important as physiological transport metabolites. Unfortunately, until now, detailed analyses of the occurrence of amygdalin in prunasin-containing plants have been lacking but our most recent studies seem to confirm that these two compounds generally co-occur.

Vicianin, a prunasin-6′-arabinoside, occurs in the seeds of certain species of the Fabaceae and in the leaves of some ferns (Lizotte and Poulton, 1986; Wajant *et al.*, 1995). In addition to prunasin, the (*S*)-epimer, sambunigrin, is present in some plants. The xylosides of these enantiomers are known as lucumin and epilucumin, respectively (Nahrstedt *et al.*, 1983). Various esters of these aromatic cyanogenic glucosides are known, e.g. prunasin-6′-malonate (Nahrstedt *et al.*, 1989), amygdalin-hydroxybenzoate (Nahrstedt *et al.*, 1990), oxyanthin-benzoate (Rockenbach *et al.*, 1992), and the *Anthemis* glycosides A and B. These compounds are complex glucosylated cinnamoyl derivatives of lucumin (Nahrstedt *et al.*, 1983). A quite unusual prunasin derivative, in which the prunasin moiety is attached to an iridoid-monoterpene, was found in *Canthium schimperianum* (Schwarz *et al.*, 1996). The biological significance of these complex structures is still unknown. Their structures are comprehensively reviewed by Seigler (1991) and Møller and Seigler (1998).

Although the biosynthetic origins of all *meta*-hydroxylated aromatic cyanogenic glucosides, such as (*R*)-holocalin or (*S*)-zierin, have not been definitely established, Nahrstedt and Schwind (1992) were able to show, at least, that zierin is derived from phenylalanine. In *Sambucus nigra*, the enantiomers, holocalin and zierin, co-occur with the corresponding glucosides, (*R*)-prunasin and (*S*)-sambunigrin. Thus, it is also likely that, in this plant, holocalin is derived from phenylalanine. Additionally glycosylated derivatives have not yet been detected in *Sambucus*. However, a zierin-xyloside is present in the seeds of *Xeranthemum cylindraceum* (Hübel *et al.*, 1982). This plant also contains xeranthin, one of the most complex structures of the cyanogenic glycosides known. Xeranthin is a zierin-xyloside to which an apiose residue is attached; and that unit is subsequently esterified with a glucosylated caffeoyl acid residue (Schwind *et al.*, 1990).

3.2.2.5 Tyrosine-derived cyanogenic glycosides

While the *m*-hydroxylated aromatic glucosides are derived from phenylalanine, the *p*-hydroxylated aromatic cyanogenic glucosides, such as (*S*)-dhurrin or (*R*)-taxiphyllin, are synthesized from tyrosine. These glycosides occur commonly in monocotyledonous angiosperms but are found in many families of dicotyledonous plants (Hegnauer, 1986; Saupe, 1981). As with other cyanogenic glycosides, glycosylated derivatives are also known for the tyrosine-derived compounds. Thus, the presence of a dhurrin-6′-glucoside was shown in *Sorghum bicolor* (Selmar *et al.*, 1996). In addition to the unusual cyanogen, *p*-glucosyloxymandelonitrile, the corresponding caffeoyl ester, referred to as nandinine, is found in *Nandina domestica.*

The cyanogenic glucoside, triglochinin, reveals a quite unusual structure (Fig. 3.1). Indeed, triglochinin does not represent an aromatic compound but appears to be derived from tyrosine (Nahrstedt *et al.*, 1984). Biosynthetic details, especially the reactions involved in ring-opening, are unknown. Isotriglochinin, a *Z*-isomer of triglochinin, and triglochinin-methylester have been reported but both appear to be produced as artifacts during isolation (Conn, 1981).

3.2.2.6 Acalyphin

The cyanogenic glucoside, acalyphin (Fig .3.1), found in *Acalypha indica*, appears to be derived from nicotinic acid metabolism (Nahrstedt *et al.*, 1982). Acalyphin is homologous to four noncyanogenic 3-cyanopyridones, including ricinine, that have also been isolated from various Acalypheae (Nahrstedt, 1987).

3.2.2.7 Related compounds

Due to homologies in structures and biosynthesis, some minor groups of natural products seem to be related to cyanogenic glucosides. These compounds, i.e. cyanogenic lipids, nitrile- and nitro-compounds, are briefly presented in the present chapter.

Cyanogenic lipids. Cyanogenic lipids are present in the seeds of various species of Sapindaceae. These substances consist of a α-hydroxynitrile that is stabilized by esterification with long fatty acids (C18 or C20); one example is presented in Figure 3.2 (Seigler, 1973; Mikolajczak, 1977). The α-hydroxynitrile is identical to that of proacacipetalin. Since corresponding leucine-derived glucosides occur in the leaves of these plants, it is assumed that the α-hydroxynitrile of cyanogenic lipids is also synthesized from leucine (Møller and Seigler, 1998). In addition to these cyanogenic lipids, analogous esters of related β-hydroxynitriles occur.

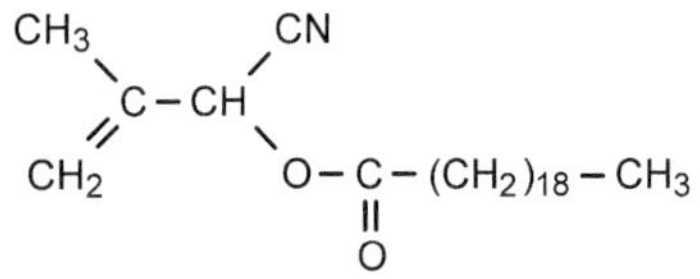

```
CH3          CN
   \        /
    C - CH
   //       \
CH2          O - C - (CH2)18 - CH3
                 ||
                 O
```

cyanogenic lipid (type 1)

Figure 3.2 General structure of cyanogenic lipids.

Due to the higher stability of β-hydroxynitrile, the related lipids do not evolve HCN when hydrolyzed (Seigler, 1991).

In the seeds of *Ungnadia speciosa*, which contain very high concentrations of cyanogenic lipids, an esterase is present that efficiently hydrolyzes the cyanogenic lipids present (Selmar, 1991a). Thus, when the seeds are injured, the esterase gains access to the cyanogenic lipids, which are rapidly cleaved. The unstable hydroxynitriles thus produced dissociate and HCN is liberated (see section 3.2.3). In addition to their hydrolysis in the course of postmortem cyanogenesis, cyanogenic lipids are also decomposed in intact plants. During seedling development of *Ungnadia speciosa*, these substances are metabolized to noncyanogenic compounds or are converted to various cyanogenic glucosides of the heterodendrin family, mainly to *p*-coumaroylcardiospermin (Selmar *et al.*, 1990).

Nitrile-glucosides. The group of so-called nitrile-glucosides consists of several noncyanogenic compounds that have a nitrile group. Due to their structural similarities to intermediates in cyanogenic glycoside biosynthesis, it has been suggested that these compounds are related to cyanogenic glucosides.

The leucine-derived cyanogenic glucoside, epiheterodendrin, which corresponds to the (*R*)-epimer of (*S*)-heterodendrin, occurs in various Rosaceae. In addition, several structurally-related noncyanogenic nitriles, such as sutherlandin (Fig. 3.3) and osmaronin, co-occur (Lechtenberg *et al.*, 1996). A second group of nitrile compounds includes those related to acalyphin, e.g. ricinine (Fig. 3.3). The third group of nitrile compounds resembles dhurrin and comprises compounds such as menisdaurin (Nakanishi *et al.*, 1994), bauhinin (Chen *et al.*, 1985) and simmondsin (van Boven *et al.*, 1994). As an example, menisdaurin is presented in Figure 3.3. Because of its occurrence in jojoba products, simmondsin has been studied intensively. Simmondsin accounts for more than 30% of the nonprotein nitrogen in jojoba seeds (Wolf *et al.*, 1994). This large accumulation is similar to that of many cyanogenic glycosides. A number

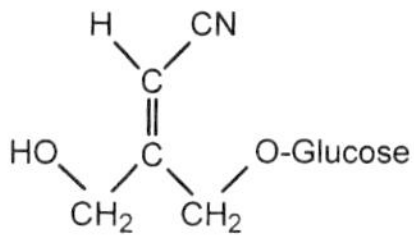

sutherlandin

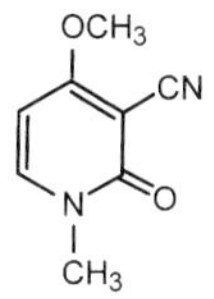

ricinine

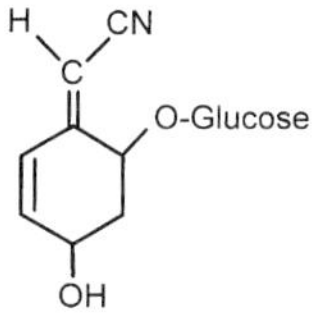

menisdaurin

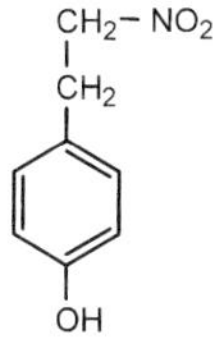

1-(-4`hydroxyphenyl)-
2-nitroethane

Figure 3.3 Structure of cyano- and nitro-compounds.

of derivatives of simmondsin have been described, e.g. the corresponding feruloyl ester (van Boven *et al.*, 1995).

Nitro-compounds. Another group of compounds that appear to be somehow related to cyanogenic glucosides are the so-called nitro-compounds (Conn, 1988). Cell suspension cultures of *Eschscholtzia californica* produce 1-(4′-hydroxyphenyl)-2-nitroethane (Fig. 3.3) (Hösel *et al.*, 1985). Analogous to the cyanogenic glucosides, triglochinin and dhurrin, which are also present in the plant, the nitro-compound is synthesized from tyrosine. A glucosyltransferase, which glucosylates the nitro-compound, also occurs in the cell cultures. But, the occurrence of nitro-compounds is not restricted to cell cultures. Various derivatives of 3-nitropropionic acid are present in a number of plants, e.g. from the genera *Coronilla*, *Indigofera*, and *Viola* (for review see Møller and Seigler, 1998).

3.2.3 Cyanogenesis

Apart from the small amounts of HCN that are produced in all plants during ethylene production (Yang and Hoffmann, 1984), intact cyanogenic plants do not liberate HCN. In living cells, the cyanogenic glucosides are accumulated in the vacuole and are, thus, spatially separated from their hydrolytic enzymes. This compartmentation is abolished only when the cells are destroyed. The catabolic enzymes, namely β-glucosidases and hydroxynitrile lyases, then mix with their substrates and the postmortem process of cyanogenesis is initiated (Fig. 3.4).

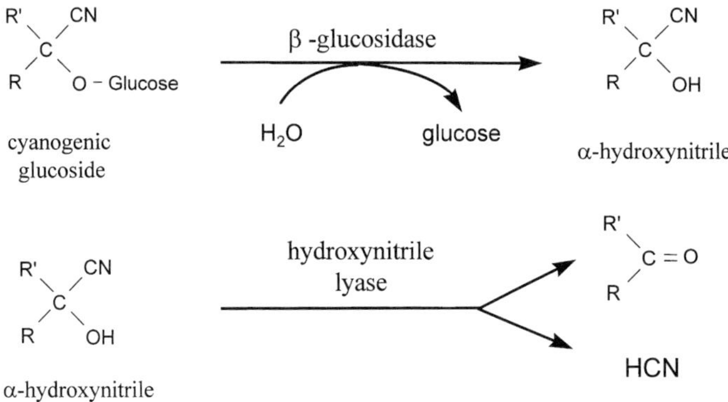

Figure 3.4 Cyanogenesis in plants.

In the first step, cyanogenic glucosides are cleaved by β-glucosidases. The resulting α-hydroxynitriles are unstable and dissociate to produce a carbonyl compound and HCN. In many plants, the dissociation of the cyanohydrins is accelerated by a hydroxynitrile lyase. In plants that accumulate diglucosidic compounds, the hydrolysis of these substances can be achieved by either a sequential or a simultaneous mechanism (Kuroki *et al.*, 1984) (Fig. 3.5).

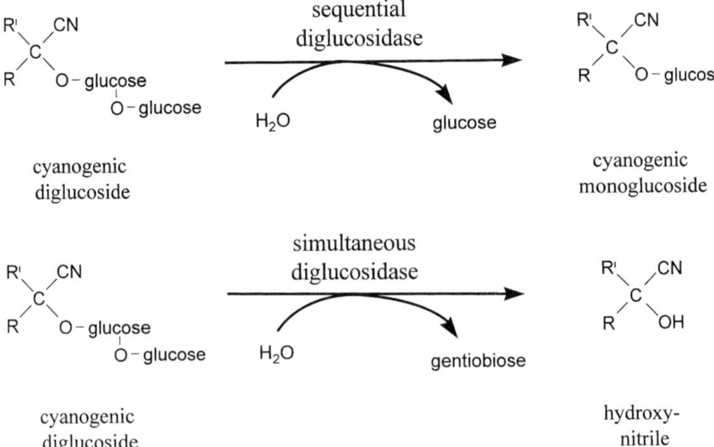

Figure 3.5 The hydrolysis of cyanogenic diglucosides by diglucosidases. Cleavage of cyanogenic diglucosidase is performed by either a sequential or simultaneous mechanism.

In injured seeds of *Prunus serotina*, hydrolysis of the diglucoside, amygdalin, occurs sequentially. Initially, amygdalin hydrolase splits off the terminal glucose, forming prunasin, which is hydrolyzed by prunasin hydrolase (Poulton, 1988). An analogous sequential hydrolysis of linustatin occurs in injured flax seeds. Both of the enzymes involved, linustatinase and linamarase, have been purified by Fan and Conn (1985). In contrast, in injured leaves of the fern *Davallia trichomanoides*, the diglycosidic cyanogen, vicianin, is hydrolyzed by a diglycosidase, which splits off both sugars simultaneously to form the saccharide known as vicianose (Kuroki *et al.*, 1984).

3.2.3.1 Ecological significance of cyanogenesis

HCN or cyanide, is relatively toxic and inhibits numerous metabolic processes in all organisms (for review see Solomonson, 1981). Due to the great impact of cyanide on the respiratory chain in particular, it is highly toxic for all animals. Based on this toxicity, it seems obvious that cyanogenesis should repel potential herbivores. Some investigations have verified this assumption. Whilst some repellent effects were detected for a few intact cyanogenic glucosides (Kaethler *et al.*, 1982; Braekman *et al.*, 1982), in most cases, the repellent effect for herbivores was due to the HCN liberated from cyanogenic glucosides (Woodhead and Bernays, 1977; Bernays *et al.*, 1977). Moreover, carbonyl compounds produced during cyanogenesis, e.g. benzaldehyde, were also deterrents (Peterson, 1986). Consequently, the repellent effect of cyanogenic plants is attributed mainly to the process of cyanogenesis and formation of the decomposition products of cyanogenic glucosides (Dirzo and Harper, 1982; Compton and Jones, 1985; Nahrstedt, 1985). In this context, we have to consider that the enzymes involved in cyanogenesis are also important ecological factors, since they accelerate the velocity of production of the repelling components.

Plant effectiveness in repelling herbivores is strongly influenced by the feeding strategy of the animals; therefore, the efficiency of protection by cyanogens varies greatly, depending on the combination of plants and herbivores studied (Compton and Jones, 1985). Despite the fact that more comprehensive studies on the ecological significance of cyanogenic glucosides are required, it is generally accepted that cyanogenic glucosides and the HCN liberated provide a protective function for cyanogenic plants (for review see Nahrstedt, 1985; Jones, 1988; Seigler, 1991).

In contrast to protection against herbivores, no clear picture can be drawn of the ecological significance of cyanogenic glucosides with regard to interactions of plants with microorganisms. In most cases, the presence of cyanogenic glucosides appears to have negative effects for the plant. There has only been one study in which cyanide appears to have a protective role against fungi; Timonin (1941) showed that isolated pathogens of flax roots were inhibited by HCN. In all other cases, the presence of cyanogenic glucosides or cyanide had a deleterious effect on the plant (Lüdtke and Hahn, 1953; Trione, 1960; Lieberei, 1988). The toxicity of HCN to most microorganisms is not very pronounced. In contrast to animals, most microorganisms can cope with HCN because of their ability to use the cyanide insensitive 'alternative respiratory pathway' (Henry, 1981) or their ability to detoxify HCN. However, HCN is also toxic for plants, e.g. by inhibiting photosynthesis (Lieberei *et al.*, 1989) and other important metabolic processes (Solomonson, 1981). In general, when pathogens attack plants, a hypersensitive reaction is induced. In cyanogenic plants, this is accompanied by cyanogenesis. The HCN liberated inhibits tanning reactions.

In addition, HCN acts on neighbouring cells. Lieberei and co-workers (1992) showed that the HCN that is liberated during the infection of leaves of the rubber tree (*Hevea brasiliensis*) with *Microcyclus ulei* inhibits phytoalexin production in adjacent cells (Lieberei *et al.*, 1992). This explains why strongly cyanogenic *Hevea* species are apparently much more sensitive to the infecting fungi than weakly cyanogenic varieties (Lieberei, 1988). Since production of phytoalexin and the provision of assimilates via photosynthesis are major factors in plant resistance against pathogens, this situation may apply for nearly all plant-pathogen systems. Thus, due to the reduced capacity of cyanogenic plants to cope with cyanide in comparison to microorganisms, these plants seem to be less resistant than acyanogenic plants. This has been confirmed in other plant-pathogen relationships; the occurrence of the cyanogenic glucoside, heterodendrin (Erb *et al.*, 1979), increased the susceptibility of barley (*Hordeum vulgare*) to mildew (*Erysiphe graminis*) (Pourmohseni and Ibenthal, 1991). A similar situation has been reported for flax (Lüdtke and Hahn, 1953).

3.2.3.2 Compartmentation

In intact cells, cyanogenic glucosides are apparently spatially separated from their hydrolyzing enzymes. Saunders and Conn (1977) showed that dhurrin is quantitatively localized in the vacuoles of *Sorghum* leaves. This type of localization was confirmed by the work of Gruhnert *et al.* (1994), who showed that linamarin is quantitatively localized in the vacuoles of *Hevea* leaves. While there is a lack of further data on the subcellular localization of cyanogenic glucosides, it is generally accepted that—in analogy to many other secondary plant products—cyanogenic glucosides are accumulated in the vacuoles. Nevertheless, vacuolar localization has only been proved for the cyanogenic monoglucosides, linamarin and dhurrin. It is likely that cyanogenic diglucosides are also located in vacuoles, e.g. in the case of large amounts of amygdalin stored in seeds of several *Prunus* species (Poulton, 1988). Nonetheless, because of their metabolic role as transport metabolites (see section 3.2.5.2), cyanogenic diglucosides must occur in the cytosol and apoplast, for a short time at least.

By separating vacuoles isolated from mesophyll and epidermal tissue of *Sorghum* leaves, Kojima and co-workers (1979) showed that the cyanogenic glucoside, dhurrin, is preferentially localized in the epidermal layer. The epidermal localization of leucine-derived cyanogenic glucosides was also reported for barley leaves (Pourmohseni *et al.*, 1993).

Cyanogenesis is initiated following the hydrolysis of cyanogenic glucosides by β-glucosidases, which are often referred to as 'cyanogenic β-glucosidases'. Such enzymes are localized in the apoplasm, in protein bodies or in chloroplasts. For many cyanogenic plants (e.g. *Trifolium repens, Phaseolus, Manihot esculenta, Hevea brasiliensis*), an apoplastic localization of the β-glucosidases involved in cyanogenesis has been reported (Table 3.2). Whereas the apoplastic β-glucosidases do not exhibit distinct substrate-specificity, the β-glucosidase localized in the chloroplast of *Sorghum* leaves (Thayer and Conn, 1981) is relatively specific for dhurrin, the cyanogenic glucoside that occurs in this plant (Hösel *et al.*, 1987). Using immunogold-labelled antibodies, Swain and co-workers (1992) elegantly demonstrated that, in seeds of *Prunus serotina*, the specific prunasin hydrolase occurs exclusively in protein bodies. However, the cyanogenic glucoside, prunasin, is also hydrolyzed by apoplastic enzymes that are present in *Prunus domestica* (Selmar, 1993a). Obviously, in addition to the specific prunasin hydrolase present in the protein bodies, another β-glucosidase capable of hydrolysing prunasin is located in the apoplastic space. In all cyanogenic plants investigated so far, β-glucosidases capable of hydrolyzing the cyanogenic (mono)-glucosides are present in the apoplastic space.

3.2.3.3 β-Glucosidases

Emulsin, the amygdalin-splitting β-glucosidase of bitter almonds, was the first enzyme shown to be present in plants by Wöhler and Liebig. Since that time, many β-glucosidases from cyanogenic plants have been studied. Their biochemical properties differ drastically. In plants like *Alocasia* or *Triglochin*, the β-glucosidases are strictly specific for the cyanogenic glucoside, triglochinin, that occurs in these plants (Table 3.2). In contrast, the cyanogenic β-glucosidases of *Sorghum* or *Prunus* reveal moderate specificity. In addition to hydrolyzing the cyanogenic glucosides present in these plants, they are able to hydrolyse various other glucosides. In flax, cassava and *Hevea*, the related cyanogenic β-glucosidases are rather non-specific and are capable of hydrolyzing a large variety of different glucosides. Because little information about the molecular biology of these enzymes is available, no firm conclusions can be drawn on any relationship between gene structure and substrate-specificity of the

Table 3.2 Substrate specificity and localization of cyanogenic β-glucosidases

Plant species	Cyanogenic glucoside	Specificity	Localization	References
Alocasia macrorrhiza	triglochinin	+ + +	?	Hösel and Nahrstedt (1975)
Triglochin maritima	triglochinin	+ + +	?	Nahrstedt *et al.* (1979)
Sorghum bicolor	dhurrin	+ +	chloroplasts	Hösel *et al.* (1987); Thayer and Conn (1981)
Prunus serotina	prunasin	+ +	protein bodies	Kuroki and Poulton (1987); Swain and Poulton (1992)
Trifolium repens	linamarin	±	apoplastic space	Butler *et al.* (1965); Kakes (1985)
Linum usitatissimum	linamarin	±	?	Fan and Conn (1985)
Hevea brasiliensis	linamarin	±	apoplastic space	Selmar *et al.* (1987); Kurzhals *et al.* (1989)
Manihot esculenta	linamarin	±	apoplastic space	Yeoh (1989) Mkpong *et al.* (1990); Kurzhals *et al.* (1989)
Lotus coniculatus	linamarin	?	apoplastic space	Rissler and Millar (1977)
Phaseolus lunatus	linamarin	?	apoplastic space	Frehner and Conn (1987)
Dimorphotheca sinuata	linamarin	?	apoplastic space	Grützmacher *et al.* (1990)

β-glucosidases involved in cyanogenesis. Despite the differences observed in their substrate-specificity, all these β-glucosidases share one important feature, i.e. they do not hydrolyze cyanogenic glycosides that contain two sugar moieties. The inability to hydrolyse cyanogenic diglucosides is of importance with regard to the translocation of cyanogenic glucosides (see section 3.2.5.2).

Only a few cyanogenic β-glucosidases have been cloned and sequenced. The complementary deoxyribonucleic acids (c-DNAs) of linamarase from *Trifolium repens* (Oxtoby *et al.*, 1991), of cassava linamarase (Hughes *et al.*, 1992) and of dhurrinase from *Sorghum* (Cicek and Esens, 1995) have been found to be highly homologous. These cyanogenic glucosidases are similar to other plant β-glucosidases and belong to the family A1. The cassava enzyme is glycosylated, having high mannose-type *N*-asparagine-linked oligosaccharides. Consistent with this structure and the extracellular localization of the active enzyme is the identification of an *N*-terminal signal peptide (Hughes *et al.*, 1992).

3.2.3.4 Hydroxynitrile lyases

Cleavage of cyanogenic glucosides leads to α-hydroxynitriles, also called cyanohydrins (Fig. 3.4). While these compounds are relatively stable in acids, under physiological conditions or in alkaline media they dissociate spontaneously to yield a carbonyl compound and HCN, respectively (Cooke, 1978; Conn, 1980). In some plants, this dissociation is catalyzed by special enzymes, the hydroxynitrile lyases, whose activity was first described by Rosenthaler (1908). Many publications report that this enzyme is involved in cyanogenesis upon tissue disruption (Kojima *et al.*, 1979; Conn, 1981) but, in contrast to the intensive investigation of β-glucosidases, only a few papers have dealt with hydroxynitrile lyases. This may be due to the assumption that hydroxynitrile lyases are not apparently essential for successful cyanogenesis. Bové and Conn (1961) proposed that this enzyme might also be involved in the catalysis of the back reaction, i.e. to form hydroxynitriles that have dissociated spontaneously during the biosynthesis of cyanogenic glucosides.

Several hydroxynitrile lyases have been purified and biochemically characterized. In general, their optimum pH is between 5.4 and 6.0 and they exhibit no distinct substrate-specificity (for review see Poulton; 1988; Hickel *et al.*, 1996; Wajant and Effenberger, 1996).

The importance of hydroxynitrile lyases for rapid cyanogenesis has been demonstrated by Selmar and co-workers (1989). Comparison of the rates of cyanogenesis with hydroxynitrile lyases present and absent clearly showed that the velocity of HCN liberation is accelerated enzymatically up to 20-fold (Selmar *et al.*, 1989). As mentioned above, the rapid velocity of cyanogenesis is essential for the protective function of cyanogenic glucosides. Thus, β-glucosidases and hydroxynitrile lyases are both important factors for successful protection by cyanogenesis.

During the last ten years, much research has been conducted on the biochemistry and molecular biology of hydroxynitrile lyases, not so much for understanding of the biological significance of these enzymes but to make use of their excellent catalytic abilities in chemical synthesis. Over 30 years ago, a partially purified hydroxynitrile lyase from bitter almonds was used to synthesize special, stereospecific hydroxynitriles (Becker and Pfeil, 1966; Aschhoff and Pfeil, 1970). The desired stereoselectivity was very high, especially when the reaction was rapid. However, when substrates were converted relatively slowly, racemates were produced due to spontaneous, base-catalyzed cyanohydrin production (Effenberger, 1994). An important advance in the enzyme-catalyzed stereoselective synthesis of hydroxynitriles was achieved with the introduction of nonaqueous media. This suppressed the spontaneous, nonstereoselective reaction, and the use of high carbonyl concentrations resulted in high yields of stereospecific hydroxynitriles (Effenberger *et al.*, 1987, 1988; Ziegler *et al.*, 1990). Because of their effectiveness, hydroxynitrile lyases of various plants have been intensively analyzed. The c-DNA of hydroxynitrile lyases of five plants have been cloned and sequenced: *Prunus serotina* (Cheng and Poulton, 1993); *Manihot esculenta* (Hughes *et al.*, 1994); *Sorghum bicolor* (Wajant *et al.*, 1994); *Hevea brasiliensis* (Hasslacher *et al.*, 1996); and *Linum usitatissimum* (Trummler and Wajant, 1997). Recently, Hu and Poulton (1997) presented the first genomic clone of the mandelonitrile lyase from *Prunus serotina*. Based on this work, Hu and Poulton (1998) were able to show that the mandelonitrile lyase of *Prunus serotina* exists as several isoforms. The chemical nature and physiological significance of these are still unclear. They exhibit 75–88% amino acid identity and appear to represent members of a multigene family (Hu and Poulton, 1998).

In contrast to the high homologies found among the cyanogenic β-glucosidases, the situation is completely different for the hydroxynitrile lyasses isolated from various plants. The enzyme from *Sorghum*, which does not show any significant homology to the enzymes from *Prunus* or *Linum*, is apparently related to the lyases from *Hevea* and *Manihot*. However, this sorghum lyase is highly homologous to carboxypeptidases (Wajant *et al.*, 1994). In contrast, the lyases from *Hevea brasiliensis* exhibit high homologies to a rice protein of unknown function (Trummler and Wajant, 1997). It appears that these two groups of hydroxynitrile lyases have different direct ancestors, i.e. carboxypeptidases and a protein X of unknown function, respectively. Nevertheless, they seem to have developed from a common but more ancient protein bearing an α/β-hydrolase fold and a catalytic triad (Fig. 3.6). The

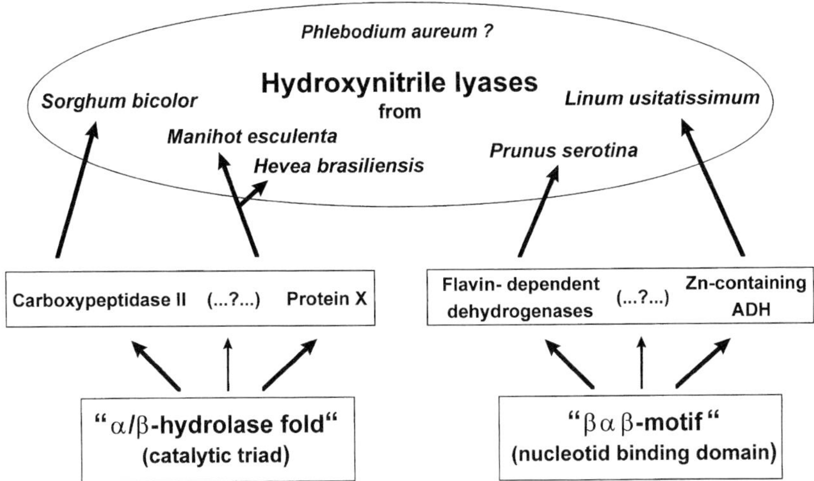

Figure 3.6 Evolutionary relationships between hydroxynitrile lyases and their apparent ancestors according to Trummler and Wajant. Abbreviation: ADH, alcoholdehydrogenases.

sequence comparison of the hydroxynitrile lyases from *Prunus* and *Linum* points in a similar direction. The hydroxynitrile lyases of these plants reveal only slight homologies to each other. Whereas the lyase from *Prunus* is strongly homologous to flavine-dependent dehydrogenases, the lyase from flax has strong homologies to Zn-containing alcohol dehydrogenases (Trummler and Wajant, 1997). Both groups of dehydrogenases have their origin in a common putative ancestor, sharing a nucleotide-binding sequence and a βαβ-motif. From these data, Trummler and Wajant (1997) deduce that hydroxynitrile lyases have developed convergently at least four times.

3.2.4 Biosynthesis of cyanogenic glucosides

The biosynthesis of cyanogenic glucosides has been intensively investigated in the laboratory of Eric E. Conn. Scientific work from this laboratory has resulted in a thorough knowledge of the precursors and the major biosynthetic steps of the pathway. In more recent work, new techniques in biochemistry and molecular biology have allowed in-depth investigation of the enzymes involved in the biosynthesis of cyanogenic glucosides. Much research, utilizing these approaches and focusing on the isolation and characterization of the enzymes themselves and on the nature of the genes that control their biosynthesis, has been carried out in the laboratory of Birger L. Møller. These molecular-based approaches have led to a clearer picture of the mechanisms of cyanogenic glucoside biosynthesis. This complex field, focused on the related molecular biology, has been comprehensively reviewed by Møller and Seigler, 1998.

3.2.4.1 Classical studies

Most early work on the elucidation of the biosynthetic pathway of cyanogenic glucosides involved feeding studies using cherry laurel (*Prunus laurocerasus*), flax (*Linum usitatissimum*) and sorghum (*Sorghum bicolor*) (Conn, 1981, 1983; Cutler and Conn, 1981). By the application of radioactively-labelled precursors it was shown that: in sorghum seedlings, dhurrin is synthesized from tyrosine (Koukoul *et al.*, 1962; McFarlane *et al.*, 1975); in cherry laurel, prunasin is built from phenylalanine (Tapper and Butler, 1971); and in flax, linamarin is derived from valine (Cutler and Conn, 1985). Subsequently, by using microsomal fractions (see section 3.2.4.2) isolated from various plants, it was shown that cyanogenic glucosides, in general, are synthesized from five protein amino acids: valine, leucine, isoleucine, phenylalanine and tyrosine, and from the nonprotein amino acid, cyclopentenylglycine, respectively (for reviews see Conn, 1980, 1988; Møller and Seigler, 1998). Up to now, the only exception to this scheme is acalyphin, which is putatively derived from nicotinic acid (Nahrstedt *et al.*, 1982).

Experiments with doubly-labelled amino acids revealed that the C-N bond of the amino acid is not broken during biosynthesis of cyanogenic glucosides and that all intermediates contain nitrogen (Uribe and Conn, 1966). Although the feeding of radioactively-labelled amino acids to whole plants resulted in extremely high incorporation of label into cyanogenic glucosides, it was not possible to isolate any labelled intermediates (Reay and Conn, 1970). In order to gain access to the major intermediates and to identify them as *N*-hydroxyamino acids, aldoximes and nitriles, *in vitro* studies with active microsomes had to be performed (Møller and Conn, 1979, 1980; Cutler *et al.*, 1985; Halkier *et al.*, 1988; Halkier and Møller, 1989).

3.2.4.2 Studies with microsomal fractions

A major breakthrough in identifying the intermediates involved was the use of microsomal fractions for biosynthetic studies. This particular fraction, obtained from etiolated sorghum seedlings, was able to convert tyrosine *in vitro* to *p*-hydroxymandelonitrile, the aglycone of dhurrin. In addition to the amino acid, the microsomes required nicotinamide adenine dinucleotide phosphate (reduced form) (NADPH), oxygen and a reductant, such as mercaptoethanol or dithiothreitol (McFarlane *et al.*, 1975; Møller and Conn, 1979). When the assays were performed without these thiol reagents, later steps in the pathway were inactivated and *Z-p-*

hydroxyphenylacetaldoxime accumulated. During *in vitro* biosyntheses with isolated microsomes (as was observed in *in vivo* studies) only very small amounts of intermediates were detectable. The most successful method for isolation of the postulated intermediates was the use of trapping experiments. In addition to introduction of ^{14}C-labelled tyrosine, varying amounts of non-labelled putative intermediates were added to microsomal fractions from sorghum (Møller and Conn, 1980; Conn, 1981; Halkier *et al.*, 1988). In this way, all intermediates involved in dhurrin biosynthesis were isolated and identified (Fig. 3.7). In the sorghum system, the only intermediate that equilibrated freely when added externally, was the *Z*-oxime (*Z*-*p*-hydroxyphenylacetaldoxime) (Halkier *et al.*, 1989). The observed lack of accumulation of other intermediates was attributed to the presence of a highly-organized multienzyme complex, in which the product of one enzyme is used as a substrate by the next enzyme without leaving the complex. This channelled biosynthetic process was thought to be necessary in order to protect labile intermediates from wasteful and deleterious side-reactions.

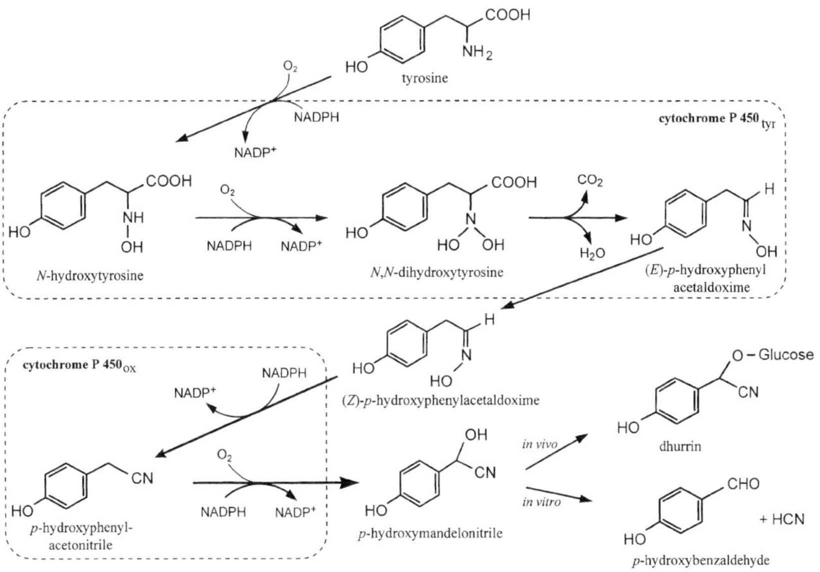

Figure 3.7 Biosynthesis of cyanogenic glucosides, e.g. the biosynthetic pathway for dhurrin. The biosynthesis of the aglycone is catalyzed by two cytochrome P_{450}-dependent monooxygenases. Abbreviations: $NADP^+$, nicotinamide adenine dinucleotide phosphate; NADPH, NADP reduced form.

Biosynthetically-active microsomes were also obtained from various other cyanogenic plants, e.g. *Triglochin maritima* (Hösel and Nahrstedt, 1980), *Linum usitatissimum* (Cutler and Conn, 1981), *Trifolium repens*

(Collinge and Hughes, 1982), *Eschscholtzia californica* (Hösel *et al.*, 1985) and *Manihot esculenta* (Koch *et al.*, 1992). The data obtained from these experiments confirmed the postulated scheme for biosynthesis of cyanogenic glucosides, based on the biosynthesis of dhurrin in sorghum. In all plants so far tested, cyanogenic glucosides appear to be synthesized by a similar channelled pathway that must be of ancient origin.

3.2.4.3 New approaches

Biosynthesis of dhurrin in sorghum plays an important role as a model system for obtaining further insight into the enzymology and molecular biology of the biosynthesis of cyanogenic glucosides.

As mentioned previously, microsomal activity depends on the presence of oxygen and NADPH. Stoichiometric studies revealed that three molecules of oxygen are consumed as one molecule of tyrosine is converted to dhurrin or to its aglycone *p*-hydroxymandelonitrile (Halkier and Møller, 1990). This is consistent with the involvement of three hydroxylation steps (Fig. 3.7). Two molecules of oxygen are consumed in the conversion of tyrosine to the aldoxime and one is required for the conversion of the aldoxime to the cyanohydrin (Halkier and Møller, 1990). Unfortunately, $NADP^+$-CN adducts interfered with the spectrophotometric methods used to quantify NADPH at 340 nm (Colowick *et al.*, 1951), so that stoichiometric measurements of the consumption of NADPH could not be performed. Nonetheless, for the conversion of an amino acid to a hydroxynitrile, four NADPH molecules are required and, at the same time, three oxygen molecules are reduced. The predicted stoichiometry has been confirmed by various investigations, either with microsomes or with partially purified enzyme systems (Halkier and Møller, 1989; Halkier and Møller, 1990). Using $^{18}O_2$, Halkier and co-workers (1991) postulated that *N*,*N*-dihydroxytyrosine is an intermediate and that two oxygen atoms of the two *N*-hydroxyl groups originated from different oxygen molecules. As expected, when amino acid substrates were incubated with $^{18}O_2$, the hydroxyl group of the aldoxime produced was labelled entirely with ^{18}O. However, when hydroxytyrosine was used as substrate, the same recovery was observed (Halkier *et al.*, 1991). This was surprising because one would expect a 50% loss of ^{18}O incorporation during the second hydroxylation due to free rotation around the C-N bond. This observation could only be explained by the fact that all reactions involved in aldoxime synthesis are catalyzed by one enzyme, a multifunctional cytochrome P_{450} (see below). Apparently, decarboxylation and dehydration proceed in a concerted step, in which hydrogen abstraction from *N*-hydroxytyrosine occurs but while the nitrogen atom is still bound to the active iron-oxo complex (Halkier *et al.*, 1991). These results, in combination with the consumption of two molecules of oxygen, exclude 1-*p*-hydroxyphenyl-2-nitroethane (Fig. 3.3) as an intermediate. Consequently, the small amounts of 1-*p*-hydroxyphenyl-2-nitroethane that can be detected when sorghum microsomes are incubated with tyrosine (Halkier *et al.*, 1991) must be side-products of the pathway.

The use of partially-purified enzyme systems, instead of microsomal fractions, was the first step in acquiring the actual enzyme proteins involved in the biosynthesis of cyanogenic glucosides (Halkier and Møller, 1989). Initially, only two steps of dhurrin biosynthesis were shown to be catalyzed by cytochrome P_{450} enzymes: firstly, an *N*-hydroxylase that converts tyrosine into *N*-hydroxytyrosine; and secondly, a C-hydroxylase converting *p*-hydroxyphenylacetonitrile into *p*-hydroxymandelonitrile (Halkier and Møller, 1991). Further investigation revealed that these P_{450} enzymes correspond to two multifunctional membrane-bound enzymes that catalyze the entire conversion of tyrosine to *p*-hydroxymandelonitrile (Fig. 3.7). The first P_{450}, designated $P_{450,\,\mathrm{tyr}}$, catalyzes the conversion of tyrosine to *Z*-*p*-hydroxyphenylacetaldoxime (Koch *et al.*, 1995a; Sibbesen *et al.*, 1994, 1995), whereas the second, designated $P_{450\,\mathrm{ox}}$, catalyzes the conversion of *Z*-*p*-hydroxyphenylacetaldoxime to *p*-hydroxymandelonitrile (Kahn *et al.*, 1997). In order to function, an NADPH-cytochrome oxidoreductase must be present to establish electron flow from NADPH via cytochrome to the oxygen (Sibbesen *et al.*, 1995; Kahn *et al.*, 1997). The multifunctionality of $P_{450,\,\mathrm{tyr}}$ and $P_{450,\,\mathrm{ox}}$ was confirmed by reconstitution experiments. When the two isolated cytochromes and the purified NADPH-cytochrome oxidoreductase were inserted into artificial membranes constructed with L-α-dilauroylphosphatidylcholine, these membranes catalyzed the conversion of tyrosine to *p*-hydroxymandelonitrile in the presence of NADPH. This clearly demonstrated that all membrane-bound reactions of cyanogenic glucoside biosynthesis are performed by only two multifunctional cytochromes. When a soluble glucosyltransferase was added to the reconstitution mixture, *p*-hydroxymandelonitrile was glucosylated to dhurrin in the presence of uridine diphosphate glucose (UDPG). Thus, the entire biosynthetic pathway for cyanogenic glucosides was carried out *in vitro* by using isolated enzymes (Kahn *et al.*, 1997).

Based on a monospecific polyclonal antibody and oligonucleotide probes, designed on the basis of amino acid sequences of tryptic fragments derived from the isolated cytochrome $P_{450,\,\mathrm{tyr}}$, the enzyme was cloned (Koch *et al.*, 1995a). By comparison with published sequences, the greatest homologies were found to be a 3′,5′-flavanoid hydroxylase of petunia (Holton *et al.*, 1993) and a cytochrome P_{450} of unknown function from avocado (Christofferson *et al.*, 1995). Cytochrome $P_{450,\,\mathrm{tyr}}$ was efficiently expressed in *Escherichia coli* (Halkier *et al.*, 1995). As known for other recombinant P_{450}s (Barnes *et al.*, 1991), the recombinant $P_{450,\,\mathrm{tyr}}$

expressed in *E. coli* was also active when used in reconstitution experiments (Halkier *et al.*, 1995). The final proof that only the two cytochromes are needed for biosynthesis of cyanogens was also provided in the laboratory of Birger Møller. Recently, both cytochromes have been successfully expressed in *Nicotiana tabacum*. In contrast to the original *Nicotiana* plants, the related transgenic plants are highly cyanogenic (Møller, personal communication).

3.2.4.4 Glucosyltransferases

The last step in the biosynthesis of cyanogenic glucosides is the glucosylation of the labile hydroxynitriles. In general, UDPG is required as a glucose donor. In contrast to the membrane-bound biosynthesis of the aglycones, glucosylation is catalyzed by soluble enzymes. Up to now, only a few such glucosylating enzymes have been examined. The first cyanogenic glucosyltransferase was purified from flax seedlings by Hahlbrock and Conn (1970). This enzyme catalyzes the glucosylation of acetone cyanohydrin and 2-hydroxy-2-methylbutyronitrile to yield linamarin and lotaustralin, respectively. A similar enzyme was partially purified by Mederacke and co-workers (1996) from cassava leaves. In addition to the highly specific glucosyltransferase, which is thought to be responsible for the linamarin biosynthesis in cassava, two other UDPG transferases are detectable. These last enzymes are able to catalyze glucosylation of cyanohydrins but also glucosylate anthocyanidins and other flavanoids (Mederacke *et al.*, 1995). Glucosyltransferases that catalyze the glucosylation of aromatic cyanohydrins have been purified from sorghum (Reay and Conn, 1974) and from *Triglochin maritima* (Hösel and Schiel, 1984). These enzymes catalyze the synthesis of dhurrin and taxiphyllin, respectively. Whereas both of these enzymes exhibit distinct substrate specificity, the glucosyltransferase from black cherries, which is responsible for prunasin biosynthesis, is relatively unspecific (Poulton and Shin, 1983).

The glucosyltransferase from *Triglochin maritima* only glucosylates (*R*)-hydroxy-mandelonitrile and not its (*S*)-isomer (Hösel and Schiel, 1984). In contrast, the corresponding flax enzyme uses both (*R*)- and (*S*)-forms of hydroxy-2-methylbutyronitrile (Zilg and Conn, 1974). While it could be argued that the stereospecificity of the glucosyltransferase may determine the ratio of enantiomers present *in vivo* (see section 3.2.2), it is known that, in the course of biosynthesis, only a particular enantiomer is produced. Thus, if the (*R*)-hydroxynitrile is synthesized, glucosylation could not yield the (*S*)-form. Only if the labile hydroxynitriles were to dissociate and reassociate prior to glucosylation—and thus become racemic—would the specificity of the glucosyltransferase influence the enantiomeric ratio in the plant. Indeed, in the slightly alkaline media in which cyanogenic glucosyltransferases are active, the dissociation equilibrium of hydroxynitriles is established immediately. This was demonstrated by incubation of glucosyltransferases with carbonyl compounds and HCN instead of the preformed hydroxynitriles, resulting in nearly the same reaction velocity as in the usual assay, where undissociated hydroxynitriles were involved (Mederacke *et al.*, 1996). This clearly shows that enantiomeric hydroxynitriles are racemized *in vitro* prior to glucosylation.

Unfortunately, no data are available for the corresponding situation *in vivo*. Nevertheless, one can draw some solid conclusions from these observations. When hydroxynitriles dissociate, a small amount of HCN is always liberated to the atmosphere. Such HCN may be refixed by the plant via β-cyanoalanine synthase, assuming that the activity of this enzyme is sufficient (see section 3.2.5.1). However, as the activity of β-cyanoalanine synthase is not significantly enhanced in tissues synthesizing cyanogenic glucosides, e.g. in etiolated sorghum seedlings (Wurtele *et al.*, 1982), quantitative refixation of the HCN liberated can be excluded. Since intact tissues of cyanogenic plants do not liberate HCN, it can be concluded that the unstable hydroxynitriles do not dissociate in the course of biosynthesis. Thus, they must be glucosylated directly following their synthesis, without having any chance to dissociate. This indicates a close association between the soluble glucosyltransferase and the membrane-bound cytochrome $P_{450,\,ox}$, ensuring that the biosynthesized hydroxynitriles are utilized directly by the associated glucosyltransferase. Further research is still required to fully understand the cooperation of membrane-bound cytochromes and soluble glucosyltransferases.

In contrast to the glucosyltransferases that are responsible for biosynthesis of cyanogenic monoglucosides, no information is yet available concerning the related enzymes that catalyze the synthesis of diglucosidic cyanogens. Indeed, it is not known whether cyanogenic diglycosides are synthesized by glycosylation of monoglucosides (as is described below for the synthesis of diglucosidic transport metabolites) or whether disaccharides might be directly transferred to hydroxynitriles.

3.2.5 *Metabolism of cyanogenic glycosides*

A few studies have shown that cyanogenic glycosides, like other secondary plant products, are metabolized *in vivo*.

3.2.5.1 *Turnover*

The first indication that, in addition to cyanogenesis upon tissue disruption, cyanogenic glucosides are also metabolized *in vivo* was provided as early as 1927 by Godwin and Bishop, who showed that the cyanogenic glucosides present in cherry laurel could also decline in the living plant. Subsequently, several papers were published describing changes in the content of cyanogenic glucosides during development (Stafford, 1969; Clegg *et al.*, 1979). However, these investigations failed to prove that no HCN was liberated to the atmosphere during the decrease of cyanogens in the plant. Thus, it cannot be deduced unequivocally that cyanogenic glucosides were metabolized because a related *in vivo* cyanogenesis and loss of HCN could not be excluded. Bough and Gander (1971) were first to demonstrate a true turnover of dhurrin in sorghum. This was confirmed by further studies by Adewusi (1990). Even in these investigations, it remained unclear whether the turnover observed was caused by complete endogenous conversion of cyanogenic glucosides to noncyanogenic compounds or by concomitant processes of *de novo* synthesis and of hydrolysis of cyanogenic glucosides followed by liberation of HCN to the atmosphere.

Authentic conversion of cyanogenic glucosides to noncyanogenic compounds, referred to as metabolization, was demonstrated for the first time by analyses of developing seedlings of rubber trees (*Hevea brasiliensis*) (Lieberei *et al.*, 1985; Selmar *et al.*, 1988). *Hevea* seeds contain large amounts of linamarin (up to 250 μmol per seed). During seedling development, the amount of cyanogenic glucosides was found to decrease sharply without significant liberation of HCN into the atmosphere. Consequently, linamarin must have been converted to noncyanogenic compounds. The obvious reaction known for the decomposition of cyanogenic glucosides is their hydrolysis by hydrolytic enzymes (Fig. 3.5). Because no significant amounts of HCN were liberated, the HCN produced from dissociating hydroxynitriles must have been efficiently refixed by the plant. In plants, two different reactions are known for such cyanide fixation, i.e. the production of either thiocyanide or β-cyanoalanine (Fig. 3.8). These reactions are catalyzed by rhodanese and β-cyanoalanine synthase, respectively (Chew, 1973; Blumenthal *et al.*, 1968). The β-cyanoalanine produced can subsequently be hydrolyzed to asparagine (Castric *et al.*, 1972).

In some early reports, rhodanese activity was reported to be significant in cyanogenic plants (Chew, 1973). However, careful analysis of assay methods for rhodanese revealed that most of the putative activity was due to artefacts, leading to erroneous values. The correct determination of rhodanese requires many controls (Lieberei and Selmar, 1990). Using accurate analytical procedures, recent studies have shown that rhodanese activity in plants is very low in comparison to β-cyanoalanine synthase (Kakes and Hakvoort, 1992; Nambisam and Sundaresan, 1994; Elias *et al.*, 1997). Assuming that intermediate hydroxynitriles are produced during conversion of cyanogenic glucosides to noncyanogenic com-

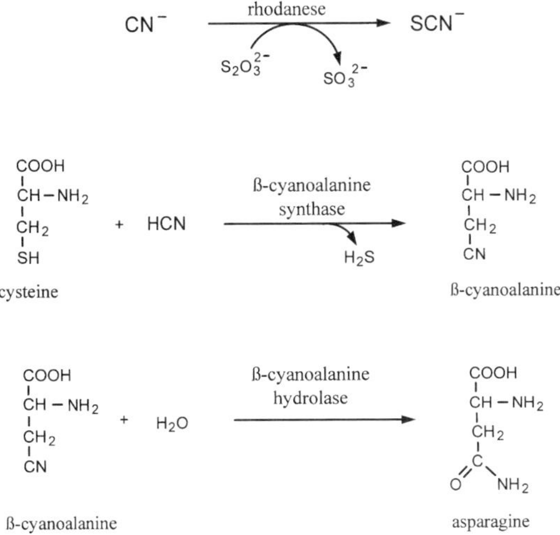

Figure 3.8 Detoxification of HCN in plants. Abbreviations: HCN, hydrogen cyanide; SCN, potassium, thiocyanate.

pounds and that these subsequently dissociate, the refixation of the corresponding HCN seems to be catalyzed by β-cyanoalanine synthase.

In *Hevea*, the amount of cyanogenic glucosides converted to noncyanogenic compounds may be very large (up to 200 μmol per seed). Thus, in addition to the significance of cyanogenic glucosides in plant defence, these compounds may also function as storage forms for reduced nitrogen (Selmar *et al.*, 1988). Similar conditions have been reported for the utilization of cyanogenic lipids in *Ungnadia speciosa* (Selmar *et al.*, 1990) and for the utilization of amygdalin in *Prunus serotina* seedlings (Swain and Poulton, 1995).

3.2.5.2 Transport of cyanogenic glucosides

As is true for many other natural products, cyanogenic glucosides are translocated within the plant. This was first reported by DeBruijn (1973) in work that involved ringing experiments with cassava stems. Similar observations were made by Clegg and co-workers (1979), who showed that, in seedlings of lima beans (*Phaseolus lunatus*), the content of linamarin drastically decreases in the cotyledons, whereas it increases in the same manner in the growing primary leaves. Additional support for translocation of cyanogenic glucosides was obtained from investigation of the metabolization of cyanogenic glucosides in *Hevea* seedlings; whereas the cyanogens are stored in the endosperm, the enzymes responsible for metabolization (i.e. β-cyanoalanine synthase) are located in the growing leaves. Thus, before metabolization, the compounds must be translocated from the endosperm into the seedling. This transport doubtless includes passage across the apoplast between endosperm and cotyledons. As high activities of linamarin-splitting β-glucosidases are present in the apoplastic space, direct transport of the monoglucoside is impossible. As mentioned above, apoplastic β-glucosidases are quite nonspecific but they are unable to hydrolyse diglucosides, which have been postulated to be important transport metabolites (Selmar *et al.*, 1988).

Further investigations with *Hevea*, *Linum* and *Manihot* have indicated that the corresponding diglucoside, linustatin, does indeed function as a transport metabolite for linamarin and is part of the so-called 'linustatin pathway' (Selmar *et al.*, 1988; Selmar, 1993b). Nevertheless, substances must pass through the apoplast, not only during seedling development but also in the course of any long distance transport. This is true for xylem transport, which is entirely apoplastic, or for apoplastic phloem loading (Van Bel, 1989). Consequently, cyanogenic monoglucosides also have to be protected against hydrolysis by apoplastic β-glucosidases during long distance transport (Selmar, 1993a). The involvement of linustatin in the long distance transport of linamarin was confirmed by detecting linustatin in phloem sap of *Hevea* and cassava (Selmar, 1993b, 1994). Since the apoplastic occurrence of nonspecific β-glucosidases is a general feature of plants, the conditions outlined for linamarin transport in *Hevea* and cassava are likely to be valid for all cyanogenic glucosides (for review see Selmar, 1993a).

From corresponding changes in the pattern of cyanogenic mono- and diglucosides described by Frehner *et al.* (1990), it could be deduced that, in developing seeds of *Prunus amygdalus*, *Linum usitatissimum* and *Phaseolus lunatus*, translocation of cyanogens is also performed via diglucosides. Moreover, in the cyanogenic plants so far investigated, when special attention was paid to the detection of low quantities of cyanogenic metabolites during these analyses, in addition to the corresponding monoglucosides, small amounts of the corresponding cyanogenic diglucosides could always be detected. Such diglucosides, e.g. the dhurrin-6′-glucoside in sorghum (Selmar *et al.*, 1996), presumably represent potential transport metabolites.

3.2.5.3 Cleavage of transport metabolites and their metabolic fate

In general, the diglucosidic transport metabolites are hydrolyzed immediately after their import into the 'source' tissue. As in the case of cyanogenesis resulting from tissue disruption, the cleavage of diglucosides can occur via either a sequential or a simultaneous process (Fig. 3.5). In the former case, the original cyanogenic monoglucosides are reformed, resulting in simple translocation of cyanogenic monoglucosides from 'source' to 'sink' tissues by means of diglucosidic transport metabolites.

However, when both glucose moieties are split-off simultaneously, hydroxynitriles are formed. In contrast to cyanogenesis following tissue disruption, in this case, the hydroxynitriles are formed within the living tissue of the plant. In living cells, the HCN produced on dissociation of hydroxynitriles can easily be refixed by β-cyanoalanine synthase (Elias *et al.*, 1997). As mentioned previously, β-glucosidases capable of hydrolyzing linamarin are localized exclusively in the apoplasmic cell wall (see section 3.2.3.3). Since linamarase is absent from the living cell, a direct cleavage of linamarin *in vivo* without destroying the cell can be excluded. Therefore, the sequential cleavage of imported linustatin always results in a translocation of cyanogenic glucosides, whereas simultaneous cleavage initiates the conversion of cyanogens into noncyanogenic compounds (Fig. 3.9).

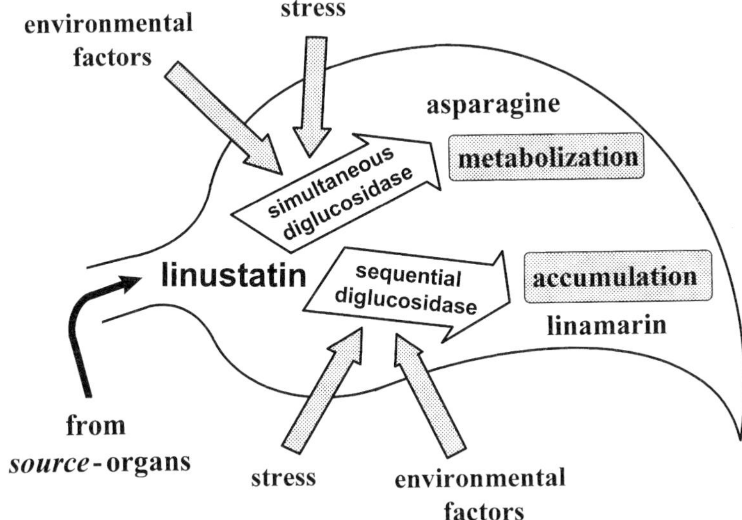

Figure 3.9 Cleavage of linustatin imported into 'sink' organs. Depending on environmental factors, the activity of sequential and simultaneous diglucosidase is modified. Cleavage by simultaneous diglucosidase initiates the conversion of cyanogenic glucosides into noncyanogenic compounds. Cleavage by sequential diglucosidase leads to accumulation of linamarin and, thus, to translocation of cyanogenic glucosides from 'source' to 'sink' organs.

As is known for many other enzymes, the activity of sequential and simultaneous diglucosidases is strongly dependent on the physiological status of the leaves. In *Hevea*, the activity of both diglucosidases is highest in young and growing 'sink' tissue (Hillmar and Selmar, unpublished data). Varying ratios of simultaneous to sequential diglucosidase activity should result in different rates of translocation and metabolization of translocated cyanogenic glucosides. Such differences are observed in seedlings of varieties of *Hevea brasiliensis* as well as in other *Hevea* species. Whilst, in some varieties, over 80% of the cyanogens formerly stored in the endosperm are converted to noncyanogenic compounds after translocation into the cotyledons, in other varieties, linamarin is simply translocated (as linustatin) from the endosperm into the cotyledons (Selmar *et al.*, 1991).

The spatial conditions for the metabolization of cyanogenic glucosides in the course of their translocation are the same in principle as those for the processes decribed as turnover. Turnover requires controlled cleavage of cyanogenic glucosides. Due to the absence of symplastic linamarase in linamarin-containing plants, turnover also requires the involvement of diglucosidic metabolites, i.e. linustatin. Basic turnover requires both biosynthesis and catabolism of cyanogenic glucosides. Moreover, translocation of metabolites interferes with these processes. Depending on the relative amount of each process that occurs, the content of cyanogenic glucosides in a certain organ increases, decreases or remains constant.

It is well known that various abiotic factors influence the cyanogenicity of plants. Contradictory findings are reported with regard to the influence of light on cyanogenic potential. On the one hand, light-grown flax plants were found to contain a far higher level of cyanogenic glucosides than etiolated ones (Trione, 1960; Xu *et al.*, 1988) but, on the other hand, a negative effect of light intensity on the cyanogen content in *Trifolium repens* has been reported (Vickery *et al.*, 1987). Temperature also influences cyanogenicity. In clover plants grown at 27°C, the content of cyanogens was about half that of plants grown at 19°C (Hughes, 1981). Water potential is another important factor. Bokanga *et al.* (1994) reported that the water content of soil strongly influences the linamarin content of cassava tubers. Gershenzon (1984) noted that the content of cyanogenic glucosides is generally higher when plants suffer water stress. These differences in cyanogenicity obviously depend on changes in the relative amounts of biosynthesis, catabolism and translocation. Unfortunately, little information is available to clarify how these individual processes are influenced by different environmental factors.

3.2.5.4 Cyanogenic glycosides in cell and tissue cultures

Whilst extensive information is available on the occurrence of cyanogenic glucosides in plants, little is known about the presence of these compounds in cell and tissue cultures. Suspension cultures of the California poppy (*Eschscholtzia californica*) contain several cyanogenic compounds (Hösel *et al.*, 1985). However, the cyanogenic glucosides present in cell cultures of this plant are different from triglochinin and taxiphyllin found in intact *Eschscholtzia* plants and are still unknown.

The amount of these unknown cyanogens could be significantly enhanced by applying osmotic stress to the cultures. In addition, 1-(4′-hydroxvphenyl)-2-nitroethane was present in the cultures. This compound is thought to be a side-product of cyanogenic glucoside biosynthesis (see section 3.2.4).

In contrast, the cyanogenic glucosides occurring in calli of the South African plant, *Schlechteria mitosemmatoides* (Passifloraceae), are the same as those present in the intact plant (Jäger *et al.*, 1995). The compounds that occur in established suspension cultures have to be synthesized in the cultured cells themselves. However, the cyanogens present in young callus could also be due to remains of cyanogens that were originally present in the tissues used for callus production. Without *de novo* biosynthesis, the content of these compounds will steadily decrease during continued culture. Such an effect was detected for cyanogenic glucosides in calli of *Phaseolus lunatus* (Istock *et al.*, 1990). From this observation, the authors concluded that the dedifferentiated callus cells do not synthesize cyanogenic glucosides. An analogous suppression of cyanogenic glucoside biosynthesis has also been reported for the suspension cultures of *P. lunatus* (Istock *et al.*, 1990).

3.2.6 Cyanogenic glycosides and foods

Various aspects of the occurrence of cyanogenic glucosides in food have been comprehensively reviewed by Poulton (1989) and by Nahrstedt (1993). In the present chapter, only the most important aspects are mentioned briefly in order to give an overview of this important subject.

3.2.6.1 Occurrence of cyanide

Almost all plants used for human nutrition contain cyanogenic glucosides and, thus, nearly all of our food contains cyanide, which arises from endogenous cyanogenic glucosides during food preparation (Lang, 1990). However, the cyanide concentration is usually small, often in the ppb range; examples are given in Table 3.3. Cyanide is certainly moderately toxic but, because of the low concentration in most of our foods, does not cause serious problems. Due to an efficient detoxification system, man is able to deal with much larger amounts of cyanide than those actually encountered (see section 3.2.6.1). In contrast, if food is prepared from strongly cyanogenic plants, e.g. bamboo, cassava or lima beans (Table 3.4), the resulting concentrations of cyanide can be dangerous. Therefore, these plants must be properly processed and detoxified before consumption. In principle, such processing is relatively simple and is outlined, in brief, for cassava in section 3.2.6.3. In all cases, plant material

Table 3.3 Cyanide content in various foods

Product	HCN potential (μg/kg)*
Oatmeal	16
Flour (rye)	15
Flour (barley)	24
Rice	1
Cornflakes	8
White bread	11
Beer	3–160
Apple juice	60
Plum juice	2100
Orange juice	20
Cherry juice	500–1900

*The HCN-potential corresponds to the total amount of cyanide that will be liberated after complete hydrolysis of cyanogenic glucosides. (Values according to Lang, 1990).

Table 3.4 HCN potential of highly cyanogenic food plants

Plant	Tissue	Content of cyanogenic glycosides (mmol/kg)	HCN potential* (mg/kg)
Cassava	tubers	2–8	50–200
(*Manihot esculenta*)	(maximal range)	(1–25)	(25–650)
	flour (gari)	0.02–11	0.5–300
Bamboo (*Bambus vulgaris*)	sprouts	up to 300	up to 8000
Lima beans (*Phaseolus lunatus*)	seeds	2–75	500–2000
Vetch (*Vicia sativa*)	seeds	2–20	50–500
Flax (*Linum unsitatissimum*)	seeds	10–20	250–500

*The HCN potential corresponds to the total amount of cyanide that will be liberated after complete hydrolysis of cyanogenic glucosides.

must be macerated in order to initiate cyanogenesis; subsequently, the cyanide must be removed by evaporation.

3.2.6.2 Cyanide and health

The acute toxicity of HCN and cyanide is a consequence of the affinity of these substances for various heavy metals, such as iron or copper, by forming cyano complexes. The effect on cytochromes, which results in an efficient inhibition of respiration, is most important. In addition, numerous other metabolic processes are affected (for review see Solomonson, 1981). The lethal dose of cyanide for humans is considered to be about 1 mg per kg body weight (Montgomery, 1969). In mammals, cyanide is detoxified in the liver by the enzyme, rhodanese (Westley, 1981), which catalyzes the transfer of cyanide to a sulfane-sulfur (e.g. the sulfur atom from thiosulfate) to yield thiocyanate, sometimes called rhodanide (Fig. 3.8). The potassium thiocyanate (SCN) produced in this fashion is excreted in urine (Rosling, 1994). Due to this efficient detoxification system, humans are able to tolerate moderate amounts of cyanide (a few milligrams per day) without any problem. However, the intake of larger amounts of HCN leads to enhanced SCN concentrations in the blood, which can result in severe health problems. These disorders are due mainly to the interference of SCN with iodine metabolism (Rosling, 1994). Thus, human exposure to HCN in significant concentrations causes or aggravates iodine deficiency disorders, expressed mainly as goitre and cretinism.

Several investigations have suggested that consumption of residual cyanide in cassava products causes paralytic disorders, such as konzo (Tylleskär, 1994; Spencer, 1994) and tropical ataxic neuropathy (Osuntokun, 1994; Spencer, 1994). In both conditions, the pathogenic mechanism is still unknown. In addition, there are indications that the long-term effects of increased cyanide consumption might include diabetes (Akanji, 1994).

3.2.6.3 Cyanide in cassava

In the tropics, more than 400 million people depend on cassava tubers (*Manihot esculenta*) as a staple food. Many people consume as much as one kilogram of cassava products daily. As the tubers are strongly cyanogenic, they must be carefully detoxified. In principle, such processing is simple and numerous methods are used (Oke, 1994; Dufour, 1994); the compartmentation is destroyed by grinding or grating the tubers and cyanogenesis is initiated. Provided that subsequent heating is not performed too soon after tissue disruption and that the β-glucosidase is not destroyed before all cyanogenic glucosides are hydrolyzed, roasting guarantees complete hydrolysis of cyanohydrins and evaporation of the prussic acid produced. In this manner, safe cassava products are produced from the toxic tubers. Unfortunately, such detoxification is often incomplete due to short-cuts in processing. Consequently, HCN intoxication and related disorders caused by thiocyanate are widespread, especially in arid regions of Africa.

There is a strong demand for cassava plants that produce acyanogenic tubers or tubers with low concentrations of cyanogenic glucosides. Up till now, no acyanogenic cassava plants have been produced by classical plant breeding. Some low cyanogenic varieties are available but they taste much sweeter than commonly cultivated varieties and this seems to be an undesired characteristic. The bitter taste, which is preferred by most cassava consumers, is not directly attributed to the presence of cyanogenic glucosides. There are some good correlations of bitterness and content of cyanogenic glucosides (Sundaresan *et al.*, 1987); however, there are several sweet varieties that contain the same concentration of cyanogens as bitter-tasting varieties (Bokanga, 1994; Nye, 1991) and some have even more (Pereire *et al.*, 1981). A compound that is putatively responsible for the bitter taste has been identified as isopropylapiosyl-glucoside (King and Bradbury, 1995).

As classical breeding has not been successful in accomplishing the goal of producing acyanogenic cassava plants, molecular biology and gene technology are thought to be the best tools. Such efforts should first concentrate on the biosynthetic pathway. A total 'knockout' of the two cytochromes involved in biosynthesis of cyanogenic glucosides should yield acyanogenic cassava plants (Koch *et al.*, 1994). Apart from their cyanogenic character, these plants should not differ from the standard varieties. However, due to the lack of chemical protection provided by cyanogenic compounds, acyanogenic plants may be attacked extensively by generalist herbivores. Thus, cultivation of these transgenic plants may become difficult.

Using a second strategy, transgenic plants may be generated in which the content of cyanogenic glucosides is drastically reduced only in the tubers. This might be achieved by modifying the transport of cyanogens (Selmar, 1994). While tubers are able to synthesize some cyanogens (Du *et al.*, 1995b), most of the cyanogenic glucosides present in the tubers are synthesized in the leaves (Bediako *et al.*, 1981; Makame *et al.*, 1987) and are subsequently translocated into the tubers (De Bruijn, 1973). After import of the transport metabolite, linustatin, into the cassava tubers, this diglucoside is hydrolyzed preferentially by a sequential diglucosidase, yielding linamarin, which accumulates in the tubers (Selmar, 1994) (Fig. 3.9). Tuber-specific suppression of the sequential diglucosidase and concomitant overexpression of the simultaneous diglucosidase should change the metabolic fate of linustatin imported into the tubers, causing it to be metabolized into noncyanogenic compounds. The other enzymes required for this process, β-cyanoalanine synthase and cyanoalanine hydrolase, are present naturally in cassava tubers of the original varieties (Nartey, 1968).

3.2.7 Perspectives

Many major questions related to the biosynthesis of cyanogenic glycosides have been solved by the well-known work of Eric E. Conn,

Birger L. Møller and their co-workers. Nevertheless, additional, important, basic research questions, as well as problems of applied botany, remain to be solved. Molecular biology offers many possibilities for examination of these problems. Various aspects of the regulation of biosynthesis, of subcellular localization of the enzymes involved and of interaction of membrane-bound cytochromes and soluble glucosyltransferases need to be clarified. Access to the genes involved will permit creation of transgenic plants with modified cyanogenic properties. Such plants could be the means to provide proof of the protective role of cyanogenic glucosides. Moreover, these plants will almost certainly contribute to our understanding of the overall significance of cyanogenic compounds in plants.

The biosynthetic pathway for synthesis of cyanogenic glucosides is present in many unrelated families throughout the plant kingdom. Thus, the character of cyanogenicity must be ancient and conservative. Hydoxynitrile lyases evolved much later (see section 3.2.3.4). Ancient plants must have been able to synthesize cyanogenic glucosides but were not able to liberate HCN rapidly, due to the lack of hydroxynitrile lyase. Because effective and rapid cyanogenesis upon tissue disruption is the basis for the protective function of cyanogenic glucosides (see section 3.2.3.1), the significance of cyanogenic glucosides in these ancient plants must have been different from that of plant protection by cyanogenesis. This alternative function may also be manifested in modern plants that contain only low amounts of cyanogens, inadequate to repel herbivores. To understand this interesting situation, new ideas and vigorous application of the principles of plant physiology, biochemistry and molecular biology will be required.

3.3 Glucosinolates

3.3.1 General aspects

Glucosinolates resemble cyanogenic compounds in many aspects; however, this group of compounds contains sulfur atoms in the molecule. They are characterized by the liberation of thiocyanates (mustard oils) or related nitrile compounds after being decomposed (for review see Bones and Rossiter, 1996). Degradation takes place when tissues of glucosinolate-containing plants are damaged and cells are destroyed. Analogous to cyanogenesis, this postmortem process is initiated by the loss of cell integrity, leading to contact between glucosinolates and their hydrolytic enzymes. In contrast to widespread cyanogenic glucosides, the occurrence of glucosinolates is restricted. Most of these compounds are found in the Capparales; however, sporadic occurrences have also been recorded for members of other families, e.g. Caricaceae, Euphorbiaceae and Sterculiaceae (Rodman *et al.*, 1991).

Glucosinolates and their degradation products are important factors in plant defence against herbivores, as well as against pathogens (for review see Louda and Mole, 1991). In addition, they have significant allelopathic potential and are thought to be effective in defence against ephemeral, unapparent plants or plant parts (Feeny, 1977).

The presence of glucosinolates in the agriculturally important crop plant, rape (*Brassica napus*), is of great economic significance, because glucosinolates drastically reduce the feeding quality of rapeseed meal. However, with regard to our health, glucosinolates also reveal positive effects based on their anticarcinogenic potential. As a consequence of the wide range of interest, glucosinolates are now being studied in many different fields of biology, biochemistry, agriculture and medicine. Several recent reviews have focused on different aspects of glucosinolate research, such as: taxonomy (Rodman *et al.*, 1996); chemistry and ecology (Louda and Mole, 1991); biosynthesis (Halkier, 1999); degradation (Bones and Rositer, 1996); methodology (Poulton and Møller, 1993); and anticarcinogenic potential (Jongen, 1996; Verhoeven *et al.*, 1997). A comprehensive review dealing with the entire field of glucosinolate research has been presented by Wallsgrove and co-workers (1998). As these recent reviews cover the whole range of research on glucosinolates and provide much detailed information, the present chapter will give only a brief overview of the biology and biochemistry of these natural products.

3.3.2 *Structures*

Glucosinolates are composed of a β-thioglucose moiety, a sulfonated oxime moiety and a variable side chain. The parent compound, 'glucosinolate', according to the semisystematic nomenclature introduced by Ettlinger and Dateo (1961) is presented in Figure 3.10, where R = H. The various glucosinolates are derived by naming the side chain R as a prefix. Some examples are presented in Table 3.5. Because of the low p*K*-value of the sulfonic group and the instability of glucosinolates in strong acids, these substances invariably occur in nature in the anionic form.

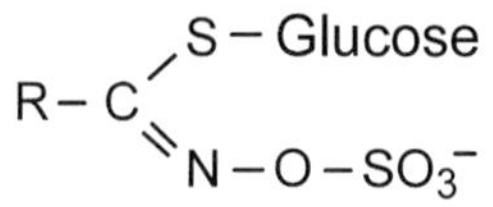

$$R-C{\overset{\diagup\ S-\text{Glucose}}{\underset{\diagdown\!\!\diagdown\ N-O-SO_3^-}{}}}$$

Figure 3.10 General structure of glucosinolates.

Table 3.5 Glucosinolates and related isothiocyanates

Glucosinolates	Isothiocyanates
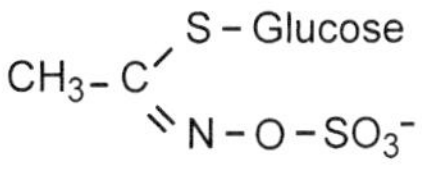 $CH_3-C(=N-O-SO_3^-)-S-Glucose$ Methylglucosinolate (=Glucocapparin)	$CH_3-N=C=S$ Methylisothiocyanate
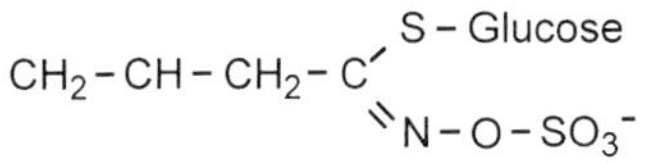 $CH_2-CH-CH_2-C(=N-O-SO_3^-)-S-Glucose$ Allylglucosinolate(=Sinigrin)	$CH_2-CH-CH_2-N=C=S$ Allylisothiocyanate
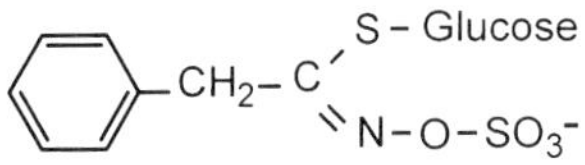 $C_6H_5-CH_2-C(=N-O-SO_3^-)-S-Glucose$ Benzylglucosinolate (=Glucotropaeolin)	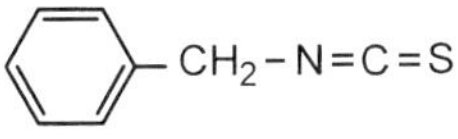 $C_6H_5-CH_2-N=C=S$ Benzylisothiocyanate
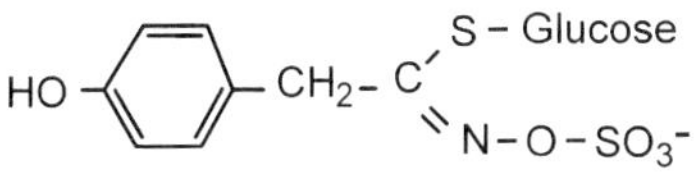 $HO-C_6H_4-CH_2-C(=N-O-SO_3^-)-S-Glucose$ Hydroxybenzylglucosinolate (=Sinalbin)	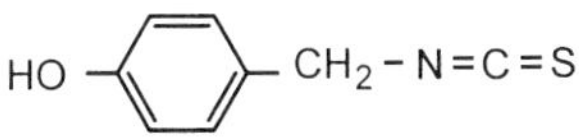 $HO-C_6H_4-CH_2-N=C=S$ 4-Hydroxybenzylisothiocyanate
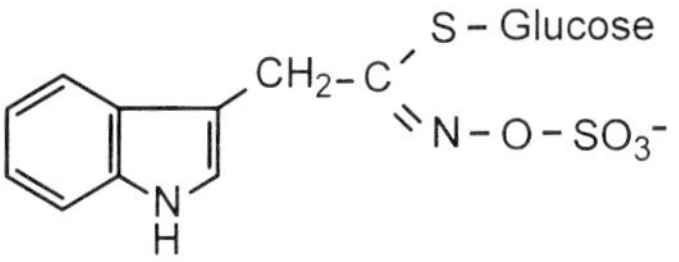 Indol-3-yl$-CH_2-C(=N-O-SO_3^-)-S-Glucose$ 3-Indolylmethylglucosinolate (=Glucobrassicin)	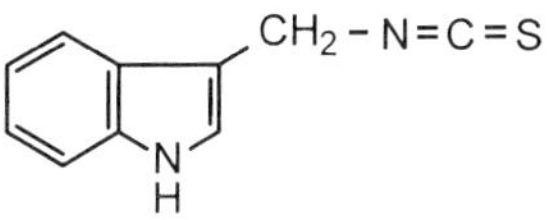 Indol-3-yl$-CH_2-N=C=S$ 3-Indolylmethylisothiocyanate

About 100 different glucosinolate structures are known. Presumably, all are derived biosynthetically from amino acids (Kutachek *et al.*, 1962; Underhill and Chisholm, 1964). Analogous to the biosynthesis of cyanogenic glucosides the carboxyl group is lost and the α-carbon is transformed into the central carbon of the glucosinolates (see section 3.3.3). The side chain R is therefore identical to the substituent of the α-carbon of the amino acid. Only seven glucosinolates correspond directly to protein amino acids. In addition to the five amino acids that are utilized for cyanogen biosynthesis (valine, leucine, isoleucine, phenylalanine and tyrosine), alanine and tryptophan also serve as precursors for glucosinolates. The large variety of additional glucosinolates is either a consequence of modification of the side chains, apparently taking place at the glucosinolate level, or has its origin in NPAAs that are produced from protein amino acids by chain-lengthening processes. For example, 2-phenylethylglucosinolate is synthesized from homophenylalanine, which, in turn, is derived from phenylalanine by chain elongation (Underhill *et al.*, 1962).

Glucosinolates synthesized from methionine by side chain elongation may have up to 11 methylene-groups introduced (Kjær and Schuster, 1972a, b). In addition, oxidation of the methionine sulfur to a sulfinyl or a sulfonyl group (Fig 3.11) (Dalgaard *et al.*, 1977) or the loss of the methylthio group accompanied by the introduction of a terminal double-bond can lead to further modifications. These modifications at the amino acid level alone result in four series of methionine-derived glucosinolates (Fig. 3.11). Additionally, glucosinolate side chains may be altered by hydroxylation, desaturation or methoxylation. Further diversifications are achieved by esterification or acylation of the hydroxyl groups of the side chain. This can be demonstrated by the pattern of glucosinolates present in *Arabidopsis thaliana*; 23 of the glucosinolates identified correspond to various benzoyl esters of the hydroxyl groups of the side chain (Hogge *et al.*, 1988). In the most comprehensive list of structures, Ettlinger and Kjær (1968) presented 74 different glucosinolates.

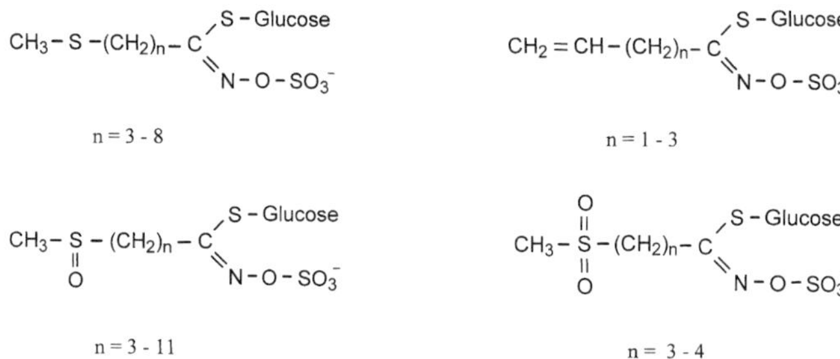

Figure 3.11 Glucosinolates from chain-elongated and oxidized methionine.

In contrast to cyanogenic glucosides, variations of the sugar moiety are not common in glucosinolates. All known glucosinolates contain glucose bound as a thioglucose derivative. The only variations known to occur within the sugar moiety are esterifications with several organic acids, e.g. sinapinic acid (Linscheid *et al.*, 1980; Sørensen, 1990); and, in a very few cases, additional glycosylation is observed. In *Hesperis matronalis*, various apiosyl derivatives of hydroxybenzyl- and dihydroxybenzylglucosinolates have been detected. Interestingly, these compounds with a substituted thioglucose moiety are not hydrolyzed by myrosinases. The fact that these compounds are protected against hydrolysis may be significant (Sørensen, 1990). Thus, in analogy to the diglucosidic cyanogens, these compounds might represent metabolites that can occur within the apoplastic space without being hydrolyzed, e.g. in the course of translocation processes.

3.3.3 Biosynthesis

The biosynthesis of glucosinolates includes three independent stages: firstly, the chain-elongation of amino acids; secondly, conversion of the precursor amino acid into glucosinolates; and, finally, further modifications of the resulting glucosinolates. Detailed information on glucosinolate biosynthesis has been given in the excellent review by Halkier (1999).

3.3.3.1 Side chain elongation of precursor amino acids

Elongation of amino acid side chains prior to glucosinolate biosynthesis has been studied in several plants. The mechanisms involved are believed to be similar to the formation of leucine from valine and acetate (Fig. 3.12). Through transamination, the amino acid is converted to the corresponding α-keto acid, followed by incorporation of an acetyl residue from acetyl coenzyme A (AcCoA). After isomerization, the compounds are oxidized. In the course of this NAD-mediated oxidation, the intermediate is decarboxylated. The α-keto acid produced is transaminated to yield an amino acid that, in comparison to the original compound, is elongated by a methylene group. The biochemical evidence for this scheme is based on the analysis of ^{14}C-labelled glucosinolates

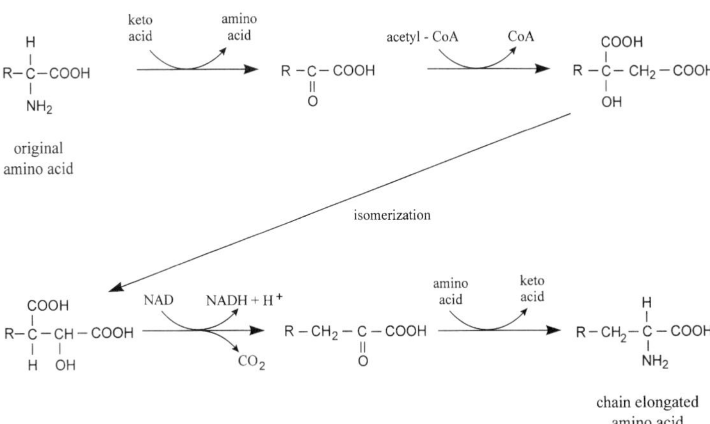

Figure 3.12 Side chain elongation of amino acids. In analogy to the conversion of valine to leucine, the methene group (CH_2) is introduced to various other amino acids, which subsequently serve as precursors of glucosinolates. Abbreviations: NAD, nicotinamide adenine dinucleotide; NADH, reduced NAD; CoA, co-enzyme A.

isolated from plants to which either ^{14}C-labelled protein amino acids or [2-^{14}C] acetate had been administered (Matsuo and Yamazaki, 1964; Chisholm and Wetter, 1964).

3.3.3.2 Biosynthesis of basic glucosinolates

In contrast to the biosynthesis of cyanogenic glucosides, the intermediates involved in the conversion of the amino acids to glucosinolates have not yet been unequivocally identified. However, *in vivo* studies with seedlings from various plants have indicated that *N*-hydroxyamino acids, nitro-compounds, oximes, thiohydroximates and desulphoglucosinolates are putative precursors of glucosinolates (for review see Underhill *et al.*, 1973; Larsen, 1981). Despite these data, the involvement of the nitro-compound in the biosynthetic pathway of glucosinolates is doubtful. It must be considered that, in analogy to cyanogenic glucoside biosynthesis, the occurrence of related nitro-compounds might correspond to artefactual side-products that arise only under experimental conditions.

Based on various experimental data, it is evident that aldoximes are the final products of the first set of reactions leading to glucosinolates (Bennett *et al.*, 1993; Du *et al.*, 1995a). Nevertheless, the subsequent steps in the biosynthetic pathway have not been elucidated; the intermediates between aldoximes and thiohydroximates have not been identified and no biochemical evidence is available for the potential enzymes involved in this transformation (Halkier, 1999). Moreover, the sulfur donor for the thiol sulfur is not known, although thioglucose can be excluded (Wetter and Chisholm, 1968). *In vivo* studies have revealed that several inorganic and organic sulfur compounds are incorporated into thiohydroximates. Since cysteine was incorporated most efficiently in these experiments, this amino acid is thought to be the sulfur donor (Wetter and Chisholm, 1968). Following the introduction of sulfur, the thiohydroximates produced are glucosylated by a soluble UDPG-dependent transferase. In the final step of glucosinolate biosynthesis, the resulting thioglucoside is sulfurylated by 3′-phosphoadenosine-5′-phosphosulfate (PAPS). The putative biosynthetic pathway of glucosinolates is outlined in Figure 3.13.

Conversion of amino acids to oximes. Independent studies of various glucosinolate-containing plants have indicated that, depending on the species, different enzyme systems are involved in conversion of the amino acids into aldoximes.

Analysis of microsomes isolated from young leaves of *Brassica napus* has established that chain-elongated amino acids are converted into the related aldoximes (Dawson *et al.*, 1993; Bennett *et al.*, 1993). As this reaction is not inhibited by carbon monoxide or other cytochrome inhibitors, nor by antisera toward NADPH-cytochrome P_{450}-reductase,

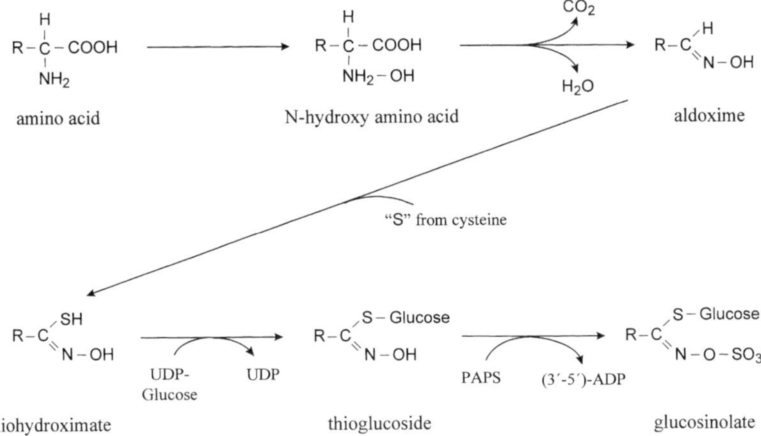

Figure 3.13 Biosynthesis of glucosinolates. Abbreviations: UDP, uridine diphosphate; UDPG, uridine diphosphate glucose; PAPS, 3′-phosphoadenosine-5′-phosphosulfate; ADP, adenosine diphosphate.

involvement of a cytochrome P_{450} could be excluded. However, inhibitors of flavin-dependent enzymes (e.g. copper salts, diphenyl iodonium sulfate) were effective in inhibiting aldoxime synthesis (Bennett *et al.*, 1993; Bennett *et al.*, 1995a). Based on these results, it is concluded that, at least in the biosynthesis of chain-elongated glucosinolates in *Brassica napus*, flavin-containing monooxygenases are involved. Further characterization using a variety of substrates has indicated that chain-elongated methionine homologues competitively inhibit oxidation of homophenylalanine. In contrast, the oxidation of chain-elongated methionine homologues was not influenced by the corresponding aromatic and aliphatic amino acids. Thus, in *Brassica napus*, at least two flavin-containing monooxygenases are involved in the biosynthesis of glucosinolates: one being responsible for the oxidation of elongated aromatic and aliphatic amino acids; and the other being specific for oxidation of chain-elongated methionine derivatives.

In contrast, the corresponding enzyme systems isolated from young seedlings of *Sinapis alba* and *Tropaeolum majus* have turned out to be cytochrome P_{450} monooxygenases (Du *et al.*, 1995a; Du and Halkier 1996). These enzymes have now been purified and cloned. These data and corresponding conclusions on the evolutionary relationships have been presented in detail by Bak and co-workers (1998). Based on the great homology to cytochrome $P_{450,\,tyr}$ involved in the biosynthesis of cyanogenic glucosides, it can be assumed that the reaction mechanisms of these two enzymes are very similar. Since the aldoxime synthesis involved in cyanogenic glucoside biosynthesis is perfomed via *N,N*-dihydroxyamino acids (see section 3.2.4.3), the aldoxime synthesis leading to glucosinolates, which is catalyzed by similar cytochrome monooxygenases from *S. alba* and *T. majus*, should also include *N,N*-dihydroxyamino acids as intermediates (Halkier, 1999).

In seedlings of Chinese cabbage (*Brassica campestris*), conversion of tryptophan into indole acetaldoxime, representing the first step in the biosynthesis of indole glucosinolates, is catalyzed by a membrane-bound peroxidase (Ludwig-Müller and Hilgenberg, 1988). The corresponding enzymatic activity was also detected in several species that do not contain glucosinolates; therefore, it was concluded that the enzyme involved in the biosynthesis of indole acetic acid in Chinese cabbage is also involved in indole acetaldoxime production (Ludwig-Müller *et al.*, 1990). Various comparative studies have demonstrated a good correlation between the content of indolyl glucosinolates and peroxidase activity on the one hand and the concentration of chain-elongated glucosinolates and the activity of flavin-containing monooxygenase on the other. These correlations suggest that aldoxime production in the biosynthesis of the two different groups of glucosinolates present in *Brassica* is catalyzed by distinct enzyme systems (Ludwig-Müller *et al.*, 1990; Bennett *et al.*, 1995b). It appears that the enzymes catalyzing conversion of amino acids into aldoximes within the glucosinolate pathway have evolved at least three times in a non-homologous manner. This has given rise to much speculation and discussion concerning the evolutionary origin of glucosinolate biosynthesis and the manner by which it was optimized (Bak *et al.*, 1998).

Glucosylation and sulfation of thiohydroximates. The final steps in glucosinolate biosynthesis are represented by the glucosylation of the sulfydryl group of the thiohydroximates and subsequent attachment of sulfate to the aldoxime function. Glucosylation is performed by a soluble UDPG: thiohydroximate glucosyltransferase. Corresponding enzymes from *Brassica juncea* (Jain *et al.*, 1990b), *Brassica napus* (Reed *et al.*, 1993) and *Arabidopsis thaliana* (Guo and Poulton, 1994) have been purified and characterized. Whilst these enzymes appear to be specific for thiohydroximates, they do not reveal a marked substrate-specificity with regard to differences in the side chain.

Little is known about sulfation of desulfoglucosinolates. The sulfate is introduced by PAPS. Only two corresponding sulfotransferases have been detected and purified: firstly, from cress seedlings, *Lepidium sativum* (Glendening and Poulton, 1988); and, secondly, from *Brassica juncea* cell cultures (Jain *et al.*, 1990a). Both of the enzymes investigated have very similar properties; they catalyze the sulfation of several different desulfoglucosinolates. Despite their low substrate-specificity for desulfoglucosinolates, they do not catalyze the transfer of sulfate to other potential substrates, e.g. flavonoids, and phenylacetaldoximes.

3.3.3.3 Side chain modification of basic glucosinolates

In general, side chain modifications of glucosinolates consist of hydroxylations and transformations of methylthio groups into methylsulfinyl groups, into methylsulfonyl groups, and, by elimination, into terminal double-bonds (Fig. 3.11). The enzymes involved in these modifications have not been identified. Based on comprehensive genetic studies, it can be deduced that chain modifications of aliphatic glucosinolates depend on three loci (Parkin *et al.*, 1994; Mithen *et al.*, 1995; Giamoustaris and Mithen, 1996): 1) the *Gsl-oxid* locus is responsible for the oxidation of methylthio groups; 2) a gene product of *Gsl-alk* catalyzes elimination of the sulfinyl group yielding alkenyl homologues; and 3) *Gsl-oh* corresponds to the hydroxylation of alkenyl glucosinolates. In spite of the great variation in aliphatic side chain structures, the genetic results indicate that the diversity is the result of genetic variations in only three major loci, *Gsl-oxid, Gsl-alk and Gsl-oh.*

Biochemical studies indicate that the enzyme that is responsible for the hydroxylation of 3-butenylglucosinolate to yield 2-hydroxy-3-butenylglucosinolate in *Brassica napus* corresponds to a cytochrome P_{450} monooxygenase (Rossiter *et al.*, 1990).

3.3.4 Mustard oil formation

All plants containing glucosinolates also contain enzymes that are capable of decomposing these compounds. These β-glucosidases are generally called myrosinases. The enzymatically-catalyzed loss of glucose to give thiohydroxamate-*O*-sulfonates is normally followed by a Loessen-type rearrangement, with a concerted loss of sulfate to yield isothiocyanates. However, not only isothiocyanates but also the corresponding nitriles are formed in greater or lesser amounts along with the concomitant liberation of elemental sulfur (Fig. 3.14). Nitrile formation is favoured by low pH values and is also promoted by ferrous ions (for review see Larsen, 1981).

Under postmortem conditions after tissue disruption, isothiocyanates are normally the predominant products, accompanied by lesser amounts of nitriles. In contrast, the aglycones of some glucosinolates (e.g. allyl, benzyl and 4-(methylthio)-butyl glucosinolates) undergo enzymatic degradation to thiocyanates. The mechanism for thiocyanate formation is still unknown. The enzyme that is presumably responsible for the corresponding rearrangement to yield thiocyanates has not been isolated or properly characterized. The presence of β-hydroxylated side chains

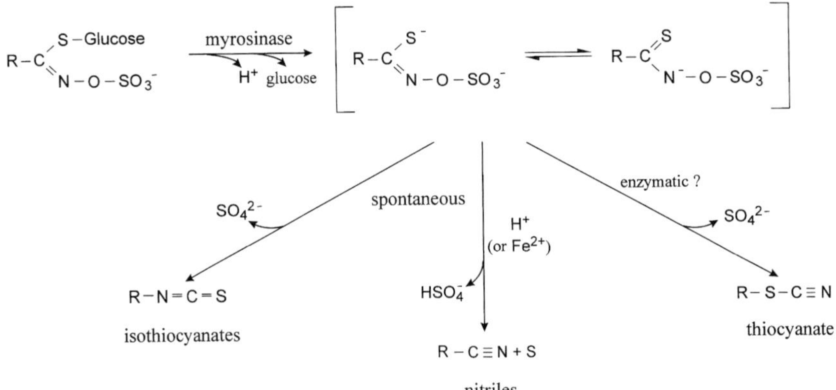

Figure 3.14 Mustard oil formation. After hydrolysis of glucosinolates, the unstable intermediates rearrange. In general, the main reaction products are isothiocyanates but nitriles and thiocyanates are also produced.

results in spontaneous cyclization of isothiocyanates to produce oxazolidine-2-thiones. A terminal double-bond in the side chain may result in the formation of epithionitriles, although for this reaction an epithiospecifier protein is necessary (Fig. 3.15).

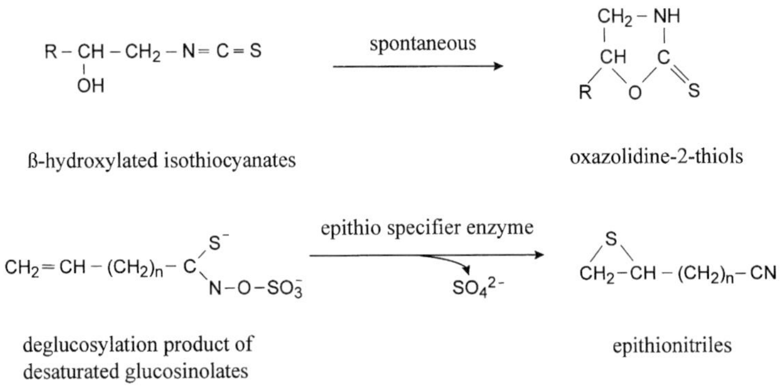

R-CH(OH)-CH$_2$-N=C=S — spontaneous → oxazolidine-2-thiols

ß-hydroxylated isothiocyanates

oxazolidine-2-thiols

CH$_2$=CH-(CH$_2$)$_n$-C(S$^-$)=N-O-SO$_3^-$ — epithio specifier enzyme, SO$_4^{2-}$ → CH$_2$-CH(S)-(CH$_2$)$_n$-CN

deglucosylation product of desaturated glucosinolates

epithionitriles

Figure 3.15 Formation of unusual toxic degradation products from glucosinolate decomposition products.

When tissues of glucosinolate-containing plants are injured and cells are disrupted, myrosinases and glucosinolates come into contact and mustard oil formation is initiated. This process has been graphically described as a 'mustard oil bomb' (Matile, 1980). Consequently, under *in vivo* conditions, hydrolytic enzymes and glucosinolates are efficiently partitioned. Glucosinolates are localized in vacuoles (Grob and Matile,

1979; Helmlinger *et al.*, 1983). In contrast, the localization of myrosinase has remained unclear. It has long been known that myrosinases are localized in special cells, so-called 'myrosin cells' (Guignard, 1980). Myrosin cells are scattered thoughout most tissues of glucosinolate-containing plants. As myrosin cells contain special granular structures, called myrosin grains, and the presence of myrosinase activity was detected in vacuolar fractions (Matile, 1980), it was concluded that myrosinase is localized inside the myrosin grains. The localization of myrosinase in myrosin cells has been confirmed by immunocytochemical studies. Although myrosinase is associated with the membrane surface of myrosin grains, it is localized in the cytosol (Thangstad *et al.*, 1990, 1991). Apart from the presence of myrosinase in the cytosol, enzyme activity can also be detected in cell walls, corresponding to an apoplastic localization (Matile, 1980).

Degradation of glucosinolates is initiated by the mixing of enzymes and substrates; however, mustard oil formation is accelerated by concomitant activation of the myrosinase by ascorbic acid, which is localized in the vacuoles of intact cells. Stimulation by ascorbic acid appears to be due to conformational changes of the enzyme, probably as a consequence of the reduction of disulfide bridging in the protein (Bones and Rossiter, 1996). Interestingly, various other proteins have been identified in relation to myrosinases, namely myrosinase-binding proteins, myrosinase-binding protein-related proteins and myrosinase-associated proteins (Falk *et al.*, 1995; Taipalensuu *et al.*, 1996). The localization and putative function of these proteins has not yet been clarified but it has been speculated that they are important for the activation process of myrosinase as cell integrity is destroyed (Geshi and Brandt, 1997).

Myrosinases are the only known *S*-glucosidases; they exhibit a pronounced substrate-specificity towards glucosinolates. The hydrolysis of other *S*- or *O*-glucosides is only poorly catalyzed by these enzymes (Lein, 1972; Durham and Poulton, 1990). Ascorbic acid activates most myrosinases at concentrations of about 1 mmol/l, whereas higher concentrations inhibit myrosinase activity (Ohtsuru and Hata, 1973). In the meantime, cDNAs of several myrosinases have been cloned and sequenced, e.g. from *Sinapis alba* (Xue *et al.*, 1992) *Brassica napus* (Thangstad *et al.*, 1993) and *Arabidopsis thaliana* (Chadchawan *et al.*, 1993). Myrosinases are encoded by multigene families; 14 genes have been estimated to be present in *Brassica napus* (Thangstad *et al.*, 1993). Recently, a myrosinase from *Sinapis alba* was crystallized (Burmeister *et al.*, 1997). This enzyme folds into a structure very similar to that of cyanogenic β-glucosidases from white clover (Barrett *et al.*, 1995), which supports the assumption that myrosinases have been evolved from ancestral *O*-glucosidases (Burmeister *et al.*, 1997).

3.3.5 Ecological significance of glucosinolates

In a manner similar to cyanogenic glucosides, glucosinolates can be considered as preformed defence chemicals that are activated in case of emergency. Many experimental data demonstrate the protective role of glucosinolates and their degradation products (for review see Louda and Mole,1991; Oleszek, 1995). The pungent smell and taste of glucosinolates reduce the palatability of plants that contain them to generalist herbivores, e.g. birds, slugs and insects (Chew, 1988; Glen *et al.*, 1990). Because isothiocyanates can easily penetrate biomembranes, they can interact with epidermal and mucosal skin, leading to painful irritations. In addition, isothiocyanates can lead to various complaints (e.g. bronchitis, pneumonia, gastroenteritis and kidney disorders). Consequently, high concentrations of glucosinolates and isothiocyanates are toxic to animals; although adapted specialists, such as the cabbage white butterfly (*Pieris brassicae*), can generally handle these toxins (Siemens and Mitchell-Olds, 1996). Indeed, for the imagines of these specialized butterflies, glucosinolates are attractants that stimulate oviposition. Interestingly, the oviposition stimulus has its origin in the glucosinolates rather than in the isothiocyanates. This was clearly demonstrated by application of allyl glucosinolate and allyl isothiocyanate to nonhost plants of the butterfly (Stadler, 1978).

In addition to their protective function against herbivores, glucosinolates and their degradation products are important factors in the interactions of plants with microorganisms. In most cases reported, the presence of glucosinolates enhances the resistance of the plant against numerous pests (Giamoustaris and Mithen, 1996; Mayton *et al.*, 1996). In *Brassica napus*, the content of glucosinolates significantly increased after being infected with various pathogens (Doughty *et al.*, 1991). However, the resistance is not caused by the glucosinolates themselves, but by their degradation products, i.e. the isothiocyanates (Mayton *et al.*, 1996; Manici *et al.*, 1997). In contrast to the numerous data on the protective function of glucosinolates against pathogens, there have also been contradictory findings: high glucosinolate contents in Chinese cabbage enhanced its susceptibility to *Plasmodiophora brassicae*, the causal organism of the clubroot disease. The reason for these contradictions is not understood and may be attributed to differences in the specificity of the pathogens involved.

Glucosinolates have been reported to have a significant allelopathic potential and are thought to be involved in the defence of ephemeral, unapparent plants or plant parts (Feeny, 1976). Several studies have indicated that, in analogy to other ecological effects, this allelopathic impact is caused by isothiocyanates rather than by the intact glucosinolates (Brown and Morra, 1995; Bialy *et al.*, 1990; Oleszek,

1995). In contrast, some studies have suggested that neither glucosinolates nor isothiocyanates have significant allelopathic potential (Choesin and Boerner, 1991). These differences may be explained by the use of different plant species for the evaluation of the allelopathic potential.

3.3.6 Glucosinolates and nutrition

Many glucosinolate-containing plants (e.g. cabbage, kale, broccoli, Brussels sprouts, cauliflower, and horseradish) are used by man as foods or spices. Thus, human metabolism is often affected by glucosinolates and their degradation products. These natural products are precursors of compounds with goitrogenic action in animals and humans. The active antithyroid compounds include: isothiocyanates as direct products of glucosinolate hydrolysis; and thiocyanate ions as final decomposition products. As mentioned above, rhodanide affects thyroid functions (van Etten, 1969). Moreover, in some plants, the goitrogenic effects of glucosinolates are strongly enhanced by specific degradation products, such as oxazolidine-2-thiones (e.g. progoitrin, glucoconringin). These compounds inhibit the uptake of iodine, which strongly affects thyroid function.

Based on their toxic properties and their pungent taste, glucosinolates are often classified as antinutritive compounds. However, the special taste of glucosinolates and their degradation products is often desired by the consumer. Thus, numerous glucosinolate-containing plants are extensively consumed and represent important vegetables. Generally, glucosinolate levels in fresh plant parts (stems, leaves), based on fresh weight, are 0.1% or less (van Etten *et al.*, 1976a, 1976b). These moderate concentrations do not create health problems when glucosinolate-containing vegetables or cole crops are consumed.

In addition to the negative properties of glucosinolates and their degradation products on human nutrition, these compounds also appear to have positive effects. The consumption of glucosinolate-containing vegetables apparently reduces the risk of developing cancer. Most evidence concerning the anticarcinogenic effects of glucosinolate hydrolysis products comes from studies in animals (for review see Verhoeven *et al.*, 1997; Jongen, 1996). However, epidemiological data concerning the cancer-preventive effects of *Brassica* vegetables, including cabbage, kale, broccoli, Brussels sprouts and cauliflower, also support this assumption (Verhoeven *et al.*, 1997). The exact mechanism by which glucosinolates and their degradation products are involved in cancer prevention is not completely understood. The anticarcinogenic effects of isothiocyanates appear to be mediated by tandem and cooperating mechanisms. The activation of carcinogens by cytochrome P_{450} is suppressed, probably by a combination of downregulation of enzyme levels and direct inhibition of their catalytic activities. These effects lower the level of carcinogens ultimately formed. In addition, these compounds promote the induction of phase II enzymes, such as glutathione transferases and NAD(P)H: quinone reductase, enzymes that detoxify any residual electrophilic metabolites generated by phase I enzymes. In this manner, phase II enzymes destroy the ability of these residual compounds to damage DNA (Zhang and Talalay, 1994; Zhang *et al.*, 1994). 4-Methylsulfinylbutyl isothiocyanate (sulforaphane), isolated from broccoli, was found to be a potent anticarcinogen. The isolated compound effectively induces phase II enzymes (Zhang *et al.*, 1992). In contrast to a protective action, a few isothiocyanates apparently have mutagenetic potential in mammalian cells and in bacteria (Verhoeven *et al.*, 1997). Nevertheless, as isothiocyanates block carcinogenesis by dual mechanisms and are present in substantial quantities in human diets, these agents are ideal candidates for the development of effective chemoprotection schemes for humans against cancer (Zhang and Talalay, 1994). Consequently, glucosinolate hydrolysis products are considered to be good candidates for creating 'functional foods' designed to prevent cancer, e.g. by enhancement of the concentration of 4-methylsulfinylbutyl isothiocyanate in cole plants.

In contrast to green plant parts, the concentration of total glucosinolates in seeds may be much higher. Levels up to 10% dry weight have been reported (Josefsson, 1973, van Etten *et al.*, 1974). Due to their general toxicity, these plant parts are not used for nutritional purposes. However, rapeseed meal, a side-product of rapeseed oil production, is used as fodder for various animals. Strong efforts have been made to breed *Brassica napus* varieties that contain small amounts of glucosinolates in the seeds. As classical breeding strategies have had only limited success, this goal may be achieved by gene technology, e.g. by knocking out the biosynthetic pathway.

3.3.7 Conclusion

In recent years, much scientific work has focused on the biochemistry of glucosinolates. Significant progress has been made in elucidating glucosinolate pathways and the steps of biosynthesis. However, due to the multiple enzyme systems present, i.e. both cytochrome P_{450} monooxygenases and flavine-dependent oxygenases that produce glucosinolates in different plants by distinct routes, and the numerous mechanisms of modifications of precursors and products of these biosynthetic pathways, many questions related to the biosynthesis of glucosinolates cannot yet be answered. In order to establish a solid basis for obtaining glucosinolate plants with the desired properties, much basic research is still required. It seems feasible to increase the level of 4-methylsulfinylbutyl glucosinolate in order to increase the anticarcinogenic potential and also to create seeds that contain only traces of glucosinolates. Unfortunately, and in contrast to the metabolism of cyanogenic glucosides, there is almost no information on the *in vivo* metabolism of glucosinolates. Related knowledge about the accumulation, translocation and turnover processes of glucosinolates is an important precondition for understanding those metabolic processes that will be modified in the corresponding transgenic plants. More knowledge about glucosinolates and their metabolism is required for the development of successful biotechnological approaches.

3.4 Nonprotein amino acids

Proteins of all organisms are based on the 20 common L-amino acids, generally referred to as protein amino acids. In some cases, these amino acids are modified post-translationally, e.g. the hydroxyproline moieties in several cell wall proteins. Apart from these protein amino acids, numerous other amino acids occur in plants. Some of them are known to be intermediates in various pathways of primary metabolism, e.g. ornithine as a metabolite in arginine biosynthesis, δ-aminolevulinic acid as a precursor of chlorophyll, and *O*-acetylserine as an *S*-acceptor to yield cysteine. In addition, about 900 other amino acids, which are not thought to be involved in primary metabolism, have been isolated from plants. These nonprotein amino acids (NPAAs) are regarded as typical secondary metabolites with corresponding ecological functions.

3.4.1 General aspects

In contrast to the comprehensive knowledge of cyanogenic glucosides and glucosinolates discussed above, far less is known about the biology and biochemistry of NPAAs. Based on phytochemical research, the structures of many NPAAs have been elucidated. In several cases, their toxicity for animals or microorganisms has been determined. Based on their toxicity and related antinutritive properties, NPAAs represent significant ecological factors that have the potential to interfere with the metabolism of herbivores and microorganisms.

Whereas much information is available about the biosynthesis of protein amino acids, little is known about the biosynthesis of NPAAs. Moreover, most of these studies are related to the metabolism of the NPAAs involved in primary metabolism. Few data have been published that deal with the biosynthesis of those NPAAs that are typical secondary plant products. In most cases, our knowledge is based on precursor studies. There is little information about the enzymes apparently involved in the biosynthesis of NPAAs.

Comprehensive reviews of these different aspects of NPAAs have been produced by Bell (1980), Fowden (1981), Rosenthal (1982, 1990); and Hunt (1985). During the last decade, few additional studies have been published. Consequently, this chapter gives a brief basic overview of important aspects of the biology and biochemistry of NPAAs and reviews some recently published studies concerning more detailed examination of the origin of these compounds.

3.4.2 Structures

Amino acids are characterized by the concurrent presence of an amino and a carboxyl group. In protein amino acids, the amino group is linked at the α-carbon, i.e. the carbon-2 atom of the acid. In NPAAs, the amino group can be attached to the β-C atom, e.g. in 3-alanine (see Fig. 3.16), or to the γ-C-atom, e.g. in 4-aminobutyric acid (see Fig. 3.16). Particular compounds may be found widely distributed within the families of the plant kingdom, e.g. homoserine, 4-aminobutyric acid (see Fig. 3.16), but, more generally, NPAAs have restricted distribution, frequently being found only within a closely-related group of plants, such as a genus or a few allied genera of a family. Comprehensive reviews on the structures of NPAAs have been published by Fowden (1981) and Bell (1980).

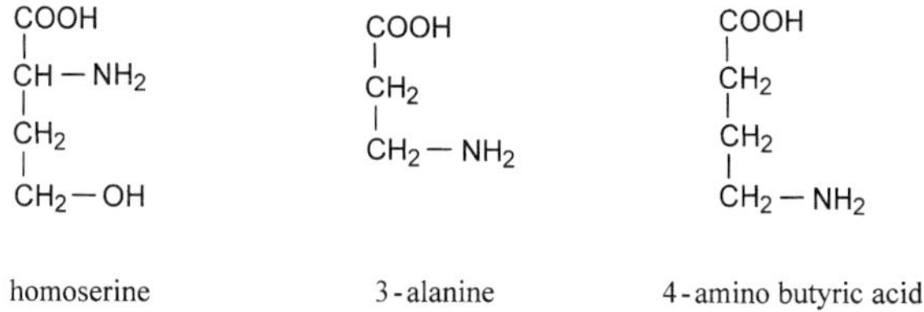

Figure 3.16 Stuctures of simple nonprotein amino acids.

Some NPAAs are simple homologues of protein amino acids. Such compounds have similar properties, sometimes mimicking the behaviour of standard amino acids and sometimes acting as metabolic antagonists or inhibitors. Structural differences other than those of homology are also consistent with analogue behaviour. Related isostere compounds may result from replacement of one atom or group of atoms by another of similar size and polarity. Many such compounds have been isolated and characterized, for example, canavanine is an effective analogue of arginine (Fig. 3.17).

In the following paragraphs, a brief overview of the structural variety of NPAAs is given by presenting selected structural groups of these natural products.

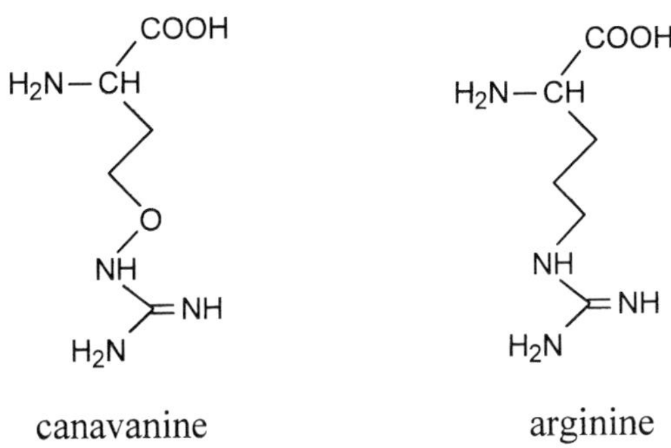

Figure 3.17 Structure of canavanine, an analogue of arginine.

3.4.2.1 Acidic amino acids

Most of these compounds have two carboxyl groups, as in the protein amino acids, aspartic and glutamic acid. Both aspartic and glutamic acid are universally distributed as protein constituents. However, the majority of acidic NPAAs are structurally related only to glutamic acid or to glutamine. The simplest types are hydroxylated or methylated derivatives of glutamic acid, e.g. γ-hydroxy-glutamic acid present in *Phlox decussata* and certain ferns, and γ-methylglutamic acid (Fig. 3.18) isolated from *Phyllitis scolopendrium*. Another group of amino acids is related to aromatic amino acids that possess two carboxyl groups. These compounds, characteristic for some members of the Iridaceae and Resedaceae, contain a carboxyl group attached to a phenyl ring in the *meta*-position. As an example, 3-carboxyphenylalanine is presented in Figure 3.18. A third group of dicarboxylic amino acids, such as *S*-carboxyethyl-cysteine (Fig. 3.18) and *S*-carboxyisopropyl-cysteine from various *Acacia* and *Albizia* species, corresponds to *S*-substituted cysteines.

3.4.2.2 Imino acids

Proline is the only protein imino acid. In some proteins, proline is post-translationally hydroxylated to hydroxyproline. Such modifications occur

γ-methyglutamic acid

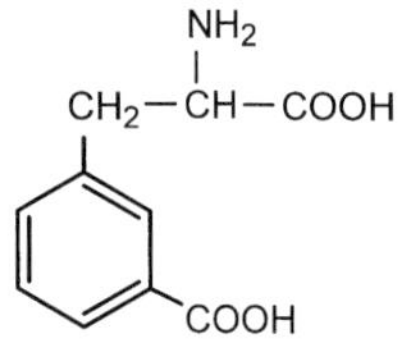

3-carboxyphenylalanine

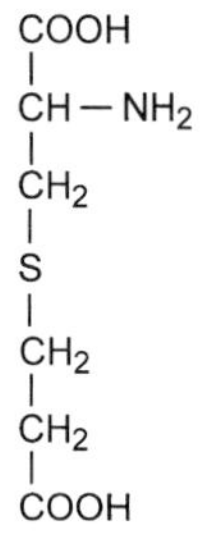

S-carboxyethylcysteine

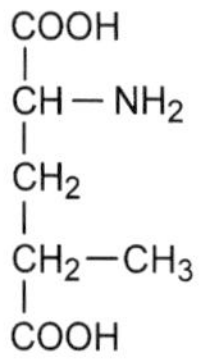

Figure 3.18 Structures of acidic nonprotein amino acids.

to a large extent in hydroxyproline-rich glycoproteins (HPRG), which are involved in cell wall construction (Moore *et al.*, 1991). Apart from the presence of proline in proteins, this amino acid also occurs in significant concentrations in various tissues. In particular, proline is accumulated as a compatible solute under water stress (Yoshiba *et al.*, 1997). The lower homologue of proline, azetidine-2-carboxylic acid (Fig. 3.19) was first isolated from various members of the Liliaceae, e.g. *Convallaria majalis*

azetidine-2-carboxylic acid

nicotianamine

proline

pipecolic acid

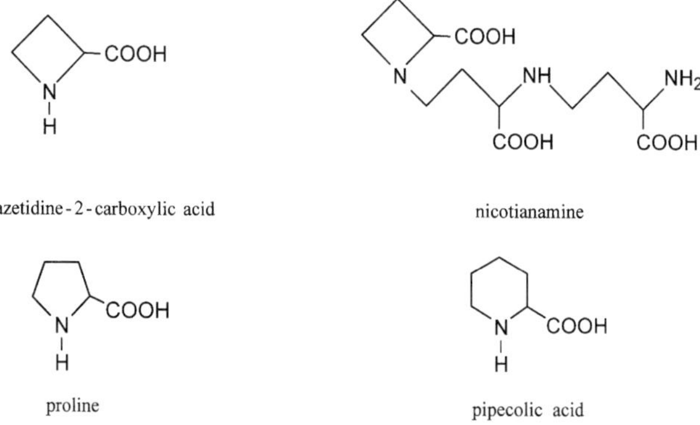

Figure 3.19 Structure of imino acids.

and *Polygonatum multiflorum*. A certain derivative, nicotianamide, is an important chelator that is required for iron uptake and iron metabolism (Pich and Scholz, 1993; Stephan *et al.*, 1996). The corresponding six-atom *N*-heterocyclic compound, pipecolic acid, has also been detected in several plants. Various derivatives of these basic structures have been isolated and characterized (for review see Fowden, 1981).

3.4.2.3 γ-Substituted alanines

γ-Substituted alanines comprise a heterogeneous group of NPAAs. These compounds are characterized chemically by the attachment of a phenyl group or a heterocyclic ring to the β-carbon atom of alanine. Whereas only four protein amino acids of this series occur (phenylalanine, tyrosine, tryptophan and histidine), several hundred NPAAs are known. In addition to the 3-carboxyphenyl-alanine, already mentioned as an acidic amino acid, an analogous 3-aminomethylphenyl-alanine, (Fig. 3.20) has also been

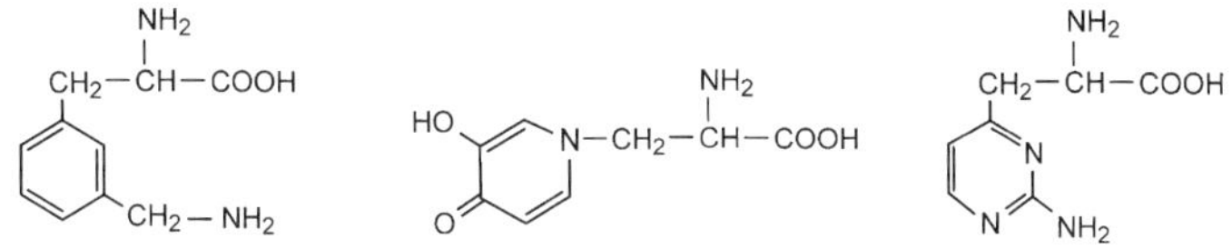

3-aminomethylphenylalanine mimosine lathyrine

Figure 3.20 Structures of β-substituted nonprotein amino acids.

isolated. Many hydroxylated and methylated derivatives of the basic structures have been described (Bell, 1980; Fowden, 1981). In addition, a large number of alanine derivatives with heterocyclic β-substitutions are known, including mimosine and lathyrine (Fig. 3.20). Mimosine was first isolated from *Mimosa pudica*. In *Leucaena leucocephala*, this amino acid constitutes about 2–5% the dry matter of the leaf.

3.4.2.4 Branched-chain and cyclopropyl amino acids

Various amino acids containing a cyclopropyl residue have been found in members of the Sapindaceae, Hippocastanaceae and Aceraceae. The same plants often contain a range of C_6- and C_7-amino acids, with a noncyclic branched carbon skeleton. The position of branching suggests possible biogenetic relationships to cyclopropane-containing amino acids. Variation of the basic structures mentioned in Figure 3.21 is achieved by different chain lengths and by the introduction of double- and triple-bonds (Fowden, 1981).

In contrast to the restricted occurrence of the secondary metabolites mentioned above, all plants contain 1-amino-cyclopropane-1-carboxylic acid. This amino acid is the precursor of ethylene. In the course of the biosynthesis of this gaseous phytohormone, 1-aminocyclopropane-1-carboxylic acid is oxidized and decomposed to yield ethylene, HCN and water (John, 1997).

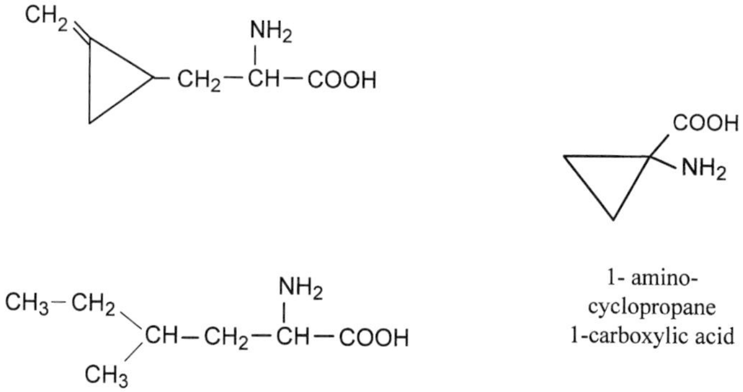

CH_2 (methylenecyclopropyl)–$CH_2-CH(NH_2)-COOH$

$CH_3-CH_2-CH(CH_3)-CH_2-CH(NH_2)-COOH$

(cyclopropane with COOH and NH_2)

1- amino-
cyclopropane
1-carboxylic acid

Figure 3.21 Structures of branched-chain and cyclopropyl nonprotein amino acids.

3.4.3 Biosynthesis and metabolism

Relatively little work has been reported on the biosynthesis of NPAAs. In principle, there are two different possibilities. Firstly, a protein amino acid is modified, e.g. by the introduction of various functional groups or, secondly, a particular α-keto acid is transaminated to yield the corresponding amino acid. The chain-elongation process described previously for amino acids that are precursors for certain glucosinolates (see Fig. 3.13, section 3.3.3.1) represents an intermediate mechanism. As mentioned previously, most of our knowledge about the biosynthesis of NPAAs is based on precursor studies. Little specific information is available concerning the pathways and enzymes involved. Moreover, our picture of the biosynthesis of NPAAs becomes even less clear due to the finding that similar, or even identical, amino acids are thought to be synthesized by different processes in different plants.

3.4.3.1 Precursor studies

Based on their close structural relationship to glutamic acid, γ-hydroxyglutamic acid and γ-methylglutamic acid may be regarded as simple derivatives of glutamic acid. However, it has been shown that these amino acids are not derived from glutamic acid by simple hydroxylation or methylation, respectively. A simple hypothesis explaining the formation of γ-substituted glutamic acids has been advanced. Two molecules of pyruvate condense to yield the α-keto acid corresponding to γ-hydroxy-γ-methylglutamic acid. Transamination could then be envisaged as the final step in the formation of the related amino acid. However, this biosynthetic pathway must be excluded in the legume, *Gleditsia triacanthos*. Precursor studies using various ^{14}C-labelled amino acids have clearly shown that γ-methylglutamic acid is derived from leucine in *Gleditsia*. Seemingly, one of the terminal methyl groups of leucine is oxidized to a carboxyl group (Peterson and Fowden, 1972).

The carbon skeleton common to C_6-cyclopropyl amino acids suggests an origin from either leucine or isoleucine by ring closure mechanisms. At present, no experimental evidence is available to confirm this hypothesis. However, the finding that isoleucine is the biogenetic precursor of branched-chain amino acids (Fig. 3.21), believed to be closely related to cyclopropyl amino acids, supports the theory that cyclopropane amino acids are also derived from this amino acid. Application of ^{14}C-amino acid precursors to *Aesculus californica* revealed that, in this plant, branched-chain amino acids (e.g. 2-amino-4-methylhex-4-enoic acid) are indeed derived from isoleucine. In addition, ^{14}C-labelled acetate was also incorporated into these amino acids (Fowden and Mazelis, 1971). Obviously, by analogy to the processes mentioned for chain-lengthening of glucosinolate precursors (section 3.3.3.1, Fig. 3.12), branched-chain amino acids are synthesized by lengthening α-keto-β-methylvaleric acid, the α-keto acid derived from isoleucine by transamination. In contrast, 1-aminocyclopropane-1-carboxylic acid, the precursor of ethylene, is synthesized from methionine (Yang and Hoffmann, 1984).

3.4.3.2 Enzymatic approaches

Little information is available on the enzymes involved in the biosynthesis of NPAAs. This chapter presents new data concerning the synthase involved in lathyrine biosynthesis, cysteine synthase, which catalyzes the formation of β-(pyrazole-1-yl)-alanine, and the metabolism of canavaline.

In contrast to the limited information available concerning the biosynthesis of most other NPAAs, comprehensive knowledge of the biosynthesis of lathyrine (Fig. 3.20) exists. Precursor studies have shown that all atoms of the alanine side chain of the pyrimidyl amino acid, lathyrine, are derived as one unit from serine. Furthermore, isotope incorporation studies have identified the precursor of the pyrimidine moiety as 2-amino-4-carboxypyrimidine. Studies with enzymic extracts of *Lathyrus tingitanus* seedlings have demonstrated the presence of a pyridoxal phosphate-dependent lathyrine synthase that simultaneously decarboxylates the pyrimidine precursor and alanylates the heterocycle in C-4 position. Unlike a number of other plant synthases catalyzing the formation of heterocyclic β-substituted alanines, lathyrine synthase requires serine and not *O*-acetylserine, as a substrate. The action of this synthase has been successfully modelled in a non-enzymic pyridoxal-catalysed reaction in the presence of Al^{3+} (Brown and Mohamad, 1990). The enzyme was partially purified (150-fold) by using an assay in which the activity of the lathyrine synthase was determined by incorporation of

[3-^{14}C]-serine into lathyrine. In addition to a requirement for pyridoxal 5-monophosphate, the enzyme is stimulated by biotin and inhibited by avidin. Lathyrine synthase exhibits a bimodal pH optimum curve with a major peak at pH 4.5 and a secondary peak at pH 7.2 (Brown and Mohamad, 1994). ^{14}C-Labelling experiments in *Lathyrus tingitanus* indicate that the serine acceptor, 2-amino-4-carboxypyrimidine, is derived from uracil and that carboxylation precedes amination (Brown and Turan, 1995).

As mentioned above, serine is the donor for the alanine residue of lathyrine (Brown and Mohamad, 1990). In contrast, the alanine side chain of mimosine (Fig. 3.20) and related derivatives (e.g. pyrazole-1-yl-alanine) has its origin in *O*-acetylserine. The enzyme responsible for the transfer of the alanine residue was named pyrazolealanine synthase and corresponds to an *O*-acetylserine lyase. A corresponding reaction is involved in cysteine biosynthesis. In this example, the serine residue is transferred to sulfide by the action of an *O*-acetylserine-(thio)-lyase, called cysteine synthase. Characterization of an enzyme from *Leucaena leucocephala*, putatively involved in mimosine biosynthesis, provided evidence that mimosine synthase corresponds to a cysteine synthase (Ikegami *et al.*, 1990). *In vitro* studies of the formation of pyrazole-1-yl-alanine revealed that in watermelons (*Citrullus vulgaris*) this NPAA is also generated by cysteine synthase (Noji *et al.*, 1993). The cDNA for cysteine synthase was cloned and, together with an expression vector driven by the lacZ promoter, it was overexpressed in *E. coli*. To confirm the responsibility of cysteine synthase for the formation of pyrazole-derived NPAAs *in vivo*, pyrazole and serine or *O*-acetylserine were applied to the transformed *E. coli* culture. The production of pyrazole-1-yl-alanine by the culture unequivocally confirmed that the cloned cysteine synthase of watermelon catalyzes the formation of pyrazole-1-yl-alanine. This finding suggests that pyrazolealanine synthase is identical to cysteine synthase in plants of the Cucurbitaceae (Noji *et al.*, 1993; Saito *et al.*, 1997).

In addition to compounds related to mimosine, other NPAAs are synthesized by transfer of an alanine residue catalyzed by cysteine synthase, e.g. the formation of isoxazolin-5-on-2yl-alanine in *Lathyrus sativus* (Ikegami *et al.*, 1993). Moreover, partial purification of cysteine synthase from *Allium tuberosum* revealed that this enzyme also catalyzes the formation of cysteine derivatives, such as *S*-allylcysteine (Ikegami *et al.*, 1993). The various aspects of the formation of NPAAs by cysteine synthase are presented by Noji *et al.* (1993) and Ikegami and Murakoshi (1994).

3.4.3.3 Metabolism

Information about the metabolism of NPAAs is rare. As various NPAAs are accumulated to high levels, they are sometimes regarded as storage compounds for reduced nitrogen; in *Dioclea megacarpa*, up to 8% of the dry weight of the seeds corresponds to canavanine. In other legumes, azetidine-2-carboxylic acid or mimosine content may exceed 5% dry weight (Rosenthal, 1991).

The nitrogen of canavanine, which is accumulated in the seeds of jack beans (*Canavalia ensiformis*) to high levels, is reintroduced into basic nitrogen metabolism during seedling development (Rosenthal *et al.*, 1988; Rosenthal and Berge, 1989). Using ^{14}C-canavanine, which was applied to *Canavalia* cotyledons, it could be shown that canavanine is translocated from the cotyledons into the growing tissue (Rosenthal and Rhodes, 1984). Before the nitrogen of canavanine can be reintroduced into the general nitrogen metabolism of the seedling, translocation of the amino acid from the seeds into the primary leaves takes places. Canavanine is hydrolyzed by an arginase to yield canaline and urea. Whereas urea is degraded quite rapidly (Rosenthal and Rhodes, 1984), the poisonous canaline is either detoxified by the formation of a stable oxime between canaline and glyoxylic acid (Rosenthal *et al.*, 1989) or is cleaved by canaline reductase. This NADPH-dependent enzyme catalyzes the reductive cleavage of canaline to homoserine and ammonia (Rosenthal, 1992). By this pathway, all nitrogen atoms previously incorporated into canavanine are reintroduced into general nitrogen metabolism. An analogous storage function of nonprotein is also postulated for azetidine-2-carboxylic acid, for mimosine or for δ-acetylornithine in the rhizomes of *Bistorta bistortoides*. The last compound accounts for more than 12% of the total nitrogen of the rhizomes of *B. bistortoides* (Lipson *et al.*, 1996). In contrast to the information relating to the potential storage function NPAAs, no further data are available concerning their general metabolism.

3.4.4 *Ecological aspects*

There is no doubt that the ecological significance of toxic NPAAs is related to their protective function. These compounds are potent toxicants, capable of protecting plants against predation and disease and improving a plant's ability to compete for resources with other plants. Due to their structural homology to primary amino acids, NPAAs may strongly influence basic metabolism. The inhibitory effects of such structural analogues can be very intense and unusual, e.g. the toxic effects of mimosine. Mules and horses that consume mimosine-containing plant parts often lose their manes and the hair of their tails. However, mimosine damage is limited to active hair growth and does not affect hair that has already been produced (for review see Rosenthal, 1991).

As outlined above, numerous amino acids are highly toxic to most organisms. As a result, the plant part that accumulates these toxins is protected against herbivory. However, certain animal species can overcome the toxic property by detoxifying or otherwise dealing with the toxin. A graphic example of such specialization is given by the bruchid beetle, *Caryedes brasiliensis*, which in Costa Rica feeds exclusively on seeds of *Dioclea megacarpa*. As mentioned previously, the seeds of this leguminous plant accumulate high levels of canavanine. Canavanine is a structural analogue of arginine (Fig. 3.17). This structural similarity accounts for the ability of arginyl-t-RNA synthase to activate and attach canavanine to the t-RNA that normally carries arginine to the protein assembly site. Replacement of arginine in a protein by the less basic amino acid, canavanine, affects interactions between the amino acid residues. This results in alteration or even disruption of the tertiary and quarternary structures of the proteins, which are essential for their normal functions. The metabolic consequences of the uptake of canavanine are discussed in detail by Rosenthal (1991). Thus, canavanine corresponds to a general toxin. However, in the course of evolution, *Caryedes brasiliensis* became adapted to this toxin. The specificity of the arginyl-t-RNA-synthase of the specialized bruchid beetle is significantly higher than corresponding enzymes of other organisms, and this enzyme is able to distinguish perfectly between arginine and canavanine.

The toxic effects of NPAAs are numerous and mostly still unknown. Nevertheless, it is generally accepted that accumulation of toxic NPAAs makes the plant parts in which these compounds are accumulated less palatable to generalist herbivores. This apparently results in protection against such animals. Although this is a commonly observed phenomenon, far more experimental evidence is required to establish the validity and basis of these empirical observations.

In addition to their significance for protection of plants from herbivores, NPAAs may be important factors for defence against pathogens and in allelopathy. Based on the structural analogy mentioned above, NPAAs may also affect the metabolism of microorganisms. In this manner, these secondary plant products also have significance for defence against pathogens. Unfortunately, few data have been reported on the involvement of NPAAs in resistance mechanisms. Mimosine, isolated from seeds of *Leucaena leucocephala*, caused drastic inhibition of the growth of various fungi. This antifungal effect was detectable even when crude extracts of *Leucaena* seeds were diluted tenfold (Murugesan and Radha, 1994). No comprehensive studies of particular plant-pathogen systems are available, nor is there much information concerning the fungitoxicity of common NPAAs.

Furthermore, as mentioned previously, little information is available about the allelopathic effects of NPAAs. 3-Isoxazolin-5-on-2-ylalanine has been shown to be the active allelopathic compound in root exudates of pea seedlings. When germinated in the presence of this amino acid, the roots of grasses and of *Lactuca sativa* were significantly affected; a pronounced reduction in root length and necroses of the root tips was observed (Schenk and Werner, 1991). In contrast to the interactions between plants and herbivores or plants and pathogens, a general precondition for interaction between plants is the necessity for exudation of the active compounds. If NPAAs indeed have allelopathic effects, screening root exudates for potential allelochemicals should result in the detection of active amino acids.

3.4.5 Perspectives

As mentioned previously, much new research is required to gain further insight into the biology and biochemistry of nonprotein amino acids. Considering the strong competitive effects of nonprotein amino acids on enzymes and receptors, these compounds could become valuable tools for analysis of biochemical reactions as well as for development of new medicaments. This possibility has been impressively demonstrated by the use of azaserine and methionine sulfoximine, two amino acids which specifically inhibit glutamate synthetase and glutamine synthase, respectively (Wang and Nicholas, 1985). By inhibiting the refixation of ammonia produced during photorespiration, new approaches for the elucidation of the complex photorespiratory pathway were devised (Berger *et al.*, 1986).

The utilization of nonprotein amino acids in medical research, e.g. the use of various glutamine derivatives for investigation of kainate-receptor-mediated cell death (Brauner-Osborne *et al.*, 1997), and their increasing use in studies of oligopeptide chemistry and in the development of new pharmaceutical applications (Kreuzfeld *et al.*, 1996) underscores the requirement for detailed and comprehensive information about their biology and biochemistry.

Acknowledgements

I wish to thank Dr Eric E. Conn and Dr David S. Seigler for critical reading of the manuscript and helpful suggestions related to the scientific content, as well as for linguistic improvements. I also thank Dr Birger L. Møller, Dr David S. Seigler and Dr Barbara A. Halkier for access to their manuscripts before publication.

References

Adewusi, S.R.A. (1990) Turnover of dhurrin in green *Sorghum* seedlings. *Plant Physiol.*, **94** 1219-24.

Akanji, A.O. (1994) Cassava intake and the risk of diabetes in humans. *Acta Horticulture*, **375** 349-59.

Aschhoff, H.J. and Pfeil, U. (1970) Auftrennung und Charakterisierung der Isoenzyme von D-Hydroxynitril-Lyase (D-Oxynitrilase) aus Mandeln. *Hoppe-Seyler's Z. Physiol. Chem.*, **351** 818-26.

Bak, S., Nielsen, H.L. and Halkier, B.A. (1998) The presence of CYP79 homologues in glucosinolate-producing plants shows evolutionary conservation of the enzymes in the conversion of amino acids to aldoxime in the biosynthesis of cyanogenic glucosides and glucosinolates. *Plant Mol. Biol.*, **38** 725-34.

Barnes, H.J., Arlotto, M.P. and Waterman, M.R. (1991) Expression and enzymatic activity of recombinant cytochrome P_{450} 17-α-hydroxylase in *Escherichia coli. Proc. Nat. Acad. Sci. USA*, **88** 5597-601.

Barrett, T., Suresh, C.G., Tolley, S.P., Sodson, E.J. and Hughes, M.A. (1995) The crystal structure of cyanogenic β-glucosidase from white clover, a family 1-glycosyl hydrolase. *Structure*, **3** 951-60.

Becker, W. and Pfeil, E. (1966) Über das Flavinenzym D-Oxynitrilase. *Biochem. Z.*, **346** 301-22.

Bediako, M.K.B., Tapper, B.A. and Pritchard, G.G. (1981) Metabolism, synthetic site and translocation of cyanogenic glycosides in cassava, in *Tropical Root Crops: Research Strategies for the 1980s* (eds. E.R. Terry, K.A. Oduro and F. Caveness), International Development Research Centre, Ottawa, Canada, pp. 143-48.

Bell, E.A. (1980) Nonprotein amino acids in plants, in *Encyclopaedia of Plant Physiology*, *Vol. 8*, Secondary Plant Products. Springer Verlag, Heidelberg, pp. 401-32.

Bennett, R.N., Donald, A.M., Dawson, G.W., Hick, A.J. and Wallsgrove, R.M. (1993) Aldoxime-forming microsomal enzyme systems involved in the biosynthesis of glucosinolates in oilseed rape leaves. *Plant Physiol.*, **102** 1307-12.

Bennett, R.N., Ludwig-Müller, J., Kiddle, G., Hilgenberg, W. and Wallsgrove, R.M. (1995a) Developmental regulation of aldoxime formation in seedlings and mature plants of Chinese cabbage (*Brassica campestris* sp. *Pekinensis*) and oilseed rape (*Brassica napus*): glucosinolate and IAA biosynthetic enzymes. *Planta*, **114** 239-44.

Bennett, R.N., Dawson, G.W., Hick, A.J. and Wallsgrove, R.M. (1995b) Glucosinolate biosynthesis: further characterization of the aldoxime-forming microsomal monooxygenases in oilseed rape leaves. *Plant Physiol.*, **109** 299-305.

Berger, M.G., Sprengart, M.L., Kusnan, M. and Fock, H.P. (1986) Ammonia fixation via glutamine synthetase and glutamate synthase in the crassulacean acid metabolism plant, *Cissus quadrangularis. Plant Physiol.*, **81** 356-60.

Bernays, E.A., Chapman, R.F., Leather, E.M., McCaffery, A.R. and Modder, W.W.D. (1977) The relationship of *Zonocerus variegatus* with cassava. *Bull. Ent. Res.*, **67** 391-404.

Bialy, Z., Oleszek, W., Lewis, J. and Fenwick, G.R. (1990) Allelopathic potential of glucosinolates (mustard oil glycosides) and their degradation products against wheat. *Plant Soil*, **129** 277-82.

Blumenthal, G.S., Hendrickson, H.R., Abrol, Y.P. and Conn, E.E. (1968) Cyanide metabolism in higher plants. *J. Biol. Chem.*, **243** 5302-307.

Bokanga, M. (1994) Distribution of cyanogenic potential in cassava germplasm. *Acta Horticulture*, **375** 117-23.

Bokanga, M., Ekanayake, I.J., Dixon, A.G.O. and Porto, M.C.M. (1994) Genotype-environment interactions for cyanogenic potential in cassava. *Acta Horticulture*, **375** 131-39.

Bones, A.M. and Rossiter, J.T. (1966) The myrosinase-glucosinolate system, its organisation and biochemistry. *Physiologia Plantarum*, **97** 194-208.

Bough, W.A. and Gander, J.E. (1971) Exogenous L-tyrosine metabolism and dhurrin turnover in *Sorghum* seedlings. *Phytochemistry*, **10** 67-77.

Bové, C. and Conn, E.E. (1961) Metabolism of aromatic compounds in higher plants. II. Purification and properties of the oxynitrilase of *Sorghum vulgare*. *J. Biol. Chem.*, **236** 207-10.

Braekman, L.D., Daloze, D. and Pasteels, J.M. (1982) Cyanogenic and other glucosides in a Neo-Guinean bug. *Leptococris isolata*. *Biochem. System.*, **10** 97-130.

Brauner-Osborne, H., Nielson, B., Stensbol, T.B., Johanson, T.N. and Skjaerbaek, N. (1997) Molecular pharmacology of 4-substituted glutamic acid analogues at ionotropic and metatropic excitatory amino acid receptors. *Eur. J. Pharmacol.*, **335** R1-R3.

Brinker, A.M. and Seigler, D.S. (1992) Determination of cyanide and cyanogenic glycosides, in *Modern Methods of Plant Analysis New Series*, Vol. 13, Plant Toxin Analysis (eds. H.F. Linskens and J.F. Jackson), Springer, Berlin, pp. 359-81.

Brown, E.G. and Mohamad, J. (1990) Biosynthesis of lathyrine: a novel synthase activity. *Phytochemistry*, **29** 3117-22.

Brown, E.G. and Mohamad, J. (1994) Partial purification and properties of lathyrine synthase. *Phytochemistry*, **36** 285-87.

Brown, E.G. and Turan, Y. (1995) Pyrimidine metabolism and secondary product formation: biogenesis of albizziine, 4-hydroxyhomoarginine and 2,3-diaminopropanoic acid. *Phytochemistry*, **40** 763-71.

Brown, P.D. and Morra, M.J. (1995) Glucosinolate-containing plant tissues as bioherbicides. *J Agric. Food Chem.*, **43** 3070-74.

Burmeister, W.P., Cottaz, S., Driguez, H., Iori, R., Palmieri, S. and Henrissat, B. (1997) The crystal structures of *Sinapis alba* myrosinase and a covalent glycosyl-enzyme intermediate provide insights into the substrate recognition and active-site machinery of an *S*-glycosidase. *Structure*, **5** 663-75.

Butler, G.W., Baily, R.W. and Kennedy, L.D. (1965) Studies on the glucosidase 'linamarase'. *Phytochemistry*, **4** 369-81.

Castric, P.A., Farnden, K.F. and Conn, E.E. (1972) Cyanide metabolism in higher plants. 5. The formation of asparagine from β-cyanoalanine. *Arch. Biochem. Biophys.*, **152** 62-69.

Chadchawan, S., Bishop, J., Thangstad, O.P., Bones, A.M., Mitchell-Olds, T. and Bradley, D. (1993) *Arabidopsis* cDNA sequence encoding myrosinase. *Plant Physiol.*, **103** 671-72.

Chen, C.C., Chen, Y.P., Hsu, H.Y., Lee, K.H., Tani, S. and McPhail, A.T. (1985) Bauhinin, a new nitrile glucoside from *Bauhinia championii*. *J. Nat. Prod.*, **48** 933-37.

Cheng, I.P. and Poulton, J.E. (1993) Cloning of cDNA of *Prunus serotina* (R)-(+)-mandelonitrile lyase and identification of a putative FAD-binding site. *Plant Cell Physiol.*, **34** 1139-43.

Chew, F.S. (1988) Biological effects of glucosinolates, in *Biologically Active Natural Products Potenial Use in Agriculture* (ed. H.G. Cutler), American Chemical Society Press, Washington, pp. 155-81.

Chew, M.Y. (1973) Rhodanese in higher plants. *Phytochemistry*, **12** 2365-67.

Choesin, D.N. and Boerner, E.J. (1991) Allyl isothiocyanate release and the allelopathic potential of *Brassica napus* (Brassicaceae). *Am. J. Bot.*, **78** 1083-90.

Chisholm, M.D. and Wetter, L.R. (1964) Biosynthesis of mustard oil glucosides. IV. The administration of methionine-C^{14} and related compounds to horseradish. *Can. J. Biochem.*, **42** 1033-40.

Christoffersen, R.E., Percival, F.W. and Bozak, K.R. (1995) Functional and DNA sequence divergence of the CYP71 gene family in higher plants. *Drug Metab. Drug Interact.*, **12** 207-19.

Cicek, M. and Esens, A. (1995) Cloning and sequencing of a cDNA coding for β-glucosidase (dhurrinase) from *Sorghum bicolor* (L.). Moench. *Plant Physiol.*, **109** 1497.

Clegg, D.O., Conn, E.E. and Janzen, D.H. (1979) Developmental fate of the cyanogenic glucoside, linamarin, in Costa Rican wild lima bean seeds. *Nature*, **278** 343-44.

Collinge, D.B. and Hughes, M.A. (1982) *In vitro* characterization of the Ac-locus in white clover (*Trifolium repens*). *Arch. Biochem. Biophys.*, **218** 38-45.

Colowick, S.P., Kaplan, N.O. and Ciotti, M.M. (1951) The reaction of pyridine-nucleotide with cyanide and its analytical use. *J. Biol. Chem.*, **191** 447-59.

Compton, S.G. and Jones, D.A. (1985) An investigation of the response of herbivores to cyanogenesis in *Lotus corniculatus* (L.). *Biol. J. Linnean Soc.*, **26** 21-38.

Conn, E.E. (1980) Cyanogenic compounds. *Annu. Rev. Plant Physiol.*, **31** 433-51.

Conn, E.E. (1981) Cyanogenic glycosides, in *Secondary Plant Products*, Vol. 7 (ed. E.E. Conn). *The Biochemistry of Plants* (eds. P.K. Stumpf and E.E. Conn), Academic Press, New York, pp. 479-500.

Conn, E.E. (1983) Cyanogenic glucosides: a possible model for the biosynthesis of natural products, in *The New Frontiers in Plant Biochemistry* (eds. T. Akazawa, T. Ashai and H. Imaseki), Japan Scientific Societies Press, Tokyo, pp. 11-22.

Conn, E.E. (1988) Biosynthetic relationship among cyanogenic glycosides, glucosinolates and nitro-compounds, in *Biologically Active Natural Products: Potential Use in Agriculture* (ed. G.Cutler), American Chemical Society, Washington, pp. 143-54.

Cooke, R.D. (1978) An enzymatic assay for the total cyanide content of Cassava (*Manihot esculenta*). *J. Sci. Food Agric.*, **29** 345-52.

Cutler, A.J. and Conn, E.E. (1981) The biosynthesis of cyanogenic glucosides in *Linum usitatissimum* (linen flax) *in vitro*. *Arch. Biochem. Biophys.*, **212** 468-74.

Cutler, A.J., Sternberg, M. and Conn, E.E. (1985) Properties of a microsomal enzyme system from *Linum usitatissimum* (linen flax), which oxidizes valine to acetone cyanohydrin and isoleucine to 2-methylbutanone cyanohydrin. *Arch. Biochem. Biophys.*, **238** 272-79.

Dalgaard, L., Nawaz, R. and Sørensen, H. (1977) 3-Methylthiopropylamine and (*R*)-3-methylsulphinylpropylamine in *Iberis amara*. *Phytochemistry*, **16** 931-32.

Dawson, G.W., Hick, A.J., Bennett, R.N., Donald, A.M. and Wallsgrove, R.M. (1993) Synthesis of glucosinolate precursors and investigations into the biosynthesis of phenylalkyl- and methylthioalkylglucosinolates. *J. Biol. Chem.*, **268** 27154-59.

De Bruijn, G.H. (1973) The cyanogenic character of cassava (*Manihot esculenta*), in *Chronic Cassava Toxicity* (eds. B. Nestel and R. MacIntyre), International Development Research Centre, Ottawa, Canada, pp. 43-48.

Dirzo, R. and Harper, J.L. (1982) Experimental studies on slug-plant interactions. III. Differences in the acceptability of individual plants of *Trifolium repens* to slugs and snails. *J. Ecol.*, **70** 101-17.

Doughty, K.J., Porter, A.J.R., Morton, A.M., Kiddle, G. and Bock, C.H. (1991) Variation in the glucosinolate content of oilseed rape (*Brassica napus* L.) leaves. II. Response to infection by *Alternaria brassicae* (Berk.) Sacc. *Annal. Appl. Biol.*, **118** 469-78.

Du, L. and Halkier, B.A. (1996) Isolation of a microsomal enzyme system involved in glucosinolate biosynthesis from seedlings of *Tropaeolum majus* (L.). *Plant Physiol.*, **111** 831-37.

Du, L., Lykkesfeldt, J., Olsen, C.-E. and Halkier, B.A. (1995a) Involvement of cytochrome P_{450} in oxime production in glucosinolate biosynthesis as demonstrated by an *in vitro* microsomal enzyme system isolated from jasmonic acid-induced seedlings of *Sinapis alba* (L.). *Proc. Nat. Acad. Sci. North Am.*, **92** 12505-509.

Du, L., Bokanga, M., Moller, B.L. and Halker, B.A. (1995b) The biosynthesis of cyanogenic glucosides in roots of cassava. *Phytochemistry*, **39** 323-26.

Dufour, D.L. (1994) Cassava in Amazonia: lessons in utilization and safety from native people. *Acta Horticulture*, **375** 175-82.

Dürham, P.L. and Poulton, J.E. (1990) Enzyme properties of purified myrosinase from *Lepidium sativum* seedlings. *Z. Naturforsch.*, **45c** 173-78.

Effenberger, F. (1994) Synthese und Reaktion optisch aktiver Cyanohydrine. *Angew. Chem.*, **106** 1009-19.

Effenberger, F., Ziegler, T. and Förster, S. (1987) Enzyme-catalyzed reaction. 15. Preparation of (*R*)-2-(sulfonyloxy)-nitriles and their reactions with acetates: inversion of the configuration of optically active cyanohydrins. *Chemische Berichte*, **126** 779-86.

Elias, M., Nambisan, B. and Sudhakaran, P.R. (1997) Catabolism of linamarin in cassava (*Manihot esculenta* Crantz). *Plant Sci.*, **126** 155-62.

Erb, N., Zinsmeister, H.D., Lehmann, G. and Nahrstedt, A. (1979) Epiheterodendrin: a new cyanogenic glucoside from *Hordeum vulgare*. *Phytochemistry*, **18** 1515-17.

Ettlinger, M.G. and Dateo, G.P. (1961) Studies of mustard oil glucosides. Final Report Contract DA19-129-QM-1059, US Army Natick Laboratories, Natick, Massachusetts.

Ettlinger, M.G. and Kjær, A. (1968) Sulfur compounds in plants. *Rec. Adv. Phytochem.*, **1** 59-144.

Falk, A., Taipalensuu, J., Lenman, M. and Rask, L. (1995) Characterization of rapeseed myrosinase-binding protein. *Planta*, **195** 387-95.

Fan, T.W.-M. and Conn, E.E. (1985) Isolation and characterization of two β-glucosidases from Flax seeds. *Arch. Biochem. Biophys.*, **243** 361-73.

Feeny, P. (1976) Glucosinolates, in *Biochemical Interaction Between Plants and Insect*s (eds. J. Wallace and R. Mansell), American Chemical Society, Washington.

Fowden, L. (1981) Nonprotein amino acids, in *The Biochemistry of Plants* (eds. P.K. Stumpf and E.E. Conn), Vol. 7, Secondary Plant Products, pp. 215-47.

Fowden, L. and Mazelis, M. (1971) Biosynthesis of 2-amino-4-methylnex-4-enoic acid in *Aesculus californica*: the precursor role of isoleucine. *Phytochemistry*, **10** 359-65.

Frehner, M. and Conn, E.E. (1987) The linamarin β-glucosidase in Costa Rican wild bean (*Phaseolus lunatus* L.) is apoplastic. *Plant Physiol.*, **84** 1296-300.

Frehner, M., Scalet, M. and Conn, E.E. (1990) Pattern of the cyanide-potential in developing fruits. *Plant Physiol.*, **94** 28-34.

Gershenzon, J. (1984) Changes in the levels of plant secondary metabolites under water and nutrient stress, in *Recent Advances in Phytochemistry. 18. Phytochemical Adaptations to Stress* (eds. B.N. Timmermann, C. Steelink and F.A. Loewus), Plenum Press, New York, pp. 273-320.

Geshi, N. and Brandt, A. (1997) Two jasmonate inducible proteins from *Brassica napus* seedlings homologous to myrosinase-binding proteins and jacalin. *Planta*, **204** 295-304.

Giamoustaris, A. and Mithen, R. (1996) Genetics of aliphatic glucosinolates. IV. Side-chain modification in *Brassica oleracea. Theor. Appl. Gen.*, **93** 1006-10.

Glen, D.M., Jones, H. and Fieldsend, J.K. (1990) Damage to oilseed rape seedlings by the field slug, *Deroceras reticulaum*, in relation to glucosinolate concentration. *Annal. Appl. Biol.*, **117** 197-207.

Glendening, T.M. and Poulton, J.E. (1988) Glucosinolate biosynthesis. sulfation of desulfoglucosinolate by cell-free extracts of cress (*Lepidium sativum* L.) seedling. *Plant Physiol.*, **86** 319-21.

Godwin, H. and Bishop, L.R. (1927) The behaviour of the cyanogenic glucosides of cherry laurel during starvation. *New Phytol.*, **26** 295-315.

Grob, K. and Matile, P.H. (1979) Vacuolar location of glucosinolates in horseradish root cells. *Plant Sci. Lett.*, **14** 327-35.

Grob, K. and Matile, P.H. (1980) Compartmentation of ascorbic acid in vacuoles of horseradish root cells: note on vacuolar peroxidase. *Z. Pflanzenphys.*, **98** 235-43.

Gruhnert, Ch., Biehl, B. and Selmar, D. (1994) Compartmentation of cyanogenic glucosides and their degrading enzymes. *Plant Physiol.*, **195** 36-42.

Grützmacher, H., Biehl, B., Czygan, F.C. and Selmar, D. (1990) Variations in HCN potential in *Dimorphotheca sinuata. Planta Med.*, **56** 610-11.

Guignard, L. (1980) Recherches sur la localisation des principles actifs des cruciferes. *J. Botanique*, **4** 385-94.

Guo, I. and Poulton, J.E. (1994) Partial purification and characterization of *Arabidopsis thaliana* UDPG: thiohydroximate glucosyltransferase. *Phytochemistry*, **36** 1133-38.

Hahlbrock, K. and Conn, E.E. (1970) The biosynthesis of cyanogenic glycosides in higher plants: purification and properties of a uridine diphosphate-glucose-ketone cyanohydrin β-glucosyltransferase from *Linum usitatissimum* (L.). *J. Biol. Chem.*, **245** 917-22.

Halkier, B.A. (1999) Glucosinolates, in *Naturally Occurring Glycosides* (ed. R. Ikan), Wiley and Sons, Chichester, UK, pp. 193-223.

Halkier, B.A. and Møller, B.L. (1989) Biosynthesis of the cyanogenic glucoside, dhurrin, in seedlings of *Sorghum bicolor* (L.). Moench. and partial purification of the enzyme system involved. *Plant Physiol.*, **90** 1552-59.

Halkier, B.A. and Møller, B.L. (1990) The biosynthesis of the cyanogenic glucosides in higher plants: identification of three hydroxylation steps in the biosynthesis of dhurrin in seedlings of *Sorghum bicolor* (L.). Moench. and the involvement of 1-*aci*-nitro-2-(*p*-hydroxyphenyl)-ethane as intermediate. *J. Biol. Chem.*, **265** 21114-21.

Halkier, B.A. and Møller, B.L. (1991) Involvement of cytochrome P_{450} in the biosynthesis of dhurrin in *Sorghum bicolor* (L.). Moench. *Plant Physiol.*, **96** 10-17.

Halkier, B.A., Scheller, H.V. and Møller, B.L. (1988) Cyanogenic glucosides: the biosynthetic pathway and the enzyme system involved, in *Cyanide Compounds in Biology* (eds. D. Everett and S. Harnett). Wiley and Sons, Chichester, UK, pp. 49-61.

Halkier, B.A., Olsen, C.E. and Møller, B.L. (1989) The biosynthesis of cyanogenic glucosides in higher plants: The (*E*)- and (*Z*)-isomers of *p*-hydroxyphenyl-acetaldehyde oxime as intermediates in the biosynthesis of dhurrin in *Sorghum bicolor* (L.). Moench. *J. Biol. Chem.*, **264** 19487-94.

Halkier, B.A., Lykkesfeldt, J. and Møller, B.L. (1991) 2-Nitro-3-(*p*-hydroxyphenyl) propionate and *aci*-1-nitro-2-(*p*-hydroxyphenyl)ethane, two intermediates in the biosynthesis of the cyanogenic glucoside, dhurrin, in *Sorghum bicolor* (L.). Moench. *Proc. Nat. Acad. Sci.*, **88** 487-91.

Halkier, B.A., Nielsen, H.L., Koch, B. and Møller, B.L. (1995) Purification and characterization of recombinant cytochrome $P_{450,\ tyr}$ expressed at high levels in *Escherichia coli. Arch. Biochem. Biophys.*, **322** 369-77.

Hasslacher, M., Schall, M., Hayn, M., Griengl, H., Kohlwein, S.D. and Schwalb, H. (1996) Molecular cloning of the full-length cDNA of (*S*)-hydroxynitrile lyase from *Hevea brasiliensis. J. Biol. Chem.*, **271** 5884-91.

Hegnauer, R. (1986) *Chemotaxonomie der Pflanzen*, Vol. VII, Birkhäuser Verlag, Basel-Stuttgart, p. 345ff.

Helmlinger, J., Rausch, T. and Hilgenberg, W. (1983) Localization of newly synthesized indole-3-methylglucosinolate (=glucobrassicin) in vacuoles from horseradish (*Armoracia rusticana*). *Physiologia Plantarum*, **58** 302-10.

Henry, M.F. (1981) Bacterial cyanide-resistant respiration: a review, in *Cyanide in Biology* (eds. B. Vennesland, E.E. Conn, C.J. Knowles, J. Westley and F.Wissing). Academic Press, London, pp. 415-36.

Hickel, A., Hasslacher, M. and Griengl, M.H.A. (1996) Hydroxynitrile lyases: functions and properties. *Physiologia Plantarum*, **98** 891-98.

Hogge, L.R., Reed, D.W., Underhill, E.W. and Haughn, G.W. (1988) HPLC separation of glucosinolates from leaves and seeds of *Arabidopsis thaliana* and their identification using thermospray liquid chromatography/mass spectrometry. *J. Chromatogr. Sci.*, **26** 551-56.

Holton, T.A., Brugliera, F., Lester, D.R., Tanaka, Y., Hyland, C.D., Menting, J.G.T., Lu, C.Y., Farcy, E., Stevenson, T.W. and Cornish, E.C. (1993) Cloning and expression of cytochromic P_{450} genes controlling flower colour. *Nature* (*Land*), **366** 276-79.

Hösel, W. and Nahrstedt, A. (1975) Spezifische Glucosidasen für das Cyanglucosid Triglochinin, Reinigung und Charakterisierung von β-Glucosidasen aus *Alocasia macrorrhiza*, Schott. *Hoppe-Seyler's Z. Physiol. Chem.*, **356** 1265-75.

Hösel, W. and Nahrstedt, A. (1980) *In vitro* biosynthesis of the cyanogenic glucoside, taxiphyllin, in *Triglochin maritima. Arch. Biochem. Biophys.*, **203** 753-57.

Hösel, W. and Schiel, O. (1984) Biosynthesis of the cyanogenic glucosides: *in vitro* analysis of the glucosylation step. *Arch. Biochem. Biophys.*, **229** 177-86.

Hösel, W., Berlin, J., Hanzlik, T.N. and Conn, E.E. (1985) *In vitro* biosynthesis of 1-(4'-hydroxyphenyl)-2-nitroethane and production of cyanogenic compounds in osmotically stressed cell suspension cultures of *Eschscholtzia californica. Planta*, **166** 176-181.

Hösel, W., Tobler, I., Eklund, S.H. and Conn, E.E. (1987) Characterization of β-glucosidases with high specificity for the cyanogenic glucoside, dhurrin, in *Sorghum bicolor* (L.). Moench seedlings. *Arch. Biochem. Biophys.*, **252** 152-62.

Hu, Z. and Poulton, J.E. (1997) Sequencing, genomic organization and preliminary promotor analysis of black cherry (*R*)-(+)-mandelonitrile lyase gene. *Plant Physiol.*, **115** (4) 1359-69.

Hu, Z. and Poulton, J.E. (1999) Members of the multigene family encoding black cherry (*Prunus serotina*) (*R*)-(+)-mandelonitrile lyase are differentially expressed. *Plant Physiol.*, (in press).

Hughes, M.A. (1981) The genetic control of plant cyanogenesis, in *Cyanide in Biology* (eds. B. Vennesland, E.E. Conn, C.J. Knowles, J. Westley and F.Wissing), Academic Press, London, pp. 495-508.

Hübel, W., Nahrstedt, A., Fikenscher, L.H. and Hegnauer, R. (1982) Zierinxylosid, eine neues cyanogenes Glykosid aus *Xeranthemum cylindraceum. Planta Med.*, **44** 178-80.

Hughes, J., de Carvalho, F.J.P. and Hughes, M.A. (1994) Purification, characterization and cloning of α-hydroxynitrile lyase from cassava (*Manihot esculenta* Crantz). *Arch. Biochem. Biophys.*, **311** 496-502.

Hughes, M.A., Brown, K., Pancoro, A., Murray, B.S., Oxtoby, E. and Hughes, J. (1992) A molecular and biochemical analysis of the structure of the cyanogenic β-glucosidase (linamarase) from cassava (*Manihot esculenta* Cranz) *Arch. Biochem. Biophys.*, **295** 273-79.

Hunt, S. (1985) Nonprotein amino acids, in *Chemistry and Biochemistry of Amino Acids* (ed. G.C. Barrett), Chapman and Hall, London.

Ikegami, F., Mizuno, M. and Murakoshi, I. (1990) Enzymatic synthesis of the thyrotoxic amino acid, mimosine, by cysteine synthase. *Phytochemistry*, **29** 3461-66.

Ikegami, F., Itagaki, S. and Murakoshi, I. (1993) Purification and characterization of two forms of cysteine synthase from *Allium tuberosum. Phytochemistry*, **32** 31-34.

Ikegami, F. and Murakoshi, I. (1994) Enzymatic synthesis of nonprotein β-substituted alanines and some higher homologues in plants. *Phytochemistry*, **35** 1089-104.

Istock, U., Lieberei, R. and Harms, H. (1990) Pattern of enzymes involved in cyanogenesis and HCN metabolism in cell cultures of *Phaseolus lunatus* (L.). varieties. *Plant Cell Tiss. Org. Cult.*, **22** 105-12.

Jäger, A.K., McAlister, B.G. and Staden, J. (1995) Cyanogenic glycosides in leaves and callus cultures of *Schlechterina mitostemmatoides. S. Afr. J. Bot.*, **61** (5) 274-75.

Jain, J.C., GrootWassink, J.W.D., Kolenovsky, A.D. and Unterhill, E.W. (1990a) Purification and properties of 3′-phosphoadenosine-5′-phosphosulphate: desulphoglucosinolate sulphotransferase from *Brassica juncea* cell cultures. *Phytochemistry*, **29** 1425-28.

Jain, J.C., GrootWassink, J.W.D., Reed, D.W. and Underhill, E.W. (1990b) Persistent co-purification of enzymes catalyzing the sequential glucoxylation and sulfation step in glucosinolate biosynthesis. *J. Plant Physiol.*, **136** 356-61.

Jaroszewski, J.W. and Fog, E. (1989) Sulfate esters of cyclopentenoid cyanohydrin glycosides. *Phytochemistry*, **28** 1527-28.

John, P. (1997) Ethylene biosynthesis: the role of 1-aminocyclopropane-1-carboxylate (ACC) oxidase and its possible evolutionary origin. *Physiologia Plantarum*, **100** 583-92.

Jones, D.A. (1988) Cyanogenesis in animal-plant interactions, in *Cyanide Compounds in Biology* (eds. D. Everett and S. Harnett), Wiley & Sons, Chichester, pp. 151-65.

Jones, D.A. (1998) Why are so many food plants cyanogenic? *Phytochemistry*, **47** 155-62.

Jongen, W.M.F. (1996) Glucosinolates in *Brassica*: occurrence and significance as cancer-modulating agents. *Proc. Nutr. Soc.*, **55** 433-46.

Josefsson, E. (1973) Studies on the biochemical background to differences in glucosinolate content in *Brassica napus* (L.). III. Further studies to localize metabolic blocks. *Plant Physiol.*, **29** 28-32.

Kaethler, F., Pree, D.J. and Brown, A.W. (1982) HCN: a feeding deterrent in peach to the oblique-banded leafroller. *Annal. Entomol. Soc. Am.*, **75** 568-73.

Kahn, R.A., Bak, S., Svendsen, I., Halkier, B.A. and Moller, B.L. (1997) Isolation and reconstitution of cytochrome $P_{450,ox}$ and *in vitro* reconstitution of the entire biosynthetic pathway of the cyanogenic glucoside, dhurrin, from sorghum. *Plant Physiol.*, **115** 1661-70.

Kakes, P. (1985) Linamarase and other β-glucosidases are present in the cell walls of *Trifolium repens* leaves. *Planta*, **166** 156-60.

Kakes, P. (1990) Properties and function of the cyanogenic system in higher plants. *Euphytica*, **48** 25-43.

Kakes, P. and Hakvoort, H. (1992) Is there rhodanese activity in plants? *Phytochemistry*, **31** 1501-505.

King, N.L.R. and Bradbury, J.H. (1995) Bitterness of cassava: identification of a new apiosyl glucoside and other compounds that affect its bitter taste. *J. Sci. Food Agric.*, **68** 223-30.

Kjær, A. and Schuster, A. (1972a) Glucosinolates in seeds of *Arabis hirsuta* (L). *Acta Chem. Scand.*, **26** 8-14.

Kjær, A. and Schuster, A. (1972b) Glucosinolates in seeds of *Neslia paniculata. Phytochemistry*, **11** 3045-48.

Koch, B., Nielsen, V.S., Halkier, B.A. and Møller, B.L. (1992) The biosynthesis of cyanogenic glucosides in seedlings of cassava (*Manihot esculenta* Crantz). *Arch. Biochem. Biophys.*, **292** 141-50

Koch, B.M., Sibbesen, O., Swain, E., Kahn, R.A., Liangcheng, D., Bak, S., Halkier, B.A., Svendsen, I. and Møller, B.L. (1994) Possible use of a biotechnological approach to optimize and regulate the content and distribution of cyanogenic glucosides in cassava to increase food safety. *Acta Horticulture*, **375** 45-60.

Kojima, M., Poulton, J.E., Thayer, S.S. and Conn, E.E. (1979) Tissue distribution of dhurrin and enzymes involved in its metabolism in leaves of *Sorghum bicolor. Plant Physiol.*, **67** 617-22.

Koukol, J., Miljanich, P. and Conn, E.E. (1962) The metabolism of aromatic compounds in higher plants. VI. Studies on the biosynthesis of dhurrin, the cyanogenic glucoside of *Sorghum bicolor. J. Biol. Chem.*, **237** 3223-28.

Kreuzfeld, H.J., Doebler, C., Schmidt, U. and Krause, H.K. (1996) Synthesis of non-proteinogenic (D)- or (L)-amino acids by asymmetric hydrogenation. *Amino Acids*, **11** 269-82.

Kuroki, G.W. and Poulton, J.E. (1987) Isolation and characterization of multiple forms of prunasin hydrolase from black cherry, (*Prunus serotina* Ehrh.) seeds. *Arch. Biochem. Biophys.*, **255** 19-26.

Kuroki, G., Lizotte, P.A. and Poulton, J.E. (1984) Catabolism of (*R*)-amygdalin and (*R*)-vicianin by partially purified β-glucosidases from *Prunus serotina* Ehrh. and *Davallia trichomanoides. Z. Naturforsch.*, **39** 232-39.

Kurzhals, C., Grützmacher, H., Selmar, D. and Biehl, B. (1990) Linustatin, the linamarin glucoside protected against cleavage by apoplastic linamarase. *Planta Med.*, **55** 673.

Kutachek, M., Prochazka, Z. and Veres, K. (1962) Biogenesis of glucobrassicin, the *in vitro* precursor of ascorbigen. *Nature*, **104** 393-94.

Lang, I. (1990) Cyanogene Verbindungen in Nahrungs, Gewürz- und Genuβmittelpflanzen sowie in Nahrungs- und Genuβmitteln. Master Thesis (Diplomarbeit), Faculty of Biology, University of Saarbrücken.

Larsen, P.O. (1981) Glucosinolates, in *The Biochemistry of Plants* (eds. P.K. Stumpf and E.E. Conn), Vol. 7, Secondary Plant Products, pp. 501-25.

Lechtenberg, M., Nahrstedt, A. and Fronczek, F.R. (1996) Leucine-derived nitrile glucosides in the Rosaceae and their systematic significance. *Phytochemistry*, **41** 779-85.

Lein, K.-A. (1972) Zur quantitativen Bestimmungen des Glucosinolatgehaltes in *Brassica*-Samen. I. Gewinnung und Reinigung der Myrosinase. *Z. Angew. Botanik*, **46** 137-59.

Lenman, M., Falk, A., Xue, J. and Rask, L. (1993) Characterization of a *Brassica napus* myrosinase pseudogene: myrosinases are members of the BGA family of β-glycosidases. *Plant Mol. Biol.*, **21** 463-74.

Lieberei, R. (1988) Relationship of cyanogenic capacity (HCN-c) of the rubber tree *Hevea brasiliensis* to susceptibility to *Microcyclus ulei*, the agent causing South American leaf blight. *J. Phytopathol.*, **122** 54-67.

Lieberei, R. and Selmar, D. (1990) Determination of rhodanese in plants. *Phytochemistry*, **29** 1421-24.

Lieberei, R., Selmar, D. and Biehl, B. (1985) Metabolization of cyanogenic glycosides in *Hevea brasiliensis*. *Plant System. Evol.*, **105** 49-63.

Lieberei, R., Biehl, B., Giesemann, A. and Junqueira, N.T.V. (1989) Cyanogenesis inhibits active defense reactions in plants. *Plant Physiol.*, **90** 33-36.

Lieberei, R., Fock, H. and Biehl, B. (1992) Cyanogenesis inhibits active pathogen defence in plants: inhibition by gaseous HCN of photosynthetic CO_2 fixation and respiration in intact leaves. *J. Appl. Bot.*, **70** 230-38.

Linscheid, M., Wendisch, D. and Strack, D. (1980) The structures of sinapic acid esters and their metabolism in cotyledons of *Raphanus sativus*. *Z. Naturforsch.*, **35c** 907.

Lipson, D.A., Bowman, W.D. and Monson, R.K. (1996) Luxury uptake and storage of nitrogen in the rhizomatous alpine herb, *Bistorta bistortoides*. *Ecology*, **77** 1277-85.

Lizotte, P.A. and Poulton, J.E. (1986) Identification of (*R*)-vicianin in *Davallia trichomanoides*. *Z. Naturforsch., Sektion C, Biosciences*, **41** 5-8.

Louda, S. and Mole, S. (1991) Glucosinolates, in *Herbivores: Their Interactions with Secondary Plant Metabolites*, Vol. 1, The Chemical Participants (eds. G.A. Rosenthal and M.R. Berenbaum), Academic Press, London, pp. 124-64.

Lüdtke, M. and Hahn, H. (1953) Über den Linamaringehalt gesunder und von *Colletotrichum befallener* junger Leinpflanzen. *Biochem. Z.*, **324** 433-42.

Ludwig-Müller, J. and Hilgenberg, W. (1988) A plasma membrane-bound enzyme oxidases L-tryptophan to indole-3-acetaldoxime. *Physiologia Plantarum*, **74** 240-50.

Ludwig-Müller, J., Rausch, T., Lang, S. and Hilgenberg, W. (1990) Plasma membrane-bound high plant isoenzymes convert tryptophan to indole-3-acetaldoxime. *Phytochemistry*, **29** 1397-400.

Manici, L.M., Lazzeri, L. and Palmieri, S. (1997) *In vitro* fungitoxic activity of some glucosinolates and their enzyme-derived products towards plant pathogenic fungi. *J. Agric. Food Chem.*, **45** 2768-73.

Makame, M., Akoroda, M.O. and Hahm, S.K. (1987) Effects of reciprocal stem grafts on translocation in cassava. *J. Agric. Sci. Camb.*, **109** 605-608.

Matile, P.H. (1980) 'Die Senfölbombe': Zur Kompartimentierung des Myrosinase systems. *Biochem. Physiol. Pflanzen*, **14** 327-35.

Matsuo, M. and Yamazaki, M. (1964) Biosynthesis of siringin. *Chem. Pharm. Bull.*, **12** 1388-89.

Mayton, H.S., Olivier, C., Vaughn, S.F. and Loria, R. (1996) Correlation of fungicidal activity of *Brassica* species with allyl isothiocyanate production in macerated leaf tissue. *Phytopathology*, **86** 267-71.

McFarlane, I.J., Less, E.M. and Conn, E.E. (1975) The *in vitro* biosynthesis of dhurrin, the cyanogenic glucoside of *Sorghum bicolor*. *J. Biol. Chem.*, **250** 4708-13.

Mederacke, H., Biehl, B. and Selmar, D. (1995) Glucosyltransferases in Cassava *Manihot esculenta*. *J. Appl. Bot.*, **69** 119-24.

Mederacke, H., Biehl, B. and Selmar, D. (1996) Characterization of two cyano- glucosyltransferases from cassava leaves. *Phytochemistry*, **42** 1517-22.

Mikolajczak, K.L. (1977) Cyanolipids. *Prog. Chem. Fats Lipids*, **15** 97-130.

Mithen, R., Clarke, J., Lister, C. and Dean, C. (1995) Genetics of aliphatic glucosinolates. III. Side chain structure of aliphatic glucosinolates in *Arabidopsis thaliana*. *Heredity*, **74** 210-15.

Mkpong, O.E., Yan, H., Chism, G. and Sayre, R.T. (1990) Purification, characterization and localization of linamarase in cassava. *Plant Physiol.*, **93** 176-81.

Møller, B.L. and Conn, E.E. (1979) The biosynthesis of cyanogenic glucosides in higher plants: *N*-hydroxytyrosine as an intermediate in the biosynthesis of dhurrin by *Sorghum bicolor*. *J. Biol. Chem.*, **254** 8575-83.

Møller, B.L. and Conn, E.E. (1980) The biosynthesis of cyanogenic glucosides in higher plants: channeling of intermediates in dhurrin biosynthesis by a microsomal system from *Sorghum bicolor*. *J. Biol. Chem.*, **255** 3049-56.

Møller, B.L. and Seigler, D.S. (1998) Biosynthesis of cyanogenic glucosides, cyanolipids and related compounds, in *Plant Amino Acids: Biochemistry and Biotechnology* (ed B. Singh) Decker, New York, pp. 563-609.

Montgomery, R.D. (1969) Cyanogens, in *Toxic Constituents of Plant Foodstuffs* (ed. I.E. Liener), Academic Press, London.

Moore, P.J., Swords, K.M.M., Lynch, M.A. and Staehelin, L.A. (1991) Spatial organization of the assembly pathway of glycoproteins and complex polysaccharides in golgi apparatus of plants. *J. Cell Biol.*, **112** 589-602.

Murugesan, K. and Radha, A. (1994) Biochemical mechanism of mimosine toxicity to fungi. *Int. J. Trop. Plant Dis.*, **12** 171-76.

Nartey, F. (1968) Studies on cassava, Manihot usitatissimun. *Phytochemistry*, **20** 1311-14.

Nahrstedt, A. (1985) Cyanogenic compounds as protecting agents for organisms. *Plant Syst. Evol.*, **105** 35-47.

Nahrstedt, A. (1987) Recent developments in chemistry, distribution and biology of the cyanogenic glycosides, in *Annual Proceedings of the Phytochemical Society of Europe. 24. Biologically Active Natural Products* (eds. K. Hostettmann and P.J. Lea) Oxford University Press, Oxford, pp. 213-34.

Nahrstedt, A. (1992) The biology of the cyanogenic glycosides: new developments, in *Annual Proceedings of the Phytochemical Society of Europe. 29. Nitrogen Metabolism in Plants* (eds. K. Mengel and D.J. Pilbeam), Oxford University Press, Oxford, pp. 249-69.

Nahrstedt, A. (1993) Cyanogenesis in food plants, in *Annual Proceedings of the Phytochemical Society of Europe: Phytochemistry and Agriculture* (eds. T.A. van Beek and H. Breteler) Oxford University Press, Oxford, pp. 107-29.

Nahrstedt, A. (1996) Relationships between the defense systems of plants and insects, in *Phytochemical Diversity and Redundancy in Ecological Interactions* (eds. J.T. Romeo, J.A. Saunders and P. Barbosa), Plenum Press, New York, pp. 217-30.

Nahrstedt, A., Hösel, W. and Walter, A. (1979) Characterization of cyanogenic glucosides and β-glucosidases in *Triglochin maritima* seedlings. *Phytochemistry*, **18** 1137-41.

Nahrstedt, A., Kant, J.D. and Wray, V. (1982) Acalyphin, a new cyanogenic glucoside from *Acalypha indica* (Euphorbiaceae). *Phytochemistry*, **21** 101-104.

Nahrstedt, A., Wray, V., Grotjahn, L., Fikenscher, L.H. and Hegnauer, R. (1983) New acylated cyanogenic diglycosides from fruits of *Anthemis cairica* and *A. altissima*. *Planta Med.*, **49** 143.

Nahrstedt, A., Kant, J.D. and Hösel, W. (1984) Aspects of the biosynthesis of the cyanogenic glucoside, triglochinin, in *Triglochin maritima*. *Planta Med.*, **50** 394-98.

Nahrstedt, A., Jensen, P.S. and Wray, V. (1989) Prunasin-6′-malonate, a cyanogenic glucoside from *Merremia dissecta*. *Phytochemistry*, **28** 623-24.

Nahrstedt, A., Sattar, E.A. and El-Zalabani, S.M.H. (1990) Amygdalin acyl derivatives: cyanogenic glycosides from the seeds of *Merremia dissecta*. *Phytochemistry*, **29** 1179-82.

Nahrstedt, A. and Schwind, P. (1992) Phenylalanine is the biogenetic precursor of *meta*-hydroxylated zierin, the aromatic cyanogenic glucoside of unripe achenes of *Xeranthemum cylindraceum*. *Phytochemistry*, **31** 1997-2001.

Nakanishi, T., Nishi, M., Somekawa, M., Murata, H., Mizuno, M., Iinuma, M., Tanaka, T., Murata, J., Lang, F.A. and Inada, A. (1994) Structures of new and known cyanoglucosides from a North American plant, *Purshia tridentata* DC. *Chem. Pharm. Bull.*, **42** 2251-55.

Nambisan, B. and Sundaresan, S. (1994) Distribution of linamarin and its metabolising enzymes in cassava tissues. *J. Sci. Food Agric.*, **66** 503-507.

Noji, M., Murakoshi, I. and Saito, K. (1993) Evidence for identity of β-pyrazolealanine synthase with cysteine synthase in watermelon: formation of beta-pyrazolealanine by cloned cysteine synthase *in vitro* and *in vivo*. *Biochem. Biophys. Res. Commun.*, **197** 1111-17.

Nye, M.M. (1991) The mis-measure of manioc (*Manihot esculenta*, Euphorbiaceae. *Econ. Bot.*, **45** 47-57.

Ohtsuru, M. and Hata, T. (1973) Studies on the activation mechanism of the myrosinase methylthioalkylglucosinolates. *J. Biol. Chem.*, **268** 27154-59.

Oke, O.L. (1994) Eliminating cyanogens from cassava through processing: technology and tradition. *Acta Horticulture*, **375** 163-74.

Olafsdottir, S., Andersen, J.V. and Jaroszewski, J.W. (1989) Cyanohydrin glycosides of *Passifloraceae*. *Phytochemistry*, **28** 127-32.

Oleszek, W. (1995) Glucosinolates: occurrence and ecological significance. *Wiadomosci Botaniczne*, **39** 49-58.

Osuntokun, B.O. (1994) Chronic cyanide intoxication of dietary origin and degenerative neuropathy in Nigeria. *Acta Horticulture*, **375** 61.

Oxtoby, E., Dunn, M.A., Pancoro, A. and Hughes, M.A. (1991) Nucleotide and derived amino acid sequence of the cyanogenic β-glucosidase (linamarase) from white clover (*Trifolium repens* L.). *Plant Mol. Biol.*, **17** 209-20.

Parkin, I., Magrath, R., Keith, D., Sharpe, A., Mithen, R. and Lydiate, D. (1994) Genetics of aliphatic glucosinolates. II. Hydroxylation of alkenyl glucosinolates in *Brassica napus*. *Heredity*, **72** 594-98.

Pereira, J.F., Seigler, D.S. and Splttstoesser, W.E. (1981) Cyanogenesis in sweet and bitter cultivars of cassava. *Hortscience*, **16** 776-77.

Peterson, P.J. and Fowden, L. (1972) The biosynthesis of L-γ-substituted glutamic acids in *Gleditsia triacanthos*. *Phytochemistry*, **11** 663-67.

Peterson, S.C. (1986) Breakdown products of cyanogenesis. repellency and toxicity to predatory ants. *Naturwissenchaften*, **73** 627-28.

Pich, A. and Scholz, G. (1993) The relationship between the activity of various iron-containing and iron-free enzymes and the presence of nicotianamine in tomato seedlings. *Physiologia Plantarum*, **88** 172-78.

Pitsch, C., Keller, M., Zinsmeister, H.D. and Nahrstedt, A. (1984) Cyanogenic glycosides from *Triticum monococcum*. *Planta Med.*, **50** 388-90.

Poulton, J.E. (1988) Localization and catabolism of cyanogenic glucosides, in *Cyanide Compounds in Biology* (eds. D. Everett and S. Harnett), Wiley & Sons, Chichester, pp. 67-81.

Poulton, J.E. (1989) Toxic compounds in foodstuffs: cyanogens in *Food Proteins* (eds. J.E. Kinsella and W.G. Soucie) American Oil Chemists' Society, Champaign, IL, pp. 381-401.

Poulton, J.E. (1990) Cyanogenesis in plants. *Plant Physiol.*, **94** 401-405.

Poulton, J.E. and Shin, S.I. (1983) Prunasin biosynthesis by cell-free extracts from black cherry (*Prunus serotina* Ehrh.) fruits and leaves. *Z. Naturforsch.*, **38c** 369-74.

Poulton, J.E. and Møller, B.L. (1993) Glucosinolates. *Methods of Plant Biochemistry*, **9** 209-37.

Pourmohseni, H. and Ibenthal, W.D. (1991) Novel β-glucosides in the epidermal tissue of barley and their possible role in barley-powdery mildew interaction. *Angew. Botanik*, **65** 341-50.

Pourmohseni, H., Ibenthal, W.D., Machinek, R. and Remberg, G. and Wray, V. (1993) Cyanoglucosides in the epidermis of *Hordeum vulgare*. *Phytochemistry*, **33** 295-97.

Reay, P.F. and Conn, E.E. (1970) Dhurrin synthesis in excised shoots and roots of sorghum seedlings. *Phytochemistry*, **9** 1825-27.

Reay, P.F. and Conn, E.E. (1974) The purification and properties of a uridine diphosphate glucose: aldehyde cyanohydrin β-glucosyltransferase from sorghum seedlings. *Arch. Biochem. Biophys.*, **249** 5826-30.

Reed, D.W., Davin, L., Jain, J.C., Deluca, V., Nelson, L. and Unterhill, E.W. (1993) Purification and properties of UDP-glucose: thiohydroximate glucosyltranserase from *Brassica napus* (L.). seedlings. *Arch. Biochem. Biophys.*, **305** 526-32.

Rockenbach, J., Nahrstedt, A. and Wray, V. (1992) Cyanogenic glycosides from *Psydrax*. *Phytochemistry*, **31** 567-70.

Rodman, J.E. (1991) A taxonomic analysis of glucosinolate producing plants, Part 1. *Phenetics Syst. Bot.*, **16** 598-618.

Rodman, J.E., Karol, K.G., Price, R.A. and Sytsma, K.J. (1996) Molecules, morphology and Dahlgren's expanded order Capparales. *System. Bot.*, **21** 289-307.

Rosenthal, G.A. (1982) *Plant Nonprotein Amino Acids and Imino Acids: Biological, Biochemical and Toxicological Properties*. Academic Press, New York.

Rosenthal, G.A. (1991) Nonprotein amino acids, in *Herbivores: Their Interaction with Secondary Plant Metabolites*, Vol. 1, The Chemical Participants (eds. G.A. Rosenthal and M.R. Berenbaum) Academic Press, San Diego, pp. 1-34.

Rosenthal, G.A. (1992) Purification and characterization of the higher plant enzyme L-canaline reductase. *Academy of Sciences of the United States of America*, **89** 1780-84.

Rosenthal, G.A. and Rhodes, D. (1984) L-Canavanine transport and utilization in developing jack bean, *Canavalia ensiformis* (Leguminosae). *Plant Physiol.*, **76** 541-44.

Rosenthal, G.A. and Berge, M.A. (1989) Catabolism of L-canavanine and L-canaline in the jack bean, *Canavalia ensiformis* (L.). *J. Agric. Food Chem.*, **37** 591-95.

Rosenthal, G.A., Berge, M.A., Ozinskas, A.J. and Hughes, C.G. (1988) Ability of L-canavanine to support nitrogen metabolism in the jack bean, *Canavalia ensiformis* (L.). *J. Agric. Food Chem.*, **36**, 1159-63.

Rosenthal, G.A., Berge, M.A. and Bleiler, J.A. (1989) A novel mechanism for detoxification of L-canaline. *Biochem. System. Ecol.*, **17** 203-206.

Rosenthaler, L. (1908) Durch Enzyme bewirkte asymetrische synthesen. *Biochemische Zeitschrift*, **14** 238-53.

Rossiter, J.T., James, D.C. and Atkins, N. (1990) Biosynthesis of 2-hydroxy-3-butenylglucosinolate and 3-butenylglucosinolate in *Brassica napus*. *Phytochemistry*, **29** 2509-12.

Rosling, H. (1994) Measuring effects in humans of dietary cyanide exposure from cassava. *Acta Horticulture*, **375** 271-83.

Saito, K., Kimura, N., Ikegami, F. and Noji, M. (1997) Production of plant nonprotein amino acids by recombinant enzymes of sequential biosynthetic reactions in bacteria. *Biol. Pharmaceut. Bull.*, **20** 47-53.

Saunders, J.A. and Conn, E.E. (1977) Subcellular localization of the cyanogenic glucoside in *Sorghum* by autoradiography. *Plant Physiol.*, **59** 647-52.

Saupe, S.G. (1981) Cyanogenic compounds and angiosperm phylogeny, in *Phytochemistry and Angiosperm Phylogeny* (eds. D.A. Young and D.S. Seigler) Praeger, New York, pp. 80-116.

Schenk, S.U. and Werner, D. (1991) β-(3-isoxazolin-5-on-2-YL)-alanine from *Pisum*: allelopathic properties and antimycotic bioassay. *Phytochemistry*, **30** 467-70.

Schwarz, B., Wray, V. and Proksch, P. (1996) A cyanogenic glycoside from *Canthium schimperianum*. *Phytochemistry*, **42** 633-36.

Schwind, P., Wray, V. and Nahrstedt, A. (1990) Structure elucidation of an acylated cyanogenic triglycoside and further cyanogenic constituents from *Xeranthemum cylindraceum*. *Phytochemistry*, **29** 1903-12.

Seigler, D. (1973) Determination of cyanolipids in seed oils of the Sapindaceae by the means of their NMR spectra. *Phytochemistry*, **13** 841-43.

Seigler, D.S. (1991) Cyanide and cyanogenic glycosides, in *Herbivores: Their Interaction with Secondary Plant Metabolites*, Vol. 1, The Chemical Participants (eds. G.A. Rosenthal and M.R. Berenbaum) Academic Press, San Diego, pp. 35-77.

Selmar, D. (1991a) The cleavage of cyanogenic lipids. *Physiologia Plantarum*, **83** 63-66.

Selmar, D. (1993a) Apoplastic occurrence of cyanogenic β-glucosidases and consequences for the metabolism of cyanogenic glucosides, in *The Biochemistry and Molecular Biology of β-Glucosidases* (ed. A. Esen), American Chemical Society, Washington, pp. 191-204.

Selmar, D. (1993b) Transport of cyanogenic glucosides: linustatin uptake by *Hevea* cotyledons. *Planta*, **191** 191-99.

Selmar, D. (1994) Translocation of cyanogenic glucosides in cassava. *Acta Horticulture*, **375** 61-67.

Selmar, D., Lieberei, R., Biehl, B. and Voigt, J. (1987) Linamarase in *Hevea*, a nonspecific β-glycosidase. *Plant Physiol.*, **83** 557-63.

Selmar, D., Lieberei, R. and Biehl, B. (1988) Mobilization and utilization of cyanogenic glycosides: the linustatin pathway. *Plant Physiol.*, **86** 711-16.

Selmar, D., Lieberei, R., Biehl, B. and Conn, E.E. (1989) α-Hydroxynitrile lyase in *Hevea brasiliensis* and its significance for rapid cyanogenesis. *Physiologia Plantarum*, **75** 97-101.

Selmar, D., Grocholewski, S. and Seigler, D.S. (1990) Cyanogenic lipids: utilization during seedling development of *Ungnadia speciosa*. *Plant Physiol.*, **93** 631-36.

Selmar, D., Lieberei, R., Junqueira, N. and Biehl, B. (1991) Changes in the cyanogenic glucoside content in seeds and seedlings of *Hevea* species. *Phytochemistry*, **30** 2135-40.

Selmar, D., Irandoost, S. and Wray, V. (1996) Dhurrin-6′-glucoside, a new cyanogenic diglucoside from *Sorghum bicolor* (L.). *Phytochemistry*, **43** 569-72.

Sibbesen, O., Koch, B., Halkier, B.A. and Moller, B.L. (1994) Isolation of the heme-thiolate enzyme cytochrome P-450-TYR, which catalyzes the committed step in the biosynthesis of the cyanogenic glucoside, dhurrin, in *Sorghum bicolor* (L.). Moench. *Proc. Natl. Acad. Sci. USA*, **91** 9740-44.

Sibbesen, O., Koch, B., Halkier, B.A. and Møller, B.L. (1995) Cytochrome P-450-TYR is a multifunctional heme-thiolate enzyme catalyzing the conversion of L-tyrosine to *p*-hydroxy-phenylacetaldehyde oxime in the biosynthesis of the cyanogenic glucoside, dhurrin, in Sorghum bicolor (L.). Moench. *J, Biol. Chem.*, **270** 3506-11.

Siemens, D.H. and Mitchell-Olds, T. (1996) Glucosinolates and herbivory by specialists (Coleoptera: Chrysomelidae; Lepidoptera: Plutellidae): consequences of concentration and induced resistance. *Environ. Entomol.*, **25** 1344-53.

Solomonson, L.P. (1981) Cyanide as a metabolic inhibitor, in *Cyanide in Biology* (eds. B. Vennesland, E.E. Conn, C.J. Knowles, J. Westley and F.Wissing), Academic Press, London, pp. 11-28.

Sørensen, H. (1990) Glucosinolates: structure, properties and function, in *Canola and Rapeseed: Production, Chemistry, Nutrition and Processing Technology* (ed. R. Shahidi), Van Nostrand Reinhold, New York, pp. 149-72.

Spencer, K.C. and Seigler, D.S. (1985) Passibiflorin, epipassibiflorin and passitrifasciatin: cyclopentenoid cyanogenic glucosides from *Passiflora*. *Phytochemistry*, **24** 981-86.

Spencer, P. (1994) Human consumption of plant material with neurotoxic potential. *Acta Horticulture*, **375** 341-48.

Stadler, E. (1978) Chemoreception of host plant chemicals by oviposting females of *Delia* (*Hylema*) brassicae. *Entomol. Exp. Appl.*, **24** 711-20.

Stafford, H.A. (1969) Changes in phenolic compounds content and related enzymes in young plants of *Sorghum*. *Phytochemistry*, **8** 743-52.

Stephan, U.W., Schmidke, I., Stephan, V.W. and Scholz, G. (1996) The nicotianamine molecule is made-to-measure for complexation of metal micronutrients in plants. *Biometals*, **9** 84-90.

Sundaresan, S., Nambisan, B. and Amma, C.S.F. (1987) Bitterness in cassava in relation to cyanoglucoside content. *Ind. J. Agric. Sci.*, **57** 37-40.

Swain, E. and Poulton, J.E. (1995) Utilization of amygdalin during seedling development of *Prunus serotina*. *Plant Physiol.*, **106** 437-45.

Swain, E., Li, C.P. and Poulton, J.E. (1992) Tissue and subcellular localization of enzymes catabolizing (*R*)-amygdalin in mature *Prunus serotina* seeds. *Plant Physiol.*, **100** 291-300.

Taipalensuu, J., Falk, A. and Rask, L. (1996) A wound- and methyl jasmonate-inducible transcript coding for a myrosinase-associated protein with similarities to an early nodulin. *Plant Physiol.*, **110** 483-91.

Tapper, B.A. and Butler, G.W. (1971) *Biochem. J.*, **124** 935-41.

Thangstad, O.P., Iversen, T.-H., Slupphaug, G. and Bones, A. (1990) Immunocytochemical localization of myrosinase in *Brassica napus* (L.). *Planta*, **180** 245-48.

Thangstad, O.P., Evjen, K. and Bones, A. (1991) Immunogold-EM localization of myrosinase in Brassicaceae. *Protoplasma*, **161** 85-93.

Thangstad, O.P., Winge, P., Husebye, H. and Bones, A. (1993) The thioglucoside glucohydrolase (myrosinase) gene family in Brassicaceae. *Plant Mol. Biol.*, **23** 511-24.

Thayer, S.S. and Conn, E.E. (1981) Subcellular localization of dhurrin β-glucosidase and hydroxynitrile lyase in the mesophyll cells of *Sorghum* leaf blades. *Plant Physiol.*, **67** 617-22.

Timonin, M.I. (1941) The interaction of higher plants and soil microorganisms. III. Effects of byproducts of plant growth on activity of fungi and actinomycetes. *Soil Sci.*, **52** 395-413.

Trione, E. J. (1960) The HCN content of flax in relation to flax wilt resistance. *Phytopathology*, **50** 482-86.

Trummler, K. and Wajant, H. (1997) A novel class of hydroxynitrile lyases. *J. Biol. Chem.*, **272** 4770-74.

Tylleskär, T. (1994) The association between cassava and the paralytic disease, konzo. *Acta Horticulture*, **375** 331-39.

Underhill, E.W. and Chisholm, M.D. (1964) Biosynthesis of mustard oil glucosides. *Biochem. Biophys. Res. Commun.*, **14** 425-30.

Underhill, E.W., Chisholm, M.D. and Wetter, L.R. (1962) Biosynthesis of mustard oil glucosides: administration of ^{14}C-labelled compounds to horseradish, nasturtium and watercress. *Can. J. Biochem. Physiol.*, **40** 1505-14.

Underhill, E.W., Wetter, L.R. and Chisholm, M.D. (1973) Biosynthesis of glucosinolates. *Biochem. Soc. Symp.*, **38** 303-26.

Uribe, E. and Conn, E.E. (1966) The origin of the nitrile nitrogen atom of dhurrin. *J. Biol. Chem.*, **241** 92-94.

Van Bel, A.J.E. (1989) The challenge of symplastic phloem loading. *Botanica Acta*, **102** 183-85.

Van-Boven, M., Toppet, S., Cokelaere, M.M. and Daenens, P. (1994) Isolation and structural identification of a new simmondsin ferulate from jojoba meal. *J. Agric. Food Chem.*, **42** 1118-21.

Van Boven, M., Daenens, P. and Cokelaere, M. (1995) New simmondsin 2′-ferrulates from jojoba meal. *J. Agric. Food Chem.*, **43** 1193-97.

Van Etten, C.H. (1969) Goitrogens, in *The Toxic Consituents of Plant Foodstuff* (ed. I.E. Leiner). Academic Press, London, pp. 103-42.

Van Etten, C.H., Daxenbichler, M.E., Williams, P.H. and Kwolek, W.F. (1974) Glucosinolates and derived products in cruciferous vegetables: analysis of the edible part from twenty two varieties of cabbage. *J. Agric. Food Chem.*, **24** 452-55.

Van Etten, C.H., McGrew, C.E. and Daxenbichler, M.E. (1976) Glucosinolate determination in cruciferous seeds and meals by means of enzymatically-released glucose. *J. Agric. Food Chem.*, **22** 483-87.

Verhoeven, D.ThH., Verhagen, H., Goldbohm, R.A., van den Brandt, P.A. and van Poppel, G. (1997) A review of mechanisms underlying anticarcinogenicity by *Brassica* vegetables. *Chem. Biol. Interact.*, **103** 79-129.

Vickery, P.J., Wheeler, J.L. and Mulcahy, C. (1987) Factors affecting the hydrogen cyanide potential of white clover (*Trifolium repens* L.). *Aust. J. Agric. Res.*, **38** 1053-59.

Wajant, H. and Effenberger, F. (1996) Hydroxynitrile lyases of higher plants. *Biol. Chem.*, **377** 611-17.

Wajant, H., Mundry, K.W. and Pfizenmaier, K. (1994) Molecular cloning of hydroxynitrile lyase from *Sorghum bicolor* (L.): homologies to serine carboxypeptidases. *Plant Mol. Biol.*, **26** 735-46.

Wajant, H., Foerster, S., Selmar, D., Effenberger, F. and Pfizenmaier, K. (1995) Purification and characterization of a novel (*R*)-mandelonitrile lyase from the fern *Phlebodium aureum. Plant Physiol.*, **109** 1231-38.

Wallsgrove, R.M., Doughty, K. and Bennett, R.N. (1998) Glucosinolates, in *Plant Amino Acids: Biochemistry and Biotechnology* (ed. B. Singh), Dekker Inc., New York, pp. 523-61.

Wang, R. and Nicholas, D.J.D. (1985) Some properties of glutamine synthetase and glutamate synthase from *Derxia gummosa. Phytochemistry*, **24** 1133-40.

Wetter, L.R. and Chisholm, M.D. (1968) Sources of sulfur in the thioglucosides of various higher plants. *Can. J. Biochem.*, **46** 931-35.

Wolf, W.J., Schaer, M.L. and Abbott, T.P. (1994) Nonprotein nitrogen content of defatted jojoba meals. *J. Sci. Food Agric.*, **65** 277-88.

Woodhead, S. and Bernays, E. (1977) Changes in release rates of cyanide in relation to palatability of *Sorghum* to insects. *Nature*, **279** 235-36.

Wurtele, E.S., Thayer, S.S. and Conn, E.E. (1982) Subcellular localization of a UDP-glucose: aldehyde cyanohydrin β-glucosyl transferase in epidermal plastids of *Sorghum* leaf blades. *Plant Physiol.*, **10** 1732-37.

Westley, J. (1981) Cyanide and sulphane sulfur, in *Cyanide in Biology* (eds. B. Vennesland, E.E. Conn, C.J. Knowles, J. Westley and F. Wissing). Academic Press, London, pp. 61-76.

Xu, L.L., Singh, B.K. and Conn, E.E. (1988) Purification and characterization of acetone cyanohydrin lyase from *Linum usitatissimum. Arch. Biochem. Biophys.*, **263** 256-64.

Xue, J., Lenman, M., Falk, A. and Rask, L. (1992) The glucosinolate-degrading enzyme myrosinase in Brassicaceae is encoded by a gene family. *Plant Mol. Biol.*, **18** 387-98.

Yang, S.F. and Hoffmann, N.E. (1984) Ethylene biosynthesis and its regulation in higher plants. *Annu. Rev. Plant Physiol.*, **35** 155-89.

Yeoh, H.-H. (1989) Kinetic properties of β-glucosidase from Cassava. *Phytochemistry*, **28** 721-24.

Yoshiba, Y., Kiyosue, T., Nakashima, K., Yamaguchi-Shinozaki, K. and Shinozaki, K. (1997) Regulation of levels of proline as an osmolyte in plants under water stress. *Plant Cell Physiol.*, **38** 1095-102.

Zhang, Y. and Talalay, P. (1994) Anticarcinogenic activities of organic isothiocyanates: chemistry and mechanisms. *Cancer Res.*, **54** 1976S-81S.

Zhang, Y., Talalay, P., Cho, C.G. and Posner, G.H. (1992) A major inducer of anticarcinogenic protective enzymes from broccoli: isolation and elucidation of structure. *Proc. Natl. Acad. Sci. USA*, **89** 2399-403.

Zhang, Y., Kensler, T.W., Cho, C.G., Posner, G.H. and Talalay, P. (1994) Anticarcinogenic activities of sulforaphane and structurally-related synthetic norbornylisothiocyanates. *Proc. Natl. Acad. Sci. USA*, **91** 3147-50.

Ziegler, T., Hörsch, B. and Effenberger, F. (1990) Ein einfacher Zugang zu (*R*)-α-Hydroxycarbonsäuren und (*R*)-1-Amino-2-alkoholen aus (*R*)-Cyanhydrinen. *Synthesis*, **7** 575-78.

Zilg, H. and Conn, E.E. (1974) Stereochemical aspects of lotaustralin biosynthesis. *J. Biol. Chem.*, **249** 3112-15.

4 Biosynthesis of phenylpropanoids and related compounds

Maike Petersen, Dieter Strack and Ulrich Matern

4.1 Introduction

The biosyntheses of phenylpropanoids and the natural compounds derived from them are among the most thoroughly investigated biosynthetic pathways in plant natural products. All of the enzymes involved in the biosynthesis of a number of compounds are known and genes or complementary deoxyribonucleic acid (cDNA) clones have been isolated for several of them. Nowadays, research is focused mainly at the molecular and genetic level, elucidating the regulatory principles of the biosyntheses and the functions of natural products for their producers. We are just beginning to understand the importance of natural compounds in the interactions of plants with their environment. The biosyntheses of other natural compounds are on the brink of being understood, but for a number of compounds evidence at the enzymatic level is still missing. This review provides a broad overview of our knowledge of the biosynthesis and molecular biology of a number of compounds related to phenylpropanoid metabolism. It is not meant to be comprehensive and the reader is referred to other recent reviews to answer specific questions.

4.2 General phenylpropanoid pathway and hydroxycinnamate conjugates

Phenylpropanoids, i.e. in a narrower sense phenolic compounds with a C_6-C_3 skeleton, are products of the general phenylpropanoid (phenylalanine/hydroxycinnamate) pathway, which includes reactions from L-phenylalanine to the hydroxycinnamates (HCAs). The latter occur ubiquitously in higher plants, caffeate being the most common, followed by 4-coumarate, ferulate and sinapate. They are usually activated as coenzyme A (CoA) thioesters or 1-*O*-acylglucosides, being the precursors of a vast number of HCA conjugates accumulating in plants. The most common types of such conjugates are esters and amides, rarely glycosides. Conjugating moieties can be carbohydrates, peptides, lipids, amino acids, amines, hydroxycarboxylic acids, terpenoids, alkaloids or flavonoids. In addition, insoluble forms of HCAs occur bound to polymers, such as cutins and suberins, lignins or polysaccharides in cell wall fractions.

Numerous biochemical and molecular studies of the phenylpropanoid pathway and the enzymology of conjugate formation have been published in recent years; however, important questions remain regarding the enzymes involved. The present chapter reviews some recent and earlier biochemical and molecular work on the phenylpropanoid pathway and the mechanisms involved in the formation of HCA esters and amides. A brief summary of the possible role of HCA conjugates in plants is also included.

4.2.1 *The phenylalanine/hydroxycinnamate pathway*

4.2.1.1 *Phenylalanine ammonia-lyase*

Phenylpropanoids are derived from L-phenylalanine by the action of phenylalanine ammonia-lyase (PAL), an enzyme detected in some fungi and all higher plants investigated. Figure 4.1 illustrates the key position of this reaction in the overall scheme of the general phenylpropanoid pathway. The enzyme catalyzes a non-oxidative deamination of L-phenylalanine to form (*E*)-cinnamate. Induction of PAL and regulation of its activity plays an important role in plant development. It has been shown that activation of PAL is controlled by MYB-related transcription factors. The role of two of these factors in the regulation of phenylpropanoid and lignin biosynthesis has recently been reported (Tamagnone *et al.*, 1998), thus extending their well-known function in flavonoid metabolism (Jackson *et al.*, 1991; Sablowski *et al.*, 1994, 1995; Moyano *et al.*, 1996). Through the action of PAL, ammonia is generated in large amounts, especially in lignifying tissues, and might be reassimilated through the action of glutamine synthetase (Lam *et al.*, 1995). This hypothesis is supported by the vascular bundle-specific immunolocalization of cytosolic glutamine synthetase in rice leaves (Kamachi *et al.*, 1992). However, by application of ^{15}N-labelled precursors to lignifying *Pinus taeda* cell cultures, Van Heeren and co-workers (1996) showed that the ammonia liberated is rapidly recycled to regenerate phenylalanine.

PAL generally occurs as a tetrameric structure (Havir and Hanson, 1973). In some plants PAL exists as a single enzyme, e.g. in some gymnosperms. Multiple forms (tetrameric isoenzymes) are characteristic of angiosperms (see review by Whetten and Sederoff, 1995). The isoenzymes may differ with respect to kinetic properties (Bollwell *et al.*, 1985). Reports on tissue-specific expression of their genes (Lois and Hahlbrock, 1992; Shufflebottom *et al.*, 1993) may indicate different functions for different isoforms. Appert and co-workers (1994) cloned

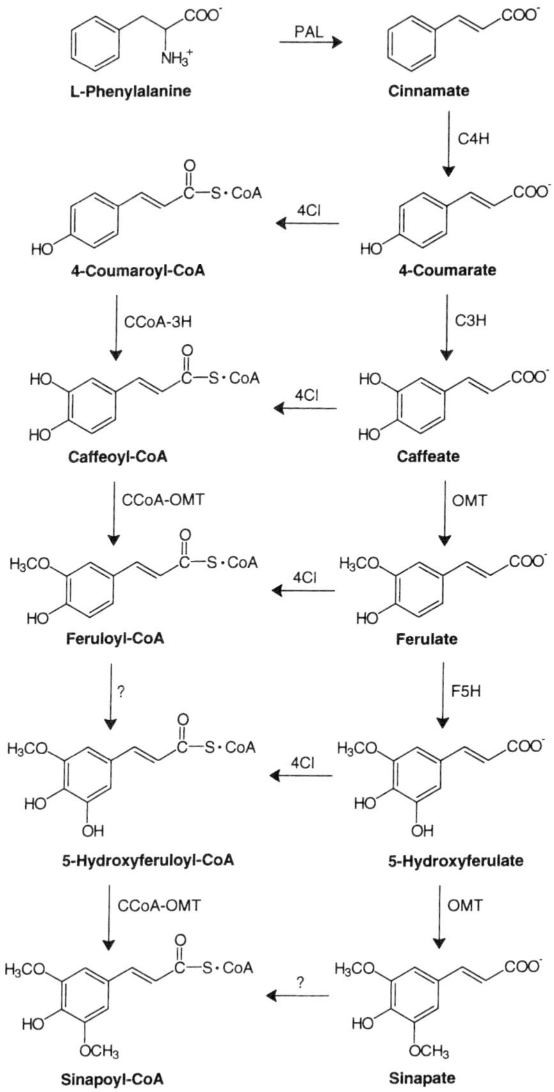

Figure 4.1 Scheme of the general phenylpropanoid pathway. The activation reactions leading through the action of UDP-glucose:HCA glucosyltransferase to the HCA 1-*O*-acylglucosides as an alternative to the HCA-CoAs are not included. Abbreviations: PAL, phenylalanine ammonia-lyase; C4H, cinnamate 4-hydroxylase; C3H, 4-coumarate 3-hydroxylase; OMT, *O*-methyltransferase; F5H, ferulate 5-hydroxylase; 4CL, 4-coumarate:CoA ligase; CCoA-3H, 4-coumaroyl-CoA 3-hydroxylase; CCoA-OMT, caffeoyl-CoA *O*-methyltransferase; UDP, uridine diphosphate; HCA, hydroxycinnamate.

cDNAs encoding four PAL isoenzymes in parsley, which were then expressed in *Escherichia coli* and characterized. Since the isoenzymes exhibited similar properties, the authors suggest that the occurrence of multiple genes should have a function other than expressing different enzyme kinetics. However, specific metabolic roles for the individual PAL isoenzymes have not yet been demonstrated.

4.2.1.2 Hydroxylation

There are two types of hydroxylase involved in the phenylalanine/hydroxycinnamate pathway: 1) the membrane-bound (microsomal) cytochrome P_{450}-dependent monooxygenases that catalyze hydroxylation of cinnamate (cinnamate 4-hydroxylase; C4H) and ferulate (ferulate 5-hydroxylase; F5H); and 2) the soluble phenolase that catalyzes hydroxylation of 4-coumarate (4-coumarate 3-hydroxylase; C3H).

C4H has been cloned and constitutes a distinct class of P_{450}s (e.g. Fahrendorf and Dixon, 1993). The enzyme appears to be closely associated with PAL in the microsomal compartment (Hrazdina and Wagner, 1985). Cinnamate generated by PAL is preferentially transferred (channelled) to C4H, apparently preventing its release into the cytosol.

In contrast to this well-characterized and widely-accepted specific reaction, it is still a matter of dispute to what extent phenolase activity (non-specific?), characterized in earlier studies (Vaughan and Butt, 1969; Bolwell and Butt, 1983), is involved in the second hydroxylation step leading to caffeate. Arguments against the involvement of a non-specific phenolase, i.e. a copper-containing polyphenol oxidase, might arise from its plastidic localization, while the other enzymes of the phenylpropanoid pathway are localized in the cytosol or at the endoplasmic reticulum. Studies of this enzymatic reaction have provided evidence that three hydroxylation pathways exist: one that operates at the level of the free acids; the second at the level of the coenzyme A esters; and a third that uses HCA conjugates.

In vivo inhibition studies with the fungal cyclic tetrapeptide, tentoxin (Kojima and Takeuchi, 1989) have suggested that, at least in mung beans, a specific C3H is involved in the 3-hydroxylation of 4-coumarate, excluding non-specific phenolase activities. An alternative reaction, accepting 4-coumaroyl-CoA, has been described (Kamsteeg *et al.*, 1981; Kneusel *et al.*, 1989). However, both the free acid and the CoA thioester may be accepted by the same enzyme (Boniwell and Butt, 1986; Kneusel *et al.*, 1989). Wang and co-workers (1997) purified a 4-coumaroyl-CoA 3-hydroxylase from cell cultures of *Lithospermum erythrorhizon*, which also accepted free 4-coumarate with about the same efficiency as the CoA ester. Properties of this enzyme resemble those of a 4-coumaroyl-glucose 3-hydroxylase from sweet potato (*Ipomoea batatas*), which was reported by Tanaka and Kojima

(1991) to be involved in chlorogenate biosynthesis. However, comparison with the properties of polyphenol oxidase suggests that the active enzymes from *Lithospermum* and sweet potato are polyphenol oxidases rather than specific enzymes of phenylpropanoid metabolism.

The third hydroxylation step is catalyzed by F5H, which like C4H was reported to be a P_{450}-dependent monooxygenase (Grand, 1984). The enzyme was found to be highly sensitive to detergents, prohibiting its purification as a prerequisite to clone the F5H gene. However, Meyer and co-workers (1996) were able to clone the gene by using a mutant defective in the accumulation of sinapate esters. They cloned the gene using transferred deoxyribonucleic acid (T-DNA) tagging and confirmed its identity by complementation of the mutant phenotype. They found that the highest degree of identity between the F5H and previously sequenced P_{450}s was only 34%. Thus, F5H constitutes a new P_{450} subfamily.

There are reports suggesting that the final substitution pattern of the aromatic rings of HCAs can be established with HCA conjugates. Kühnl and co-workers (1987) and Heller and Kühnl (1985) described a cytochrome P_{450}-dependent monooxygenase from carrot and parsley cell cultures, respectively, hydroxylating 5-*O*-(4-coumaroyl)-quinate and -shikimate to the respective caffeate esters. Petersen (1997) described the formation of the caffeoyl moiety of rosmarinic acid (caffeoyl-3′,4′-dihydroxyphenyllactate) in *Coleus blumei* cell cultures from 4-coumaroyl-4′-hydroxyphenyllactate or 4-coumaroyl-3′,4′-dihydroxyphenyllactate via the activity of cytochrome P_{450}-dependent hydroxylases (Petersen *et al.*, 1993; Petersen, 1997).

4.2.1.3 O-Methylation

S-Adenosyl-L-methionine (SAM)-dependent *O*-methylation of caffeate and 5-hydroxyferulate to yield ferulate and sinapate, respectively, has been reported to be catalyzed by an *O*-methyltransferase (OMT) purified from *Brassica oleracea* leaves (De Carolis and Ibrahim, 1989). Edwards and Dixon (1991) were able to isolate two OMT isoforms from cultured alfalfa cells, with equal affinities towards caffeate. Gowri *et al.* (1991) isolated an OMT cDNA clone from alfalfa. Southern blots indicated that this OMT is encoded by at least two genes. Whether one or two enzymes are involved in the formation of ferulate and sinapate depends on the plant system studied. OMT activities have been classified in relation to lignin biosynthesis on the basis of substrate specificity of OMTs of gymnosperms (softwoods) and angiosperm dicots (hardwoods). The angiosperm dicot OMTs catalyze, at least *in vitro*, the *O*-methylation of caffeate and 5-hydroxyferulate (bispecific OMTs), while the gymnosperm OMTs preferentially catalyze the *O*-methylation of caffeate and are inefficient at accepting 5-hydroxyferulate (monospecific OMTs) (Bugos *et al.*, 1992, and literature cited therein). Atanassova and co-workers (1995) demonstrated the importance of OMT for the monomeric composition of lignin. They modified tobacco lignin by genetic engineering. Antisense expression of sequences encoding OMT led to a marked decrease of syringyl units and the appearance of 5-hydroxy guaiacyl units. These features are also characteristic of natural maize mutants that have an improved digestibility compared to wild lines.

As shown for hydroxylase reactions, *O*-methylations can also occur with the CoA esters. A caffeoyl-CoA 3-*O*-methyltransferase (CCoA-OMT) has been identified in plant species in the course of defence reactions (Kühnl *et al.*, 1989; Pakusch *et al.*, 1989). The coding gene was cloned from parsley (Schmitt *et al.*, 1991; Grimmig and Matern, 1997); and *cis*-active promoter elements typical of inducible phenylpropanoid pathway genes classified this methyltransferase as an enzyme of the phenylpropanoid pathway. A respective cDNA has been cloned from elicited *Vitis vinifera* cell cultures and expressed in *E. coli* (Busam *et al.*, 1997). The protein revealed 85–94% identity with those from several other plants, i.e. *Petroselinum crispum* (Schmitt *et al.*, 1991), *Zinnia elegans* (Ye *et al.*, 1994), *Medicago sativa* (Sewalt *et al.*, 1995) and *Populus tremuloides* (Meng and Campbell, 1996).

A novel multifunctional OMT from loblolly pine has been cloned and expressed in yeast (Li *et al.*, 1997). The enzyme catalyzed the methylation of caffeate and 5-hydroxyferulate, as well as caffeoyl-CoA and 5-hydroxyferuloyl-CoA, with similar specific activities. The authors suggested that this activity might mediate a dual methylation pathway in lignin biosynthesis in loblolly pine xylem.

4.2.1.4 Formation of CoA thioester

The last step of the general phenylpropanoid pathway is the carboxyl activation of HCAs, generally catalyzed by HCA:CoA ligase or by the action of *O*-glucosyltransferase (formation of 1-*O*-acylglucosides). Whereas the acylglucosides are involved in the formation of HCA *O*-esters (see section 4.2.2), the HCA-CoA thioesters enter various biosynthetic pathways of plant phenolics, such as: condensation with malonyl-CoA leading to the flavonoids; nicotinamide adenine dinucleotide phosphate (reduced form) (NADPH)-dependent reductions leading to lignins or lignans (see section 4.4); or conjugation reactions in ester and amide formation (for a review focusing on the CoA ligase with regard to regulation by environmental and developmental signals, see Douglas *et al.*, 1992).

The enzymes catalyzing the formation of HCA-CoA thioesters are collectively called 4-coumarate:CoA ligase (4CL). The enzyme may preferentially activate different HCAs, thus controlling subsequent phenylpropanoid branch pathways (Douglas *et al.*, 1992). Some interesting molecular work on this subject has recently been published.

4CLs from hybrid poplar and recombinant 4CLs converted HCAs in the order 4-coumarate > ferulate > caffeate with similar specificities but did not accept sinapate (Allina *et al.*, 1998). It is likely that sinapoyl-CoA is formed via the alternative pathway involving hydroxylation and *O*-methylation of the HCA-CoAs (Ye *et al.*, 1994). Two functionally similar 4CLs and their cDNAs have been described from parsley (Lozoya *et al.*, 1988) and tobacco (Lee and Douglas, 1996).

Arabidopsis 4CL is encoded by a single gene, with expression patterns correlated to lignification of stems and defence against pathogens (Lee *et al.*, 1995). In the gymnosperm, loblolly pine, a single 4CL gene with two alleles at one locus has been characterized (Voo *et al.*, 1995). A more complex organization of 4CL has recently been suggested by the identification of two distinct 4CL genes in *Populus tremuloides*, which differ in structure, function (substrate-specificity of enzymes encoded) and expression (Hu *et al.*, 1998).

Antisense suppression of 4CL in *Arabidopsis* led to considerable alterations in lignin composition, i.e. a strong decrease in guaiacyl units, whereas levels of syringyl units remained unchanged (Lee *et al.*, 1997). This result indicates a hitherto non-characterized route to sinapyl alcohol, which seems to be independent of 4CL.

4.2.2 Formation of hydroxycinnamate conjugates

There are two major groups of HCA conjugates that are accumulated in plants, the HCA amides and the HCA *O*-esters. Up to now, amide formation has been considered to proceed exclusively via the CoA thioesters (Strack and Mock, 1993). Several additions to CoA-dependent transferases, leading to HCA amides as well as HCA *O*-esters, have been reported in recent years, of which just three examples will be given. Reinhard and Matern (1989) reported the elicitor-induction of anthranilate *N*-benzoyltransferase activity from carnation, which was recently cloned (Yang *et al.*, 1997) and shown to represent a HCA transferase. Hedberg and co-workers (1996) described the formation of spermine and spermidine amides via the HCA-CoA thioester, with protein preparations from the apical stems of *Aphelandra tetragona*. Ishihara and co-workers (1997) reported the induction of HCA-CoA:hydroxyanthranilate *N*-HCA-transferase activity in oat leaves by victorin C, a host-specific toxin produced by *Helminthosporium victoriae*. Another example of elicitor-induced HCA amide formation is discussed below in more detail, i.e. the *Phytophthora infestans*-induced formation of tyramine amides in potato.

An interesting transferase activity involved in the *O*-acylation of suberin with ferulate was reported by Lotfy and co-workers (1994). The enzyme transfers ferulate from feruloyl-CoA to ω-hydroxypalmitate and to several 1-alkanols. In a study on the distribution of this enzyme among 21 species investigated, 17 plants from 11 different families of angiosperms and gymnosperms showed HCA-CoA: ω-hydroxypalmitate *O*-HCA-transferase activity (Lotfy *et al.*, 1995).

The HCA transferases catalyzing the formation of *O*-esters may accept the CoA thioester in one plant or the 1-*O*-acylglucoside in another (Strack and Mock, 1993). The involvement of the energy-rich thioesters in such reactions is plausible. It was found, however, that the same holds true for the 1-*O*-acylglucosides, indicated by the free reversibility of uridine diphosphate (UDP)-glucose-dependent formation of these acylglucosides (this has also been found for various phenolic glucosides; as cited by Mock and Strack, 1993). The free energy of hydrolysis for the HCA acylglucosides has been calculated to be −36 kJ/mol (Mock and Strack, 1993), being in the range of high-energy acyl donors.

The pathway utilized is not dependent on the nature of the conjugating moiety but rather on the source of enzyme used, i.e. the plant species investigated. A good example of converging lines in the formation of HCA esters is that of caffeoylglutarate. In *Secale cereale* (Poaceae), the biosynthesis proceeds via caffeoyl-CoA (Strack *et al.*, 1987); in *Cestrum elegans* (Solanaceae), however, via 1-*O*-caffeoylglucose (Strack *et al.*, 1988). In addition, transacylation of HCA esters is possible. For example, in *Lycopersicon esculentum* caffeoylglutarate is synthesized via 5-*O*-caffeoylquinate (chlorogenate) (Strack and Gross, 1990). The latter is another example of such alternative pathways. Chlorogenate is usually formed via caffeoyl-CoA, as found in various species (Ulbrich and Zenk, 1979), but it may also be formed via 1-*O*-caffeoylglucose, e.g. in *Ipomoea batatas* (Convolvulaceae) (Villegas and Kojima, 1986).

Aromatic acylation of flavonoids usually proceeds via the HCA-CoAs (Heller and Forkmann, 1988), although the 1-*O*-acylglucosides have also been found to serve as acyl donors (Gläßgen and Seitz, 1992). The respective acylation of betacyanins appears to proceed exclusively via the 1-*O*-acylglucosides (compare Chapter 2, on alkaloids and betalains in the present volume). One interesting example of another 1-*O*-acylglucoside-dependent formation of HCA *O*-esters has recently been reported in fruits of *Physalis peruviana* (Latza and Berger, 1997). Methyl and ethyl cinnamate esters, which are aroma volatiles in these fruits, are apparently formed via the 1-*O*-acylglucoside of cinnamate. The enzyme accepted both the HCA 1-*O*-acylglucoside and the respective gentiobioside.

4.2.3 Functions of hydroxycinnamate conjugates

It is increasingly understood that HCA conjugates are of prime ecological importance for plant survival: 1) there is strong evidence that plants are protected against DNA-damaging ultraviolet (UV-B) light by HCA conjugates; 2) acylation of anthocyanins with HCAs has a copigmentation effect (intramolecular copigmentation) and protects these pigments against degradation by water; and 3) soluble conjugates and cell wall-bound HCAs may participate in plant defence against microbial infection. These roles will be exemplified with the following case studies.

1) Earlier investigations with *Raphanus sativus* seedlings (Strack *et al.*, 1985) showed that sinapate esters, with sinapoylmalate as the major component, accumulate primarily in the upper epidermis of the cotyledons, presumably as a protection against UV light. This has been demonstrated by Li and co-workers (1993), who described highly UV-sensitive *Arabidopsis thaliana* mutants that not only lack flavonoids but also have lower amounts of sinapate esters in their leaves compared to the wild type. Landry and co-workers (1995) reported that an *Arabidopsis* ferulate hydroxylase mutant, unable to synthesize sinapate esters, showed an extreme UV-B sensitivity, despite the ability to accumulate UV-absorbing flavonoids. This clearly demonstrates the importance of HCA conjugates as UV-B protectants in some plants.
2) Anthocyanins can exist in various structural forms, depending on the pH. At pH 4–6, which is the range existing in most plant vacuoles, hydration of the anthocyanidin nucleus leads to the colourless carbinol pseudobase (Brouillard and Dangles, 1994). Thus, there must be a mechanism for protecting anthocyanins against hydration. The most effective protection is achieved by intermolecular copigmentation, either with non-covalently bound colourless flavonoids or HCA conjugates, e.g. chlorogenate, or with aromatic acyl groups (namely HCAs) that are part of the anthocyanin structure, e.g. sandwich-type intramolecular association (Brouillard and Dangles, 1994). The intramolecular copigmentation of complex anthocyanin structures (polyglycosylated and polyacylated) shows an *in vivo* conformation with the acyl groups on either side of the anthocyanidin nucleus, thus avoiding nucleophilic water addition. The driving forces in this conformation are hydrophobic interactions between the anthocyanidin and the aromatic acyl groups. There are numerous descriptions of highly complex anthocyanin structures (Strack and Wray, 1994), stabilized by intramolecular copigmentation. Ternatin A1 from flowers of *Clitoria ternatea* is one of the largest monomeric anthocyanins yet known (Terahara *et al.*, 1990). It is composed of delphinidin, with seven molecules of glucose, four molecules of 4-coumarate and one molecule of malonate, and with a

molecular-ion peak at *m/z* 2107 as a flavylium ion corresponding to $C_{96}H_{107}O_{53}^{+}$ in its fast atom bombardment mass spectrometry (FAB-MS) spectrum.

3) The phenylpropanoid pathway plays a pivotal role in the defence reactions of plants upon microbial infection (Hahlbrock and Scheel, 1989). It is known that in some plants phenylpropanoids are required for formation of phytoalexins (Matern, 1991). There is increasing knowledge about pathogen-induced cell wall incorporation of HCAs, most often 4-coumarate and ferulate, and their conjugates. This should lead to increased rigidity and decreased digestibility of the cell wall by pathogenic cell wall-degrading enzymes (Nicholson and Hammerschmidt, 1992; Matern *et al.*, 1995). For example, potato (*Solanum tuberosum*) responds to infections by the late blight-causing oomycete, *Phytophthora infestans*, with stimulation of the phenylpropanoid pathway. This results in increased cell wall incorporation of various phenolics, with 4-hydroxybenzaldehyde, 4-hydroxybenzoate and tyramine amides of 4-coumarate and ferulate as the predominant components (Keller *et al.*, 1996; Schmidt *et al.*, 1998). The induced amide accumulation was preceeded by rapid and transient increases in the activities of phenylalanine ammonia-lyase (PAL) and tyrosine decarboxylase (TyrDC), providing the HCA-CoA:tyramine HCA-transferase (THT) with substrates (Schmidt *et al.*, 1998). Large amounts of the tyramine amides in elicited potato cell cultures were excreted into the culture medium (Schmidt *et al.*, 1998). This may indicate apoplastic secretion of these amides in infected intact potato leaves, thus directly inhibiting hyphal growth of a potential fungal invader, as shown for arbuscular mycorrhizal roots (Grandmaison *et al.*, 1993). The importance of phenylpropanoid-related defence reactions has been demonstrated by inhibitor studies. Treatment of potato leaves with the PAL inhibitor, L-2-aminooxy-3-phenylpropionate (AOPP), prior to *Phytophthora infestans* infection resulted in a collapse of late blight resistance (Parker *et al.*, 1991).

THT was discovered in tobacco mosaic virus (TMV)-inoculated tobacco leaves (Negrel and Martin, 1984) and has frequently been studied with regard to increased biotic and abiotic elicitor- and stress-stimulated activity in tobacco and other plants (Negrel and Javelle, 1997, and the literature cited therein). A recent example of wounding- and elicitor-induced accumulation of 4-coumaroyl- and feruloyltyramine in tomato leaves (Pearce *et al.*, 1998) supports the assumption that these tyramine conjugates play an important role in protecting plants against pathogen and herbivore attack.

The THTs from tobacco (Negrel and Javelle, 1997) and potato (Hohlfeld *et al.*, 1996) have been purified to apparent homogeneity. Partial amino acid sequencing of the potato THT and molecular cloning and expression of a potato cDNA clone encoding this enzyme has recently been achieved (Schmidt *et al.*, 1999). The availability of the THT cDNA will ultimately permit transgenic manipulation of the potato defence mechanism to enhance resistance to *Phytophthora infestans.*

4.3 Coumarins

4.3.1 Current points of interest and classification

Naturally occurring coumarins comprise a large group of compounds classified by the 2*H*-1-benzopyran-2-one (benzo-α-pyrone) core structure, which may accumulate as such or in the form of glycosidic conjugates (Murray *et al.*, 1982; O'Kennedy and Thornes, 1997). Most of these metabolites have been isolated from plant sources. Some noteworthy examples have also been described from microorganisms, e.g. the highly toxic aflatoxins from *Aspergillus* spp. or the substituted 4-hydroxycoumarins, novobiocin, clorobiocin and coumermycin, from *Streptomyces* spp., which are potent DNA gyrase inhibitors (Sekiguchi *et al.*, 1996; Tsai *et al.*, 1997). Irrespective of their pharmacological impact, the latter metabolites will not be considered any further, since both aflatoxins and 4-hydroxycoumarins are produced via the polyketide pathway (Singh and Hsieh, 1977; Inoue *et al.*, 1989), in contrast to most plant coumarins (Matern *et al.*, 1999; Murray *et al.*, 1982).

Two perspectives appear to have fuelled coumarin research for many years. The remarkable and highly versatile bioactivities of various coumarins caused random screenings of coumarin-producing plants for medicinal purposes and numerous novel structures are being reported each year (Estévez-Braun and González, 1997; Murray, 1997). Along these lines, activity-guided screenings have disclosed new applications of coumarins, such as inhibition of human immunodeficiency virus (HIV) reverse transcriptase by the calanolides (McKee *et al.*, 1995) and inhibition of a central nervous system receptor (Bergendorff *et al.*, 1997). On the other hand, the ecological and physiological implications of coumarins for plant-insect or plant-fungi interactions have occupied much attention in recent years (Berenbaum and Zangerl, 1996; Stanjek *et al.*, 1997a). For example, fungi and caterpillars that colonize plants like celery or wild parsnip are capable of tolerating or degrading the toxic furanocoumarins of their host plants and details of the mechanism of degradation have been investigated (Hung *et al.*, 1996, 1997; Spencer *et al.*, 1990). Compared to these studies, the biosynthesis of coumarins has received less attention over the last decade, as documented by Keating and O'Kennedy (1997), and major progress has been accomplished only very recently. It is obvious that the capacity for furanocoumarin biosynthesis must have evolved independently several times in the plant kingdom, since identical compounds recur in multiple unrelated families (*cf.* Berenbaum and Zangerl, 1996). Thus, the possibility exists that pivotal enzymes of furanocoumarin biosynthesis are related to ubiquitous enzymes of the general plant phenolic metabolism.

The nomenclature of coumarins is occasionally problematical, since ambiguous trivial names are used and the literature does not always follow the international rules of carbon numbering (Murray *et al.*, 1982). For convenience, most authors use a biogenetically-related classification, based on the number and position of oxygen atoms attached directly to the coumarin nucleus (Estévez-Braun and González, 1997; Keating and O'Kennedy, 1997; Murray, 1997). Accordingly, the biosynthetic principles are considered separately for 'simple' coumarins, subsuming all hydroxylated, alkoxylated and alkylated derivatives of coumarin (Fig. 4.2), for furano- or pyranocoumarins and for oxygenated furanocoumarins, and the carbon skeleton is numbered as in Figure 4.2. Only recent findings are addressed in detail and the reader is referred

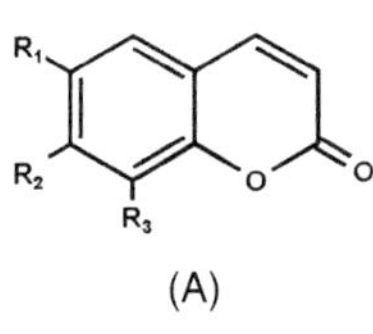

(A)

R_1	R_2	R_3	Compound
OH	OH	H	Esculetin
H	OH	OH	Daphnetin
H	OCH_3	H	Herniarin
OCH_3	OH	H	Scopoletin
OCH_3	OCH_3	H	Scoparone
Methylene-dioxy		H	Ayapin
OCH_3	OH	OH	Fraxetin
OCH_3	OH	OCH_3	Isofraxidine
OCH_3	OCH_3	OH	Fraxidine
OCH_3	OCH_3	OCH_3	Trimethoxycoumarin

(B)

R_1	R_2	Compound
OH	H	Bergaptol
OCH_3	H	Bergapten
OCH_3	OH	8-Hydroxybergapten
H	OH	Xanthotoxol
H	OCH_3	Xanthotoxin
OH	OCH_3	5-Hydroxyxanthotoxin
OH	OH	5,8-Dihydroxypsoralen
OCH_3	OCH_3	Isopimpinellin

Figure 4.2 Designation of simple coumarins (A) and of linear furanocoumarins (B).

to previous articles for more general information (Murray *et al.*, 1982; Matern *et al.*, 1988a, 1999; Hakamatsuka *et al.*, 1991).

4.3.2 *Simple coumarins*

4.3.2.1 *Coumarin and umbelliferone*

Precursor feeding studies demonstrated many years ago that the biosynthesis of coumarin and umbelliferone proceeds from L-phenylalanine via *trans*-cinnamic and *trans*-4-coumaric acids (Fig. 4.2) (*cf.* Murray *et al.*, 1982), which are generated by the shikimate and general phenylpropanoid pathways from primary metabolites (Strack, 1997). Although the shikimate pathway has been assigned to the plastids (Weaver and Herrmann, 1997), the subcellular topology of subsequent reactions has remained unclear, since two of the three enzymes of the general phenylpropanoid pathway, phenylalanine ammonia-lyase and 4-coumarate:CoA ligase, are soluble (Douglas, 1996; Lozoya *et al.*, 1991) and cinnamate 4-hydroxylase is a cytochrome P_{450} monooxygenase associated with the endoplasmic reticulum (*cf.* Schuler, 1996). No bottleneck enzyme for coumarin biosynthesis has yet been identified (Ahl Goy *et al.*, 1993; Hamdi *et al.*, 1995), which points to cyclization as the overall rate-limiting step, and it remains to be established whether CoA-ester substrates are required.

In contrast to mammals (Shimada *et al.*, 1996), only a few plant species, e.g. *Catharanthus roseus* and *Conium maculatum* (*cf.* Murray *et al.*, 1982) are capable of hydroxylating coumarin to umbelliferone (Fig. 4.2) and two routes have been proposed for the pivotal benzo-2-pyrone cyclization reaction of 4-coumaric acid (Fig. 4.3). The oxidative cyclization via a spirodienone intermediate (*cf.* Matern *et al.*, 1988b) would yield umbelliferone, in which the lactone oxygen is derived from the carboxyl group. Although the lactone oxygen of novobiocin was traced back to the carboxyl function (*cf.* Murray *et al.*, 1982), this is no precedent for the biosynthesis of common plant coumarins, since novobiocin probably arises as a polyketide. It appears possible, however, that particular plant phenoloxidase activities might be capable of catalyzing such an oxidative cyclization. Alternatively, the 2′-hydroxylation of cinnamic or 4-coumaric acid may be followed by *trans* to *cis* isomerization and lactonization; provided that the hydroxylation is catalyzed by a cytochrome P_{450} monooxygenase, molecular oxygen should be incorporated into the lactone ring. Benzoate 2-hydroxylase from tobacco (León *et al.*, 1995) might be considered as a model enzyme for such hydroxylation but neither option has been supported or ruled out for plant coumarins. In *Melilotus*, the 2′-*O*-glucoside of *trans*-2′-hydroxycinnamate is translocated through the tonoplast followed by

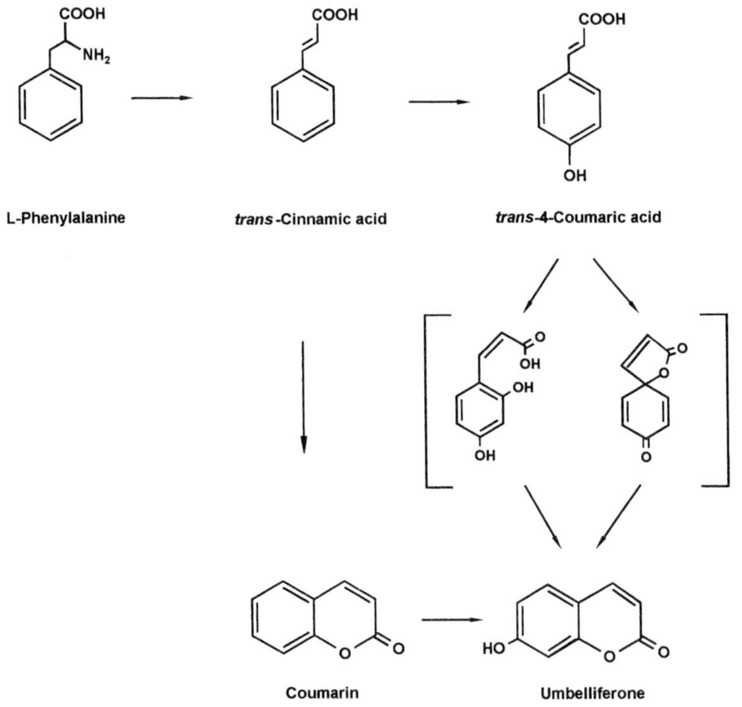

Figure 4.3 Proposed routes for the conversion of *trans*-cinnamic acid to umbelliferone.

light-independent conversion to the *cis*-configuration in the vacuole (Rataboul *et al.*, 1985). About 20 years ago, three laboratories independently reported the 2′-hydroxylation of cinnamic acids *in vitro* by chloroplast preparations from *Melilotus*, *Hydrangea* or *Petunia* (*cf.* Matern *et al.*, 1988a,b). Unfortunately, while these reports seemed to support the plastids as the site of biosynthesis of all simple coumarins, the results could not be reliably reproduced (Conn, 1984, *cf.* Matern, 1991). Nevertheless, the *ortho*-hydroxylation remains plausible in *Melilotus*, since the glucoside of 2′-hydroxycinnamate (coumarinic acid) rather than coumarin is the true metabolite. Under these premises, however, neither the correct substrate nor the mechanism of cyclization to simple coumarins can be specified.

4.3.2.2 Alkylated umbelliferone

Umbelliferone is the mother compound for various sets of substituted simple coumarins as well as for furano- and pyranocoumarins. O-alkylation (methylation, prenylation) was observed in only a few instances, whereas the capacity for C-alkylation is more abundant in higher plants. The 6-C- or 8-C-prenylation to demethylsuberosin and osthenol, respectively, often initiates the synthesis of linear or angular furano- and pyranocoumarins. Occasionally, as in the case of *Ammi majus* (Hamerski *et al.*, 1990a,b; Elgamal *et al.*, 1993), plants catalyze all three prenylation reactions. The dimethylallyl transferase of *Ruta graveolens*, mediating prenylation of position 6 of umbelliferone by dimethylallyl pyrophosphate, was the first plant prenyltransferase purified and studied *in vitro* (Ellis and Brown, 1974; Dhillon and Brown, 1976). This enzyme is position-specific, has high specificity for isoprenoid chain length and requires a free 7-hydroxyl function. Furthermore, the authors assigned the particulate enzyme to chloroplast membranes.

The latter point is supported by recent data from other plant systems. The accumulation of coumarins can be triggered in various Apiaceae cell cultures by treatment with fungal elicitors (see section 4.3.3.2), and two inducible membrane-bound umbelliferone 6-C- and 7-*O*-dimethylallyl transferases were isolated from elicited *Ammi majus* cells (Hamerski *et al.*, 1990b). In this study, the membranes were not fractionated sufficiently to allow more detailed differentiation. In intact celery plants, however, Stanjek and co-workers (1999b) demonstrated that the isoprenoid chain for the biosynthesis of linear furanocoumarins in celery originated from desoxy-D-xylulose, a pathway (Rohmer pathway) that was assigned to the plastids (Sprenger *et al.*, 1997). This strengthens the argument for a major role of chloroplasts in the synthesis of prenylated simple coumarins as well as of related coumarins and, in retrospect, probably explains the extremely low rates of incorporation of mevalonic acid into furanocoumarins observed in earlier feeding studies with *Pimpinella*, *Thamnosma* or *Pastinaca* species (*cf.* Murray *et al.*, 1982). In this context, it has to be recalled that an elicitor-inducible flavonoid dimethylallyl transferase was also located in the chloroplasts of bean and soybean (Biggs *et al.*, 1990).

4.3.2.3 Polyoxygenated coumarins

Formally, the hydroxylation or methoxylation of umbelliferone in 6- and/or 8-position leads to the most common polyoxygenated coumarins, esculetin, daphnetin, herniarin, scopoletin, fraxetin or isofraxidin (Fig. 4.2). Two routes can be envisaged to esculetin, scopoletin, fraxetin and isofraxidin, assuming either the cyclization of caffeic, ferulic, 5-hydroxyferulic and sinapic acid, respectively, or the stepwise hydroxylation and methylation of umbelliferone. Evidence was presented for the cyclization of caffeic acid to esculetin in *Saxifraga* (Sato, 1967) and *Petroselinum* (Kneusel, 1987), and of ferulic acid to scopoletin in tobacco (*cf.* Murray *et al.*, 1982). More recently, however, the hydroxylation of umbelliferone to daphnetin (Brown, 1986) and the conversion of umbelliferone to scopoletin via esculetin (Brown *et al.*, 1988) were reported from *Daphne mezereum* and *Agathosma puberula*, respectively. Furthermore, sunflower was reported to express an *O*-methyltransferase (OMT) activity that converts esculetin to scopoletin (Gutierrez *et al.*, 1995). However, it is difficult to evaluate the *in vivo* significance of substrate specificities of OMTs measured *in vitro*, since activities from *Ailanthus altissima* cell cultures were also reported as methylating esculetin to scopoletin or isoscopoletin, isoscopoletin to scoparone, fraxetin to isofraxidine, and fraxidine to 6,7,8-trimethoxycoumarin (Fig. 4.2), although the cells produced only low levels of isofraxidin and scopoletin (Osoba and Roberts, 1994).

Several recent reports have documented the revived interest in both the regulation of accumulation and the functions of esculetin and scopoletin derivatives. In addition to the lipoxygenase inhibitor activity exploited for antioedematic therapy, esculetin was shown to exert antiproliferative effects on vascular smooth muscle cells partly mediated through inhibition of protein tyrosine kinase (Huang *et al.*, 1993). In leafy galls of tobacco, the induced accumulation of 7-methylesculin was observed, and it was proposed that this unusual metabolite controls excessive cell growth (Vereecke *et al.*, 1997). Thus, esculetin and its derivatives may possess ‘hormone-like’ activities. On the other hand, a surprisingly large number of plants produce umbelliferone, scopoletin and the related ayapin or scoparone (Fig. 4.2) as phytoalexins upon challenge with biotic or abiotic elicitors, e.g. wild carrot (Coxon *et al.*, 1973), potato (Andreae and Andreae, 1949), sweet potato (Minamikawa *et al.*, 1963), *Platanus* (El Modafar *et al.*, 1993), rubber tree (Giesemann *et al.*, 1986; Garcia *et al.*, 1995), sunflower (Tal and Robeson, 1986; Gutierrez *et al.*, 1995), citrus (Sulistyowati *et al.*, 1990), elm tree (Valle *et al.*, 1997) and tobacco (Ahl Goy *et al.*, 1993). Scoparone also accumulated in the peel of grapefruit following gamma-irradiation or stress upon curing (*cf.* Sulistyowati *et al.*, 1990). The relevance of scopoletin for the expression of disease resistance was genetically corroborated in tobacco (Ahl Goy *et al.*, 1993). Furthermore, the involvement of cytokinin in the control of coumarin accumulation was demonstrated in tobacco tissues transformed with the isopentenyl transferase gene, and cytokinin was assumed to mediate the stress responses (Hamdi *et al.*, 1995). In $CuCl_2$–treated sunflower, the tissue-dependent and developmentally-regulated induction of scopoletin biosynthesis was reported (Gutiérrez-Mellado *et al.*, 1996). Maximal levels of scopoletin and ayapin were observed rather late in these studies (72 h and beyond), which corresponds to the elicitor induction of furanocoumarins in other plant cells (see section 4.3.3.1). Furthermore, a peroxidase was concomitantly induced in sunflower that metabolized scopoletin but not ayapin (Edwards *et al.*, 1997).

4.3.3 Furanocoumarins

4.3.3.1 Formation of the furanocoumarin nucleus

More than 20 years ago, precursor feeding studies, conducted primarily with *Pimpinella magna* and *Pastinaca sativa* plants or *Thamnosma montana* cell cultures, suggested that linear and angular furanocoumarins were derived from umbelliferone prenylated in the 6- (demethylsuberosin) and 8-position (osthenol), respectively (Murray *et al.*, 1982) (Fig. 4.4). Much later, linear furanocoumarins were described as phytoalexins from various umbelliferous cell cultures (*Ammi majus*, *Petroselinum crispum*, *Arracacia xanthorrhiza*) that had been treated with fungal elicitor (Matern *et al.*, 1988a,b; Matern, 1991), and such cell cultures proved to be reliable enzyme sources for relevant *in vitro* investigations.

Microsomal fractions of induced *Petroselinum* or *Ammi* cells cyclized demethylsuberosin to (+)-marmesin in the presence of NADPH and molecular oxygen, and the 'marmesin synthase' was identified as a cytochrome P_{450} monooxygenase (Matern *et al.*, 1988b). P_{450} monooxygenases are formally considered to catalyze the epoxidation of olefins by insertion of an 'oxen' (Akhtar and Wright, 1991; Bollwell *et al.*, 1994), and the reactive product of this reaction often inactivates the enzyme by alkylation of the prosthetic heme group (*cf.* Halkier, 1996). However, no intermediate was released from the marmesin synthase reaction, and it is likely that the 7-hydroxyl group of demethylsuberosin delocalizes the double bond electrons and favours the instantaneous cyclization to the dihydrofuranocoumarin. Model mechanisms proposed for the primary interaction of the catalytic P_{450} oxo-derivative, formed by heterolytic cleavage of the oxygen-oxygen bond in the ferric-hydroperoxy species, with aliphatic double bonds (Halkier, 1996) are compatible with such a cyclization of demethylsuberosin to (+)-marmesin, avoiding the formation of an intermediate epoxide. It appears feasible that the synthesis of linear dihydropyrano- or pyronocoumarins, such as graveolone, which may be produced concomitantly with furanocoumarins (Beier *et al.*, 1994), occurs in a very similar mode from demethylsuberosin. The formation of (−)-columbianetin from osthenol (Fig. 4.4) is probably catalyzed in an analogous fashion but this has not yet been supported experimentally. In contrast to the linear furanocoumarins, angular furanocoumarins are not induced as readily in infected umbelliferous plants; the induction has been reported from celery only (Heath-Pagliuso *et al.*, 1992; Afek *et al.*, 1995). Nevertheless, jasmonate was recently

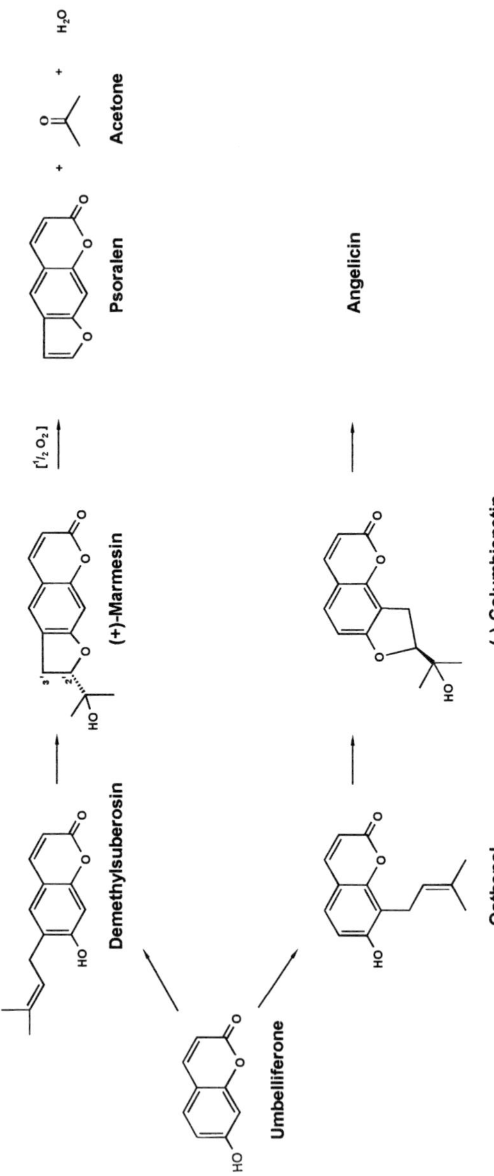

Figure 4.4 Biosynthesis of linear and angular furanocoumarins from umbelliferone.

shown to induce the biosynthesis of angelicin in *Heracleum mantegazzianum* (Stanjek and Boland, 1998), a system that may be used further.

The conversion of (+)-marmesin to psoralen (Fig. 4.4) was proposed to proceed by the generation of a carbocation at C-4′ of (+)-marmesin followed by 1,3-elimination to yield acetone and psoralen (*cf.* Murray *et al.*, 1982). The release of acetone is rather unusual in biosynthetic reactions and, therefore, an alternative, two-step oxidation and removal of one and two carbons was considered (Stanjek *et al.*, 1999a) in analogy to C-C bond cleavage in steroid metabolism (Akhtar and Wright, 1991; Halkier, 1996). However, microsomes from elicited *Ammi majus* cells contained a cytochrome P_{450} monooxygenase that catalyzed the one-step conversion of (+)-marmesin to psoralen (Matern *et al.*, 1988a) without the release of intermediates, and the products formed *in vitro* from (+)-marmesin labelled in the isopropyloxy side chain supported the one-step mechanism (Stanjek *et al.*, 1999a). Extensive inhibitor studies (Matern *et al.*, 1988b) have revealed the psoralen synthase to be an enzyme distinct from other monooxygenases, e.g. marmesin synthase or psoralen 5-monooxygenase (Hamerski and Matern, 1988). In accordance with the general mechanism of P_{450} monooxygenases (Halkier, 1996), psoralen synthase might catalyze the initial 3′-hydroxylation of (+)-marmesin by an oxygen-rebound process followed by base-catalyzed anti-elimination (Matern *et al.*, 1988a). An alternative mechanism could involve the homolytic abstraction of one of the 3′-hydrogens of (+)-marmesin and the disproportionation of the primary radical to psoralen, releasing the isopropyloxy side chain radical, which recombines with the hydroxyl radical to yield acetone and water (Hakamatsuka *et al.*, 1991).

Stereoselectively deuterated (±)-marmesin and (±)-acetyl-2′,3′-dihydropsoralen were recently synthesized (Stanjek *et al.*, 1997a) and used to study psoralen synthase catalysis with *Ammi majus* microsomes (Stanjek *et al.*, 1999a). Both the substrate and pseudosubstrate were converted to psoralen and the syn-elimination only was observed (Figs. 4.4 and 4.5). In control incubations, synthetic tetraphenyl-^{21}H,^{23}H-porphin-Fe^{III}-complex, activated with iodosobenzene, also converted both compounds to psoralen, but both the syn- and anti-elimination were observed under these conditions. The porphin-Fe^{III} model complex does not deliver the ferri-hydroperoxy species, and thus the elimination must have been initiated by the oxo-iron radical species (Akhtar and Wright, 1991). Unequivocal proof for the type of carbonyl compound produced during psoralen synthase catalysis was achieved by trapping experiments employing *O*-(2,3,4,5,6-pentafluorobenzyl)-hydroxylamine, which revealed the stoichiometric release of acetone and psoralen from (+)-marmesin (Stanjek *et al.*, 1999a). The syn-elimination observed probably results from abstraction of one hydrogen atom from carbon-3′ of

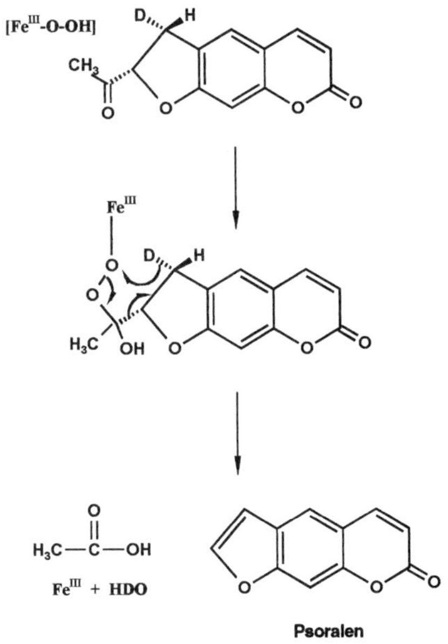

Figure 4.5 Mechanism proposed for the psoralen synthase reaction.

(+)-marmesin by the P_{450} oxo-Fe^{IV}-porphyrin radical (which acts like an alkoxy radical) and loss of the side chain isopropyl by disproportionation, which coincidentally recombines with the hydroxyl radical to give psoralen, acetone and water (Fig. 4.4). The identification of psoralen synthase as a P_{450} monooxygenase, the syn-elimination mechanism and the lack of any intermediate strongly argue against (+)-3′-hydroxymarmesin as an intermediate in the reaction. Overall, catalysis by psoralen synthase proceeds with remarkably high stereoselectivity, which is probably provided by a combination of steric and electronic effects (*cf.* Groves, 1997). The angular furanocoumarin corresponding to psoralen, angelicin, is probably generated in an analogous fashion from the angular dihydrofuranocoumarin, (−)-columbianetin. This was recently supported by precursor feeding studies in *Heracleum mantegazzianum* (Stanjek and Boland, 1998), whereas psoralen synthase from *Ammi majus* did not accept (±)-columbianetin.

4.3.3.2 Oxygenated psoralens

Bergaptol, xanthotoxol and the 5,8-dihydroxypsoralen (Fig. 4.2) are formed by hydroxylation of psoralen in the 5 and/or 8-position. The labile hydroquinone 5,8-dihydroxypsoralen, was presumed to be the precursor of isopimpinellin but the sequence of hydroxylations has not yet been determined (Murray *et al.*, 1982). Psoralen 5-monoxygenase was identified as a particulate cytochrome P_{450} monooxygenase from elicited *Ammi majus* cells (Hamerski and Matern, 1988). Since bergaptol was the only product observed in *in vitro* assays, an additional one or two enzymes appear to be required for the formation of 8-hydroxypsoralen (xanthotoxin) and 5,8-dihydroxypsoralen.

The methoxylated psoralens, bergapten, xanthotoxin and isopimpinellin (Fig. 4.2), are the major final products of the coumarin pathway in many umbelliferous plants. The *O*-methyltransferases (OMTs) catalyzing the methylation of bergaptol or xanthotoxol to bergapten (BMT) and xanthotoxin (XMT), respectively, were extensively purified from *Ruta graveolens* (Murray *et al.*, 1982) and *Petroselinum crispum* (*cf.* Lozoya *et al.*, 1991). *Ruta* converted both xanthotoxin and bergapten to isopimpinellin, as revealed by precursor feeding studies, with slight bias towards xanthotoxin. The XMT activity of *Petroselinum* exclusively methylated xanthotoxol, whereas the BMT activity catalyzed the 5-*O*-methylation of bergaptol (5-hydroxypsoralen) as well as the sequential 5- and 8-*O*-methylations of 5,8-dihydroxypsoralen. The strong preference of BMT for the substrate 5-hydroxyxanthotoxin over bergaptol suggested that the parsley cells contained an additional unidentified OMT for the methylation of 8-hydroxybergapten (Fig. 4.2). Thus, the specificities of the OMTs are insufficient to support either pathway for isopimpinellin biosynthesis, and the ambiguity is as great as in those OMT studies concerned with the biosynthesis of simple coumarins.

The accumulation of furanocoumarins in umbelliferous plant cell cultures induced by fungal elicitors or other stress conditions (Eckey-Kaltenbach *et al.*, 1997) provided convenient access to the mechanism, enzymology and regulation of biosynthesis, and the cDNA of one coumarin-specific enzyme (BMT) has been cloned (*cf.* Lozoya *et al.*, 1991). It is noteworthy that maximal levels of coumarin-specific enzyme activities and transcript abundance upon induction of the cells were observed rather late at 25 h and beyond, whereas the activities and transcript amounts of the enzymes of the general phenylpropanoid pathway, e.g. PAL and 4CL, passed their transient maxima much earlier (*cf.* Lozoya *et al.*, 1991). These diverse kinetics suggest a low degree of correlation of these pathways, which is compatible with the proposal that PAL activity is not rate-limiting for coumarin biosynthesis (Ahl Goy *et al.*, 1993; Hamdi *et al.*, 1995).

4.4 Lignans

Lignans are phenylpropanoid dimers linked by a C-C-bond between carbons 8 and 8′ in the side chain (Haworth, 1942). Dimers linked by other carbon atoms are named neolignans; here 3,3′-, 8,3′- or 8-*O*-4′-linkages are most frequently found (Davin and Lewis, 1992). Higher oligomers also occur: sesquilignans and dilignans (Dewick, 1989). Lignans can be divided into several subgroups, depending on other linkages and substitution patterns introduced into the original coniferyl alcohol dimer. Lignans and neolignans are widely distributed in the plant kingdom. More than 55 plant families contain lignans (Dewick, 1989), mainly gymnosperms and dicotyledonous angiosperms, but hornworts already contain lignan-like compounds (Takeda *et al.*, 1990). Since the same precursors are used for lignan and lignin biosynthesis and the linkages in both groups are essentially the same, lignin and lignan biosyntheses were considered to be parallel pathways. In contrast to lignin, however, lignans in plants usually have considerably lower molecular mass and are optically pure. This makes a stereoselective biosynthetic system necessary. The biosynthesis of lignans was first studied by feeding radioactively-labelled precursors (phenylalanine, ferulic acid, coniferyl aldehyde, coniferyl alcohol) to lignan-containing plants. This revealed two phenylpropanoid units with a ferulic acid substitution pattern, most probably coniferyl alcohol, to be the lignan precursor (Ayres, 1969; Stöckigt and Klischies, 1977; Ayres *et al.*, 1981; Rahman *et al.*, 1990a; Umezawa *et al.*, 1991; Kato *et al.*, 1998; Miyauchi and Ozawa, 1998). In recent studies, specific enzymes have been detected that are involved in the dimerization and subsequent transformation reactions.

Several reviews on monolignol formation, lignans and lignan biosynthesis have recently been published (e.g. Ayres and Loike, 1990; Lewis and Yamamoto, 1990; Davin and Lewis, 1992; Lewis and Davin, 1994; Lewis *et al.*, 1995; Ward, 1997; Gang *et al.*, 1997).

4.4.1 Biosynthesis of monolignols

Monolignols are the hydroxycinnamoyl alcohol monomers entering lignan and lignin biosynthesis, e.g. 4-coumaroyl, coniferyl and sinapyl alcohol. They are directly derived from the general phenylpropanoid pathway (see section 4.2) by reduction of the coenzyme A-thioesters of 4-coumaric, ferulic and sinapic acid to the corresponding alcohols via the respective aldehydes. The enzymes involved are cinnamoyl-CoA:NADPH oxidoreductase (E.C. 1.2.1.44) and cinnamoyl alcohol dehydrogenase (E.C. 1.1.1.195). These enzymes have been characterized mainly in relation to lignin biosynthesis. Until today, separate pathways providing the monolignols for lignin and lignan pathways or channelling of monolignols into one of the two pathways have not been described. Further steps involved in monolignol formation are the glucosylation of monolignols for storage and/or transport and the cleavage by β-glucosidases.

Reviews that include aspects of monolignol biosynthesis have been published by, for example, Lewis and Yamamoto (1990), Davin and Lewis (1992), Whetten and Sederoff (1995) and Boudet (1998).

4.4.1.1 *Cinnamoyl-CoA:NADPH oxidoreductase*

Cinnamoyl-CoA:NADPH oxidoreductase (cinnamoyl-CoA reductase, CCR) converts CoA-activated cinnamic acids to the corresponding aldehydes, preferentially using NADPH as reductant (Fig. 4.6). The

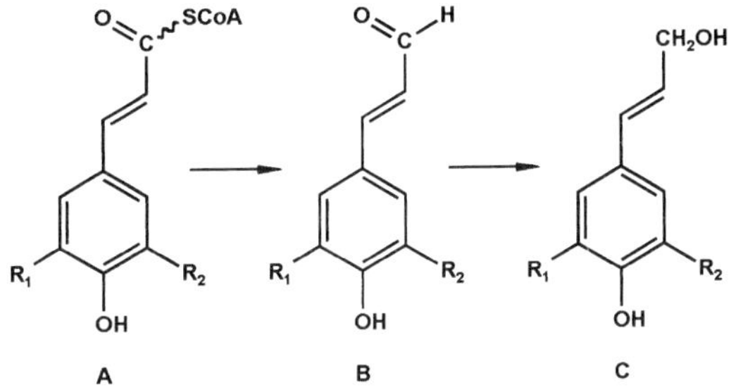

	A	B	C
$R_1 = R_2 = H$	4-coumaroyl-CoA	4-coumaraldehyde	4-coumaroyl alcohol
$R_1 = H$, $R_2 = OCH_3$	feruloyl-CoA	coniferaldehyde	coniferyl alcohol
$R_1 = R_2 = OCH_3$	sinapoyl-CoA	sinapaldehyde	sinapyl alcohol.

Figure 4.6 Formation of monolignols from hydroxycinnamic acid coenzyme A thioesters by cinnamoyl-CoA reductase (CCR) and cinnamoyl alcohol dehydrogenase (CAD).

reaction is readily reversible. The enzyme has been detected, characterized and, in some cases, purified from several sources; e.g. *Forsythia* (Gross and Kreiten, 1975), swede root (Rhodes and Wooltorton, 1975), *Glycine max* (Wengenmayer *et al.*, 1976), *Picea abies* (Lüderitz and Grisebach, 1981), *Populus x euamericana* (Sarni *et al.*, 1984), *Eucalyptus gunnii* (Goffner *et al.*, 1994) and lignan-accumulating cell cultures of *Linum album* (Alfermann and Windhövel, unpublished results; Windhövel, 1998). The cinnamoyl-CoA reductases from soybean, spruce, poplar and *Eucalyptus* have been purified. The enzyme is a monomer of 36–38 kDa molecular mass. The substrate preferences were slightly different from different sources but feruloyl-CoA was usually the preferred substrate followed by sinapoyl-CoA, although 4-coumaroyl-CoA was also accepted. cDNA and genomic clones for the *Eucalyptus* enzyme have recently been isolated (Lacombe *et al.*, 1997) and transformation with antisense constructs of CCR from tobacco have been used for modification of tobacco lignin composition (Piquemal *et al.*, 1998).

cDNAs for CCR from *Zea mays* and putative CCR-cDNAs from *Mesembryanthemum crystallinum* and *Arabidopsis thaliana* have been entered into databases. cDNA clones for CCR from *Eucalyptus gunnii* revealed an open reading frame of 1008 nucleotides coding for a protein of 336 amino acids with a calculated molecular mass of 36,500 Da (Lacombe *et al.*, 1997). The cDNA was functionally expressed in *E. coli.* The genomic clone showed the presence of four introns. Interestingly, the gene for CCR showed high homologies and similarities with plant dihydroflavonol 4-reductase and, furthermore, with bacterial cholesterol dehydrogenase and UDP-galactose 4-epimerase, as well as mammalian 3β-hydroxysteroid dehydrogenase. This indicates that CCR belongs to the mammalian 3β-hydroxysteroid dehydrogenase/plant dihydroflavonol dehydrogenase superfamily (Baker *et al.*, 1990; Baker and Blasco, 1992). CCR is expressed in young lignifying xylem of poplar (Lacombe *et al.*, 1997) but also in leaves that are not highly lignified. It was, therefore, proposed that expression of CCR might not occur exclusively during lignification but that CCR products may also be destined for other biosynthetic pathways, e.g. biosynthesis of lignans and/or neolignans.

Table 4.1 Examples of cinnamoyl alcohol dehydrogenase (CAD) from angiosperm and gymnosperm sources

Plant source	Molecular mass	Reference
Forsythia suspensa	80 kDa	Mansell *et al.*, 1974
Glycine max	43 and 69 kDa	Wyrambik and Grisebach, 1975
Populus X euamericana	40 kDa	Sarni *et al.*, 1984
Picea abies	72 kDa	Lüderitz and Grisebach, 1981
	63 kDa (dimer 2 × 42 kDa)	Galliano *et al.*, 1993b
Pinus thunbergii	67 kDa	Kutsuki *et al.*, 1982
Sorghum bicolor		Pillonel *et al.*, 1991
Wheat	3 isoenzymes	Pillonel *et al.*, 1992
Poplar	40 kDa	Tamura *et al.*, 1992
Pinus taeda	82 kDa (dimer 2 × 44 kDa)	O'Malley *et al.*, 1992
Eucalyptus gunnii	38 and 83 kDa	Goffner *et al.*, 1992
	34 and 84 kDa	Hawkins and Boudet, 1994
Nicotiana tabacum	two subunits of 42.5 and 44 kDa	Halpin *et al.*, 1992
Aralia cordata	72 kDa (heterodimer, 2 × appr. 39 kDa)	Hibino *et al.*, 1993b
Phaseolus vulgaris	34 and 40 kDa	Grima-Pettenati *et al.*, 1994

4.4.1.2 Cinnamoyl alcohol dehydrogenase

The second reduction step is catalyzed by cinnamoyl alcohol dehydrogenase (CAD), which uses NADPH for the reduction of cinnamoyl aldehydes to the respective alcohols (Fig. 4.6). Again, this reaction is readily reversible and is often assayed by measuring the formation of coniferyl aldehyde from coniferyl alcohol in the presence of NADP. The enzyme was first described by Mansell and co-workers (1974) in cell-free extracts from

Table 4.2 Entries for cinnamoyl alcohol dehydrogenase (CAD) in the SWISSPROT database

Identification	Plant source	Amino acid residues	Calculated molecular mass	Reference
CAD2 ARATH	*Arabidopsis thaliana*	357	38215	Kiedrowski *et al*., 1992
CAD3 ARATH	*Arabidopsis thaliana*	359	38942	Kiedrowski *et al*., 1992
CADH PETCR	*Petroselinum crispum*	337	36209	Kiedrowski *et al*., 1992
CAD4 TOBAC	*Nicotiana tabacum*	357	38906	Knight *et al*., 1992
CAD9 TOBAC	*Nicotiana tabacum*	357	38760	Knight *et al*., 1992
CAD1 ARACO	*Aralia cordata*	360	39129	Hibino *et al*., 1993a
CAD2 EUCGU	*Eucalyptus gunnii*	356	38791	Grima-Pettenati *et al*., 1993
CADH PICAB	*Picea abies*	357	38777	Galliano *et al*., 1993a
CADH EUCBO	*Eucalyptus botrydoides*	355	38679	Hibino *et al*., 1994
CAD1 ARATH	*Arabidopsis thaliana*	360	38907	Somers *et al*., 1995
CAD4 ARATH	*Arabidopsis thaliana*	365	39098	Baucher *et al*., 1995
CADH MEDSA	*Medicago sativa*	358	38948	Van Doorsselaere *et al*., 1995
CADH PINTA	*Pinus taeda*	357	38847	MacKay *et al*., 1995
CADH POPDE	*Populus deltoides*	357	39034	Van Doorsselaere *et al*., 1995

Forsythia suspensa and has been investigated much more intensively than CCR since its first description. CAD has been characterized and purified from several angiosperm and gymnosperm sources (see Table 4.1). Depending on the plant source, one to three isoforms have been described, some of them monomeric and others dimeric. The substrate specificities of CAD from different sources and of the different CAD isoenzymes from the same plant vary. Generally, coniferyl aldehyde (coniferyl alcohol) is accepted by CAD. 4-Coumaroyl and sinapyl aldehydes (alcohols) are mostly accepted; however, some enzymes were not able to use sinapyl aldehyde (alcohol), e.g. CAD from *Picea abies* (Lüderitz and Grisebach, 1981) and *Pinus thunbergii* (Kutsuki *et al*., 1982) or CAD1 from *Eucalyptus gunnii* (Goffner *et al*., 1992). A novel CAD isoenzyme from parsley was expressed during defence responses; this CAD accepted cinnamaldehyde, 4-coumaraldehyde and coniferaldehyde but not syringaldehyde, which was accepted by the other CAD isoenzymes from parsley (Logemann *et al*., 1997). CAD from cell cultures of *Linum* species has been characterized with respect to the biosynthesis of podophyllotoxin and related compounds

(Alfermann and coworkers, unpublished results; Kalenberg, 1994; Schönell, 1996). A number of CAD cDNA and genomic sequences have been published (Table 4.2). Sequence comparisons have shown high similarities between the sequences from different sources as well as the grouping of CAD into the family of zinc-containing alcohol dehydrogenases. CAD is expressed mainly in lignifying tissues, showing the main function of CAD in the formation of lignin monomers. However, in some cases, CAD activities or expression were detected in tissues with little or no lignin content, e.g. CAD1 in pods of *Phaseolus vulgaris* (Grima-Pettenati *et al.*, 1994) or *Eucalyptus* xylem (Goffner *et al.*, 1992). The monolignols formed in these cases were proposed to be functional for biosyntheses of compounds other than lignin (Baudracco *et al.*, 1993).

4.4.1.3 UDP-glucose:hydroxycinnamyl alcohol glucosyltransferase and β-glucosidase

Monomers for lignin biosynthesis are supposed to be glucosylated for storage or transport across the plasma membrane and deglycosylated prior to polymerization in the cell wall, although the exact function of the glucosylated monolignols is still under discussion (Lewis and Yamamoto, 1990; Davin and Lewis, 1992). Specific glucosyltransferases (UDP-glucose:coniferyl alcohol glucosyltransferase, E.C. 2.4.1.111) have been described for the formation of glucocoumaroylalcohol, syringin and coniferin, transferring the glucose unit from UDP-glucose to the aromatic hydroxyl group in the para-position of the side chain of the monolignols (Ibrahim and Grisebach, 1976; Ibrahim, 1977; Schmid and Grisebach, 1982b; Schmid *et al.*, 1982; Alfermann and coworkers, unpublished results). The glucosylation of the side chain hydroxyl function (e.g. the formation of isoconiferin) occurs much more rarely. Cell wall-associated β-glucosidases (coniferin β-glucosidase; E.C. 3.2.1.126) have been found mainly in lignifying cells, indicating the role of monolignol release for lignification (e.g. Marcinowski and Grisebach, 1978; Marcinowski *et al.*, 1979; Burmeister and Hösel, 1981; Hösel *et al.*, 1982). The importance of glucosylation and glucosylated precursors for lignan biosynthesis is not yet known. Some aspects will be discussed in section 4.4.2.8.

4.4.2 Lignan biosynthesis

Plant lignans occur mainly as stereochemically pure (+)- or (−)-enantiomers. However, different enantiomers are found in different plant species, e.g. (+)-pinoresinol in *Forsythia* spp. and (−)-pinoresinol in *Zanthoxylum ailanthoides* (Katayama *et al.*, 1997). It has been concluded that dimerization of monolignols would occur either by a non-specific peroxidase followed by stereoselective biosynthetic steps or that the dimerization is already stereospecific.

4.4.2.1 Formation of phenylpropanoid dimers

Most known phenylpropanoid coupling enzymes (peroxidases, phenoloxidases, laccases) catalyze the racemic coupling of phenylpropanoids, e.g. *E*-coniferyl alcohol giving rise to (+/−)-pinoresinols, (+/−)-dehydrodiconiferyl alcohols and (+/−)-*erythro*/*threo*-guajacylglycerol-8-*O*-4′-coniferyl alcohol ethers (Gang *et al.*, 1997). Dimers of caffeic and ferulic acid linked 8,8′ were formed by a specific peroxidase (glycoprotein, MW 38 kDa) from leaves of *Bupleurum salicifolium* after addition of H_2O_2 (Frias *et al.*, 1991). Cell-free extracts from *Larix leptolepis* callus catalyzed the formation of pinoresinol with enantiomeric excess for (−)-pinoresinol (−/+0.74) after addition of H_2O_2 (Nabeta *et al.*, 1991). This shows an enantioselective component in the otherwise unspecific peroxidase-catalyzed pinoresinol synthesis.

A stereoselective 8,8′-dimerization of monolignols is catalyzed by '(+)-pinoresinol synthase' from *Forsythia suspensa* (Fig. 4.7). This enzyme was

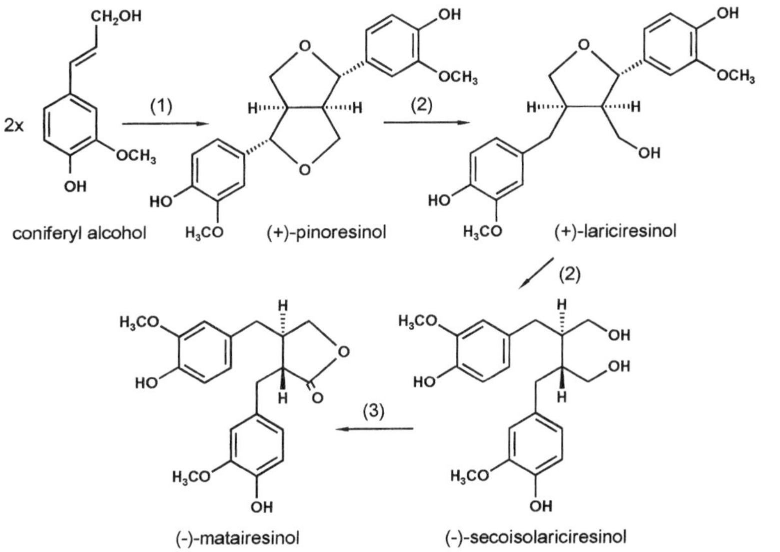

Figure 4.7 Enzymatic steps leading from two molecules of coniferyl alcohol to (−)-matairesinol in *Forsythia* spp. (1) = '(+)-pinoresinol synthase'; (2) = pinoresinol/lariciresinol reductase; (3) = (−)-secoisolariciresinol dehydrogenase.

first detected in 'crude cell wall preparations', where it catalyzed the stereospecific formation of (+)-pinoresinol from two molecules of *E*-coniferyl alcohol, in contrast to non-specific soluble enzymes catalyzing the formation of racemic pinoresinol (Davin *et al.*, 1992; Paré *et al.*,

1994). '(+)-Pinoresinol synthase' has recently been purified and characterized, showing an enzyme system consisting of two proteins, an oxidase and a dirigent protein, without catalytic activity (Davin *et al.*, 1997). Both proteins have been solubilized from cell wall enriched homogenates and purified. The last purification step yielded four fractions: fraction I did not have significant dimerization activity, whereas fraction III catalyzed unspecific coupling of *E*-coniferyl alcohol to (+/−)-pinoresinol and other dimers. Combination of the two fractions resulted in the original '(+)-pinoresinol synthase' activity with full regio- and stereospecificity. An oxidase, most probably a plant laccase generating free radicals of *E*-coniferyl alcohol, was found in fraction III. Fraction I contained a protein with an approximate MW of 78 kDa, possibly a trimer of 27 kDa subunits. Isoelectric focusing resolved six isoforms. The protein has no catalytically active centre. Since this protein determines the regio- and stereospecificity without having any catalytic properties, it was named 'dirigent protein'. It was shown that chemical formation of coniferyl alcohol radicals, with the help of flavin mononucleotide (FMN), flavin adenine dinucleotide (FAD) or ammonium peroxidisulfate, was sufficient to form (+)-pinoresinol in the presence, but not in the absence, of the 'dirigent protein'. Therefore, it was proposed that the phenoxy radicals formed by the oxidase (fraction III) are captured by the 'dirigent protein', leading to a stereospecific and regiospecific coupling of the monomers. '(+)-Pinoresinol synthase' was strictly specific for coniferyl alcohol; 4-coumaroyl and sinapoyl alcohols were not accepted. Formation of (+)-pinoresinol in *Forsythia*, therefore, is made possible by concomitant action of two proteins. However, it is doubtful whether the dirigent protein also plays a role in lignin biosynthesis, as stated by Boudet (1998). There are strong indications that lignans are synthesized in the cytoplasm and stored in the vacuole (Henges *et al.*, 1996), whereas lignin is an extracellular compound. Lignin and lignan biosyntheses, therefore, seem to be separate biosynthetic pathways only using the same precursors.

4.4.2.2 Pinoresinol/lariciresinol reductase

Incubation of cell-free extracts from *Forsythia intermedia* and *F. koreana* with coniferyl alcohol in the presence of H_2O_2 and NAD(P)H resulted in the formation of (−)-secoisolariciresinol, the enantiomer that also occurs naturally in *Forsythia* (Umezawa *et al.*, 1990, 1991, 1994; Katayama *et al.*, 1992 and 1993). The naturally occurring (+)-secoisolariciresinol (about 20% enantiomer excess) was formed with cell-free extracts from *Arctium lappa* (Umezawa and Shimada, 1996). Soluble peroxidases present in the crude cell-free extracts first catalyzed the H_2O_2-dependent coupling of two coniferyl alcohol moieties to racemic pinoresinol. Only one enantiomer was further converted by NAD(P)H-dependent reductases. This led to an accumulation of (−)-pinoresinol (that does not occur naturally in *Forsythia intermedia*) in the cell-free assay, due to metabolization of (+)-pinoresinol (Katayama *et al.*, 1992). The reduction of (+)-pinoresinol led to the formation of (−)-secoisolariciresinol via the intermediary (+)-lariciresinol in protein preparations from *Forsythia intermedia* (Katayama *et al.*, 1993) (Fig. 4.7). (+)-Lariciresinol was not reoxidized to (+)-pinoresinol when it was incubated with cell-free extracts and NADP.

Pinoresinol/lariciresinol reductase has recently been characterized, purified and cloned from *Forsythia intermedia* (Chu *et al.*, 1992; Dinkova-Kostova *et al.*, 1996). During all of the purification steps of this soluble enzyme, the reductase activities with pinoresinol and lariciresinol could not be separated, although two isoforms were resolved. Both isoforms revealed the same activities towards pinoresinol and lariciresinol and also similar kinetic properties. The hydride transfer from NADPH to the lignans is highly stereospecific. Only the 4 *pro-R* hydrogen from NADPH was transferred to the *pro-R* position at the C-7 and/or C-7′ of (+)-pinoresinol/(+)-lariciresinol (Chu *et al.*, 1992; Dinkova-Kostova *et al.*, 1996). Any mechanism in which the hydride is delivered randomly to a planar quinonemethide could, therefore, be ruled out.

Pinoresinol/lariciresinol reductase was cloned from a *Forsythia intermedia* cDNA library. The cDNA was heterologously expressed in *E. coli* and the protein exhibited the expected pinoresinol/lariciresinol reductase activity. The polypeptide deduced has 312 amino acids and a calculated MW of 34.9 kDa. Interestingly, the sequence of pinoresinol/lariciresinol reductase showed considerable similarity to isoflavone reductases, indicating a possible evolutionary relationship (Dinkova-Kostova *et al.*, 1996; Gang *et al.*, 1997).

Stereospecific reduction of (+)-pinoresinol from racemic pinoresinol to (+)-lariciresinol with the help of NADPH was demonstrated with cell-free extracts of *Zanthoxylum ailanthoides* (Katayama *et al.*, 1997). No further conversion to (−)-secoisolariciresinol occurred, although the latter is the lignan accumulated naturally in this plant species.

4.4.2.3 Formation of (−)-matairesinol from (−)-secoisolariciresinol

Matairesinol differs from secoisolariciresinol in the lactone ring. Feeding of racemic secoisolariciresinol to shoots of *Forsythia intermedia* resulted in the stereospecific formation of (−)-matairesinol (Umezawa *et al.*, 1991). This was confirmed by experiments with cell-free extracts from the same plant, which specifically converted (−)-secoisolariciresinol into (−)-matairesinol in the presence of NAD(P) (Fig. 4.7). The activity of the dehydrogenase involved was a little greater with NAD than with NADP.

4.4.2.4 Methylation reactions

Methylation of matairesinol with cell-free extracts of *Forsythia intermedia* leads to the formation of arctigenin and isoarctigenin (Ozawa *et al.*, 1993); (Fig. 4.8). *S*-adenosyl-L-methionine (SAM) served as methyl

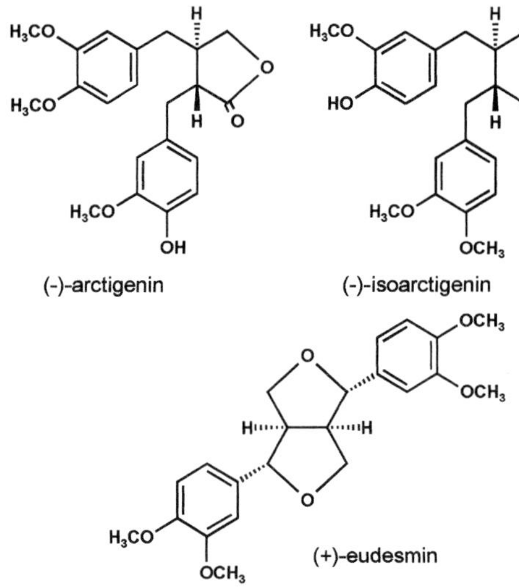

(-)-arctigenin

(-)-isoarctigenin

(+)-eudesmin

Figure 4.8 Structural formula of (−)-arctigenin, (−)-isoarctigenin and (+)-eudesmin.

donor. With racemic matairesinol as substrate, racemic arctigenin and isoarctigenin were formed, with a slight preference for the (−)-enantiomers. The reaction, therefore, is not enantiospecific and regiospecific. Only one methyl group was transferred to matairesinol. It was proposed that the formation of arctigenin proceeds from matairesinol via matairesinoside (matairesinol-glucoside) and arctiin to arctigenin. Intermediary glucosylation protects the free 4-OH group in the pendant ring and methylation takes place only in the second aromatic ring.

The non-phenolic furofuran lignan, (+)-eudesmin, from *Magnolia kobus* var. *borealis* is formed from pinoresinol by two SAM-dependent methylation steps (Miyauchi and Ozawa, 1998). Cell-free extracts catalyzed the successive non-stereospecific methylation both of (+)- and (−)-pinoresinol. Thus, the stereospecificity has to be established in an earlier step.

4.4.2.5 Steps from matairesinol to deoxypodophyllotoxin and 4′-demethyldeoxypodophyllotoxin

Little information is available concerning biosynthetic steps from matairesinol to deoxypodophyllotoxin and 4′-demethyldeoxypodophyllotoxin (Fig. 4.9). It is supposed that the transformation proceeds via

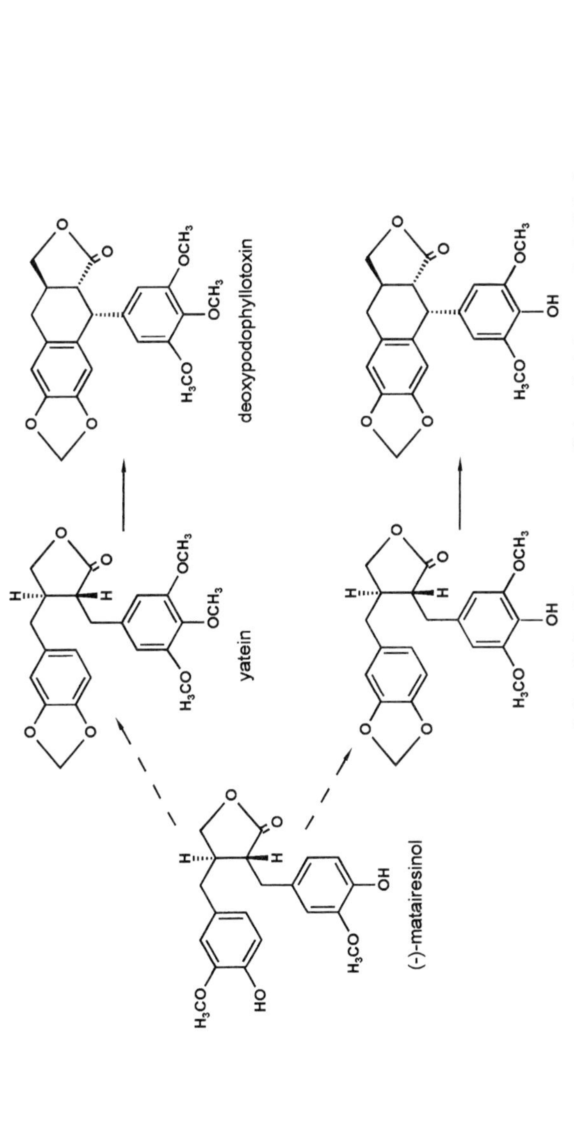

Figure 4.9 Formation of yatein and 4′-demethylyatein from (−)-matairesinol, and further transformation to deoxypodophyllotoxin and 4′-demethyldeoxypodophyllotoxin.

yatein and the reactions include ring closure, the formation of the methylenedioxy bridge and hydroxylation and methylation reactions in the pendant ring. Matairesinol is regarded as the key intermediate leading to two separate groups of lignans: those with a 3′,4′,5′-trimethoxy and those with a 4′-hydroxy-3′,5′-dimethoxy substitution pattern in the pendant ring (Kamil and Dewick, 1986a). Feeding of yatein or deoxypodophyllotoxin to *Podophyllum hexandrum* plants led to the formation of podophyllotoxin, whereas feeding of 4′-demethyldeoxypodophyllotoxin gave rise to 4′-demethylpodophyllotoxin. No interconversion occurred, indicating that the two groups arise separately from a common precursor (Jackson and Dewick, 1984; Kamil and Dewick, 1986b). Matairesinol was incorporated into both groups of lignans (Broomhead *et al.*, 1991) and may, therefore, represent the branch-point compound. The two groups of lignans then arise from yatein and 4′-demethylyatein, respectively.

4.4.2.6 Formation of methylenedioxy bridges

A number of common lignans contain methylenedioxy bridges linked to aromatic rings, e.g. yatein, podophyllotoxin and its derivatives and some lignans from *Sesamum indicum* (Ogasawara *et al.*, 1997; Kato *et al.*, 1998). Enzymes catalyzing the formation of these methylenedioxy bridges in lignan biosynthesis have not yet been described. However, feeding experiments with *Sesamum indicum* showed their sequential introduction: (+)-pinoresinol is transformed to (+)-piperitol and further to (+)-sesamin (Kato *et al.*, 1998) (Fig. 4.10). Although no experimental evidence exists, there might be a parallel between the biosynthesis of lignans and isoquinoline alkaloids. In the latter biosynthetic pathway, the formation of methylenedioxy bridges is catalyzed by cytochrome P_{450}-dependent monooxygenases (e.g. Bauer and Zenk, 1989, 1991; Rueffer and Zenk, 1994).

4.4.2.7 Biosynthesis of podophyllotoxin, β-peltatin and 5-methoxypodophyllotoxin

Deoxypodophyllotoxin is regarded as a precursor for podophyllotoxin, β-peltatin and 5-methoxypodophyllotoxin (Fig. 4.11). 4-Hydroxylation of deoxypodophyllotoxin results in podophyllotoxin, whereas 5-hydroxylation leads to β-peltatin. The formation of 5-methoxypodophyllotoxin requires either 5-hydroxylation and methylation of podophyllotoxin or 4-hydroxylation and 5-methylation of β-peltatin. The latter reaction sequence is supposed to be the pathway in *Linum flavum* (Van Uden *et al.*, 1997b). Biotransformation experiments with plants and plant cell cultures indicated the interconversions shown in Figure 4.11.

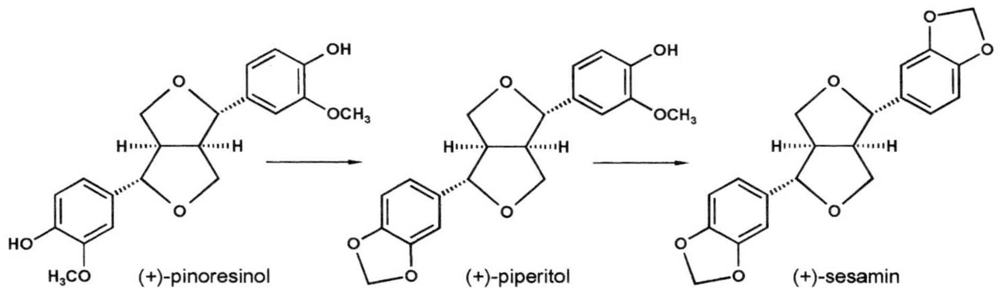

Figure 4.10 Sequential introduction of methylenedioxy bridges into (+)-pinoresinol, leading to (+)-piperitol and (+)-sesamin in *Sesamum indicum*.

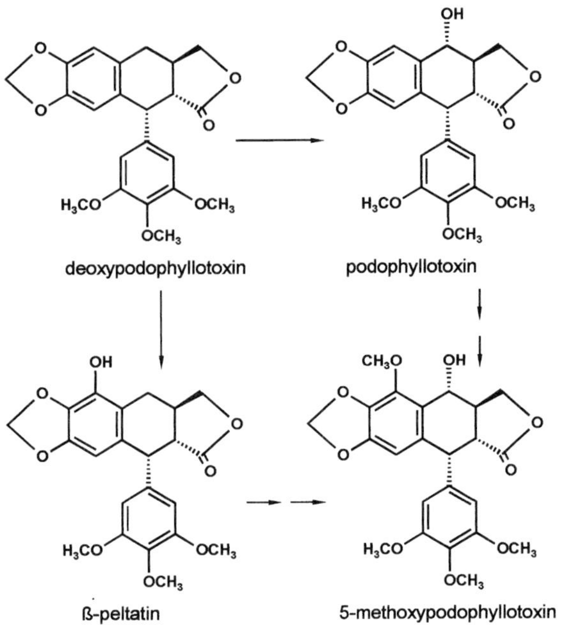

deoxypodophyllotoxin

podophyllotoxin

ß-peltatin

5-methoxypodophyllotoxin

Figure 4.11 Podophyllotoxin is formed from deoxypodophyllotoxin by 4-hydroxylation, β-peltatin by 5-hydroxylation by the cytochrome P_{450}-dependent deoxypodophyllotoxin 5-hydroxylase. 5-Methoxypodophyllotoxin is probably synthesized from β-peltatin by 4-hydroxylation and methyl transfer.

Deoxypodophyllotoxin was incorporated into podophyllotoxin after feeding to *Podophyllum hexandrum* plants (Jackson and Dewick, 1984; Kamil and Dewick, 1986b). This was also shown for cell cultures of *Podophyllum hexandrum*; here podophyllotoxin β-glucoside was isolated as well as podophyllotoxin. In *Linum flavum* suspension cultures, deoxypodophyllotoxin and β-peltatin were converted to 5-methoxypodophyllotoxin and the respective β-glucosides (Van Uden *et al.*, 1995, 1997a,b).

The first known enzyme involved in these reactions is deoxypodophyllotoxin 5-hydroxylase, which converts deoxypodophyllotoxin into β-peltatin (Molog *et al.*, 1998). The hydroxylation is catalyzed by a cytochrome P_{450}-dependent monooxygenase, dependent on NADPH and O_2. The optimum pH is 7.4. The participation of cytochrome P_{450} was demonstrated by the inhibition of the hydroxylase activity in an atmosphere consisting of 17% O_2, 20% CO and 63% N_2 by 72% in darkness, and the partial reversion of this inhibition by illuminating the assay with light at wavelength 450 nm (restored activity 45%). The enzyme has high affinities towards deoxypodophyllotoxin as well as NADPH.

4.4.2.8 Glucosylation reactions

Monolignols as well as lignans occur as glycosides. However, very active β-glucosidases are ubiquitously present in plants and, therefore, after extraction mainly the lignan aglyca are found, unless very cautious extraction methods are used.

Coniferin (the β-D-glucoside of coniferyl alcohol) is accumulated prior to lignin formation and in lignan-synthesizing cell cultures (e.g. Berlin *et al.*, 1986; Van Uden *et al.*, 1991; Smollny *et al.*, 1998). Coniferin and lignan contents were found to be inversely correlated in cell cultures. However, there is no direct proof for a transformation of stored coniferin into lignans. Feeding of coniferin resulted in an enhanced podophyllotoxin accumulation in cell cultures of *Podophyllum hexandrum* (Van Uden *et al.*, 1990).

The first description of coniferin biosynthesis by a UDP-glucose:coniferyl alcohol glucosyltransferase was reported from rose cell cultures. In addition to coniferin, where the phenolic hydroxyl group is glucosylated, isoconiferin was also formed (side chain glucosylation). UDP-glucose:-coniferyl alcohol glucosyltransferase (E.C. 2.4.1.111) is widely distributed in the plant kingdom, which correlates with its supposed function in lignin biosynthesis in formation of the storage and/or transport compound, coniferin (Ibrahim and Grisebach, 1976; Ibrahim, 1977). A coniferin-glucosyltransferase was demonstrated in lignan-accumulating cell cultures of *Linum nodiflorum* (Gisler-Ziebarth, 1997). Coniferin is stored in the vacuoles of *Pinus banksiana* and *Pinus strobus* cells (Leinhos and Savidge, 1993).

Coniferin and syringin are hydrolyzed by cell wall-associated β-glucosidases in lignifying tissues (e.g. Marcinowski and Grisebach, 1978; Marcinowski *et al.*, 1979; Burmeister and Hösel, 1981; Leinhos *et al.*, 1994; Dharmawardhana *et al.*, 1995). Similar enzymes involved in lignan biosynthesis have not so far been described, although β-glucosidase activities towards coniferin and lignan glycosides have been observed in lignan-accumulating cell cultures of *Linum* (Smollny *et al.*, 1998). In *Linum*, at least part of the coniferin was localized in the vacuole (Henges and Alfermann, unpublished results); therefore, vacuolar or cytoplasmic β-glucosidases might be involved in the hydrolysis.

Podophyllotoxin, 5-methoxypodophyllotoxin, and α- and β-peltatin are present as glucosides (e.g. Berlin *et al.*, 1988; Broomhead and Dewick, 1990; Heyenga *et al.*, 1990; Van Uden *et al.*, 1993, 1994; Wichers *et al.*, 1991; Smollny *et al.*, 1998) and the feeding of lignan agylca resulted in the formation of glucosides (Van Uden *et al.*, 1995, 1997a,b). Glucosylation takes place at the free 4- and 5-hydroxyl groups but the enzymes responsible are not known. Arctigenin, matairesinol, phillygenin and epipinoresinol have been isolated as glucosides (arctiin, matairesinoside, phillyrin and epipinoresinol glucoside, respectively) from *Forsythia* (Rahman *et al.*, 1986, 1990b; Ozawa *et al.*, 1993); in these cases, the *para*-located hydroxyl group in one of the aromatic rings was glucosylated. In *Sesamum indicum*, hexoses are linked to pinoresinol and sesaminol at the free *para*- or *ortho*-hydroxyl groups (Ogasawara *et al.*, 1997). Again, the glycosyltransferases are unknown. The isolation of glycosylated lignans together with aglyca or the complete loss of glycosylated products is probably due to β-glucosidases, and it must be assumed that all, or at least part, of the lignans is present in the glycosidic form in the plant itself.

4.5 Gallotannins and ellagitannins

Tannins are a heterogeneous group of secondary plant products characterized by their ability to bind and precipitate proteins. Two major groups of tannins are distinguished: the condensed tannins, flavonoid-derived compounds, also called proanthocyanidins; and the hydrolyzable tannins, characterized by a central polyol moiety (mostly glucose, but also hamamelose, shikimic and quinic acid or cyclitols are found) esterified with gallic acid moieties (Gross, 1999). The latter group can be subdivided into the gallotannins and the ellagitannins. The basic molecule of both groups is 1,2,3,4,6-pentagalloylglucose. In the gallotannins, this molecule is further galloylated with up to 10–12 galloyl moieties per molecule, whereas in the ellagitannins, additional C-C-bonds are introduced into the pentagalloylglucose. Higher oligomers of these compounds also occur. Tannins are widespread in the plant kingdom and a high structural variability has been found (e.g. Haddock *et al.*, 1982; Bate-Smith, 1984; Haslam and Cai, 1994; Gross, 1999).

The biosynthesis of hydrolyzable and condensed tannins must be treated separately, although derivatives of the shikimic acid pathway are involved in both biosynthetic schemes. Since the condensed tannins belong to the flavonoid group, the biosynthesis of these compounds will be addressed in the respective section (see section 4.6).

Investigations on the enzymes involved in the biosynthesis of hydrolyzable tannins and the intermediates involved therein started in the early 1980s. Reviews on the classification and the biosynthesis of hydrolyzable tannins have been published by, for example, Haslam (1989, 1992) and Gross (1994, 1999).

The basic molecule for the biosynthesis of gallo- and ellagitannins is β-glucogallin (1-*O*-galloyl-β-D-glucose) (Fig. 4.12), which is further galloylated to 1,2,3,4,6-pentagalloylglucose. Investigations into this biosynthetic pathway, mainly by Gross and co-workers, using cell-free

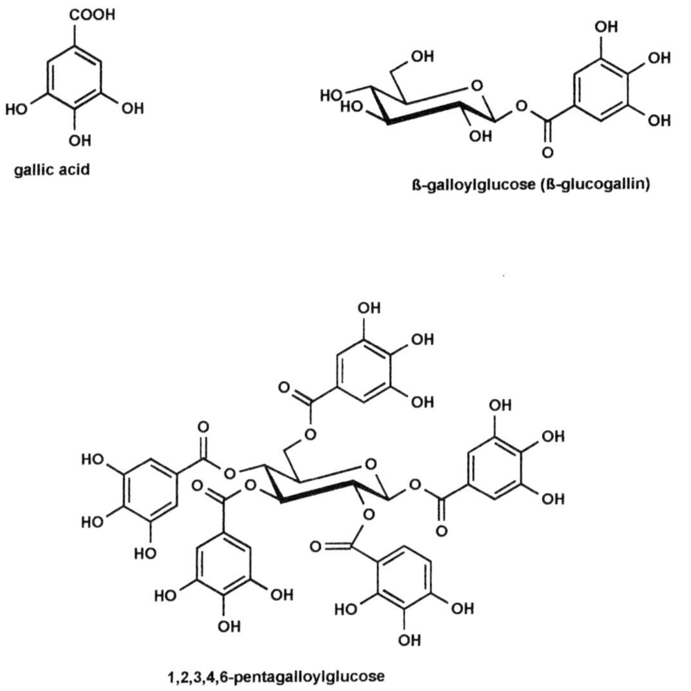

gallic acid

ß-galloylglucose (ß-glucogallin)

1,2,3,4,6-pentagalloylglucose

Figure 4.12 Structural formulae of gallic acid, β-galloylglucose (β-glucogallin) and 1,2,3,4,6-pentagalloyl-glucose.

extracts from *Quercus* spp. and *Rhus* spp., showed that β-glucogallin as well as higher galloylated glucose can act as gallic acid donor and acceptor.

4.5.1 Biosynthesis of β-glucogallin and 1,2,3,4,6-pentagalloyl-β-D-glucose

β-Glucogallin (Fig. 4.12) is formed from gallic acid and UDP-glucose by a glucosyltransferase, which was partially purified (45-fold) from young oak leaves (Gross, 1982, 1983a). In addition to gallic acid (K_m = 1.1 mM), the enzyme accepted several benzoic acids, vanillic acid being the best substrate (K_m = 0.57 mM) and, to a lesser extent, cinnamic acids. UDP-glucose was the sole glucose donor; the K_m-value for this substrate was 2.3 mM. The enzyme had an apparent MW of 68 kDa and an optimum pH of 6.5–7.0. Although gallic acid was not the best substrate, it was proposed that this enzyme was functional in the formation of β-glucogallin for the biosynthesis of gallotannins.

A question that has not been fully resolved is the origin of gallic acid (Fig. 4.12). It might be formed either directly from 3-dehydroshikimic acid by dehydrogenation or from a cinnamic acid or cinnamoyl-CoA by side chain cleavage.

β-Oxidation of 4-coumarate via 4-coumaroyl-CoA was demonstrated in cell-free extracts from cell cultures of *Lithospermum erythrorhizon* and 4-hydroxybenzoate was formed (Löscher and Heide, 1994). 4-Coumaroyl-CoA is cleaved, dependent on NAD, into 4-hydroxybenzoyl-CoA and acetyl-CoA, which are hydrolyzed into 4-hydroxybenzoate and acetate. On the other hand, French and co-workers (1976), Yazaki and co-workers (1991) and Schnitzler and co-workers (1992) have reported the formation of 4-hydroxybenzoate from 4-coumarate, without the intermediary activation as CoA-ester and with 4-hydroxybenzaldehyde as intermediate. In addition to the problem of side chain shortening, the introduction of the 3,4,5-trihydroxy substitution pattern of gallic acid is also a problem, since a cinnamic acid with this pattern has never been reported.

It has been proposed that aromatization of 3-dehydroshikimate occurs during the formation of gallic acid. This was shown by feeding experiments and inhibition experiments with L-2-aminooxy-3-phenylpropionic acid (L-AOPP) and glyphosate. L-AOPP inhibits the oxidative deamination of phenylalanine to cinnamic acid by phenylalanine ammonia-lyase, whereas glyphosate (*N*-phosphonomethyl-glycine) inhibits the formation of 3-enolpyruvylshikimate-5-phosphate, an important step in the formation of chorismate, the precursor for aromatic amino acids. It was suggested that the dehydrogenation of 3-dehydroshikimate contributes, at least partially, to the formation of gallic acid, if it is not the main pathway (Gross, 1999).

The transfer of galloyl moieties to β-glucogallin (Gross, 1983b) with the final formation of 1,2,3,4,6-pentagalloylglucose (Fig. 4.12) was clarified by Gross and co-workers in *Quercus* spp. and *Rhus typhina*. The main biosynthetic pathway follows the successive transfer of galloyl moieties to the hydroxyl groups of β-glucogallin, with β-glucogallin as galloyl donor; free glucose is released. The sequence of galloylation is very specific: 1-OH→6-OH→2-OH→3-OH→4-OH. Each of these steps is catalyzed by a specific enzyme. Some characteristics of these enzymes are summarized in Table 4.3.

In addition to the galloylation sequence described above, it was shown that higher galloylated glucoses can also act as galloyl donors. For example, two molecules of 1,6-digalloylglucose can disproportionate to 1,2,6-trigalloylglucose and 6-galloylglucose. 1,6-Digalloyl-glucose:1,6-digalloylglucose 2-*O*-galloyltransferase was purified from leaves of *Rhus typhina*. It has a native MW of 56 kDa, an optimum pH of 5.9 and an optimum temperature of 40°C (Denzel and Gross, 1991). Galloylglucoses with three and four galloyl groups were also effective as donors of their 1-*O*-galloyl group (Denzel and Gross, 1991).

Table 4.3 Characteristics of enzymes involved in the biosynthesis of 1,2,3,4,6-pentagalloylglucose

Reaction	Optimum pH	Optimum temperature	Native molecular mass	Reference
2 β-galloylGlc → 1,6-digalloylGlc + Glc	6.5	30°C	400 kDa	Gross, 1983b; Schmidt *et al.*, 1987; Gross *et al.*, 1990
1,6-digalloylGlc + β-galloylGlc → 1,2,6-trigalloylGlc + Glc	5.0–5.5	50°C	450 kDa	Denzel *et al.*, 1988; Gross and Denzel, 1991
1,2,6-trigalloylGlc + β-galloylGlc → 1,2,3,6-tetragalloylGlc + Glc	6.0	55°C	380 kDa	Hagenah and Gross, 1993
1,2,3,6-tetragalloylGlc + β-galloylGlc → 1,2,3,4,6-pentagalloylGlc + Glc	6.3	40°C	260 kDa (homotetramer, subunit 65 kDa)	Cammann *et al.*, 1989; Gross, 1999

In all cases, the donor of gallic acid is β-glucogallin (β-galloylGlc) and glucose (Glc) is released.

4.5.2 Biosynthesis of gallotannins

Gallotannins are synthesized from 1,2,3,4,6-pentagalloylglucose by further transfer of galloyl moieties in the characteristic *meta*-depside bond. β-Glucogallin serves as the galloyl donor. Enzyme extracts from leaves of *Rhus typhina* catalyzed the formation of hexa-, hepta-, octa-, nona- and decagalloylglucose (Hofmann and Gross, 1990). β-Glucogallin:1,2,3,4,6-pentagalloyl-β-D-glucose (3-*O*-galloyl)-galloyltransferase, the enzyme catalyzing the first step from pentagalloylglucose to gallotannins, was purified more than 500-fold from sumac leaves (Niemetz and Gross, 1998). The enzyme had an optimum pH of 4.0–4.5, an optimum temperature of 25°C and a native molecular mass of 170 kDa. Since sodium dodecyl sulphate-polyacrylamide gel electrophoresis (SDS-PAGE) showed a single band at 42 kDa, it was concluded that the native enzyme is a homotetramer. The main reaction product was 3-*O*-digalloyl-1,2,4,6-tetra-*O*-galloyl-β-D-glucose but other hexagalloylglucoses as well as hepta- and octagalloylglucoses were found in lower concentrations.

4.5.3 Biosynthesis of ellagitannins

The ellagitannin group comprises hexahydroxydiphenoyl and dehydrohexahydroxydiphenoyl esters formed from pentagalloylglucose, as well as dimers and higher oligomers of these compounds (Haslam and Cai, 1994). This group is structurally very diverse and more than 500 different structures have been elucidated. Schmidt and Mayer (1956) postulated that the different ellagitannin structures arise by oxidative coupling of galloyl esters, with the formation of new C-C- and C-O-bonds and oxidative and hydrolytic derivatization. A hypothetical biosynthetic scheme postulated the intramolecular C-C-coupling between galloyl residues of pentagalloylglucose giving rise to hexahydroxydiphenoyl and dehydrohexahydroxydiphenoyl esters, which can further combine to higher oligomers by C-O-bonding (Haslam, 1982; Haslam and Cai, 1984). However, no enzyme has yet been isolated from higher plants catalyzing this postulated oxidative coupling. Therefore, the biosynthesis of even the most simple ellagitannis remains unresolved. The peroxidative coupling of gallic acid to ellagic acid could be observed after addition of extracellular proteins of grapevine suspension cultures in the presence of H_2O_2 (Barcelo *et al.*, 1994). The report of a soluble enzyme from *Tellima grandiflora* that catalyzed the formation of ellagitannins from pentagalloylglucose in the presence of FMN subsequently proved to be due to enzymatic and chemical side-reactions in the enzyme assay (Gross, 1994, 1999). In alkaloid biosynthetic pathways, however, it has been shown that coupling of C-C- and C-O-bonds can be catalyzed not only by laccase- or peroxidase-like enzymes but also by cytochrome P_{450}-dependent monooxygenases. Berbamunine synthase, a cytochrome P_{450} enzyme from *Berberis* spp., catalyzes the dimerization of *N*-methylcoclaurines to berbamunine by establishing a C-O-C-bond between aromatic rings (Zenk *et al.*, 1989; Stadler and Zenk, 1993). A C-C-bond is established in the transformation of (*R*)-reticuline to salutaridine, again by a cytochrome P_{450} from *Papaver* spp. (Zenk *et al.*, 1989; Gerardy and Zenk, 1993). Participation of similar cytochrome P_{450} enzyme systems in ellagitannin biosynthesis, however, remains speculative.

4.6 Flavonoids, anthocyanins, proanthocyanidins, condensed tannins and isoflavonoids

Flavonoids, in the broadest sense (including, e.g. anthocyanins, isoflavonoids, proanthocyanins, catechins and condensed tannins), are widespread compounds in the plant kingdom with the exception of algae and Anthocerotales. More than 4000 different structures have been reported. They are formed by two different secondary pathways: the general phenylpropanoid pathway and the polyketide pathway. Phenylalanine gives rise to 4-coumaroyl-CoA or, in some cases, cinnamoyl-, caffeoyl- or feruloyl-CoA, by the enzymes of the general phenylpropanoid pathway (see section 4.2). To 4-coumaryol(caffeoyl)-CoA, three molecules of malonyl-CoA are condensed under release of three CO_2 by the key enzyme of flavonoid biosynthesis, chalcone synthase (CHS). The first C_{15}-condensation product, the chalcone (mostly the 4,2′,4′,6′-tetrahydroxychalcone), gives rise to a great variety of flavonoids, isoflavonoids, aurones, anthocyanins, proanthocyanidins and condensed tannins.

The chalcone has two aromatic rings, A and B, which are linked by a C_3-bridge (Fig. 4.13). In all other flavonoid classes, this bridge gives rise to the heterocyclic ring C, which shows various degrees of oxidation and substitution in the different flavonoid classes (see Fig. 4.13). Ring closure is catalyzed by chalcone isomerase (CHI), leading to the flavanones. Migration of the B-ring catalyzed by the cytochrome P_{450} enzyme, isoflavone synthase (Hagmann and Grisebach, 1984; Kochs and Grisebach, 1986a), opens the pathway towards the isoflavonoids and pterocarpans, which are important in plant-microbe interactions. Further variation within the flavonoid classes is introduced by different degrees of oxidation of the two aromatic rings and further substitution.

The enzymes involved in the formation of the different classes of flavonoids, isoflavonoids and anthocyanins are mostly known and

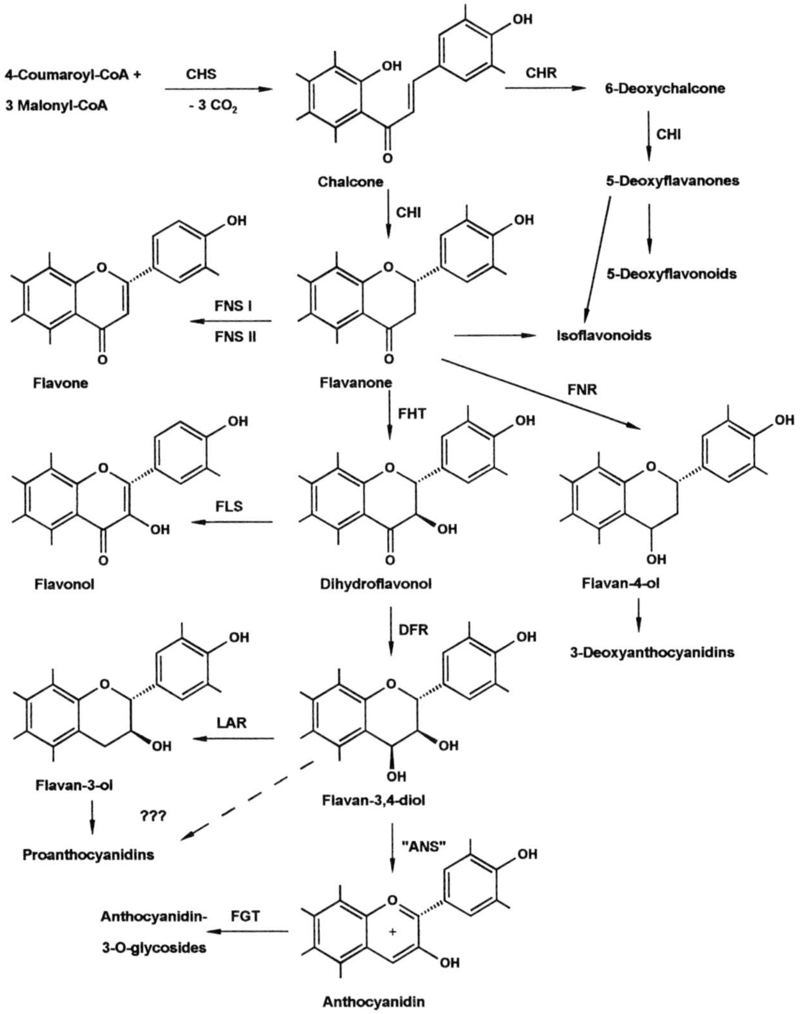

Figure 4.13 Scheme of flavonoid classes and their biosynthetic pathways. Abbreviations: CHS, chalcone synthase; CHI, chalcone isomerase; CHR, chalcone reductase; FNS, flavone synthase; FHT, flavanone 3β-hydroxylase; FNR, flavanone 4-reductase; DFR, dihydroflavonol 4-reductase; FLS, flavonol synthase; LAR, leucoanthocyanidin reductase; 'ANS', anthocyanidin synthase; FGT, flavonoid glucosyltransferase.

characterized. For most of them, cDNA or genomic clones have been isolated and regulation has been studied at the enzyme as well as the gene level. Very few enzymes are still missing, e.g. the last enzyme of anthocyanin formation 'anthocyanidin synthase'. Additionally, the formation of aurones is still not clarified at the enzymatic level. Flavonoid biosynthesis is one of the best reviewed topics of plant natural product biosynthesis and for detailed information the reader is referred to the numerous excellent and comprehensive reviews published during recent years (e.g. Stafford, 1991; Heller and Forkmann, 1993; Koes *et al.*, 1994; Holton and Cornish, 1995; Shirley, 1996; Forkmann and Heller, 1999). Therefore, only a short overview will be given here.

4.6.1 *Enzymes of flavonoid and anthocyanin biosynthesis*

4.6.1.1 *Chalcone synthase (CHS) and chalcone reductase (CHR; chalcone ketide reductase, CHKR)*

The first description of chalcone synthase (CHS) was from cell cultures of parsley, *Petroselinum crispum* (Kreuzaler and Hahlbrock, 1972). Among lower plants, CHS was detected in the liverwort *Marchantia polymorpha* (Fischer *et al.*, 1995). As stated above, CHS condenses three molecules of malonyl-CoA to 4-coumaroyl-CoA, with release of three CO_2 and the formation of the C_{15}-compound 4,2′,4′,6′-tetrahydroxychalcone. It is believed that the condensation reaction is similar to the condensation reaction of fatty acid biosynthesis, where malonyl-CoA units are also condensed with release of CO_2. A common ancestry of chalcone synthase and the enzymes involved in fatty acid biosynthesis has been proposed (Verwoert *et al.*, 1992). During recent years, a number of plant enzymes involved in similar condensation reactions in the biosyntheses of different natural products have been described, which are biochemically and/or genetically related to chalcone synthase (Schröder, 1997), e.g. acridone synthase (Junghanns *et al.*, 1995), stilbene synthase (Schröder and Schröder, 1990; Tropf *et al.*, 1994), benzophenone synthase (Beerhues, 1996), styrylpyrone synthase (Beckert *et al.*, 1997; Herderich *et al.*, 1997) or the enzyme involved in hop bitter acid formation (Zuurbier *et al.*, 1995). Generally, 4-coumaroyl-CoA serves as a substrate for CHS, which in some cases could also accept cinnamoyl-, caffeoyl-CoA or feruloyl-CoA. In most cases, however, the introduction of further substituents into the B-ring occurs at the C_{15}-level. CHS is a dimeric enzyme of subunits of 40–44 kDa. The enzyme has been purified from numerous plant sources and CHS genes from many plant species have been cloned; CHS is often encoded by a small gene family. CHS is usually considered a cytosolic enzyme but several studies have shown that it might be associated with membranes of the endoplasmic reticulum or the vacuole (Hopp *et al.*, 1985; Hrazdina *et al.*, 1987; Beerhues *et al.*, 1988; Hrazdina and Jensen, 1992).

Concomitant action of CHS and CHR leads to the formation of 6′-deoxychalcones, which are the precursors for a number of important phytoalexins (isoflavonoids, pterocarpans), e.g. in leguminous plants. The formation of 6′-deoxychalcones was first demonstrated in cell-free extracts from *Glycyrrhiza echinata* (Ayabe *et al.*, 1988a,b). CHR acts together with CHS and needs NADPH as cofactor. The enzyme was first purified and cloned from cell cultures of *Glycine max* (Welle and Grisebach, 1988a, 1989; Welle and Schröder, 1992). It is supposed that the reduction takes place at an enzyme-bound polyketide intermediate and the enzyme is, therefore, also named chalcone polyketide reductase (CHKR).

4.6.1.2 Chalcone isomerase (CHI)

Although chalcones can isomerize spontaneously to the respective flavanones under suitable conditions, it is now generally accepted that this reaction is catalyzed by chalcone isomerase (CHI) in the plant, where (2*S*)-flavanones are exclusively formed (see Fig. 4.13). This enzyme was detected more than 30 years ago by Moustafa and Wong (1967) in soybean. Two types of CHI exist, one accepting only 6′-hydroxychalcones and the other accepting 6′-deoxychalcones, forming 5-hydroxy- and 5-deoxyflavanones, respectively (see Heller and Forkmann, 1993; Forkmann and Heller, 1999). Chalcone glycosides cannot be transformed by CHI. CHI is a monomeric enzyme with a molecular mass of 24–29 kDa. It has been purified and cloned from a number of plant sources. Interestingly, the homology of CHI from different plant sources can be as low as 44% of the amino acid residues (Forkmann and Heller, 1999).

4.6.1.3 Flavone synthase I and II (FNS I, FNS II)

Flavones are formed from flavanones by the introduction of a double bond between C_2 and C_3 of the heterocycle (Fig. 4.13). Formally, this reaction is the abstraction of two hydrogens from the flavanone; enzymatically, it is performed by hydroxylases of either the cytochrome P_{450}-dependent monooxygenase (FNS II) or the 2-oxoglutarate-dependent dioxygenase (FNS I) type. The former type of reaction was detected in *Antirrhinum majus* (Stotz and Forkmann, 1981). The monooxygenase is typically membrane-bound and dependent on NADPH and molecular oxygen. FNS II was characterized from cell cultures of *Glycine max* (Kochs and Grisebach, 1986b). FNS I, on the other hand, is a soluble enzyme dependent on 2-oxoglutarate, molecular oxygen and Fe^{2+} and enhanced in its activity by ascorbate. This enzyme was first detected in *Petroselinum crispum* (Sutter *et al.*, 1975; Britsch *et al.*, 1981) and seems to be restricted to Apiaceae. FNS I has been purified by Britsch (1990a); it is a dimer of subunits of 24–25 kDa. Flavanones but not dihydroflavonols are accepted as substrates.

4.6.1.4 Flavanone 3ß-hydroxylase (FHT)

Another possible reaction acting on flavanones is the hydroxylation in position 3 of the hetercycle, giving rise to dihydroflavonols. This reaction was first detected in *Matthiola incana* (Forkmann *et al.*, 1980) and classified as a 2-oxoglutarate-dependent dioxygenase with 2-oxoglutarate, Fe^{2+} and ascorbate as cofactors. FHT is widespread in the plant kingdom. The enzyme was found to be extremely unstable and the molecular mass could only be determined after extreme caution during its purification from *Petunia* (Britsch and Grisebach, 1986; Britsch, 1990b). The molecular mass is 41–42 kDa, which corresponds to the molecular mass deduced from the cDNA clone (Britsch *et al.*, 1992). *In vivo*, the enzyme acts as a dimer. Essential amino acid residues of the putative active site have been identified by site-directed mutagenesis (Lukacin and Britsch, 1997).

4.6.1.5 Flavonol synthase (FLS)

Another 2-oxoglutarate-dependent dioxygenase acts on dihydroflavonols and introduces the C_2C_3-double-bond of the heterocycle forming flavonols. This is a parallel reaction to the reaction of flavone synthase (see section 4.6.1.3) but takes place specifically with dihydroflavonols. FLS was first described in enzyme preparations from cell cultures of parsley (Britsch *et al.*, 1981) but seems not to be restricted to the Apiaceae, since it was detected in a number of species belonging to different families (see Heller and Forkmann, 1993; Forkmann and Heller, 1999). Corresponding cDNA/genomic clones have been isolated from several plant species (see Forkmann and Heller, 1999).

4.6.1.6 Flavanone 4-reductase (FNR) and dihydroflavonol 4-reductase (DFR)

The carbonyl group in position 4 of flavanones and dihydroflavonols can be reduced by NADPH-dependent enzymes to OH-groups. The reduction of flavanones to flavan-4-ols (FNR) was first demonstrated with enzyme preparations from *Sinningia cardinalis* (Stich and Forkmann, 1988). FNR activity was detected mainly in plants producing 3-deoxyanthocyanidins. DFR activity was first shown in *Pseudotsuga menziesii* (Stafford and Lester, 1982). DFR catalyzes the reduction of dihydroflavonols to the respective flavan-3,4-diols, also called leucoanthocyanidins. Both enzymatic activities, FNR and DFR, are widespread in the plant kingdom. DFR from different plant sources shows distinct substrate specificity, correlated to the B-ring substitution patterns of the main flavonoids/anthocyanins accumulated in the respective plants. In some but not all cases, DFR also catalyzes the reduction of flavanones and FNR the reduction of dihydroflavonols (see Heller and Forkmann, 1993; Forkmann and Heller, 1999). It is not yet unequivocally clear whether FNR and DFR are the same enzymes or coded by different genes. DFR was purified from *Dahlia variabilis* (MW 41 kDa) (Fischer *et al.*, 1988) and cloned from several plant sources. Transformation of *Petunia*, which cannot usually accumulate pelargonidin-derivatives, with DFR from maize led to a changed flower colour due to the altered substitution pattern of the anthocyanins (Meyer *et al.*, 1987).

4.6.1.7 'Anthocyanidin synthase (ANS)', leucoanthocyanidin dioxygenase (LDOX)

Interestingly, there is still no *in vitro* enzymatic evidence for the formation of anthocyanidins from flavan-3,4-diols or leucoanthocyanidins, although it has been demonstrated that these are the correct precursors. From several plant sources (see Forkmann and Heller, 1999; Pelletier *et al.*, 1997), genes have been cloned which are supposed to code for 'anthocyanidin synthase' and the amino acid sequences deduced indicate that the enzyme is a 2-oxoglutarate-dependent dioxygenase. The direct product, the anthocyanidin, may be extremely unstable. However, even in the presence of suitable glucosyltransferases (see section 4.6.1.8), ANS enzyme activities have not so far been detected.

4.6.1.8 UDP-glucose:flavonoid 3-O-glucosyltransferase (FGT)

In anthocyanidins, and often in the other flavonoid classes, the hydroxyl group at C_3 of the heterocycle is glycosylated in order to stabilize the structure. UDP-activated sugars, in many cases UDP-glucose, are generally used as sugar donors. Other sugars, e.g. galactose, can also be attached as the first sugar (Gläβgen *et al.*, 1992, 1998; Rose *et al.*, 1996). FGT activity was first demonstrated in maize pollen (see Forkmann and Heller, 1999). Further sugar moieties, as well as acyl residues, may be attached to the primary sugar moiety. Glucosyltransferases have been characterized, purified and cloned from several plant sources (see Heller and Forkmann, 1993; Forkmann and Heller, 1999). The glycosylation is regarded as necessary for a vacuolar accumulation of flavonoids and anthocyanins.

4.6.2 Formation of proanthocyanidins and condensed tannins

Flavan-3,4-diols (leucoanthocyanidins) are reduced to flavan-2,3-*trans*-3-ols by a NADPH-dependent leucoanthocyanidin 4-reductase (LAR), which was first isolated from *Pseudotsuga menziesii* (Stafford and Lester, 1984). The enzyme transforms leucocyanidin to (+)-catechin and leucodelphinidin to (+)-gallocatechin. The parallel enzymes forming the flavan-2,3-*cis*-3-ols, epicatechin and epigallocatechin, are not yet known. A spatial restriction of LAR activity was observed in flower petals, where anthocyanins were synthesized and accumulated only in epidermal cells, whereas proanthocyanidins were synthesized and accumulated in parenchymatic tissue (Skadhauge *et al.*, 1997).

There is so far no enzymatic evidence for the formation of condensed tannins, that is the formation of oligomers of proanthocanidins, despite their wide occurrence in the plant kingdom.

4.6.3 Modification of flavonoids and anthocyanins

Rings A and B are generally modified in naturally occurring flavonoids and anthocyanins. The modifications include: hydroxylation, methylation, glycosylation (C- and O-), acylation (with aliphatic or aromatic acids), prenylation and sulfation. This section presents a short overview of these modifications, which have been reviewed in detail by Heller and Forkmann (1993) and Forkmann and Heller (1999).

Hydroxylation. In addition to the hydroxyl groups in positions 5 and 7 (A-ring) and 4′ (B-ring), which are formed during the establishment of the C_{15}-skeleton, hydroxyl groups can be introduced into positions 6 and 8 of ring A and 2′, 3′ and 5′ of ring B. All the known hydroxylases involved in these hydroxylation reactions are cytochrome P_{450}-dependent monooxygenases, e.g. the newly discovered flavonol 6- and 8-hydroxylases (see Forkmann and Heller, 1999), flavonoid 3′-hydroxylase, first established in *Haplopappus gracilis* (Fritsch and Grisebach, 1975) and flavonoid 3′,5′-hydroxylase, first detected in *Verbena hybrida* (Stotz and Forkmann, 1982). Flavonoid 3′,5′-hydroxylase has been cloned from several plant species (see Forkmann and Heller, 1999). The introduction of the rare 2′-OH-groups is not clarified at the enzymatic level for flavonoids, although it is well-known for isoflavonoids (see section 4.6.4.4). Hydroxylation of 6′-deoxychalcones in position 3 of the aromatic ring derived from 4-coumaroyl-CoA to butein is catalyzed by a specific cytochrome P_{450}-monooxygenase (‘chalcone 3-hydroxylase’), which is different from flavonoid 3′-hydroxylase (Wimmer *et al.*, 1998).

Methylation. Generally, all hydroxyl groups in rings A, B and the heterocycle of flavonoids, isoflavonoids and anthocyanins can be O-methylated. C-methylated flavones (positions 6 and 8 of the A-ring) have been observed, but the respective methyltransferases are not known. The ubiquitous methyl donor is *S*-adenosyl-L-methionine (SAM). The methyltransferases can be rather unspecific with respect to their substrates or very specific. In the latter case, only specific substrates are accepted and consecutive methylation at different positions takes place in a strict sequence, mostly at later stages of the biosynthesis. A novel *O*-methyltransferase was cloned from *Chrysosplenium americanum*, which methylates phenylpropanoids as well as flavonoids, thus showing a very broad substrate pattern (Gauthier *et al.*, 1998).

Glycosylation. In addition to glycosylation at the C_3 hydroxyl group of the heterocycle, which is essential for anthocyanin stability (see section 4.6.1.8), all other hydroxyl groups (*O*-glycosylation at positions 3, 5, 7, 2′, 3′, 4′, 5′) of anthocyanins and flavonoids can be glycosylated with one or more sugar moieties. C-glycosides (positions 6 and 8 of ring A) also occur. Generally, UDP-activated sugars or sugar acids (e.g. glucose, galactose, xylose, rhamnose and glucuronic acid) are used by the mostly soluble glycosyltransferases (see Heller and Forkmann, 1993; Forkmann and Heller, 1999). Further sugar residues can be attached to the primary sugars (e.g. Rose *et al.*, 1996; Gläßgen *et al.*, 1998) and these can be further substituted by acyl residues. Glycosylation of flavonol 3-*O*-glycosides in position 2″ is catalyzed by a membrane-bound galactosyltransferase in *Petunia* pollen (Vogt and Taylor, 1995). It has been shown that the correct glycosylation and acylation pattern is essential for the transport of the anthocyanin into the vacuole (Hopp and Seitz, 1987).

C-glycosylation at C_6 or C_8 of flavanones was demonstrated with enzyme preparations from *Fagopyrum esculentum* (Kerscher and Franz, 1987, 1988).

Acylation. Two different kinds of acylation can be found for flavonoids: the transfer of aliphatic or aromatic acids to glycosyl substituents; or the sulfation of phenolic hydroxyl groups of flavones and flavonols. The most common aliphatic organic acids are acetate, malonate or succinate, which are transferred via their coenzyme A-thioesters to OH-groups of sugar residues. Aromatic acids, such as differently substituted cinnamic acids, can be activated as CoA-esters or as 1-*O*-glucose esters (Gläßgen and Seitz, 1992). Several specific acyltransferases have been characterized from different plant species. The reader is referred to recent reviews for further details (Heller and Forkmann, 1993; Forkmann and Heller, 1999).

Sulfation. Flavonoid sulfotransferases have been detected in enzyme extracts from *Flaveria* spp. (Varin *et al.*, 1987; Barron *et al.*, 1988). Different positions can be sulfated: flavonols in position 3, further flavonol-3-sulfates in positions 3′ and 4′ in ring B and 7 in ring A. 3′-Phosphoadenosine 5′-phosphosulfate (PAPS) is the ubiquitous sulfate donor. Different sulfotransferases have been purified from *Flaveria* and cDNA clones for two of them have been isolated (Varin and Ibrahim, 1989, 1991, 1992; Varin *et al.*, 1992).

Glutathione transfer. The transfer of glutathione to anthocyanins has been shown to be essential for the transport of these compounds into the vacuole by a glutathione pump in maize (Marrs *et al.*, 1995; Marrs, 1996).

Prenylation. The transfer of dimethylallylpyrophosphate to C_8 of kaempferol is catalyzed by enzyme extracts from *Epimedium diphyllum* (Yamamoto *et al.*, 1997).

4.6.4 *Biosynthesis of isoflavonoids and pterocarpans*

Isoflavonoids and the pterocarpans which are derived from isoflavones differ from flavonoids in the position of the aromatic B-ring, which is attached in position 3 of the heterocycle. The important reaction for isoflavonoid biosynthesis, therefore, is the migration of the B-ring, which is catalyzed by isoflavone synthase and the concomitant action of a dehydratase. Isoflavonoids and pterocarpans occur as 5-hydroxy- as well as 5-deoxy-derivatives. They play crucial roles in plant-microbe interactions, e.g. the establishment of the *Rhizobium symbiosis* in leguminous plants or as phytoalexins in the defence against pathogens.

4.6.4.1 *Isoflavone synthase (IFS) and dehydratase (IFD)*

Isoflavone synthase (IFS), in coaction with a soluble dehydratase, was first demonstrated in soybean, catalyzing B-ring migration (Hagmann and Grisebach, 1984; Kochs and Grisebach, 1986a). (2*S*)-Naringenin is transformed to 2-hydroxyisoflavanone by a cytochrome P_{450}-mediated reaction, and further to genistein by dehydration (Fig. 4.14). The reaction requires molecular oxygen and NADPH. (2*S*)-Liquiritigenin is transformed to daidzein accordingly (Fig. 4.14).

4.6.4.2 *4′-O-Methyltransferase*

Biosynthesis of pterocarpan phytoalexins in chickpea requires the 4′-*O*-methylation of daidzein and genistein to formononetin and biochanin A, respectively (Fig. 4.14). In contrast, the glyceollins in soybean have a free 4′-OH-group. 4′-*O*-Methylation of isoflavones has not yet been unequivocally demonstrated *in vitro*; activities measured in protein preparations from *Pisum sativum* were very low (Dixon *et al.*, 1995). Interestingly, only methylation of the 7-OH-group was observed, although corresponding

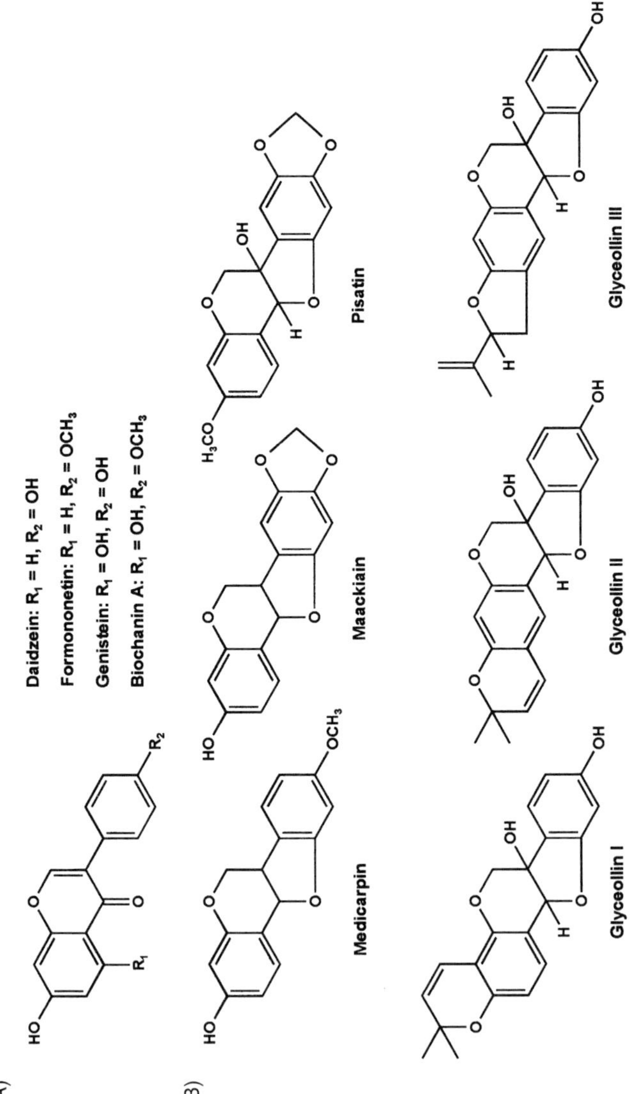

Figure 4.14 Examples of some important isoflavones (A) and pterocarpan phytoalexins (B).

products have not been detected in alfalfa or chickpea. The 7-*O*-methyltransferase was cloned from *Medicago sativa* and the enzyme expressed in *E. coli* catalyzed only 7-*O*-methylation and not methylation in position 4′ (He *et al.*, 1998).

4.6.4.3 Glucosylation and malonylation

Vacuolar storage of isoflavones (daidzein and genistein in soybean, formononetin and biochanin A in chickpea) (Fig. 4.14) as 7-*O*-glucoside 6″-*O*-malonate conjugates has been observed. Isoflavones are thus conjugated by a UDP-glucose-dependent 7-*O*-glucosyltransferase (IGT) and a malonyl-CoA-dependent malonyl transferase (IMT). The conjugates are transported into the vacuole and can be released from there after cleavage by a membrane-associated malonyl esterase (IEST) and an isoflavone glucoside-specific β-glucosidase (IGLC) (Barz and Welle, 1992).

4.6.4.4 Isoflavone 2′- and 3′-hydroxylase (I2′H, I3′H) and isoflavone reductase (IFR)

Two cytochrome P_{450}-dependent microsomal hydroxylases open the pathway towards the pterocarpans. Daidzein or formononetin are hydroxylated in position 2′ to 2′-hydroxydaidzein and 2′-hydroxyformononetin, respectively (Hinderer *et al.*, 1987; Clemens *et al.*, 1993). Formononetin can first be hydroxylated in position 3′ (Hinderer *et al.*, 1987; Clemens *et al.*, 1993) followed by methylenedioxy bridge formation and 2′-hydroxylation leading to 2′-hydroxypseudobaptigenin. These isoflavones are further reduced to the respective isoflavanones by the NADPH-dependent isoflavone reductases (Tiemann *et al.*, 1987; Fischer *et al.*, 1990a; Preisig *et al.*, 1990; Paiva *et al.*, 1991). The stereochemistry of the pterocarpans of different plant species is determined by these species-specific oxidoreductases.

4.6.4.5 Pterocarpan synthase (PTS)

Isoflavanones are further converted to pterocarpans by closing the C-O-C-bridge between the heterocycle and ring B. The pterocarpan synthases have been isolated from *Cicer arietinum* (Bless and Barz, 1988) and *Glycine max* (Fischer *et al.*, 1990b). They are soluble enzymes, dependent on NADPH. In chickpea, this is the final step of pterocarpan phytoalexin synthesis, giving rise to the plant-specific compounds, maackiain and medicarpin (Fig. 4.14), which can be stored in the vacuole as malonylglucosides (Weidemann *et al.*, 1991). In *Glycine max* and *Pisum sativum*, the pterocarpans (3,9-dihydroxypterocarpan and maackiain, respectively) will be further converted to the species-specific phytoalexins.

4.6.4.6 Pterocarpan 6a-hydroxylase

Pterocarpans hydroxylated in position 6 are the main products in soybean and pea. The introduction of this hydroxyl group in position 6a of (–)-3,9-dihydroxypterocarpan is catalyzed by pterocarpan 6a-hydroxylase, a cytochrome P_{450}-dependent monooxygenase first detected in soybean (Hagmann *et al.*, 1984). The reaction is dependent on O_2 and NADPH and the reaction product is (–)-glycinol. Pterocarpan 6a-hydroxylase has been purified to homogeneity from soybean cell cultures (Kochs and Grisebach, 1989). The parallel hydroxylation in pea seems to incorporate oxygen from water into (+)-maackiain (6a*S*) in order to yield (+)-6a-hydroxymaackiain (Matthews *et al.*, 1987).

*4.6.4.7 Pterocarpan 3-*O*-methyltransferase*

Methylation in position 3 of the A-ring of 6a-hydroxymaackiain leads to the major phytoalexin of *Pisum sativum*, (+)-pisatin (Fig. 4.14) (Preisig *et al.*, 1989). A cDNA clone for this (+)-6a-hydroxymaackiain 3-*O*-methyltransferase has recently been isolated (Wu *et al.*, 1997).

4.6.4.8 Pterocarpan prenylation and cyclization

Dimethylallylpyrophosphate is transferred (under release of pyrophosphate) by membrane-bound prenyltransferases to either position 2 or 4 of glycinol in *Glycine max* (Welle and Grisebach, 1991) or to position 10 of 3,9-dihydroxypterocarpan in *Phaseolus vulgaris* (Biggs *et al.*, 1987, 1990), leading to the precursors of the glyceollins and phaseollin, respectively. Another prenyltransferase prenylating positions 6, 8 and 3′ of isoflavones was isolated from lupin, *Lupinus albus* (Laflamme *et al.*, 1993).

Cyclization of the glyceollidins I and II to the final glyceollins I, II and III (Fig. 4.14) is catalyzed by prenylcyclases, which are cytochrome P_{450}-monooxygenase(s) (Welle and Grisebach, 1988b).

References

Afek, U., Carmeli, S. and Aharoni, N. (1995) Columbianetin, a phytoalexin associated with celery resistance to pathogens during storage. *Phytochemistry*, **39** 1347-50.

Ahl Goy, P., Signer, H., Reist, R., Aichholz, R., Blum, W., Schmidt, E. and Kessmann, H. (1993) Accumulation of scopoletin is associated with the high disease resistance of the hybrid *Nicotiana glutinosa* x *Nicotiana debneyi*. *Planta*, **191** 200-206.

Akhtar, M. and Wright, J.N. (1991) A unified mechanistic view of oxidative reactions catalyzed by P_{450} and related Fe-containing enzymes. *Natural Prod. Rep.*, **8** 527-51.

Allina, S.M., Pri-Hadash, A., Theilmann, D.A., Ellis, B.E. and Douglas, C.J. (1998) 4-Coumarate:coenzyme A ligase in hybrid poplar: properties of native enzymes, cDNA cloning and analysis of recombinant enzymes. *Plant Physiol.*, **116** 743-54.

Andreae, S.R. and Andreae, W.A. (1949) The metabolism of scopoletin by healthy and virus-infected potato tubers. *Can. J. Res.*, **27** 15-22.

Appert, C., Logemann, E., Hahlbrock, K., Schmid, J. and Amrhein, N. (1994) Structural and catalytic properties of the four phenylalanine ammonia-lyase isoenzymes from parsley (*Petroselinum crispum* Nym.). *Eur. J. Biochem.*, **225** 491-99.

Atanassova, R., Favet, N., Martz, F., Chabbert, B., Tollier, M.T., Monties, B., Fritig, B. and Legrand, M. (1995) Altered lignin composition in transgenic tobacco expressing *O*-methyltransferase sequences in sense and antisense orientation. *Plant J.*, **8** 465-77.

Ayabe, S., Udagawa, A. and Furuya, T. (1988a) Stimulation of chalcone synthase activity by yeast extract in cultured *Glycyrrhiza echinata* cells and 5-deoxyflavone formation by isolated protoplasts. *Plant Cell Rep.*, **7** 35-38.

Ayabe, S., Udagawa, A. and Furuya, T. (1988b) NADP(H)-dependent 6′-deoxychalcone synthase activity in *Glycyrrhiza echinata* cells induced by yeast extract. *Arch. Biochem. Biophys.*, **261** 458-62.

Ayres, D.C. (1969) Incorporation of L-[U-^{14}C]-β-phenylalanine into the lignan podophyllotoxin. *Tetrahedron Lett.*, **11** 883-86.

Ayres D.C. and Loike, J.D. (1990) Lignans: Chemical, Biological and Clinical Properties. Cambridge University Press, Cambridge, UK.

Ayres, D.C., Farrow, A. and Carpenter, B.G. (1981) Lignans and related polyphenols. Part 16. The biogenesis of podophyllotoxin. *J. Chem. Soc. Perkin Trans.*, **1** 2134-36.

Baker, M.E. and Blasco, R. (1992) Expansion of the mammalian 3β-hydroxysteroid dehydrogenase/plant dihydroflavonol reductase superfamily to include a bacterial cholesterol dehydrogenase, a bacterial UDP-galactose 4-epimerase, and open reading frames in vaccinia virus and fish lymphocystis disease virus. *FEBS Lett.*, **301** 89-93.

Baker, M.E., Luu-The, V., Simard, J. and Labrie, F. (1990) A common ancestor for mammalian 3β-hydroxysteroid dehydrogenase and plant dihydroflavonol reductase. *Biochem. J.*, **269** 558-59.

Barcelo, A.R., Zapata, J.M. and Calderon, A.A. (1994) Oxidation of gallic acid to ellagic acid by the extracellular protein fraction from grapevine (*Vitis vinifera* L.) cell suspension cultures. *Wein-Wiss.*, **49** 83-85.

Barron, D., Varin, L., Ibrahim, R.K., Harborne, J.B. and Williams, C.A. (1988) Sulphated flavonoids: an update. *Phytochemistry*, **27** 2375-95.

Barz, W. and Welle, R. (1992) Biosynthesis and metabolism of isoflavones and pterocarpan phytoalexins in chickpea, soybean and phytopathogenic fungi, in *Phenolic Metabolism in Plants* (eds. H.A. Stafford and R.K. Ibrahim), Plenum Press, New York, pp. 139-64.

Bate-Smith, E.C. (1984) Age and distribution of gallolyl esters, iridoids and certain other repellents in plants. *Phytochemistry*, **23** 945-90.

Baucher, M., Van Doorsselaere, J., Gielen, J., Inze, D., Van Montagu, M. and Boerjan, W. (1995) Genomic nucleotide sequence of an *Arabidopsis thaliana* gene encoding a cinnamyl alcohol dehydrogenase. *Plant Physiol.*, **107** 285-86.

Baudracco, S., Grima-Pettenati, J., Boudet, A.M. and Gahan, P.B. (1993) Quantitative cytochemical localization of cinnamyl alcohol dehydrogenase activity in plant tissues. *Phytochem. Anal.*, **4** 205-209.

Bauer, W. and Zenk, M.H. (1989) Formation of both methylenedioxy groups in the alkaloid (*S*)-stylopine is catalyzed by cytochrome P_{450} enzymes. *Tetrahedron Lett.*, **30** 5257-60.

Bauer, W. and Zenk, M.H. (1991) Two methylenedioxy bridge-forming cytochrome P_{450}-dependent enzymes are involved in (*S*)-stylopine biosynthesis. *Phytochemistry*, **30** 2953-61.

Beckert, C., Horn, C., Schnitzler, J.P., Lehning, A., Heller, M. and Veit, M. (1997) Styrylpyrone biosynthesis in *Equisetum arvense*. *Phytochemistry*, **44** 275-83.

Beerhues, L. (1996) Benzophenone synthase from cultured cells of *Centaurium erythraea*. *FEBS Lett.*, **383** 264-66.

Beerhues, L., Robenek, H. and Wiermann, R. (1988) Chalcone synthases from spinach (*Spinacia oleracea* L.). II. Immunofluorescence and immunogold localization. *Planta*, **173** 544-53.

Beier, R.C., Ivie, G.W. and Oertli, E.H. (1994) Linear furanocoumarins and graveolone from the common herb parsley. *Phytochemistry*, **36** 869-72.

Berenbaum, M.R. and Zangerl, A.R. (1996) Phytochemical diversity: adaption or random variation? *Rec. Adv. Phytochem.*, **30** 1-24.

Bergendorff, O., Dekermendjian, K., Nielsen, M., Shan, R., Witt, R., Ai, J. and Sterner, O. (1997) Furanocoumarins with affinity to brain benzodiazepine receptors *in vitro*. *Phytochemistry*, **44** 1121-24.

Berlin, J., Wray, V., Mollenschott, C. and Sasse, F. (1986) Formation of β-peltatin-A methylether and coniferin by root cultures of *Linum flavum*. *J. Nat. Prod.*, **49** 435-39.

Berlin, J., Bedorf, N., Wray, V. and Höfle, G. (1988) On the podophyllotoxins of root cultures of *Linum flavum*. *Planta Med.*, **54** 204-206.

Biggs, D.R., Welle, R., Visser, F.R. and Grisebach, H. (1987) Dimethylallylpyrophosphate:3,9-dihydroxypterocarpan 10-dimethylallyl transferase from *Phaseolus vulgaris*. *FEBS Lett.*, **220** 223-26.

Biggs, D.R., Welle, R. and Grisebach, H. (1990) Intracellular localization of prenyltransferases of isoflavonoid phytoalexin biosynthesis in bean and soybean. *Planta*, **181** 244-48.

Bless, W. and Barz, W. (1988) Isolation of pterocarpan synthase, the terminal enzyme of pterocarpan phytoalexin biosynthesis in cell suspension cultures of *Cicer arietinum* (L.). *FEBS Lett.*, **235** 47-50.

Bollwell, G.P. and Butt, V.S. (1983) Photoinduced changes of *o*-diphenol oxidase and *p*-coumarate hydroxylase activities in spinach beet seedlings and leaves. *Phytochemistry*, **22** 37-45.

Bollwell, G.P., Bell, J.N., Cramer, C.L., Schuch, W., Lamb, C. and Dixon, R.A. (1985) L-Phenylalanine ammonia-lyase from *Phaseolus vulgaris*: characterization and differential induction of multiple forms from elicitor-treated cell suspension cultures. *Eur. J. Biochem.*, **149** 411-19.

Bollwell, G.P., Bozak, K. and Zimmerlin, A. (1994) Plant cytochrome P_{450}. *Phytochemistry*, **37** 1491-506.

Boniwell, J.M. and Butt, V.S. (1986) Flavin nucleotide-dependent 3-hydroxylation of 4-hydroxyphenylpropanoid carboxylic acids by particulate preparations from potato tubers. *Z. Naturforsch.*, **41c** 56-60.

Boudet, A.M. (1998) A new view of lignification. *Trends Plant Sci.*, **3** 67-71.

Britsch, L. (1990a) Purification and characterization of flavone synthase I, a 2-oxoglutarate-dependent desaturase. *Arch. Biochem. Biophys.*, **282** 152-60.

Britsch, L. (1990b) Purification of flavanone 3β-hydroxylase from *Petunia hybrida*: antibody preparation and characterization of a chemogenetically-defined mutant. *Arch. Biochem. Biophys.*, **276** 348-54.

Britsch, L. and Grisebach, H. (1986) Purification and characterization of (2*S*)-flavanone 3-hydroxylase from *Petunia hybrida*. *Eur. J. Biochem.*, **156** 569-77.

Britsch, L., Heller, W. and Grisebach, H. (1981) Conversion of flavanone to flavone, dihydroflavonol and flavonol with an enzyme system from cell cultures of parsley. *Z. Naturforsch.*, **36c** 742-50.

Britsch, L., Ruhnau-Brich, B. and Forkmann, G. (1992) Molecular cloning, sequence analysis, and *in vitro* expression of flavanone 3β-hydroxylase from *Petunia hybrida*. *J. Biol. Chem.*, **267** 5380-87.

Broomhead, A.J. and Dewick, P.M. (1990) Aryltetralin lignans from *Linum flavum* and *Linum capitatum*. *Phytochemistry*, **29** 3839-44.

Broomhead, A.J., Rahman, M.M.A., Dewick, P.M., Jackson, D.E. and Lucas, J.A. (1991) Matairesinol as precursor of *Podophyllum* lignans. *Phytochemistry*, **30** 1489-92.

Brouillard, R. and Dangles, O. (1994) Flavonoids and flower colour, in *The Flavonoids* (ed. J.B. Harborne), Chapman & Hall, London, pp. 565-88.

Brown, S.A. (1986) Biosynthesis of daphnetin in *Daphne mezereum* (L.). *Z. Naturforsch.*, **41c** 247-52.

Brown, S.A., March, R.E., Rivett, D.E.A. and Thompson, H.J. (1988) Intermediates in the formation of puberulin by *Agathosma puberula. Phytochemistry*, **27** 391-95.

Bugos, R.C., Chiang, V.L.C. and Campbell, W.H. (1992) Characterization of bispecific caffeic acid/5-hydroxyferulic acid *O*-methyltransferase from aspen. *Phytochemistry*, **31** 1495-98.

Burmeister, G. and Hösel, W. (1981) Immunohistological localization of β-glucosidases in lignin and isoflavone metabolism in *Cicer arietinum* (L.) seedlings. *Planta*, **152** 578-86.

Busam, G., Junghanns, K.T., Kneusel, R.E., Kassemeyer, H.-H. and Matern, U. (1997) Characterization and expression of caffeoyl-coenzyme A 3-*O*-methyltransferase proposed for the induced resistance response of *Vitis vinifera* (L.). *Plant Physiol.*, **115** 1039-48.

Cammann, J., Denzel, K., Schilling, G. and Gross, G.G. (1989) Biosynthesis of gallotannins: β-glucogallin-dependent formation of 1,2,3,4,6-pentagalloylglucose by enzymatic galloylation of 1,2,3,6-tetragalloylglucose. *Arch. Biochem. Biophys.*, **273** 58-63.

Chu, A., Dinkova, A., Davin, L.B., Bedgar, D.L. and Lewis, N.G. (1992) Stereospecificity of (+)-pinoresinol and (+)-lariciresinol reductases from *Forsythia intermedia. J. Biol Chem.*, **268** 27026-33.

Clemens, S., Hinderer, W., Wittkampf, U. and Barz, W. (1993) Characterization of cytochrome P_{450}-dependent isoflavone hydroxylases from chickpea. *Phytochemistry*, **32** 653-57.

Conn, E.E. (1984) Compartmentation of secondary compounds. *Annu. Proc. Phytochem. Soc. Eur.*, **24** 1-28.

Coxon, D.T., Curtis, R.F., Price, K.R. and Levett, G. (1973) Abnormal metabolites produced by *Daucus carota* roots stored under conditions of stress. *Phytochemistry*, **12** 1881-85.

Davin, L.B. and Lewis, N.G. (1992) Phenylpropanoid metabolism: biosynthesis of monolignols, lignans and neolignans, lignins and suberins, in *Phenolic Metabolism in Plants* (eds. H.A. Stafford and R.K. Ibrahim), Plenum Press, New York, pp. 325-75.

Davin, L.B., Bedgar, D.L., Katayama, T. and Lewis, N.G. (1992) On the stereoselective synthesis of (+)-pinoresinol in *Forsythia suspensa* from its achiral precursor, coniferyl alcohol. *Phytochemistry*, **31** 3869-74.

Davin, L.B., Wang, H.B., Crowell, A.L., Bedgar, D.L., Martin, D.M., Sarkanen, S. and Lewis, N.G. (1997) Stereoselective bimolecular phenoxy radical coupling by an auxiliary (dirigent) protein without an active center. *Science*, **275** 362-66.

De Carolis, E. and Ibrahim, R.K. (1989) Purification and kinetics of phenylpropanoid *O*-methyltransferase activities from *Brassica oleracea. Biochem. Cell Biol.*, **67** 763-69.

Denzel, K. and Gross, G.G. (1991) Biosynthesis of gallotannins: enzymatic 'disproportionation' of 1,6-digalloylglucose to 1,2,6-trigalloylglucose and 6-galloylglucose by an acyltransferase from leaves of *Rhus typhina* (L.). *Planta*, **184** 285-89.

Denzel, K., Schilling, G. and Gross, G.G. (1988) Biosynthesis of gallotannins: enzymatic conversion of 1,6-digalloylglucose to 1,2,6-trigalloylglucose. *Planta*, **176** 135-37.

Dewick, P.M. (1989) Biosynthesis of lignans, in *Studies in Natural Products Chemistry*, Vol. 5, Structure Elucidation (Part B) (ed. Atta-ur-Rahman), Elsevier, Amsterdam, Oxford, New York, Tokyo, pp. 459-503.

Dharmawardhana, D.P., Ellis, B.E. and Carlson, J.E. (1995) A β-glucosidase from lodgepole pine xylem specific for the lignin precursor coniferin. *Plant Physiol.*, **107** 331-39.

Dhillon, D.S. and Brown, S.A. (1976) Localization, purification and characterization of dimethylallylpyrophosphate:umbelliferone dimethylallyl transferase from *Ruta graveolens. Arch. Biochem. Biophys.*, **177** 74-83.

Dinkova-Kostova, A.T., Gang, D.R., Davin, L.B., Bedgar, D.L., Chu, A. and Lewis, N.G. (1996) (+)-Pinoresinol/(+)-lariciresinol reductase from *Forsythia intermedia*: protein purification, cDNA cloning, heterologous expression and comparison to isoflavone reductase. *J. Biol. Chem.*, **46** 29473-82.

Dixon, R.A., Harrison, M.J. and Paiva, N.L. (1995) The isoflavonoid phytoalexin pathway: from enzymes to genes to transcription factors. *Physiologia Plantarum*, **93** 385-92.

Douglas, C.J. (1996) Phenylpropanoid metabolism and lignin biosynthesis: from weeds to trees. *Trends Plant Sci.*, **1** 171-76.

Douglas, C.J., Ellard, M., Hauffe, K.D., Molitor, E., Moniz de Sa, M., Reinold, S., Subramaniam, R. and Williams, F. (1992) General phenylpropanoid metabolism: regulation by environmental and developmental signals, in *Phenolic Metabolism in Plants* (ed. H.A. Stafford and R.K. Ibrahim), Plenum Press, New York, pp. 63-89.

Eckey-Kaltenbach, H., Kiefer, E., Grosskopf, E., Ernst, D. and Sandermann Jr., H. (1997) Differential transcript induction of parsley pathogenesis-related proteins and of a small heat shock protein by ozone and heat shock. *Plant Mol. Biol.*, **33** 343-50.

Edwards, R. and Dixon, R.A. (1991) Purification and characterization of *S*-adenosyl-L-methionine:caffeic acid 3-*O*-methyltransferase from suspension cultures of alfalfa (*Medicago sativa* L.). *Arch. Biochem. Biophys.*, **287** 372-79.

Edwards, R., Stones, S.M., Gutiérrez-Mellado, M.C. and Jorrin, J. (1997) Characterization and inducibility of a scopoletin-degrading enzyme from sunflower. *Phytochemistry*, **45** 1109-14.

Elgamal, M.H.A., Shalaby, N.M.M., Duddeck, H. and Hiegemann, M. (1993) Coumarins and coumarin glucosides from the fruits of *Ammi majus*. *Phytochemistry*, **34** 819-23.

Ellis, B.E. and Brown, S.A. (1974) Isolation of dimethylallylpyrophosphate:umbelliferone dimethylallyl transferase from *Ruta graveolens*. *Can. J. Biochem.*, **52** 734-38.

El Modafar, C., Clerivet, A., Fleuriet, A. and Macheix, J.J. (1993) Inoculation of *Platanus acerifolia* with *Ceratocystis fimbriata* f. sp. *platani* induces scopoletin and umbelliferone accumulation. *Phytochemistry*, **34** 1271-76.

Estévez-Braun, A. and González, A.G. (1997) Coumarins. *Nat. Prod. Rep.*, **14** 465-57.

Fahrendorf, T. and Dixon, R.A. (1993) Stress responses in alfalfa (*Medicago sativa* L.). 18. Molecular cloning and expression of the elicitor-inducible cinnamic acid 4-hydroxylase cytochrome P_{450}. *Arch. Biochem. Biophys.*, **305** 509-15.

Fischer, D., Stich, K., Britsch, L. and Grisebach, H. (1988) Purification and characterization of (+)-dihydroflavonol (3-hydroxyflavanone) 4-reductase from flowers of *Dahlia variabilis*. *Arch. Biochem. Biophys.*, **264** 40-47.

Fischer, D., Ebenau-Jehle, C. and Grisebach, H. (1990a) Phytoalexin synthesis in soybean: purification and characterization of NADPH:2′-hydroxydaidzein oxidoreductase from elicitor-challenged soybean cell cultures. *Arch. Biochem. Biophys.*, **276** 390-95.

Fischer, D., Ebenau-Jehle, C. and Grisebach, H. (1990b) Purification and characterization of pterocarpan synthase from elicitor-challenged soybean cell cultures. *Phytochemistry*, **29** 2879-82.

Fischer, S., Böttcher, U., Reuber, S., Anhalt, S. and Weissenböck, G. (1995) Chalcone synthase in the liverwort *Marchantia polymorpha*. *Phytochemistry*, **39** 1007-12.

Forkmann, G. and Heller, W. (1999) Biosynthesis of flavonoids, in *Comprehensive Natural Products Chemistry* (eds. D.H.R. Barton, K. Nakanishi and O. Meth-Coon), Vol. 1, Polyketides and Other Secondary Metabolites Including Fatty Acids and Their Derivatives (ed. U. Sankawa), Elsevier Science, Oxford, 713-48.

Forkmann, G., Heller, W. and Grisebach, H. (1980) Anthocyanin biosynthesis in flowers of *Matthiola incana*: flavanone 3- and flavonoid 3′-hydroxylase. *Z. Naturforsch.*, **35c** 691-95.

French, C.J., Vance, C.P. and Towers, G.H.N. (1976) Conversion of *p*-coumaric acid to *p*-hydroxybenzoic acid by cell-free extracts of potato tubers and *Polyporus hispidus*. *Phytochemistry*, **15** 564-66.

Frias, I., Siverio, J.M., Gonzalez, C., Trujillo, J.M. and Perez, J.A. (1991) Purification of a new peroxidase catalysing the formation of lignan-type compounds. *Biochem. J.*, **273** 109-13.

Fritsch, H. and Grisebach, H. (1975) Biosynthesis of cyanidin in cell cultures of *Haplopappus gracilis*. *Phytochemistry*, **14** 2437-42.

Galliano, H., Cabane, M., Eckerskorn, C., Lottspeich, F., Sandermann Jr., H. and Ernst, D. (1993a) Molecular cloning, sequence analysis and elicitor-/ozone-induced accumulation of cinnamyl alcohol dehydrogenase from Norway spruce (*Picea abies* L.). *Plant Mol. Biol.*, **23** 145-56.

Galliano, H., Heller, W. and Sandermann, H. (1993b) Ozone induction and purification of spruce cinnamyl alcohol dehydrogenase. *Phytochemistry*, **32** 557-63.

Gang, D.R., Dinkova-Kostova, A.T., Davin, L.B. and Lewis, N.G. (1997) Phylogenetic links in plant defense systems: lignans, isoflavonoids and their reductases, in *Phytochemicals for Pest Control*, ACS Symposium Series 658, American Chemical Society, Washington DC, pp. 58-89.

Garcia, D., Sanier, C., Macheix, J.J. and D'Auzac, J. (1995) Accumulation of scopoletin in *Hevea brasiliensis* infected by *Microcyclus ulei* (P. Henn.) V. Arx and evaluation of its fungitoxicity for three leaf pathogens of rubber tree. *Physiol. Mol. Plant Pathol.*, **47** 213-23.

Gauthier, A., Gulick, P.J. and Ibrahim, R.K. (1998) Characterization of two cDNA clones which encode *O*-methyltransferases for the methylation of both flavonoid and phenylpropanoid compounds. *Arch. Biochem. Biophys.*, **351** 243-49.

Gerardy, R. and Zenk, M.H. (1993) Formation of salutaridine from (*R*)-reticuline by a membrane-bound cytochrome P_{450} enzyme from *Papaver somniferum*. *Phytochemistry*, **32** 79-86.

Giesemann, A., Biehl, B. and Lieberei, R. (1986) Identification of scopoletin as a phytoalexin of the rubber tree *Hevea brasiliensis*. *J. Phytopathol.*, **117** 373-76.

Gisler-Ziebarth, B. (1997) Biosynthese und Akkumulation von Coniferin und Lignanen in Zellkulturen von *Linum nodiflorum*. Diploma thesis, University of Düsseldorf, Germany.

Gläβgen, W.E. and Seitz, H.U. (1992) Acylation of anthocyanins with hydroxycinnamic acids via 1-*O*-acylglucosides by protein preparations from cell cultures of *Daucus carota* (L.). *Planta*, **186** 582-85.

Gläβgen, W.E., Wray, V., Strack, D., Metzger, J.W. and Seitz, H.U. (1992) Anthocyanins from cell suspension cultures of *Daucus carota*. *Phytochemistry*, **31** 1593-601.

Gläβgen, W.E., Rose, A., Madlung, J., Koch, W., Gleitz, J. and Seitz, H.U. (1998) Regulation of enzymes involved in anthocyanin biosynthesis in carrot cell cultures in response to treatment with ultraviolet light and fungal elicitors. *Planta*, **204** 490-98.

Goffner, D., Joffroy, I., Grima-Pettenati, J., Halpin, C., Knight, M.E., Schuch, W. and Boudet, A.M. (1992) Purification and characterization of isoforms of cinnamyl alcohol dehydrogenase from *Eucalyptus* xylem. *Planta*, **188** 48-53.

Goffner, D., Campbell, M.M., Campargue, C., Clastre, M., Borderies, G., Boudet, A. and Boudet, A.M. (1994) Purification and characterization of cinnamoyl-coenzyme A:NADP oxidoreductase in *Eucalyptus gunnii*. *Plant Physiol.*, **106** 625-32.

Gowri, G., Bugos, R.C., Campbell, W.H., Maxwell, C.A. and Dixon, R.A. (1991) Stress responses in alfalfa (*Medicago sativa* L.). X. Molecular cloning and expression of *S*-adenosyl-L-methionine:caffeic acid 3-*O*-methyltransferase, a key enzyme of lignin biosynthesis. *Plant Physiol.*, **97** 7-14.

Grand, C. (1984) Ferulic acid 5-hydroxylase: a new cytochrome P_{450}-dependent enzyme from higher plant microsomes involved in lignin synthesis. *FEBS Lett.*, **169** 7-11.

Grandmaison, J., Olah, G.M., Van Calsteren, M.-R. and Furlan, V. (1993) Characterization and localization of plant phenolics likely involved in the pathogen resistance expressed by endomycorrhizal roots. *Mycorrhiza*, **3** 155-64.

Grima-Pettenati, J., Feuillet, C., Goffner, D., Borderies, G. and Boudet, A.M. (1993) Molecular cloning and expression of a *Eucalyptus gunnii* cDNA clone encoding cinnamyl alcohol dehydrogenase. *Plant Mol. Biol.*, **21** 1085-95.

Grima-Pettenati, J., Campargue, C., Boudet, A. and Boudet, A.M. (1994) Purification and characterization of cinnamyl alcohol dehydrogenase isoforms from *Phaseolus vulgaris*. *Phytochemistry*, **37** 941-47.

Grimmig, B. and Matern, U. (1997) Structure of the parsley caffeoyl-CoA *O*-methyltransferase gene, harbouring a novel elicitor responsive *cis*-acting element. *Plant Mol. Biol.*, **33** 323-41.

Gross, G.G. (1982) Synthesis of β-glucogallin from UDP-glucose and gallic acid by an enzyme preparation from oak leaves. *FEBS Lett.*, **148** 67-70.

Gross, G.G. (1983a) Partial purification and properties of UDP-glucose:vanillate 1-*O*-glucosyl transferase from oak leaves. *Phytochemistry*, **22** 2179-82.

Gross, G.G. (1983b) Synthesis of mono-, di- and trigalloyl-β-D-glucose by β-glucogallin-dependent galloyltransferases from oak leaves. *Z. Naturforsch.*, **38c** 519-23.

Gross, G.G. (1994) *In vitro* studies on the biosynthesis of gallotannins and ellagitannins. *Acta Hortic.*, **381** 74-80.

Gross, G.G. (1999) Biosynthesis of hydrolyzable tannins, in *Comprehensive Natural Products Chemistry* (eds. D.H.R. Barton, K. Nakanishi and O. Meth-Coon), Vol. 3, Carbohydrates and Their Derivatives Including Tannins, Cellulose, and the Related Lignins (ed. P.M. Pinto), Elsevier, Oxford, (in press).

Gross, G.G. and Kreiten, W. (1975) Reduction of coenzyme A thioesters of cinnamic acids with an enzyme preparation from lignifying tissue of *Forsythia. FEBS Lett.*, **54** 259-62.

Gross, G.G. and Denzel, K. (1991) Biosynthesis of gallotannins. β-glucogallin-dependent galloylation of 1,6-digalloylglucose to 1,2,6-trigalloylglucose. *Z. Naturforsch.*, **46c** 389-94.

Gross, G.G., Denzel, K. and Schilling, G. (1990) Enzymatic synthesis of di-*O*-phenylcarboxyl-β-D-glucose esters by an acyltransferase from oak leaves. *Z. Naturforsch.*, **45c** 37-41.

Groves, J.T. (1997) The importance of being selective. *Nature*, **389** 329-30.

Gutierrez, M.C., Parry, A., Tena, M., Jorrin, J. and Edwards, R. (1995) Abiotic elicitation of coumarin phytoalexins in sunflower. *Phytochemistry*, **38** 1185-91.

Gutiérrez-Mellado, M.C., Edwards, R., Tena, M., Cabello, F., Serghini, K. and Jorrin, J. (1996) The production of coumarin phytoalexins in different plant organs of sunflower (*Helianthus annuus* L.). *J. Plant Physiol.*, **149** 261-66.

Haddock, E.A., Gupta, R.K., Al-Shafi, S.M.K., Layden, K., Haslam, E. and Magnolato, D. (1982) The metabolism of gallic acid and hexahydroxydiphenic acid in plants: biogenetic and molecular taxonomic considerations. *Phytochemistry*, **21** 1049-62.

Hagenah, S. and Gross, G.G. (1993) Biosynthesis of 1,2,3,6-tetra-*O*-galloyl-β-D-glucose. *Phytochemistry*, **32** 637-41.

Hagmann, M. and Grisebach, H. (1984) Enzymatic rearrangement of flavanone to isoflavone. *FEBS Lett.*, **175** 199-202.

Hagmann, M.L., Heller, W. and Grisebach, H. (1984) Induction of phytoalexin biosynthesis in soybean: stereospecific 3,9-dihydroxypterocarpan 6a-hydroxylase from elicitor-induced soybean cell cultures. *Eur. J. Biochem.*, **142** 127-31.

Hahlbrock, K. and Scheel, D. (1989) Physiology and molecular biology of phenylpropanoid metabolism. *Annu. Rev. Plant Physiol. Plant Mol. Biol.*, **40** 347-69.

Hakamatsuka, T., Hashim, M.F., Ebizuka, Y. and Sankawa, U. (1991) P_{450}-dependent oxidative rearrangement in isoflavone biosynthesis: reconstitution of P_{450} and NADPH:P_{450} reductase. *Tetrahedron*, **47** 5969-78.

Halkier, B.A. (1996) Catalytic reactivities and structure/function relationships of cytochrome P_{450} enzymes. *Phytochemistry*, **43** 1-21.

Halpin, C., Knight, M.E., Grima-Pettenati, J., Goffner, D., Boudet, A.M. and Schuch, W. (1992) Purification and characterization of cinnamyl alcohol dehydrogenase from tobacco stems. *Plant Physiol.*, **98** 12-16.

Hamdi, S., Créche, J., Garnier, F., Mars, M., Decendit, A., Gaspar, T. and Rideau, M. (1995) Cytokinin involvement in the control of coumarin accumulation in *Nicotiana tabacum*: investigations with normal and transformed tissues carrying the isopentenyl transferase gene. *Plant Physiol. Biochem.*, **33** 283-88.

Hamerski, D. and Matern, U. (1988) Biosynthesis of psoralens: psoralen 5-monooxygenase activity from elicitor-treated *Ammi majus* cells. *FEBS Lett.*, **239** 263-65.

Hamerski, D., Beier, R.C., Kneusel, R.E., Matern, U. and Himmelspach, K. (1990a) Accumulation of coumarins in elicitor-treated *Ammi majus* (L.) cell suspension cultures. *Phytochemistry*, **29** 1137-42.

Hamerski, D., Schmitt, D. and Matern, U. (1990b) Induction of two prenyltransferases for the accumulation of coumarin phytoalexins in elicitor-treated *Ammi majus* cell suspension cultures. *Phytochemistry*, **29** 1131-35.

Haslam, E. (1982) The metabolism of gallic acid and hexahydroxydiphenic acid in higher plants. *Prog. Chem. Org. Nat. Prod.*, **41** 1-46.

Haslam, E. (1989) *Plant Polyphenols: Vegetable Tannins Revisited.* Cambridge University Press, Cambridge, UK.

Haslam, E. (1992) Gallic acid and its metabolites. *Basic Life Sci.*, **59** 169-94.

Haslam, E. and Cai, Y. (1994) Plant polyphenols (vegetable tannins): gallic acid metabolism. *Nat. Prod. Rep.*, **11** 41-66.

Havir, E. A. and Hanson, K. R. (1973) L-Phenylalanine ammonia-lyase (maize and potato): evidence that the enzyme is composed of four subunits. *Biochemistry*, **12** 1583-91.

Hawkins, S.W. and Boudet, A.M. (1994) Purification and characterization of cinnamyl alcohol dehydrogenase isoforms from the periderm of *Eucalyptus gunnii* Hook. *Plant Physiol.*, **104** 75-84.

Haworth, R.D. (1942) The chemistry of the lignan group of natural products. *J. Chem. Soc.*, 448-56.

He, X.Z., Reddy, J.T. and Dixon, R.A. (1998) Stress responses in alfalfa (*Medicago sativa* L.). XXII. cDNA cloning and characterization of an elicitor-inducible isoflavone 7-*O*-methyltransferase. *Plant Mol. Biol.*, **36** 43-54.

Heath-Pagliuso, S., Matlin, S.A., Fang, N., Thompson, R.H. and Rappaport, L. (1992) Stimulation of furanocoumarin accumulation in celery and celeriac tissues by *Fusarium oxysporum* f.sp. *apii. Phytochemistry*, **31** 2683-88.

Hedberg, C., Hesse, M. and Werner, C. (1996) Spermine and spermidine hydroxycinnamoyl transferases in *Aphelandra tetragona. Plant Sci.*, **113** 149-56.

Heller, W. and Forkmann (1988) Biosynthesis, in *The Flavonoids: Advances in Research Since 1980* (ed. J. B. Harborne), Chapman & Hall, London, pp. 399-425.

Heller, W. and Kühnl, T. (1985) Elicitor induction of a microsomal 5-*O*-(4-coumaroyl)shikimate 3′-hydroxylase in parsley cell suspension cultures. *Arch. Biochem. Biophys.*, **241** 453-60.

Heller, W. and Forkmann, G. (1993) Biosynthesis of Flavonoids, in *The Flavonoids: Advances in Research since 1986* (ed. J.B. Harborne), Chapman & Hall, London, pp. 499-35.

Henges, A., Petersen, M. and Alfermann, A.W. (1996) Localization of lignans in suspension-cultured cells of *Linum album* during the culture period. Abstract at the "Botanikertagung Düsseldorf', Düsseldorf, Germany.

Herderich, M., Beckert, C. and Veit, M. (1997) Establishing styrylpyrone synthase activity in cell-free extracts obtained from gametophytes of *Equisetum arvense* by high-performance liquid chromatography tandem mass spectrometry. *Phytochem. Anal.*, **8** 194-97.

Heyenga, A.G., Lucas, J.A. and Dewick, P.M. (1990) Production of tumour-inhibitory lignans in callus cultures of *Podophyllum hexandrum. Plant Cell Rep.*, **9** 382-85.

Hibino, T., Shibata, D., Chen, J.Q. and Higuchi, T. (1993a) Cinnamyl alcohol dehydrogenase from *Aralia cordata*: cloning of the cDNA and expression of the gene in lignified tissues. *Plant Cell Physiol.*, **34** 659-65.

Hibino, T., Shibata, D., Umezawa, T. and Higuchi, T. (1993b) Purification and partial sequences of *Aralia cordata* cinnamyl alcohol dehydrogenase. *Phytochemistry*, **32** 565-67.

Hohlfeld, H., Scheel, D. and Strack, D. (1996) Purification of hydroxycinnamoyl-CoA:tyramine hydroxycinnamoyltransferase from cell-suspension cultures of *Solanum tuberosum* (L.) cv. Datura. *Planta*, **199** 166-68.

Hibino, T., Chen, J.Q., Shibata, D. and Higuchi, T. (1994) Nucleotide sequence of a *Eucalyptus botrydoides* gene encoding cinnamyl alcohol dehydrogenase. *Plant Physiol.*, **104** 305-306.

Hinderer, W., Flentje, U. and Barz, W. (1987) Microsomal isoflavone 2′- and 3′-hydroxylases from chickpea (*Cicer arietinum* L.) cell suspension cultures induced for pterocarpan phytoalexin formation. *FEBS Lett.*, **214** 101-106.

Hohlfeld, M., Veit, M. and Strack, D. (1996) Hydroxycinnamoyltransferases involved in the accumulation of caffeic acid esters in gametophytes and sporophytes of *Equisetum arvense*. *Plant Physiol.*, **111** 1153-59.

Holton, T.A. and Cornish, E.C. (1995) Genetics and biochemistry of anthocyanin biosynthesis. *Plant Cell*, **7** 1071-83.

Hopp, W. and Seitz, H.U. (1987) The uptake of acylated anthocyanin into isolated vacuoles from a cell suspension culture of *Daucus carota*. *Planta*, **170** 74-85.

Hopp, W., Hinderer, W., Petersen, M. and Seitz, H.U. (1985) Anthocyanin-containing vacuoles isolated from protoplasts of *Daucus carota* cell cultures, in *The Physiological Properties of Plant Protoplasts* (ed. P.E. Pilet), Springer, Berlin, Heidelberg, pp. 122-32.

Hösel, W., Fiedler-Preiss, A. and Borgmann, E. (1982) Relationship of coniferin β-glucosidase to lignification in various plant cell suspension cultures. *Plant Cell Tiss. Org. Cult.*, **1** 137-48.

Hrazdina, G. and Wagner, G.J. (1985) Metabolic pathways as enzyme complexes: evidence for the synthesis of phenylpropanoids and flavonoids on membrane-associated enzyme complexes. *Arch. Biochem. Biophys.*, **237** 88-100.

Hrazdina, G. and Jensen, R.A. (1992) Spatial organization of enzymes in plant metabolic pathways. *Annu. Rev. Plant Physiol. Plant Mol. Biol.*, **43** 241-67.

Hrazdina, G., Zobel, A.M. and Hoch, H.C. (1987) Biochemical, immunological, and immunocytochemical evidence for the association of chalcone synthase with endoplasmic reticulum membranes. *Proc. Natl. Acad. Sci. USA*, **84** 8966-70.

Hu, W.J., Kawaoka, A., Tsai, C.J., Lung, J., Osakabe, K., Ebinuma, H. and Chiang, V.L. (1998) Compartmentalized expression of two structurally and functionally distinct 4-coumarate ligase genes in aspen (*Populus tremuloides*). *Proc. Nat. Acad. Sci. USA*, **95** 5407-12.

Hofmann, A.S. and Gross, G.G. (1990) Biosynthesis of gallotannins: formation of polygalloylglucoses by enzymatic acylation of 1,2,3,4,6-penta-*O*-galloylglucose. *Arch. Biochem. Biophys.*, **283** 530-32.

Huang, H.C., Lai, M.W., Wang, H.R., Chung, Y.L., Hsieh, L.M. and Chen, C.C. (1993) Antiproliferative effect of esculetin on vascular smooth muscle cells: possible roles of signal transduction pathways. *Eur. J. Pharmacol.*, **237** 39-44.

Hung, C.F., Holzmacher, R., Conolly, E., Berenbaum, M.R. and Schuler, M.A. (1996) Conserved promoter elements in the *CYP6B* gene family suggest common ancestry for cytochrome P_{450} monooxygenases mediating furanocoumarin detoxification. *Proc. Natl. Acad. Sci. USA*, **93** 12200-205.

Hung, C.F., Berenbaum, M.R. and Schuler, M.A. (1997) Isolation and characterization of CYP6B4, a furanocoumarin-inducible cytochrome P_{450} from a polyphagous caterpillar (Lepidoptera: Papilionidae). *Insect Biochem. Mol. Biol.*, **27** 377-85.

Ibrahim, R.K. (1977) Glucosylation of lignin precursors by uridine diphosphate glucose:coniferyl alcohol glucosyltransferase from suspension cultures of Paul's Scarlet Rose. *Arch. Biochem. Biophys.*, **176** 700-708.

Ibrahim, R.K. and Grisebach, H. (1976) Purification and properties of UDP-glucose:coniferyl alcohol glucosyltransferase from suspension cultures of Paul's Scarlet Rose. *Z. Pflanzenphysiol.*, **85** 253-62.

Inoue, T., Toyonaga, T., Nagumo, S. and Nagai, M. (1989) Biosynthesis of 4-hydroxy-5-methylcoumarin in a *Gerbera jamesonii* hybrid. *Phytochemistry*, **28** 2329-30.

Ishihara, A., Matsukawa, T., Miyagawa, H., Ueno, T., Mayama, S. and Iwamura, H. (1997) Induction of hydroxycinnamoyl-CoA:hydroxyanthranilate *N*-hydroxycinnamoyltransferase (HHT) activity in oat leaves by victorin C. *Z. Naturforsch.*, **52c** 756-60.

Jackson, D.E. and Dewick, P.M. (1984) Biosynthesis of *Podophyllum* lignans. II. Interconversions of aryltetralin lignans in *Podophyllum hexandrum*. *Phytochemistry*, **23** 1037-42.

Jackson, D., Culianez-Macia, F., Prescott, A. G., Roberts, K. and Martin, C. (1991) Expression pattern of *myb* genes from *Antirrhinum* flowers. *The Plant Cell*, **3** 115-25.

Junghanns, K.T., Kneusel, R.E., Baumert, A., Maier, W., Gröger, D. and Matern, U. (1995) Molecular cloning and heterologous expression of acridone synthase from elicited *Ruta graveolens* (L.) cell suspension cultures. *Plant Mol. Biol.*, **27** 681-92.

Kalenberg, S. (1994) Untersuchungen zur Enzymatik der Coniferinbiosynthese in Zellkulturen von *Linum album*. Diploma thesis, University of Düsseldorf.

Kamachi, K., Yamay, T., Hayakawa, T., Mae, T. and Ojima, K. (1992) Vascular bundle-specific localization of cytosolic glutamine synthetase in rice leaves. *Plant Physiol.*, **99** 1481-86.

Kamil, W.M. and Dewick, P.M. (1986a) Biosynthesis of the lignans, α- and β-peltatin. *Phytochemistry*, **25** 2089-92.

Kamil, W.M. and Dewick, P.M. (1986b) Biosynthetic relationship of aryltetralin lactone lignans to dibenzylbutyrolactone lignans. *Phytochemistry*, **25** 2093-102.

Kamsteeg, J., Van Brederode, J., Verschuren, P.M. and Van Nigtevecht, G. (1981) Identification, properties and genetic control of *p*-coumaroyl-coenzyme A, 3-hydroxylase isolated from petals of *Silene dioica*. *Z. Pflanzenphys.*, **102** 435-42.

Katayama, T., Davin, L.B. and Lewis, N.G. (1992) An extraordinary accumulation of (−)-pinoresinol in cell-free extracts of *Forsythia intermedia*: evidence for enantiospecific reduction of (+)-pinoresinol. *Phytochemistry*, **31** 3875-81.

Katayama, T., Davin, L.B., Chu, A. and Lewis, N.G. (1993) Novel benzylic ether reductions in lignan biogenesis in *Forsythia intermedia*. *Phytochemistry*, **33** 581-91.

Katayama, T., Masaoka, T. and Yamada, H. (1997) Biosynthesis and stereochemistry of lignans in *Zanthoxylum ailanthoides*. I. (+)-Lariciresinol formation by enzymatic reduction of (+/−)-pinoresinols. *Mokuzai Gakkaishi*, **43** 580-88.

Kato, M.J., Chu, A., Davin, L.B. and Lewis, N.G. (1998) Biosynthesis of antioxidant lignans in *Sesamum indicum* seeds. *Phytochemistry*, **47** 583-91.

Keating, G.J. and O'Kennedy, R. (1997) The chemistry and occurrence of coumarins, in *Coumarins: Biology, Applications and Mode of Action* (eds. R. O'Kennedy and R.D. Thornes), Wiley, New York, pp. 23-66.

Keller, H., Hohlfeld, H., Wray, V., Hahlbrock, K., Scheel, D. and Strack, D. (1996) Changes in the accumulation of soluble and cell wall-bound phenolics in elicitor-treated cell suspension cultures and fungus-infected leaves of *Solanum tuberosum*. *Phytochemistry*, **42** 389-96.

Kerscher, F. and Franz, G. (1987) Biosynthesis of vitexin and isovitexin: enzymatic synthesis of the C-glucosylflavones, vitexin and isovitexin, with an enzyme preparation from *Fagopyrum esculentum* M. seedlings. *Z. Naturforsch.*, **42c** 519-24.

Kerscher, F. and Franz, G. (1988) Isolation and some properties of a UDP-glucose:2-hydroxyflavanone-6(or 8)-C-glucosyltransferase from *Fagopyrum esculentum* M. cotyledons. *J. Plant Physiol.*, **132** 110-15.

Kiedrowski, S., Kawalleck, P., Hahlbrock, K., Somssich, I.E. and Dangl, J.L. (1992) Rapid inactivation of a novel plant defense gene is strictly dependent on the *Arabidopsis* RPM1 disease resistance locus. *EMBO J.*, **11** 4677-84.

Kneusel, R.E. (1987) Phenolische Verbindungen in der pflanzlichen Abwehr: Eine 4-Cumaroyl-CoA 3-Hydroxylase und eine S-Adenosyl-L-methionin:Kaffeoyl-CoA 3-*O*-Methyltransferase in Zellsuspensionskulturen von Petersilie (*Petroselinum crispum*). Diploma Thesis, University of Freiburg, F.R.G.

Kneusel, R.E., Matern, U. and Nicolay, K. (1989) Formation of *trans*-caffeoyl-CoA from *trans*-4-coumaroyl-CoA by Zn^{+}-dependent enzymes in cultured plant cells and its activation by an elicitor-induced pH shift. *Arch. Biochem. Biophys.*, **269** 455-62.

Knight, M.E., Halpin, C. and Schuch, W. (1992) Identification and characterisation of cDNA clones encoding cinnamyl alcohol dehydrogenase from tobacco. *Plant Mol. Biol.*, **19** 793-801.

Kochs, G. and Grisebach, H. (1986a) Enzymic synthesis of isoflavones. *Eur. J. Biochem.*, **155** 311-18.

Kochs, G. and Grisebach, H. (1986b) Induction and characterization of a NADPH-dependent flavone synthase from cell cultures of soybean. *Z. Naturforsch.*, **42c** 343-48.

Kochs, G. and Grisebach, H. (1989) Phytoalexin synthesis in soybean: purification and reconstitution of cytochrome P_{450} 3,9-dihydroxypterocarpan 6a-hydroxylase and separation from cytochrome P_{450} cinnamate 4-hydroxylase. *Arch. Biochem. Biophys.*, **273** 543-53.

Koes, R.E., Quattrocchio, F. and Mol, J.N.M. (1994) The flavonoid biosynthetic pathway in plants: function and evolution. *BioEssays*, **16** 123-32.

Kojima, M. and Takeuchi, W. (1989) Detection and characterization of *p*-coumaric acid hydroxylase in mung bean, *Vigna muno*, seedlings. *J. Biochem.*, **105** 265-70.

Kreuzaler, F. and Hahlbrock, K. (1972) Enzymic synthesis of aromatic compounds in higher plants: formation of naringenin (5,7,4′-trihydroxy-flavanone) from *p*-coumaroyl-coenzyme A and malonyl-coenzyme A. *FEBS Lett.*, **28** 69-72.

Kühnl, T., Koch, U., Heller, W. and Wellmann, E. (1987) Chlorogenic acid biosynthesis: characterization of a light-induced microsomal 5-*O*-(4-coumaroyl)-D-quinate/shikimate 3′-hydroxylase from carrot (*Daucus carota* L.) cell suspension cultures. *Arch. Biochem. Biophys.*, **258** 226-32.

Kühnl, T., Koch, U., Heller, W. and Wellmann, E. (1989) Elicitor-induced *S*-adenosyl-methionine:caffeoyl-CoA 3-*O*-methyltransferase from carrot cell suspension cultures. *Plant Sci.*, **60** 21-25.

Kutsuki, H., Shimada, M. and Higuchi, T. (1982) Regulatory role of cinnamyl alcohol dehydrogenase in the formation of guaiacyl and syringyl lignins. *Phytochemistry*, **21** 19-23.

Lacombe, E., Hawkins, S., Van Doorsselaere, J., Piquemal, J., Goffner, D., Poeydomenge, O., Boudet, A.M. and Grima-Pettenati, J. (1997) Cinnamoyl CoA reductase, the first committed enzyme of the lignin branch biosynthetic pathway: cloning, expression and phylogenetic relationships. *Plant J.*, **11** 429-41.

Laflamme, P., Khouri, H., Gulick, P. and Ibrahim, R.K. (1993) Enzymatic prenylation of isoflavones in white lupin. *Phytochemistry*, **34** 147-51.

Lam, H.-M., Coschigano, K., Schultz, C., Melo-Oliveira, R., Tjaden, G., Oliveira, I., Ngai, N., Hsieh, M.-H. and Coruzzi, G. (1995) Use of *Arabidopsis* mutants and genes to study amino acid biosynthesis. *The Plant Cell*, **7** 887-98.

Landry, L.G., Chapple, C.C.S. and Last, R.L. (1995) *Arabidopsis* mutants lacking phenolic sunscreens exhibit enhanced ultraviolet-B injury and oxidative damage. *Plant Physiol.*, **109** 1159-66.

Latza, S. and Berger, R.G. (1997) 1-*O*-*trans*-Cinnamoyl-β-D-glucopyranose:alcohol cinnamoyl-transferase activity in fruits of cape gooseberry (*Physalis peruviana* L.). *Z. Naturforsch.*, **52c** 747-55.

Lee, D. and Douglas, C.J. (1996) Two divergent members of a tobacco 4-coumarate:coenzyme A ligase (4CL) gene family: cDNA structure, gene inheritance and expression and properties of recombinant proteins. *Plant Physiol.*, **112** 193-205.

Lee, D., Ellard, M., Wanner, L.A., Davis, K.R. and Douglas, C.J. (1995) The *Arabidopsis thaliana* 4-coumarate:CoA ligase (4CL) gene: stress and developmentally regulated expression and nucleotide sequence of its cDNA. *Plant Mol. Biol.*, **28** 871-84.

Lee, D., Meyer, K., Chapple, C. and Douglas, C.J. (1997) Antisense suppression of 4-coumarate:coenzyme A ligase activity in *Arabidopsis* leads to altered lignin subunit composition. *The Plant Cell*, **9** 1985-98.

Leinhos, V. and Savidge, R.A. (1993) Isolation of protoplasts from developing xylem of *Pinus banksiana* and *Pinus strobus*. *Can. J. For. Res.*, **23** 343-48.

Leinhos, V., Udagama-Randeniya, P.V. and Savidge, R.A. (1994) Purification of an acidic coniferin-hydrolyzing β-glucosidase from developing xylem of *Pinus banksiana*. *Phytochemistry*, **37** 311-15.

León, J., Shulaev, V., Yalpani, N., Lawton, M.A. and Raskin, I. (1995) Benzoic acid 2-hydroxylase, a soluble oxygenase from tobacco, catalyzes salicylic acid biosynthesis. *Proc. Natl. Acad. Sci. USA*, **92** 10413-417.

Lewis, N.G. and Yamamoto, E. (1990) Lignin: occurrence, biogenesis and biodegradation. *Annu. Rev. Plant Physiol. Plant Mol. Biol.*, **41** 455-96.

Lewis, N.G. and Davin, L.B. (1994) Evolution in lignan and neolignan biochemical pathways, in *Evolution of Natural Products* (ed. D. Nes), ACS Symposium Series 562, American Chemical Society, Washington DC, pp. 202-46.

Lewis, N.G., Kato, M.J., Lopes, N. and Davin, L.B. (1995) Lignans: diversity, biosynthesis and function, in *Chemistry of the Amazon: Biodiversity, Natural Products and Environmental Issues* (eds. P.R. Seidel, O.R. Gottlieb and M.A.C. Kaplan), ACS Symposium Series 588, American Chemical Society, Washington DC, pp. 135-67.

Li, J., Ou-Lee, T.-M., Raba, R., Amundson, R.G. and Last, R.L. (1993) *Arabidopsis* flavonoid mutants are hypersensitive to UV-B irradiation. *The Plant Cell*, **5** 171-79.

Li, L., Popko, J.L., Zhang, X.-H., Osakabe, K., Tsai, C.-J., Joshi, C.P. and Chiang, V.L. (1997) A novel multifunctional *O*-methyltransferase implicated in a dual methylation pathway associated with lignin biosynthesis in loblolly pine. *Proc. Nat. Acad. Sci. USA*, **94** 5461-66.

Logemann, E., Reinold, S., Somssich, I.E. and Hahlbrock, K. (1997) A novel type of pathogen defense-related cinnamyl alcohol dehydrogenase. *Biol. Chem.*, **378** 909-13.

Lois, R. and Hahlbrock, K. (1992) Differential wound activation of members of the phenylalanine ammonia-lyase and 4-coumarate:CoA ligase gene families in various organs of parsley plants. *Z. Naturforsch.*, **47c** 90-94.

Löscher, R. and Heide, L. (1994) Biosynthesis of *p*-hydroxybenzoate from *p*-coumarate and *p*-coumaroyl-coenzyme A in cell-free extracts of *Lithospermum erythrorhizon* cell cultures. *Plant Physiol.*, **106** 271-79.

Lotfy, S., Negrel, N. and Javelle, F. (1994) Formation of ω-feruloylpalmitic acid by an enzyme from wound-healing potato tuber discs. *Phytochemistry*, **35** 1419-24.

Lotfy, S., Javelle, F. and Negrel, J. (1995) Distribution of hydroxycinnamoyl-CoA: ω-hydroxypalmitic acid *O*-hydroxycinnamoyltransferase in higher plants. *Phytochemistry*, **40** 389-91.

Lozoya, E., Hoffmann, H., Douglas, C., Schulz, W., Scheel, D. and Hahlbrock, K. (1988) Primary structures and catalytic properties of isoenzymes encoded by the two 4-coumarate:CoA ligase genes in parsley. *Eur. J. Biochem.*, **176** 661-67.

Lozoya, E., Block, A., Lois, R., Hahlbrock, K. and Scheel, D. (1991) Transcriptional repression of light-induced flavonoid synthesis by elicitor treatment of cultured parsley cells. *Plant J.*, **1** 227-34.

Lüderitz, T. and Grisebach, H. (1981) Enzymic synthesis of lignin precursors: comparison of cinnamoyl-CoA reductase and cinnamyl alcohol:$NADP^+$ dehydrogenase from spruce (*Picea abies* L.) and soybean (*Glycine max* L.). *Eur. J. Biochem.*, **119** 115-24.

Lukacin, R. and Britsch, L. (1997) Identification of strictly conserved histidine and arginine residues as part of the active site in *Petunia hybrida* flavanone 3β-hydroxylase. *Eur. J. Biochem.*, **249** 748-57.

MacKay, J.J., Liu, W., Whetten, R., Sederoff, R.R. and O'Malley, D.M. (1995) Genetic analysis of cinnamyl alcohol dehydrogenase in loblolly pine: single gene inheritance, molecular characterization and evolution. *Mol. Gen. Genet.*, **247** 537-45.

Mansell, R.L., Gross, G.G., Stöckigt, J., Franke, H. and Zenk, M.H. (1974) Purification and properties of cinnamyl alcohol dehydrogenase from higher plants involved in lignin biosynthesis. *Phytochemistry*, **13** 2427-35.

Marcinowski, S. and Grisebach, H. (1978) Enzymology of lignification: cell wall-bound β-glucosidases for coniferin from spruce (*Picea abies*) seedlings. *Eur. J. Biochem.*, **87** 37-44.

Marcinowski, S., Falk, H., Hammer, D.K., Hoyer, B. and Grisebach, H. (1979) Appearance and localization of a β-glucosidase hydrolyzing coniferin in spruce (*Picea abies*) seedlings. *Planta*, **144** 161-65.

Marrs, K.A. (1996) The functions and regulation of glutathione *S*-transferases in plants. *Annu. Rev. Plant Physiol. Plant Mol. Biol.*, **47** 127-58.

Marrs, K.A., Alfenito, M.R., Lloyd, A.M. and Walbot, V. (1995) A glutathione *S*-transferase involved in vacuolar transfer encoded by the maize gene *Bronze-2*. *Nature*, **375** 397-400.

Matern, U. (1991) Coumarins and other phenylpropanoid compounds in the defense response of plant cells. *Planta Med.*, **57** S15-S20.

Matern, U., Strasser, H., Wendorff, H. and Hamerski, H. (1988a) Coumarins and furanocoumarins, in *Cell Culture and Somatic Cell Genetics of Plants*, Vol. 5; Phytochemicals in Plant Cell Cultures (eds. F. Constabel and I.K. Vasil), Academic Press, New York, pp. 3-21.

Matern, U., Wendorff, H., Hamerski, D., Pakusch, A.E. and Kneusel, R.E. (1988b) Elicitor-induced phenylpropanoid synthesis in *Apiaceae* cell cultures. *Bulletin de Liaison du Groupe Polyphenols*, **14** 173-84.

Matern, U., Grimmig, B. and Kneusel, R.E. (1995) Plant cell wall reinforcement in the disease resistance response: molecular composition and regulation. *Can. J. Bot.*, **73** 511-17.

Matern, U., Lüer, P. and Kreusch, D. (1999) Biosynthesis of coumarins, in *Comprehensive Natural Products Chemistry*, Vol. 1 (ed. U. Sankawa), Elsevier Science, Oxford, 623-37.

Matthews, D.E., Weiner, E.J., Matthews, P.S. and Van Etten, H.D. (1987) Role of oxygenases in pisatin biosynthesis and in the fungal degradation of maackiain. *Plant Physiol.*, **83** 365-70.

McKee, T.C., Cardellina II, J.H., Dreyer, G.B. and Boyd, M.R. (1995) The pseudocalanolides: structure revision of calanolides C and D. *J. Nat. Prod.*, **58** 916-20.

Meng, H. and Campbell, W. H. (1996) Characterization and site-directed mutagenesis of aspen lignin-specific *O*-methyltransferase expressed in *Escherichia coli*. *Arch. Biochem. Biophys.*, **330** 329-41.

Meyer, P., Heidmann, I., Forkmann, G. and Saedler, H. (1987) A new petunia flower colour generated by transformation of a mutant with a maize gene. *Nature*, **330** 677-78.

Meyer, K., Cusumano, J.C., Somerville, C. and Chapple, C.C.S. (1996) Ferulate-5-hydroxylase from *Arabidopsis thaliana* defines a new family of cytochrome P_{450}-dependent monooxygenase. *Proc. Nat. Acad. Sci. USA*, **93** 6869-74.

Minamikawa, T., Akazawa, T. and Iritani, I. (1963) Analytical study of umbelliferone and scopoletin synthesis in sweet potato roots infected by *Ceratocystis fimbriata*. *Plant Physiol.*, **38** 493-97.

Miyauchi, T. and Ozawa, S. (1998) Formation of (+)-eudesmin in *Magnolia kobus* DC. var. *borealis* Sarg. *Phytochemistry*, **47** 665-70.

Mock, H.-P. and Strack, D. (1993) Energetics of the uridine 5′-diphosphoglucose:hydroxycinnamic acid acyl-glucosyltransferase reaction. *Phytochemistry*, **32** 575-79.

Molog, G., Petersen, M., Alfermann, A.W. and Van Uden, W. (1998) Desoxypodophyllotoxin 5-Hydroxylase, ein Cytochrom P_{450}-abhängiges Enzym der Lignanbiosynthese aus Zellkulturen von *Linum flavum*. Poster and short lecture at the DECHEMA Meeting '10. Irseer Naturstofftage', Irsee, Germany.

Moustafa, E. and Wong, E. (1967) Purification and properties of chalcone-flavanone isomerase from soybean seed. *Phytochemistry*, **6** 625-32.

Moyano, E., Martinez-Garcia, J.F. and Martin, C. (1996) Apparent redundancy in *myb* gene function provides gearing for the control of flavonoid biosynthesis in *Antirrhinum* flowers. *The Plant Cell*, **8** 1519-32.

Murray, R.D.H. (1997) Naturally occurring plant coumarins. *Prog. Chem. Org. Nat. Prod.*, **72** 1-119.

Murray, R.D.H., Méndez, J. and Brown, S.A. (eds) (1982) *The Natural Coumarins: Occurrence, Chemistry and Biochemistry*, Wiley, New York.

Nabeta, K., Nakahara, K., Yonekubo, J., Okuyama, H. and Sasaya, T. (1991) Lignan biosynthesis in *Larix leptolepis* callus. *Phytochemistry*, **30** 3591-93.

Negrel, J. and Martin, C. (1984) The biosynthesis of feruloyltyramine in *Nicotiana tabacum*. *Phytochemistry*, **23** 2797-801.

Negrel, J. and Javelle, F. (1997) Purification, characterization and partial amino acid sequencing of hydroxycinnamoyl-CoA:tyramine *N*-(hydroxycinnamoyl)transferase from tobacco cell-suspension cultures. *Eur. J. Biochem.*, **347** 1127-35.

Nicholson, R.L. and Hammerschmidt, R. (1992) Phenolic compounds and their role in disease resistance. *Annu. Rev. Phytopathol.*, **30** 369-89.

Niemetz, R. and Gross, G.G. (1998) Gallotannin biosynthesis: purification of β-glucogallin:1,2,3,4,6-pentagalloyl-β-D-glucose galloyltransferase from sumac leaves. *Phytochemistry*, **49** 327-32.

Ogasawara, T., Chiba, K. and Tada, M. (1997) *Sesamum indicum* (L.) (Sesame): *in vitro* culture, and the production of naphthoquinone and other secondary metabolites, in *Biotechnology in Agriculture and Forestry. 41. Medicinal and Aromatic Plants X* (ed. Y.P.S. Bajaj), Springer, Berlin, Heidelberg, pp. 366-93.

O'Kennedy, R. and Thornes, R.D. (1997) Coumarins: Biology, Applications and Mode of Action. Wiley & Sons, Chichester.

O'Malley, D.M., Porter, S. and Sederoff, R.R. (1992) Purification, characterization and cloning of cinnamyl alcohol dehydrogenase in loblolly pine (*Pinus taeda* L.). *Plant Physiol.*, **98** 1364-71.

Osoba, O.A. and Roberts, M.F. (1994) Methyltransferase activity in *Ailanthus altissima* cell suspension cultures. *Plant Cell Rep.*, **13** 277-81.

Ozawa, S., Davin, L.B. and Lewis, N.G. (1993) Formation of (–)-arctigenin in *Forsythia intermedia*. *Phytochemistry*, **32** 643-52.

Paiva, N.L., Edwards, R., Sun, Y., Hrazdina, G. and Dixon, R.A. (1991) Stress responses in alfalfa (*Medicago sativa* L.). 11. Molecular cloning and expression of alfalfa isoflavone reductase, a key enzyme of isoflavonoid phytoalexin biosynthesis. *Plant Mol. Biol.*, **17** 653-67.

Pakusch, A.-E., Kneusel, R.E. and Matern, U. (1989) *S*-Adenosyl-methionine:*trans*-caffeoyl-coenzyme A 3-*O*-methyltransferase from elicitor-treated parsley cell suspension cultures. *Arch. Biochem. Biophys.*, **271** 488-94.

Paré, P.W., Wang, H.B., Davin, L.B. and Lewis, N.G. (1994) (+)-Pinoresinol synthase: a stereoselective oxidase catalysing 8,8′-lignan formation. *Tetrahedron Lett.*, **35** 4731-34.

Parker, J.E., Knogge, W. and Scheel, D. (1991) Molecular aspects of host-pathogen interactions in *Phytophthora*, in *Phytophthora* (eds. J.A. Lucas, R.C. Shattock, D.S. Shaw and L.R. Cooke), Cambridge University Press, Cambridge, UK, pp. 90-103.

Pearce, G., Marchand, P.A., Griswold, J., Lewis, N.G. and Ryan, C.A. (1998) Accumulation of feruloyltyramine and *p*-coumaroyltyramine in tomato leaves in response to wounding. *Phytochemistry*, **47** 659-64.

Pelletier, M.K., Murrell, J.R. and Shirley, B.W. (1997) Characterization of flavonol synthase and leucoanthocyanidin dioxygenase genes in *Arabidopsis*: further evidence for differential regulation of 'early' and 'late' genes. *Plant Physiol.*, **113** 1437-45.

Petersen, M. (1997) Cytochrome P_{450}-dependent hydroxylation in the biosynthesis of rosmarinic acid in *Coleus*. *Phytochemistry*, **45** 1165-72.

Petersen, M., Häusler, E., Karwatzki, B. and Meinhard, J. (1993) Proposed biosynthetic pathway for rosmarinic acid in cell cultures of *Coleus blumei* Benth. *Planta*, **189** 10-14.

Pillonel, C., Mulder, M.M., Boon, J.J., Forster, B. and Binder, A. (1991) Involvement of cinnamyl-alcohol dehydrogenase in the control of lignin formation in *Sorghum bicolor* (L.) Moench. *Planta*, **185** 538-44.

Pillonel, C., Hunziker, P., Binder, A. (1992) Multiple forms of the constitutive wheat cinnamyl alcohol dehydrogenase. *J. Exp. Bot.*, **43** 299-305.

Piquemal, J., Lapierre, C., Myton, K., O'Connell, A., Schuch, W., Grima-Pettenati, J. and Boudet, A.M. (1998) Downregulation of cinnamoyl-CoA reductase induces significant changes of lignin profiles in transgenic tobacco plants. *Plant J.*, **13** 71-83.

Preisig, C.L., Matthews, D.E. and Van Etten, H.D. (1989) Purification and characterization of *S*-adenosyl-L-methionine:6a-hydroxymaackiain 3-*O*-methyltransferase from *Pisum sativum. Plant Physiol.*, **91** 559-66.

Preisig, C.L., Bell, J.N., Sun, Y., Hrazdina, G., Matthews, D.E. and Van Etten, H.D. (1990) Biosynthesis of the phytoalexin pisatin: isoflavone reduction and further metabolism of the product, sophorol, by extract of *Pisum sativum. Plant Physiol.*, **94** 1444-48.

Rahman, M., Dewick, P.M., Jackson, D.E. and Lucas, J.A. (1986) Lignans in *Forsythia* leaves and cell cultures. *J. Pharm. Pharmacol.*, **38** (Suppl.) 15P.

Rahman, M.M.A., Dewick, P.M., Jackson, D.E. and Lucas, J.A. (1990a) Biosynthesis of lignans in *Forsythia intermedia. Phytochemistry*, **29** 1841-46.

Rahman, M.M.A., Dewick, P.M., Jackson, D.E. and Lucas, J.A. (1990b) Production of lignans in *Forsythia intermedia* cell cultures. *Phytochemistry*, **29** 1861-66.

Rataboul, P., Alibert, G., Boller, T. and Boudet, A.M. (1985) Intracellular transport and vacuolar accumulation of *o*-coumaric acid glucoside in *Melilotus alba* mesophyll cell protoplasts. *Biochim. Biophys. Acta*, **816** 25-36.

Reinhard, K. and Matern, U. (1989) The biosynthesis of phytoalexins in *Dianthus caryophyllus* (L.) cell cultures: induction of benzoyl-CoA:anthranilate *N*-benzoyltransferase activity. *Arch. Biochem. Biophys.*, **275** 295-301.

Rhodes, M.J.C. and Wooltorton, L.S.C. (1975) Enzymes involved in the reduction of ferulic acid to coniferyl alcohol during the aging of disks of swede root tissue. *Phytochemistry*, **14** 1235-40.

Rose, A., Gläβgen, W.E., Hopp, W. and Seitz, H.U. (1996) Purification and characterization of glycosyltransferase involved in anthocyanin biosynthesis in cell-suspension cultures of *Daucus carota* (L.) *Planta*, **198** 397-403.

Rueffer, M. and Zenk, M.H. (1994) Canadine synthase from *Thalictrum tuberosum* cell cultures catalyses the formation of the methylenedioxy bridge in berberine synthesis. *Phytochemistry*, **36** 1219-23.

Sablowski, R.W.M., Moyano, E., Culianez-Macia, F.A., Schuch, W., Martin, C. and Bevan, M. (1994) A flower-specific Myb protein activates transcription of phenylpropanoid biosynthetic genes. *EMBO J.*, **13** 128-37.

Sablowski, R.W.M., Baulcombe, D.C. and Bevan, M. (1995) Expression of a flower-specific Myb protein in leaf cells using a viral vector causes ectopic expression of a target promoter. *Proc. Nat. Acad. Sci. USA*, **92** 6901-905.

Sarni, F., Grand, C. and Boudet, A.M. (1984) Purification and properties of cinnamoyl-CoA reductase and cinnamyl alcohol dehydrogenase from poplar stems (*Populus X euamericana*). *Eur. J. Biochem.*, **139** 259-65.

Sato, M. (1967) Metabolism of phenolic substances by the chloroplasts. III. Phenolase as an enzyme concerning the formation of esculetin. *Phytochemistry*, **6** 1363-73.

Schmid, G. and Grisebach, H. (1982a) Enzymic synthesis of lignin precursors: purification and properties of UDP-glucose:coniferyl alcohol glucosyltransferase from cambial sap of spruce (*Picea abies* L.). *Eur. J. Biochem.*, **123** 363-70.

Schmid, G., Hammer, D.K., Ritterbusch, A. and Grisebach, H. (1982b) Appearance and immunohistochemical localization of UDP-glucose:coniferyl alcohol glucosyltransferase in spruce (*Picea abies* (L.) Karst.) seedlings. *Planta*, **156** 207-12.

Schmidt, A., Scheel, D. and Strack, D. (1998) Elicitor-stimulated biosynthesis of hydroxycinnamoyltyramines in cell suspension cultures of *Solanum tuberosum. Planta*, **205** 51-55.

Schmidt, A., Grimm, R., Schmidt, J., Scheel, D., Strack, D. and Rosahl, S. (1999) *J. Biol. Chem.*, **274** 4273-80.

Schmidt, O.T. and Mayer, W. (1956) Natürliche Gerbstoffe. *Angew. Chemie*, **68** 103-15.

Schmidt, S.W., Denzel, K., Schilling, G. and Gross, G.G. (1987) Enzymatic synthesis of 1,6-digalloylglucose from β-glucogallin by β-glucogallin:β-glucogallin 6-*O*-galloyltransferase from oak leaves. *Z. Naturforsch.*, **42c** 87-92.

Schmitt, D., Pakusch, A.-E. and Matern, U. (1991) Molecular cloning, induction and taxonomic distribution of caffeoyl-CoA 3-*O*-methyltransferase, an enzyme involved in disease resistance. *J. Biol. Chem.*, **266** 17416-23.

Schnitzler, J.P., Madlung, J., Rose, A. and Seitz, H.U. (1992) Biosynthesis of *p*-hydroxybenzoic acid in elicitor-treated carrot cell cultures. *Planta*, **188** 594-600.

Schönell, B. (1996) Enzyme der Coniferinbiosynthese in Zellkulturen von *Linum album*. Diploma Thesis, University of Düsseldorf, Germany.

Schröder, J. (1997) A family of plant-specific polyketide synthases: facts and predictions. *Trends Plant Sci.*, **2** 373-78.

Schröder, J. and Schröder, G. (1990) Stilbene and chalcone synthases: related enzymes with key functions in plant specific pathways. *Z. Naturforsch.*, **45c** 1-8.

Schuler, M.A. (1996) Plant cytochrome P_{450} monooxygenases. *Crit. Rev. Plant Sci.*, **15** 235-84.

Sekiguchi, J., Stivers, J.T., Mildvan, A.S. and Shuman, S. (1996) Mechanism of inhibition of vaccinia DNA topoisomerase by novobiocin and coumermycin. *J. Biol. Chem.*, **271** 2313-22.

Sewalt, V.J.H., Ballance, G.M., Ni, W. and Dixon, R.A. (1995) Developmental and elicitor-induced expression of alfalfa COMT and CCOMT, methylating enzymes in parallel pathways for monolignol synthesis. *Plant Physiol.*, **108** S74.

Shimada, T., Yamazaki, H. and Guengerich, F.P. (1996) Ethnic-related differences in coumarin 7-hydroxylation activities catalyzed by cytochrome P_{4502A6} in liver microsomes of Japanese and Caucasian populations. *Xenobiotica*, **26** 395-403.

Shirley, B.W. (1996) Flavonoid biosynthesis: 'new' functions for an 'old' pathway. *Trends Plant Sci.*, **1** 377-82.

Shufflebottom, D., Edwards, K., Schuch, W. and Bevan, M. (1993) Transcription of two members of a gene family encoding phenylalanine ammonia-lyase leads to remarkably different cell specifities and induction patterns. *Plant J.*, **3** 835-45.

Singh, R. and Hsieh, D.P.H. (1977) Aflatoxin biosynthetic pathway: elucidation by using blocked mutants of *Aspergillus parasiticus*. *Arch. Biochem. Biophys.*, **178** 285-92.

Skadhauge, B., Gruber, M.Y., Thomsen, K.K. and von Wettstein, D. (1997) Leucocyanidin reductase activity and accumulation of proanthocyanidins in developing legume tissues. *Am. J. Bot.*, **84** 494-503.

Smollny, T., Wichers, H., Kalenberg, S., Shahsavari, A., Petersen, M. and Alfermann, A.W. (1998) Accumulation of podophyllotoxin and related lignans in cell suspension cultures of *Linum album*. *Phytochemistry*, **48** 975-79.

Somers, D.A., Nourse, J.P., Manners, J.M., Abrahams, S. and Watson, J.M. (1995) A gene encoding a cinnamyl alcohol dehydrogenase homolog in *Arabidopsis thaliana*. *Plant Physiol.*, **108** 1309-10.

Spencer, G.F., Desjardins, A.E. and Plattner, R.D. (1990) 5-(2-Carboxyethyl)-6-hydroxy-7-methoxybenzofuran, a fungal metabolite of xanthotoxin. *Phytochemistry*, **29** 2495-97.

Sprenger, G.A., Schörken, U., Wiegert, T., Grolle, S., De Graaf, A.A., Taylor, S.V., Begley, T.P., Bringer-Meyer, S. and Sahm, H. (1997) Identification of a thiamine-dependent synthase in *Escherichia coli* required for the formation of the 1-deoxy-D-xylulose 5-phosphate precursor to isoprenoids, thiamine and pyridoxol. *Proc. Natl. Acad. Sci. USA*, **94** 12857-62.

Stadler, R. and Zenk, M.H. (1993) The purification and characterization of a unique cytochrome P_{450} enzyme from *Berberis stolonifera* plant cell cultures. *J. Biol. Chem.*, **268** 823-31.

Stafford, H.A. (1991) Flavonoid evolution: an enzymic approach. *Plant Physiol.*, **96** 680-85.

Stafford, H.A. and Lester, H.H. (1982) Enzymic and non-enzymic reduction of (+)-dihydroquercetin to its 3,4-diol. *Plant Physiol.*, **70** 695-98.

Stafford, H.A. and Lester, H.H. (1984) Flavan-3-ol biosynthesis: the conversion of (+)-dihydroquercetin and flavan-3,4-*cis*-diol (leucocyanidin) to (+)-catechin by reductases extracted from cell suspension cultures of douglas fir. *Plant Physiol.*, **76** 184-86.

Stanjek, V. and Boland, W. (1998) Biosynthesis of angular furanocoumarins: mechanism and stereochemistry of the oxidative dealkylation of columbianetin to angelicin in *Heracleum mantegazzianum* (Apiaceae). *Helv. Chim. Acta,* **81** 1596-607.

Stanjek, V., Miksch, M. and Boland, W. (1997a) Stereoselective syntheses of deuterium-labelled marmesins; valuable metabolic probes for mechanistic studies in furanocoumarin biosynthesis. *Tetrahedron,* **53** 17699-710.

Stanjek, V., Herhaus, C., Ritgen, U., Boland, W. and Städler, E. (1997b) Changes in the leaf surface chemistry of *Apium graveolens* (Apiaceae) stimulated by jasmonic acid and perceived by a specialist insect. *Helv. Chim. Acta,* **80** 1408-19.

Stanjek, V., Miksch, M., Lüer, P., Matern, U. and Boland, W. (1999a) Biosynthesis of Psoralen: mechanism of a cytochrome P_{450} catalyzed oxidative bond cleavage. *Angew. Chemie,* Int. Ed., **38** 400-402.

Stanjek, V., Piel, J. and Boland, W. (1999b) Mevalonat-independent biosynthesis of linear furanocoumarins in *Apium graveolens* (*Apiaceae*). *Phytochemistry,* (in press).

Stich, K. and Forkmann, G. (1988) Biosynthesis of 3-deoxyanthocyanins with flower extracts from *Sinningia cardinalis. Phytochemistry,* **27** 785-89.

Stöckigt, J. and Klischies, M. (1977) Biosynthesis of lignans. Part I. Biosynthesis of arctiin and phillyrin. *Holzforsch.,* **31** 41-44.

Stotz, G. and Forkmann, G. (1981) Oxidation of flavanones to flavones with flower extracts of *Antirrhinum majus* (snapdragon). *Z. Naturforsch.,* **36c** 737-41.

Stotz, G. and Forkmann, G. (1982) Hydroxylation of the B-ring of flavonoids in the 3′- and 5′-position with enzyme extracts from flowers of *Verbena hybrida. Z. Naturforsch.,* **37c** 19-23.

Strack, D. (1997) Phenolic metabolism, in *Plant Biochemistry* (eds. J.B. Harborne and P.M. Dey), Academic Press, New York, pp. 387-416.

Strack, D. and Gross, W. (1990) Properties and activity changes of chlorogenic acid:glucaric acid caffeoyltransferase from tomato (*Lycopersicon esculentum*). *Plant Physiol.,* **92** 41-47.

Strack, D. and Mock, H.-P. (1993) Hydroxycinnamic acids and lignins, in *Methods in Plant Biochemistry* (eds. P.M. Dey and J.B. Harborne), Vol. 9, Enzymes of Secondary Metabolism (ed. P.J. Lea), Academic Press, London, pp. 45-97.

Strack, D. and Wray, V. (1994) The anthocyanins, in *The Flavonoids* (ed. J.B. Harborne), Chapman & Hall, London, pp. 1-22.

Strack, D., Pieroth, M., Scharf, H. and Sharma, V. (1985) Tissue distribution of phenylpropanoid metabolism in cotyledons of *Raphanus sativus. Planta,* **164** 507-11.

Strack, D., Keller, H. and Weissenböck, G. (1987) Enzymatic synthesis of hydroxycinnamic acid esters of sugar acids and hydroaromatic acids by protein preparations from rye (*Secale cereale*) primary leaves. *J. Plant Physiol.,* **131** 61-73.

Strack, D., Gross, W., Heilemann, J., Keller, H. and Ohm, S. (1988) Enzymic synthesis of hydroxycinnamic acid esters of glucaric acid and hydroaromatic acids from the respective 1-*O*-hydroxycinnamoylglucoside and hydroxycinnamoyl-coenzyme-A thioester as acyldonors with a protein preparation from *Cestrum elegans* leaves. *Z. Naturforsch.,* **43c** 32-36.

Sulistyowati, L., Keane, P.J. and Anderson, J.W. (1990) Accumulation of the phytoalexin, 6,7-dimethyoxycoumarin, in roots and stems of citrus seedlings following inoculation with *Phytophthora citrophthora. Physiol. Mol. Plant Pathol.,* **37** 451-61.

Sutter, A., Poulton, J. and Grisebach, H. (1975) Oxidation of flavanone to flavone with cell-free extracts from young parsley leaves. *Arch. Biochem. Biophys.,* **170** 547-56.

Takeda, R., Hasegawa, J. and Sinozaki, K. (1990) The first isolation of lignans, megacerotonic acid and anthocerotonic acid, from non-vascular plants, Anthocerotae (hornworts). *Tetrahedron Lett.,* **31** 4159-62.

Tal, B. and Robeson, D.J. (1986) The induction by fungal inoculation of ayapin and scopoletin biosynthesis in *Helianthus annuus. Phytochemistry,* **25** 77-79.

Tamagnone, L., Merida, A., Parr, A., Mackay, S., Culianez-Macia, F.A., Roberts, K. and Martin, C. (1998) The AmMYB308 and AmMYB330 transcription factors from *Antirrhinum* regulate phenylpropanoid and lignin biosynthesis in transgenic tobacco. *The Plant Cell*, **10** 135-54.

Tamura, R., Kawai, S., Katayama, Y. and Morohoshi, N. (1992) Purification and characterization of cinnamyl alcohol dehydrogenase derived from woody plant. *Tokyo Noko Daigaku Nogakubu Enshurin Hokoku*, **30** 1-4.

Tanaka, M. and Kojima, M. (1991) Purification and characterization of *p*-coumaroyl-D-glucose hydroxylase of sweet potato (*Ipomoea batatas*) roots. *Arch. Biochem. Biophys.*, **284** 151-57.

Terahara, N., Saito, N., Honda, T., Toki, K. and Osajima, Y. (1990) Structure of ternatin A1, the largest ternatin in the major blue anthocyanins from *Clitoria ternatea* flowers. *Tetrahedron Lett.*, **31** 2921-24.

Tiemann, K., Hinderer, W. and Barz, W. (1987) Isolation of NADPH:isoflavone oxidoreductase, a new enzyme of pterocarpan phytoalexin biosynthesis in cell suspension cultures of *Cicer arietinum*. *FEBS Lett.*, **213** 324-28.

Tropf, S., Lanz, T., Rensing, S.A., Schröder, J. and Schröder, G. (1994) Evidence that stilbene synthases have developed from chalcone synthases several times in the course of evolution. *J. Mol. Evol.*, **38** 610-18.

Tsai, F.T.F., Singh, O.M.P., Skarzynski, T., Wonacott, A.J., Weston, S., Tucker, A., Pauptit, R.A., Breeze, A.L., Poyser, J.P., O'Brien, R., Ladbury, J.E. and Wigley, D.B. (1997) The high-resolution crystal structure of a 24 kDA gyrase B fragment from *E. coli* complexed with one of the most potent coumarin inhibitors, clorobiocin. *Proteins: Structure, Function, and Genetics*, **28** 41-52.

Ulbrich, B. and Zenk, M.H. (1979) Partial purification and properties of hydroxycinnamoyl-CoA:quinate hydroxycinnamoyl transferase from higher plants. *Phytochemistry*, **18** 929-33.

Umezawa, T. and Shimada, M. (1996) Formation of the lignan (+)-secoisolariciresinol by cell-free extracts of *Arctium lappa*. *Biosci. Biotech. Biochem.*, **60** 736-37.

Umezawa, T., Davin, L.B. and Lewis, N.G. (1990) Formation of the lignan, (–)-secoisolarici-resinol, by cell-free extracts of *Forsythia intermedia*. *Biochem. Biophys. Res. Commun.*, **171** 1008-14.

Umezawa, T., Davin, L.B. and Lewis, N.G. (1991) Formation of lignans (–)-secoisolariciresinol and (–)-matairesinol with *Forsythia intermedia* cell-free extracts. *J. Biol. Chem.*, **266** 10210-17.

Umezawa, T., Kuroda, H., Isohata, T., Higuchi, T. and Shimada, M. (1994) Enantioselective lignan synthesis by cell-free extracts of *Forsythia koreana*. *Biosci. Biotech. Biochem.*, **58** 230-34.

Valle, T., López, J.L., Hernández, J.M. and Corchete, P. (1997) Antifungal activity of scopoletin and its differential accumulation in *Ulmus pumila* and *Ulmus campestris* cell suspension cultures infected with *Ophiostoma ulmi* spores. *Plant Sci.*, **125** 97-101.

Van Doorsselaere, J., Baucher, M., Feuillet, C., Boudet, A.M., Van Montagu, M. and Inze, D. (1995) Isolation of cinnamyl alcohol dehydrogenase cDNAs from two important economic species; alfalfa and poplar: demonstration of a high homology of the gene within angiosperms. *Plant Physiol. Biochem.*, **33** 105-109.

Van Heeren, P.S., Towers, G.H.N. and Lewis, N.G. (1996) Nitrogen metabolism in lignifying *Pinus taeda* cell cultures. *J. Biol. Chem.*, **271** 12350-55.

Van Uden, W., Pras, N. and Malingré, T.M. (1990) On the improvement of the podophyllotoxin production by phenylpropanoid precursor feeding to cell cultures of *Podophyllum hexandrum* Royle. *Plant Cell Tiss. Org. Cult.*, **23** 217-24.

Van Uden, W., Pras, N., Batterman, S., Visser, J.F. and Malingré, T.M. (1991) The accumulation and isolation of coniferin from a high-producing cell suspension of *Linum flavum*. *Planta*, **183** 25-30.

Van Uden, W., Oeij, H., Woerdenbag, H.J. and Pras, N. (1993) Glucosylation of cyclodextrin-complexed podophyllotoxin by cell cultures of *Linum flavum* (L.). *Plant Cell Tiss. Org. Cult.*, **34** 169-75.

Van Uden, W., Pras, N. and Woerdenbag, H.J. (1994) *Linum* species (Flax): *in vivo* and *in vitro* accumulation of lignans and other metabolites, in *Biotechnology in Agriculture and Forestry. 26. Medicinal and Aromatic Plants. VI* (ed. Y.P.S. Bajaj), Springer, Berlin, Heidelberg, pp. 219-44.

Van Uden, W., Bouma, A.S., Bracht Walker, J.F., Middel, O., Wichers, H.J., De Waard, P., Woerdenbag, H.J., Kellogg, R.M. and Pras, N. (1995) The production of podophyllotoxin and its 5-methoxy derivative through bioconversion of cyclodextrin-complexed desoxypodophyllotoxin by plant cell cultures. *Plant Cell Tiss. Org. Cult.*, **42** 73-79.

Van Uden, W., Bos, J.A., Boeke, G.M., Woerdenbag, H.J. and Pras, N. (1997a) The large-scale isolation of deoxypodophyllotoxin from rhizomes of *Anthriscus sylvestris* followed by its bioconversion into 5-methoxypodophyllotoxin β-D-glucoside by cell cultures of *Linum flavum*. *J. Nat. Prod.*, **60** 401-403.

Van Uden, W., Lalbahadoersing, R., Molog, G.A., Petersen, M., Woerdenbag, H.J., Alfermann, A.W. and Pras, N. (1997b) The isolation of β-peltatin from podophyllin and its bioconversion into 5-methoxypodophyllotoxin-β-D-glucoside by cell cultures of *Linum flavum*. Poster at the 45th Annual Congress of the Society for Medicinal Plant Research, Regensburg, Germany.

Varin, L. and Ibrahim, R.K. (1989) Partial purification and characterization of three flavonol-specific sulfotransferases from *Flaveria chloraefolia*. *Plant Physiol.*, **90** 977-81.

Varin, L. and Ibrahim, R.K. (1991) Partial purification and some properties of flavono 7-sulphotransferase from *Flaveria bidentis*. *Plant Physiol..*, **95** 1254-58.

Varin, L. and Ibrahim, R.K. (1992) Novel flavonol 3-sulfotransferase: purification, kinetic properties and partial amino acid sequence. *J. Biol. Chem.*, **267** 1858-63.

Varin, L., Barron, D. and Ibrahim, R.K. (1987) Enzymatic synthesis of sulphated flavonols in *Flaveria*. *Phytochemistry*, **26** 135-38.

Varin, L., DeLuca, V., Ibrahim, R.K. and Brisson, N. (1992) Molecular characterization of two plant flavonol sulfotransferases (*Flaveria chloraefolia*). *Proc. Natl. Acad. Sci. USA*, **89** 1286-90.

Vaughan, P.F.T. and Butt, V.S. (1969) The hydroxylation of *p*-coumaric acid by an enzyme from leaves of spinach beet (*Beta vulgaris* L.). *Biochem. J.*, **113** 109-15.

Vereecke, D., Messens, E., Klarskov, K., De Bruyn, A., Van Montagu, M. and Goethals, K. (1997) Patterns of phenolic compounds in leafy galls of tobacco. *Planta*, **201** 342-48.

Verwoert, I.I.G.S., Verbree, E.C., Van der Linden, K.H., Nijkamp, H.J.J. and Stuitje, A.R. (1992) Cloning, nucleotide sequence and expression of the *Escherichia coli* fabD gene, encoding malonyl-coenzyme A-acyl carrier protein transacylase. *J. Bact.*, **174** 2851-57.

Villegas, R.J.A. and Kojima, M. (1986) Purification and characterization of hydroxycinnamoyl D-glucose: quinate hydroxycinnamoyl transferase in the root of sweet potato, *Ipomoea batatas* Lam. *J. Biol. Chem.*, **261** 8729-33.

Vogt, T. and Taylor, L.P. (1995) Flavonol 3-*O*-glycosyltransferases associated with petunia pollen produce gametophyte-specific flavonol diglycosides. *Plant Physiol.*, **108** 903-11.

Voo, K.S., Whetten, R.W., O'Malley, D.M. and Sederoff, R.R. (1995) 4-Coumarate:coenzyme A ligase from loblolly pine xylem: isolation, characterization and complementary DNA cloning. *Plant Physiol.*, **108** 85-97.

Wang, Z.-X., Li, S.-M., Löscher, R. and Heide, L. (1997) 4-Coumaroyl coenzyme-A 3-hydroxylase activity from cell cultures of *Lithospermum erythrorhizon* and its relationship to polyphenol oxidase. *Arch. Biochem. Biophys.*, **347** 249-55.

Ward, R.S. (1997) Lignans, neolignans and related compounds. *Nat. Prod. Rep.*, **14** 43-74.

Weaver, L.M. and Herrmann, K.M. (1997) Dynamics of the shikimate pathway in plants. *Trends Plant Sci.*, **2** 346-51.

Weidemann, C., Tenhaken, R., Höhl, U. and Barz, W. (1991) Medicarpin and maackiain 3-*O*-glucoside-6′-*O*-malonate conjugates are constitutive compounds in chickpea (*Cicer arietinum* L.) cell cultures. *Plant Cell Rep.*, **10** 371-74.

Welle, R. and Grisebach, H. (1988a) Isolation of a novel NADPH-dependent reductase which coacts with chalcone synthase in the biosynthesis of 6′-deoxychalcone. *FEBS Lett.*, **236** 221-25.

Welle, R. and Grisebach, H. (1988b) Induction of phytoalexin synthesis in soybean: enzymatic cyclization of prenylated pterocarpans to glyceollin isomers. *Arch. Biochem. Biophys.*, **263** 191-98.

Welle, R. and Grisebach, H. (1989) Phytoalexin synthesis in soybean cells: elicitor induction of reductase involved in biosynthesis of 6′-deoxychalcone. *Arch. Biochem. Biophys.*, **272**, 97-102.

Welle, R. and Grisebach, H. (1991) Properties and solubilization of the prenyltransferase of isoflavonoid phytoalexin biosynthesis in soybean. *Phytochemistry*, **30** 479-84.

Welle, R. and Schröder, J. (1992) Expression cloning in *Escherichia coli* and preparative isolation of the reductase coacting with chalcone synthase during the key step in the biosynthesis of soybean phytoalexins. *Arch. Biochem. Biophys.*, **293** 377-81.

Wengenmayer, H., Ebel, J. and Grisebach, H. (1976) Enzymic synthesis of lignin precursors: purification and properties of a cinnamoyl-CoA:NADPH reductase from cell suspension cultures of soybean (*Glycine max*). *Eur. J. Biochem.*, **65** 529-36.

Whetten, R. and Sederoff, R. (1995) Lignin biosynthesis. *Plant Cell*, **7** 1001-13.

Wichers, H.J., Versluis-De Haan, G., Marsman, J.W. and Harkes, M.P. (1991) Podophyllotoxin-related lignans in plants and cell cultures of *Linum flavum*. *Phytochemistry*, **30** 3601-604.

Wimmer, G., Halbwirth, H., Wurst, F., Forkmann, G. and Stich, K. (1998) Enzymatic hydroxylation of 6′-deoxychalcones with protein preparations from petals of *Dahlia variabilis*. *Phytochemistry*, **47** 1013-16.

Windhövel, J. (1998) Coniferinbiosynthese in Zellkulturen von *Linum album*: Untersuchungen zur Cinnamoyl-CoA:NADP Oxidoreduktase. Diploma Thesis, University of Düsseldorf, Germany.

Wu, Q.D., Preisig, C.L. and Van Etten, H.D. (1997) Isolation of the cDNAs encoding (+)-6a-hydroxymaackiain 3-*O*-methyltransferase, the terminal step for the synthesis of the phytoalexin pisatin in *Pisum sativum*. *Plant Mol. Biol.*, **35** 551-60.

Wyrambik, D. and Grisebach, H. (1975) Purification and properties of isoenzymes of cinnamyl-alcohol dehydrogenase from soybean cell suspension cultures. *Eur. J. Biochem.*, **59** 9-15.

Yamamoto, H., Kimata, J., Senda, M. and Inoue, K. (1997) Dimethylallyl diphosphate:kaempferol 8-dimethylallyl transferase in *Epimedium diphyllum* cell suspension cultures. *Phytochemistry*, **44** 23-28.

Yang, Q., Reinhard, K., Schiltz, E. and Matern, U. (1997) Characterization and heterologous expression of hydroxycinnamoyl/benzoyl-CoA:anthranilate *N*-hydroxycinnamoyl/benzoyl transferase from elicited cell cultures of carnation, *Dianthus caryophyllus* (L.). *Plant Mol. Biol.*, **35** 777-89.

Yazaki, K., Heide, L. and Tabata, M. (1991) Formation of *p*-hydroxybenzoic acid from *p*-coumaric acid by cell-free extracts of *Lithospermum erythrorhizon* cell cultures. *Phytochemistry*, **30** 2233-36.

Ye, Z.H., Kneusel, R.E., Matern, U. and Varner, J.E. (1994) An alternative methylation pathway in lignin biosynthesis in *Zinnia*. *The Plant Cell*, **6** 1427-39.

Zenk, M.H., Gerardy, R. and Stadler, R. (1989) Phenol oxidative coupling of benzylisoquinoline alkaloids is catalysed by regio- and stereoselective cytochrome P_{450}-linked plant enzymes: salutaridine and berbamunine. *J. Chem. Soc. Chem. Commun.*, 1725-27.

Zuurbier, K.W.M., Fung, S.Y., Scheffer, J.J.C. and Verpoorte, R. (1995) Formation of aromatic intermediates in the biosynthesis of bitter acids in *Humulus lupulus*. *Phytochemistry*, **38** 77-82.

5 Biochemistry of terpenoids: monoterpenes, sesquiterpenes, diterpenes, sterols, cardiac glycosides and steroid saponins

Jonathan Gershenzon and Wolfgang Kreis

5.1 The basic pathway of terpenoid biosynthesis and the formation and function of C_5-C_{20} terpenoid metabolites

5.1.1 Introduction

The largest class of plant secondary metabolites is undoubtedly that of the terpenoids or isoprenoids. Over 22,000 individual members of this class have been reported (Connolly and Hill, 1991) and new structures are currently being added at the rate of about 1000 every year. Compilations of newly-described terpenoids appear periodically in *Natural Product Reports* (e.g. Grayson, 1997; Fraga, 1997; Hanson, 1997 and Connolly and Hill, 1997). Terpenoids are not only numerous but also extremely variable in structure, exhibiting hundreds of different carbon skeletons and a large assortment of functional groups. In spite of such diversity, all terpenoids are unified by a common mode of biosynthesis: the fusion of C_5 units with an isopentenoid structure.

Since the origins of organic chemistry, terpenoids have been a source of fascination for many practitioners of this discipline. However, the basic structural unity of terpenoids has only been appreciated since the end of the last century, when pioneers, such as the German, Otto Wallach, discovered that some members of this class could be pyrolyzed to give isoprene, a C_5 diene with an isopentenoid skeleton (Fig. 5.1). These studies gave rise to the so-called isoprene rule, which states that all terpenoids are derived from the ordered, head-to-tail joining of isoprene units. More recent workers have refined the original concept, recognizing that non head-to-tail condensations of isoprene units also occur and that substantial structural rearrangements can occur during biosynthesis. Nevertheless, the original isoprene rule was a very useful concept in determining the structures of many unknown substances and assessing their biogenetic origin. In this context, terpenoids have frequently been referred to as isoprenoids, and the terms isoprenoids, terpenoids and terpenes are now used interchangeably.

The classification of terpenoids is based on the number of isoprenoid units present in their structure. The largest categories are those made up of compounds with two isoprenoid units (monoterpenes), three

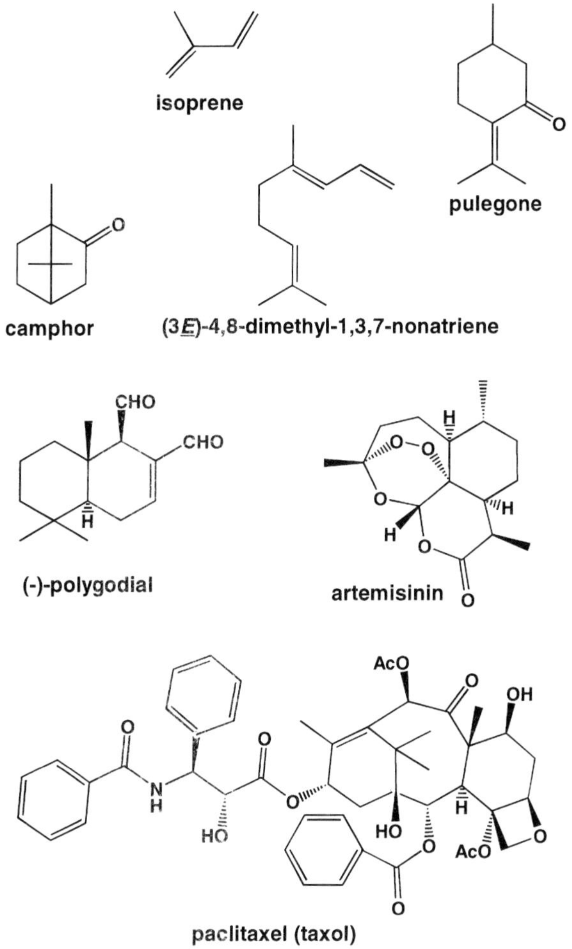

isoprene

pulegone

camphor

(3*E*)-4,8-dimethyl-1,3,7-nonatriene

(-)-polygodial

artemisinin

paclitaxel (taxol)

Figure 5.1 Examples of terpenoids that are of commercial importance or whose functional role in plants has recently been investigated. Isoprene may stabilize membranes at high temperatures. Camphor, artemisinin and paclitaxel (taxol) are valuable pharmaceuticals. The other three compounds appear to be involved in plant defence: pulegone is toxic to herbivores; polygodial is a herbivore feeding deterrent; and (3*E*)-4,8-dimethyl-1,3,7-nonatriene, a C_{11} homoterpene, functions to attract herbivore enemies to herbivore-damaged plants.

isoprenoid units (sesquiterpenes), four isoprenoid units (diterpenes), six isoprenoid units (triterpenes) and eight isoprenoid units (tetraterpenes) (Table 5.1). Although biosynthesis is based on a unit of five carbon atoms, terpenoid nomenclature is based on a unit of ten carbon atoms, since the C_{10} terpenoids were once thought to be the smallest naturally occurring representatives of this class. Designation of the C_{10} terpenoids

Table 5.1 The classification of terpenoids is based on the number of C_5 isoprenoid units in their structures

Isoprene units *n*	Carbon atoms *n*	Name	Example
1	5	Hemiterpenes	Isoprene
2	10	Monoterpenes	Pulegone
3	15	Sesquiterpenes	Polygodial
4	20	Diterpenes	Paclitaxel
6	30	Triterpenes	β-Amyrin
8	40	Tetraterpenes	β-Carotene
9–30000	>40	Polyterpenes	Rubber

as mono-('one')-terpenes made it necessary to name the subsequently described C_5 terpenes as hemi-('half')-terpenes, the C_{15} terpenes as sesqui-('one-and-a-half')-terpenes, and so on. In this section, the biosynthesis and functional significance of the lower (C_5–C_{20}) terpenes are surveyed, with emphasis on the major advances in the last five years. Triterpenes (C_{30}), cardiac glycosides and steroid saponins are treated in the following section. A recent monograph of outstanding coverage and quality (Cane, 1998) and several excellent individual reviews (Chappell, 1995; McGarvey and Croteau, 1995) have covered many aspects of this subject.

5.1.2 Function

The enormous structural diversity of the terpenoids is almost matched by their functional variability. Terpenoids have well-established roles in almost all basic plant processes, including growth, development, reproduction and defence. Among the best known lower (C_5–C_{20}) terpenes are the gibberellins, a large group of diterpene plant hormones involved in the control of seed germination, stem elongation and flower induction (Hedden and Kamiya, 1997). Another terpenoid hormone, the C_{15} compound, abscisic acid, is not properly considered a lower terpenoid, since it is formed from the oxidative cleavage of a C_{40} carotenoid precursor (Schwartz *et al.*, 1997).

Several important groups of plant compounds, including cytokinins, chlorophylls and the quinone-based electron carriers (the plastoquinones and ubiquinones), have terpenoid side chains attached to a non-terpenoid nucleus. These side chains facilitate anchoring to or movement within membranes. In the past decade, proteins have also been found to have terpenoid side chains attached. In fact, all eukaryotic cells appear to contain proteins that have been post-translationally modified by the attachment of C_{15} and C_{20} terpenoid side chains via a thioether linkage.

Prenylation substantially increases protein hydrophobicity and serves to target proteins to membranes or direct protein-protein interactions (Zhang and Casey, 1996). In plants, prenylated proteins may be involved in the control of the cell cycle (Morehead *et al.*, 1995; Qian *et al.*, 1996), nutrient allocation (Zhou *et al.*, 1997) and abscisic acid (ABA) signal transduction (Cutler *et al.*, 1996).

The most abundant hydrocarbon emitted by plants is the hemiterpene (C_5) isoprene, 2-methyl-1,3-butadiene (Fig. 5.1). Emitted from many taxa, especially woody species, isoprene has a major impact on the redox balance of the atmosphere, affecting levels of ozone, carbon monoxide and methane (Lerdau *et al.*, 1997). The release of isoprene from plants is strongly influenced by light and temperature, with the greatest release rates typically occurring under conditions of high light and high temperature (Monson *et al.*, 1992). Although the function of isoprene in plants has been a mystery for many years, there are now indications that it may serve to prevent cellular damage at high temperatures, perhaps by reacting with free radicals to stabilize membrane components (Singsaas *et al.*, 1997). Instead of isoprene, some plant species emit large amounts of monoterpene (C_{10}) hydrocarbons, which may function in a similar fashion (Loreto *et al.*, 1998).

Most of the thousands of terpenoids produced by plants have no discernible role in growth and development and are, therefore, often classified as 'secondary' metabolites. Although comparatively few of these substances have been investigated in depth, they are thought to serve primarily in ecological roles, providing defence against herbivores or pathogens, and acting as attractants for animals that disperse pollen or seeds and as inhibitors of the germination and growth of neighbouring plants (Harborne and Tomas-Barberan, 1991; Langenheim, 1994). One of the best known examples of a lower terpene involved in plant defence is polygodial, a drimane-type sesquiterpene dialdehyde found in *Polygonum hydropiper* (Fig. 5.1). Among the most potent deterrents to insect feeding known, polygodial has been shown to inhibit the feeding of a diverse assortment of herbivorous insects (van Beek and de Groot, 1986). The deterrent effect appears to be a direct result of the action of polygodial on taste receptors. In lepidopteran larvae, polygodial and other drimane dialdehydes block the stimulatory effects of glucose and sucrose on chemosensory receptor cells found on the mouthparts (Frazier, 1986; Jansen and de Groot, 1991).

Although few lower terpenes have been studied in as much detail as polygodial, many other members of this group serve as toxins, feeding deterrents or oviposition deterrents to herbivores, and so are also thought to function in plant defence. As toxins or deterrents, these substances possess many diverse modes of action on herbivores. For example: the monoterpenoid ketone, pulegone (Fig. 5.1), is a liver toxin in mammals (Nelson *et al.*, 1992); the pyrethrins, monoterpene esters, function as insect nerve poisons; sesquiterpene juvenile hormone analogues disrupt endocrine-mediated processes in insects, including metamorphosis and reproduction (Bowers, 1991); and the diterpene, atractyloside, inhibits oxidative phosphorylation in mitochondria (Obatomi and Bach, 1998).

In the last few years, a new role for lower terpenes in plant defence has emerged. Certain plant species respond to herbivore attack by emitting volatile terpenes that attract the enemies of herbivores. For example, lima bean (*Phaseolus lunatus*) plants damaged by the spider mite, *Tetranychus urticae*, emit a mixture of monoterpenes, C_{11} and C_{16} homoterpenes (Fig. 5.1) and methyl salicylate, which attracts a carnivorous mite, *Phytoseiulus persimilis*, that preys on spider mites (Dicke, 1994; Dicke *et al.*, 1990). When maize or cotton is fed upon by lepidopteran larvae, a blend of monoterpenes, sesquiterpenes, homoterpenes and other compounds is released, which attracts parasitic wasps that oviposit on the larvae (Turlings *et al.*, 1990, 1995). The majority of these volatiles are emitted only by arthropod-damaged plants and not by unattacked or artificially-damaged plants. The terpenoids released are largely synthesized *de novo* following initial herbivore attack (Pare and Tumlinson, 1997) and are released systemically throughout the plant (Dicke *et al.*, 1993; Rose *et al.*, 1996). The use of volatile terpenoids to attract the enemies of herbivores may be a valuable complement to the more direct modes of anti-herbivore defence.

The functions of the lower terpenes are not limited to the natural world. Many play important roles in human society, such as the myriad of monoterpene and sesquiterpene flavour and fragrance agents that are added to foods, beverages, perfumes, soaps, toothpaste, tobacco and other products (Verlet, 1993). Some lower terpenes find use in industry as raw materials in the manufacture of adhesives, coatings, emulsifiers and speciality chemicals, whilst others, such as limonene and the pyrethrins, are of increasing commercial importance as insecticides because of their low toxicity to mammals and lack of persistence in the environment. The pharmaceutical importance of plant lower terpenes has steadily increased in the last decade. In addition to the well-known roles of camphor (Fig. 5.1) and cineole in preparations to relieve the pain of burns, strains and other inflammations, the last few years have seen the acceptance of artemisinin, a sesquiterpene endoperoxide derived from the traditional Chinese medicinal plant, *Artemisia annua* (Fig. 5.1), as a valuable antimalarial compound (Butler and Wu, 1992), and the development of paclitaxel (Fig. 5.1), a highly functionalized diterpene from yew (*Taxus* spp.), as a new drug for the treatment of ovarian and breast cancer (Hezari and Croteau, 1997). Paclitaxel, also known as taxol, enhances the polymerization of tubulin, a protein component of the microtubules of the mitotic spindle, resulting in stabilized, nonfunctional tubules and blocking the cell cycle. The potential of other lower terpenes in the therapy and prevention of cancer is currently under active investigation (Gould, 1995).

5.1.3 Biosynthesis

The biosynthetic pathway to terpenoids (Fig. 5.2) is conveniently treated as comprising four stages, the first of which involves the formation of

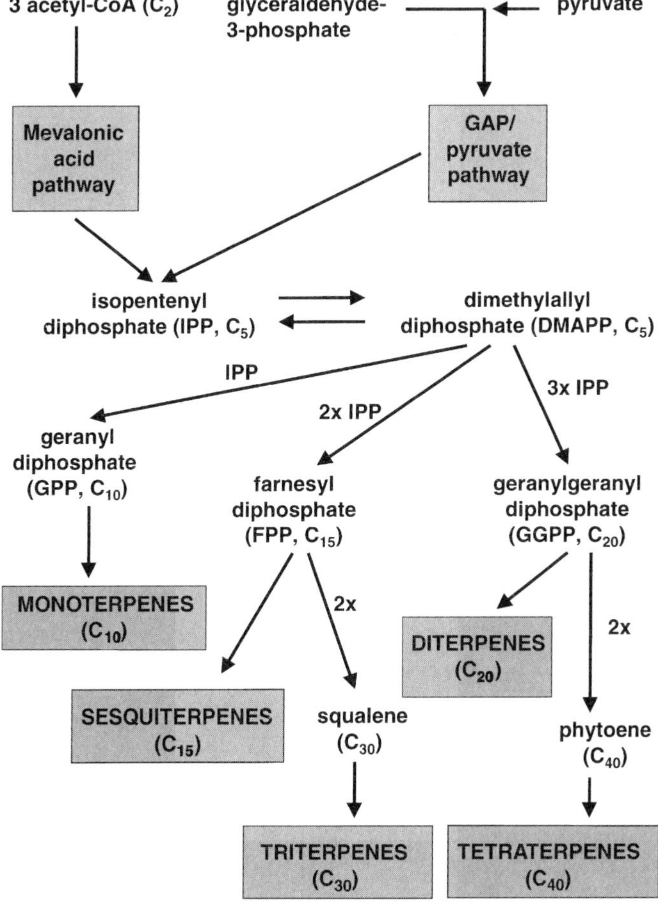

Figure 5.2 Overview of terpenoid biosynthesis in plants, showing the basic stages of this process and major groups of end-products. Abbreviations: CoA, coenzyme A; GAP, glyceraldehyde-3-phosphate.

isopentenyl diphosphate (IPP), the biological C_5 isoprene unit. Plants synthesize IPP and its allylic isomer, dimethylallyl diphosphate (DMAPP), by one of two routes: the well-known mevalonic acid pathway; or the newly-discovered glyceraldehyde phosphate/pyruvate pathway. In the second stage, the basic C_5 units condense to generate three larger prenyl diphosphates, geranyl diphosphate (GPP, C_{10}), farnesyl diphosphate (FPP, C_{15}) and geranylgeranyl diphosphate (GGPP, C_{20}). In the third stage, the C_{10}–C_{20} diphosphates undergo a wide range of cyclizations and rearrangements to produce the parent carbon skeletons of each terpene class. GPP is converted to the monoterpenes, FPP is converted to the sesquiterpenes and GGPP is converted to the diterpenes. FPP and GGPP can also dimerize in a head-to-head fashion to form the precursors of the C_{30} and the C_{40} terpenoids, respectively. The fourth and final stage encompasses a variety of oxidations, reductions isomerizations, conjugations and other transformations, by which the parent skeletons of each terpene class are converted to thousands of distinct terpene metabolites. This section discusses the latest findings concerning each of the four stages of terpenoid biosynthesis in plants. The portions of the third and fourth stages that are not involved in the formation of the lower (C_5–C_{20}) terpenes are dealt with in section 5.2.

5.1.3.1 Formation of the basic C_5 unit: the mevalonate pathway

The classic route for the formation of the C_5 building blocks of terpenoid biosynthesis in plants is via the reactions of the mevalonate pathway, first demonstrated in yeast and mammals. This well-characterized sequence (Fig. 5.3) involves the stepwise condensation of three molecules of acetyl coenzyme A (AcCoA) to form the branched C_6 compound, 3-hydroxy-3-methylglutaryl-CoA (HMG-CoA). Following the reduction of HMG-CoA to mevalonic acid, two successive phosphorylations and a decarboxylation-elimination yield the C_5 compound, isopentenyl diphosphate (IPP).

Among the most recent developments in mevalonate pathway research is the first successful cloning of the plant genes for the initial two steps of the pathway, acetoacetyl-CoA thiolase (Vollack and Bach, 1996) and HMG-CoA synthase (Montamat *et al.*, 1995). The two sequences are separate and distinct from each other, in contrast to an earlier report suggesting that in plants, in contrast to animals and microorganisms, both reactions are catalyzed by a single protein (Weber and Bach, 1994). Each sequence is highly homologous to that of corresponding genes in the mevalonate pathways of mammals and microbes.

The third step of the mevalonic acid pathway is the conversion of HMG-CoA to mevalonic acid, a two-step, nicotinamide adenine diphosphate (reduced form) (NADPH)-requiring reduction catalyzed by HMG-CoA reductase (HMGR) (Fig. 5.3). Researchers have lavished considerable attention on HMGR, since it catalyzes a critical, rate-determining step in the biosynthesis of sterols in animals, and has been assumed to play a role of similar importance in the formation of plant terpenoids. Plant HMGR is a membrane-bound enzyme, a feature that has greatly hindered efforts to purify and characterize it. However, now that HMGR genes from more than ten species have been cloned and analyzed (Table 5.2A), our knowledge of this important catalyst has increased substantially. All plant genes isolated so far encode polypeptides of 60–65 kDa each, with three distinct regions: a very divergent NH_2-terminal domain: a more conserved membrane-binding region with two membrane-spanning sequences; and a highly-conserved COOH-terminal domain containing the catalytic site.

Experiments with cloned genes have contributed to the resolution of a long-standing controversy concerning the subcellular location of HMGR in plants. Over the last 25 yrs, it has been claimed that HMGR is present in the endoplasmic reticulum (ER), the plastids and the mitochondria (Bach *et al.*, 1991). However, HMGR gene products from both *Arabidopsis thaliana* (Campos and Boronat, 1995; Enjuto *et al.*, 1994) and tomato (Denbow *et al.*, 1996) have recently been demonstrated to be co-translationally inserted into ER-derived microsomal membranes *in vitro*. Since insertion is mediated by the two transmembrane regions (Denbow *et al.*, 1996; Enjuto *et al.*, 1994; Re *et al.*, 1997) whose sequences are conserved among all plant HMGR genes so far isolated, it seems probable that all known plant HMGRs are targeted to the ER (Campos and Boronat, 1995). Nevertheless, claims regarding the plastidial localization of HMGR have continued to appear (Bestwick *et al.*, 1995; Kim *et al.*, 1996; Nakagawara *et al.*, 1993). While an as yet uncharacterized HMGR may be present in plastids, reports of plastidial localization are more likely to be due to contamination of plastid fractions with microsomes (Gray, 1987). Marker enzymes or electron microscopy have seldom been used to verify the purity of subcellular fractions in such studies.

Evidence for the regulatory role of HMGR in the formation of plant terpenoids comes from numerous studies that have demonstrated a close correlation between changes in HMGR activity and alterations in the rate of terpenoid biosynthesis. For example, Heide and co-workers (Gaisser and Heide, 1996; Lange *et al.*, 1998a) have been studying the formation of shikonin, a napthoquinone pigment constructed from a benzenoid ring and a molecule of GPP. In *Lithospermum erythrorhizon* cultures, they showed that increases in the level of HMGR enzyme activity under various light and inhibitor treatments were associated with greater

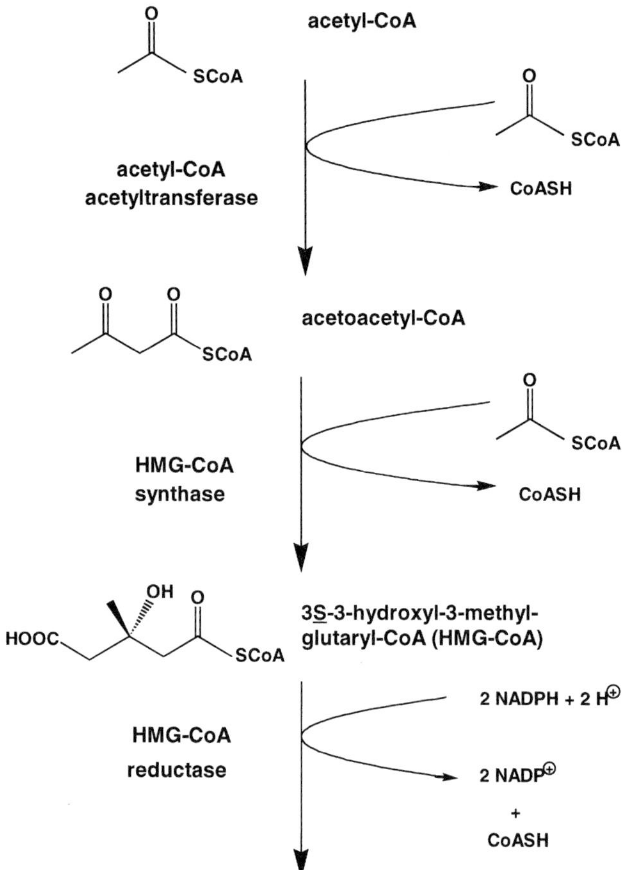

Figure 5.3 Outline of the mevalonate pathway for the formation of C_5 isoprenoid units. Most research has focused on HMG-CoA reductase (HMGR), the rate-determining step in terpenoid biosynthesis in mammals. P indicates a phosphate moiety. Abbreviations: HMG-CoA, 3-hydroxy-3 methylglutaryl coenzyme A; NADPH, nicotinamide adenine dinucleotide phosphate (reduced form); SCoA, S-Coenzyme A (to which acetate is attached); CoASH, free coenzyme A.

accumulation of shikonin and its derivatives. Other recent examples include correlations between the level of HMGR and the formation of: sesquiterpenes in lettuce (Bestwick *et al.*, 1995); sesquiterpenes in cotton (Joost *et al.*, 1995); triterpenes in *Tabernaemontana divaricata* (Fulton *et al.*, 1994); and rubber in guayule (Ji *et al.*, 1993).

To obtain more rigorous proof of the regulatory role of plant HMGR, researchers have used constitutive promoters to overexpress HMGR in various species. For example, tobacco transformed with a constitutively-

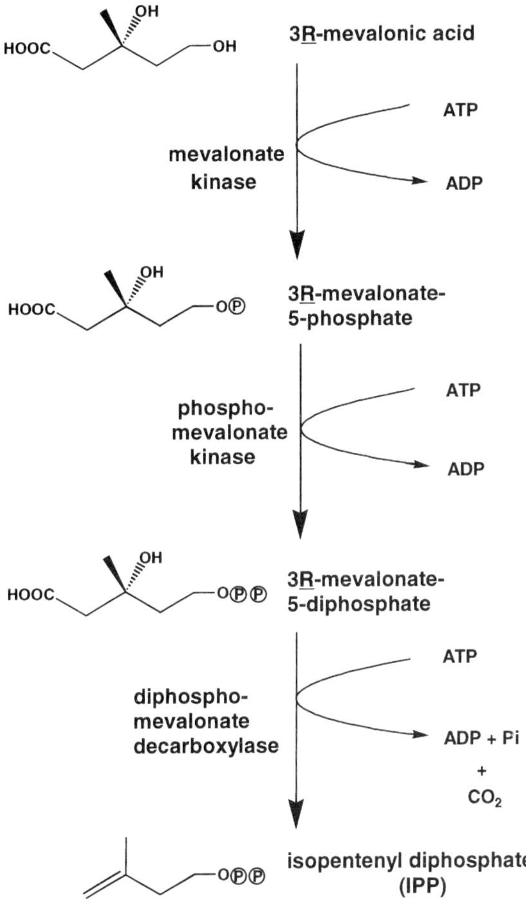

Figure 5.3 (Continued).

expressed HMGR construct showed a 3–8 fold increase in HMGR enzyme activity and a 3–10 fold increase in total sterols (Chappell *et al.*, 1995; Schaller *et al.*, 1995). However, there was no change in the level of other terpenoid end-products, including sesquiterpenes, phytol (the C_{20} side chain of chlorophyll) and carotenoids. Curiously, the sterol composition of these HMGR-overexpressing plants differed from that of untransformed tobacco in having a much higher proportion of biosynthetic intermediates, such as cycloartenol (often conjugated as esters), rather than end-products, such as sitosterol or stigmasterol. A mutant tobacco cell line resistant to a sterol inhibitor showed a very similar phenotype (Gondet *et al.*, 1994, 1992). Taken together, these

Table 5.2 Isolated genes encoding several major classes of enzymes in terpene biosynthesis

Enzyme	Species	Reference
A) HMG-CoA reductase	*Arabidopsis thaliana*	Caelles *et al.*, 1989
		Enjuto *et al.*, 1994
		Learned and Fink, 1989
	Camptotheca acuminata	Burnett *et al.*, 1993
	Catharanthus roseus	Maldonado-Mendoza *et al.*, 1992
	Gossypium barbadense	Joost *et al.*, 1995
	Gossypium hirsutum	
	Hevea brasiliensis	Chye *et al.*, 1992
	Lycopersicon esculentum	Narita and Gruissem, 1989
		Park *et al.*, 1992
	Nicotiana sylvestris	Genschik *et al.*, 1992
	Oryza sativa	Nelson *et al.*, 1994
	Pisum sativum	Monfar *et al.*, 1990
	Raphanus sativus	Wettstein *et al.*, 1989
		Vollack *et al.*, 1994
	Solanum tuberosum	Bhattacharyya *et al.*, 1995
		Choi *et al.*, 1992
		Korth *et al.*, 1997
		Oosterhaven *et al.*, 1993
		Yang *et al.*, 1991
	Triticum aestivum	Aoyagi *et al.*, 1993
B) Prenyltransferases		
FPP synthase	*Arabidopsis thaliana*	Delourme *et al.*, 1994
	Artemisia annua	Matsushita *et al.*, 1996
	Capsicum annuum	Hugueney *et al.*, 1996
	Hevea brasiliensis	Adiwilaga and Kush, 1996
	Lupinus albus	Attucci *et al.*, 1995
	Oryza sativa	Sanmiya *et al.*, 1997
	Parthenium argentatum	Pan *et al.*, 1996
	Zea mays	Li and Larkins, 1996
GGPP synthase	*Arabidopsis thaliana*	Scolnick and Bartley, 1996
		Scolnick and Bartley, 1994
	Brassica campestris	Lim *et al.*, 1996
	Capsicum annuum	Badillo *et al.*, 1995
		Kuntz *et al.*, 1992
	Catharanthus roseus	Bantignies *et al.*, 1996
	Lupinus albus	Aitken *et al.*, 1995
C) Terpene synthases	*Abies grandis*	Bohlmann *et al.*, 1997
		Bohlmann *et al.*, 1998a
		Steele *et al.*, 1998a
		Vogel *et al.*, 1996
	Arabidopsis thaliana	Corey *et al.*, 1993
		Sun and Kamiya, 1994
		Yamaguchi *et al.*, 1998
	Clarkia brewerii	Dudareva *et al.*, 1996
	Cucurbita maxima	Yamaguchi *et al.*, 1996
	Gossypium arboreum	Chen *et al.*, 1995
		Chen *et al.*, 1996
	Hyoscyamus muticus	Back and Chappell, 1995

Table 5.2 (Continued).

Enzyme	Species	Reference
	Lycopersicon esculentum	Colby *et al.*, 1998
	Mentha x piperita	Crock *et al.*, 1997
	Mentha spicata	Colby *et al.*, 1993
	Nicotiana tabacum	Facchini and Chappell, 1992
	Perilla frutescens	Yuba *et al.*, 1996
	Pisum sativum	Ait-Ali *et al.*, 1997
	Ricinus communis	Mau and West, 1994
	Salvia officinalis	Wise *et al.*, 1998
	Taxus brevifolia	Wildung and Croteau, 1996
	Zea mays	Bensen *et al.*, 1995

Abbreviations: HMG-COA, 3-hydroxy-3 methylglutaryl coenzyme A; FPP, farnesyl diphosphate; GGPP, geranylgeranyl diphosphate.

results make a strong case for HMGR being a rate-determining step, at least in the formation of sterols, although later enzymes in the pathway also have a significant influence on the rate of sterol biosynthesis. However, this conclusion may not be applicable to all plant species, since the overexpression of HMGR in *Arabidopsis thaliana* had no effect on the accumulation of sterols and other terpenoids (Re *et al.*, 1995).

If HMGR activity limits the rate of terpenoid formation, it is important to understand the mechanism of this control. In mammals, HMGR activity is subject to feedback inhibition by sterols that regulates the rates of transcription and translation, and post-translational controls involving allosteric effects and reversible phosphorylation (Goldstein and Brown, 1990). HMGR activity in plants appears to be modulated in similar ways, although we are only just beginning to understand the mechanisms of control. The close correlation of HMGR activity with the abundance of HMGR mRNA in *L. erythrorhizon* (Lange *et al.*, 1998a), tomato (Yang *et al.*, 1991) and other species (Stermer *et al.*, 1994) is good evidence for transcriptional control. At the post-translational level, HMGR from *Brassica oleracea* was shown to be inactivated by reversible phosphorylation, mediated by a specific kinase (Dale *et al.*, 1995; MacKintosh *et al.*, 1992). Since plants produce a much wider assortment of terpenoid end-products than mammals do, they might be expected to regulate HMGR in unique ways not found in mammals. While only a single HMGR gene is known from each of the mammal species studied so far, all plants examined possess a small gene family with as many as nine members (Bhattacharyya *et al.*, 1995; Joost *et al.*, 1995). Detailed studies in tomato and potato reveal that different HMGR genes may be expressed in different organs or under different environmental conditions (Choi *et al.*, 1994; Daraselia *et al.*, 1996; Enjuto *et al.*,

1995), raising the possibility that differential expression of HMGR genes could serve as a major mechanism for the control of HMGR activity.

Mevalonic acid, the product of HMGR, is converted to isopentenyl diphosphate (IPP) by the sequential action of three enzymes: mevalonate kinase, phosphomevalonate kinase and diphosphomevalonate decarboxylase (Fig. 5.3). These three catalysts have not previously been considered to be important control points in plant terpenoid biosynthesis, and little new information has appeared to alter this view. The activities of all three enzymes were shown to be higher than that of HMGR (Bianchini *et al.*, 1996), similar to each other (Sandmann and Albrecht, 1994), and unrelated to fluctuations in the rate of terpenoid formation (Bianchini *et al.*, 1996; Ji *et al.*, 1993). A cDNA encoding mevalonate kinase was recently isolated from *Arabidopsis thaliana* by genetic complementation in yeast (Riou *et al.*, 1994). The lack of a transit peptide and the presence of only a single gene, as deduced from Southern blotting, make it appear that plant mevalonate kinase, like HMGR, is a cytosolic enzyme.

5.1.3.2 Formation of the basic C_5 unit: the glyceraldehyde phosphate-pyruvate pathway

The most exciting recent advance in the field of plant terpenoid biosynthesis is the discovery of a second route for making the basic C_5 building block of terpenes, completely distinct from the mevalonate pathway (Lichtenthaler *et al.*, 1997a). This new route, which starts from glyceraldehyde phosphate and pyruvate (Fig. 5.4), has also been detected in bacteria and other microorganisms. With the advantage of hindsight, one can list many observations made during the last 30 yrs that, taken together, should have persuaded researchers of the existence of a non-mevalonate pathway to terpenoids in higher plants. For example, it was demonstrated numerous times that mevalonate itself is a very poor precursor for many classes of terpenoids (Charlwood and Banthorpe, 1978; Croteau and Loomis, 1972). However, there was no reasonable alternative to the mevalonate pathway prior to the pioneering investigations of terpenoid biosynthesis in eubacteria, carried out by Michel Rohmer, Hermann Sahm and co-workers. These investigators discovered that the incorporation of ^{13}C-labelled precursors, such as glucose, acetate and pyruvate, into bacterial terpenoids (hopanoids and ubiquinones) was not consistent with the operation of the mevalonate pathway (Flesch and Rohmer, 1988; Rohmer *et al.*, 1993). In addition, when intermediates of the mevalonate pathway were fed to species such as *Escherichia coli*, they were not incorporated (Horbach *et al.*, 1993). Analysis of the ^{13}C incorporation patterns from labelled glucose and acetate allowed the deduction that a C_3 unit from glycolysis and a C_2 unit from pyruvate

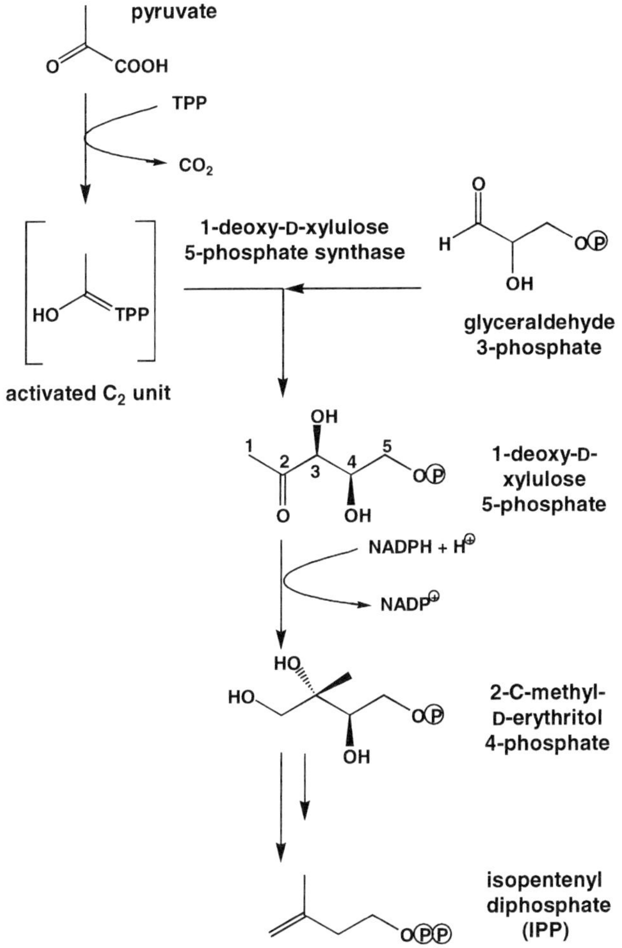

Figure 5.4 Outline of the newly-discovered glyceraldehyde phosphate/pyruvate pathway for the formation of C_5 isoprenoid units. None of the intermediates after 2-C-methyl-D-erythritol 4-phosphate are known. P indicates a phosphate moiety. Abbreviations: TPP, thiamine pyrophosphate; NADP, nicotinamide adenine dinucleotide phosphate.

combined in some manner to form the basic C_5 isopentenoid unit (Rohmer *et al.*, 1993). Subsequent experiments with *E. coli* mutants, blocked in specific steps of triose phosphate metabolism, pointed to glyceraldehyde phosphate and pyruvate as the actual precursors of this new pathway (Rohmer *et al.*, 1996).

The existence of a similar non-mevalonate route to terpenoids in plants was first reported in 1994. When Duilio Arigoni and co-workers fed different ^{13}C-labelled forms of glucose to *Ginkgo biloba* embryos, the ^{13}C-nuclear magnetic resonance (NMR) spectra of the resulting diterpenes were not what would have been expected from the normal operation of the mevalonate pathway (Cartayrade *et al.*, 1994) but showed an incorporation pattern identical to that seen with the *E. coli* terpenoids. Subsequent studies employing similar methodology have demonstrated that an assortment of terpenoids from angiosperms, gymnosperms and bryophytes, including monoterpenes (Adam *et al.*, 1998; Eisenreich *et al.*, 1997), diterpenes (Eisenreich *et al.*, 1996; Knoss *et al.*, 1997), carotenoids (Lichtenthaler *et al.*, 1997b), and the side chains of chlorophyll (phytol) and quinones (Adam *et al.*, 1998; Lichtenthaler *et al.*, 1997b) are formed in non-mevalonate fashion, while the labelling of sesquiterpenes and sterols was consistent with their origin from the mevalonate pathway (Adam *et al.*, 1998; Lichtenthaler *et al.*, 1997b; Schwarz, 1994).

Several research groups are now actively involved in elucidating the sequence of the new pathway. In 1996, Rohmer and co-workers refined their concept of the first step, proposing that hydroxyethylthiamine diphosphate, a C_2 unit derived from pyruvate, condenses with glyceraldehyde-3-phosphate to form 1-deoxy-D-xylulose 5-phosphate (Rohmer *et al.*, 1996) (Fig. 5.4). This hypothesis was based on the pattern of labelling in terpenoids formed from [^{13}C]-pyruvate, [^{13}C]-glycerol and various [^{13}C]-glucoses, and the natural occurrence of 1-deoxy-D-xylulose, a precursor of the enzyme cofactors thiamine (vitamin B_1) diphosphate and pyridoxal (vitamin B_6) 5′-phosphate. Additional support comes from the high rate of 1-deoxy-D-xylulose incorporation into terpenoids measured in *E. coli* (Broers, 1994) and several plant species (Arigoni *et al.*, 1997; Sagner *et al.*, 1998b; Zeidler *et al.*, 1997). More rigorous proof of the nature of the first step of the non-mevalonate pathway has become available in the last year, with the isolation of cDNAs for enzymes that catalyze the conversion of glyceraldehyde phosphate and pyruvate to 1-deoxy-D-xylulose 5-phosphate from *E. coli* (Lois *et al.*, 1998; Sprenger *et al.*, 1997), *Capsicum annuum* (Bouvier *et al.*, 1998) and *Mentha* x *piperita* (Lange *et al.*, 1998b). The encoded enzymes are novel transketolases that are distinct from other members of this enzyme family, such as the well-characterized transketolases of the pentose phosphate pathway.

After 1-deoxy-D-xylulose 5-phosphate, subsequent reactions of the new pathway must transform the linear five-carbon backbone of this sugar phosphate to a branched, isopentenoid carbon skeleton. Just recently, 1-deoxy-D-xylulose 5-phosphate has been shown to be converted to 2-C-methyl-D-erythritol 4-phosphate in *E. coli* (Duvold *et al.*, 1997; Kuzuyama *et al.*, 1998; Takahashi *et al.*, 1998) (Fig. 5.4), and the same reaction was demonstrated to occur in several species of plants (Sagner *et al.*, 1998a). This intramolecular rearrangement involves the cleavage of the C3-C4 bond of the deoxyxylulose backbone and the establishment of a new bond between C2 and C4. Similar skeletal rearrangements are involved in both riboflavin and valine biosynthesis. While nothing is yet known of any additional intermediates in the pathway, several dehydration steps, reductions and at least one phosphorylation seem to be required to transform 2-C-methyl-D-erythritol 4-phosphate to IPP. Given the high level of interest in this work and the participation of several excellent research groups, it would be surprising if the remaining steps of this novel pathway were not rapidly elucidated.

The non-mevalonate route to terpenoids appears to be localized in the plastids. In plant cells, terpenoids are manufactured both in plastids and the cytosol (Gray, 1987; Kleinig, 1989). As a general rule, the plastids produce monoterpenes, diterpenes, phytol, carotenoids and the side chains of plastoquinone and α-tocopherol, while the cytosol/ER compartment produces sesquiterpenes, sterols and dolichols. In the studies discussed above, nearly all of the terpenoids labelled by deoxyxylulose (Arigoni *et al.*, 1997; Sagner *et al.*, 1998b) and 2-C-methyl erythritol feeding (Duvold *et al.*, 1997), or showing ^{13}C-patterns indicative of a non-mevalonate origin (Adam *et al.*, 1998; Cartayrade *et al.*, 1994; Eisenreich *et al.*, 1996, 1997; Lichtenthaler *et al.*, 1997b) are thought to be plastid-derived. Consistent with this generalization is the fact that the genes of the non-mevalonate pathway that have been isolated so far all encode plastid-targeting sequences (Bouvier *et al.*, 1998; Lange *et al.*, 1998b). In contrast, the mevalonate pathway appears to reside solely in the cytosol/ER compartment based on the sequence analysis and expression of genes encoding pathway enzymes, including acetoacetyl-CoA thiolase (Vollack and Bach, 1996), HMG-CoA synthase (Montamat *et al.*, 1995), HMGR (discussed in section 5.1.3.1) and mevalonate kinase (Riou *et al.*, 1994). A third subcellular compartment, the mitochondrion, also participates in terpenoid biosynthesis, making the prenyl side chain of ubiquinone, an electron transport system component found in this organelle, using IPP derived from the cytosol/ER pathway (Disch *et al.*, 1998a).

It was once difficult to reconcile the terpenoid-manufacturing capabilities of the plastids with the usual absence of detectable HMGR activity in these organelles. Models proposed that the basic reactions of terpenoid biosynthesis are confined to the cytosol, with the preformed C_5 units being transferred to other subcellular compartments (Gray, 1987; Luetke-Brinkhaus and Kleinig, 1987). However, current knowledge suggests a more accurate generalization: plastids biosynthesize terpenoids primarily via the glyceraldehyde phosphate-pyruvate pathway, while in the cytosol/ER terpenoid formation occurs largely via the mevalonate pathway. Reviewing the older literature with this paradigm in mind, it is not surprising: that mevalonate was found to be so poorly incorporated into many plastid-formed terpenoids (Charlwood and Banthorpe, 1978; Croteau and Loomis, 1972; Keene and Wagner, 1985; Rogers *et al.*, 1968); that levels of HMGR activity were often noted to be poorly correlated with the formation of plastidial terpenoids (Chappell *et al.*, 1989; Narita and Gruissem, 1989); and that the HMGR inhibitor, mevinolin, was shown to have negligible effect on the production of plastidial terpenoids (Bach, 1995; Bach and Lichtenthaler, 1983).

The existence of a non-mevalonate route to terpenoids also helps account for other puzzling observations, such as the complete failure of green algae to incorporate mevalonate into terpenoids (Lichtenthaler *et al.*, 1997a). Feeding experiments with ^{13}C-labelled glucose and acetate have now shown that all terpenoids in *Scenedesmus obliquus* (Schwender *et al.*, 1996) and other green algae (Disch *et al.*, 1998b) are formed by the glyceraldehyde-pyruvate pathway. Among other photosynthetic micro-organisms surveyed: the red alga, *Cyanidium caldarium*, and the chrysophyte, *Ochromonas danica* (Disch *et al.*, 1998b) use both pathways; *Euglena gracilis* (Disch *et al.*, 1998b) and the eubacterium, *Chloroflexus aurantiacus* (Rieder *et al.*, 1998) use only the mevalonate pathway; while the cyanobacterium, *Synechocystis* PCC 6714 (Disch *et al.*, 1998b), employs only the glyceraldehyde-pyruvate pathway, like the plastids of higher plants. These results are in accord with the endosymbiotic origin of higher plant plastids from a cyanobacterium-like symbiont.

A strict division between the mevalonate and non-mevalonate pathways may not always exist for a given end-product. The biosynthesis of certain terpenoids appears to involve the participation of both routes (Adam and Zapp, 1998; Nabeta *et al.*, 1995; Piel *et al.*, 1998; Schwarz, 1994). For example, the first two C_5 units of the sesquiterpenes of chamomile (*Matricaria recutita*) are formed via the glyceraldehyde-pyruvate pathway, while the third unit is derived from both the mevalonate pathway and the glyceraldehyde-pyruvate pathway (Adam and Zapp, 1998). Joint participation of the two pathways may be a result of the transport of prenyl diphosphate intermediates between the different sites of terpenoid biosynthesis (Heintze *et al.*, 1990; McCaskill and Croteau, 1995; Soler *et al.*, 1993), or the actual presence of both pathways in the same compartment. While the preponderance of evidence argues for the localization of the mevalonate pathway in the cytosol and the glyceraldehyde-pyruvate pathway in the plastids, as discussed above, there are some indications that the mevalonate pathway may also be found in plastids, at least in certain species (Kim *et al.*, 1996) at certain developmental stages (Heintze *et al.*, 1990, 1994).

The occurrence of both terpenoid pathways at the same subcellular site, or the exchange of prenyl diphosphates between sites, may also help explain other curious phenomena noted in previous biosynthetic studies, such as the unequal labelling of different C_5 units. Administration of mevalonate has frequently been shown to result in the IPP-derived portion of the molecule being much more heavily labelled than the portion derived from DMAPP (Charlwood and Banthorpe, 1978; Croteau and Loomis, 1972). Such asymmetry has been attributed to the existence of a large pool of DMAPP that dilutes any DMAPP formed from an exogenous, labelled precursor. However, asymmetric labelling could also be a consequence of having separate pathways to each of the two basic C_5 units. The actual C_5 product of the alternative pathway is not known, and might be DMAPP rather than IPP. If DMAPP arising from the non-mevalonate pathway condensed with mevalonate-derived IPP (produced *in situ* or transported from another compartment), this could result in the unequal labelling of C_5 units. More research is needed, not only to identify the remaining intermediates in the glyceraldehyde-pyruvate pathway but also to determine in which species, tissues and compartments it operates, and to understand its regulation.

5.1.3.3 Assembly of C_5 units into C_{10}, C_{15} and C_{20} prenyl diphosphates
The second stage of terpene biosynthesis involves the fusion of the basic C_5 building blocks to yield larger metabolic intermediates (Fig. 5.2). IPP and its more reactive allylic isomer, DMAPP, condense in a head-to-tail orientation to form C_{10}, C_{15} and C_{20} prenyl diphosphates (Fig. 5.5). The requisite DMAPP is derived directly from IPP by the action of IPP isomerase, which is also capable of catalyzing the reverse reaction. In the last three years, genes encoding this enzyme have been isolated from *Arabidopsis thaliana* (Campbell *et al.*, 1998) and *Clarkia breweri* (Blanc and Pichersky, 1995). The sequences reported exhibit high homology to the IPP isomerase gene sequences of other organisms, except at their N-termini, which seem to encode transit peptides for plastid localization. *A. thaliana* possesses an IPP isomerase gene family consisting of at least two members (Campbell *et al.*, 1998), a finding consistent with the detection of multiple forms of this enzyme in cell cultures of several plant species (Ramosvaldivia *et al.*, 1998). In *Cinchona robusta*, for example, the two isoforms of IPP isomerase had different kinetic parameters, different preferences for divalent metal ion cofactors and different patterns of occurrence; one form was present only after induction by fungal elicitor (Ramosvaldivia *et al.*, 1997c). Although there is no strong evidence that IPP isomerase has any control of flux through the terpenoid pathway (Ramosvaldivia *et al.*, 1997b), the activity of this enzyme in maize increases significantly after stimulation of carotenoid biosynthesis by

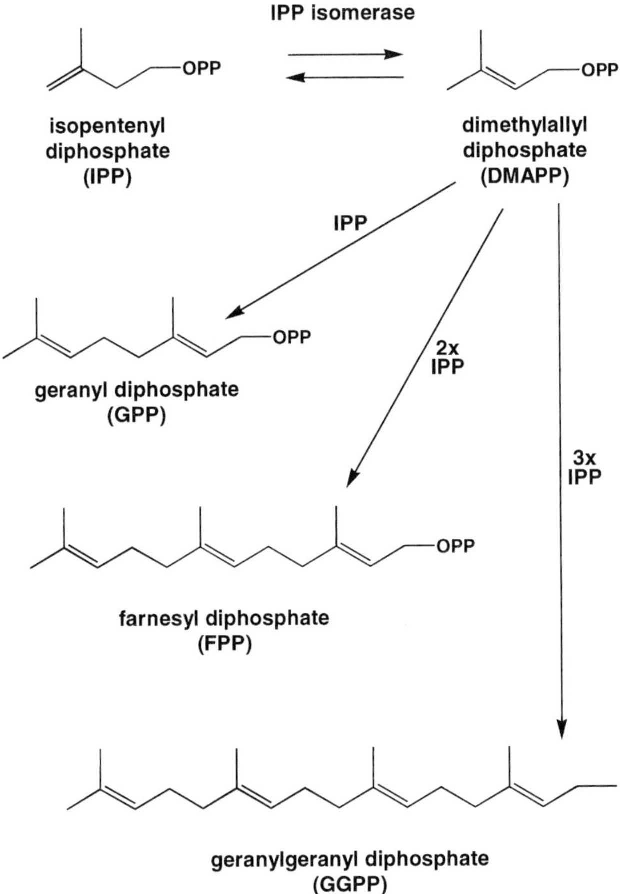

Figure 5.5 The formation of C_{10}, C_{15} and C_{20} prenyl diphosphates from the fusion of C_5 isoprenoid units. PP indicates a diphosphate moiety.

light (Albrecht and Sandmann, 1994), and activity in cell cultures of several species increases after induction of phytoalexin formation by treatment with fungal elicitors (Fulton *et al.*, 1994; Hanley *et al.*, 1992; Ramosvaldivia *et al.*, 1997a).

The substrate (IPP) and the product (DMAPP) of IPP isomerase are both involved in the fundamental reactions by which C_5 isopentenoid units are joined together. Enzymes known as prenyltransferases add varying numbers of IPP units to a DMAPP primer in sequential chain elongation steps. The initial head-to-tail (1′-4) condensation of IPP and DMAPP yields the C_{10} allylic diphosphate, geranyl diphosphate (GPP).

Further 1′-4 condensations of IPP with the enlarging allylic diphosphate chain give the C_{15} allylic diphosphate, farnesyl diphosphate (FPP), and the C_{20} allylic diphosphate, geranylgeranyl diphosphate (GGPP). In plants, FPP and GGPP are produced by well-characterized, product-specific enzymes that catalyze two- or three-step elongation sequences starting with IPP and DMAPP (Fig. 5.5). For example, GGPP synthases convert DMAPP and IPP directly to GGPP (Dogbo and Camara, 1987; Laferriere and Beyer, 1991; Spurgeon *et al.*, 1984). The reaction proceeds through the intermediacy of GPP and FPP, but under normal conditions GGPP is the first product to leave the active site. In contrast to FPP and GGPP synthases, much less attention has been devoted to GPP synthases. In fact, the very existence of this class of prenyltransferases in plants was once doubted, in the belief that amounts of GPP sufficient to sustain monoterpene biosynthesis were released during the formation of the larger allylic diphosphates (Heide and Berger, 1989). However, prenyltransferases that synthesize GPP exclusively have now been discovered in several plant species that produce monoterpenes or natural products incorporating a monoterpene unit (Clastre *et al.*, 1993; Croteau and Purkett, 1989; Heide and Berger, 1989).

In the past six years, cDNAs encoding FPP and GGPP synthases have been isolated from a diverse assortment of plant species (Table 5.2B). The amino acid sequences deduced have a high degree of similarity to the FPP and GGPP synthases of other organisms (Chen *et al.*, 1994), which means that the recent determination of the crystal structure of an avian FPP synthase has considerable value for the study of plant prenyltransferases as well. The structure of FPP synthase from avian liver consists of a novel arrangement of ten parallel α-helices positioned around a large central cavity (Tarshis *et al.*, 1994). Two aspartate-rich sequences (DDxxD) that are highly conserved among other prenyltransferases (Chen *et al.*, 1994) and essential for catalysis (Joly and Edwards, 1993; Marrero *et al.*, 1992; Song and Poulter, 1994) are found on opposite sides of the cavity, with their aspartate carboxyl side chains pointing toward the cavity centre. These aspartate residues had previously been suggested to bind the diphosphate moieties of the substrates via Mg^{2+} bridges (Marrero *et al.*, 1992). Structural analysis of a samarium-containing heavy atom derivative of avian FPP synthase (samarium commonly adheres to Mg^{2+}-binding sites in enzymes) showed samarium atoms bound to each of the two aspartate-rich regions, supporting the role of the aspartate residues in binding Mg^{2+} (Tarshis *et al.*, 1994). Work has now begun to identify other amino acid residues involved in the reaction mechanism. Prenyltransferases are one of the few groups of enzymes in which carbon-carbon bond formation results from electrophilic attack of a carbocationic species on a pre-existing double-bond (Poulter and Rilling, 1981).

The initial carbocation is formed by the ionization of the allylic substrate through hydrolysis of the diphosphate ester. Subsequently, addition to the double-bond of IPP forms a new carbocation, which is then stabilized by proton elimination.

A long-standing goal in the study of prenyltransferases is to understand how these catalysts control the length of the growing chain during the reaction sequence. The availability of cloned prenyltransferase sequences and a three-dimensional structure for this enzyme class has provided new tools to approach this problem. Random and site-directed mutagenesis of bacterial FPP and GGPP synthases has demonstrated that several amino acid residues near the conserved aspartate-rich domains were most critical in determining chain length (Ohnuma *et al.*, 1996a,b,c, 1997 Tarshis *et al.*, 1996). For example, when avian FPP synthase was altered so that two phenylalanine residues, located just to the N-terminal side of the first aspartate-rich domain, were changed to serine and alanine, the mutant enzyme produced products up to C_{70}, with an average size of $C_{35}-C_{40}$ (Tarshis *et al.*, 1996). Structural analysis carried out in parallel with the mutagenesis revealed that the mutant FPP synthase had a larger binding pocket for allylic diphosphate substrates than native FPP synthase. Other amino acid residues involved in the substrate and product specificity of prenyltransferases are being actively sought.

The prenyltransferases that catalyze the syntheses of GPP, FPP and GGPP may be important regulatory enzymes in plant terpenoid biosynthesis since they are situated at the primary branch-points of the pathway, directing flux among the various major classes of terpenoids. The level of prenyltransferase activity is, in fact, closely correlated with the rate of terpenoid formation in many experimental systems (Dudley *et al.*, 1986; Hanley *et al.*, 1992; Hugueney *et al.*, 1996) consistent with the regulatory importance of these catalysts. The localization of specific prenyltransferases in particular types of tissue or subcellular compartments may control the flux and direction of terpenoid synthesis at these sites. For example, the GPP synthase in *Salvia officinalis* is restricted to the secretory cells of the glandular trichomes, which are the sole site of monoterpene biosynthesis in this species (Croteau and Purkett, 1989).

5.1.3.4 Formation of parent carbon skeletons

The prenyl diphosphates, GPP, FPP and GGPP, are the central intermediates of terpenoid biosynthesis. Under the catalysis of monoterpene, sesquiterpene and diterpene synthases, respectively, these substances are transformed into the primary representatives of each terpene skeletal type. Recent progress in the area of terpene synthases has been remarkable. In the last six years, many novel activities have been described for the first time (Adam *et al.*, 1996; Dekraker *et al.*, 1998; Guo *et al.*, 1994; Pichersky *et al.*, 1995), over 30 terpene synthase cDNAs have been isolated from plants (Table 5.2C) and the first crystal structures of terpene synthases obtained (Lesburg *et al.*, 1997; Starks *et al.*, 1997; Wendt *et al.*, 1997). These achievements have permitted new insights into the evolutionary origin and genetic regulation of terpene synthases and have provided unprecedented opportunities for exploring the reaction mechanisms of these catalysts.

Sequence comparison of the isolated terpene synthase cDNAs suggests that all appear to be derived from a single ancestral stock (Bohlmann *et al.*, 1998b). Overall, the amino acid sequences deduced share a high degree of similarity, and the positions of many residues thought to be involved in catalysis are conserved. When genomic sequences are compared (Back and Chappell, 1995; Facchini and Chappell, 1992; Mau and West, 1994), a common pattern of intron-exon organization is evident. Within the terpene synthases, phylogenetic reconstruction divides the known sequences into six subfamilies, each of which has a minimum of 40% identity among its members (Bohlmann *et al.*, 1998b). The pattern of sequence relationships is influenced by the taxonomic affinities of plant species, as well as by the chemical similarities among enzyme products and the reaction mechanism employed. For example, the limonene synthases of *Abies grandis*, a gymnosperm, are more closely related to other gymnosperm monoterpene and sesquiterpene synthases than they are to the limonene synthases from angiosperms.

Terpene synthases, also known as terpene cyclases because most of their products are cyclic, utilize a carbocationic reaction mechanism very similar to that employed by the prenyltransferases. Numerous experiments with inhibitors, substrate analogues and chemical model systems (Cane, 1990, 1998; Croteau, 1987) have revealed that reaction usually begins with the divalent metal ion-assisted cleavage of the diphosphate moiety (Fig. 5.6). The resulting allylic carbocation may then cyclize by addition of the resonance-stabilized cationic centre to one of the other carbon-carbon double-bonds in the substrate. Cyclization is followed by a series of rearrangements that may include hydride shifts, alkyl shifts, deprotonation, reprotonation and additional cyclizations, all mediated through enzyme-bound carbocationic intermediates. The reaction cascade terminates by deprotonation of the cation to an olefin or capture by a nucleophile, such as water. Since the native substrates of terpene synthases are all configured with *trans* (*E*)-double-bonds, they are unable to cyclize directly to many of the carbon skeletons found in nature. In such cases, the cyclization process is preceded by isomerization of the initial carbocation to an intermediate capable of cyclization.

The recently published crystal structure of tobacco epi-aristolochene synthase (a sesquiterpene synthase) has provided the first look at the

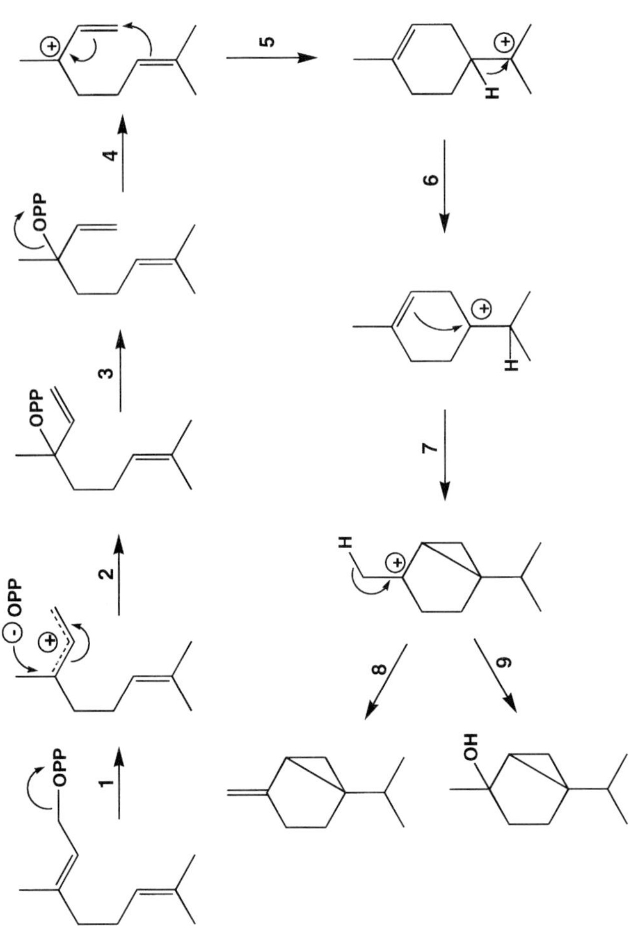

Figure 5.6 Proposed mechanism for the cyclization of geranyl diphosphate to sabinene and sabinene hydrate under catalysis by monoterpene synthases: the reaction begins with the hydrolysis of the diphosphate moiety to generate a resonance-stabilized carbocation (1); the carbocation then isomerizes to an intermediate capable of cyclization by return of the diphosphate (2); and rotation around a single bond (3); after a second diphosphate hydrolysis (4); the resulting carbocation undergoes a cyclization (5); a hydride shift (6); and a second cyclization (7); before the reaction terminates by deprotonation (8); or capture of the cation by water (9). Cyclizations, hydride shifts and a variety of other rearrangements of carbocationic intermediates are characteristic of the mechanisms of terpene synthases. No known terpene synthase actually produces both sabinene and sabinene hydrate; these are shown to indicate the possibilities for reaction termination. **PP** indicates a diphosphate moiety.

three-dimensional configuration of a plant terpene synthase (Starks *et al.*, 1997). The structure provides a physical basis for some of the proposed mechanistic features and reveals several elements responsible for controlling the course of reaction. The arrangement of the protein backbone, consisting of eight antiparallel α-helices that form a large cavity, is very similar to that reported for two other terpene synthases, a fungal sesquiterpene synthase (Lesburg *et al.*, 1997) and a bacterial triterpene synthase (Wendt *et al.*, 1997). It is also strongly reminiscent of the structure of avian liver FPP synthase (discussed in section 5.1.3.3) despite only a low level of sequence similarity, reflecting the parallels in reaction mechanism between terpene synthases and prenyltransferases. Among the notable features of the epi-aristolochene synthase structure is the presence of an aspartate-rich cluster, DDxxD, in the active site (just like those found in prenyltransferases) that serves to bind the diphosphate moiety of the substrate via a Mg^{2+} bridge. Prenyltransferases, which simultaneously bind two different diphosphate-containing substrates, have two such clusters, while epi-aristolochene synthase and other terpene synthases, which bind only one diphosphate-containing substrate, have only one. The active site of epi-aristolochene synthase also contains a variety of aromatic amino acid residues that may serve to stabilize the enzyme-bound carbocationic intermediates by π-cation interactions (Wise and Croteau, 1998). Other amino acid residues were identified that direct the released diphosphate moiety away from the active site, that complex two additional Mg^{2+} ions, and that participate in protonation and deprotonation.

Terpene synthases employ two other modes of generating the initial carbocationic intermediate in addition to hydrolysis of the diphosphate ester. Reaction may be initiated by protonation of an epoxide, as in the cyclization of oxidosqualene to sterols and triterpenes (Abe *et al.*, 1993), or by protonation of the carbon-carbon double-bond at the opposite end of the molecule from the diphosphate moiety. Mechanisms initiated by double-bond protonation are characteristic of the formation of many diterpenes, such as copalyl diphosphate (West, 1981) (Fig. 5.7). Isolated cDNA sequences encoding copalyl diphosphate synthase have some homology to the sequences of terpene synthases in which reaction is initiated by diphosphate hydrolysis but lack the characteristic DDxxD motif, possessing instead an alternate aspartate-rich motif, DxDDTA, at a very different position in the sequence (Ait-Ali *et al.*, 1997; Bensen *et al.*, 1995; Sun and Kamiya, 1994). A second category of diterpene synthases has more in common with the majority of terpene synthases discussed above, catalyzing diphosphate hydrolysis-initiated cyclizations while possessing typical DDxxD motifs (Yamaguchi *et al.*, 1996, 1998). Notable members of this group include the *ent*-kaurene synthases

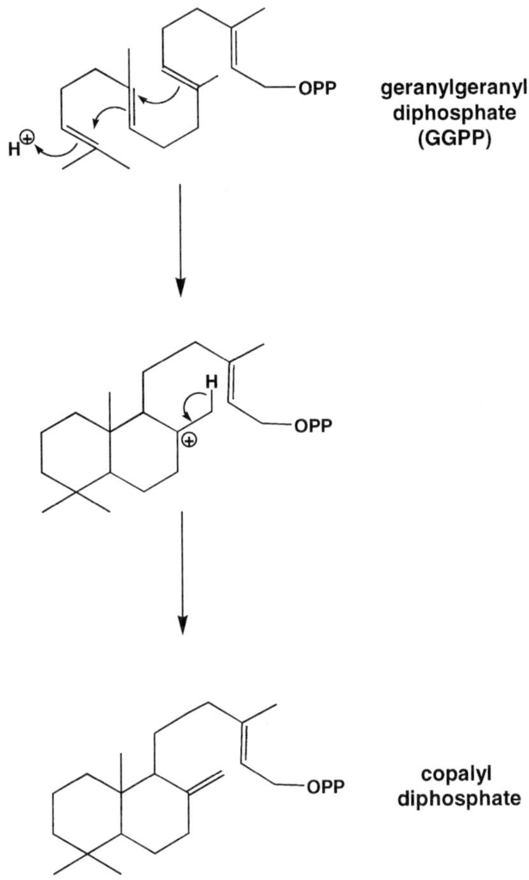

OPP geranylgeranyl diphosphate (GGPP)

OPP

OPP copalyl diphosphate

Figure 5.7 Proposed mechanism for the cyclization of geranylgeranyl diphosphate (GGPP) to the diterpene copalyl diphosphate, an example of terpene synthase-catalyzed cyclization initiated by double-bond protonation, rather than by hydrolysis of the diphosphate ester. PP indicates a diphosphate moiety.

involved in gibberellin biosynthesis, which use copalyl diphosphate as a substrate rather than a product. There is also a third type of diterpene synthase that seems to combine the properties of the other two classes. For example, abietadiene synthase from *Abies grandis* catalyzes two sequential cyclization steps: first cyclizing GGPP to copalyl diphosphate via a double-bond protonation-initiated cyclization; and then converting copalyl diphosphate to the olefin, abietadiene, via a diphosphate hydrolysis-initiated process (LaFever *et al.*, 1994). Appropriately, the

A. grandis abietadiene synthase cDNA has regions of sequence homologous to both other types of diterpene synthases and contains both DDxxD and DxDDTA elements (Vogel *et al.*, 1996).

Not all terpene synthases catalyze complex reactions. Isoprene synthase converts DMAPP to the hemiterpene (C_5), isoprene (Fig. 5.1), a comparatively simple process involving the ionization of the diphosphate group, followed by double-bond migration and proton elimination (Silver and Fall, 1991). Present in chloroplasts in both stromal and thylakoid-bound forms, isoprene synthase is a homodimer that differs from other terpene synthases in many properties, such as subunit architecture, optimum pH and kinetic parameters (Silver and Fall, 1995; Wildermuth and Fall, 1998). Its key role in the formation of isoprene, an abundant plant volatile with a major influence on atmospheric chemistry, has made it a popular target for cloning efforts.

An unusual feature of terpene synthases is the ability of a single enzyme to catalyze the formation of more than one product species. First suggested by the copurification of separate activities and differential inactivation studies, and later demonstrated by isotopically-sensitive branching experiments (Rajaonarivony *et al.*, 1992; Wagschal *et al.*, 1991), this property has been unequivocally proved by cDNA cloning. Heterologous expression of many cloned terpene synthases, such as 1,8-cineole synthase from *Salvia officinalis*, leads to a mixture of products (Wise *et al.*, 1998). In a spectacular, recently-published example, two sesquiterpene synthases from *A. grandis*, δ-selinene synthase and γ-humulene synthase, were shown to synthesize 34 and 52 different sesquiterpenes, respectively (Steele *et al.*, 1998a). The tendency of terpene synthases to form multiple products is probably a consequence of their reaction mechanisms, which involve highly reactive carbocationic intermediates that may have more than one chemical fate. Interestingly, exon-swapping experiments on epi-aristolochene synthase converted this single product sesquiterpene synthase to one making multiple products (Back and Chappell, 1996). Further correlations between elements of protein structure and features of the reaction mechanism using three-dimensional structures will increase our understanding of how terpene synthases are able to make multiple products.

Terpene synthases are likely to serve as important agents of flux control in terpene biosynthesis because they operate at metabolic branch-points where pathways diverge to different terpene types. However, there is still insufficient information available to assess the regulatory significance of these catalysts. Direct relationships between terpene synthase activity and changes in the rate of terpene formation have been noted on several occasions (Dudley *et al.*, 1986; Funk *et al.*, 1994; Gijzen *et al.*, 1991; Kuzma and Fall, 1993; Zook *et al.*, 1992), but terpene synthase activity is not always well-correlated with the accumulation of end-products of the pathway (Hezari *et al.*, 1997; Keller *et al.*, 1998a; Pichersky *et al.*, 1994). In evaluating the regulatory importance of terpene synthases, it is necessary to consider not only the level of activity but also its subcellular location. As we have noted above, monoterpenes and diterpenes are generally formed in the plastids, while sesquiterpene and triterpene biosynthesis is restricted to the cytosol (Gleizes *et al.*, 1983; Kleinig, 1989; Mettal *et al.*, 1988). Based on subcellular fractionation studies and the presence or absence of plastid transit peptides, the distribution of most terpene synthases follows this pattern. Most monoterpene and diterpene synthases are localized in plastids (Aach *et al.*, 1995, 1997; Mau and West, 1994; Vogel *et al.*, 1996; Wise *et al.*, 1998; Yamaguchi *et al.*, 1998), while sesquiterpene and triterpene synthases are cytosolic (Belingheri *et al.*, 1988; Bohlmann *et al.*, 1998a; Kleinig, 1989; Steele *et al.*, 1998a). Terpene synthase activity itself seems to be regulated by the level of the corresponding mRNA (Chen *et al.*, 1995; Dudareva *et al.*, 1996; Facchini and Chappell, 1992; Keller *et al.*, 1998a; Steele *et al.*, 1998b). Reports of multi-gene families (Back and Chappell, 1995; Colby *et al.*, 1993; Facchini and Chappell, 1992) may imply complex developmental and tissue-specific patterns of regulation or may just indicate the existence of different synthases with closely-related sequences.

In addition to terpene synthases, the construction of terpenoid carbon skeletons in plants also involves a number of prenyltransferases distinct from those that make the C_{10}, C_{15} and C_{20} diphosphates. One class of prenyltransferases catalyzes 1′-4 condensations of IPP with an FPP or GGPP starter unit to make long-chain polyterpenes, such as rubber, a linear hydrocarbon with *cis* (*Z*)-double-bonds and as many as 30,000 isoprene units. The *cis*-polyprenyltransferase participating in rubber biosynthesis has been characterized in several species of plants (Cornish, 1993; Cornish and Backhaus, 1990; Cornish and Siler, 1996) but efforts to purify this protein or clone the corresponding gene have not yet been successful. Another class of prenyltransferases mediates condensations between allylic diphosphates and non-isoprenoid substrates, in which dimethylallyl, geranyl, farnesyl or geranylgeranyl moieties are transferred to a nucleophilic acceptor. These are key reactions in the formation of many different prenylated compounds, including prenylated proteins, prenylated flavonoids, furanocoumarins, cytokinins, ubiquinone, plastoquinone and the tocopherols. Several of the enzymes responsible have been well studied, and are similar in gross properties to other prenyltransferases (Cutler *et al.*, 1996; Fellermeier and Zenk, 1998; Laflamme *et al.*, 1993; Muhlenweg *et al.*, 1998; Qian *et al.*, 1996; Yamamoto *et al.*, 1997).

5.1.3.5 *Secondary transformations*

The cyclic terpenes formed initially are subject to an assortment of further enzymatic modifications, including oxidations, reductions, isomerizations and conjugations, to produce the wide array of terpenoid end-products found in plants. Unfortunately, few of these conversions have been well studied, and there is little evidence from most of the biosynthetic routes proposed, except in the case of the gibberellin (Hedden and Kamiya, 1997) pathway. Many of the secondary transformations belong to a series of well-known reaction types that are not restricted to terpenoid biosynthesis. For example, the hydroxylation of terpenes by cytochrome P_{450}-dependent-oxygenases has been the subject of much investigation (Mihaliak *et al.*, 1993) (Fig. 5.8A). This large family of membrane-bound enzymes catalyzes the position-specific hydroxylation of many terpenoids, using molecular oxygen and NADPH (Funk and Croteau, 1994; Hallahan *et al.*, 1992; Helliwell *et al.*, 1998; Hoshino *et al.*, 1995; Kato *et al.*, 1995; Winkler and Helentjaris, 1995). The first cDNA encoding a cytochrome P_{450}-dependent terpene hydroxylase has recently been isolated (Lupien *et al.*, 1995).

A second group of oxidative enzymes, the 2-oxoglutarate-dependent dioxygenases, are soluble, nonhaeme iron-containing catalysts (Prescott and John, 1996) that participate in several reactions in terpene biosynthesis (Hedden and Kamiya, 1997; Lange *et al.*, 1994; Phillips *et al.*, 1995; Xu *et al.*, 1995) (Fig. 5.8B). Several other types of secondary transformation that have been characterized include: the oxidation of acyclic monoterpene alcohols to their corresponding aldehydes during iridoid biosynthesis in *Nepeta racemosa* (Hallahan *et al.*, 1995); the reduction of the geranylgeranyl moiety of chlorophylls, tocopherols and phylloquinone in *A. thaliana* (Keller *et al.*, 1998b); and the glucosylation of diterpene alcohols by glucosyltransferases in *Stevia rebaudiana* (Shibata *et al.*, 1995).

5.1.4 *Conclusions*

Research on the formation and function of plant terpenoids has flourished in the last five years. The greatest achievement has been the discovery of a new, non-mevalonate route for the synthesis of the C_5 building blocks of terpenoids. While many of the intermediates of the new glyceraldehyde phosphate/pyruvate pathway are still unidentified and most of the enzymes are completely unknown, such details should be rapidly eludicated setting the stage for studies on the distribution of the new pathway in plants and its relationship to the 'classical' mevalonate pathway. At present, the glyceraldehyde phosphate/pyruvate route appears to be found in the plastids of all higher plant species and is the

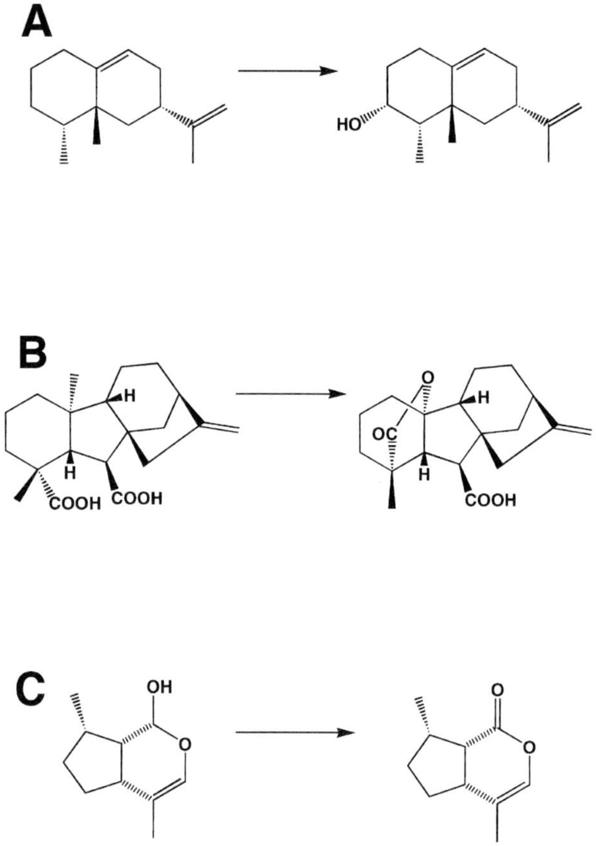

Figure 5.8 Examples of oxidative secondary transformations in terpenoid biosynthesis. A) Hydroxylation of epi-aristolochene at the 3-position by a cytochrome P_{450}-dependent terpene hydroxylase in *Capsicum annuum* (Hoshino *et al.*, 1995). B) Conversion of GA_{12} to GA_9 by a 2-oxoglutarate-dependent dioxygenase involved in gibberellin biosynthesis. A single enzyme catalyzes three successive oxidations leading to the loss of a methyl group and lactone formation (Lange *et al.*, 1994; Phillips *et al.*, 1995; Xu *et al.*, 1995). C) Oxidation of *cis*, *cis*-nepetalactol to *cis*, *cis*-nepetalactone by a nicotinamide adenine dinucleotide (NAD^+)-dependent soluble oxidoreductase in *Nepeta racemosa* (Hallahan *et al.*, 1998).

likely source of substrate for the plastid-associated terpenoids, including monoterpenes, diterpenes, phytol, plastoquinones and carotenoids. In contrast, the mevalonate pathway appears to be restricted to the cytosol/ endoplasmic reticulum based on the finding that all known pathway genes are targeted to this compartment. The mevalonate route may be the chief source of substrate for cytosolic (sesquiterpenes, triterpenes, dolichols) and mitochondrial (ubiquinone) terpenoids. Further research is urgently needed to confirm these generalizations concerning the subcellular compartmentation of terpenoid biosynthesis. The extent to which the two pathways interact must also be clarified and the existence of a cryptic mevalonate pathway in plastids, at least in certain taxa or specific developmental stages, must be investigated. With the basic features of the new, non-mevalonate pathway coming into focus, it is also time to re-evaluate the regulation of terpenoid formation in general, especially the role of HMGR, to determine which steps are the main modulators of flux.

As in most other branches of plant science, the application of molecular biology to terpenoid biosynthesis has led to enormous progress. The cloning and heterologous expression of biosynthetic enzymes has permitted new inferences about the evolution of these catalysts and has opened the door to site-specific mutagenesis and X-ray structure determination, which in turn have revealed much new information on enzyme structure and mechanism. For prenyltransferases and terpene synthases, two major groups of terpenoid-synthesizing enzymes that catalyze complex reactions involving carbocationic intermediates, we will soon achieve a detailed understanding not only of how the enzyme directs the outcome of the reaction but also how redesign of the protein can give altered product distributions.

As terpenoids constitute the largest class of plant secondary compounds, it is fitting that terpenoid metabolites play a wide assortment of roles in nearly all basic plant processes. Recent research has added to this list, suggesting new functions for terpenoids, such as isoprene (stabilizing membranes at high temperatures), prenylated proteins (control of the cell cycle, allocation of nutrients), and certain mono- and sesquiterpenes (attraction of the enemies of herbivores). Nevertheless, the roles of most terpenoids are completely unstudied. Many compounds are thought to be involved in protecting plants from herbivores and pathogens but supporting data are often fragmentary and unconvincing. In the coming years, the use of molecular techniques to make precise alterations to the levels of individual compounds should facilitate more rigorous investigation of the functional significance of terpenoids and give us a greater appreciation of their roles in plants.

5.2 Sterols, cardiac glycosides and steroid saponins

Sterols, cardiac glycosides, and steroid saponins are steroidal metabolites that may be considered to be triterpenes which have lost a minimum of three methyl groups during their biogenesis, and are thus supposed to be derived from mevalonic acid via the triterpenoid pathway. All triterpenes originate from squalene, and the cyclic representatives, including the steroids, are composed of cyclohexane and cyclopropane units annelated *trans* or *cis*, the annelation being specific for the different groups of otherwise structurally closely-related compounds (Table 5.3).

Separating triterpenes from steroids is not always easy, especially with regard to the close structural relationship between some tetracyclic structures, such as the ginsenosides, the cucurbitacins, and cycloartenol (Fig. 5.9); only by considering the biosynthetic routes it is possible to separate the two groups. Members of both groups generally arise from the initial cyclization of 3*S*-squalene-2,3-epoxide (2,3-oxidosqualene). The opening of the epoxide initiates the cyclization and it is the initial conformation of 2,3-oxidosqualene which determines the biosynthetic route to follow. Therefore, different 2,3-oxidosqualene cyclases must be involved in the formation of the more than 4000 triterpenes (including steroids) isolated from plants so far.

Cardiac glycoside and steroid saponin biosynthesis in angiosperms cannot be separated from sterol biosynthesis, which will therefore also be discussed in this chapter. In plants, triterpenoids most often occur as 3-*O*-glycosides, 3-*O*-acyl esters and/or glucose esters; the hydroxyl group in position C-3 arising from the opening of the 2,3-epoxide. It is assumed that 2,3-oxidosqualene cyclases are regulatory key enzymes in the isoprenoid pathway, with a high degree of specificity, thus orienting the biosynthetic flux towards either tetracyclic or pentacyclic structures (e.g. Henry *et al.*, 1992). Recent findings concerning the formation of ginseng saponins support this assumption. (*RS*)-(3-3H)-2,3-oxidosqualene was converted into (20*S*)-dammarenediol (= protopanaxadiol; Fig. 5.9) but not to (20*R*)-dammarenediol by a microsomal fraction prepared from hairy roots of *Panax ginseng*. The properties of the cyclase differed significantly from those of other 2,3-oxidosqualene cyclases reported from higher plants (Kushiro *et al.*, 1997).

The chemistry, biosynthesis and biological activities of triterpenoids have been described in recent publications (Luckner, 1990; and Charlwood and Banthorpe, 1991, and in a review by Mahato *et al.*, 1992). In the present chapter, emphasis will be laid on the formation of steroids in plants; the pathways leading to the tetra- and pentacyclic triterpenes will not be considered further.

Steroids are widely used as drugs and constitute anti-inflammatory, contraceptive and anticancer agents. Most are obtained by semisynthesis using natural substances, such as sterols (from plants or animals), saponins, including steroid alkaloids (from plants), and bile acids (from animals) as precursors. Plant steroids comprise sterols, steroid saponins, steroid alkaloids, pregnanes, androstanes, estranes, ectysteroids, withanolides and cardiac glycosides (Fig. 5.9), which all share the same basic skeleton. Some of them are widespread (sterols, pregnanes) in the plant

Table 5.3 Ring annelation in different steroids (after Luckner, 1990)

Group	Individual substance	Rings A/B	Substituents in position 5/10	Rings B/C	Substituents in position 8/9	Rings C/D	Substituents in position 13/14
Sterols	Lanosterol	*trans*	α/β	-	-	*trans*	α/β
	Cycloartenol	*trans*	α/β	*cis*	β/β	*trans*	α/β
	Euphol	*trans*	α/β	-	-	*trans*	α/β
	Cholesterol	-	-	*trans*	β/α	*trans*	β/α
Saponins	Smilagenin	*cis*	β/β	*trans*	β/α	*trans*	β/α
	Tigogenin	*trans*	α/β	*trans*	β/α	*trans*	β/α
	Diosgenin	-	-	*trans*	β/α	*trans*	β/α
C_{27}-Steroid alkaloids	α-Tomatine	*trans*	α/β	*trans*	β/α	*trans*	β/α
	Solasodine	-	-	*trans*	β/α	*trans*	β/α
Bile alcohols and bile acids	Allocholic acid	*trans*	α/β	*trans*	β/α	*trans*	β/α
	Cholic acid	*cis*	β/β	*trans*	β/α	*trans*	β/α
Pregnanes and allopregnanes	Urocortisol	*cis*	β/β	*trans*	β/α	*trans*	β/α
	Alloconolone	*trans*	α/β	*trans*	β/α	*trans*	β/α
	Progesterone	-	-	*trans*	β/α	*trans*	β/α
	Digipurpurogenin	-	-	*trans*	β/α	*cis*	β/β
Androstanes	Testosterone	-	-	*trans*	β/α	*trans*	β/α
	5α-Androstane-17β-ol-3-one	*trans*	α/β	*trans*	β/α	*trans*	β/α
Estranes	Estradiol	-	-	*trans*	β/α	*trans*	β/α
Cardiac glycosides	Digitoxigenin	*cis*	β/β	*trans*	β/α	*cis*	β/β
	Uzarigenin	*trans*	α/β	*trans*	β/α	*cis*	β/β
	Scillarenin	-	-	*trans*	β/α	*cis*	β/β

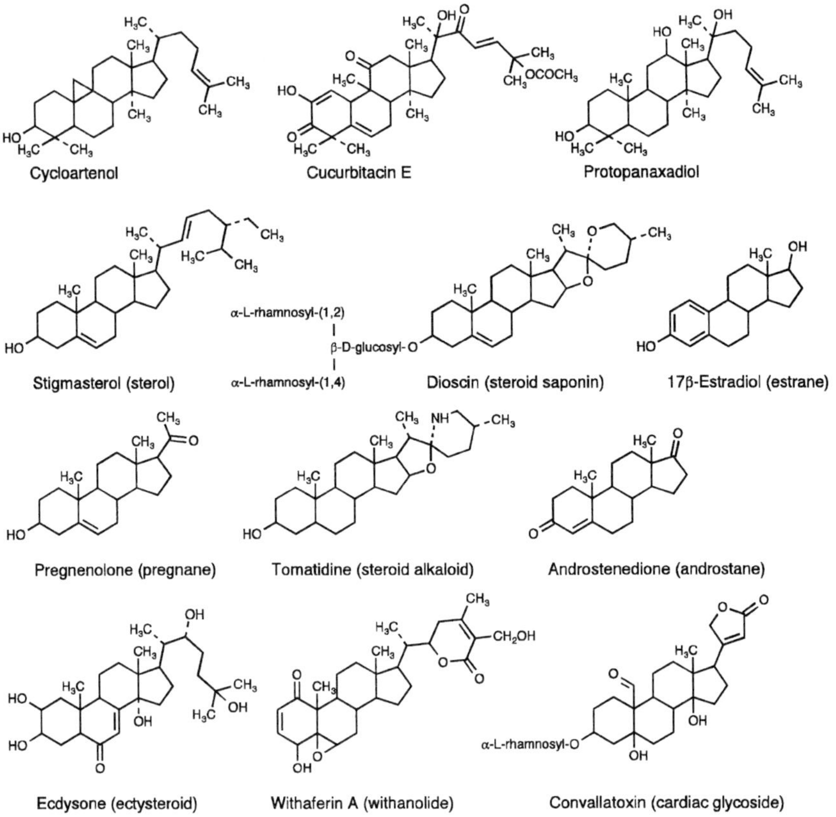
Cycloartenol
Cucurbitacin E
Protopanaxadiol
Stigmasterol (sterol)
α-L-rhamnosyl-(1,2)
β-D-glucosyl-O
α-L-rhamnosyl-(1,4)
Dioscin (steroid saponin)
17β-Estradiol (estrane)
Pregnenolone (pregnane)
Tomatidine (steroid alkaloid)
Androstenedione (androstane)
Ecdysone (ectysteroid)
Withaferin A (withanolide)
α-L-rhamnosyl-O
Convallatoxin (cardiac glycoside)

Figure 5.9 Chemical structures of plant metabolites synthesized from squalene-2,3-epoxide.

kingdom, whereas the occurrence of others (androstanes, estranes, withanolides) is limited. Estranes, for example, have been found in seeds of *Punica granatum* (Dean *et al.*, 1971) and androstenes accumulate in pollen of *Pinus sylvestris* (Saden-Krehula *et al.*, 1976).

5.2.1 Sterols

5.2.1.1 Biosynthesis

In sterol biosynthesis, squalene 2,3-epoxide can cyclize in two ways, to form lanosterol or cycloartenol, respectively. The cycloartenol pathway of steroid biosynthesis appears to be specific for photosynthetic eukaryotes, whereas the lanosterol route seems to be operative in fungi and animals. In this context, it is interesting to note that an *Arabidopsis thaliana* gene encoding cycloartenol synthase was expressed in a yeast mutant lacking lanosterol synthase. Several of the transformants were able to cyclize squalene 2,3-epoxide to cycloartenol (Corey *et al.*, 1993). Although most plant steroids are derived from cycloartenol, it has to be mentioned that lanosterol and lanosterol oligosaccharides have been detected in various plants, e.g. in the latex of different *Euphorbia* species. Since the conversion of cycloartenol to lanosterol could not be demonstrated, it is most likely that both sterol pathways are operative in these plants (Giner and Djerassi, 1995). In this context, it should be stressed that the biosynthesis of cholesterol in plants is not yet fully understood but is probably similar to the formation of the 24-alkyl sterols, i.e. via cycloartenol (Goodwin, 1985), although in animals cholesterol is only formed via the lanosterol pathway. Cholesterol contributes to the sterol pool of many plants and exogenous cholesterol can be transformed by plants to various products, including pregnanes and other steroids (e.g. Bennett and Heftmann, 1966; Caspi *et al.*, 1966). Therefore, cholesterol may also be considered as a precursor of cardiac glycosides and steroid saponins.

The biosynthesis of 24-alkyl sterols was comprehensively reviewed by Benveniste (1986). Recently, various enzymes that are involved in the formation of plant sterols have been identified and characterized. The mechanisms of enzyme action were elucidated in studies using analogues of the high-energy carbocationic intermediates supposed to be involved in the various biosynthetic steps. Additional information was provided by studies using various commercial or experimental fungicides that have been found to interfere with plant sterol biosynthesis. Morpholine-type fungicides, for example, inhibit cycloeucalenol isomerization, Δ^8/Δ^7-isomerization, Δ^{14}-reduction and Δ^7-reduction in the sterol pathway (Fig. 5.10), whereas azole fungicides were shown to block the 14α-demethylation step (see section 5.2.1.1 'Obtusifoliol 14α-demethylase') (Rahier and Taton, 1997).

Sterol methyltransferases. The enzymes involved in C-24 alkylation in plant sterol formation have already been described by Benveniste (1986). Recently, a full-length complementary deoxyribonucleic acid (cDNA) sequence was isolated from *Arabidopsis thaliana*, which contained features typical of methyltransferases in general and, in particular, showed 38% identity with a yeast gene encoding zymosterol-C-24-methyltransferase. A yeast mutant accumulating zymosterol, i.e. not capable of sterol C-24 alkylation, was transformed with the plant gene. As a result, several 24-ethyl and 24-ethylidene sterols were synthesized, indicating that the respective cDNA encodes a plant sterol C-methyltransferase able to perform two sequential methylations of the sterol side chain (Husselstein *et al.*, 1996).

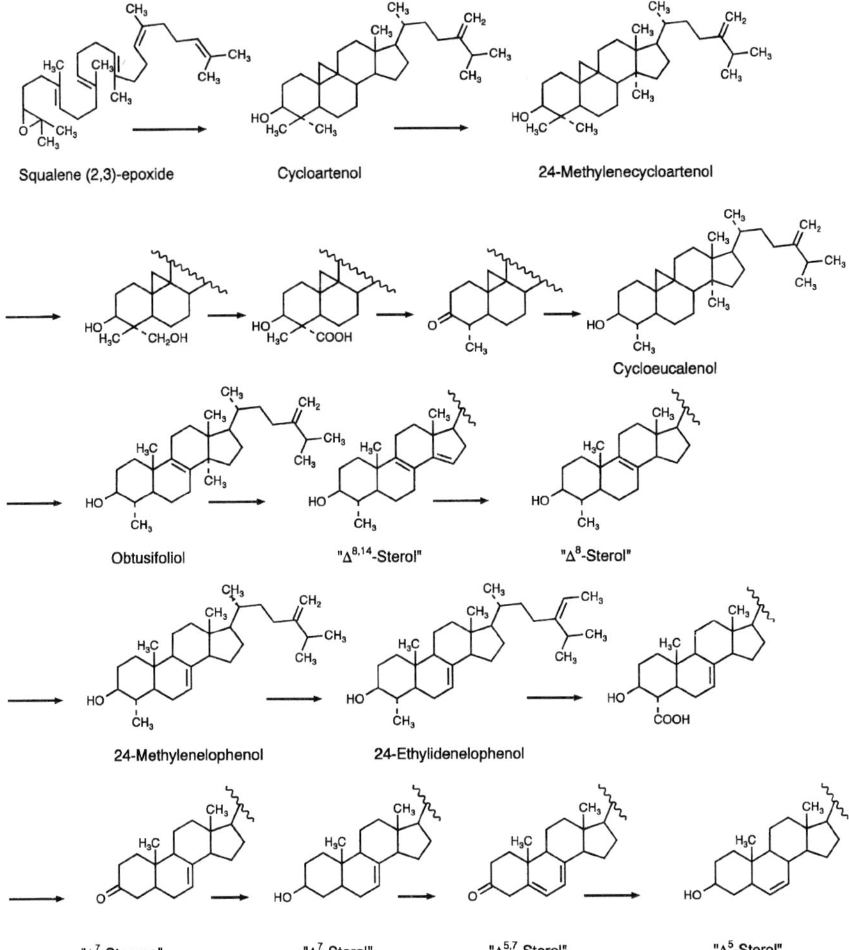

Figure 5.10 Proposed pathway for sterol biosynthesis in higher plants.

Crucial steps in the conversion of cycloartenol to sterols are the events leading to the removal of the methyl groups at C-4 and C-14. Microsomes prepared from maize (*Zea mays*) embryos or seedlings have proved to be an excellent experimental system to study sterol biosynthesis *in vitro*. The more recent results on this issue are summarized below.

4,4-Dimethyl sterol 4-demethylase (4,4-DMSO). C-4 monodemethylation of 28-(^{3}H),24-methylene cycloartanol leads to the corresponding

4α-methyl sterol, cycloeucalenol. The demethylation process requires NADPH and molecular oxygen, and was shown to involve a 4-methyl, 4-hydroxymethyl derivative. From inhibitor studies, it was concluded that the C-4 demethylation of methylene cycloartanol results from a multistep process, involving a terminal oxygenation system sensitive to cyanide that is distinct from cytochrome P_{450} (Pascal *et al.*, 1990). Immunoglobulin G (IgG), raised against plant cytochrome b_5, was used to characterize the electron-donating system further and it was found that the activities of 4,4-DMSO, 4α-methylsterol-4α-methyl oxidase, and sterol Δ^7-sterol C-5(6)-desaturase (see section 5.2.1.1 'Δ^7-Sterol C-5(6)-desaturase (5-DES)') were completely inhibited by the antibody. These results suggest that membrane-bound cytochrome b_5 is carrying electrons from NAD(P)H to the cytochrome P_{450}-independent oxidative enzymes mentioned (Rahier *et al.*, 1997).

Obtusifoliol 14α-demethylase. The 14α-methyl group of obtusifoliol is removed by the action of a cytochrome P_{450}-containing monooxygenase system (Rahier and Taton, 1986). A series of 7-oxo-obtusifoliol analogues and other compounds have been synthesized and investigated as potential inhibitors of the enzyme. Some of them were potent competitive inhibitors, binding 125–200 times more tightly than obtusifoliol. Feeding of one of the compounds synthesized, namely 7-oxo-24(25)-dihydro-29-norlanosterol, to cultured bramble cells resulted in a strong decrease of (^{14}C)-acetate incorporation into the demethyl-sterols fraction and in an accumulation of labelled obtusifoliol (Rahier and Taton, 1992). The *R*-(-) isomer of methyl 1-(2,2-dimethylindan-1-yl)imidazole-5-carboxylate (CGA 214372) inhibited obtusifoliol 14α-demethylase uncompetitively and was shown to have a high degree of selectivity for obtusifoliol 14α-demethylase (Salmon *et al.*, 1992).

Evidence is accumulating that obtusifoliol 14α-demethylase may be a good target for herbicides. For example, *Nicotiana tabacum* protoplasts have been transformed with the gene CYP51A1 encoding lanosterol-14-demethylase from *Saccharomyces cerevisiae*. Transgenic calli were killed by a phytotoxic fungicide inhibiting both plant obtusifoliol-14-demethylase and lanosterol-14-demethylase but were resistant to 7-ketotriazole, a herbicide which has been shown to inhibit obtusifoliol-14-demethylase only. It seems that lanosterol-14-demethylase can bypass the blocked obtusifoliol-14-demethylase, in this way causing the plant tissue to be resistant to a triazole herbicide (Grausem *et al.*, 1995). Screening of a wheat cDNA library with a heterologous CYP81B1 probe from *Helianthus tuberosus* led to the isolation of a cDNA coding for obtusifoliol 14α-demethylase. The cDNA was expressed in *Saccharomyces cerevisiae* and it was demonstrated that membranes isolated from yeast expressing the gene, efficiently catalyzed 14α-demethylation of obtusifoliol. From the molecular data, the enzyme was assigned to the CYP51 family (Cabello-Hurtado, 1997). The respective CYP51 from *Sorghum bicolor* was cloned and expressed in *Escherichia coli* (Bak *et al.*, 1997). The plant enzymes (but not sterol 14-demethylases from fungal or human origin) showed strict substrate specificity towards obtusifoliol. The *Sorghum* enzyme, for example, was not capable of demethylating various lanosterol derivatives, indicating that a demethylating sequence 4, 14, 4 is realized in plants (Lamb *et al.*, 1998).

4α-Methylsterol demethylase. All reactions in the process of plant sterol demethylation appear to proceed via α-face attack. In fact, after the sequential oxidative 4α-demethylation of 4,4-dimethylsterols, a 4α-monomethyl sterol is produced. However, this compound cannot be demethylated further by the action of 4α-methylsterol demethylase, since this enzyme favours 4α-methyl sterols with rigid planar conformation. These structural requirements satisfy the Δ^7-sterols that are, however, formed only after sterol 14α-demethylation (see section 5.2.1.1 'Obtusifoliol 14α-demethylase'). Extensive substrate recognition and inhibitor studies have further established that in higher plants the demethylations occur in the sequence 4, 14, 4, in contrast to animals and yeast where the sequence is 14, 4, 4 (Taton *et al.*, 1994).

NADPH:sterone reductase. Microsomes prepared from maize embryos were also shown to catalyze the reduction of various sterones to produce the corresponding 3β-hydroxy derivatives. Based on studies concerning coenzyme requirements and inhibitor susceptibility, the enzyme was classified as belonging to the family of ketone reductases. Since 4,4-dimethyl-sterones react poorly as compared to desmethyl- or 4α-monomethyl sterones, it was concluded that the reductase is a component of the microsomal sterol 4-demethylation complex (Pascal *et al.*, 1993, 1994). The enzyme may be related to the hydroxysteroid oxidoreductases involved in cardenolide biosynthesis (see section 5.2.2).

$\Delta^{8,14}$-sterol Δ^{14}-reductase. This enzymatic double-bound reduction is thought to proceed through an electrophilic addition mechanism. Using an *in vitro* assay, ammonium and iminium analogues of the putative C-14 carbonium intermediate were shown to be potent inhibitors of the reduction reaction. The relative specificity of these different series of inhibitors toward cycloeucalenol-obtusifoliol isomerase, Δ^8/Δ^7-sterol isomerase and $\Delta^{8,14}$-sterol Δ^{14}-reductase, was studied directly (Taton *et al.*, 1989).

Δ^7-Sterol C-5(6)-desaturase (5-DES). During plant sterol synthesis, the Δ^5-bond is supposed to be introduced via the sequence Δ^7-sterol $\Rightarrow$ $\Delta^{5,7}$-sterol $\Rightarrow$ Δ^5-sterol. Only recently, a microsomal enzyme system was identified that catalyzes the conversion of Δ^7-sterols to their corresponding Δ^5-sterols. Part of the sequence is catalyzed by a C-5(6)-desaturase requiring molecular oxygen and NADH. The enzyme appears to be specific for 4-desmethyl-Δ^7-sterols favouring sterols possessing a C-24 methylene or ethylidene substituent (Taton and Rahier, 1996).

$\Delta^{5,7}$-sterol Δ^7-reductase. A microsomal preparation from seedlings of *Zea mays* catalyzed the NADPH-dependent reduction of the Δ^7-bond of $\Delta^{5,7}$-cholestadienol, providing the first *in vitro* evidence for the intermediacy of $\Delta^{5,7}$-sterols in plant sterol biosynthesis. The potent inhibition of the enzyme by ammonium-containing fungicides suggests a cationic mechanism involved in this reduction reaction (Taton and Rahier, 1991).

With a view to producing $\Delta^{5(6)}$-pregnenes in yeast, the Δ^7-reductase gene from *Arabidopsis thaliana* was engineered into *Saccharomyces cerevisiae* in order to overcome the dominance of endogenous $\Delta^{5(6),7}$ sterols, such as ergosterol. Coexpression of bovine side chain cleavage $P_{450,\,scc}$ (see section 5.2.1.1 'Side chain cleavage cytochrome $P_{450,\,scc}$'), adrenodoxin and adrenodoxin reductase, led to the formation of pregnenolone, which was found to be totally absent from cell lysates or culture medium from control strains. Following additional coexpression of human NAD: Δ^5-3β-hydroxysteroid dehydrogenase, pregnenolone was further metabolized to progesterone. The majority of pregnenolone and progesterone produced remained sequestered in the yeast cells (Duport *et al.*, 1998).

Uridine diphosphate glucose (UDP-glucose) sterol glucosyltransferase (SGTase). SGTases are membrane-bound enzymes and have been isolated from various sources. When investigating the localization of SGTase, it was found that the enzyme is only associated with the plasma membrane; therefore, SGTase is now being used as a marker enzyme for plasma membranes. It was shown that delipidated protein preparations showed no SGTase activity but that enzyme activity could be restored completely when phospholipids were added. The effect of different phospholipids on recovery of SGTase activity and the kinetic parameters of the reaction was studied using a delipidated and inactive enzyme preparation obtained from maize coleoptiles. Both phosphatidylcholine and phosphatidylglycerol significantly decreased Km_{sterol} and increased V_{max} (Ullman *et al.*, 1984, 1987). SGTase was reconstituted into unilamellar lipid vesicles. This was achieved by adding phospholipids, sterols and β-octylglucoside to the solubilized enzyme and passing the mixture through Sephadex G-50. An outward orientation for the active site of the enzyme was suggested and it was demonstrated that reconstituted SGTase activity is stimulated to a large extent by negatively-charged phospholipids (Ury *et al.*, 1989).

SGTase was purified from *Avena sativa.* Polyclonal antibodies raised against *Avena* SGTase did not inhibit enzyme activity but specifically bound to the native enzyme (Warnecke and Heinz, 1994). The purified SGTase has been used for the cloning of a corresponding cDNA from *Avena sativa.* Different fragments of the cDNA obtained were expressed in *E. coli* and it was found that homogenates of the transformed cells exhibited sterol glucosyltransferase activity (Warnecke *et al.*, 1997).

SGTase was also detected in cell cultures and leaves of *Digitalis purpurea.* In the cultured cells, the enzyme was not associated with a specific subcellular fraction. However, almost 60% of the enzyme isolated from leaves was associated with the microsomal fraction. SGT was partially purified from both sources. Δ^5-steroids were good substrates for the SGTase from *Digitalis purpurea.* 5α-steroids, such as epiandrosterone and 5α-pregnan-3β-ol-20-one, were better substrates than their corresponding 5β-analogues. Digitoxigenin, a 5β-cardenolide genin (see section 5.2.2), was only a poor substrate for the SGTase (Yoshikawa and Furuya, 1979).

Evidence is accumulating that at least two SGTases are present in potato. A membrane-bound enzyme with high affinity to sitosterol and a cytosolic enzyme with high affinity to solanidine, a steroid alkaloid (see section 5.2.3.1). The membrane-bound enzyme glucosylated the substrates investigated in the following sequence: plant sterols > androstanes, pregnanes > steroid alkaloids (spirosolane type), steroid sapogenins > steroid alkaloids (solanidane type). The cytosolic SGTase clearly preferred steroid alkaloids of the solanidane type (Zimowski, 1992).

Sterol acyltransferase (SATase) and steryl ester hydrolase (SEHase). Unesterified sterols modulate the function of eukaryotic membranes. In human cells, sterol is esterified to a storage form by acyl-coenzyme A (CoA):cholesterol acyl transferase (SATase). In plants, free sterols are associated mainly with microsomal membranes, whereas the steryl esters are stored in lipid granules. The esterification process may, thus, allow regulation of the amount of free sterols in membranes by subcellular compartmentation. Enzymes involved in the esterification of sterols and hydrolysis of steryl esters were investigated in tobacco. Results obtained with a sterol-overproducing mutant indicated that both SATase and SEHase are involved in the control of the free sterol content and, more generally, in the homeostasis of free sterols in the plant cells (Bouvier-

Navé and Benveniste, 1995). Esterase(s) capable of releasing acetate from semisynthetic 3-acetoxycardenolides may be related to the steryl esterases described here (Kreis *et al.*, 1997).

Side chain cleavage cytochrome $P_{450,\,scc}$. In mammals, the first and limiting step in the biosynthesis of all C_{21} and C_{20} steroids is the conversion of cholesterol into pregnenolone. Cholesterol is also supposed to be a precursor of pregnanes, cardenolides and steroid saponins in plants. Analogous to the formation of steroids in animals, this reaction is thought to be catalyzed by side chain cleavage cytochrome $P_{450,\,scc}$. Recently, the enzyme was detected in mitochondria and microsomes prepared from proembryogenic masses, somatic embryoids and leaves of *D. lanata* (Lindemann and Luckner, 1997). Formation of pregnenolone was highest with sitosterol as the substrate, however, other sterols, including cholesterol, were also accepted.

NAD: Δ^5*-3β-hydroxysteroid dehydrogenase/*Δ^5*-*Δ^4*-ketosteroid isomerase (3β-HSD).* The conversion of pregnenolone into progesterone involves two steps. The first reaction is the NAD-dependent oxidation of the 3β-hydroxy group, yielding Δ^5-pregnen-3-one catalyzed by the Δ^5-3β-hydroxysteroid dehydrogenase. The double-bond is shifted from position 5 to position 4 by the action of Δ^5-Δ^4-ketosteroid isomerase. The enzyme was isolated from *Digitalis lanata* cell suspension cultures and characterized by Seidel and co-workers (1990), and partially purified only recently (Finsterbusch *et al.*, 1997).

Other enzymes involved in pregnane metabolism will be introduced when discussing cardenolide biosynthesis (see section 5.2.2).

5.2.1.2 Biotransformation

Exogenous organic compounds can be modified by living cells. These modifications are generally referred to as 'biotransformations'. Plant cell suspension cultures can be used for biotransformation purposes (see for example the comprehensive reviews of Kurz and Constabel, 1979 and Reinhard and Alfermann, 1980). The supply of a suitable precursor may result in the formation of a product known from the intact plant or closely-related compounds with interesting biological properties. In addition, the demonstration of a biotransformation reaction may be a first step in the elucidation of an enzyme-catalyzed conversion.

The transformations of cholesterol, progesterone, pregnenolone and pregnanes has been studied extensively with cell cultures of *Atropa belladonna*, *Brassica napus*, *Catharanthus roseus*, *Capsicum frutescens*, *Cheiranthus cheiri*, *Digitalis lanata*, *D. lutea*, *D. purpurea*, *Dioscorea deltoidea*, *Glycine max*, *Hedera helix*, *Lycopersicum esculentum*, *Nicotiana rustica*, *N. tabacum*, *Parthenocissus* spp., *Rosa* spp., *Solanum tuberosum* and *Sophora angustifolia*. The biotransformation reactions observed include: reduction of double-bonds; reduction of the 3-keto function; oxidation of the 3-hydroxyl group; reduction of the 20-keto group; 6β-, 11α- and 14α-hydroxylation; as well as 3-*O*-glucoside and 3-*O*-palmitate formation (Kurz and Constabel, 1979; Reinhard and Alfermann, 1980).

Mucuna pruriens cell cultures are known to hydroxylate a variety of phenolic compounds (Pras, 1990). The solubility of the phenolic steroid, 17β-estradiol (Fig. 5.9), is only 12 μM in culture medium and no biotransformation products could be detected after administration to freely-suspended cells, immobilized cells or partially purified *Mucuna* phenoloxidase. Complexation with β-cyclodextrin dramatically enhanced the solubility of 17β-estradiol. Alginate-entrapped cells, cell homogenates and the phenoloxidase were able to *o*-hydroxylate 17β-estradiol when supplied as the cyclodextrin complex; the most efficient biotransformation being achieved with the isolated enzyme (Woerdenbag *et al.*, 1990).

A green cell suspension culture of *Marchantia polymorpha*, a liverwort, was shown to convert testosterone to 6β-hydroxytestosterone and epitestosterone to androst-4-ene-3,17-dione (Hamada *et al.*, 1991). The same culture was able to reduce the C-17 carbonyl of androst-4-ene-3,17-dione. It seems that the enzymes responsible for the 6β-hydroxylation of testosterone and the oxidation of C-17 hydroxyls exhibit strict substrate specificity (Fig. 5.11).

With a view to synthesizing isotopically-labelled cardenolide precursors, the metabolism of 5β-pregnan-3β-ol-20-one was investigated in *Nerium oleander* cell cultures. This particular pregnane was oxidized and epimerized to its 3-keto- and the 3α-hydroxyderivative, respectively (Fig. 5.12). The latter compound was further biotransformed to its glucoside, 5β-pregnan-20-one-3α-*O*-glucoside. Interestingly, the 3β-isomer, which might be an intermediate in cardenolide biosynthesis, was not glucosylated (Paper and Franz, 1990).

5.2.2 Cardiac glycosides

Cardiac glycosides are secondary plant metabolites scattered in several unrelated angiosperm families, e.g. Apocynaceae, Asclepiadaceae, Convallariaceae, Fabaceae, Hyacynthaceae, Ranunculaceae and Scrophulariaceae. Some of the cardiac glycosides are important pharmaceuticals in the treatment of heart insufficiency. Cardiac glycosides consist of a steroid nucleus and a sugar side chain of variable length. The C and D rings of the steroid nucleus are connected *cis*, in contrast to most other steroids (Table 5.3). Another common structural feature is a hydroxyl group in position C-14β. Cardiac glycosides are divided into two groups:

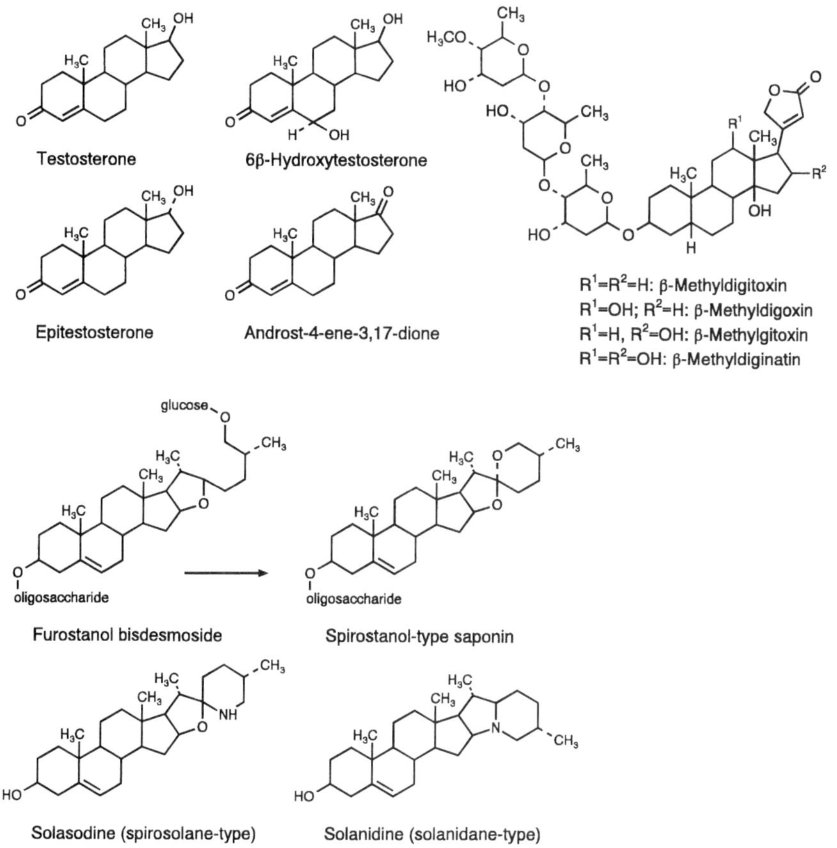
Testosterone
6β-Hydroxytestosterone
Epitestosterone
Androst-4-ene-3,17-dione
R1=R2=H: β-Methyldigitoxin
R1=OH; R2=H: β-Methyldigoxin
R1=H, R2=OH: β-Methylgitoxin
R1=R2=OH: β-Methyldiginatin
glucose
oligosaccharide
Furostanol bisdesmoside
oligosaccharide
Spirostanol-type saponin
Solasodine (spirosolane-type)
Solanidine (solanidane-type)

Figure 5.11 Chemical structures of estranes, androstanes, steroid saponins and steroid alkaloids mentioned in the text.

1) the cardenolides, carrying a five-membered lactone ring; and 2) the bufadienolides, carrying a six-membered lactone ring in position C-17β (Fig. 5.15).

5.2.2.1 Biosynthesis

The putative biosynthetic pathway (Fig. 5.12) leading to the cardiac glycosides is basically deduced from studies using radio-labelled precursors. For more details, the reader is referred to reviews by Grunwald (1980), Schütte (1987) and Kreis and co-workers (1998). The more recent identification and characterization of various enzymes involved in pregnane and cardenolide metabolism have further clarified the pathway. Since little is known about enzymes involved in the formation of

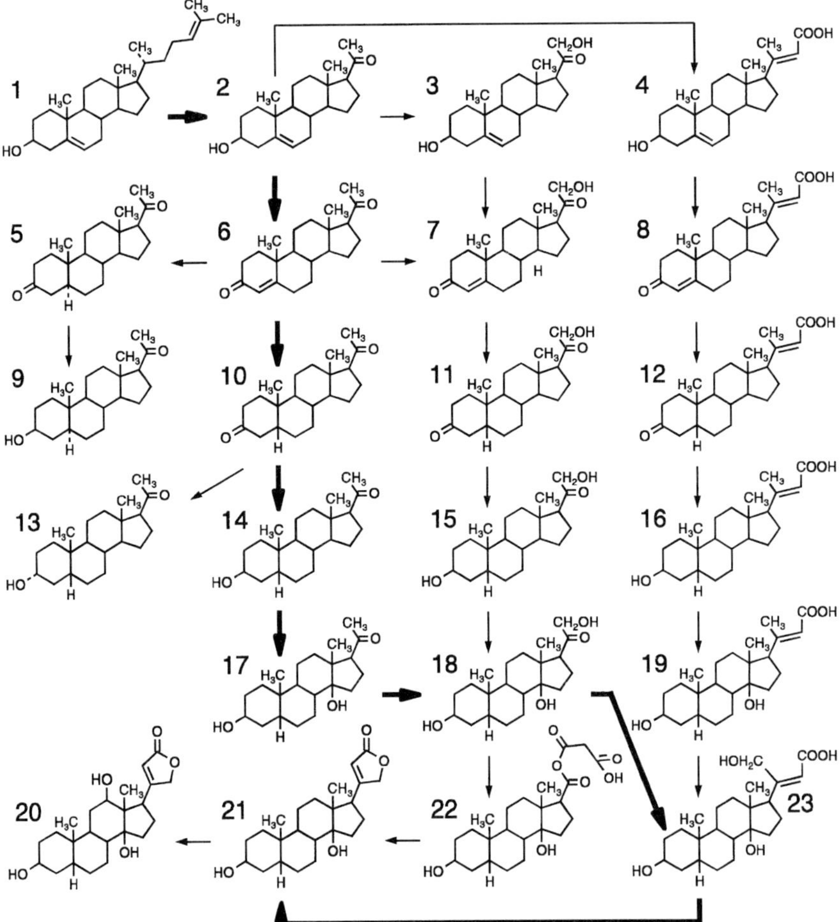

Figure 5.12 Routes for cardenolide genin formation in *Digitalis*. The putative cardenolide pathway, as depicted in standard text books, is traced with bold arrows: 1) cholesterol; 2) pregnenolone; 3) pregnen-3β,21-diol-20-one; 4) 23-nor-5,20(22)*E*-choladienic acid-3β-ol; 5) 5α-pregnane-3,20-dione; 6) progesterone; 7) cortexone; 8) 23-nor-4,20(22)*E*-choladienic acid-3-one; 9) 5α-pregnane-3β-ol-20-one; 10) 5β-pregnane-3,20-dione; 11) 5β-Pregnan-21-ol-3,20-dione; 12) 23-nor-5β-chol-20(22)*E*-enic acid-3-one; 13) 5α-pregnan-3β-ol-20-one; 14) 5β-pregnan-3β-ol-20-one; 15) 5β-pregnan-3β,21-diol-20-one; 16) 23-nor-5β-chol-20(22)*E*-enic acid-3β-ol; 17) 5β-pregnane-3β,14β-diol-20-one; 18) 5β-pregnane-3β,14β,21-triol-20-one; 19) 23-nor-5β-chol-20(22)*E*-enic acid-3β,14β-diol; 20) digoxigenin; 21) digitoxigenin; 22) 5β-pregnane-3β,14β-diol-21-*O*-malonyl hemiester; and 23) 23-nor-5β-chol-20(22)*E*-enic acid-3β,14β,21-triol.

bufadienolides, their biosynthesis will not be considered here in depth. Most of the more recent studies concerning the biosynthesis of cardiac glycosides have been conducted with enzymes isolated from *Digitalis*

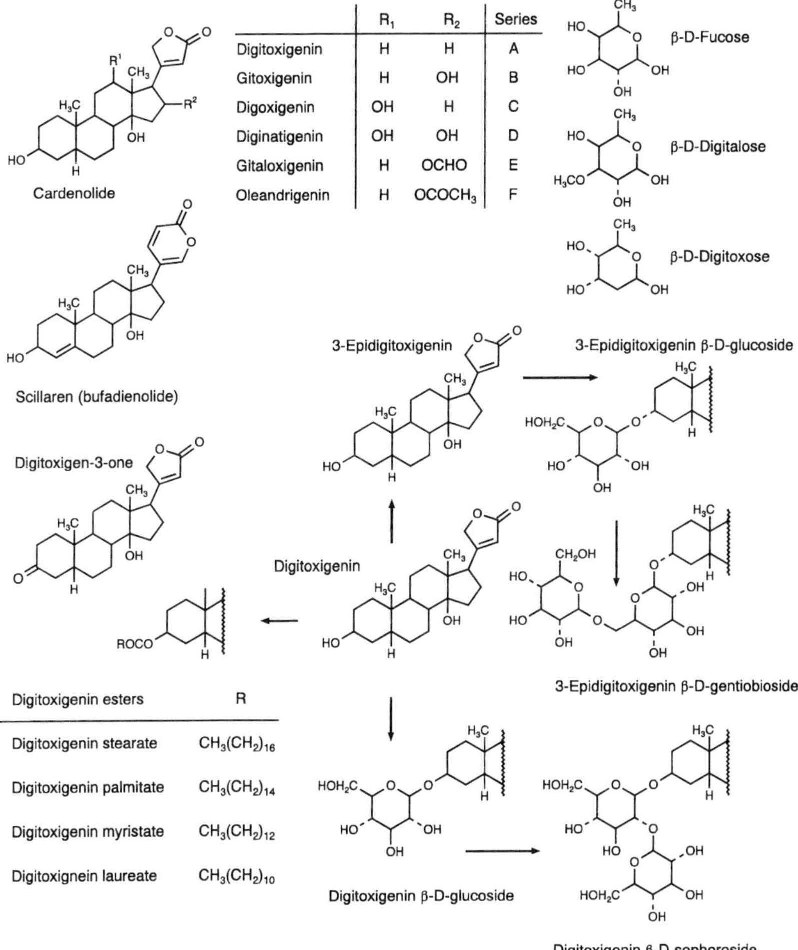

Figure 5.13 Structures of cardiac glycosides mentioned in the text and cardenolide esters and glycosides produced by biotransformation. Formation of the sugar side chain of *Digitalis* cardenolides.

plants and tissue cultures. The *Digitalis* glycosides are cardenolides classified according to the substitution patterns of their steroid moieties. The A-type glycosides (digitoxigenin derivatives) are the most abundant and the C-type glycosides (digoxigenin derivatives) are the most important cardenolides (Fig. 5.13). The sugar side chain attached in position C-3β of the steroid part is composed of up to five sugar residues, including rare 6-deoxy and 2,6-dideoxy sugars, such as D-fucose, D-digitalose and D-digitoxose (Fig. 5.13). The so-called primary glycosides carry a terminal glucose.

Cholesterol is assumed to be the sterol precursor both of cardenolides and bufadienolides. However, several studies have indicated that a route via cholesterol and progesterone is not the most significant cardenolide-forming pathway (see Kreis *et al.*, 1998, for a recent review). More recently, Maier *et al.* (1986) found that Δ^5-norcholenoic acids are incorporated into cardenolides. Further indirect evidence for a main route not involving cholesterol was provided by studies in which 5-azacycloartanol, a specific inhibitor of the *S*-adenosyl-L-methionin (SAM):cycloartenol 24-methyltransferase, was fed to *Digitalis lanata* shoot cultures. As a result, the endogenous pool of cholesterol increased, whereas the cardenolides decreased. The decrease of cardenolides was in the same range as the decrease of 24-alkylsterols, indicating that one of these sterols, but not cholesterol, may be a precursor fuelling the cardenolide pathway (Milek *et al.*, 1997). In this context, it is interesting to note that in addition to the mammalian pathway from cholesterol to pregnenolone, another route from Δ^{22}-sterols may be operative (Kerr *et al.*, 1995). In this case, the $P_{450,\,scc}$ (see section 5.2.1.1 'Side chain cleavage cytochrome $P_{450,\,scc}$') is not necessarily involved in pregnenolone formation, and stigmasterol, the main phytosterol in cardenolide-producing tissues, may be a good candidate as a cardenolide precursor in a hypothetical Δ^{22}-sterol pathway.

NADPH: progesterone 5β-reductase (5β-POR). 5β-POR catalyzes the transformation of progesterone into 5β-pregnane-3,20-dione, i.e. the rings A and B of the steroid are then connected *cis*. Therefore, one of the important structural characteristics of the *Digitalis* cardenolides appears to be accomplished at this stage. Progesterone was the preferred substrate, whereas the relative conversion rates for other steroids, such as testosterone, cortisone and cortisol, were much lower. The enzyme was purified to homogeneity from the cytosolic fraction of shoot cultures of *D. purpurea* (Gärtner *et al.*, 1990).

NADPH: progesterone 5α-reductase (5α-POR). 5α-POR, which catalyzes the reduction of progesterone to 5α-pregnane-3,20-dione, probably in a competitive situation with the 5β-POR, was isolated and characterized (Warneck and Seitz, 1990). At temperatures below 45°C, the product of the enzyme reaction, 5α-pregnane-3,20-dione, was enzymatically reduced to 5α-pregnan-3β-ol-20-one.

NADPH: 3β-hydroxysteroid 5β-oxidoreductase (3β-HS-5β-OR). The 3β-HS-5β-OR catalyzes the conversion of 5β-pregnane-3,20-dione to 5β-pregnane-3β-ol,20-one. It was found to be a soluble protein (Gärtner and Seitz, 1993). The reverse reaction was observed, yielding 5β-pregnane-

3,20-dione when using 5β-pregnane-3β-ol,20-one and NADP as a substrate and cosubstrate, respectively.

NADPH: 3α-hydroxysteroid 5β-oxidoreductase (3α-HS-5β-OR). This microsomal enzyme catalyzes the conversion of 5β-pregnane-3,20-dione to 5β-pregnan-3α-ol-20-one (Stuhlemmer *et al.*, 1993a). In a situation similar to that described for the progesterone reductases, the hydroxysteroid 5β-oxidoreductases may compete for 5β-pregnane-3-ones and, in the cardenolide pathway, part of these putative intermediates will be withdrawn due to the action of the 3α-HS-5β–OR. 3α-Cardenolides have been described in *Xysmalobium* (Asclepidiaceae) and *Isoplexis* (Scrophulariaceae) but never in the genus *Digitalis*, where the final products of the 5α-pregnane pathway may be digitonin and related saponins. The 3α-HS-5β-OR seems to be specific for 5β-pregnane-3-ones; 5α-pregnane-3-ones or Δ^4/Δ^5-pregnenes were not accepted as substrates.

Malonyl-coenzyme A:21-hydroxypregnane 21-O-malonyltransferase (MHPMT). With regard to the formation of the butenolide ring, it is hypothesized that the condensation of 5β-pregnane-3β,14β,21-triol-20-one with a dicarbon unit yields digitoxigenin. However, when the 3-β-*O*-acetate of 5β-pregnane-3β,14β,21-triol-20-one was incubated together with malonyl-coenzyme A in cell-free extracts of cardenolide-producing plants, the malonyl hemiester of the substrate was formed (Stuhlemmer and Kreis, 1996). The compound decomposes at temperatures higher than about 100°C and two products are formed, namely 5β-pregnane-14β-ol-20-one 3β-*O*-,21-*O*-diacetate and the 3-*O*-acetate of digitoxigenin. Malonyl-CoA and acetoacetyl-CoA were accepted as cosubstrates, whereas no 21-*O*-ester formation was observed with acetyl-CoA or succinyl-CoA. Pregnen-21-ol-20-one, cortexone, 5β-pregnan-21-ol-3,20-dione and 5β-pregnane-3β,21-diol-20-one were only very poor substrates (Stuhlemmer and Kreis, 1996). Butenolide formation was also studied in *Asclepias curassavica* (Groeneveld *et al.*, 1990). Excised defoliated stems incorporated radioactive acetate into various lipids, including cardenolides. Labelled cardenolides, biosynthesized from (1,2-^{13}C)-acetate were isolated. The construction of the butenolide ring by the condensation of a pregnane derivative with one molecule acetate, as proposed for the *Digitalis* cardenolides, was not confirmed by the ^{13}C NMR data. In summary, butenolide ring formation in cardenolide biosynthesis is still far from being elucidated.

As mentioned previously, little is known about the biosynthetic sequence leading to bufadienolides. It may be similar to the cardenolide pathway as far as the sequence leading to 5β-pregnane-3β,14β,21-triol-20-one is concerned. With regard to the final step, α-pyrone formation, it was reported that administration of radio-labelled oxaloacetate to *Urginea maritima* plants yielded labelled scillirosid. Chemical degradation of scillirosid indicated that the α-pyrone ring of bufadienolides is formed by the condensation of a pregnane derivative, such as 5β-pregnane-3β,14β,21-triol-20-one, with oxaloacetic acid (Galagovsky *et al.*, 1984).

Pregnane 21-hydroxylation and 14β-hydroxylation. The enzymes involved in pregnane 21-hydroxylation and pregnane 14β-hydroxylation in the course of cardenolide or bufadienolide formation have not yet been described. Concerning steroid 14β-hydroxylation, it was found that labelled 3β-hydroxy-5β-pregnan-20-one was incorporated by *Digitalis purpurea* plants into digitoxin while 3β-hydroxy-5β-pregn-8(14)-en-20-one was not. From this and previous studies, it was concluded that a route via Δ8(14) or Δ8(9) pregnenes, 14β-steroids or an 8,14-epoxide (Tschesche and Kleff, 1973; Anastasia and Ronchetti, 1977) does not appear to be operative in the cardenolide pathway. Therefore, direct hydroxylation with a change in configuration at C-14 seems to be the most probable mechanism of 14β-hydroxylation.

Digitoxin 12β-hydroxylase (D12H). This microsomal cytochrome P_{450}-dependent monooxygenase is capable of converting digitoxigenin-type cardenolides to their corresponding digoxin-type cardenolides (Petersen and Seitz, 1985). Digitoxin, β-methyldigitoxin and α-acetyldigitoxin, as well as digitoxigenin-type cardenolides with shorter or no sugar side chain, were hydroxylated (Petersen *et al.*, 1988). Gitoxigenin, k-strophanthin-β and cymarin, on the other hand, were not accepted. After immobilization in alginate, the enzyme retained 70% of its original activity. The kinetic data of D12H immobilized in alginate were the same as for the enzyme in freely-suspended microsomes (Petersen *et al.*, 1987).

The putative cardenolide pathway implies that the various sugars are attached at the cardenolide aglycone stage, although it cannot be ruled out that pregnane glycosides are obligate intermediates in cardenolide formation. Some results indicate that digitoxose is formed from glucose without rearrangement of the carbon skeleton (Franz and Hassid, 1967) and that nucleotide-bound deoxysugars are present in cardenolide-producing plants (Bauer *et al.*, 1984). Recent investigations into cardenolide biosynthesis have shown high incorporation of ^{14}C-labelled malonate into cardenolides but one third of the radioactivity disappeared after acid hydrolysis of the cardiac glycosides and was, therefore, postulated to be incorporated into the carbohydrate side chain (Groeneveld *et al.*, 1992).

To study cardenolide genin glycosylation in more detail, digitoxigenin was fed to light-grown and dark-grown *D. lanata* shoot cultures, as well as to suspension-cultured cells (Theurer, 1993). In either system, the substrate was converted to digoxigenin (Fig. 5.12), digitoxigen-3-one, 3-epidigitoxigenin, digitoxigenin 3-*O*-β-D-glucoside, 3-epidigitoxigenin 3-*O*-β-D-glucoside (Fig. 5.13), glucodigifucoside (Fig. 5.14) and additional cardenolides. Digitoxosylation was not observed in these studies. Moreover, administration of cardenolide mono- and bisdigitoxosides or cardenolide fucosides did not lead to the formation of cardenolide tridigitoxosides. These results support the hypothesis that cardenolide fucosides and digitoxosides may be formed via different biosynthetic routes and that glycosylation may be an earlier event in cardenolide biosynthesis than previously assumed. Recently, a set of pregnane and cardenolide fucosides was synthesized (Luta *et al*., 1998); and it was shown that feeding of the 3-*O*-β-D-fucoside of 21-hydroxypregnenolone to *D. lanata* shoot cultures leads to a 25-fold increase in the formation of glucodigifucoside, when compared to a control where the respective

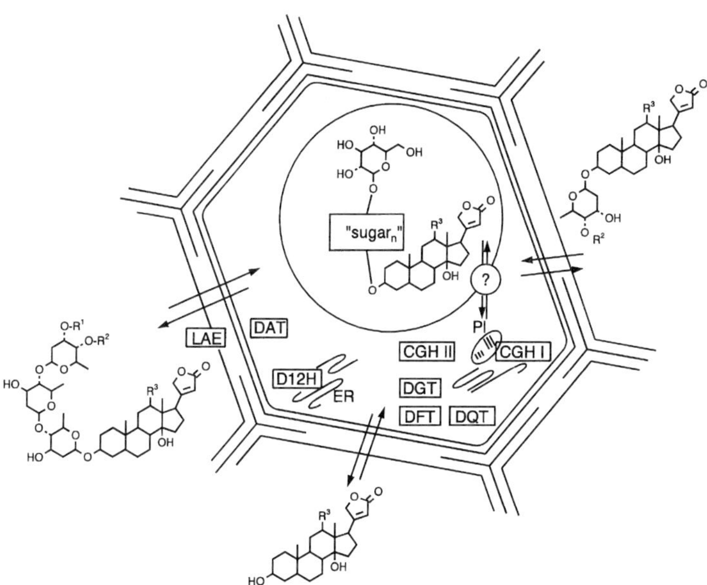

Figure 5.14 Cellular organization of cardenolide glycoside uptake, modification and storage. Exogenous cardenolides enter the cell by diffusion, after which they can be modified in several ways. Only those possessing a terminal glucose are stored in the vacuole, probably involving active transport across the tonoplast. Abbreviations: LAE, lanatoside 15′-*O*-acetylesterase; DAT, digitoxin 15′-*O*-acetyltransferase; DI2H, digitoxin 12β-hydroxylase; ER, endoplasmic reticulum; CGH I and CGH II, cardenolide 16′-*O*-glucohydrolase I and II, respectively; DGT, digitoxin 16′-*O*-glycosyltransferase; DFT, digitoxigenin 3-*O*-fucosyltransferase; DQT, digitoxigenin 3-*O*-quinovosyltransferase.

aglycone was fed (Luta *et al.*, 1997). The enzyme-catalyzed reactions involved in the formation or modification of the sugar side chain of *Digitalis* cardenolides are summarized in Figure 5.14.

*UDP-glucose: digitoxin 16′-*O*-glucosyltransferase (DGT).* The enzymatic glucosylation of secondary glycosides to their respective primary glycosides was first demonstrated by Franz and Meier (1969) in particulate preparations from *D. purpurea* leaves and was investigated in more detail in cell cultures of *D. lanata* (Kreis *et al.*, 1986). The DGT requires two substrates: a secondary cardiac glycoside and a sugar nucleotide. Of six sugar nucleotides tested, only UDP-α-D-glucose served as a glycosyl donor; other glucose nucleotides (Kreis *et al.*, 1986) and UDP-α-*D*-fucose (Faust *et al.*, 1994) were not accepted. The DGTs of different *Digitalis* species differed considerably with regard to their substrate preferences. Although 15′-*O*-acylated glycosides do not occur in *D. purpurea,* they were glucosylated to their corresponding primary glycosides by enzyme preparations from *D. purpurea* cell cultures (Kreis *et al.*, 1986). Cardenolide monodigitoxosides, such as evatromonoside, were accepted very well, whereas cardenolide genins or bisdigitoxosides were glucosylated at a much slower rate. Glucosylation was not observed when digiproside (digitoxigenin fucoside) was tried as the glucosyl acceptor, indicating that DGT accepts only substrates with an equatorial OH group in the 4′ position (Faust *et al.*, 1994).

*UDP-fucose:digitoxigenin 3-*O*-fucosyltransferase (DFT) and UDP-quinovose: digitoxigenin 3-*O*-quinovosyltransferase (DQT).* DFT is a soluble enzyme in *D. lanata* leaves and catalyzes the transfer of the sugar moiety of UDP-α-D-fucose to cardenolide genins. Gitoxigenin and digitoxigenin were much better substrates than digoxigenin (Faust *et al.*, 1994). Incubation of crude protein extracts together with digitoxigenin and UDP-α-D-fucose resulted not only in the formation of digiproside but also of digitoxigenin quinovoside, its 4′-epimer, which is a minor glycoside in *D. lanata*. It was demonstrated that the sugar is epimerized at the sugar nucleotide level and not at the glycoside stage. Neither DQT nor epimerase activity were present in purified DFT preparations.

*UDP-glucose: digiproside 4′-*O*-glucosyltransferase (DPGT).* Glucodigifucoside was formed by a soluble enzyme from young leaves of *D. lanata* in the presence of UDP-α-D-glucose and digiproside (Faust *et al.*, 1994). The enzyme is not identical with the glucosyltransferases described above; it has not yet been characterized in detail. Glucodigifucoside is a major cardenolide in *D. lanata* leaves during all stages of development and may be regarded as the end-product of the 'fucose pathway'.

*Acetyl coenzyme A: digitoxin 15′-*O*-acetyltransferase (DAT).* This soluble, cytosolic enzyme catalyzes the 15′-*O*-acetylation of cardenolide tri- and tetrasaccharides. Using acetyl coenzyme A as the acetyl donor, DAT activity was detected in partially purified protein extracts from *D. lanata* and *D. grandiflora,* both known to contain lanatosides (Sutor *et al.*, 1993).

*Lanatoside 15′-*O*-acetylesterase (LAE).* An esterase converting acetyldigitoxose-containing cardenolides to their corresponding non-acetylated derivatives was demonstrated in *D. lanata* cell suspension cultures and leaves (Sutor *et al.*, 1990). The LAE was shown to be bound to the cell wall. LAE was present in *D. lanata* leaves and cell cultures (Sutor *et al.*, 1990) but was not detectable in cell suspension cultures of *D. grandiflora* and *D. purpurea* (Kreis *et al.*, 1993), and in leaves of *D. purpurea* and *D. heywoodii* (Sutor *et al.*, 1990). Lanatosides, as well as their corresponding secondary glycosides, were good substrates; α,β-diacetyldigoxin was deacetylated to some extent, yielding small amounts of β-acetyldigoxin but not the respective α-derivative. Apigenin 7-*O*-acetylglucoside was not deacetylated. Therefore, LAE seems to be a site-specific cardenolide acetylesterase capable of removing the 15′-acetyl group of lanatosides and their deglucosylated derivatives. Meanwhile, LAE was isolated, purified and partially sequenced (Sutor and Kreis, 1996; Kandzia *et al.*, 1998).

*Cardenolide 16′-*O*-glucohydrolase* I *(CGH* I*) and cardenolide glucohydrolase* II *(CGH* II*).* CGH I was found to be associated with plastids (Bühl, 1984) and could be solubilized from leaves of various *Digitalis* species using buffers containing Triton X-100 or other detergents (Kreis and May, 1990). Considerable variations in substrate preferences were observed among the cardenolide 16′-*O*-glucosidases of the three species investigated. The enzyme of *D. lanata*, termed CGH I, was purified from young leaves. Another cardenolide glucohydrolase, termed CGH II, was isolated from *D. lanata* and *D. heywoodii* leaves and cell cultures. This soluble enzyme hydrolyzes cardenolide disaccharides with a terminal glucose and appears to be quite specific for glucoevatromonoside, which is supposed to be an intermediate in the formation of the cardenolide tetrasaccharides. The tetrasaccharides, deacetyllanatoside C and purpureaglycoside A, which are rapidly hydrolysed by CGH I (see section 5.2.2.1) were very poor substrates for CGH II (Böttigheimer and Kreis, 1995; Hornberger and Kreis, manuscript in preparation).

*Cardenolide β-*D*-fucohydrolase (CFH).* A β-D-fucosidase was isolated from young *D. lanata* leaves. This soluble enzyme catalyzes the cleavage of digiproside and synthetic pregnane 3β-*O*-D-fucosides to D-fucose (6-deoxygalactose) and the respective genin. Digitoxigenin 3β-*O*-D-galactoside was not hydrolyzed by the enzyme. It is not identical with the cardenolide glucohydrolases described above, which do not accept β-D-fucosides as substrates (Luta *et al.*, 1997).

5.2.2.2 Transport and storage

Cell suspension cultures established from different plants producing cardiac glycosides did not produce cardenolides or bufadienolides, whereas embryoids, morphogenic clumps and shoot-differentiating cultures generally contained low amounts of cardiac glycosides (Luckner and Diettrich, 1985; Seidel and Reinhard, 1987; Stuhlemmer *et al.*, 1993b). Plants obtained by organogenesis or somatic embryogenesis were found to contain the cardiac glycosides characteristic of the parent plant. Several studies have reported a positive correlation between light, chlorophyll content and cardenolide production (e.g. Hagimori *et al.*, 1982). However, chloroplast development is not sufficient for expression of the cardenolide pathway, since photomixotropic cell cultures where shown to be incapable of producing cardenolides (Reinhard *et al.*, 1975). *Digitalis* roots cultivated *in vitro* are not capable of producing cardenolides, although they do contain these compounds *in situ*.

With the exception of the 5β-POR (see section 5.2.1.1), all known enzymes of the putative biosynthetic pathway were detected in plants, organ cultures and suspension cultures of *D. lanata* (Stuhlemmer and Kreis, 1996), supporting the view that 5β-POR is a key enzyme in cardenolide biosynthesis (Gärtner and Seitz, 1993). This concept, however, was not accepted by Lindemann and Luckner (1997), who found 5β-POR expressed in a cardenolide-free embryogenic cell line of *D. lanata* and speculated that cardenolide formation is regulated mainly by the availability of cholesterol and its transport into mitochondria, where the $P_{450,\,scc}$ is assumed to be located.

Suspension-cultured *Digitalis* cells, which do not synthesize cardenolides *de novo* (Kreis *et al.*, 1993), as well as roots or shoots cultivated *in vitro* (Theurer, 1993), are able to take up exogenous cardenolides and modify them. It has been demonstrated that cardenolides may enter and leave the cells by diffusion. Only the primary cardenolides, i.e. those containing a terminal glucose, are actively transported across the tonoplast and stored in the vacuole. A model comprising the events leading to cardenolide storage has been proposed (Fig. 5.15) (Kreis *et al.*, 1993). Cardiac glycoside transport was also investigated at the organ and whole plant level. The long-distance transport of primary cardenolides from the leaves to the roots or to etiolated leaves was demonstrated. It was established that the phloem but not the xylem is a transporting tissue

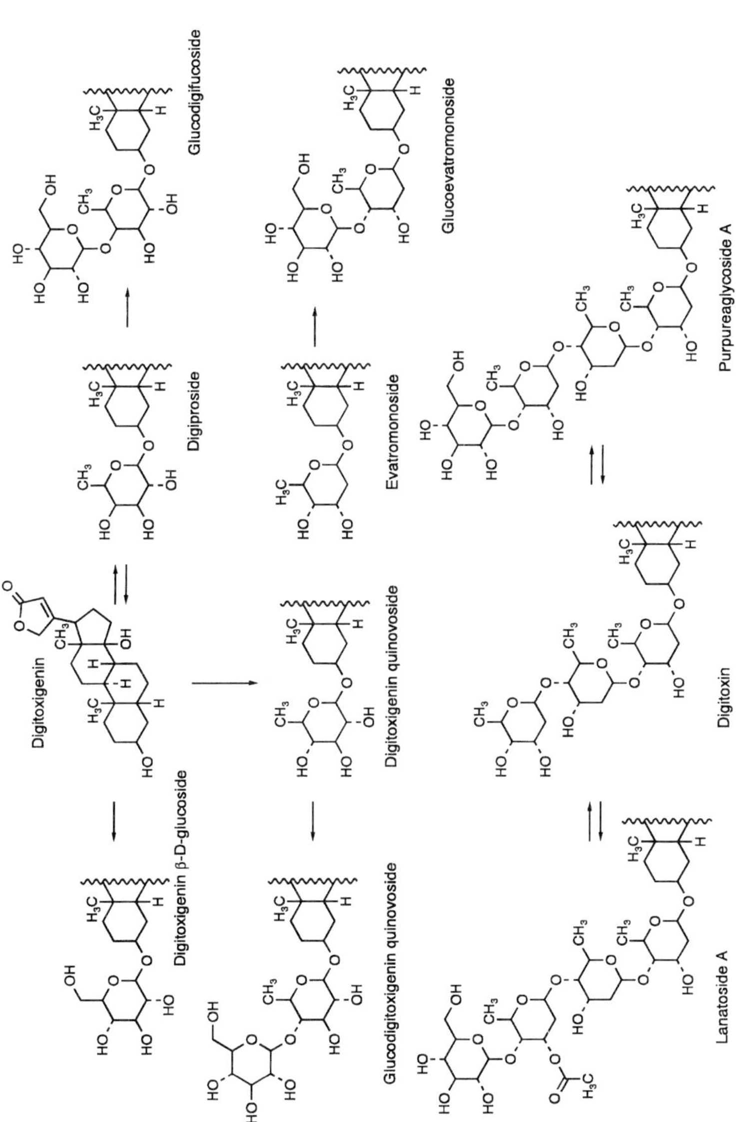

Figure 5.15 Structures of cardiac glycosides mentioned in the text and cardenolide esters and glycosides produced by biotransformation.

for cardenolides (Christmann *et al.*, 1993). To summarize, it seems that primary cardenolides may serve both as the transport and the storage form of cardenolides. After their synthesis they are either stored in the vacuoles of the source tissue or loaded into the sieve tubes and transported to various cardenolide sinks, such as roots or flowers. The mechanisms involved in remetabolization and phloem loading and unloading have not yet been investigated.

5.2.2.3 Biotransformations

During the 1970s and 1980s, investigations concerning the ability of cultured plant cells to modify exogenous cardenolides were carried out (Reinhard and Alfermann, 1980; Suga and Hirata, 1990). In these studies, cell cultures of the cardenolide-producing species *Digitalis cariensis*, *D. dubia*, *D. grandiflora*, *D. lanata*, *D. leucophaea*, *D. lutea*, *D. mertonensis*, *D. parviflora*, *D. purpurea*, *Strophanthus amboensis*, *S. intermedius*, *S. gratus*, *Thevetia neriifolia*, as well as of various cardenolide-free species, were employed.

Biotransformation of cardenolide genins. To summarize these studies, oxidation and epimerization of the 3β-hydroxyl and 5β-hydroxylation and glucosylation of the 3-hydroxyl appear to be quite common reactions, whereas other stereospecific hydroxylations as well as conjugation with deoxysugars are probably more species-specific. The combination of the biosynthetic potential of unrelated plant species and the formation of novel cardenolides by biotransformation was achieved by Furuya and co-workers (Kawaguchi *et al.*, 1990), who administered digitoxigenin to hairy root cultures of *Panax ginseng*. Four esters, namely digitoxigenin stearate, digitoxigenin palmitate, digitoxigenin myristate and digitoxigenin laureate, as well as two new glycosides, 3-epidigitoxigenin β-D-gentiobioside and digitoxigenin β-D-sophoroside, were isolated, together with six known cardenolides (Fig. 5.13).

In a more recent study, digitoxigenin was fed to light-grown and dark-grown *Digitalis lanata* shoot cultures. In either system, the substrate was converted to digoxigenin (Fig. 5.12), digitoxigen-3-one, 3-epidigitoxigenin, digitoxigenin β-D-glucoside, 3-epidigitoxigenin β-D-glucoside (Fig. 5.13) and glucodigifucoside (Fig. 5.15). Interestingly, fucosylated and digitalosylated cardenolides were formed in light-grown shoots, whereas digitoxosylation was not observed (Theurer *et al.*, 1998).

Biotransformation of cardiac glycosides. The biotransformation of cardiac glycosides has been studied extensively using *Digitalis lanata* cell and organ cultures. Side chain glucosylation, deglucosylation, acetylation, deacetylation and steroid 12β-hydroxylation, have been reported (Reinhard and Alfermann, 1980). Most important is the ability of cultured *Digitalis* cells to biotransform cardenolide tridigitoxosides of the A-series into the respective 12β-hydroxylated C-series glycosides (see section 5.2.2). *Digitalis lanata* cell lines with high 12β-hydroxylation capacity have been selected by cell-aggregate-cloning and by protoplast-cloning techniques (Reinhard and Alfermann, 1980; Baumann *et al.*, 1990; Kreis and Reinhard, 1990a). A cell culture process was developed in which a commercial digoxin-type cardenolide, namely β-methyldigoxin, can be prepared with good yields and almost no side reactions from β-methyldigitoxin (Fig. 5.11) (Alfermann *et al.*, 1983; Reinhard *et al.*, 1989). More recently, alternative approaches using *Digitalis lanata* cells to produce C-series cardenolides have been tried. Special emphasis was laid on the use of digitoxin as the substrate for biotransformation. For example, a two-stage cultivation method was employed to develop a semicontinuous biotransformation process for the production of deacetyllanatoside C on the 20 L scale using two airlift bioreactors, one for cell growth and another for deacetyllanatoside C production (Kreis and Reinhard, 1990b).

Since the pharmacological properties of cardiac glycosides may improve with the introduction of additional hydroxyl functions, attempts have been made to combine the biotransformation abilities of the cell cultures of *Digitalis lanata* (12β-hydroxylation) and *Digitalis purpurea* (16β-hydroxylation). In this approach, the target compound was β-methyldiginatin, a cardenolide not found in nature. This compound was produced using a two-step procedure. In the first step, *Digitalis purpurea* cells were used to 16β-hydroxylate β-methyldigitoxin to β-methylgitoxin, which was isolated from the bathing medium and subsequently added to cultured *Digitalis lanata* cells. These attached an additional hydroxyl function at position 12β of the molecule to yield the final product, β-methyldiginatin (Fig. 15.11) (Meiss *et al.*, 1986).

5.2.3 Steroid saponins and steroid alkaloids

5.2.3.1 Steroid saponins

Saponins may be classified into two groups, the triterpenoid saponins, which will not be considered here (for recent reviews, see Mahato *et al.*, 1991 and Conolly *et al.*, 1994), and the steroid saponins. Steroid alkaloids behave like saponins but are sometimes treated as 'alkaloids', although these compounds are formed from intermediates of the steroid saponin pathway. Steroid saponins constitute a vast group of plant-borne glycosides present almost exclusively in the monocotyledonous angiosperms, and occurring in only a few dicotyledonous families, such as the Fabaceae and Scrophulariaceae. When dissolved in water, saponins form soapy solutions and can therefore be used as detergents in the preparation of galenicals and cosmetics. Saponins can increase the permeability of biomembranes and may thus exhibit cytotoxic, haemolytic and antiviral properties; most of them are highly toxic for fish. Moreover, steroid saponins are important starting materials for the commercial production of steroid hormones.

The C_{27}-steroid saponins (including the steroid alkaloids) are probably formed from cholesterol, in such a way that ultimately one (furostanes) or two heterocyclic rings (spirostanes, spirosolanes, solanidanes) connected to C-16 and C-17 are attached to the steroid ring system. Side chain hydroxylations at C-26 or C-27 with subsequent *O*-glycosylation may be important steps in spirostane-type saponin formation. For example, 26-*O*-glycosylated oligofurostanosides may be regarded as direct precursors of dioscin and related saponins or even as 'preformed spirostanes'; once the glucose is removed, intramolecular ketalization and spiroether formation can be accomplished (Fig. 5.11). A crucial step in steroid alkaloid formation is the replacement of one of the side chain hydroxyl groups by an amino group. Subsequently, the amino nitrogen is 'trapped' by ring closure.

The withanolides (Fig. 5.9) are C_{28}-steroids and biogenetically related to the steroid saponins in that they are derived from ergostane-type sterols, in which C-22 and C-26 are oxidized and become part of a δ-lactone. These compounds appear to be specific for the Solanaceae. Their biosynthesis has not yet been studied at the enzyme level. Tracer studies have indicated that C-26 is directly derived from C-2 of mevalonolactone. From the relative incorporation rates, it was concluded that the side chain of the sterol precursor had been partially cleaved during the biosynthetic process (Veleiro *et al.*, 1985).

The saponin genins are linked to sugars at the 3-hydroxy group. Frequently, several sugar moieties are attached forming a branched oligosaccharide chain. Little is yet known about the regulation of saponin biosynthesis and the enzymes involved in saponin formation in plants. The accumulation of, for example, glycoalkaloids can be inhibited by the sterol synthesis inhibitor, tridemorph (Bergenstrahle *et al.*, 1992). Tetcyclacis, a plant growth retardant, caused a significant increase in the cholesterol content of the roots of fenugreek but a decrease of their sapogenin content. Since tetcyclacis was shown to be only a poor inhibitor of the *S*-adenosyl-L-methionine:cycloartenol-C-24-methyltransferase, cholesterol accumulation does not result from the inhibition of the sterol side chain-alkylating enzyme (Cerdon *et al.*, 1995). As in the case of cardenolides (see section 5.2.2), it remains to be determined why the increase of a putative precursor does not enhance secondary metabolite formation.

Furostanol glycoside 26-O-β-glucosidase (F26G). Some plants contain biologically inactive, bisdesmosidic furostanol saponins. Upon tissue damage, these saponins can come in contact with a β-glucosidase, which removes the glucose molecule attached to C-26, resulting in the formation of highly-active spirostanol-type saponins. These metabolites may also be formed from furostanol glycosides during postharvest treatment or storage. The F26G involved in this conversion was purified from *Costus speciosus* rhizomes. The enzyme was highly specific for cleavage of the C-26-bound glucose moiety of furostanol glycosides. The purified F26G is dimeric (subunits: 54 and 58 kDa). The N-terminal sequence of the 54 kDa protein has a high similarity to the sequences found in N-terminal regions of known plant β-glucosidases (Inoue and Ebizuka, 1996). Using primers based on sequences of F26G cDNA fragments, 5′- and 3′-end clones were isolated by rapid amplification of cDNA ends (RACE). The entire coding portion of F26G cDNA was cloned by using primers designed from sequences of the RACE products, and cell-free extracts of *E. coli* expressing F26G cDNA showed F26G activity (Inoue *et al.*, 1996). F26G activity was also detected in other plant materials, e.g. the inflorescenses of *Allium erubescens* (Vardosanidze *et al.*, 1991).

UDP-glucose:solanidine 3-O-β-D-glucosyltransferase (solanidine-GTase) and UDP-glucose:solasodine 3-O-β-D-glucosyltransferase (solasosodin-GTase). The glycosylations of the spirostanol alkaloid, solanidine, are considered to be the terminal steps in the synthesis of the potentially toxic glycoalkaloids, α-solanine and α-chaconine. As mentioned previously, at least two different enzymes responsible for steroid glucosylation are present in potato (Zimowski, 1992), and it was found that the cytosolic glucosyltransferase, termed solanidine-GTase, glycosylated solanidine with a high yield (Zimowski, 1991). Concomitant to the accumulation of glycoalkaloids in freshly cut potato tubers was an increase in the specific activity of the solanidine-GTase, whereas the activity of the sterol-specific SGTase (see above) was unaffected by either tuber slicing or addition of ethephon (Bergenstrahle *et al.*, 1992). The accumulation of glycoalkaloids can be inhibited by the ethylene-releasing substance, ethephon. Discs incubated at high levels of ethephon had a very low glycoalkaloid content and also a lower activity of solanidine-GTase than control discs. Thus, solanidine-GTase may well be involved in initiation and regulation of glycoalkaloid biosynthesis.

Solanidine-GTase was purified to near homogeneity from potato sprouts. The isolation of this enzyme was complicated by its copurification with patatin. Separation of the two proteins was finally achieved by binding the glycosylated patatin to concanavalin A, under conditions where the solanidine-GTase did not bind. In this study, no enzyme activity was detected when UDP-galactose was used as a substrate (Stapleton *et al.*, 1991). This is in contrast to other reports, where soluble enzyme preparations from potato tubers were shown to catalyze solanidine galactosylation, although with a much lower yield, using UDP-galactose as the sugar donor (Zimowski, 1991; Bergenstrahle *et al.*, 1992). After purification, solanidine glucosylating and galactosylating activities were recovered in the same fractions but with loss of most of the galactosyltransferase activity (Bergenstrahle *et al.*, 1992). The molecular weight of solanidine-GTase was about 40 kDa and the isoelectric point 4.8. With respect to substrate specificity, it was shown that the spirosolane alkaloids tomatidine and solasodine were glucosylated even better than solanidine, whereas 3β-hydroxy steroids lacking a ring nitrogen, such as cholesterol, diosgenin, digoxigenin, and β-sitosterol, did not serve as glucose acceptors. UDP-galactose was found to be a competitive inhibitor of the solanidine glucosyltransferase of potato (Bergenstrahle *et al.*, 1992).

Spirosolane-type steroid alkaloids were glucosylated by a soluble 55 kDa protein from *Solanum melongena* much better than solanidane-type compounds. The enzyme was, therefore, termed solasodine-GTase, although it may be closely related to the solanidine-GTase described above. In order to distinguish between glucosyltransferase and galactosyltransferase activity, UDP-xylose was used to block UDP-glucose 4-epimerase when using UDP-galactose as a glycosyl donor. Interestingly, spirostane-type sapogenins, such as diosgenin, tigogenin, yamogenin and hecogenin, were also glycosylated. Sterols, on the other hand, were not glycosylated by the cytosolic enzyme(s) (Paczkowski and Woiciechowski, 1994; Paczkowski *et al.*, 1997).

5.2.3.2 Transport and storage

Radio-labelled diosgenin-type saponins were isolated from different parts, such as stem, leaf, seeds, flowers and rhizomes, of *Costus speciosus* after feeding ^{14}C-labelled precursors. The results indicated that: 1) diosgenin is biosynthesized in leaves and then translocated to all the parts of the plant; and 2) glycosidation of diosgenin takes place in all parts of the plant and diosgenin glycosides are stored in rhizomes, seeds and flowers. Saponin deglycosidation was observed only in the rhizomes (Akhila and Gupta, 1987).

5.2.4 Conclusions

Plant sterols are products of primary metabolism but they may also be regarded as direct precursors of many secondary plant metabolites, such as the cardiac glycosides, saponins and steroid alkaloids. All of the compounds mentioned share the same basic skeleton; therefore, the accumulation of a particular compound can only be achieved if: 1) enzymes with a high degree of substrate-specificity are involved in their biosynthesis; 2) metabolites can be channelled efficiently to the respective pathways; and 3) products can be transported, sequestered and/or stored in specific compartments.

A detailed knowledge of the localization, properties and substrate preferences of the different enzymes involved in steroid formation in plants is necessary to understand the various pathways, their regulation and the biosynthetic relationships among the various groups of steroids. With regard to ring formation and annealing, and the biosynthetic sequence realized, initial conformation and conformational changes accomplished during biosynthesis are of utmost importance. This has been elaborated exceptionally well for sterol formation, in which specific enzymes are involved that can act only on molecules with appropriate conformation (see section 5.2.1.1). It is most likely that similar restrictions apply to, for example, 5β-cardenolide formation, where specific conformational changes are accomplished by progesterone 5β-reduction and 14β-hydroxylation, although this has not yet been clarified unambiguously. Since pregnenes are assumed to be intermediates in various pathways, several steroid-modifying enzymes, such as 3-hydroxysteroid dehydrogenases, 3-oxidoreductases and Δ5-steroid reductases (see section 5.2.2.1) may compete for the same substrate. Therefore, the various pregnane-modifying enzymes isolated from *Digitalis* may not necessarily be operative in the cardenolide pathway(s) only; progesterone 5α-oxidoreductase and progesterone 5β-oxidoreductase share the same substrate as do 3α-hydroxysteroid 5β-oxidoreductase and 3β-hydroxysteroid 5β-oxidoreductase. Moreover, one part of the intermediate pool which qualifies for further use in a specific pathway, e.g. cardenolide biosynthesis, may be removed and funnelled into known or hitherto unknown pathways. The observation that the cardenolide content of different *Digitalis lanata* shoot cultures was considerably lower than that of greenhouse plants was explained by the different activities of competing enzymes (Stuhlemmer *et al.*, 1993a, b). Bivalent cations may be involved in regulating and tuning the different hydroxysteroid pathways. It was shown, for example, that *Digitalis* 3β-hydroxysteroid 5β-oxidoreductase is inhibited by Mg^{2+} (Gärtner *et al.*, 1990), whereas the respective 3α-hydroxysteroid 5β-oxidoreductase is not. Moreover, the $NADP^{+}$-dependent enzymatic oxidation of 3α-hydroxysteroids is also strongly inhibited by Mg^{2+} (Stuhlemmer *et al.*, 1993).

The storage forms of plant sterols as well as of most of the secondary plant products derived from the cycloartenol pathway have sugars attached to the hydroxyl group at C-3 of the steroid skeleton. Some of the glycosyltransferases and glycosidases involved in the formation of various steroids have been demonstrated to exhibit a high degree of substrate-specificity. Due to these modifications, the respective molecules may be tagged, so as to be recognized and channelled into the different pathways. In fact, a branched cardenolide pathway was postulated to be operative in *Digitalis lanata* and it was assumed that cardenolide digitoxosylation has to occur at the C_{21} stage of the pathway, whereas fucosylation can be accomplished at the C_{21} and/or the C_{23} stage. These and other findings indicate that steroid glycosylation may take place at various stages and should no longer be regarded as terminal biosynthetic steps that can only be accomplished after the formation of the steroid skeleton.

Acknowledgements

J. G. would like to thank Jörg Bohlmann for valuable discussions and Angela Schneider for skillful preparation of the figures.

References

Aach, H., Bose, G. and Graebe, J.E. (1995) *Ent*-kaurene biosynthesis in a cell-free system from wheat (*Triticum aestivum*) seedlings and the localisation of *ent*-kaurene synthetase in plastids of three species. *Planta*, **197** 333-42.

Aach, H., Bode, H., Robinson, D.G. and Graebe, J.E. (1997) *Ent*-kaurene synthase is located in proplastids of meristematic shoot tissues. *Planta*, **202** 211-19.

Abe, I., Rohmer, M. and Prestwich, G.D. (1993) Enzymatic cyclization of squalene and oxidosqualene to sterols and triterpenes. *Chem. Rev.*, **93** 2189-206.

Adam, K.P. and Zapp, J. (1998) Biosynthesis of the isoprene units of chamomile sesquiterpenes. *Phytochemistry*, **48** 953-59.

Adam, K.P., Crock, J. and Croteau, R. (1996) Partial purification and characterization of a monoterpene cyclase, limonene synthase, from the liverwort *Ricciocarpos natans*. *Arch. Biochem. Biophys.*, **332** 352-56.

Adam, K.P., Thiel, R., Zapp, J. and Becker, H. (1998) Involvement of the mevalonic acid pathway and the glyceraldehyde-pyruvate pathway in terpenoid biosynthesis of the liverworts *Ricciocarpos natans* and *Conocephalum conicum*. *Arch. Biochem. Biophys.*, **354** 181-87.

Adiwilaga, K. and Kush, A. (1996) Cloning and characterization of cDNA encoding farnesyl diphosphate synthase from rubber tree (*Hevea brasiliensis*). *Plant Mol. Biol.*, **30** 935-46.

Ait-Ali, T., Swain, S.M., Reid, J.B., Sun, T.P. and Kamiya, Y. (1997) The Ls locus of pea encodes the gibberellin biosynthesis enzyme *ent*-kaurene synthase A. *Plant J.*, **11** 443-54.

Aitken, S.M., Attucci, S., Ibrahim, R.K. and Gulick, P.J. (1995) A cDNA encoding geranylgeranyl pyrophosphate synthase from white lupin. *Plant Physiol.*, **108** 837-38.

Akhila, A. and Gupta, M.M. (1987) Biosynthesis and translocation of diosgenin in *Costus speciosus*. *J. Plant Physiol.*, **130** 285-90.

Albrecht, M. and Sandmann, G. (1994) Light-stimulated carotenoid biosynthesis during transformation of maize etioplasts is regulated by increased activity of isopentenyl pyrophosphate isomerase. *Plant Physiol.*, **105** 529-34.

Alfermann, A.W., Bergmann, W., Figur, C., Helmbold, U., Schwantag, D., Schuller, I. and Reinhard, E. (1983) in *Plant biotechnology* (eds. S.H. Mantell and H. Smith), Society for Experimental Botany, Cambridge University Press, Cambridge, Seminar Series 18, pp. 67-74.

Anastasia, M. and Ronchetti, F. (1977) Mechanism of 14β-hydroxylation in the biosynthesis of cardenolides: the role of 14β-cholest-5-en-3β-ol. *Phytochemistry*, **16** 1082-83.

Aoyagi, K., Beyou, A., Moon, K., Fang, L. and Ulrich, T. (1993) Isolation and characterization of cDNAs encoding wheat 3-hydroxy-3-methylglutaryl coenzyme A reductase. *Plant Physiol.*, **102** 623-28.

Arigoni, D., Sagner, S., Latzel, C., Eisenreich, W., Bacher, A. and Zenk, M.H. (1997) Terpenoid biosynthesis from 1-deoxy-D-xylulose in higher plants by intramolecular skeletal rearrangement. *Proc. Natl. Acad. Sci. USA*, **94** 10600-605.

Attucci, S., Aitken, S.M., Gulick, P.J. and Ibrahim, R.K. (1995) Farnesyl pyrophosphate synthase from white lupin: molecular cloning, expression and purification of the expressed protein. *Arch. Biochem. Biophys.*, **321** 493-500.

Bach, T.J. (1995) Some new aspects of isoprenoid biosynthesis in plants: a review. *Lipids*, **30** 191-202.

Bach, T.J. and Lichtenthaler, H.K. (1983) Inhibition by mevinolin of plant growth, sterol formation and pigment accumulation. *Physiologia Plantarum*, **59** 50-60.

Bach, T.J., Wettstein, A., Boronat, A., Ferrer, A., Enjuto, M., Gruissem, W. and Narita, J.O. (1991) Properties and molecular cloning of plant HMG-CoA reductase, in *Physiology and Biochemistry of Sterols* (eds. G.W. Patterson and W.D. Nes), American Oil Chemists Society, Champaign, Illinois, pp. 29-49.

Back, K. and Chappell, J. (1995) Cloning and bacterial expression of a sesquiterpene cyclase from *Hyoscyamus muticus* and its molecular comparison to related terpene cyclases. *J. Biol. Chem.*, **270** 7375-81.

Back, K.W. and Chappell, J. (1996) Identifying functional domains within terpene cyclases using a domain-swapping strategy. *Proc. Natl. Acad. Sci. USA*, **93** 6841-45.

Badillo, A., Steppuhn, J., Deruere, J., Camara, B. and Kuntz, M. (1995) Structure of a functional geranylgeranyl pyrophosphate synthase gene from *Capsicum annuum*. *Plant Mol. Biol.*, **27** 425-28.

Bak, S., Kahn, R.A., Olsen, C.E. and Halkier, B.A. (1997) Cloning and expression in *Escherichia coli* of the obtusifoliol 14α-demethylase of *Sorghum bicolor* (L.) Moench, a cytochrome P_{450} orthologous to the sterol 14α-demethylases (CYP51) from fungi and mammals. *Plant J.*, **11** 191-201.

Bantignies, B., Liboz, T. and Ambid, C. (1996) Nucleotide sequence of a *Catharanthus roseus* geranylgeranyl pyrophosphate synthase gene. *Plant Physiol.*, **110** 336.

Bauer, P., Kopp, B. and Franz, G. (1984) Biosynthese von Herzglykosiden: Nachweis von nukleotidgebundenen 2,6-Didesoxy-3-*O*-methylhexosen in Blättern von *Nerium oleander*. *Planta Med.*, **50** 12-14.

Baumann, T., Kreis, W., Mehrle, W., Hampp, R. and Reinhard, E. (1990) in *Proceedings of the 4th European Symposium on Life Sciences Research in Space*, ESA Publications Div., ESTEC, Nordwijk, pp. 405-10.

Belingheri, L., Pauly, G., Gleizes, M. and Marpeau, A. (1988) Isolation by an aqueous two-polymer phase system and identification of endomembranes from *Citrofortunella mitis* fruits for sesquiterpene hydrocarbon synthesis. *J. Plant Physiol.*, **132** 80-85.

Bennett, R.D. and Heftmann, E. (1966) Biosynthesis of pregnenolone from cholesterol in *Haplopappus heterophyllus*. *Phytochemistry*, **5** 747-54.

Bensen, R.J., Johal, G.S., Crane, V.C., Tossberg, J.T., Schnable, P.S., Meeley, R.B. and Briggs, S.P. (1995) Cloning and characterization of the maize An1 gene. *Plant Cell*, **7** 75-84.

Benveniste, P. (1986) Sterol Biosynthesis. *Annu. Rev. Plant Physiol.*, **37** 275-308.

Bergenstrahle, A., Tollberg, E. and Jonsson, L. (1992a) Characterization of UDP-glucose solanidine glucosyltransferase and UDP-galactose solanidine galactosyltransferase from potato tuber. *Plant Sci.*, **84** 35-44.

Bergenstrahle, A., Tollberg, E. and Jonsson, L. (1992b) Regulation of glycoalkaloid accumulation in potato tuber discs. *J. Plant Physiol.*, **140** 269-75.

Bestwick, L., Bennett, M.H., Mansfield, J.W. and Rossiter, J.T. (1995) Accumulation of the phytoalexin lettucenin A and changes in 3-hydroxy-3-methylglutaryl coenzyme A reductase activity in lettuce seedlings with the red spot disorder. *Phytochemistry*, **39** 775-77.

Bhattacharyya, M.K., Paiva, N.L., Dixon, R.A., Korth, K.L. and Stermer, B.A. (1995) Features of the hmg 1 subfamily of genes encoding HMG-CoA reductase in potato. *Plant Mol. Biol.*, **28** 1-15.

Bianchini, G.M., Stermer, B.A. and Paiva, N.L. (1996) Induction of early mevalonate pathway enzymes and biosynthesis of end-products in potato (*Solanum tuberosum*) tubers by wounding and elicitation. *Phytochemistry*, **42** 1563-71.

Blanc, V.M. and Pichersky, E. (1995) Nucleotide sequence of a *Clarkia breweri* cDNA clone of ipi1, a gene encoding isopentenyl pyrophosphate isomerase. *Plant Physiol.*, **108** 855-56.

Bohlmann, J., Crock, J., Jetter, R. and Croteau, R. (1998a) Terpenoid-based defenses in conifers: cDNA cloning, characterization and functional expression of wound-inducible (*E*)-α-bisabolene synthase from grand fir (*Abies grandis*). *Proc. Natl. Acad. Sci. USA*, **95** 6756-61.

Bohlmann, J., Meyergauen, G. and Croteau, R. (1998b) Plant terpenoid synthases: molecular biology and phylogenetic analysis. *Proc. Natl. Acad. Sci. USA*, **95** 4126-33.

Bohlmann, J., Steele, C.L. and Croteau, R. (1997) Monoterpene synthases from grand fir (*Abies grandis*): cDNA isolation, characterization and functional expression of myrcene synthase, (−)(4*S*)-limonene synthase and (−)-(1*S*,5*S*)-pinene synthase. *J. Biol. Chem.*, **272** 21784-92.

Böttigheimer, U. and Kreis, W. (1995) Partial purification and characterization of cardenolide glucohydrolase II from *Digitalis lanata* Ehrh, in *43th Annual Congress of Medicinal Plant Research,* Halle.

Bouvier, F., d'Harlingue, A., Suire, C., Backhaus, R.A. and Camara, B. (1998) Dedicated roles of plastid transketolases during the early onset of isoprenoid biogenesis in pepper fruits. *Plant Physiol.*, **117** 1423-31.

Bouvier-Navé, P. and Benveniste, P. (1995) Sterol acyl transferase and steryl ester hydrolase activities in a tobacco mutant which overproduces sterols. *Plant Sci.*, **110** 11-19.

Bowers, W.S. (1991) Insect hormones and antihormones in plants, in *Herbivores: Their Interactions With Secondary Plant Metabolites* (eds. G.A. Rosenthal and M.R. Berenbaum) 2nd edn. Academic Press. San Diego; pp. 431-56.

Broers, S.T.J. (1994) Ueber die fruehen Stufen der Biosynthese von Isoprenoiden in *Escherichia coli* Ph.D. Thesis, Eidgenoessische Technische Hochschule, Zurich.

Bühl, W. (1984) Enzyme in Blättern von *Digitalis*-Arten unter besonderer Berücksichtigung von herzglykosidspaltender Glucosidase und Esterase, Doctoral Thesis, University of Marburg.

Burnett, R.J., Maldonado-Mendoza, I.E., McKnight, T.D. and Nessler, C.L. (1993) Expression of a 3-hydroxyl-3-methylglutaryl coenzyme A reductase gene from *Camptotheca acuminata* is differentially regulated by wounding and methyl jasmonate. *Plant Physiol.*, **103** 41-48.

Butler, A.R. and Wu, Y.-L. (1992) Artemisinin (qinghaosu): a new type of antimalarial drug. *Chem. Soc. Rev.* pp. 85-90.

Cabello-Hurtado, F., Zimmerlin, A., Rahier, A., Taton, M., Derose, R., Nedelkina, S., Batard, Y., Durst, F., Pallett, K.E. and Werck-Reichhart, D. (1997) Cloning and functional expression in yeast of a cDNA coding for an obtusifoliol 14α-demethylase (CYP51) in wheat. *Biochem. Biophys. Res. Commun.*, **230** 381-85.

Caelles, C., Ferrer, A., Balcells, L., Hegardt, F.G. and Boronat, A. (1989) Isolation and structural characterization of a cDNA encoding *Arabidopsis thaliana* 3-hydroxy-3-methylflutaryl coenzyme A reductase. *Plant Mol. Biol.*, **13** 627-38.

Campbell, M., Hahn, F.M., Poulter, C.D. and Leustek, T. (1998) Analysis of the isopentenyl diphosphate isomerase gene family from *Arabidopsis thaliana. Plant Mol. Biol.*, **36** 323-28.

Campos, N. and Boronat, A. (1995) Targeting and topology in the membrane of plant 3-hydroxy-3-methylglutaryl coenzyme a reductase. *Plant Cell,* **7** 2163-74.

Cane, D.E. (1990) Enzymatic formation of sesquiterpenes. *Chemcal Rev.*, **90** 1089-103.

Cane, D.E. (ed.) (1998) *Comprehensive Natural Products Chem: Isoprenoid Biosynthesis.* Pergamon Press, Oxford.

Cartayrade, A., Schwarz, M., Jaun, B. and Arigoni, D. (1994) Detection of two independent mechanistic pathways for the early steps of isoprenoid biosynthesis in *Ginkgo biloba*, 2nd Symposium of the European Network on Plant Terpenoids, Strasbourg, France.

Caspi, E., Lewis, D.O., Piatak, D.M., Thimann, K.V. and Winter, A. (1966) Biosynthesis of plant sterols. Conversion of cholesterol to pregnenolone in *Digitalis purpurea. Experientia,* **12** 506-507.

Cerdon, C., Rahier, A., Taton, M. and Sauvaire, Y. (1995) Effects of tetcyclacis on growth and on sterol and sapogenin content in Fenugreek. *J. Plant Growth Reg.*, **14** 15-22.

Chappell, J. (1995) Biochemistry and molecular biology of the isoprenoid biosynthetic pathway in plants. *Annu. Rev. Plant Physiol. Plant Mol. Biol.*, **46** 521-47.

Chappell, J., von Lanken, C., Vogeli, U. and Bhatt, P. (1989) Sterol and sesquiterpenoid biosynthesis during a growth cycle of tobacco cell suspension cultures. *Plant Cell Rep.*, **8** 48-52.

Chappell, J., Wolf, F., Proulx, J., Cuellar, R. and Saunders, C. (1995) Is the reaction catalyzed by 3-hydroxy-3-methylglutaryl coenzyme A reductase a rate-limiting step for isoprenoid biosynthesis in plants? *Plant Physiol.*, **109** 1337-43.

Charlwood, B.V. and Banthorpe, D.V. (1978) The biosynthesis of monoterpenes, in *Progress in Phytochemistry* (eds. L. Reinhold, J.B. Harborne and T. Swain). Pergamon Press, Oxford, pp. 65-125.

Charlwood, B.V. and Banthorpe, D.V. (eds.) (1991) *Methods in Plant Biochemsitry*, Vol. 7, Terpenoids, Academic Press, London.

Chen, A., Kroon, P.A. and Poulter, C.D. (1994) Isoprenyl diphosphate synthases: protein sequence comparisons, a phylogenetic tree and predictions of secondary structure. *Protein Sci.*, **3** 600-607.

Chen, X.Y., Chen, Y., Heinstein, P. and Davisson, V.J. (1995) Cloning, expression and characterization of (+)-delta-cadinene synthase: a catalyst for cotton phytoalexin biosynthesis. *Arch. Biochem. Biophys.*, **324** 255-66.

Chen, X.Y., Wang, M.S., Chen, Y., Davisson, V.J. and Heinstein, P. (1996) Cloning and heterologous expression of a second (+)-delta-cadinene synthase from *Gossypium arboreum. J. Nat. Prod.*, **59** 944-51.

Choi, D., Ward, B.L. and Bostock, R.M. (1992) Differential induction and suppression of potato 3-hydroxy-3-methylglutaryl coenzyme A reductase genes in response to *Phytophthora infestans* and to its elicitor arachidonic acid. *Plant Cell,* **4** 1333-44.

Choi, D., Bostock, R.M., Avdiushko, S. and Hildebrand, D.F. (1994) Lipid-derived signals that discriminate wound- and pathogen-responsive isoprenoid pathways in plants: methyl jasmonate and the fungal elicitor arachidonic acid induce different 3-hydroxy-3-methylglutaryl-coenzyme A reductase genes and antimicrobial isoprenoids in *Solanum tuberosum* (L). *Proc. Natl. Acad. Sci. USA*, **91** 2329-33.

Christmann, J., Kreis, W. and Reinhard, E. (1993) Uptake, transport and storage of cardenolides in foxglove: cardenolide sinks and occurrence of cardenolides in the sieve tubes of *Digitalis lanata. Botanica Acta*, **106** 419-27.

Chye, M.-L., Tan, C.-T. and Chua, N.-H. (1992) Three genes encode 3-hydroxy-3-methylglutaryl-coenzyme a reductase in *Hevea brasiliensis*: *hmg1* and *hmg3* are differentially expressed. *Plant Mol. Biol.*, **19** 473-84.

Clastre, M., Bantignies, B., Feron, G., Soler, E. and Ambid, C. (1993) Purification and characterization of geranyl diphosphate synthase from *Vitis vinifera* (L.) cv Muscat de Frontignan cell cultures. *Plant Physiol.*, **102** 205-11.

Colby, S.M., Alonso, W.R., Katahira, E.J., McGarvey, D.J. and Croteau, R. (1993) 4*S*-Limonene synthase from the oil glands of spearmint (*Mentha spicata*). *J. Biol. Chem.*, **268** 23016-24.

Colby, S.M., Crock, J., Dowdlerizzo, B., Lemaux, P.G. and Croteau, R. (1998) Germacrene C synthase from *Lycopersicon esculentum* cv. Vfnt cherry tomato: cDNA isolation, characterization and bacterial expression of the multiple product sesquiterpene cyclase. *Proc. Natl. Acad. Sci. USA*, **95** 2216-21.

Connolly, J.D. and Hill, R.A. (1991) *Dictionary of Terpenoids*. Chapman and Hall, London.

Connolly, J.D. and Hill, R.A. (1997) Triterpenoids. *Natl. Prod. Rep.*, **14** 661-80.

Conolly, J.D., Hill, R.A. and Ngadjui, B.T. (1994) Triterpenoids. *Natl. Prod. Rep.*, **11** 467-92.

Corey, E.J., Matsuda, S.P.T. and Bartel, B. (1993) Isolation of an *Arabidopsis thaliana* gene encoding cycloartenol synthase by functional expression in a yeast mutant lacking lanosterol synthase by the use of a chromatographic screen. *Proc. Natl. Acad. Sci. USA*, **90** 11628-32.

Cornish, K. (1993) The separate roles of plant *cis* and *trans* prenyl transferases in *cis*-1,4-polyisoprene biosynthesis. *Eur. J. Biochem.*, **218** 267-71.

Cornish, K. and Backhaus, R.A. (1990) Rubber transferase activity in rubber particles of guayule. *Phytochemistry*, **29** 3809-13.

Cornish, K. and Siler, D.J. (1996) Characterization of *cis*-prenyl transferase activity localized in a buoyant fraction of rubber particles from *Ficus elastica* latex. *Plant Physiol. Biochem.*, **34** 377-84.

Crock, J., Wildung, M. and Croteau, R. (1997) Isolation and bacterial expression of a sesquiterpene synthase cDNA clone from peppermint (*Mentha x piperita*, L.) that produces the aphid alarm pheromone (*E*)-beta-farnesene. *Proc. Natl. Acad. Sci. USA*, **94** 12833-38.

Croteau, R. (1987) Biosynthesis and catabolism of monoterpenoids. *Chem. Rev.*, **87** 929-54.

Croteau, R. and Loomis, W.D. (1972) Biosynthesis of mono- and sesquiterpenes in peppermint from mevalonate-2-^{14}C. *Phytochemistry*, **11** 1055-66.

Croteau, R. and Purkett, P.T. (1989) Geranyl pyrophosphate synthase: characterization of the enzyme and evidence that this chain-length specific prenyltransferase is associated with monoterpene biosynthesis in sage (*Salvia officinalis*). *Arch. Biochem. Biophys.*, **271** 524-35.

Cutler, S., Ghassemian, M., Bonetta, D., Cooney, S. and McCourt, P. (1996) A protein, farnesyl transferase, involved in abscisic acid signal transduction in *Arabidopsis*. *Science*, **273** 1239-41.

Dale, S., Arro, M., Becerra, B., Morrice, N.G., Boronat, A., Hardie, D.G. and Ferrer A. (1995) Bacterial expression of the catalytic domain of 3-hydroxy-3-methylglutaryl-CoA reductase (isoform hmgr1) from *Arabidopsis thaliana* and its inactivation by phosphorylation at ser577 by *Brassica oleracea* 3-hydroxy-3-methylglutaryl-CoA reductase kinase. *Eur. J. Biochem.*, **233** 506-13.

Daraselia, N.D., Tarchevskaya, S. and Narita, J.O. (1996) The promoter for tomato 3-hydroxy-3-methylglutaryl coenzyme A reductase gene 2 has unusual regulatory elements that direct high-level expression. *Plant Physiol.*, **112** 727-33.

Dean, P.D.G., Exley, D. and Goodwin, T.W. (1971) Steroid estrogens in plants: re-estimation of estrone in pomegranate seeds. *Phytochemistry*, **10** 2215-16.

Dekraker, J.W., Franssen, M.C.R., Degroot, A., Konig, W.A. and Bouwmeester, H.J. (1998) (+)-Germacrene A biosynthesis: the committed step in the biosynthesis of bitter sesquiterpene lactones in chicory. *Plant Physiol.*, **117** 1381-92.

Delourme, D., Lacroute, F. and Karst, F. (1994) Cloning of an *Arabidopsis thaliana* cDNA coding for farnesyl diphosphate synthase by functional complementation in yeast. *Plant Mol. Biol.*, **26** 1867-73.

Denbow, C.J., Lang, S. and Cramer, C.L. (1996) The N terminal domain of tomato 3-hydroxy-3-methylglutaryl-CoA reductases: sequence, microsomal targeting and glycosylation. *J. Biol. Chem.*, **271** 9710-15.

Dicke, M. (1994) Local and systemic production of volatile herbivore-induced terpenoids: their role in plant-carnivore mutualism. *J. Plant Physiol.*, **143** 465-72.

Dicke, M., van Beek, T.A., Posthumus, M.A., Ben Dom, N., van Bokhoven, H. and de Groot, A. (1990) Isolation and identification of volatile kairomone that affects acarine predator-prey interactions: involvement of host plant in its production. *J. Chem. Ecol.*, **16** 381-96.

Dicke, M., van Baarlen, P., Wessels, R. and Dijkman, H. (1993) Herbivory induces systemic production of plant volatiles that attract predators of the herbivore: extraction of endogenous elicitor. *J. Chem. Ecol.*, **19** 581-99.

Disch, A., Hemmerlin, A., Bach, T.J. and Rohmer, M. (1998a) Mevalonate-derived isopentenyl diphosphate is the biosynthetic precursor of ubiquinone prenyl side chain in tobacco by-2 cells. *Biochem. J.*, **331** (Part 2) 615-21.

Disch, A., Schwender, J., Muller, C., Lichtenthaler, H.K. and Rohmer, M. (1998b) Distribution of the mevalonate and glyceraldehyde phosphate/pyruvate pathways for isoprenoid biosynthesis in unicellular algae and the cyanobacterium *Synechocystis* PCC-6714. *Biochem. J.*, **333** 381-88.

Dogbo, O. and Camara, B. (1987) Purification of isopentenyl pyrophosphate isomerase and geranylgeranyl pyrophosphate synthase from *Capsicum* chromoplasts by affinity chromatography. *Biochim. Biophys. Acta*, **920** 140-48.

Dudareva, N., Cseke, L., Blanc, V.M. and Pichersky, E. (1996) Evolution of floral scent in *Clarkia*: novel patterns of *S*-linalool synthase gene expression in the *C. breweri* flower. *Plant Cell*, **8** 1137-48.

Dudley, M.W., Dueber, M.T. and West, C.A. (1986) Biosynthesis of the macrocyclic diterpene casbene in castor bean (*Ricinus communis* L.) seedlings: changes in enzyme levels induced by fungal infection and intracellular localization of the pathway. *Plant Physiol.*, **81** 335-42.

Duport, C., Spagnoli, R., Degryse, E. and Pompon, D. (1998) Self-sufficient biosynthesis of pregnenolone and progesterone in engineered yeast. *Nature Biotechnol.*, **16** 186-89.

Duvold, T., Cali, P., Bravo, J.M. and Rohmer, M. (1997) Incorporation of 2-C-methyl-D-erythritol, a putative isoprenoid precursor in the mevalonate-independent pathway, into ubiquinone and menaquinone of *Escherichia coli*. *Tetrahedron Lett.*, **38** 6181-84.

Eisenreich, W., Menhard, B., Hylands, P.J., Zenk, M.H. and Bacher, A. (1996) Studies on the biosynthesis of taxol: the taxane carbon skeleton is not of mevalonoid origin. *Proc. Natl. Acad. Sci. USA*, **93** 6431-36.

Eisenreich, W., Sagner, S., Zenk, M.H. and Bacher, A. (1997) Monoterpenoid essential oils are not of mevalonoid origin. *Tetrahedron Lett.*, **38** 3889-92.

Enjuto, M., Balcells, L., Campos, N., Caelles, C., Arro, M. and Boronat, A. (1994) *Arabidopsis thaliana* contains two differentially expressed 3-hydroxy-3-methylglutaryl-CoA reductase genes, which encode microsomal forms of the enzyme. *Proc. Natl. Acad. Sci. USA*, **91** 927-931.

Enjuto, M., Lumbreras, V., Marin, C. and Boronat, A. (1995) Expression of the Arabidopsis *hmg2* gene, encoding 3-hydroxy-3-methylglutaryl coenzyme A reductase, is restricted to meristematic and floral tissues. *Plant Cell*, **7** 517-27.

Facchini, P.J. and Chappell, J. (1992) Gene family for an elicitor-induced sesquiterpene cyclase in tobacco. *Proc. Natl. Acad. Sci. USA*, **89** 11088-92.

Faust, T. (1994) Synthese und Charakterisierung von Uridin-5′-diphospho-α-D-fucose sowie Nachweis, partielle Reinigung und Charakterisierung einer UDP-fucose:Digitoxigenin 3-*O*-β-D-Fucosyltransferase aus *Digitalis lanata* EHRH. Doctoral Thesis, University of Tübingen.

Faust, T., Theurer, Ch., Eger, K. and Kreis, W. (1994) Synthesis of uridine 5′-(α-D-fucopyranosyl diphosphate) and (digitoxigenin-3β-yl)-β-D-fucopyranoside and enzymatic β-D-fucosylation of cardenolide genins in *Digitalis lanata*. *Bioorg. Chem.*, **22** 140-49.

Fellermeier, M. and Zenk, M.H. (1998) Prenylation of olivetolate by a hemp transferase yields cannabigerolic acid, the precursor of tetrahydrocannabinol. *FEBS Lett.*, **427** 283-85.

Finsterbusch, A., Lindemann, P. and Luckner, M. (1997) Partial purification of Δ5-3β-hydroxysteroid dehydrogenase/Δ5-Δ4-ketosteroid isomerase of cell cultures of *Digitalis lanata*, in *45th Annual Congress on Medicinal Plant Research*, Regensburg.

Flesch, G. and Rohmer, M. (1988) Prokaryotic hopanoids: the biosynthesis of the bacteriohopane skeleton. Formation of isoprenic units from two distinct acetate pools and a novel type of carbon/carbon linkage between triterpenes and D-ribose. *Eur. J. Biochem.*, **175** 405-11.

Fraga, B.M. (1997) Natural sesquiterpenoids. *Nat. Prod. Rep.*, **14** 145-62.

Franz, G. and Meier, H. (1964) Uridine diphosphate digitoxose from the leaves of *Digitalis purpurea* (L.). *Biochim. Biophys. Acta*, **184** 658-59.

Franz, G. and Hassid, W.Z. (1967) Biosynthese of digitoxose and glucose in the purpurea glycosides of *Digitalis purpurea* (L.). *Phytochemistry*, **6** 841-44.

Franz, G. and Meier, H. (1969) Untersuchungen zur Biosynthese der Digitalisglycoside. *Planta Med.*, **4** 396-400.

Frazier, J.L. (1986) The perception of plant allelochemicals that inhibit feeding, in *Molecular Aspects of Insect-Plant Associations* (eds. L.B. Brattsten and S. Ahmad) Plenum Press, New York, pp. 1-42.

Fulton, D.C., Kroon, P.A. and Threlfall, D.R. (1994) Enzymological aspects of the redirection of terpenoid biosynthesis in elicitor-treated cultures of *Tabernaemontana divaricata*. *Phytochemistry*, **35** 1183-86.

Funk, C. and Croteau, R. (1994) Diterpenoid resin acid biosynthesis in conifers: characterization of two cytochrome P_{450}-dependent monooxygenases and an aldehyde dehydrogenase involved in abietic acid biosynthesis. *Arch. Biochem. and Biophys.*, **308** 258-66.

Funk, C., Lewinsohn, E., Vogel, B.S., Steele, C.L. and Croteau, R. (1994) Regulation of oleoresinosis in grand fir (*Abies grandis*): coordinate induction of monoterpene and diterpene cyclases and two cytochrome P_{450},-dependent diterpenoid hydroxylases by stem wounding. *Plant Physiol.*, **106** 999-1005.

Gaisser, S. and Heide, L. (1996) Inhibition and regulation of shikonin biosynthesis in suspension cultures of *Lithospermum*. *Phytochemistry*, **41** 1065-72.

Galagovsky, L.R., Porto, A.M., Burton, G. and Gros, E.G. (1984) Biosynthesis of the bufadienolide ring of scillirosid in *Scilla maritima*. *Z. Naturforsch.*, **39c** 38-44.

Gärtner, D.E. and Seitz, H.U. (1993) Enzyme activities in cardenolide-accumulating, mixotrophic shoot cultures of *Digitalis purpurea* (L.). *J. Plant Physiol.*, **141** 269-75.

Gärtner, D.E., Wendroth, S. and Seitz, H.U. (1990) A stereospecific enzyme of the putative biosynthetic pathway of cardenolides: characterization of a progesterone 5β-reductase from leaves of *Digitalis purpurea*. *FEBS Lett.*, **271** 239-42.

Genschik, P., Criqui, M.-C., Parmentier, Y., Marbach, J., Durr, A., Fleck, J. and Jamet, E. (1992) Isolation and characterization of a cDNA encoding a 3-hydroxy-3-methylglutaryl coenzyme A reductase from *Nicotiana sylvestris*. *Plant Mol. Biol.*, **20** 337-41.

Gijzen, M., Lewinsohn, E. and Croteau, R. (1991) Characterization of the constitutive and wound-inducible monoterpene cyclases of grand fir (*Abies grandis*). *Arch. Biochem. Biophys.*, **289** 267-73.

Giner, J.L. and Djerassi, C. (1995) A reinvestigation of the biosynthesis of lanosterol in *Euphorbia lathyris*. *Phytochemistry*, **39** 333-35.

Gleizes, M., Pauly, G., Carde, J.P., Marpeau, A. and Bernard-Dagan, C. (1983) Monoterpene hydrocarbon biosynthesis by isolated leucoplasts of *Citrofortunella mitis*. *Planta*, **159** 373-81.

Goldstein, J.L. and Brown, M.S. (1990) Regulation of the mevalonate pathway. *Nature*, **343** 425-30.

Gondet, L., Weber, T., Maillot-Vernier, P., Benveniste, P. and Bach, T.J. (1992) Regulatory role of microsomal 3-hydroxy-3-methylglutaryl-coenzyme A reductase in a tobacco mutant that overproduces sterols. *Biochem. Biophys. Res. Commun.*, **186** 888-93.

Gondet, L., Bronner, R. and Benveniste, P. (1994) Regulation of sterol content in membranes by subcellular compartmentation of steryl-esters accumulating in a sterol-overproducing tobacco mutant. *Plant Physiol.*, **105** 509-18.

Goodwin, T.W. (1985) Biosynthesis of plant sterols, in *Sterols and Bile Acids* (eds. H. Danielsson and J. Sjövall), New Comprehensive Biochemistry, Elsevier Science Publishers B.V., **12** 175-198.

Gould, M.N. (1995) Prevention and therapy of mammary cancer by monoterpenes. *J. Cell. Biochem.*, Suppl. **22** 139-44.

Grausem, B., Chaubet, N., Gigot, C., Loper, J.C. and Benveniste, P. (1995) Functional expression of *Saccharomyces cerevisiae* CYP51A1 encoding lanosterol-14-demethylase in tobacco results in bypass of endogenous sterol biosynthetic pathway and resistance to an obtusifoliol-14-demethylase herbicide inhibitor. *Plant J.*, **7** 761-70.

Gray, J.C. (1987) Control of isoprenoid biosynthesis in higher plants. *Adv. Bot. Res.*, **14** 25-91.

Grayson, D.H. (1997) Monoterpenoids. *Nat. Prod. Rep.*, **14** 477-522.

Groeneveld, H.W., v. Tegelen, L.J.P. and Versluis, K. (1992) Cardenolide and neutral lipid biosynthesis from malonate in *Digitalis lanata. Planta Med.*, **58** 239-44.

Groeneveld, H.W., Van den Berg, B., Elings, J.C. and Seykens, D. (1990) Cardenolide biosynthesis from malonate in *Asclepias curassavica. Phytochemistry*, **29** 3479-86.

Grunwald, C. (1980) Steroids, in *Encyclopedia of Plant Physiology*, New Series, Vol. 8, Secondary plant products (eds. E.A. Bell and B.V. Charlwood) Springer-Verlag, Berlin, Heidelberg, New York, pp. 221-56.

Guo, Z., Severson. R.F. and Wagner, G.J. (1994) Biosynthesis of the diterpene *cis*-abienol in cell-free extracts of tobacco trichomes. *Arch. Biochem. Biophys.*, **308** 103-108.

Hagimoro, M., Matsumoto, T. and Obi, Y. (1982) Studies on the production of *Digitalis* cardenolides by plant tissue culture. II. Effect of light and plant growth substances on digitoxin formation by undifferentiated cells and shoot-forming cultures of *Digitalis purpurea* (L.) grown in liquid media. *Plant Physiol.*, **69** 653-56.

Hallahan, D.L., Dawson, G.W., West, J.M. and Wallsgrove, R.M. (1992) Cytochrome P_{450}-catalyzed monoterpene hydroxylation in *Nepeta mussinii. Plant Physiol. Biochem.*, **30** 435-43.

Hallahan, D.L., West, J.M., Wallsgrove, R.M., Smiley, D.W.M., Dawson, G.W., Pickett, J.A. and Hamilton, J.G.C. (1995) Purification and characterization of an acyclic monoterpene primary alcohol-NADP(+) oxidoreductase from catmint (*Nepeta racemosa*). *Arch. Biochem. Biophys.*, **318** 105-12.

Hallahan, D.L., West, J.M., Smiley, D.W.M. and Pickett, J.A. (1998) Nepetalactol oxidoreductase in trichomes of the catmint *Nepeta racemosa. Phytochemistry*, **48** 421-27.

Hamada, H., Konishi, H., Williams, H.J. and Scott, A.I. (1991) Biotransformation of testosterone isomers by a green cell suspension cultures of *Marchantia polymorpha. Phytochemistry*, **30** 2269-70.

Hanley, K.M., Voegeli, U. and Chappell, J. (1992) A study of the isoprenoid pathway in elicitor-treated tobacco cell suspension cultures, in *Secondary-Metabolite Biosynthesis and Metabolism* (eds. R.J. Petroski and S.P. McCormick) Plenum Press, New York, pp. 329-36.

Hanson, J.R. (1997) Diterpenoids. *Nat. Prod. Rep.*, **14** 245-58.

Harborne, J.B. and Tomas-Barberan, F.A. (eds.) (1991) *Ecological Chemistry and Biochemistry of Plant Terpenoids*. Clarendon Press, Oxford, pp. 439.

Hedden, P. and Kamiya, Y. (1997) Gibberellin biosynthesis: enzymes, genes and their regulation. *Annu. Rev. Plant Physiol. Plant Mol. Biol.*, **48** 431-60.

Heide, L. and Berger, U. (1989) Partial purification and properties of geranyl pyrophosphate synthase from *Lithospermum erythrorhizon* cell cultures. *Arch. Biochem. Biophys.*, **273** 331-38.

Heintze, A., Goerlach, J., Leuschner, C., Hoppe, P., Hagelstein, P., Schulze-Siebert, D. and Schultz, G. (1990) Plastidic isoprenoid synthesis during chloroplast development: change from metabolic autonomy to division-of-labor stage. *Plant Physiol.*, **93** 1121-27.

Heintze, A., Riedel, A., Aydogdu, S. and Schultz, G. (1994) Formation of chloroplast isoprenoids from pyruvate and acetate by chloroplasts from young spinach plants: evidence for a mevalonate pathway in immature chloroplasts. *Plant Physiol. Biochem.*, **32** 791-97.

Helliwell, C.A., Sheldon, C.C., Olive, M.R., Walker, A.R., Zeevaart, J.A.D., Peacock, W.J. and Dennis, E.S. (1998) Cloning of the *Arabidopsis ent*-kaurene oxidase gene *ga3*. *Proc. Natl. Acad. Sci. USA*, **95** 9019-24.

Henry, M., Rahier, A. and Taton, M. (1992) Effect of gypsogenin 3-*O*-glucuronide pretratment of *Gypsophila paniculata and Saponaria officinalis* cell suspension cultures on the activities of microsomal 2,3-oxidosqualene cycloartenol and amyrin cyclases. *Phytochemistry*, **31** 3855-59.

Hezari, M. and Croteau, R. (1997) Taxol biosynthesis: an update. *Planta Med.*, **63** 291-95.

Hezari, M., Ketchum, R.E.B., Gibson, D.M. and Croteau, R. (1997) Taxol production and taxadiene synthase activity in *Taxus canadensis* cell suspension cultures. *Arch. Biochem. Biophys.*, **337** 185-90.

Horbach, S., Sahm, H. and Welle, R. (1993) Isoprenoid biosynthesis in bacteria: two different pathways? *FEMS Microbiol. Lett.*, **111** 135-40.

Hoshino, T., Yamaura, T., Imaishi, H., Chida, M., Yoshizawa, Y., Higashi, K., Ohkawa, H. and Mizutani, J. (1995) 5-*Epi*-aristolochene 3-hydroxylase from green pepper. *Phytochemistry*, **38** 609-13.

Hugueney, P., Bouvier, F., Badillo, A., Quennemet, J., Dharlingue, A. and Camara, B. (1996) Developmental and stress regulation of gene expression for plastid and cytosolic isoprenoid pathways in pepper fruits. *Plant Physiol.*, **111** 619-26.

Husselstein, T., Gachotte, D., Desprez, T., Bard, M. and Benvensite, P. (1996) Transformation of *Saccharomyces cerevisiae* with a cDNA encoding a sterol C-methyltransferase from *Arabidopsis thaliana* results in the synthesis of 24-ethyl sterols. *FEBS Lett.*, **381** 87-92.

Inoue, K. and Ebizuka, Y. (1996) Purification and characterization of furostanol glycoside 26-*O*-β-glucosidase from *Costus speciosus* rhizomes. *FEBS Lett.*, **378** 157-60.

Inoue, K., Shibuya, M., Yamamoto, K. and Ebizuka, Y. (1996) Molecular cloning and bacterial expression of a cDNA encoding furostanol glycoside 26-*O*-beta-glucosidase of *Costus speciosus*. *FEBS Lett.*, **389** 273-77.

Jansen, B.J.M. and de Groot, A. (1991) The occurrence and biological activity of drimane sesquiterpenoids. *Natl. Prod. Rep.*, **8** 309-18.

Ji, W., Benedict, C.R. and Foster, M.A. (1993) Seasonal variations in rubber biosynthesis, 3-hydroxy-3-methylglutaryl-coenzyme A reductase and rubber transferase activities in *Parthenium argentatum* in the Chihuahuan Desert. *Plant Physiol.*, **103** 535-42.

Joly, A. and Edwards, P.A. (1993) Effect of site-directed mutagenesis of conserved aspartate and arginine residues upon farnesyl diphosphate synthase activity. *J. Biol. Chem.*, **268** 26983-89.

Joost, O., Bianchini, G., Bell, A.A., Benedict, C.R. and Magill, C.W. (1995) Differential induction of 3-hydroxy-3-methylglutaryl CoA reductase in two cotton species following inoculation with *Verticillium*. *Mol. Plant-Microbe Interact.*, **8** 880-85.

Kandzia, R., Grimm, R., Eckerskorn, C., Lindemann, P. and Luckner, M. (1998) Purification and characterization of lanatoside 15′-*O*-acetylesterase from *Digitalis lanata* Ehrh. *Planta*, **204** 383-89.

Kato, H., Kodama, O. and Akatsuka, T. (1995) Characterization of an inducible P_{450} hydroxylase involved in the rice diterpene phytoalexin biosynthetic pathway. *Arch. Biochem. Biophys.*, **316** 707-12.

Kawaguchi, K., Hirotani, M., Yoshikawa, T. and Furuya, T. (1990) Biotransformation of digitoxigenin by ginseng hairy root cultures. *Phytochemistry*, **29** 837-44.

Keene, C.K. and Wagner, G.J. (1985) Direct demonstration of duvatrienediol biosynthesis in glandular heads of tobacco trichomes. *Plant Physiol.*, **79** 1026-32.

Keller, H., Czernic, P., Ponchet, M., Ducrot, P.H., Back, K., Chappell, J., Ricci, P. and Marco, Y. (1998a) Sesquiterpene cyclase is not a determining factor for elicitor-induced and pathogen-induced capsidiol accumulation in tobacco. *Planta*, **205** 467-76.

Keller, Y., Bouvier, F., Dharlingue, A. and Camara, B. (1998b) Metabolic compartmentation of plastid prenyllipid biosynthesis: evidence for the involvement of a multifunctional geranylgeranyl reductase. *Eur. J. Biochem.*, **251** 413-17.

Kerr, R.G., Kelly, K. and Schulman, A. (1995) A novel biosynthetic route to pregnanes in the marine sponge *Amphimedon compressa. J. Nat. Prod. — Lloydia*, **58** 1077-80.

Kim, K.K., Yamashita, H., Sawa, Y. and Shibata, H. (1996) A high activity of 3-hydroxy-3-methylglutaryl coenzyme a reductase in chloroplasts of *Stevia rebaudiana* Bertoni. *Biosci. Biotech. Biochem.*, **60** 685-86.

Kleinig, H. (1989) The role of plastids in isoprenoid biosynthesis. *Annu. Rev. Plant Physiol. Plant Mol. Biol.*, **40** 39-59.

Knoss, W., Reuter, B. and Zapp, J. (1997) Biosynthesis of the labdane diterpene marrubiin in *Marrubium vulgare* via a non-mevalonate pathway. *Biochem. J.*, **326** (Part 2) 449-54.

Korth, K.L., Stermer, B.A., Bhattacharyya, M.K. and Dixon, R.A. (1997) HMG-CoA reductase gene families that differentially accumulate transcripts in potato tubers are developmentally expressed in floral tissues. *Plant Mol. Biol.*, **33** 545-51.

Kreis, W. and May, U. (1990) Cardenolide glucosyltransferases and glucohydrolases in leaves and cell cultures of three *Digitalis* (Scrophulariaceae) species. *J. Plant Physiol.*, **136** 247-52.

Kreis, W. and Reinhard, E. (1990a) Production of deacetyllanatoside C by *Digitalis lanata* cell cultures, in *Progress in plant cellular and molecular biology* (eds H.J.J. Nijkamp, L.H.W. van der Plaas and J. van Aartrijk), Kluwer Academic Publishers, Dordrech, Boston, London, pp. 706-11.

Kreis, W. and Reinhard, E. (1990b) 12$-Hydroxylation of digitoxin by suspension-cultured *Digitalis lanata* cells: production of digoxin in 20 litre and 300 litre airlift bioreactors. *J Biotechnol.*, **16** 123-36.

Kreis, W., May, U. and Reinhard, E. (1986) UDP:glucose:digitoxin 16′-*O*-glucosyltransferase from suspension-cultured *Digitalis lanata* cells. *Plant Cell Rep.*, **5** 442-45.

Kreis, W., Hoelz, H., Sutor, R. and Reinhard, E. (1993) Cellular organization of cardenolide biotransformation in *Digitalis grandiflora. Planta*, **191** 246-51.

Kreis, W., Mangelsdorf, C., Stuhlemmer, U. and Haussmann, W. (1997) Acetoxypregnanes and acetylated cardenolides as precursors of cardiac glycosides in *Digitalis lanata* shoot cultures and the occurrence of esterases hydrolysing acetoxycardenolides, in *45th Annual Congress on Medicinal Plant Research*, Regensburg.

Kreis, W., Hensel, A. and Stuhlemmer, U. (1998) Cardenolide biosynthesis in foxglove. *Planta Med.*, (in press).

Kuntz, M., Roemer, S., Suire, C., Hugueney, P., Weil, J.H., Schantz, R. and Camara, B. (1992) Identification of a cDNA for the plastid-located geranylgeranyl pyrophosphate synthase from *Capsicum annuum*: correlative increase in enzyme activity and transcript level during fruit ripening. *Plant J.*, **2** 25-34.

Kurz, W.G.W. and Constabel, F. (1979) Plant cell cultures, a potential source of pharmaceuticals. *Adv. Appl. Microbiol.*, **25** 209-40.

Kushiro, T., Ohno, Y., Shibuya, M. and Ebizuka, Y. (1997) *In vitro* conversion of 2,3-oxidosqualene into dammarenediol by *Panax ginseng* microsomes. *Biol. Pharmaceut. Bull.*, **20** 292-94.

Kuzma, J. and Fall, R. (1993) Leaf isoprene emission rate is dependent on leaf development and the level of isoprene synthase. *Plant Physiol.*, **101** 435-40.

Kuzuyama, T., Takahashi, S., Watanabe, H. and Seto, H. (1998) Direct formation of 2-C-methyl-D-erythritol 4-phosphate from 1-deoxy-D-xylulose 5-phosphate by 1-deoxy-D-xylulose 5-phosphate reductoisomerase, a new enzyme in the non-mevalonate pathway to isopentenyl diphosphate. *Tetrahedron Lett.*, **39** 4509-12.

Laferriere, A. and Beyer, P. (1991) Purification of geranylgeranyl diphosphate synthase from *Sinapis alba* etioplasts. *Biochim. Biophys. Acta*, **1077** 167-72.

LaFever, R.E., Vogel, B.S. and Croteau, R. (1994) Diterpenoid resin acid biosynthesis in conifers: enzymatic cyclization of geranylgeranyl pyrophosphate to abietadiene, the precursor of abietic acid. *Arch. Biochem. Biophys.*, **313** 139-49.

Laflamme, P., Khouri, H., Gulick, P. and Ibrahim, R. (1993) Enzymatic prenylation of isoflavones in white lupin. *Phytochemistry*, **34** 147-51.

Lamb, D.C., Kelly, D.E. and Kelly, S.L. (1998) Molecular diversity of sterol 14α-demethylase substrates in plants, fungi and humans. *FEBS Lett.*, **425** 263-65.

Lange, B.M., Severin, K., Bechthold, A. and Heide, L. (1998a) Regulatory role of microsomal 3-hydroxy-3-methylglutaryl-coenzyme A reductase for shikonin biosynthesis in *Lithospermum erythrorhizon* cell suspension cultures. *Planta*, **204** 234-41.

Lange, B.M., Wildung, M.R., McCaskill, D. and Croteau, R. (1998b) A family of transketolases that directs isoprenoid biosynthesis via a mevalonate-independent pathway. *Proc. Natl. Acad. Sci. USA*, **95** 2100-104.

Lange, T., Hedden, P. and Graebe, J.E. (1994) Expression cloning of a gibberellin 20-oxidase, a multifunctional enzyme involved in gibberellin biosynthesis. *Proc. Natl. Acad. Sci. USA*, **91** 8552-56.

Langenheim, J.H. (1994) Higher plant terpenoids: a phytocentric overview of their ecological roles. *J. Chem. Ecol.*, **20** 1223-80.

Learned, R.M. and Fink, G.R. (1989) 3-Hydroxy-3-methylglutaryl-coenzyme A reductase from *Arabidopsis thaliana* is structurally distinct from the yeast and animal enzymes. *Proc. Natl. Acad. Sci. USA*, **86** 2779-83.

Lerdau, M., Guenther, A. and Monson, R. (1997) Plant production and emission of volatile organic compounds. *Bioscience*, **47** 373-83.

Lesburg, C.A., Zhai, G.Z., Cane, D.E. and Christianson, D.W. (1997) Crystal structure of pentalenene synthase: mechanistic insights on terpenoid cyclization reactions in biology. *Science*, **277** 1820-24.

Li, C.P. and Larkins, B.A. (1996) Identification of a maize endosperm-specific cDNA encoding farnesyl pyrophosphate synthetase. *Gene*, **171** 193-96.

Lichtenthaler, H.K., Rohmer, M. and Schwender, J. (1997a) Two independent biochemical pathways for isopentenyl diphosphate and isoprenoid biosynthesis in higher plants. *Physiologia Plantarum*, **101** 643-52.

Lichtenthaler, H.K., Schwender, J., Disch, A. and Rohmer, M. (1997b) Biosynthesis of isoprenoids in higher plant chloroplasts proceeds via a mevalonate-independent pathway. *FEBS Lett.*, **400** 271-74.

Lim, C.O., Kim, H.Y., Kim, M.G., Lee, S.I., Chung, W.S., Park, S.H., Hwang, I.H. and Cho, M.J. (1996) Expressed sequence tags of chinese cabbage flower bud cDNA. *Plant Physiol.*, **111** 577-88.

Lindemann, P. and Luckner, M. (1997) Biosynthesis of pregnane derivatives in somatic embryos of *Digitalis lanata*. *Phytochemistry*, **46** 507-13.

Lois, L.M., Campos, N., Putra, S.R., Danielsen, K., Rohmer, M. and Boronat, A. (1998) Cloning and characterization of a gene from *Escherichia coli* encoding a transketolase-like enzyme that catalyzes the synthesis of D-1-deoxyxylulose 5-phosphate, a common precursor for isoprenoid, thiamin and pyridoxol biosynthesis. *Proc. Natl. Acad. Sci. USA*, **95** 2105-10.

Loreto, F., Forster, A., Durr, M., Csiky, O. and Seufert, G. (1998) On the monoterpene emission under heat stress and on the increased thermotolerance of leaves of *Quercus ilex* (L.) fumigated with selected monoterpenes. *Plant Cell Environ.*, **21** 101-107.

Luckner, M. (1990) *Secondary Metabolism in Microorganisms, Plants, and Animals.* 3rd Edition, Gustav Fischer Verlag, Jena.

Luckner, M. and Diettrich, B. (1985) Formation of cardenolides in cell and organ cultures of *Digitalis lanata*, in *Primary and Secondary Metabolism of Plant Cell Cultures* (eds. K.H. Neumann, W. Barz and E. Reinhard), Springer-Verlag, Berlin, Heidelberg, New York, pp. 154-63.

Luetke-Brinkhaus, F. and Kleinig, H. (1987) Formation of isopentenyl diphosphate via mevalonate does not occur within etioplasts and etiochloroplasts of mustard (*Sinapis alba* L.) seedlings. *Planta*, **171** 401-406.

Lupien, S., Karp, F., Ponnamperuma, K., Wildung, M. and Croteau, R. (1995) Cytochrome P_{450} limonene hydroxylases of *Mentha* species. *Drug Metab. Drug Interact.*, **12** 245-60.

Luta, M., Hensel, A. and Kreis, W. (1997) β-D-Fucosidase and other cardenolideglycoside-modifying enzymes in *Digitalis lanata* EHRH, in *45th Annual Congress on Medicinal Plant Research*, Regensburg.

Luta, M., Hensel, A. and Kreis, W. (1998) Synthesis of cardenolide glycosides and putative biosynthesis precursors of cardenolide glycosides. *Steroids*, **63** 44-49.

MacKintosh, R.W., Davies, S.P., Clarke, P.R., Weekes, J., Gillespie, J.G., Gibb, B.J. and Hardie, D.G. (1992) Evidence for a protein kinase cascade in higher plants: 3-hydroxy-3-methylglutaryl-CoA reductase kinase. *Eur. J. Biochem.*, **209** 923-31.

Mahato, S.B., Nandy, A.K. and Roy, G. (1992) Triterpenoids, *Phytochemistry*, **31** 2199-49

Maier, M.S., Seldes, A.M. and Gros, E.G. (1986) Biosynthesis of the butenolide ring of cardenolides in *Digitalis purpurea. Phytochemistry*, **25** 1327-29.

Maldonado-Mendoza, I.E., Burnett, R.J. and Nessler, C.L. (1992) Nucleotide sequence of a cDNA encoding 3-hydroxy-3-methylglutaryl coenzyme A reductase from *Catharanthus roseus. Plant Physiol.*, **100** 1613-14.

Marrero, P.F., Poulter, C.D. and Edwards, P.A. (1992) Effects of site-directed mutagenesis of the highly conserved aspartate residues in domain II of farnesyl diphosphate synthase activity. *J. Biol. Chem.*, **267** 21873-78.

Matsushita, Y., Kang, W. and Charlwood, B.V. (1996) Cloning and analysis of a cDNA encoding farnesyl diphosphate synthase from *Artemisia annua. Gene*, **172** 207-209.

Mau, C.J.D. and West, C.A. (1994) Cloning of casbene synthase cDNA: evidence for conserved structural features among terpenoid cyclases in plants. *Proc. Natl. Acad. Sci. USA*, **91** 8497-501.

McCaskill, D. and Croteau, R. (1995) Monoterpene and sesquiterpene biosynthesis in glandular trichomes of peppermint (*Mentha* × *piperita*) rely exclusively on plastid-derived isopentenyl diphosphate. *Planta*, **197** 49-56.

McGarvey, D.J. and Croteau, R. (1995) Terpenoid metabolism. *Plant Cell*, **7** 1015-26.

Meiss, P., Sepasgosarian, J. and Reinhard, E. (1986) Production of β-methyldiginatin by *Digitalis* cell cultures. *Planta Med.*, **52** 511-13.

Mettal, U., Boland, W., Beyer, P. and Kleinig, H. (1988) Biosynthesis of monoterpene hydrocarbons by isolated chromoplasts from daffodil flowers. *Eur. J. Biochem.*, **170** 613-16.

Mihaliak, C.A., Karp, F. and Croteau, R. (1993) Cytochrome P_{450} terpene hydroxylases, in *Enzymes of Secondary Metabolism* (ed. P.J. Lea), Academic Press, London, pp. 261-79.

Milek, F., Reinhard, E. and Kreis, W. (1997) Influence of precursors and inhibitors of the sterol pathway on sterol and cardenolide metabolism in *Digitalis lanata* Ehrh. *Plant Physiol Biochem.*, **35** 111-21.

Monfar, M., Caelles, C., Balcells, L., Ferrer, A., Hegardt, F.G. and Boronat, A. (1990) Molecular cloning and characterization of plant 3-hydroxy-3-methylglutaryl coenzyme A reductase, in *Biochemistry of the Mevalonic Acid Pathway to Terpenoids* (eds. G.H.N. Towers and H.A. Stafford), Plenum Press, New York, pp. 83-97.

Monson, R., Jaeger, C.H., Adams, W.W.I., Driggers, E.M., Silver, G.M. and Fall, R. (1992) Relationships among isoprene emission rate, photosynthesis and isoprene synthase activity as influenced by temperature. *Plant Physiol.*, **98** 1175-80.

Montamat, F., Guilloton, M., Karst, F. and Delrot, S. (1995) Isolation and characterization of a cDNA encoding *Arabidopsis thaliana* 3-hydroxy-3-methylglutaryl-coenzyme A synthase. *Gene*, **167** 197-201.

Morehead, T.A., Biermann, B.J., Crowell, D.N. and Randall, S.K. (1995) Changes in protein isoprenylation during the growth of suspension-cultured tobacco cells. *Plant Physiol.*, **109** 277-84.

Muhlenweg, A., Melzer, M., Li, S.M. and Heide, L. (1998) 4-Hydroxybenzoate 3-geranyltransferase from *Lithospermum erythrorhizon*: purification of a plant membrane-bound prenyltransferase. *Planta*, **205** 407-13.

Nabeta, K., Ishikawa, T., Kawae, T. and Okuyama, H. (1995) Biosynthesis of heteroscyphic acid a in cell cultures of *Heteroscyphus planus*: nonequivalent labelling of C-5 units in diterpene biosynthesis. *J. Chem. Soc.: Series Chemical Communications*, **6** 681-82.

Nakagawara, S., Nakamura, N., Guo, Z.-J., Sumitani, K., Katoh, K. and Ohta, Y. (1993) Enhanced formation of a constitutive sesquiterpenoid in cultured cells of a liverwort, *Calypogeia granulata* Inoue during elicitation: effects of vanadate. *Plant Cell Physiol.*, **34** 421-29.

Narita, J.O. and Gruissem, W. (1989) Tomato hydroxymethylglutaryl-CoA reductase is required early in fruit development but not during ripening. *Plant Cell*, **1** 181-90.

Nelson, S.D., McClanahan, R.H., Knebel, N., Thomassen, D., Gordon, W.P. and Oishi, S. (1992) The metabolism of (*R*)-(+)-pulegone, a toxic monoterpene, in *Secondary-Metabolite Biosynthesis and Metabolism* (eds. R.J. Petroski and S.P. McCormick), Plenum Press, New York, pp. 287-96.

Nelson, A.J., Doerner, P.W., Zhu, Q. and Lamb, C.J. (1994) Isolation of a monocot 3-hydroxy-3-methylglutaryl coenzyme A reductase gene that is elicitor-inducible. *Plant Mol. Biol.*, **25** 401-12.

Obatomi, D.K. and Bach, P.H. (1998) Biochemistry and toxicology of the diterpenoid glycoside atractyloside. *Food Chem. Toxicol.*, **36** 335-46.

Ohnuma, S., Hirooka, K., Hemmi, H., Ishida, C., Ohto, C. and Nishino, T. (1996a) Conversion of product specificity of archaebacterial geranylgeranyl-diphosphate synthase: identification of essential amino acid residues for chain length determination of prenyltransferase reaction. *J. Biol. Chem.*, **271** 18831-37.

Ohnuma, S., Narita, K., Nakazawa, T., Ishida, C., Takeuchi, Y., Ohto, C. and Nishino, T. (1996b) A role of the amino acid residue located on the fifth position before the first aspartate-rich motif of farnesyl diphosphate synthase on determination of the final product. *J. Biol. Chem.*, **271** 30748-54.

Ohnuma, S.I., Nakazawa, T., Hemmi, H., Hallberg, A.M., Koyama, T., Ogura, K. and Nishino, T. (1996c) Conversion from farnesyl diphosphate synthase to geranylgeranyl diphosphate synthase by random chemical mutagenesis. *J. Biol. Chem.*, **271** 10087-95.

Ohnuma, S., Hirooka, K., Ohto, C. and Nishino, T. (1997) Conversion from archaeal geranylgeranyl diphosphate synthase to farnesyl diphosphate synthase: two amino acids before the first aspartate-rich motif solely determine eukaryotic farnesyl diphosphate synthase activity. *J. Biol. Chem.*, **272** 5192-98.

Oosterhaven, K., Hartmans, K.J. and Huizing, H.J. (1993) Inhibition of potato (*Solanum tuberosum*) sprout growth by the monoterpene *S*-carvone: reduction of 3-hydroxy-3-

3methylglutaryl coenzyme A reductase activity without effect on its mRNA level. *J. Plant Physiol.*, **141** 463-69.

Paczkowski, C. and Woiciechowski, Z.A. (1994) Glucosylation and galactosylation of diosgenin and solasodine by soluble glycosyltransferase(s) from *Solanum melongena* leaves. *Phytochemistry*, **35** 1429-34.

Paczkowski, C., Kalinowska, M. and Woiciechowski, Z.A. (1997) UDP-glucose:solasodine glucosyltransferase from eggplant (*Solanum melongena* L.) leaves: partial purification and characterization. *Acta Biochim. Polonica*, **44** 43-54.

Pan, Z.Q., Herickhoff, L. and Backhaus, R.A. (1996) Cloning, characterization and heterologous expression of cDNAs for farnesyl diphosphate synthase from the guayule rubber plant reveals that this prenyltransferase occurs in rubber particles. *Arch. Biochem. Biophys.*, **332** 196-204.

Paper, D.H. and Franz, G. (1990) Biotransformation of 5βH-pregnan-3βol-20-one and cardenolides in cell suspension cultures of *Nerium oleander* (L.). *Plant Cell Rep.*, **8** 651-55.

Pare, P.W. and Tumlinson, J.H. (1997) Induced synthesis of plant volatiles. *Nature*, **385** 30-31.

Park, H., Denbow, C.J. and Cramer, C.L. (1992) Structure and nucleotide sequence of tomato *HMG2* encoding 3-hydroxy-3-methylglutaryl coenzyme A reductase. *Plant Mol. Biol.*, **20** 327-31.

Pascal, S., Taton, M. and Rahier, A. (1990) Oxidative C4-demethylation of 24-methylenecycloartanol by a cyanide-sensitive enzymatic system from higher plant microsomes. *Biochem. Biophys. Res. Commun.*, **172** 98-106.

Pascal, S., Taton, M. and Rahier, A. (1993) Plant sterol biosynthesis: identification and characterization of two distinct microsomal oxidative enzymatic systems involved in sterol C4-demethylation. *J. Biol. Chem.*, **268** 11639.

Pascal, S., Taton, M. and Rahier, A. (1994) Plant sterol biosynthesis: identification of a NADPH-dependent sterone reductase involved in sterol 4-demethylation. *Arch. Biochem. Biophys.*, **312** 260-71.

Petersen, M. and Seitz, H.U. (1985) Cytochrome P_{450}-dependent digitoxin 12β-hydroxylase from cell cultures of *Digitalis lanata*. *FEBS Lett.*, **188** 11-14.

Petersen, M., Seitz, H.U., Alfermann, A.W. and Reinhard, E. (1987) Immobilization of digitoxin 12β-hydroxylase, a cytochrome P_{450}-dependent enzyme, from cell cultures of *Digitalis lanata* EHRH. *Plant Cell Rep.*, **6** 200-203.

Petersen, M., Seitz, H.U. and Reinhard, E. (1988) Characterization and localization of digitoxin 12β hydroxylase form cell cultures of *Digitalis lanata* EHRH. *Z. Naturforsch.*, **43c** 199-206.

Phillips, A.L., Ward, D.A., Uknes, S., Appleford, N.E.J., Lange, T., Huttly, A.K., Gaskin, P., Graebe, J.E. and Hedden, P. (1995) Isolation and expression of three gibberellin 20-oxidase cDNA clones from *Arabidopsis*. *Plant Physiol.*, **108** 1049-57.

Pichersky, E., Raguso, R.A., Lewinsohn, E. and Croteau, R. (1994) Floral scent production in *Clarkia* (Onagraceae). I. Localization and developmental modulation of monoterpene emission and linalool synthase activity. *Plant Physiol.*, **106** 1533-40.

Pichersky, E., Lewinsohn, E. and Croteau, R. (1995) Purification and characterization of *S*-linalool synthase, an enzyme involved in the production of floral scent in *Clarkia breweri*. *Arch. Biochem. Biophys.*, **316** 803-807.

Piel, J., Donath, J., Bandemer, K. and Boland, W. (1998) Mevalonate-independent biosynthesis of terpenoid volatiles in plants: induced and constitutive emission of volatiles. *Angew. Chemie*, (in press).

Poulter, C.D. and Rilling, H.C. (1981) Prenyl transferases and isomerase, in *Biosynthesis of Isoprenoid Compounds* (eds. J.W. Porter and S.L. Spurgeon), John Wiley and Sons, New York, pp. 161-224.

Pras, N. (1990) Bioconversion of precursors occurring in plants and related synthetic compounds, in *Progress in Plant Cellular and Molecular Biology* (eds. H.J.J. Nijkamp,

L.H.W. van der Plaas and J. van Aartrijk), Kluwer Academic Publishers, Dordrech, Boston, London, pp. 640-49.

Prescott, A.G. and John, P. (1996) Dioxygenases: molecular structure and role in plant metabolism. *Annu. Rev. Plant Physiol. Plant Mol. Biol.*, **47** 245-71.

Qian, D.Q., Zhou, D.F., Ju, R., Cramer, C.L. and Yang, Z.B. (1996) Protein farnesyltransferase in plants: molecular characterization and involvement in cell cycle control. *Plant Cell*, **8** 2381-94.

Rahier, A. and Taton, M. (1986) The 14α-demethylation of obtusifoliol by a cytochrome P_{450} monooxygenase from higher plants microsomes. *Biochem. Biophys. Res. Commun.*, **140** 1064-72.

Rahier, A. and Taton, M. (1992) Plant sterol biosynthesis. 7. Oxoobtusifoliol analogues as potential selective inhibitors of cytochrome P_{450}-dependent obtusifoliol 14α-demethylase. *Biochim. Biophys. Acta*, **1125** 215-22.

Rahier, A. and Taton, M. (1997) Fungicides as tools in studying postsqualene sterol synthesis in plants. *Pest. Biochem. Physiol.*, **57** 1-27.

Rahier, A., Smith, M. and Taton, M. (1997) The role of cytochrome b_5 in 4α-methyl-oxidation and C5(6) desaturation of plant sterol precursors. *Biochem. Biophys. Res. Commun.*, **236** 434-37.

Rajaonarivony, J.I.M., Gershenzon, J. and Croteau, R. (1992) Characterization and mechanism of (4*S*)-limonene synthase, a monoterpene cyclase from the glandular trichomes of peppermint (*Mentha × piperita*). *Arch. Biochem. Biophys.*, **296** 49-57.

Ramosvaldivia, A.C., Vanderheijden, R. and Verpoorte, R. (1997a) Elicitor-mediated induction of anthraquinone biosynthesis and regulation of isopentenyl diphosphate isomerase and farnesyl diphosphate synthase activities in cell suspension cultures of *Cinchona robusta* How. *Planta*, **203** 155-61.

Ramosvaldivia, A.C., Vanderheijden, R. and Verpoorte, R. (1997b) Isopentenyl diphosphate isomerase, a core enzyme in isoprenoid biosynthesis: a review of its biochemistry and function. *Nat. Prod. Rep.*, **14** 591-603.

Ramosvaldivia, A.C., Vanderheijden, R., Verpoorte, R. and Camara, B. (1997c) Purification and characterization of two isoforms of isopentenyl-diphosphate isomerase from elicitor-treated *Cinchona robusta* cells. *Eur. J. Biochem.*, **249** 161-70.

Ramosvaldivia, A.C., Vanderheijden, R. and Verpoorte, R. (1998) Isopentenyl diphosphate isomerase and prenyltransferase activities in rubiaceous and apocynaceous cultures. *Phytochemistry*, **48** 961-69.

Re, E.B., Jones, D. and Learned, R.M. (1995) Co-expression of native and introduced genes reveals cryptic regulation of HMG-CoA reductase expression in *Arabidopsis*. *Plant J.*, **7** 771-84.

Re, E.B., Brugger, S. and Learned, M. (1997) Genetic and biochemical analysis of the transmembrane domain of *Arabidopsis* 3-hydroxy-3-methylglutaryl coenzyme A reductase. *J. Cell. Biochem.*, **65** 443-59.

Reinhard, E. and Alfermann, A.W. (1980) Biotransformation by plant cell cultures. *Adv. Biochem. Eng.*, **16** 49-83.

Reinhard, E., Boy, M. and Kaiser, F. (1975) Umwandlung von *Digitalis*-Glykosiden durch Zellsuspensionskulturen. *Planta Med.*, (Suppl.) **1975** 163-68.

Reinhard, E., Kreis, W., Barthlen, U. and Helmbold, U. (1989) Semicontinuous cultivation of *Digitalis lanata* cells: production of β-methyldigoxin in a 300 L airlift bioreactor. *Biotechnol. Bioeng.*, **34** 502-508.

Rieder, C., Strauss, G., Fuchs, G., Arigoni, D., Bacher, A. and Eisenreich, W. (1998) Biosynthesis of the diterpene verrucosan-2-beta-ol in the phototrophic eubacterium *Chloroflexusaurantiacus*: a retrobiosynthetic NMR study. *J. Biol. Chem.*, **273** 18099-108.

Riou, C., Tourte, Y., Lacroute, F. and Karst, F. (1994) Isolation and characterization of a cDNA encoding *Arabidopsis thaliana* mevalonate kinase by genetic complementation in yeast. *Gene*, **148** 293-97.

Rogers, L.J., Shah, S.P.J. and Goodwin, T.W. (1968) Compartmentation of biosynthesis of terpenoids in green plants. *Photosynthetica*, **2** 184-207.

Rohmer, M., Knani, M., Simonin, P., Sutter, B. and Sahm, H. (1993) Isoprenoid biosynthesis in bacteria: a novel pathway for the early steps leading to isopentenyl diphosphate. *Biochem. J.*, **295** 517-24.

Rohmer, M., Seemann, M., Horbach, S., Bringermeyer, S. and Sahm, H. (1996) Glyceraldehyde 3-phosphate and pyruvate as precursors of isoprenic units in an alternative non-mevalonate pathway for terpenoid biosynthesis. *J. Am. Chem. Soc.*, **118** 2564-66.

Rose, U.S.R., Manukian, A., Heath, R.R. and Tumlinson, J.H. (1996) Volatile semiochemicals released from undamaged cotton leaves: a systemic response of living plants to caterpillar damage. *Plant Physiol.*, **111** 487-95.

Saden-Krehula, M., Tajic, M. and Kolbah, D. (1976) Investigation on some steroid hormones and their conjugates in pollen of *Pinus nigra*: separation of steroids by thin layer chromatography. *Biologisches Zentralblatt*, **95** 223-26.

Sagner, S., Eisenreich, W., Fellermeier, M., Latzel, C., Bacher, A. and Zenk, M.H. (1998a) Biosynthesis of 2-C-methyl-D-erythritol in plants by rearrangement of the terpenoid precursor, 1-deoxy-D-xylulose 5-phosphate. *Tetrahedron Lett.*, **39** 2091-94.

Sagner, S., Latzel, C., Eisenreich, W., Bacher, A. and Zenk, M.H. (1998b) Differential incorporation of 1-deoxy-D-xylulose into monoterpenes and carotenoids in higher plants. *Chem. Commun.*, **2** 221-22.

Salmon, F., Taton, M., Benveniste, P. and Rahier, A. (1992) Plant sterol biosynthesis novel potent and selective inhibitors of cytochrome P_{450}-dependent obtusifoliol 14α-methyldemethylase. *Arch. Biochem. Biophys.*, **297** 123-31.

Sandmann, G. and Albrecht, M. (1994) Assays for three enzymes involved in mevalonic acid metabolism. *Physiologia Plantarum*, **92** 297-301.

Sanmiya, K., Iwasaki, T., Matsuoka, M., Miyao, M. and Yamamoto, N. (1997) Cloning of a cDNA that encodes farnesyl diphosphate synthase and the blue-light-induced expression of the corresponding gene in the leaves of rice plants. *Biochim. Biophys. Acta: Gene Structure Expression*, **1350** 240-46.

Schaller, H., Grausem, B., Benveniste, P., Chye, M.L., Tan, C.T., Song, C.T. and Chua, N.H. (1995) Expression of the *Hevea brasiliensis* (*hbk*) mull arg 3-hydroxy-3-methylglutaryl-coenzyme A reductase 1 in tobacco results in sterol overproduction. *Plant Physiol.*, **109** 761-70.

Schütte, H.R. (1987) Secondary plant substances: aspects of steroid biosynthesis. *Prog. Bot.*, **49** 117-36.

Schwartz, S.H., Tan, B.C., Gage, D.A., Zeevaart, J.A.D. and McCarty, D.R. (1997) Specific oxidative cleavage of carotenoids by vp14 of maize. *Science*, **276** 1872-74.

Schwarz, M.K. (1994) Terpen-Biosynthese in *Ginkgo biloba*: Eine ueberraschende Geschichte PhD Thesis, Eidgenoessische Technische Hochschule, Zurich.

Schwender, J., Seemann, M., Lichtenthaler, H.K. and Rohmer, M. (1996) Biosynthesis of isoprenoids (carotenoids, sterols, prenyl side chains of chlorophylls and plastoquinone) via a novel pyruvate/glyceraldehyde 3-phosphate non-mevalonate pathway in the green alga *Scenedesmus obliquus*. *Biochem. J.*, **316** (Part 1) 73-80.

Scolnick, P.A. and Bartley, G.E. (1994) Nucleotide sequence of an *Arabidopsis* cDNA for geranylgeranyl pyrophosphate synthase. *Plant Physiol.*, **104** 1469-70.

Scolnick, P.A. and Bartley, G.E. (1996) Two more members of an *Arabidopsis* geranylgeranyl pyrophosphatase synthase gene family. *Plant Physiol.*, **110** 1435.

Seidel, S. and Reinhard, E. (1987) Major cardenolide glycosides in embryogenic suspension cultures of *Digitalis lanata*. *Planta Med.*, **3** 308-309.

Seidel, S., Kreis, W. and Reinhard, E. (1990) Δ5-3β-Hydroxysteroid dehydrogenase/Δ5-Δ4-ketosteroid isomerase (3β-HSD), a possible enzyme of cardiac glycoside biosynthesis, in cell cultures and plants of *Digitalis lanata* EHRH. *Plant Cell Rep.*, **8** 621-24.

Shibata, H., Sawa, Y., Oka, T., Sonoke, S., Kim, K.K. and Yoshioka, M. (1995) Steviol and steviol-glycoside—glucosyltransferase activities in *Stevia rebaudiana* Bertoni: purification and partial characterization. *Arch. Biochem. Biophys.*, **321** 390-96.

Silver, G.M. and Fall, R. (1991) Enzymatic synthesis of isoprene from dimethylallyl diphosphate in aspen leaf extracts. *Plant Physiol.*, **97** 1588-91.

Silver, G.M. and Fall, R. (1995) Characterization of aspen isoprene synthase, an enzyme responsible for leaf isoprene emission to the atmosphere. *J. Biol. Chem.*, **270** 13010-16.

Singsaas, E.L., Lerdau, M., Winter, K. and Sharkey, T.D. (1997) Isoprene increases thermotolerance of isoprene-emitting species. *Plant Physiol.*, **115** 1413-20.

Soler, E., Clastre, M., Bantignies, B., Marigo, G. and Ambid, C. (1993) Uptake of isopentenyl diphosphate by plastids isolated from *Vitis vinifera* (L.) cell suspensions. *Planta*, **191** 324-29.

Song, L. and Poulter, C.D. (1994) Yeast farnesyl-diphosphate synthase: site-directed mutagenesis of residues in highly conserved prenyltransferase domains I and II. *Proc. Natl. Acad. Sci. USA*, **91** 3044-48.

Sprenger, G.A., Schorken, U., Wiegert, T., Grolle, S., Degraaf, A.A., Taylor, S.V., Begley, T.P., Bringermeyer, S. and Sahm, H. (1997) Identification of a thiamin-dependent synthase in *Escherichia coli* required for the formation of the 1-deoxy-D-xylulose 5-phosphate precursor to isoprenoids, thiamin and pyridoxol. *Proc. Natl. Acad. Sci. USA*, **94** 12857-862.

Spurgeon, S.L., Sathyamoorthy, N. and Porter, J.W. (1984) Isopentenyl pyrophosphate isomerase and prenyltransferase from tomato fruit plastids. *Arch. Biochem. Biophys.*, **230** 446-54.

Stapleton, A., Allen, P.V., Friedman, M. and Belknap, W.R. (1991) Purification and characterization of solanidine glucosyltransferase from the potato *Solanum tuberosum*. A. *Agric. Food Chem.*, **39** 1187-93.

Starks, C.M., Back, K.W., Chappell, J. and Noel, J.P. (1997) Structural basis for cyclic terpene biosynthesis by tobacco 5-epi-aristolochene synthase. *Science*, **277** 1815-20.

Steele, C.L., Crock, J., Bohlmann, J. and Croteau, R. (1998a) Sesquiterpene synthases from grand fir (*Abies grandis*): comparison of constitutive and wound-induced activities, and cDNA isolation, characterization and bacterial expression of delta-selinene synthase and gamma-humulene synthase. *J. Biol. Chem.*, **273** 2078-89.

Steele, C.L., Katoh, S., Bohlmann, J. and Croteau, R. (1998b) Regulation of oleoresinosis in grand fir (*Abies grandis*): differential transcriptional control of monoterpene, sesquiterpene and diterpene synthase genes in response to wounding. *Plant Physiol.*, **116** 1497-504.

Stermer, B.A., Bianchini, G.M. and Korth, K.L. (1994) Regulation of HMG-CoA reductase activity in plants. *J. Lipid Res.*, **35** 1133-40.

Stuhlemmer, U. and Kreis, W. (1996a) Cardenolide formation and activity of pregnane-modifying enzymes in cell suspension cultures, shoot cultures and leaves of *Digitalis lanata*. *Plant Physiol. Biochem.*, **34** 85-91.

Stuhlemmer, U. and Kreis, W. (1996b) Does malonyl coenzyme A:hydroxypregnane 21-hydroxymalonyltransferase catalyze the first step in butenolide ring formation? *Tetrahedron Lett.*, **37** 2221-24.

Stuhlemmer, U., Haussmann, W., Milek, F., Kreis, W. and Reinhard, E. (1993a) 3α-Hydroxysteroid-5β-oxidoreductase in tissue cultures of *Digitalis lanata*. *Z. Naturforsch.*, **48c** 713-21.

Stuhlemmer, U., Kreis, W., Eisenbeiss, M. and Reinhard, E. (1993b) Cardiac glycosides in partly submerged shoots of *Digitalis lanata*. *Planta Med.*, **59** 539-45.

Suga, T. and Hirata, T. (1990) Biotransformation of exogenous substrates by plant cell cultures. *Phytochemistry*, **29** 2393-406.

Sun, T.-P. and Kamiya, Y. (1994) The *Arabidopsis* GA1 locus encodes the cyclase *ent*-kaurene synthetase A of gibberellin biosynthesis. *Plant Cell*, **6** 1509-18.

Sutor, R. and Kreis, W. (1996) Partial purification and characterization of the cell-wall-associated lanatoside 15′-*O*-acetylesterase from *Digitalis lanata* suspension cultures. *Plant Physiol. Biochem.*, **34** 763-70.

Sutor, R., Hoelz, H. and Kreis, W. (1990) Lanatoside 15′-*O*-acetylesterase from *Digitalis* (Scrophulariaceae) plants and cell cultures. *J. Plant Physiol.*, **136** 289-94.

Sutor, R., Kreis, W., Hoelz, H. and Reinhard, E. (1993) Acetyl coenzyme A:digitoxin 15′-*O*-acetyltransferase from *Digitalis* plants and suspension cultures. *Phytochemistry*, **32** 569-73.

Takahashi, S., Kuzuyama, T., Watanabe, H. and Seto, H. (1998) A 1-deoxy-D-xylulose 5-phosphate reductoisomerase catalyzing the formation of 2-C-methyl-D-erythritol 4-phosphate in an alternative non-mevalonate pathway for terpenoid biosynthesis. *Proc. Natl. Acad. Sci. USA*, **95** 9879-84.

Tarshis, L.C., Yan, M., Poulter, C.D. and Sacchettini, J.C. (1994) Crystal structure of recombinant farnesyl diphosphate synthase at 2.6-A resolution. *Biochemistry*, **33** 10871-77.

Tarshis, L.C., Proteau, P.J., Kellogg, B.A., Sacchettini, J.C. and Poulter, C.D. (1996) Regulation of product chain length by isoprenyl diphosphate synthases. *Proc. Natl. Acad. Sci. USA*, **93** 15018-23.

Taton, M., Benveniste, P. and Rahier, A. (1989) Microsomal $\Delta^{8,14}$ sterol Δ^{14}-reductase in higher plants characterization and inhibition by analogues of a presumptive carbocationic intermediate of the reduction reaction. *Eur. J. Biochem.*, **185** 605-14.

Taton, M. and Rahier, A. (1991) Identification of $\Delta^{5,7}$ sterol-Δ7-reductase in higher plant microsomes. *Biochem. Biophys. Res. Commun.*, **181** 465-73.

Taton, M., Salmon, F., Pascal, S. and Rahier, A. (1994) Plant sterol biosynthesis: recent advances in the understanding of oxidative demethylations at C4 and C14. *Plant Physiol. Biochem.*, **32** 751-60.

Taton, M. and Rahier, A. (1996) Plant sterol biosynthesis: identification and characterization of higher plant Δ7-sterol C5(6)-desaturase. *Arch. Biochem. Biophys.*, **325** 279-88.

Theurer, C., Kreis, W. and Reinhard, E. (1998) Effects of digitoxigenin, digoxigenin and various cardiac glycosides on cardenolide accumulation in shoot culters of *Digitalis lanata* Ehrh. *Planta Med.*, **64** 705-10.

Tschesche, R. and Kleff, U. (1973) Beiträge zur biochemischen 14β-Hydroxylierung von C_{21}-Steroiden zu Cardenoliden. *Phytochemistry*, **12** 2375-80.

Turlings, T.C.J., Tumlinson, J.H. and Lewis, W.J. (1990) Exploitation of herbivore-induced plant odors by host-seeking parasitic wasps. *Science*, **250** 1251-53.

Turlings, T.C.J., Loughrin, J.H., McCall, P.J., Rose, U.S.R., Lewis, W.J. and Tumlinson, J.H. (1995) How caterpillar-damaged plants protect themselves by attracting parasitic wasps. *Proc. Natl. Acad. Sci. USA*, **92** 4169-74.

Ullman, P., Rimmele, D., Benveniste, P. and Bouvier-Navé, P. (1984) Phospholipid-dependence of plant UDP-glucose-sterol-β-D-glucosyltransferase. 2. Acetone-mediated delipidation and kinetic studies. *Plant Sci. Lett.*, **36** 29-36.

Ullman, P., Bouvier-Navé, P. and Benveniste, P. (1987) Regulation by phospholipids and kinetic studies of plant membrane-bound UDP-glucose sterol β-D-glucosyltransferase. *Plant Physiol.*, **85** 51-55.

Ury, A., Benveniste, P. and Bouvier-Navé, P. (1989) Phospholipid-dependence of plant UDP-glucose-sterol-β-D-glucosyltransferase. IV. Reconstitution into small unilamellar vesicles. *Plant Physiol.*, **91** 567-73.

van Beek, T.A. and de Groot, A. (1986) Terpenoid antifeedants. Part I. An overview of terpenoid antifeedants of natural origin. *Recueil des Travaux Chimiques des Pays-Bas*, **105** 513-27.

Vardosanidze, M.G., Gurielidze, K.G., Pruidze, G.N. and Paseshnichenko, V.A. (1991) The substrate specificity of *Allium erubescens* β-glucosidase. *Biokhymia*, **56** 2025-31.

Veleiro, A.S., Burton, G. and Gros, E.G. (1985) Biosynthesis of withanolides in *Acnistus breviflorus. Phytochemistry*, **24** 2263-66.

Verlet, N. (1993) Commercial aspects, in *Volatile Oil Crops: Their Biology Biochemistry and Production.* (eds. R.K.M. Hay and P.G. Waterman), Longman Scientific and Technical, Essex, UK, pp. 137-74.

Villarreal, M.L., Arias, C., Feria-Velasco, A., Ramirez, O.T. and Quintero, R. (1997) Cell suspension culture of *Solanum chrysotrichum* (Schldl.): a plant producing an antifungal spirostanol saponin. *Plant Cell Tiss. Org. Cult.*, **50** 39-44.

Vogel, B.S., Wildung, M.R., Vogel, G. and Croteau, R. (1996) Abietadiene synthase from grand fir (*Abies grandis*): cDNA isolation, characterization and bacterial expression of a bifunctional diterpene cyclase involved in resin acid biosynthesis. *J. Biol. Chem.*, **271** 23262-68.

Vollack, K.U. and Bach, T.J. (1996) Cloning of a cDNA encoding cytosolic acetoacetyl-coenzyme A thiolase from radish by functional expression *in Saccharomyces cerevisiae. Plant Physiol.*, **111** 1097-107.

Vollack, K.-U., Dittrich, B., Ferrer, A., Boronat, A. and Bach, T.J. (1994) Two radish genes for 3-hydroxy-3-methylglutaryl-CoA reductase isozymes complement mevalonate auxotrophy in a yeast mutant and yield membrane-bound active enzyme. *J. Plant Physiol.*, **143** 479-87.

Wagschal, K., Savage, T.J. and Croteau, R. (1991) Isotopically sensitive branching as a tool for evaluating multiple product formation by monoterpene cyclases. *Tetrahedron*, **47** 5933-44.

Warneck, H.M. and Seitz, H.U. (1990) 3β-Hydroxysteroid oxidoreductase in suspension cultures of *Digitalis lanata* Ehrh. *Z. Naturforsch.*, **45c** 963-72.

Warnecke, D.C. and Heinz, E. (1994) Purification of a membrane-bound UDP-glucose: sterol β-D-glucosyltransferase based on its solubility in diethyl ether. *Plant Physiol.*, **105** 1067-73.

Warnecke, D.C., Baltrusch, M., Buck, F., Wolter, F.P. and Heinz, E. (1997) UDP-glucose:sterol glucosyltransferase: cloning and functional expression in *Escherichia coli. Plant Mol. Biol.*, **35** 597-603.

Weber, T. and Bach, T.J. (1994) Conversion of acetyl-coenzyme A into 3-hydroxy-3-methylglutarylcoenzyme A in radish seedlings: evidence of a single monomeric protein catalyzing a Fe^{II}/quinone-stimulated double condensation reaction. *Biochim. Biophys. Acta*, **1211** 85-96.

Wendt, K.U., Poralla, K. and Schulz, G.E. (1997) Structure and function of a squalene cyclase. *Science*, **277** 1811-15.

West, C.A. (1981) Biosynthesis of diterpenes, in *Biosynthesis of Isoprenoid Compounds*, (eds. J.W. Porter and S.L. Spurgeon), John Wiley and Sons, New York, pp. 376-411.

Wettstein, A., Caelles, C., Boronat, A., Jenke, H.-S. and Bach, T.J. (1989) Molecular cloning and characterization of a cDNA encoding radish 3-hydroxy-3-methylglutaryl-CoA reductase. *Biol. Chem. Hoppe-Seyler*, **370** 806-807.

Wildermuth, M.C. and Fall, R. (1998) Biochemical characterization of stromal and thylakoid-bound isoforms of isoprene synthase in willow leaves. *Plant Physiol.*, **116** 1111-23.

Wildung, M.R. and Croteau, R. (1996) A cDNA clone for taxadiene synthase, the diterpene cyclase that catalyzes the committed step of taxol biosynthesis. *J. Biol. Chem.*, **271** 9201-204.

Winkler, R.G. and Helentjaris, T. (1995) The maize dwarf3 gene encodes a cytochrome P_{450}-mediated early step in gibberellin biosynthesis. *Plant Cell*, **7** 1307-17.

Wise, M.L. and Croteau, R. (1998) Monoterpene biosynthesis, in *Comprehensive Natural Products Chemistry: Isoprenoid Biosynthesis* (ed. D.E. Cane), Pergamon Press, Oxford, UK.

Wise, M.L., Savage, T.J., Katahira, E. and Croteau, R. (1998) Monoterpene synthases from common sage (*Salvia-officinalis*): cDNA isolation, characterization and functional expression of (+)-sabinene synthase, 1,8-cineole synthase, and (+)- bornyl diphosphate synthase. *J. Biol. Chem.*, **273** 14891-99.

Woerdenbag, H.J., Pras, N., Frijlink, H.W., Lerk, C.F. and Malingré, T.M. (1990) Cyclodextrin-facilitated bioconversion of 17β-estradiol by a phenoloxidase from *Mucuna pruriens* cell cultures. *Phytochemistry*, **29** 1551-54.

Xu, Y.L., Li, L., Wu, K.Q., Peeters, A.J.M., Gage, D.A. and Zeevaart, J.A.D. (1995) The ga5 locus of *Arabidopsis thaliana* encodes a multifunctional gibberellin 20-oxidase: molecular cloning and functional expression. *Proc. Natl. Acad. Sci. USA*, **92** 6640-44.

Yamaguchi, S., Saito, T., Abe, H., Yamane, H., Murofushi, N. and Kamiya, Y. (1996) Molecular cloning and characterization of a cDNA encoding the gibberellin biosynthetic enzyme *ent*-kaurene synthase B from pumpkin (*Cucurbita maxima* L). *Plant J.*, **10** 203-13.

Yamaguchi, S., Sun, T.P., Kawaide, H. and Kamiya, Y. (1998) The ga2 locus of *Arabidopsis thaliana* encodes *ent*-kaurene synthase of gibberellin biosynthesis. *Plant Physiol.*, **116** 1271-78.

Yamamoto, H., Kimata, J., Senda, M. and Inoue, K. (1997) Dimethylallyl diphosphate: kaempferol 8-dimethylallyl transferase in *Epimedium diphyllum* cell suspension cultures. *Phytochemistry*, **44** 23-28.

Yang, Z., Park, H., Lacy, G.H. and Cramer, C.L. (1991) Differential activation of potato 3-hydroxy-3-methylglutaryl coenzyme A reductase genes by wounding and pathogen challenge. *Plant Cell*, **3** 397-405.

Yoshikawa, T. and Furuya, T. (1979) Purification and properties of sterol UDP-glucose glucosyl transferase in cell culture of *Digitalis purpurea*. *Phytochemistry*, **18** 239-42.

Yuba, A., Yazaki, K., Tabata, M., Honda, G. and Croteau, R. (1996) cDNA cloning, characterization, and functional expression of 4*S*-(−)-limonene synthase from *Perilla frutescens*. *Arch. Biochem. Biophys.*, **332** 280-87.

Zeidler, J.G., Lichtenthaler, H.K., May, H.U. and Lichtenthaler, F.W. (1997) Is isoprene emitted by plants synthesized via a novel isopentenyl pyrophosphate pathway? *Z. Naturforsch.*, **52c** 15-23.

Zhang, F.L. and Casey, P.J. (1996) Protein prenylation: molecular mechanisms and functional consequences. *Annu. Rev. Biochem.*, **65** 241-69.

Zimowski, J. (1991) Occurrence of a glucosyltransferase specific for solanidine in potato plants. *Phytochemistry*, **30** 1827-32.

Zimowski, J. (1992) Specificity and some other properties of cytosolic and membranous UDP-glucose 3β-hydroxysteroid glucosyltransferases from *Solanum tuberosum* leaves. *Phytochemistry*, **31** 2977-81.

Zhou, D.F., Qian, D.Q., Cramer, C.L. and Yang, Z.B. (1997) Developmental and environmental regulation of tissue- and cell-specific expression for a pea protein farnesyltransferase gene in transgenic plants. *Plant J.*, **12** 921-30.

Zook, M.N., Chappell, J. and Kuc, J.A. (1992) Characterization of elicitor-induction of sesquiterpene cyclase activity in potato tuber tissue. *Phytochemistry*, **31** 3441-45.

6 Chemotaxonomy in relation to molecular phylogeny of plants

Michael Wink and Peter G. Waterman

6.1 Introduction

To some degree, man has been practising chemotaxonomy with respect to plants for a very long time. The senses of taste, smell and colour have all been used to gather information about the chemistry of an organism and, thus, to classify it in terms that are important. While it is a very difficult subject to research, it can now be stated unequivocally that the ability to classify is shared by many organisms, particularly in relation to selection of plants or plant parts for feeding and reproduction (Harborne, 1993). However, the outcome of such classification is entirely phenetic, associating plants on the basis of use, danger, etc. but telling us little, if anything, about the phylogenetic or evolutionary relationships between them.

While the potential value of plant secondary metabolites to taxonomy has been recognised for nearly 200 years (Candolle, 1804; Abbott, 1886), their practical application has been restricted to this century and predominantly to the last 35 yrs. The first extensive advocacy of chemical taxonomy came from McNair (1935), who studied the distribution of volatile oils, fixed oils and alkaloids in the Angiospermae. At the same time, the first comparative analyses were being reported, most of which involved the volatile oils of the Myrtaceae, notably *Eucalyptus* (Penfold and Morrison, 1927). While these studies confirmed the distinctiveness of the chemistry of different taxa, even at this early stage, they illustrated the possibility for intraspecies variation in chemistry.

6.2 The establishment of chemotaxonomy as a research discipline

The key technical development that allowed chemotaxonomic studies to develop was paper chromatography. This procedure allowed multiple samples to be extracted and compared for the presence or absence of specific metabolites (Bate-Smith, 1948; Alston and Turner, 1959). The flavonoids and related phenolic compounds proved to be particularly suitable for examination by paper and, subsequently, thin-layer chromatography. It was the distribution of some common phenolics that was first examined in some detail across the whole of the Angiospermae (Bate-Smith, 1958, 1962).

The subject really came of age in the early 1960s, with the publication of several seminal works, notably those of Alston and Turner (1963) and Swain (1963, 1966), encompassing the discipline as a whole, and specialist works on flavonoids and other phenolics by Harborne (1964, 1967). Hegnauer had already embarked on his epic series, *Chemotaxonomie der Pflanzen*, in which, with great thoroughness, he compiled the current information on occurrence and distribution of metabolites within and between plant families (Hegnauer, 1962–1990; Hegnauer and Hegnauer, 1992–1996). By this time, sufficient data had been gathered concerning the occurrence of a wide range of secondary metabolites to allow for generalisations to be made on the taxonomic range of their distribution. This was accompanied by a rapidly growing library of experimental data dealing with the biosynthesis of these compounds (Geissmann and Crout, 1969), which allowed distribution to be placed in the context of a dynamic biosynthetic phylogeny.

During this period, a number of very exciting discoveries were made, which boded well for the impact that chemotaxonomy could have in unravelling Angiosperm evolution. These discoveries included the following.

6.2.1 *Amino acids*

The Leguminosae (Fabaceae) are a major source of 'nonprotein amino acids (NPAAS)', such as albizine, canavanine and lathyrine (Fig. 6.1). These have proved to be useful taxonomic markers throughout the family, albizine being characteristic of the Mimosoideae, while lathyrine can be used to distinguish species of *Lathyrus* from *Vicia*. The distribution of canavanine in the Papilionoideae was examined very extensively and has been used in the compilation of phylogenies for that subfamily (Bell *et al.*, 1978; Polhill *et al.*, 1981a,b).

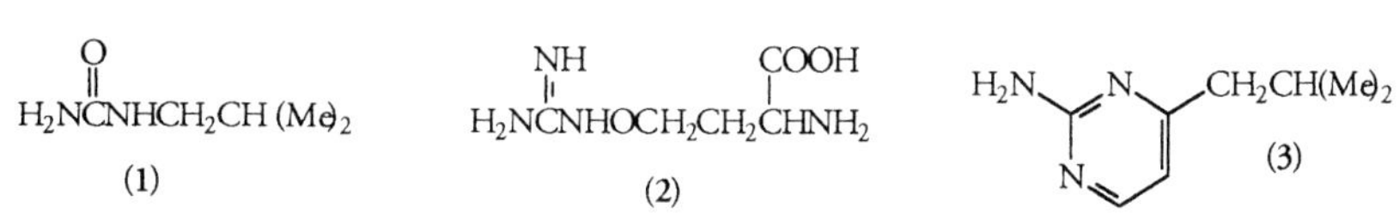

$H_2NC(=O)NHCH_2CH(Me)_2$ (1)

$H_2NC(=NH)NHOCH_2CH_2CH(COOH)NH_2$ (2)

H_2N–pyrimidine–$CH_2CH(Me)_2$ (3)

Figure 6.1 Structures of the non-protein amino acid albizine (1), canavine (2) and lathyrine (3).

6.2.2 *Flavonoids*

The flavonoids (Fig. 6.2) form one of the largest and most widespread groups of secondary metabolites. An extensive range of structural variants has been found, based on the combination of a phenylpropenyl unit with three acetate units, including polymeric condensed tannins, ubiquitous glycosidic forms, isoflavonoids and neoflavonoids. Flavonoids have received more attention from the chemotaxonomist than any other class of compound because of their ubiquity and their accessibility through relatively simple methods of analysis (Mabry *et al.*, 1970). In his monumental survey of the plant kingdom, Bate-Smith (1962) revealed changes in substitution patterns that had broad correlation with taxonomic 'advancement', and suggested that a simplification in substitution patterns had occurred as part of the evolutionary process. Harborne (1966) proposed a series of primitive and advanced flavonoid characters that could be used to assess the phylogenetic position of a taxon.

The Leguminosae have also featured as a family with interesting flavonoid distribution. The isoflavonoids (Fig 6.2) are a particular feature of the Papilionoideae, where they occur as both constitutive metabolites and phytoalexins (Ingham, 1983). The neoflavonoids (Fig 6.2) represent an alternative mode of cyclisation of the phenylpropene and triketide precursor. They occur in the Papilionoideae (in the tribe Dalbergieae), but are also to be found in some genera of the Guttiferae (Clusiaceae) (Donnelly, 1985).

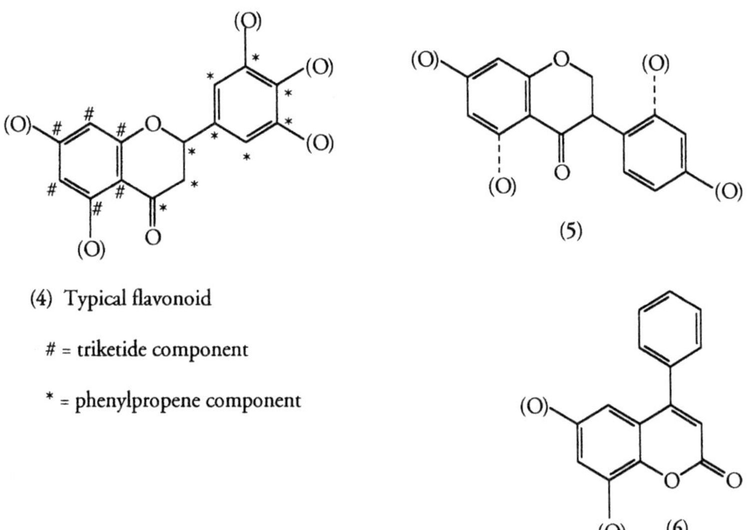

Figure 6.2 Structures of flavonoids; typical flavonoid (4), isoflavonoid (5) and neoflavonoid (6).

6.2.3 *Xanthones*

Whereas flavonoids are the product of a C_6C_3 and a triketide precursor, the xanthones (Fig. 6.3) originate from a triketide linked with a C_6C_1

unit. There are two apparently unrelated centres of xanthone production in the Angiospermae, the Guttiferae (Clusiaceae) and the Gentianaceae. With respect to the former, the occurrence of xanthones in such genera as *Bonnetia* and *Archytaea* has been cited as powerful evidence for allying them to the Guttiferae rather than the Theaceae (Kubitzki *et al.*, 1978).

6.2.4 *Coumarins*

The simple coumarin nucleus (Fig 6.3), which is derived by lactone formation of an *ortho*-hydroxy-*cis* cinnamic acid, is a common metabolite in higher plants and is often found in glycosidic form. However, proliferation of coumarins to the status of major chemical markers occurs in only a few cases, most notably, but not exclusively, in the Umbelliferae (subfamily Apioideae) and in the Rutaceae (Gray and Waterman, 1978; Murray *et al.*, 1982). In these cases, the coumarin nucleus has almost invariably been embellished by the addition of a prenyl unit leading to furocoumarin (Fig 6.3) and pyranocoumarin structures.

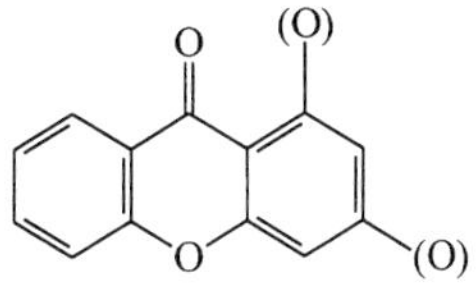

O (O) O (O) (7)

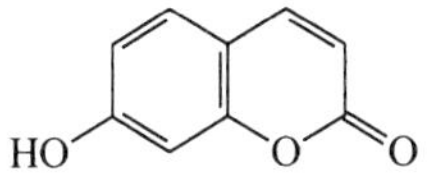

HO O O (8)

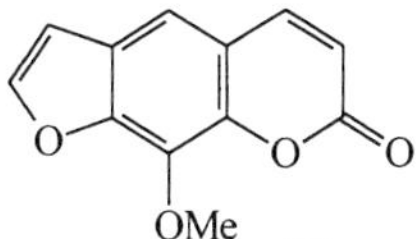

O O O OMe (9)

Figure 6.3 Structures of xanthones and coumarins: xanthone (7), coumarin (8) and furocoumarin (9).

6.2.5 *Fixed oils, fats and waxes*

When gas chromatography became established as an analytical technique, certain classes of metabolite proved particularly amenable to study. These were volatile oils (see monoterpenes), the constituents of leaf surface waxes and, in the form of their methyl esters, the fatty acid components of fixed oils and fats, particularly those occurring in seeds. Structural variation within each of these types of compound proved to be somewhat less pronounced than with many other groups of metabolites. Nevertheless, the classification of plant families on the basis of the chain length and degree of unsaturation of the predominant fatty acids was proposed (Smith, 1976).

The polyacetylenes, which have a common origin with fatty acids, showed a far more restricted distribution (Bohlmann *et al.*, 1973). Falcarinol (Fig 6.4) and allied structures were cited as being diagnostic of the Araliales (Araliaceae, Umbelliferae, Pittosporaceae), while another major centre of production was found in the Asteraceae, where sulphur-containing polyacetylenes occurred.

6.2.6 *Cyclic polyketides*

The tricyclic polyketide, anthrone (Fig 6.4) had been noted as a feature of *Aloe* and some related genera in the monocot family, Liliaceae, and in the dicots, *Rumex* (Polygonaceae) and *Cassia* (Leguminosae).

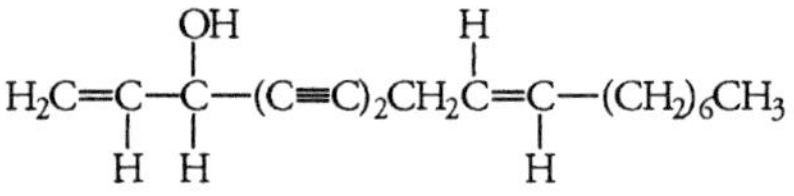

$H_2C{=}C(H){-}C(H)(OH){-}(C{\equiv}C)_2CH_2C(H){=}C(H){-}(CH_2)_6CH_3$

(10)

(O) O (O) (O) CH_3

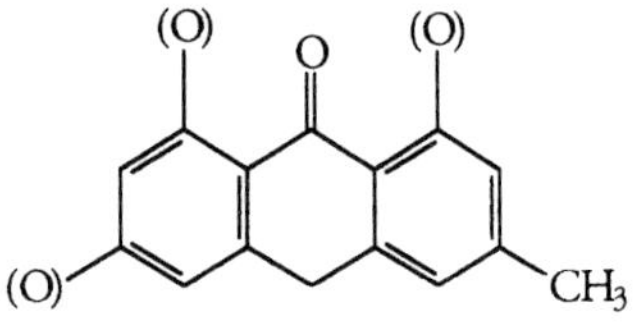

(11)

Figure 6.4 Structures of the polyacetylene, falcarinol (10), and the tricyclic polyketide, anthrone (11).

6.2.7 *Monoterpenes and sesquiterpenes (volatile oils)*

Because of the ease of qualitative analysis, firstly through distillation to isolate major components and, subsequently, through gas-liquid chromatography (GLC), volatile oils have consistently attracted the attention of chemotaxonomists. These oils are almost invariably complex mixtures, in which monoterpenes and/or sesquiterpenes usually predominate, although the biosynthetically-unrelated phenylpropenes can also be important. Some of the earliest studies on the genetic control of secondary metabolites involved the oils of mints, *Mentha* (Murray, 1960). Volatile oils yielded the first properly documented examples of chemical races (Penfold and Morrison, 1927; Sutherland and Park, 1967), while Zavarin and co-workers (1971) provided clear evidence for the impact of environmental factors on the composition of volatile oil. Because of the comparative nature of GLC analysis, volatile oils were among the first compounds to be extensively studied at the population level and to be subjected to numerical analysis. The work of Adams on *Juniperus* in south-eastern USA and northern Mexico was an excellent early example of the exploitation of numerical techniques (Adams and Turner, 1970; Adams, 1972).

Among the sesquiterpenes, there are also some more highly oxidised non-volatile compounds. The best examples are the sesquiterpene lactones, which were found to be distributed quite widely in the Asteraceae but rarely elsewhere (Herout and Sorm, 1969).

6.2.8 *Iridoids*

The iridoids are an atypical structural form of monoterpenes, exemplified by the two compounds, loganin and secologanin (Fig. 6.5). Their relatively high level of oxidation and the regular occurrence of glycosides made these bitter-tasting compounds less tractable to study than the 'normal' volatile monoterpenes. However, it rapidly became obvious that their distribution was limited to a relatively small number of families, many of which were clearly of close affinity to one another. Jensen and co-workers (1975) formerly proposed that the iridoid-producing families were a monophyletic group.

COOMe H HO H O O-glc (12)

COOH H OHC O H O-glc (13)

Figure 6.5 Structures of loganin (12) and secologanin (13).

6.2.9 *Triterpenes, sterols and carotenoids*

The common members of these classes, such as α-amyrin, β-sitosterol and β-carotene, occur very widely and were soon recognised to be of no taxonomic value. A number of rarer classes of triterpenes and sterols such as the withanolides, the cardiac glycosides of the Apocynaceae, Asclepidaceae and Scrophulariaceae and the limonoids and quassinoids of the Rutales (Fig. 6.6), were noted for their limited distribution. Some families, notably the Leguminosae, are able to produce triterpenes linked to several sugars to form a surfactant saponin, the presence of which could readily be detected by simple tests, such as blood cell haemolysis.

6.2.10 *Nitrogen-containing terpenes*

Each class of terpene was found to associate with nitrogen to form alkaloid-like compounds, for which Hegnauer (1963) coined the term 'pseudoalkaloid'. The most interesting of these are 'diterpene alkaloids',

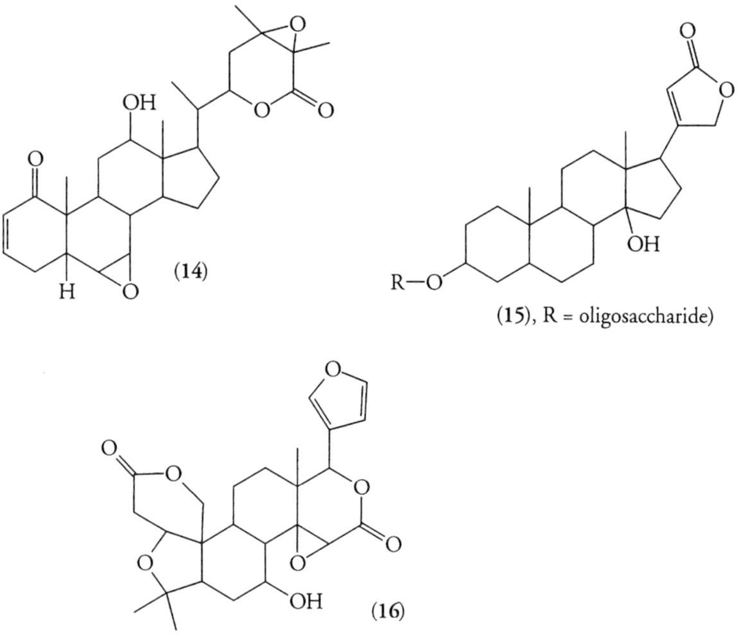

Figure 6.6 Structures of the withanolides (14), cardiac glycosides (15) and limonoids (16).

which are found in *Delphinium* and *Aconitum* (Ranunculaceae), where they were recognised as supporting a close relationship between those genera (Jensen, 1968). 'Steroidal alkaloids' were identified as being significant markers in a number of families, notably the Apocynaceae, Asclepiadaceae, Buxaceae, Solanaceae and Liliaceae. Some of these families were also found to be major sources of true alkaloids.

6.2.11 *Alkaloids*

The alkaloids have long been recognised as an important group of metabolites because of their biological activity but they, more than any other major group of metabolites, needed the technical revolutions in chromatography and spectroscopy to allow for an assessment of their distribution. In chemotaxonomic terms, alkaloids were defined by Hegnauer (1963), who distinguished 'true alkaloids' from other nitrogen-containing metabolites on the basis of their origin from amino acids, their basic nature and their limited distribution. Hegnauer defined the major classes of alkaloid in terms of their biosynthesis from precursor amino acids rather than their final structure. For example, quinine was recognised as an indole-monoterpene alkaloid arising from the same biosynthetic route as reserpine but different from that leading to 6-methoxyflindersine, with which quinine shares a quinoline nucleus (Fig. 6.7). The major classes recognised are listed in Table 6.1.

In the 1950s and 1960s, there were several notable successes involving the use of alkaloids as taxonomic markers. These included the acceptance

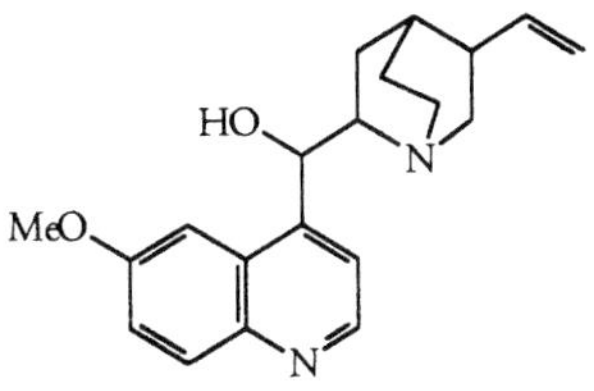

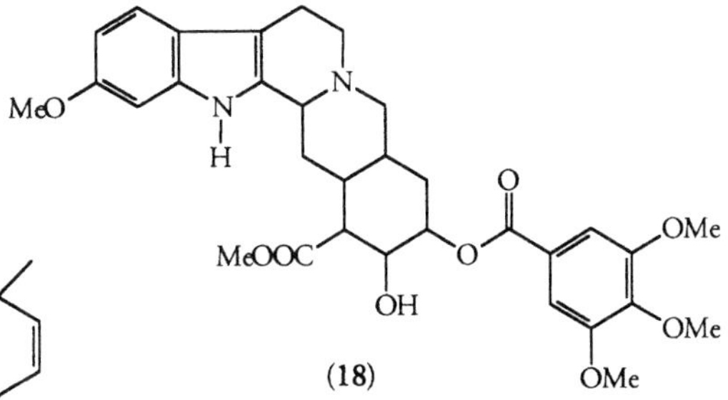

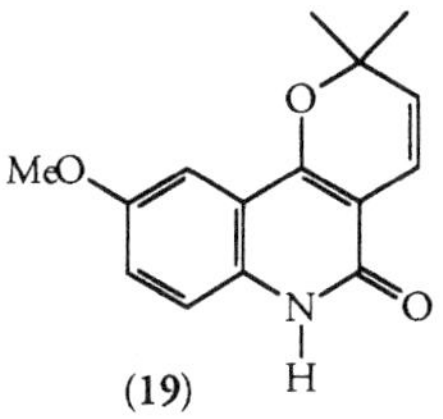

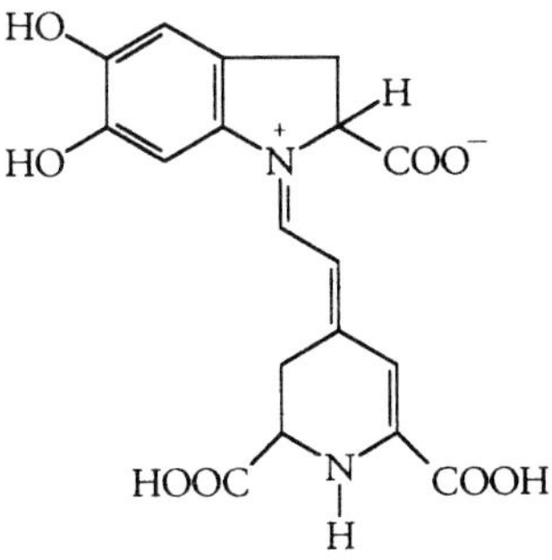

Figure 6.7 Structures of quinine (17), reserpine (18), 6-methoxyflindersine (19) and betanidin (20).

Table 6.1 Biogenetic classification and principal centres of production of major alkaloid groups

Amino acid	Condensation group	Alkaloid type	Some major sources
Tyrosine or phenylalanine	Deaminated tyrosine or phenylalanine unit (C_6C_2)	1-Benzyltetrahydro-isoquinolines	Families of the Ranales or Polycarpicae (Menispermaceae, Annonaceae, Lauraceae Magnoliaceae, Monomiaceae), Berberidaceae, Papaveraceae, Fumariaceae, Rutaceae (in part), Fabaceae (in part)
	Deaminated tyrosine or phenylalanine unit (C_6C_1)		Monocotyledenous, families, notably Amaryllidaceae
	Tyrosine or proline	Betalains	Families of the Centrospermae (e.g. Cactaceae, Aizoaceae, Portulacaceae, Phytolacaceae)
Anthranilic acid	Mono and triketides	Quinolines	Rutaceae
Tryptophan	Seco-loganic acid	Indole-monoterpene	Loganiaceae, Apocynaceae, Rubiaceae
Histidine	Acetate?	Imidazole	Rutaceae (in part), Fabaceae (in part)
Ornithine	Diketide	Tropane	Solanaceae, Erythroxylaceae, Convolvulaceae
Ornithine	Deaminated ornithine	Pyrrolizidine	Boraginaceae, Asteraceae (in part), Fabaceae (in part), Ranunculaceae
Lysine	Deaminated lysine	Quinolizidine	Fabaceae (Papilionoideae)

of the proposition of Hegnauer (1961), to the effect that the Papaveraceae and Fumariaceae were misplaced in the Rhoedales *sensu* Wettstein and were better placed in or adjacent to the Polycarpicae. Central to this argument was the co-occurrence of 1-benzyltetrahydroisoquinoline (1-btiq) alkaloids in these two families and in many of the major families of the Polycarpicae (see Table 6.1). The Polycarpicae were themselves the focus of considerable attention because of the occurrence of 1-btiq alkaloids in many of the major families. However, as noted by Hegnauer (1963), this distribution did not encompass all of the families of the Polycarpicae and some were alkaloid-free. This raised the question of whether the ability to produce these alkaloids was ancestral in the order or had arisen during its evolution. No satisfactory answer could be proposed.

Another fascinating class of compounds that originate from tyrosine are the betalains. These highly-coloured substances, typified by betanidin (Fig. 6.7), were often referred to as pigments but, biogenetically, they are alkaloids in every sense other than in the relative absence of pharmacological activity. Betalains were found to be restricted in distribution to several families that were placed together in the order Centrospermae (Mabry *et al.*, 1966). However, as with the 1-btiq alkaloids in the Ranales, the distribution of betalains within the Centrospermae did not encompass all families, the Caryophyllaceae being the most notable exception. Once again, the dilemma of an ancestral or derived origin for these compounds became a major point of debate.

The large class of indole alkaloids, based on the combination of tryptamine and the monoterpene *seco*-loganin (Fig. 6.5), also offered considerable opportunities for the chemotaxonomist. Unravelling the biosynthesis and biogenetic relationships between these alkaloids offers ample evidence of the skills of those working in this area (Geissmann and Crout, 1969), and exemplifies the capacity of plants to generate extraordinary structural diversity from one set of precursors. As noted previously, *seco*-loganin is an iridoid and it is among a subset of the iridoid-producing families that this group of alkaloids occur most widely, notably in the Apocynaceae, Loganiaceae and Rubiaceae. The Rubiaceae were often classified separately from the other two families, a course of action that was questioned on the basis of alkaloid distribution.

Of all the alkaloid-producing families, one of the most prolific is the Rutaceae (Waterman, 1975). The alkaloids obtained included 1-btiq, simple tryptophan derivatives, imidazoles and, most commonly, quinoline alkaloids originating from anthranilic acid. The Rutaceae was the only family in which the direct use of anthranilic acid in alkaloid production occurred to any extent.

6.3 Developments in small molecule chemotaxonomy over the past 25 years

6.3.1 Dahlgren's phylogenetic framework

By the beginning of the 1970's chemotaxonomy had made a considerable impact on plant systematics and new systems of classification were being developed that took account of the distribution of secondary metabolites (Thorne, 1968, 1976; Dahlgren, 1980). This, in many respects, marked a high point for the use of low molecular weight secondary metabolites as taxonomic markers. In particular, the system produced by Dahlgren placed some emphasis on the distribution of these metabolites and it was presented in a way that Dahlgren called a '2-dimensional framework', in which the orders of plants were clustered to show proposed phylogenetic relationships (Fig. 6.8).

Dahlgren's framework allowed chemotaxonomists the opportunity to plot out known distribution patterns against a phylogenetic system of classification for the Angiospermae. The results of such analyses were very revealing and more than a little disconcerting for many chemotaxonomists. In Figure 6.9, the distribution (to the family level) of three classes of alkaloids, the 1-benzyltetrahydroisoquinolines (Guinaudeau and Bruneton, 1993), tropanes (Woolley, 1993) and pyrrolizidines (Robins, 1993), has been plotted onto Dahlgren's framework.

In each case, major centres of production can be seen: the Magnoliiflorae and Ranunculiiflorae in the case of the 1-btiq alkaloids; the Solaniflorae for the tropanes; and the Solaniflorae, Asteriflorae, Fabiflorae and Liliiflorae for the pyrrolizidine alkaloids in their various forms. However, it is equally the case that for each alkaloid class a considerable number of other orders have also been found to yield examples, in many cases from either a single or a very limited number of taxa. This is a pattern that would be repeated for almost all classes of metabolite mentioned in the present chapter, with the notable exception of the betalains, which do appear to remain restricted to the Caryophylliflorae.

The inevitable conclusion drawn from these observations is that the expression of secondary metabolites of a given structural type has almost invariably arisen on a number of occasions. Consequently, the co-occurrence of a structural class of metabolite in two taxa cannot be taken to imply a monophyletic relationship. This means that the systematic value of chemical characters becomes a matter for interpretation by a systematicist in the same way as traditional morphological markers, despite the fact that they can be defined unambiguously in terms both of origin and structure. Given that the chemical record is usually only

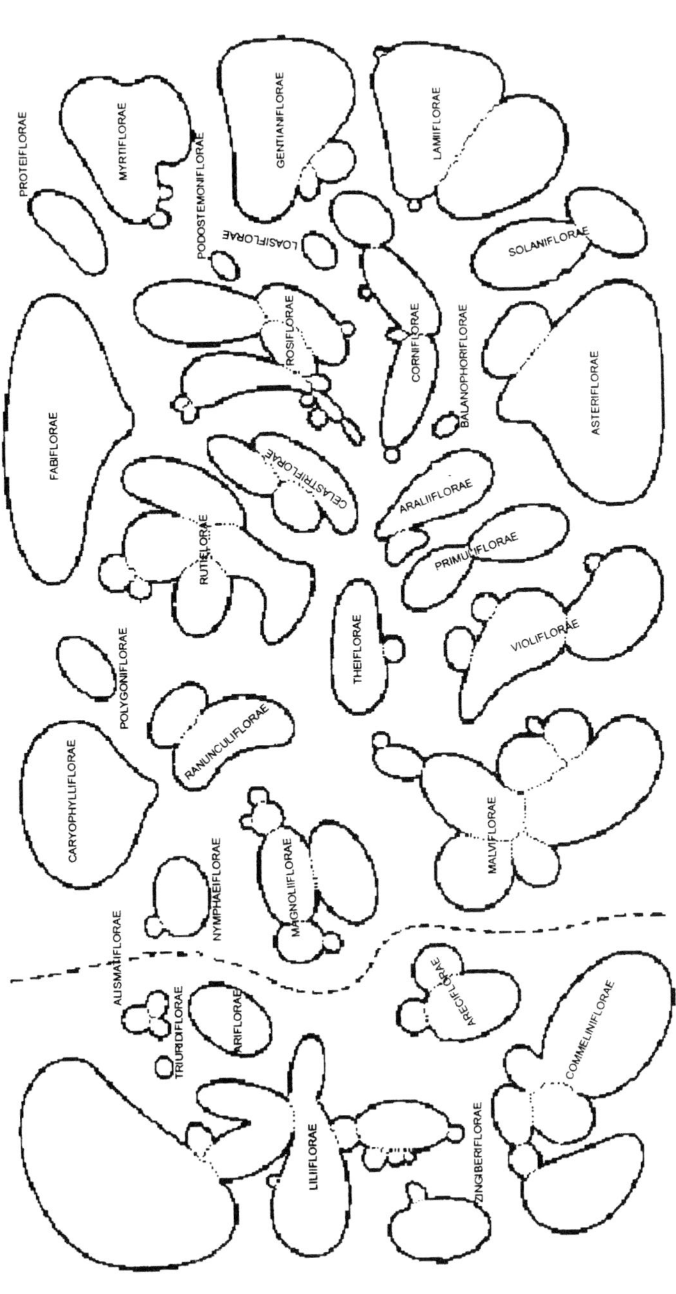

Figure 6.8 The superorders of the angiosperms, illustrated as clusters of orders in a two-dimensional framework (reprinted from the Botanical Journal of the Linnean Society, **80**, "A revised system of classification of the angiosperms", pp. 91-124, 1980, by permission of the publisher Academic Press).

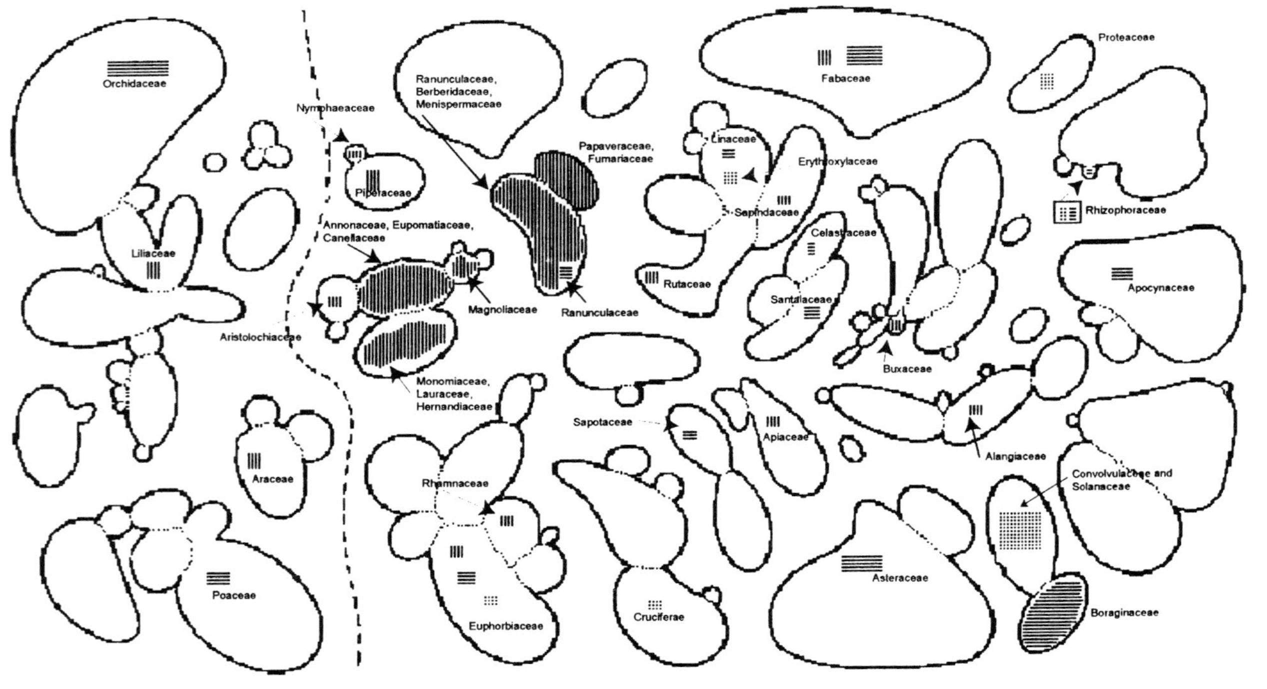

Figure 6.9 The superorders of the angiosperms, illustrated as clusters of orders in a two-dimensional framework, with the distribution of three classes of alkaloids superimposed. Key: [vertical hatching], 1-benzyltetrahydroisoquinoline alkaloids; [horizontal hatching], pyrrolizidine alkaloids, [dotted pattern], tropane alkaloids. Reprinted from the Botanical Journal of the Linnean Society, **80**, "A revised system of classification of the angiosperms", pp. 91-124, 1980, by permission of the publisher Academic Press.

fragmentary for any taxon under investigation, this makes them of limited value as markers in studies at higher hierarchical levels.

6.3.2 Quantifying chemical data for numerical taxonomy

One advantage that secondary metabolites should have is that when biosynthetic pathways are known it is possible to identify events that have evolutionary implications. It has always been attractive, therefore, to consider the use of numerical methods in assessing the implications of chemical profiles. An early example of this was an analysis of the flavonoids of *Geranium* by Bate-Smith (1973), in which 'flavonoid scores' were produced for each species based on the presence or absence of individual flavonoids. These scores were used to identify the 'relative advancement' of individual species.

The major exponents of reducing chemical data to numbers have been Gottlieb and co-workers (Gottlieb, 1982). The approach adopted has been to identify structural skeletons and then, by recognising modifying events, such as additional oxidation or substitution, to allocate scores, either positive or negative, that relate to the relevant advancement of each compound selected. Unfortunately, such interpretations are generally difficult to follow, particularly for the non-chemist. Selection of compounds to be included is based on the literature available rather than a consistent approach to data-gathering that is equivalent across the taxa under analysis, and this clearly causes bias in the results. This approach has not gained a wide level of acceptance among practising systematicists.

On the other hand, there has been an increasing employment of analytical methods to assess 'degrees of similarity' between comparable sets of chemical data produced from a series of taxa. Expansion of this approach has gone hand-in-hand with access to computing facilities. Some of the earliest examples came from work on volatile oils, an excellent example being the analysis of similarity between populations of *Juniperus ashei*, based on the comparison of 54 terpenoid characters (Adams, 1975). Such studies are, today, fairly commonplace and usually involve either volatile oils or flavonoids as it is relatively easy to establish data matrices on the presence, absence and abundance of individual compounds with little ambiguity. It is now not unusual to see comprehensive cladistic analyses incorporating some chemical data.

6.3.3 What is the future of small molecule chemotaxonomy?

It is difficult not to conclude that we have now identified most, if not all, major insights that systematics will gain from studying the distribution of low molecular weight metabolites. The examples cited in reviews by Harborne and Turner (1984) and Waterman and Gray (1988), in the most recent volumes of *Chemotaxonomie der Pflanzen* (Hegnauer, 1987–1990) and by Waterman (1997) all persist in emphasising these early findings, largely because little of equal importance has happened since.

Life for the chemical taxonomist became more complicated as it emerged that that the distribution map for almost every structural type of compound was expanding as methods for detection and identification improved. Increasingly, new findings had to be rationalised in terms of parallel or convergent evolution, so making systematic relevance more difficult to establish. The advent and rapid development of molecular biology led to the recognition that the genetic infrastructure for the production of a given structure or structural skeleton was likely to be retained as part of the genome, even after expression ceased. This allowed for the option of re-expression to be triggered at some latter point, so that the reappearance of a compound might well not even represent a 're-invention' of a structure or the apparatus for its production. A further complication was the increasing recognition that there were considerable external pressures influencing the production of secondary metabolites, usually relating to the interaction of the producer with environmental factors (Waterman and Mole, 1989). For example, where two unrelated plant taxa were faced with similar problems in relation to seed dispersal, it was to be expected that the stratagem would evolve along similar lines, so involving the production of similar compounds for seed protection and the attraction of appropriate seed dispersal agents.

These confounding factors clearly have a greater impact at higher taxonomic levels. At lower taxonomic levels, the picture has been far more encouraging. The discipline remains bedevilled with practical problems of experimental design and practice that often fail to take account of aspects critical to taxonomic studies, even such elementary factors as adequate vouchering of material. Consequently, an appreciable amount of the body of literature which purports to be of systematic value has in fact no credibility. However, there remains a healthy flow of studies throwing light on relationships between taxa through the use of low molecular weight compounds.

6.4 Molecular biology and plant taxonomy

In the past few years, the development of techniques to allow rapid sequencing of genetic material has opened up a whole new area of chemotaxonomic endeavour. There is now an opportunity to examine similarities and dissimilarities in the genetic material itself, with the generation of cladograms expressing levels of comparability that are likely to have evolutionary significance. This introduces possibilities for a reanalysis of micromolecular data and, in the rest of this chapter, these possibilities will be examined.

6.5 Comparison between patterns of secondary metabolites and molecular phylogeny

6.5.1 Use of molecular markers in plant systematics

Systematic and phylogenetic analyses are traditionally based on macroscopic and microscopic morphological characters (for example flower and pollen morphology, embryology or cytology), which are nowadays often evaluated phenetically or cladistically. Recent decades have seen the advent of chemical characters such as structures of secondary metabolites or of macromolecules, as additional systematic tools, as outlined in the first part of this review. Since the genome contains the basic information of the evolutionary past of all organisms, progress in molecular systematics depends on the ability to decipher the complexity of the corresponding genomes. This approach has profited tremendously from the rapid progress of molecular biology in general. Starting with chromosome analysis and serology of seed proteins, the field moved rapidly via DNA-DNA hybridisation and restriction fragment length polymorphism (RFLP) analyses to the sequence analysis of marker genes.

The analysis of DNA sequences, among them chloroplast DNA or nuclear DNA (Soltis *et al.*, 1992; Doyle, 1993), has increasingly been employed to reconstruct the phylogeny both of higher and lower plants. This approach provides the best phylogenetic resolution so far and has been facilitated by: rapid DNA amplification techniques, such as polymerase chain reaction (PCR); rapid DNA sequencing methods (manual and increasingly automatic sequencing systems); and powerful computation with software programs, such as phylogenetic analysis using parsimony (PAUP), phylogenetic interference package (PHYLIP) or molecular evolutionary genetics analysis (MEGA) (Felsenstein, 1985; Kumar *et al.*, 1993; Swofford, 1993). All of these have been developed during the last 10-20 years. In the legumes and also in other higher plants (Chase *et al.*, 1993), sequences of the chloroplast gene, *rbc*L, and the nuclear internal transcribed spacer (ITS) regions have been demonstrated to be valuable tools through which to infer phylogeny, from family to species level (Doyle, 1995; Sanderson and Liston, 1995; Käss and Wink, 1995, 1996, 1997a,b; Doyle, 1994; Doyle and Doyle, 1993; Doyle *et al.*, 1996).

Although in a strict sense, trees constructed from sequence data can only be gene trees, there is convincing evidence that gene trees very often reflect species trees (Doyle, 1992). Since phylogenetic relationships that are inferred from sequence data are not as much impaired by convergent traits as morphological characters, molecular phylogenies provide a valuable framework that allows the comparison and placement of many other experimental data in a phylogenetic or taxonomic context.

Since many secondary metabolites show a restricted occurrence in apparently related groups of plants (as demonstrated in the first part of this review), it is tempting to use the distribution of secondary metabolites as a systematic marker. The basic questions with regard to the distribution of secondary metabolites are: If a group of species, genera, tribes or families share common ancestry, should we expect that all members of a monophyletic clade should share common apomorphic characters? and if secondary metabolites were non-adaptive traits, which is one of the basic assumptions made in using them as taxonomic markers, should we expect all members of such a clade to produce a particular metabolite?

In the second part of this review, the phylogenetic framework provided by *rbc*L sequences is used to discuss the distribution of a number of secondary metabolites within the plant kingdom, within the Leguminosae and within the genus *Lupinus*. The *rbc*L sequences used (1400 bp) derive from: Chase *et al.* (1993); Käss and Wink, 1997a,b; and M. Wink, E. Käss, F. Merino and G. Mohamed (unpublished data). Trees were reconstructed with maximum parsimony (Swofford, 1993), which are almost congruent with trees built by distance methods, such as neighbour joining (Felsenstein, 1985). Trees that cover large phylogenetic groups cannot be correct in all branches but, for the sake of the present analysis, it is assumed that deviations from the true tree will be of minor importance.

6.5.2 Distribution of pyrrolizidine alkaloids, cardiac glycosides and glucosinolates in the plant kingdom

Pyrrolizidine alkaloids (PAs), of which more than 370 structures are known, affect muscarinic and serotonergic neuroreceptors (Schmeller *et al.*, 1997). In the liver of vertebrates, PAs are converted to toxic pyrrolic derivatives, which are alkylating compounds responsible for the long-term toxicity of PAs, and which through binding to proteins and DNA can cause mutations or even cancer (Mattocks, 1972; McLean, 1970; Roeder, 1995). PAs are produced as chemical defence compounds, mainly in the Asteraceae (tribes Eupatorieae, Senecioneae), Boraginaceae,

Leguminosae (mainly genus *Crotalaria*) and Orchidaceae. Other families include the Apocynaceae, Celastraceae, Convolvulaceae, Poaceae, Ranunculaceae, Rhizophoraceae, Santalaceae and Sapotaceae (Hartmann and Witte, 1995; Roeder, 1995).

As can be seen from Figures 6.9 and 6.10, PA-producing families are distributed all over the plant kingdom and are obviously unrelated. This implies that PA formation in unrelated plant families could be a convergent trait and, thus, not useful as a taxonomic marker at the family level. Even within PA-producing families, PAs do not necessarily occur in all their member taxa. Although these members share common ancestry, the trait is probably either not evolved or biosynthetic processes have been turned-off in these instances. Usually, other defence chemicals are then found instead.

Plant-derived pyrrolizidine alkaloids have been detected in a number of specialised insects, which often advertise their unpalatability by aposematic coloration and/or pyrazines (Brown and Trigo, 1995; Hartmann and Witte, 1995; Rothschild *et al.*, 1979). Examples include: aphids, e.g. *Aphis jacobaeae*, *A. cacaliae*; beetles, e.g. *Oreina cacaliae, O. speciosissima* (Rowell-Rahier *et al.*, 1991); grasshoppers, e.g. *Zonocerus* (Bernays *et al.*, 1977); and many moths and butterflies, especially within the families Arctiidae and Nymphalidae (subfamilies Danainae and Ithomiinae) (Brown and Trigo, 1995; Hartmann and Witte, 1995; Rothschild *et al.*, 1979). Using sequences of the mitochondrial 16S ribosomal ribonucleic acid (rRNA), it has recently been shown that PA sequestration in insects also appears to be a convergent trait that has evolved independently in each order of insects. Even within the Lepidoptera, PA sequestration evolved independently in Nymphalidae and Arctiidae (Wink and von Nickisch-Rosenegk, 1997). Thus, we find a similar theme both in plants and in herbivorous insects.

Cardiac glycosides (CGs) inhibit the Na^+, K^+-adenosine triphosphatases (ATPases) and, thus, destroy the ion gradients which are necessary for many cellular functions, including neuronal activity, secondary active transport and muscle contraction. CGs therefore provide potent chemical defence against herbivores. As can be seen from Figure 6.10, cardiac glycosides are produced in a limited number of genera in many unrelated plant families, such as the Scrophulariaceae, Apocynaceae, Asclepiadaceae, Ranunculaceae, Brassicaceae, Hyacinthaceae, Liliidae, Celastraceae and a few others. Even some animals, such as toads and beetles, can produce their own CGs. With the exception of the Apocynaceae and Asclepiadaceae, all CG-producing plant families are unrelated, implying that cardiac glycosides are not a good phylogenetic marker at the family level, since they appear to have evolved independently on a number of occasions.

Analogous to the situation with PAs, a number of specialised insects (often aposematically coloured) are able to take up and store plant-derived CGs. Examples are: grasshoppers, e.g. *Poekilocerus and Phytmaeteus* (Rothschild, 1966, 1972); aphids, e.g. *Aphis nerium* (Rothschild *et al.*, 1970)); lygaeid bugs, e.g. *Oncopeltus*, *Caenocoris*, *Spilostethus*, *Lygaeus*, *Apterola*, *Arocatus*, *Aspilocoryphus*, *Aulacopeltus*, *Graptostethus*, *Haemobaphus*, *Lygaeospilus*, *Melanerythrus*, *Microspilus* and *Horvathiolus* (Malcolm, 1990; Rothschild, 1972; Rothschild *et al.*, 1971); beetles e.g. *Tetraopes* and *Epicauta* (Rothschild, 1972); Diptera, *Zenilla* (Rothschild, 1972); and again Lepidoptera, e.g. *Danaus*, *Syntomeida*, *Euchaetias*, *Arctia* and *Empyreuma* (Nickisch-Rosenegk von *et al.*, 1990; Rothschild, 1972; Rothschild *et al.*, 1970a, 1973). Insects sequestering CGs are usually protected from predators, such as birds (Brower *et al.*, 1975; Rothschild, 1966). Using 16S rRNA sequences, it was recently shown that CG sequestration in Lepidoptera apparently evolved independently in Nymphalidae and Arctiidae (Wink and von Nickisch-Rosenegk, 1997), which corresponds to the situation in plants.

Glucosinolates are glycosides that are stored in the vacuole of plant cells. Upon wounding or infection, the cellular compartmentation breaks down, which brings together glucosinolates and corresponding glucosidases. As a result, mustard oils are released that show antimicrobial and herbivore-deterrent activities. Glucosinolates are produced by members of the Brassicaceae, Capparaceae, Resedaceae, Moringaceae, Tovariaceae, Limnanthaceae and Caricaceae. These plant families, of which some are traditionally grouped into the Capparidales, are phylogenetically related and form a monophyletic clade (Fig. 6.10). Interestingly, the Caricaceae, which had not been placed in the Capparidales in classical systematics, are united with this group based both on molecular and phytochemical reasoning (Fig. 6.10). It is therefore likely that the production of glucosinolates once evolved in an ancestor of this group and was maintained as a potent defence strategy by most of its members. This would be a good example of the usefulness of secondary molecules for taxonomy, if it were not for the fact that glucosinolates are also produced by members of the Euphorbiaceae, Gyrostemonaceae, and Salvadoraceae (Teuscher and Lindequist, 1994), which are unrelated to the Capparidales. This provides a dilemma seen in most groups of secondary metabolites.

Summarising the examples of Figure 6.9 and 6.10, it is apparent that most of these groups of compounds are of very limited value as a taxonomic marker at the higher hierarchical level. Partial exceptions are the glucosinolates, which occur in seven plant families that are indeed related as a monophyletic clade, or the 1-btiq alkaloids, which occur in the ancestral orders of Dicotyledonae, i.e. Piperales, Aristolochiales,

Magnoliales and Ranunculales (Figures 6.9 and 6.10). However, because of their occurrence in other unrelated families, glucosinolates and 1-btiq alkaloids do not provide a consistent marker. It has been argued above that the most likely explanation for the occurrence of PAs and CGs in unrelated families is convergent evolution. Since these metabolites appear to provide a strong selective advantage for the taxa producing them (as defence chemicals against microbes and/or herbivores) and since they affect important basic molecular targets in herbivores, they could have evolved randomly and been selected because of their biological activity (Wink and von Nickisch-Rosenegk, 1997; Wink *et al.*, 1998; Wink, 1998).

However, another explanation might be possible: quinolizidine alkaloids (QAs) (Fig. 6.11) are typical secondary metabolites in some phylogenetically-related tribes of the Leguminosae (Fig. 6.12A) but they have also been found in other unrelated taxa, e.g. the families Chenopodiaceae, Berberidaceae, Ranunculaceae, Scrophulariaceae and Solanaceae (Teuscher and Lindequist, 1994). Since traces of QAs can be detected in plants and cell cultures of even more taxa, it has been postulated (Wink and Witte, 1983) that the genes which encode the basic pathway leading to these alkaloids must have evolved early during evolution, that they are present but turned-off in most instances, and that they are turned-on again in plants that use the alkaloids as chemical defence substances (Wink 1988, 1992). This hypothesis can be tested as soon as the genes that encode the biosynthesis of PAs, CGs, glucosinolates or QAs have been isolated. We suspect, however, that no single evolutionary scenario will be found for all groups of compounds but that convergent and phylogenetically-conserved traits will co-occur (see distribution of glucosinolates in this section).

6.5.3 Phytochemical traits of the Leguminosae

It might be argued that secondary metabolites are better and more reliable markers within families, tribes or genera than at the higher order level. The Leguminosae have been selected as an example to examine, since this very large plant family with 650 genera and more than 18,000 species have been extensively studied phytochemically. Several types of alkaloids, non-protein amino acids (NPAAs), amines, flavonoids, isoflavones, coumarins, anthraquinones, di-, sesqui- and triterpenes, cyanogenic glycosides, protease inhibitors and lectins have been described in this family. Most of these compounds are thought to function as defence chemicals or as signal compounds (see reviews and compilations in Harborne *et al.*, 1971; Polhill *et al.*, 1981b; Stirton, 1987; Hegnauer and Hegnauer, 1994; Southon, 1994; Sprent and McKey, 1994; Kinghorn and

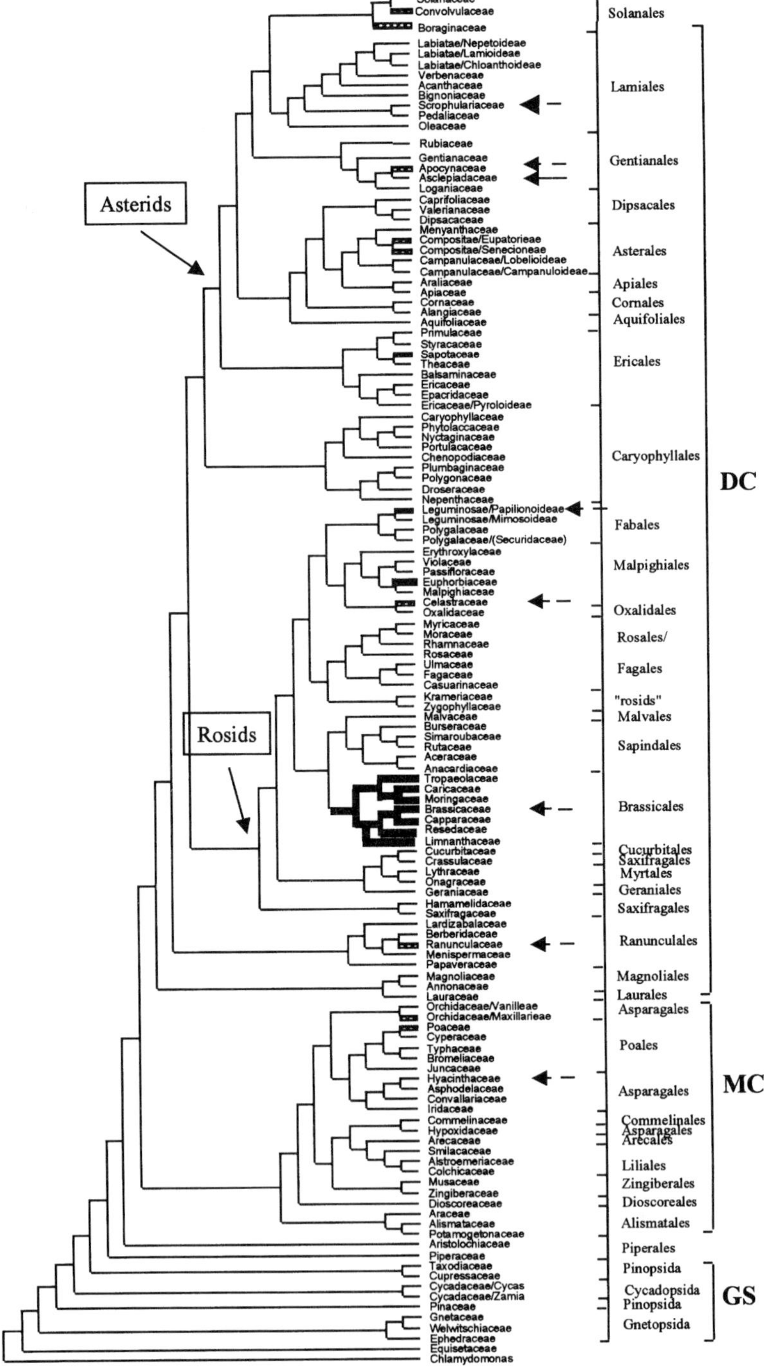
Asterids
Rosids
Solanaceae
Convolvulaceae
Boraginaceae
Labiatae/Nepetoideae
Labiatae/Lamioideae
Labiatae/Chloanthoideae
Verbenaceae
Acanthaceae
Bignoniaceae
Scrophulariaceae
Pedaliaceae
Oleaceae
Rubiaceae
Gentianaceae
Apocynaceae
Asclepiadaceae
Loganiaceae
Caprifoliaceae
Valerianaceae
Dipsacaceae
Menyanthaceae
Compositae/Eupatorieae
Compositae/Senecioneae
Campanulaceae/Lobelioideae
Campanulaceae/Campanuloideae
Araliaceae
Apiaceae
Cornaceae
Alangiaceae
Aquifoliaceae
Primulaceae
Styracaceae
Sapotaceae
Theaceae
Balsaminaceae
Ericaceae
Epacridaceae
Ericaceae/Pyroloideae
Caryophyllaceae
Phytolaccaceae
Nyctaginaceae
Portulacaceae
Chenopodiaceae
Plumbaginaceae
Polygonaceae
Droseraceae
Nepenthaceae
Leguminosae/Papilionoideae
Leguminosae/Mimosoideae
Polygalaceae
Polygalaceae/(Securidaceae)
Erythroxylaceae
Violaceae
Passifloraceae
Euphorbiaceae
Malpighiaceae
Celastraceae
Oxalidaceae
Myricaceae
Moraceae
Rhamnaceae
Rosaceae
Ulmaceae
Fagaceae
Casuarinaceae
Krameriaceae
Zygophyllaceae
Malvaceae
Burseraceae
Simaroubaceae
Rutaceae
Aceraceae
Anacardiaceae
Tropaeolaceae
Caricaceae
Moringaceae
Brassicaceae
Capparaceae
Resedaceae
Limnanthaceae
Cucurbitaceae
Crassulaceae
Lythraceae
Onagraceae
Geraniaceae
Hamamelidaceae
Saxifragaceae
Lardizabalaceae
Berberidaceae
Ranunculaceae
Menispermaceae
Papaveraceae
Magnoliaceae
Annonaceae
Lauraceae
Orchidaceae/Vanilleae
Orchidaceae/Maxillarieae
Poaceae
Cyperaceae
Typhaceae
Bromeliaceae
Juncaceae
Hyacinthaceae
Asphodelaceae
Convallariaceae
Iridaceae
Commelinaceae
Hypoxidaceae
Arecaceae
Smilacaceae
Alstroemeriaceae
Colchicaceae
Musaceae
Zingiberaceae
Dioscoreaceae
Araceae
Alismataceae
Potamogetonaceae
Aristolochiaceae
Piperaceae
Taxodiaceae
Cupressaceae
Cycadaceae/Cycas
Cycadaceae/Zamia
Pinaceae
Gnetaceae
Welwitschiaceae
Ephedraceae
Equisetaceae
Chlamydomonas
Solanales
Lamiales
Gentianales
Dipsacales
Asterales
Apiales
Cornales
Aquifoliales
Ericales
Caryophyllales
Fabales
Malpighiales
Oxalidales
Rosales/
Fagales
"rosids"
Malvales
Sapindales
Brassicales
Cucurbitales
Saxifragales
Myrtales
Geraniales
Saxifragales
Ranunculales
Magnoliales
Laurales
Asparagales
Poales
Asparagales
Commelinales
Asparagales
Arecales
Liliales
Zingiberales
Dioscoreales
Alismatales
Piperales
Pinopsida
Cycadopsida
Pinopsida
Gnetopsida
DC
MC
GS

Balandrin, 1984; Wink, 1993c; Wink *et al.*, 1995). Furthermore, *rbc*L sequences have been obtained for over 300 legumes (Käss and Wink, 1995, 1996, 1997a,b; M. Wink, E. Käss, F. Merino, G. Mohamed, unpublished data), so providing a DNA-based phylogenetic framework to analyse the distribution of secondary metabolites within the family.

About 100 genera that cover most tribes of the Leguminosae have been selected. In most cases, *rbc*L sequences of these genera cluster in a way which is consistent within their traditional grouping in tribes and

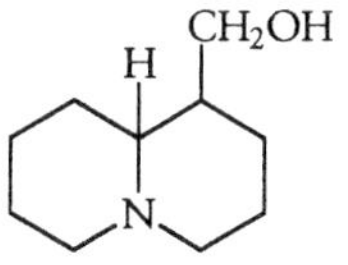

(21) Lupinine

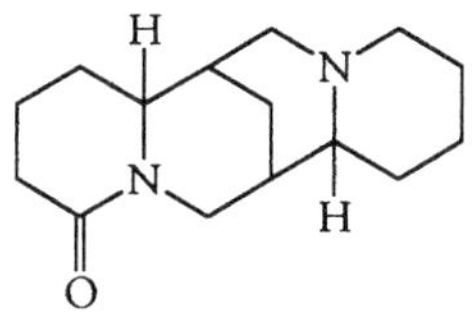

(22) Lupanine

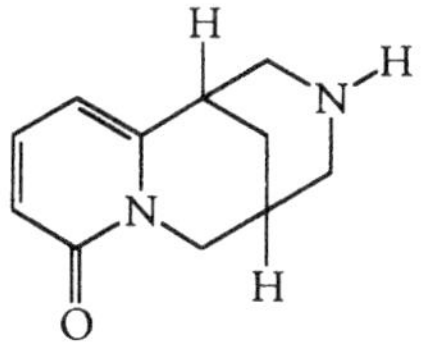

(23) Cytisine

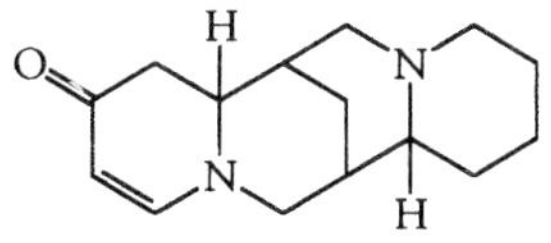

(24) Multiflorine

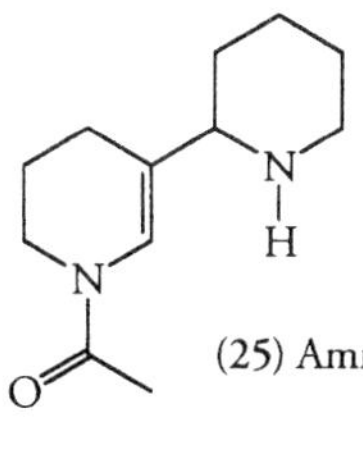

(25) Ammodendrine

Figure 6.11 Structures of the quinolizidine alkaloids, lupinine (21), lupanine (22), cytisine (23) and multiflorine (24) and of a dipiperidine alkaloid of the ammodendrine type (25).

Figure 6.10 (Facing page) Families and orders of higher plants, placed in a phylogenetic framework reconstructed from nucleotide sequences of the *rbc*L gene. The illustration is presented as a cladogram of a strict consensus of the two most parsimonious trees calculated by heuristic search. Branches leading to families which accumulate glucosinolates, pyrrolizidine alkaloids and cardiac glycosides are marked. Abbreviations: GS, Gymnospermae; MC, Monocotyledonae; DC, Dicotyledonae. Key to the occurrence of: glucosinolates, ▬; pyrrolizidine alkaloids, ▒; cardiac glycosides, ◄—.

subfamilies (Polhill, 1994). Members of the Caesalpinioideae cluster at the base of the legume tree, which is in agreement with the fossil record (Herendeen and Dilcher, 1992). Members of the Mimosoideae derive unambiguously from the Caesalpinioideae (Doyle, 1994; Wink *et al.*, 1993; Käss and Wink, 1995, 1996, 1997a) and are not ancestral, as had sometimes been assumed. Also, the groupings within the Papilionoideae, which form a monophyletic clade, are mostly congruent with traditional systematics (Polhill *et al.*, 1981a; Polhill, 1994), starting with Sophoreae at the base and leading to Genisteae as the more advanced tribes.

6.5.4 Nitrogen-containing secondary metabolites

Quinolizidine alkaloids (Fig. 6.11) are the most prominent group of alkaloids in legumes, being present in members of the subfamily Papilionoideae in the tribes Genisteae, Crotalarieae, Podalyrieae, Thermopsideae, Liparieae, Euchresteae, Bossiaeeae, and Sophoreae (Kinghorn and Balandrin, 1984; Wink, 1993a). Dipiperidine alkaloids of the ammodendrine type (Fig. 6.11), which also derive from lysine as a precursor, exhibit a comparable distribution pattern). As can be seen from Figure 6.12A, these tribes, with the exception of the Sophoreae, are apparently monophyletic and nearly all taxa in this assemblage accumulate QAs. Obvious exceptions are members of the large genus *Crotalaria*, which sequester either pyrrolizidine alkaloids (Fig. 6.12A) or NPAAs (Fig. 6.12B). In *Lotononis*, a genus closely allied to *Crotalaria*, some taxa produce QAs and others PAs. *Crotalaria* and *Lotononis* derive from ancestors that definitely produced QAs but not PAs, therefore, the general ability to make QAs must have been present but the corresponding genes are either lost or completely turned-off in *Crotalaria* and partially turned-off in *Lotononis*. The formation of PAs rather than QAs appears to be a new acquisition for chemical defence, which evolved convergently (compare Fig. 6.10 and related discussion); the occurrence of simple PAs in *Laburnum* and *Adenocarpus* might be interpreted

Figure 6.12A (Facing page) Genera and tribes of the Leguminosae, placed in a phylogenetic framework reconstructed from nucleotide sequences of the *rbc*L gene. The illustrations (Fig. 6.12A–6.12F) are presented as cladograms of a strict consensus of the six most parsimonious trees calculated by heuristic search. Due to space limitations, a few tribal names are not listed in the figures but are abbreviated by numbers after the genus name: 1 = Liparieae; 2 = Bossiaeeae; 3 = Abreae; 4 = Carmichaelieae; 5 = Millettieae; 6 = Psoraleae; 7 = Desmodieae; 8 = Tephrosieae (Millettieae); 9 = Galegeae; 10 = Indigofereae; 11 = Adesmieae; 12 = Amorpheae; 13 = Dalbergieae; 14 = Mimoseae; 15 = Ingeae; 16 = Parkieae; 17 = Acacieae; 18 = Cassieae; 19 = Caesalpinieae; 20 = Detarieae; 21 = Cercideae. Figure 6.12A shows the occurrence of alkaloids. Key to branches leading to families that accumulate: quinolizidines, ▬; pyrrolizidines (No. 1; see arrows) 1; Erythrina (No. 3) 3; indolizidines (No. 4) 4; β-carbolines (No. 5) 5; or simple indoles (No. 2) 2 are marked.

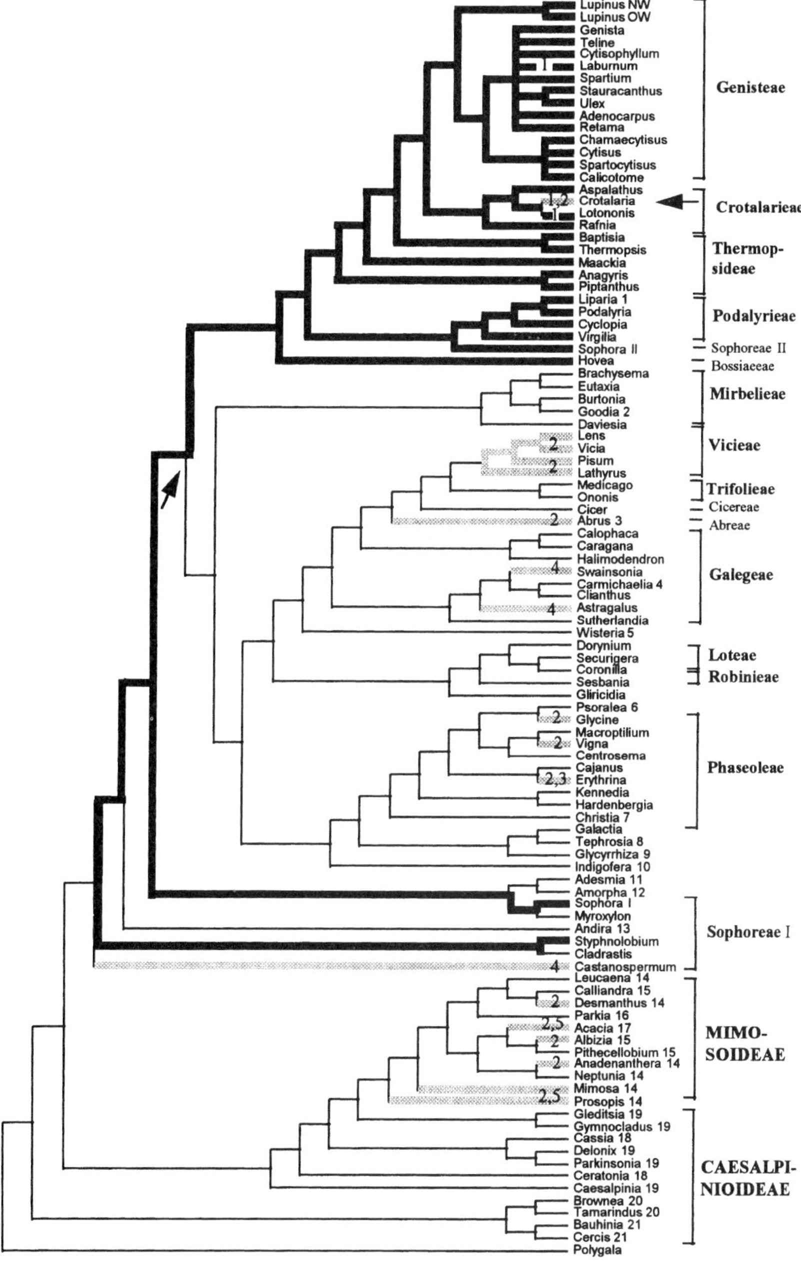

Lupinus NW
Lupinus OW
Genista
Teline
Cytisophyllum
Laburnum
Spartium
Stauracanthus
Ulex
Adenocarpus
Retama
Chamaecytisus
Cytisus
Spartocytisus
Calicotome
Aspalathus
Crotalaria
Lotononis
Rafnia
Baptisia
Thermopsis
Maackia
Anagyris
Piptanthus
Liparia 1
Podalyria
Cyclopia
Virgilia
Sophora II
Hovea
Brachysema
Eutaxia
Burtonia
Goodia 2
Daviesia
Lens
Vicia
Pisum
Lathyrus
Medicago
Ononis
Cicer
Abrus 3
Calophaca
Caragana
Halimodendron
Swainsonia
Carmichaelia 4
Clianthus
Astragalus
Sutherlandia
Wisteria 5
Dorynium
Securigera
Coronilla
Sesbania
Gliricidia
Psoralea 6
Glycine
Macroptilium
Vigna
Centrosema
Cajanus
Erythrina
Kennedia
Hardenbergia
Christia 7
Galactia
Tephrosia 8
Glycyrrhiza 9
Indigofera 10
Adesmia 11
Amorpha 12
Sophora I
Myroxylon
Andira 13
Styphnolobium
Cladrastis
Castanospermum
Leucaena 14
Calliandra 15
Desmanthus 14
Parkia 16
Acacia 17
Albizia 15
Pithecellobium 15
Anadenanthera 14
Neptunia 14
Mimosa 14
Prosopis 14
Gleditsia 19
Gymnocladus 19
Cassia 18
Delonix 19
Parkinsonia 19
Ceratonia 18
Caesalpinia 19
Brownea 20
Tamarindus 20
Bauhinia 21
Cercis 21
Polygala
1
1,2
1
2
2
2
4
4
2
2
2,3
4
2
2,5
2
2
2,5
Genisteae
Crotalarieae
Thermop-
sideae
Podalyrieae
Sophoreae II
Bossiaeeae
Mirbelieae
Vicieae
Trifolieae
Cicereae
Abreae
Galegeae
Loteae
Robinieae
Phaseoleae
Sophoreae I
MIMO-
SOIDEAE
CAESALPI-
NIOIDEAE

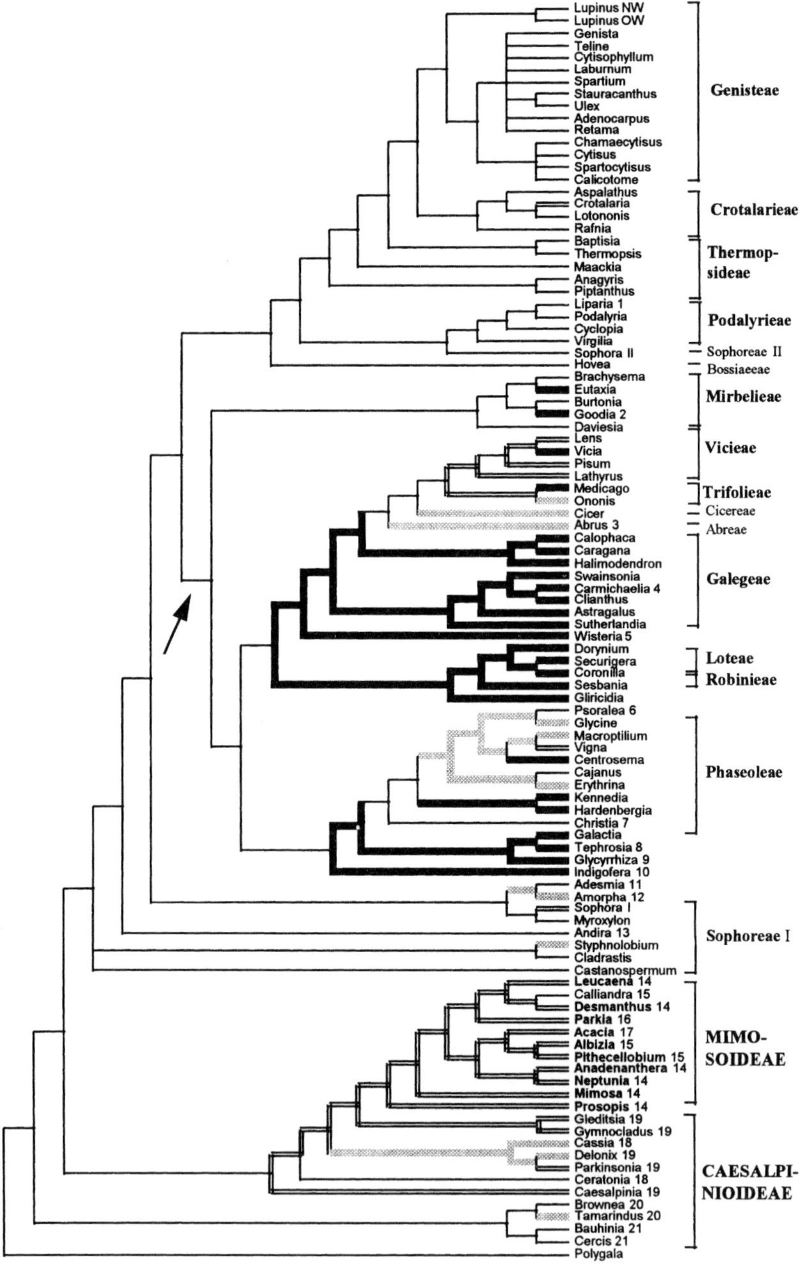

Figure 6.12B Occurrence of nonprotein amino acids (NPAAs). Key to branches leading to families that accumulate: pipecolic acid and derivatives (═══ Lens); pipecolic acid and djenkolic acids (═══ Acacia); canavanine (▬▬); others NPAAs (░░░). See also legend to Figure 6.12A.

accordingly. In a few taxa that cluster within QA-accumulating genera, QAs are hardly detectable or levels are very low, such as in *Ulex*, *Calicotome* or *Spartocytisus*. These taxa have in common extensive spines that have apparently supplanted chemical defence. In such cases, the presence or absence of QAs is clearly a trait reflecting different ecological strategies rather than taxonomic relationships.

The Sophoreae, and in particular the genus *Sophora*, appear(s) to be polyphyletic and need(s) thorough revision (Polhill *et al.*, 1981b; Stirton, 1987; Käss and Wink, 1995, 1996, 1997a). Part of the QA-producing genera *Sophora* (here *Sophora* II) and *Maackia* always cluster outside the Sophoreae, as part of the Podalyrieae and Liparieae or Thermopsideae (Fig. 6.12A). More ancestral Sophoreae include *Sophora secundiflora* (*Sophora* I) and related taxa, which cluster as a sister taxon to *Myroxylon*, while *Sophora japonica* is related to *Cladrastis* and *Castanospermum*. *S. japonica* has recently been removed from the genus *Sophora* into the genus *Styphnolobium*, thus recognising this obvious discrepancy. *Sophora* I and *Styphnolobium* accumulate QAs as major and minor secondary constituents, respectively, indicating that the genetic capacity to make QAs must be present in the very early members of the Papilionoideae. An alternative explanation of a parallel evolution of QAs in early and later Papilionoideae appears less likely. As with *Crotalaria*, which no longer accumulates QAs, we can assume that all the other tribes of the Papilionoideae that diverge at the branch that is indicated by an arrow (Fig. 6.12A) had, at that point, the capacity to synthesise QAs. This ability has subsequently been lost or the corresponding genes have simply been turned-off. As shown below, these QA-deficient tribes accumulate other defence compounds instead.

In addition to QAs, legumes accumulate a wide range of other alkaloids, deriving from different precursors. Most of them have distributions that are restricted to a few, often non-related taxa. For example, *Erythrina* alkaloids, which derive from tyrosine as a precursor, are typical of members of the large genus *Erythrina* and have not been found elsewhere in the plant kingdom. Indolizidine alkaloids, which inhibit hydrolytic enzymes, have been reported in *Swainsonia, Astragalus* (tribe Galegeae) and *Castanospermum* (Sophoreae). β-Carboline alkaloids have been detected in a few mimosoid taxa of the tribes Mimoseae and Acacieae. A number of simple phenylethylamine or simple indole alkaloids have been found, usually in taxa that do not accumulate QAs (Fig. 6.12A). Interestingly, the occurrence of quinolizidines and other alkaloids is usually mutually exclusive, indicating the parsimonious utilisation of chemical defence strategies.

The distribution of protease inhibitors (PIs) (Fig. 6.12C) (i.e. trypsin and chymotrypsin inhibitors) exhibit an almost complementary pattern to

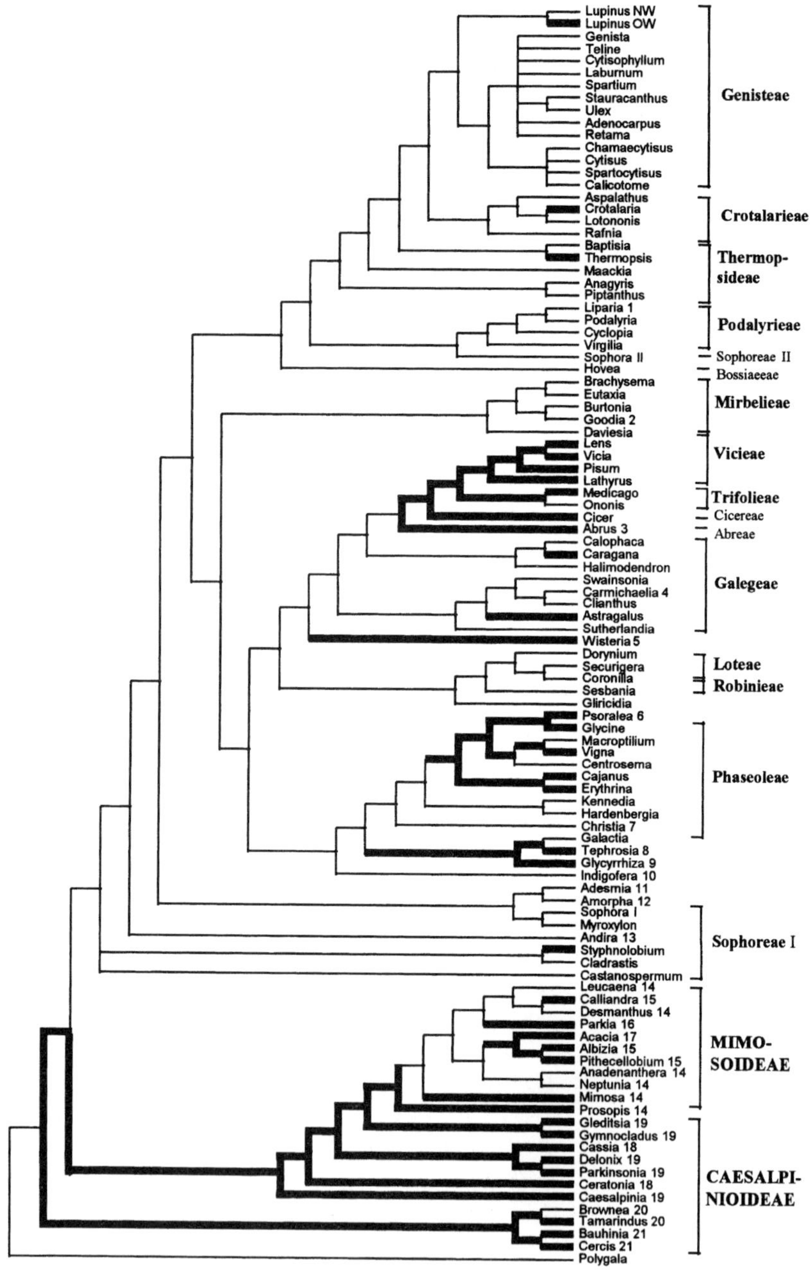

Figure 6.12C Occurrence of protease inhibitors. Key to branches leading to families that accumulate protease inhibitors (▬). See also legend to Figure 6.12A.

quinolizidine alkaloids. Most Caesalpinoideae and many Mimosoideae accumulate PIs in their seeds, where they serve concomitantly as chemical defence and nitrogen storage compounds. It is unclear whether some genera of the Mimosoideae have secondarily lost this trait or whether they have not been studied in sufficient detail. Within the Papilionoideae, PIs are prominent in the tribes Vicieae, Trifolieae, Cicereae, Abreae, Galegeae, Loteae, Phaseoleae and Tephrosieae but have not been detected in the Mirbelieae. According to Figure 6.12C, PI formation in Caesalpinioideae/Mimosoideae and Papilionoideae could be based on common ancestry. This would mean, however, that the trait has been turned-off in a number of papilionoid tribes, which produce QAs and other secondary metabolites instead. Alternatively, PI formation could have evolved independently in these legume subfamilies. Since the genes for PIs are known, it would be challenging to analyse whether PI genes are present or absent in non-PI-producing taxa.

If all NPAAs with different structures and activities are grouped together (Fig. 6.12B) the pattern of NPAA accumulation is again almost complementary to the distribution of QAs. Like PIs and QAs, NPAAs are thought to serve at least two purposes, as chemical defence compounds and as mobile nitrogen storage compounds of seeds, which are used as a nitrogen source for the seedling. Considering different structural types of NPAAs, however, a more differentiated picture becomes apparent. At least three groups of NPAAs are common in legumes, based on canavanine, pipecolic acid and derivatives, and the sulfur-containing djencolic acids. Canavanine is common in the tribes Galegeae, Loteae, Tephrosieae, Robinieae and in some Phaseoleae, and it might be assumed that the trait of canavanine accumulation was acquired by an ancestor (see arrow in Fig. 6.12B) from which all the other tribes derived. If this were so, then the canavanine genes are turned-off in the Vicieae, Trifolieae, Cicereae and Abreae, which produce pipecolic acids instead. Whether pipecolic acid biosynthesis was independently invented in Caesalpinioideae/Mimosoideae and in the papilionoid tribes, Vicieae and Trifolieae, or whether the canavanine genes were only inactivated in Vicieae and Trifolieae is open to debate, analogous to the situation of PIs (Fig. 6.12C). As strict taxonomic markers, both canavanine and pipecolic acid derivatives are of limited value, since they would place the wrong groups together in several instances. By contrast, djencolic acids appear more appropriate as a taxonomic marker, since taxa that accumulate them all belong to the Mimosoideae. Several other NPAAs have been described from legumes (Harborne *et al.*, 1971; Polhill *et al.*, 1981b; Stirton, 1987; Hegnauer and Hegnauer, 1994; Southon, 1994; Sprent and McKey, 1994), most of which have a more restricted occurrence and presence or absence in phylogenetically-related taxa is a common theme.

Cyanogenic glycosides appear to be more common in the ancestral legume tribes (Fig. 6.12D). Whether the occurrence of cyanogenic glycosides is based on common genes that are turned-off in most instances and turned-on in a few, cannot yet be answered; both convergent and independent evolution are plausible scenarios.

In summary, the numerous nitrogen-containing metabolites seem to function both as chemical defence and nitrogen storage compounds in legumes, and are thus open to natural selection. Although they appear as plausible taxonomic markers in a few parts of the legume free, they fail to do so in others. Their occurrence appears to reflect different evolutionary and life strategies, rather than taxonomic stringency.

6.5.5 Nitrogen-free secondary metabolites

Are non-nitrogenous secondary metabolites better taxonomic markers? Whereas flavonoids are found in all three subfamilies, and are thus of limited value at the family/tribal level, isoflavones are obviously restricted to the subfamily Papilionoideae (Fig. 6.12E). With the exception of a few tribes and genera, among which are several Australian taxa, all Papilionoideae accumulate isoflavones and derivatives, including phytoalexines of the pterocarpan type (Fig. 6.12E). It remains an open question as to whether the Australian taxa have not been studied appropriately to identify these compounds or whether they are absent due to the fact that a loss of biosynthetic capacity occurred in ancestors when colonising Australia. Catechins and proanthocyanins or galloylcatechins occur in all three subfamilies; their occurrence reflects life style, i.e. growth as trees, rather than taxonomic relatedness. In the Caesalpinioideae and Mimosoideae, both traits are almost congruent, since woody life style dominates in both subfamilies.

Coumarins and furanocoumarins, which serve as potent defence compounds in the Apiaceae and Rutaceae, occur in a few, mostly unrelated, species. Only in the genus *Psoralea*, do they have a wide distribution. Anthraquinones, which are potent Na^+, K^+-ATPase inhibitors and strong purgatives, occur widely in the genus *Cassia* but otherwise only occasionally in *Andira* and *Abrus*.

All classes of terpenoids have been found in legumes. The known distribution of triterpenes and triterpene and steroidal saponins (including cardiac glycosides in *Securigera* and *Coronilla*, both Loteae) is illustrated in Figure 6.12F. Triterpenes and saponins, which are again considered to be powerful defence compounds against microbes and herbivores, are more common in the ancestral Caesalpinioideae/ Mimosoideae and in the basal tribes of the Papilionoideae but are also

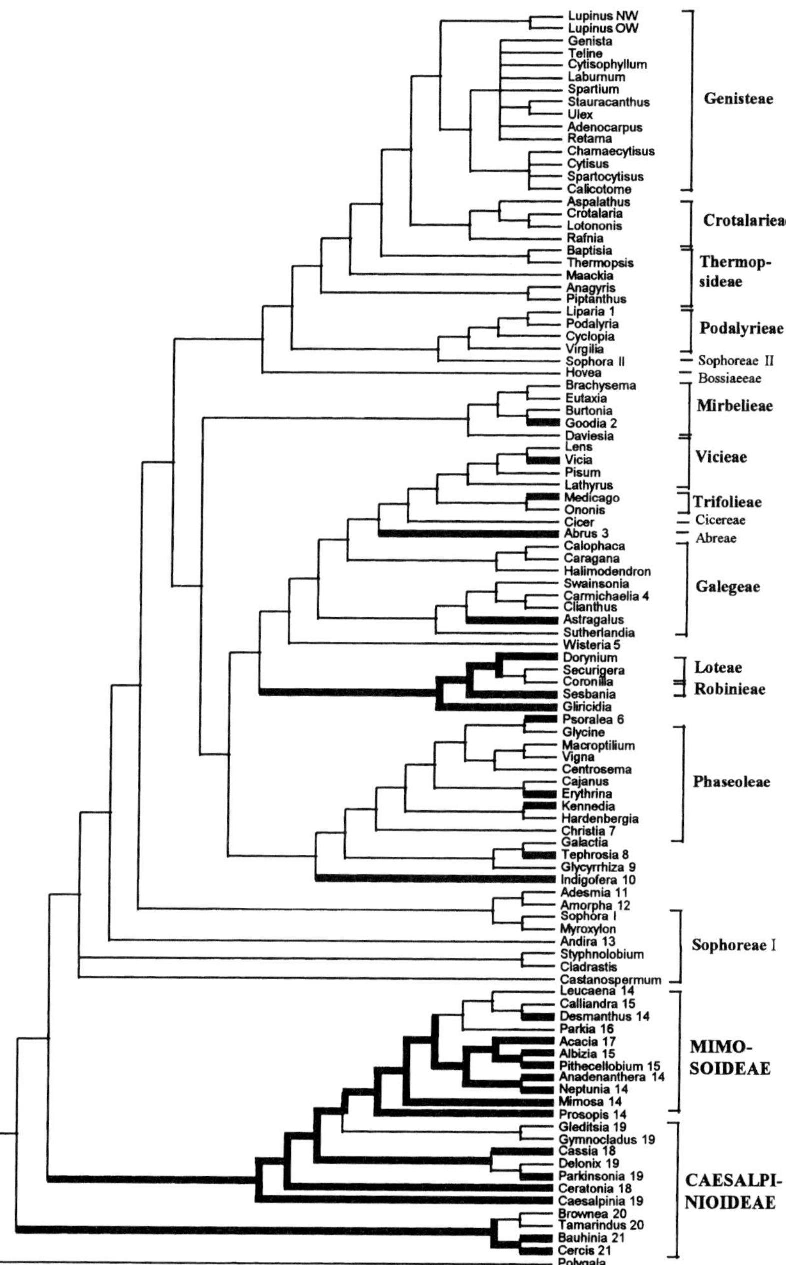

Figure 6.12D Occurrence of cyanogenic glycosides. Key to branches leading to families that accumulate cyanogens (▬). See also legend to Figure 6.12A.

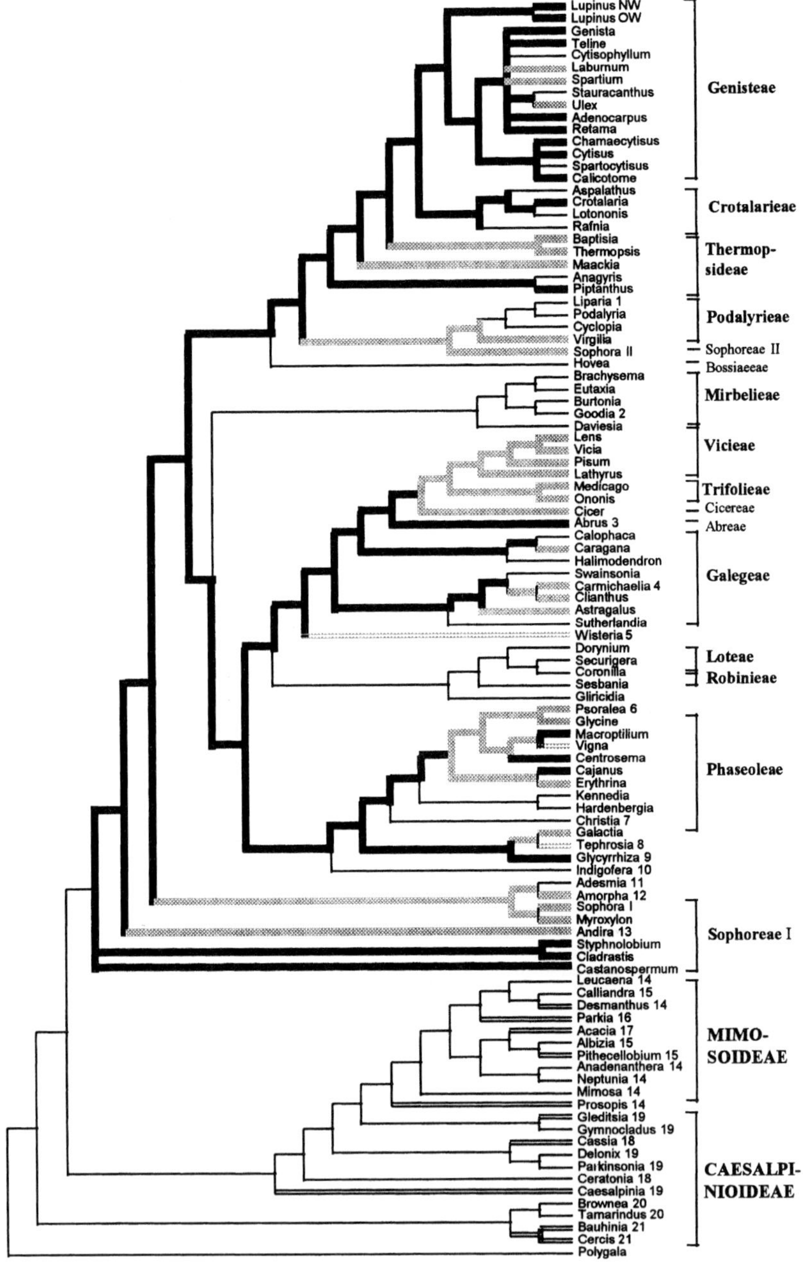

Figure 6.12E Occurrence of flavonoids. Key to branches leading to families that accumulate: isoflavones (▬); isoflavones and pterocarpans (▒); catechins/proanthocyanins (═). See also legend to Figure 6.12A.

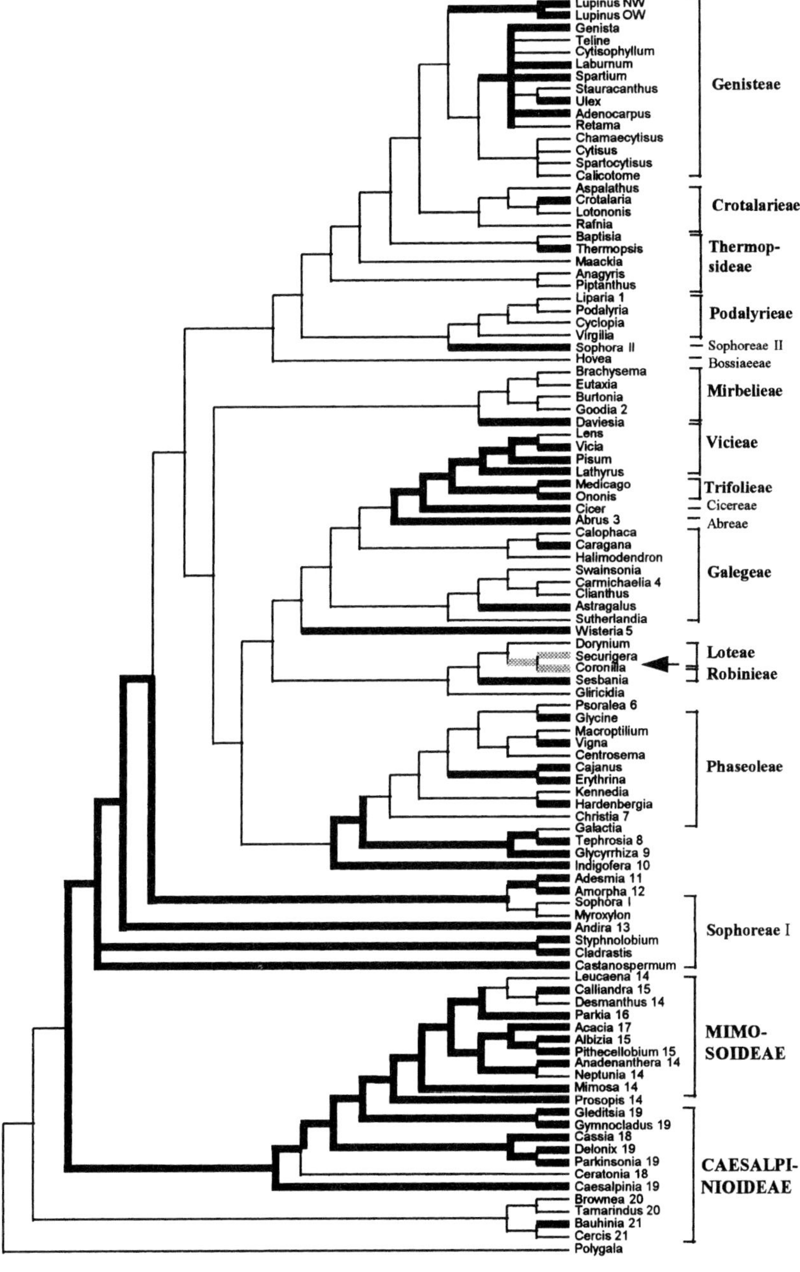

Figure 6.12F Occurrence of triterpenes and cardiac glycosides. Key to branches leading to families that accumulate: triterpenes/triterpene saponins (▬); cardiac glycosides (░). See also legend to Figure 6.12A.

important in the Vicieae, Trifolieae, Cicereae and Phaseoleae. Whether they have arisen independently in different taxa, which seems probable as there is no clear nodal link, or whether the genes evolved at the beginning of legume evolution but have switched-on or switched-off according to ecological needs, cannot be answered with certainty. The wide distribution of triterpenes and triterpene saponins in the plant kingdom and their common basic structures favours the latter possibility.

As seen in Figures 6.12A–6.12F, a particular group of secondary metabolites is confined to a systematically-related group of species or genera. Are, therefore, patterns of secondary metabolites better markers at the genus level? To assess this possibility, the occurrence of quinolizidine alkaloids in the genus *Lupinus* has been analysed.

6.5.6 *Quinolizidine alkaloids in the genus Lupinus*

For a finer phylogenetic resolution, the nuclear ITS1 and ITS2 regions have been chosen to reconstruct the phylogeny of Genisteae and some other papilionid tribes (Käss and Wink, 1997a,b). Overall, tree topology is congruent between ITS and *rbc*L trees, indicating that reticulate evolution is not a major problem in this part of the Leguminosae (Käss and Wink, 1997a).

The genus *Lupinus* comprises several hundred more or less well-defined species, 12 in the Old World and the others in the New World of North, Central and South America. Sequence data indicate that New World lupins apparently derived from Old World species. Long distance dispersal from Old World origin seems to have led to the colonisation of the Atlantic part of South America (clade with *L. aureonitens*, *L. albescens* and *L. paraguarensis*) and of North America (see Fig. 6.13A) (Käss and Wink, 1997b).

The biosynthesis of QAs proceeds from lysine via cadaverine to tetracyclic alkaloids, such as lupanine or sparteine. Lupanine/sparteine is a precursor for tricyclic alkaloids, such as angustifoline, or the α-pyridone alkaloids, such as anagyrine or cytisine. Most species of lupins exhibit typical profiles of QA that could, potentially, work as taxonomic markers. In Figures 6.13A–6.13C, the branches leading to taxa which accumulate a certain structural type of QA have been marked. All taxa show alkaloids of the sparteine/lupanine type, at least as minor alkaloids; their occurrence would be congruent to the picture shown in Figure 6.12A.

α-pyridone alkaloids are apparently present in the more ancestral tribes of the Papilionoideae but they also occur in the more advanced *Cytisus*/*Genista* complex of the Genisteae. This suggests that the ancestors of lupins, which represent a sister clade to the modern Genisteae, must have possessed the biosynthetic capacity to produce

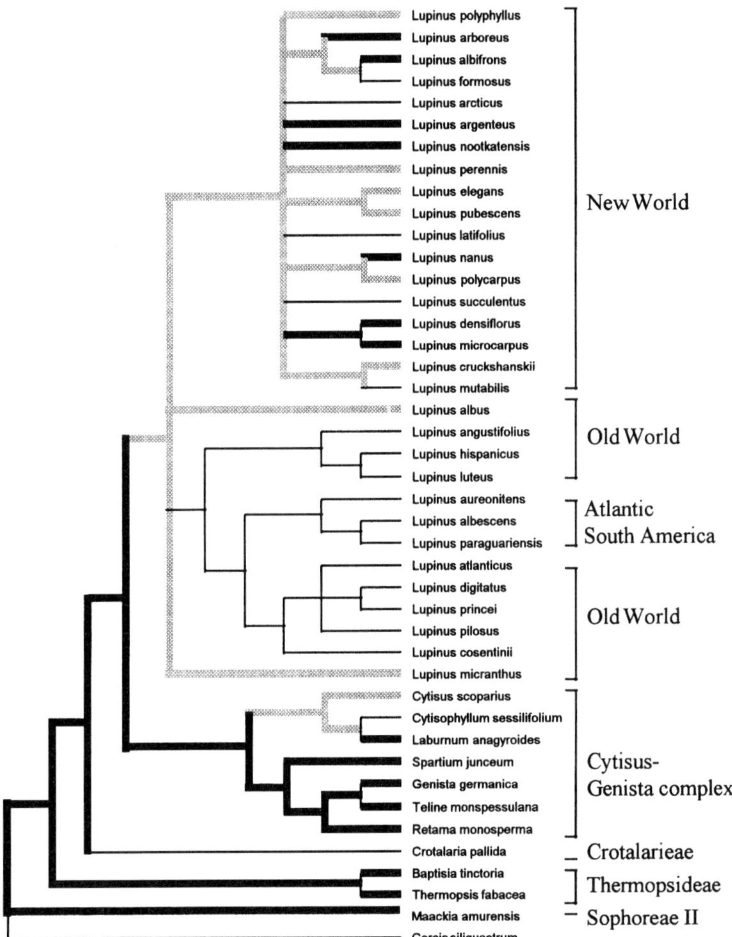

Figure 6.13A Occurrence of quinolizidine alkaloids in the genus *Lupinus*, and some other papilionoid tribes. Genera and species of the Papilionoideae were placed in a phylogenetic framework reconstructed from nucleotide sequences of the ITS1 and ITS2 regions. The illustrations are presented as cladograms of a strict consensus of the 20 most parsimonious trees calculated by heuristic search. This panel shows the distribution of 5,6-dehydrolupanine and α-pyridone alkaloids (such as anagyrine, cytisine). Key to branches leading to species that accumulate 5,6-dehydrolupanine (grey bar); 5,6-dehydrolupanine, anagyrine and other pyridones (black bar).

these alkaloids. However, anagyrine and related alkaloids have been found in comparably few lupins of North America and they are definitely absent from Old World lupins (Fig. 6.13A). The occurrence of alpha pyridones in North American taxa is sporadic and apparently not helpful

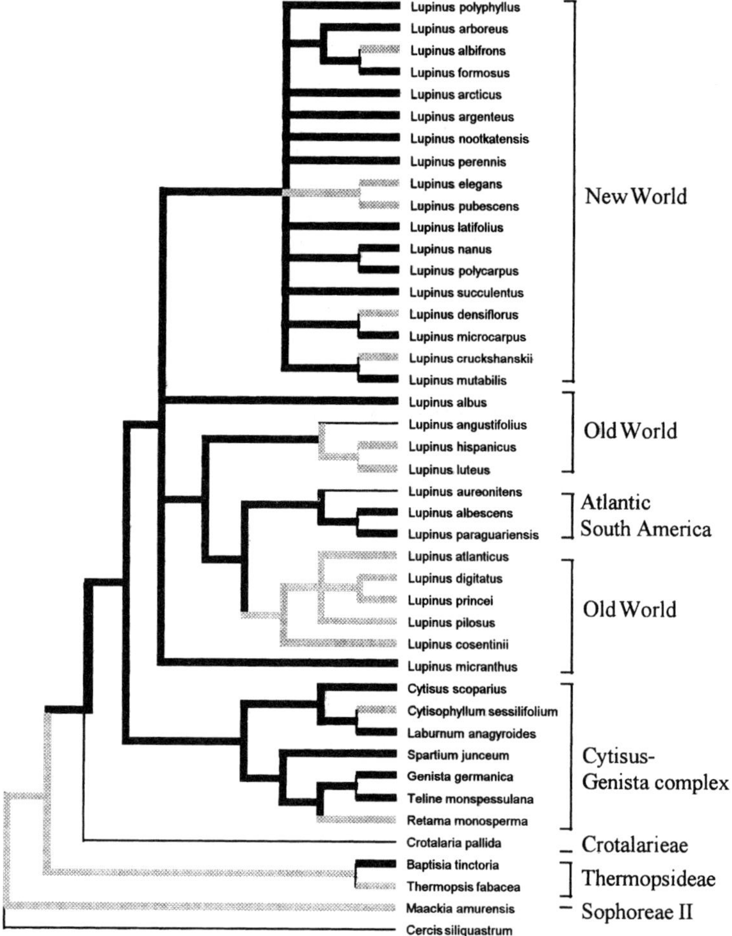

Figure 6.13B Distribution of the bipiperidine alkaloid ammodendrine and derivatives and of the bicyclic lupinine. Key to branches leading to species that accumulate: ammodendrine and derivatives (▬); bipiperidines and lupinine and derivatives (▒). See also legend to Figure 6.13A.

as a taxonomic marker. 5,6-Dehydrolupanine is an intermediate between lupanine and alpha pyridone alkaloids. Surprisingly, many more lupins have been detected that accumulate this alkaloid, at least as a minor component. As can be seen from Figure 6.13A, two Old World and most North and Central American taxa show this trait. This suggests that the pathway leading to α-pyridone alkaloids is present at the genomic level but is not expressed in most lupins. Since α-pyridone alkaloids, such as

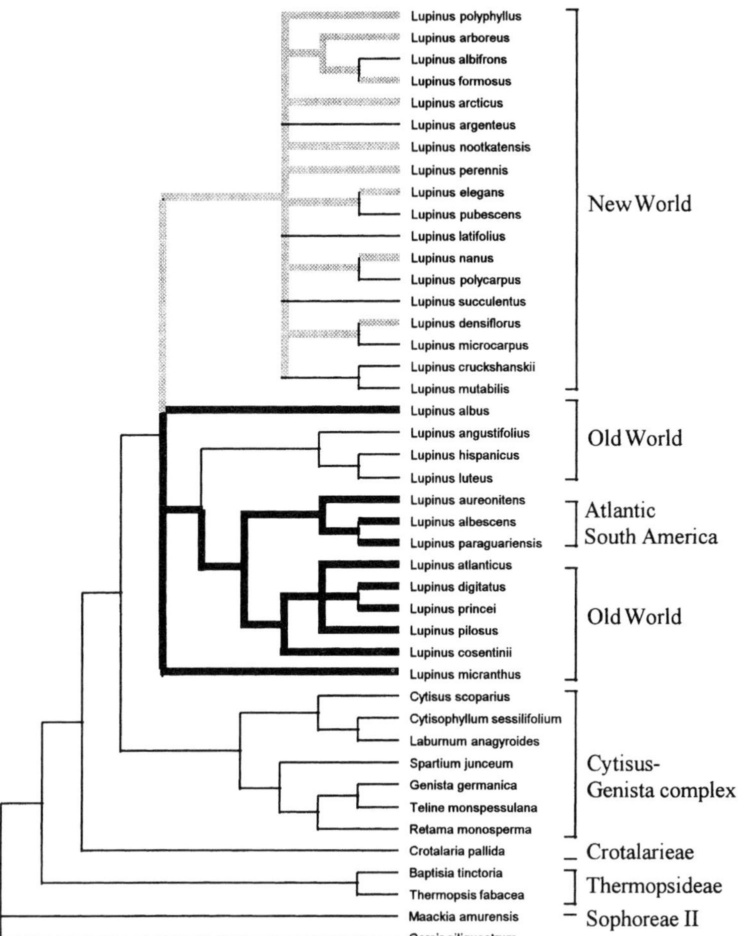

Figure 6.13C Distribution of tetracyclic multiflorine type alkaloids. Key to branches leading to species that accumulate: major constituent (▬); minor constituent (▒). See also legend to Figure 6.13A.

cytisine and *N*-methylcytisine, are strong agonists at nicotinic acetylcholine receptors (Schmeller *et al.*, 1994) or even induce mutations, it is surprising that more lupins fail to express these defence compounds rather than the tetracyclic alkaloids and their esters.

Bicyclic QAs, such as lupinine and derivatives, already occur in the more ancestral tribes, such as Thermopsideae and Podalyrieae. They are rarely found in members of the *Cytisus*/*Genista* complex but are typical for lupins of the subgroup, Scabrispermae (*L. atlanticus, L. digitatus, L. princei, L. pilosus, L. cosentinii*), and of the closely-related *L. luteus/L. hispanicus* pair. In North American lupins, bicyclic QAs occur only sporadically as minor components.

Alkaloids of the multiflorine type (multiflorine, albine) have been recorded only from lupins. They are major constituents of Old World species of the subgroup, Scabrispermae, and of *L. albus/L.micranthus* (Fig. 6.13C). They also occur as major alkaloids in South American lupins with an Atlantic distribution, which cluster as a sister taxon to the Old World Scabrispermae. Multiflorine has been sporadically recorded as a minor component in North American lupins. Dipiperidine alkaloids (DPA), such as ammodendrine and derivatives, derive from lysine, as do QAs. The distribution of DPAs resembles that of QAs, and ammodendrine is a minor component of most QA plants (Fig. 6.13B). In a few lupins, such as in *Lupinus sulphureus*, DPAs figure as major constituents.

In conclusion, when analyzing the alkaloid profiles within a genus, we observe the same phenomenon as found for other secondary metabolites at the tribe or family level. In some instances, all members of a monophyletic clade share a chemical characteristic (this would favour their use as a taxonomic marker); in other instances not. Since a good marker should work in all instances, the main question is, What were the selective forces to activate the corresponding genes in one taxon and to turn them off in another? Since secondary metabolites play a vital role as defence or signal compounds, their occurrence apparently reflects adapations and particular life strategies rather then taxonomic relationships. Studying the distribution of secondary metabolites in plants, thus, offers information on the underlying evolutionary, ecological and systematic processes and strategies but their value as taxonomic markers is constrained by the reticulate nature of their metabolic expression.

Acknowledgements

M. W. thanks his coworkers E. Kaess, F. Merino and G. Mohamed for cooperation in the molecular analysis of legumes.

References

Abbott, H.C. de S. (1886) Certain chemical constituents of plants in relation to their morphology and evolution. *Bot. Gazz.*, **11** 270-72.

Adams, R.P. (1972) Chemosystematic and numerical studies of natural populations of *Juniperus pinchoti* Sudw. *Taxon*, **21** 407-27.

Adams, R.P. (1975) Gene flow *versus* selection pressure and ancestral differentiation in the composition of species: analysis of population variation in *Juniperus ashei* Buch. using terpenoid data. *J. Mol. Evol.*, **5** 177-85.

Adams, R.P. and Turner, B.L. (1970) Chemosystematic and numerical studies of natural populations of *Juniperus ashei* Buch. *Taxon,* **19** 728-51.

Alston, R.E. and Turner, B.L. (1959) Applications of paper chromatography to systematics: recombination of parental biochemical components in a *Baptisia* hybrid population. *Nature (Lond.),* **184** 285-86.

Alston, R.E. and Turner, B.L. (1963) *Biochemical Systematics.* Prentice-Hall, New Jersey.

Bate-Smith, E.C. (1948) Paper chromatography of anthocyanins and related substances in petal extracts. *Nature (Lond.),* **161** 835-38.

Bate-Smith, E.C. (1958) Plant phenolics as taxonomic guides. *Proc. Linn. Soc.,* **169** 198-211.

Bate-Smith, E.C. (1962) The phenolic constituents of plants and their taxonomic significance. *Bot. J. Linn. Soc.,* **58** 95-173.

Bate-Smith, E.C. (1973) Chemotaxonomy of *Geranium. Bot. J. Linn. Soc.,* **67** 347-59.

Bell, E.A., Lackey, J.A. and Polhill, R.M. (1978) Systematic significance of canavanine in the Papilionoideae. *Biochem. Syst. Ecol.,* **6** 201-12.

Bernays, E., Edgar, J.A. and Rothschild, M. (1977) Pyrrolizidine alkaloids sequestered and stored by the aposematic grasshopper, *Zonocerus variegatus. J. Zool. (Lond.),* **182** 85-87.

Bohlmann, F., Burkhardt, T. and Zdero, C. (1973) *Naturally Occurring Polyacetylenes.* Academic Press, London.

Brower, L.P., Edmunds, M. and Moffitt, C.M. (1975) Cardenolide content and palatability of a population of *Danaus chrysippus* butterflies from West Africa. *J. Ent.,* **49** 183-96.

Brown, K.S. and Trigo, J.R. (1995) The ecological activity of alkaloids, in *The Alkaloids* (ed. G.A. Cordell), Academic Press, New York, pp. 227-54.

Candolle, A.P. de (1804) *Essai sur les propriétés medicales des Plantes, comparées avec leur formes extéieures et leur classification naturelle.* Edn. 1, Méquignon, Paris.

Chase, M.W., Soltis, D.E., Olmstead, R.G., Morgan, D., Les, D.H., Mishler, B.D. *et al.* (1993) Phylogenetics of seed plants: an analysis of nucleotide sequences from the plastid gene, *rbc*L. *Ann. Missouri Bot. Gard.,* **80** 528-80.

Crisp, M.D. and Doyle, J.J. (1995) *Advances in Legume Systematics.* Part 7. Phylogeny. The Royal Botanical Gardens, Kew, London, UK.

Dahlgren, R.M.T. (1980) A revised system of classification of the angiosperms. *Bot. J. Linn. Soc.,* **80** 91-124.

Donnelly, D.M.X. (1985) Neoflavonoids, in *The Biochemistry of Plant Phenolics* (eds. C.F. van Sumere and P.J. Lea), Clarendon Press, Oxford, pp. 199-220.

Doyle, J. (1992) Gene trees and species trees: molecular systematics as one-character taxonomy. *Syst. Bot.,* **17** 144-63.

Doyle, J.J. (1993) DNA, phylogeny and the flowering of plant systematics. *Bio. Sci.,* **43** 380-89.

Doyle, J.J. (1994) Phylogeny of the Legume family: an approach to understanding the origins of nodulation. *Annu. Rev. Ecol. Syst.,* **25** 325-49.

Doyle, J.J. (1995) DNA data and legume phylogeny: a progress report, in *Advances in Legume Systematics,* Part 7, Phylogeny. The Royal Botanical Gardens, Kew, pp. 11-40.

Doyle, J.J. and Doyle, J.L. (1993) Chloroplast DNA phylogeny of the papilionid legume tribe, Phaseoleae. *Syst. Bot.,* **18** 309-27.

Doyle, J.J., Doyle, J.L., Ballenger, J.A. and Palmer, J.D. (1996) The distribution and phylogenetic significance of a 50 kb chloroplast DNA inversion in the flowering plant family, Leguminosae. *Molec. Phylog. Evol.,* **5** 429-38

Felsenstein, J. (1985) Phylogenies and the comparative method. *Am. Nat.,* **125** 1-15.

Ferguson, I.K. and Tucker, S.C. (1994) *Advances in Legume Systematics,* Part 6, Structural biology. The Royal Botanical Gardens, Kew.

Geissmann, T.A. and Crout, D.H.G. (1969) *Organic Chemistry of Secondary Plant Metabolism.* Freeman Cooper and Co., San Francisco.

Gottlieb, O.R. (1982) *Micromolecular Evolution, Systematics and Ecology*. Springer Verlag, Berlin.

Gray, A.I. and Waterman, P.G. (1978) Coumarins in the Rutaceae. *Phytochemistry*, **17** 845-64.

Guinaudeau, H. and Bruneton, J. (1993) Isoquinoline alkaloids. in *Methods in Plant Biochemistry* (ed. P.G. Waterman), Vol. 8, Academic Press, London, pp. 373-419.

Harborne, J.B. (1993) *Introduction to Ecological Biochemistry*, 4th Ed., Academic Press, London.

Harborne, J.B. (ed.) (1964) *Biochemistry of Phenolic Compounds*. Academic Press, London.

Harborne, J.B. (1966) The evolution of flavonoid pigments in plants, in *Comparative Phytochemistry* (ed. T. Swain), Academic Press, London, pp. 271-95.

Harborne, J.B. (ed.) (1967) *Comparative Biochemistry of the Flavonoids*. Academic Press, London.

Harborne, J.B. and Turner, B.L. (1984) *Plant Chemosystematics*. Academic Press, London.

Harborne, J.B., Boulter, D. and Turner, B.L. (eds.) (1971) *Chemotaxonomy of the Leguminosae*. Academic Press, London.

Hartmann, T. and Witte, L. (1995) Chemistry, biology and chemoecology of the pyrrolizidine alkaloids. in *Alkaloids: Chemical and Biological Perspectives* (ed. S.W. Pelletier), Pergamon Press, Oxford, pp. 155-233.

Hegnauer, R. (1961) Die Gliederung der Rhoedales *sensu* Wettstein im Licht der Inhaltstoffe. *Planta Medi.*, **9** 37-46.

Hegnauer, R. (1963) The taxonomic significance of alkaloids. in *Chemical Plant Taxonomy* (ed. T. Swain), Academic Press, London, pp. 389-427.

Hegnauer, R. (1962–1990) *Chemotaxonomie der Pflanzen*, Vol. 1–9, Birkhäuser, Basle.

Hegnauer, R. and Hegnauer, M. (1992–1996) *Chemotaxonomie der Pflanzen*, Vol. 10, 11a and 11b, Birkhäuser, Basle.

Hegnauer, R. and Hegnauer, M. (1994) *Chemotaxonomie der Pflanzen*. Vol. XIa, Leguminosae, Birkhäuser Verlag, Basle.

Herendeen, P.S. and Dilcher, D.L. (1992) *Advances in Legume Systematics*, Part 4, The fossil record. The Royal Botanical Gardens, Kew.

Herout, V. and Sorm, F. (1969) Chemotaxonomy of the sesquiterpenes of the Compositae. in *Perspectives in Phytochemistry* (eds. J.B. Harborne and T. Swain), Academic Press, London, pp. 139-65.

Ingham, J.L. (1983) Naturally occurring isoflavonoids. *Fortschr. Chem. Org. Naturstoffe*, **43** 1-266.

Jensen, S.R., Nielsen, B. and Dahlgren, R. (1975) Iridoid compounds, their occurrence and systematic importance on the angiosperms. *Bot. Notiser.*, **128** 148-80.

Jensen, U. (1968) Serologische Beiträge zur Systematik der Ranunculaceae. *Bot. Jahrb.*, **88** 204-68.

Käss, E. and Wink, M. (1995) Molecular phylogeny of the Papilionoideae (family Leguminosae): *rbc*L gene sequences *versus* chemical taxonomy. *Bot. Acta*, **108** 149-62.

Käss, E. and Wink, M. (1996) Molecular evolution of the Leguminosae: Phylogeny of the three subfamilies based on *rbc*L-sequences. *Biochem. Syst. Ecol.*, **24** 365-78.

Käss, E. and Wink, M. (1997a) Phylogenetic relationships in the papilionoideae (family Leguminosae) based on nucleotide sequences of cpDNA (*rbc*L) and ncDNA (ITS1 and 2). *Molec. Phylog. Evol.*, **8** 65-88.

Käss, E. and Wink, M. (1997b) Molecular phylogeny and phylogeography of the genus *Lupinus* (family Leguminosae) inferred from nucleotide sequences of the *rbc*L gene and ITS 1+2 sequences of rDNA. *Plant Syst. Evol.*, **208** 139-67.

Kinghorn, A.D. and Balandrin, M.F. (1984) Quinolizidine alkaloids of the Leguminosae: structural types, analysis, chemotaxonomy and biological activities (ed. W.S. Pelletier) in *Alkaloids: Chemical and Biological Perspectives*, Wiley, New York, pp. 105-48.

Kubitzki, K., Mesquita, A.A.L. and Gottlieb, O.R. (1978) Chemosystematic implications of xanthones in *Bonnetia* and *Archyteae*. *Biochem. Syst. Ecol.*, **6** 185-87.

Kumar, S., Tamura, K. and Nei, M. (1993) MEGA: Molecular Evolutionary Genetics Analysis. Version 1.0, Pennsylvania State University, PA, USA.

Mabry, T.J. (1966) The betacyanins and betaxanthins. in *Comparative Phytochemistry* (ed. T. Swain), Academic Press, London, pp. 231-44.

Mabry, T.J., Markham, K.R. and Thomas, M.B. (1970) *The Systematic Identification of Flavonoids*. Springer Verlag, Berlin.

Malcolm, S.B. (1990) Chemical defence in chewing and sucking insect herbivores: plant-derived cardenolids in the Monarch butterfly and oleander aphid. *Chemoecol.*, **1** 12-21.

Mattocks, A.R. (1972) Acute hepatotoxicity and pyrrolic metabolites in rats dosed with pyrrolizidine alkaloids. *Chem. Biol. Interact.*, **5** 227-42.

McLean, E. (1970) The toxic actions of pyrrolizidine (*Senecio*) alkaloids. *Pharmacol. Rev.*, **22** 430-83.

McNair, J.B. (1935) Angiosperm phylogeny on a chemical basis. *Bull. Torrey Bot. Club*, **62** 515-32.

Murray, M.J. (1960) The genetic basis for the conversion of menthone to menthol in Japanese mint. *Genetics*, **45** 925-29.

Murray, R.D.H., Mendez, J. and Brown, S.A. (1982) *The Natural Coumarins*. Wiley Interscience, New York.

Nickisch-Rosenegk von, E., Detzel, A., Wink, M. and Schneider, D. (1990) Carrier-mediated uptake of digoxin by larvae of the cardenolide sequestering moth, *Syntomeida epilais*. *Naturwissenschaften*, **77** 336-38.

Penfold, A.R. and Morrison, F.R. (1927) The occurrence of a number of varieties of *Eucalyptus dives* as determined by chemical analysis of the essential oils. *J. Proc. Roy. Soc. N.S.W.*, **61** 54-67.

Polhill, R.M. (1994) Classification of the Leguminosae. in *Phytochemical Dictionary of the Leguminosae* (ed. I.W. Southon), Chapman & Hall, London, pp. 35-57.

Polhill, R.M., Raven, P.H. and Stirton, C.H. (1981a) Evolution and systematics of the Leguminosae. in *Advances in Legume Systematics*, Part 1, Royal Botanic Gardens, Kew, pp. 1-26.

Polhill, R.M., Raven, P.H., Crisp, M.D. and Doyle, J.J. (1981b) *Advances in Legume Systematics*, Part 2, The Royal Botanical Gardens, Kew.

Robins, D.J. (1993) Pyrrolizidine alkaloids, in *Methods in Plant Biochemistry* (ed. P.G. Waterman), Vol. 8, Academic Press, London, pp. 175-95.

Roeder, E. (1995) Medicinal plants in Europe containing pyrrolizidine alkaloids. *Pharmazie*, **50** 83-98.

Rothschild, M. (1966) Experiments with captive predators and the poisonous grasshopper, *Poekilocerus bufonius*. *Proc. Roy. Entomol. Soc. Lond.*, **31** 32-33.

Rothschild, M. (1972) Secondary plant substances and warning coloration in insects. in *Insect/Plant Relationships* (ed. H.E. van Emden), Blackwell, Oxford, pp. 59-83.

Rothschild, M., Reichstein, T., Euw, J. and Alpin, R. (1970a) Toxic Lepidoptera. *Toxicon*, **8** 293-99.

Rothschild, M., Von Euw, J. and Reichstein, T. (1970b) Cardiac glycosides in the oleander aphid, *Aphis nerii*. *Insect Physiol.*, **16** 1141-45.

Rothschild, M., Von Euw, J. and Reichstein, T. (1971) Heart poisons (cardiac glycosides) in the lygaeid bugs, *Caenocoris nerii* and *Spilostethus pandorus*. *Insect Biochem.*, **1** 373-84.

Rothschild, M., Von Euw, J. and Reichstein, T. (1973) Cardiac glycosides, heart poisons in the Polka-Dot moth, *Syntomeida epilais* (Ctenuchidae Lepidoptera). *Proc. R. Soc. Lond. B Biol. Sci.*, **183** 227-47.

Rothschild, M., Aplin, R.T., Cockrum, P.A., Edgar, J.A., Fairweather, P. and Lees, R. (1979) Pyrrolizidine alkaloids in arctiid moths. *Biol. J. Linn. Soc.*, **12** 305-26.

Rowell-Rahier, M., Witte, L., Ehmke, A. and Hartmann, T. (1991) Sesquestration of plant pyrrolizidine alkaloids by chrysomelid beetles and selective transfer into the defensive secretions. *Chemoecol.*, **2** 41-48.

Sanderson, M.J. and Liston, A. (1995) Molecular phylogenetic systematics of Galegeae, with special reference to *Astragalus*, in *Advances in Legume Systematics*, Part 7, Phylogeny. The Royal Botanical Gardens, Kew, pp. 331-50.

Schmeller, T., Sauerwein, M., Sporer, F., Müller, W.E. and Wink, M. (1994) Binding of quinolizidine alkaloids to nicotinic and muscarinic receptors. *J. Nat. Prod.*, **57** 1316-19.

Schmeller, T., El-Shazly, A. and Wink, M. (1997) Allelochemical activities of pyrrolizidine alkaloids: interactions with neuroreceptors and acetylcholine-related enzymes. *J. Chem. Ecol.*, **23** 399-416.

Smith, P.M. (1976) *The Chemotaxonomy of Plants*. E. Arnold Ltd, London, U.K.

Soltis, P., Soltis, D.E. and Doyle, J.J. (1992) *Molecular Systematics of Plants*. Chapman and Hall, London, UK.

Southon, I.W. (1994) Phytochemical dictionary of the Leguminosae. Chapman & Hall, London, UK.

Sprent, J.I. and McKey, D. (1994) *Advances in Legume Systematics*, Part 5, The nitrogen factor. The Royal Botanical Gardens, Kew.

Stirton, C.H. (1987) *Advances in Legume Systematics*, Part 3, The Royal Botanical Gardens, Kew.

Sutherland, M.D. and Park, R.J. (1967) Sesquiterpenes and their biogenesis in *Myoporum desertii* A. Cunn. in *Terpenoids in Plants* (ed. J. Pridham). Academic Press, London, pp. 147-57.

Swain, T. (ed.) (1963) *Chemical Plant Taxonomy*. Academic Press, London.

Swain, T. (ed.) (1966) *Comparative Phytochemistry*. Academic Press, London.

Swofford, D.L. (1993) PAUP: phylogenetic analysis using parsimony. Version 3.1.1., Illinois Natural History Survey, Champaign.

Teuscher, E. and Lindequist, U. (1994) *Biogene Gifte. Biologie, Chemie, Pharmakologie*. G. Fischer, Stuttgart.

Thorne, R.F. (1968) Synopsis of a putative phylogenetic classification of the flowering plants. *Aliso*, **6** 57-66.

Thorne, R.F. (1976) A phylogenetic classification of the Angiospermae. *Evol. Biol.*, **9** 35-106.

Waterman, P.G. (1975) Alkaloids of the Rutaceae: their distribution and systematic significance. *Biochem. Syst. Ecol.*, **3** 149-80.

Waterman, P.G. (1997) Chemical taxonomy, in *The Alkaloids* (ed. G.A. Cordell), Vol. 50, Academic Press, New York, pp. 537-65.

Waterman, P.G. and Gray, A.I. (1988) Chemical systematics. *Nat. Prod. Rep.*, **4** 175-203.

Waterman, P.G. and Mole, S. (1989) Extrinsic factors influencing production of secondary metabolites in plants, in *Insect-Plant Interactions* (ed. E.A. Bernays), CRC Press, Boca Raton, pp. 107-34.

Wink, M. (1988) Plant breeding: importance of plant secondary metabolites for protection against pathogens and herbivores. *Theoret. Appl. Genet.*, **75** 225-33.

Wink, M. (1992) The role of quinolizidine alkaloids in plant-insect interactions. in *Insect-Plant Interactions* (ed. E.A. Bernays) CRC Press, Boca Raton, pp. 131-66.

Wink, M. (1993a) Quinolizidine alkaloids, in *Methods in Plant Biochemistry* (ed. P.G. Waterman). Academic Press, London, pp. 197-239.

Wink, M. (1993b) The plant vacuole: a multifunctional compartment. *J. Exp. Bot.*, **44** (Suppl.) 231-46.

Wink, M. (1993c) Allelochemical properties and the raison d'être of alkaloids. in *The Alkaloids* (ed. G.A. Cordell), Academic Press, New York, pp. 1-118.

Wink, M. (1997) Interference of alkaloids with neuroreceptors and ion channels, in *Bioactive natural products* (ed. Atta-Ur-Rahman), Elsevier, Amsterdam, pp 1-123.

Wink, M. and Witte, L. (1983) Evidence for a widespread occurrence of the genes of quinolizidine alkaloid biosynthesis. *FEBS Lett.*, **159** 196-200.

Wink, M., Kaufmann, M. and Kaess, E. (1993) Molecular *versus* chemical taxonomy. *Planta Medica*, **59** (Suppl. 7) A594-A595.

Wink, M. and von Nickisch-Rosenegk, E. (1997) Sequence data of mitochondrial 16S rDNA of Arctiidae and Nymphalidae (Lepidoptera): evidence for a convergent evolution of pyrrolizidine alkaloid and cardiac glycoside sequestration. *J. Chem. Ecol.*, **23** 1549-68.

Wink, M., Meißner, C. and Witte, L. (1995) Patterns of quinolizidine alkaloids in 56 species of the genus *Lupinus*. *Phytochemistry*, **38** 139-53.

Wink, M., Schmeller, T. and Latz-Brüning, B. (1998) Modes of action of allelochemical alkaloids: interaction with neuroreceptors, DNA and other molecular targets. *J. Chem. Ecol.*, **24** 1881-1937.

Woolley, J.G. (1993) Tropane alkaloids. in *Methods in Plant Biochemistry* (ed. P.G. Waterman), Vol. 8, Academic Press, London, pp. 133-73.

Zavarin, E., Cobb, F.W., Bergot, J. and Bawber, H.W. (1971) Variation of the *Pinus ponderosa* needle oil with season and age. *Phytochemistry*, **10** 3107-14.

Index

ARABIDOPSIS

Annual Plant Reviews, Volume 1

Edited by Mary Anderson, Director of the *Arabidopsis* Stock Centre, University of Nottingham and Jeremy A Roberts, Reader in Plant Biology, University of Nottingham.

This volume brings together reviews from many of the most outstanding contributors to this area, who discuss recent advances in *Arabidopsis* research, including construction of the physical map, sequencing of the genome, and strategies for structure-function analysis. The power of mutagenesis as a tool to gain insights into plant developmental processes is illustrated in a range of stages in the life cycle of *Arabidopsis*, including embryogenesis, vegetative development, flowering, reproduction and cell death. In addition, the control of metabolism, secretion and biological rhythms is examined and the ways in which development is regulated by such stimuli as plant hormones and light are evaluated.

A prime source of reference for researchers and postgraduates in plant physiology, development, biochemistry, molecular biology, genetics and crop biotechnology.

- The most up-to-date review of the biology of *Arabidopsis*, which is the favoured model system for flowering plants.
- Emphasis on the use of mutations and genetics to unravel biological processes.
- The most comprehensive review of the present status of genome project.

CONTENTS

The *Arabidopsis* thaliana genome: towards a complete physical map - R Schmidt. **Unravelling the genome by genome sequencing and gene function analysis** - W J Stiekema and A Pereira. **Biochemical genetic analysis of metabolic pathways** - C S Cobbett. **Hormone regulated development** - M Bennett, J Kieber, J Giraudat and P Morris. **The secretory system and machinery for protein targeting** - S Gal. **Sexual reproduction: from sexual differentiation to fertilisation** - Hen-ming Wu and A Y Cheung. **Embryogenesis** - R A Torres Ruiz. **Patterns in vegetative development** - R Martienssen and L Dolan. **Genetic control of floral induction and floral patterning** - I Lee, D Weigel and F Parcy. **Light regulation and biological clocks** - G C Whitelam and A J Millar. **Programmed cell death in plants** - J Gray and G S Johal. **References. Index.**

ISBN 1-85075-890-5 / ISSN 1460-1494

U.S.A. and Canada only: ISBN 0-8493-9732-4 / ISSN 1097-7570

Hardback, 234 x 156 mm, 421 pages

FUNCTIONS OF PLANT SECONDARY METABOLITES AND THEIR EXPLOITATION IN BIOTECHNOLOGY

Annual Plant Reviews, Volume 3

Edited by Michael Wink, Institut für Pharmazeutische Biologie, Universität Heidelberg, Germany.

Secondary metabolites may function as signal molecules in plant-plant, plant-herbivore, plant-microbe, animal-animal, and animal-predator relationships. More often, they serve as chemical defence compounds against herbivores and predators, microbes, viruses or competing plants. They are therefore of ultimate importance for the fitness of the organisms producing or sequestering them.

FUNCTIONS OF PLANT SECONDARY METABOLITES AND THEIR EXPLOITATION IN BIOTECHNOLOGY
Annual Plant Reviews, Volume 3
Edited by Michael Wink

To understand the structural variability of secondary metabolites, their ecological function and their potential exploitation in biotechnology, detailed information is required on their biochemistry, pharmacology and ecology. This volume starts with on overview of the modes of action of defensive secondary metabolites, followed by detailed surveys of chemical defence in marine ecosystems, the biochemistry of induced defence, plant-microbe interactions, and medical applications. A chapter is included on biotechnological aspects of producing valuable secondary metabolites in plant cell and organ cultures.

The book is designed for use by advanced students, researchers and professionals in plant biochemistry, physiology, molecular biology, genetics, pharmacology, medicine, pharmacy and agriculture working in the academic and industrial sectors, including the pesticide and pharmaceutical industries.

CONTENTS

ISBN 1-84127-008-3 / ISSN 1460-1494

U.S.A. and Canada only: ISBN 0-8493-4086-1 / ISSN 1097-7570

Hardback, 234 x 156 mm, c 376 pages